A Kingdom Divided

To Steve Reginald, my editor and friend,
with thanks for the help you've offered, the direction you've given,
and the chances you've taken with my work.
Philippians 1:3 sums it up from me to you.

Castles

MAIDENS MEET THEIR KNIGHTS IN FOUR NOVELS

TRACIE PETERSON

BARBOUR
PUBLISHING

Published by Barbour Publishing, Inc., P.O. Box 719, Uhrichsville, Ohio 44683, www.barbourbooks.com.

Our mission is to publish and distribute inspirational products offering exceptional value and biblical encouragement to the masses.

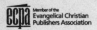 Member of the
Evangelical Christian
Publishers Association

Printed in the United States of America.
5

TRACIE PETERSON

Tracie Peterson, best-selling author of nearly fifty fiction titles and one nonfiction title, lives and works in Montana. As a Christian, wife, mother, and writer (in that order), Tracie finds her slate quite full.

First published as a columnist for the *Kansas Christian* newspaper, Tracie resigned that position to turn her attention to novels. After signing her first contract with Barbour Publishing in 1992, her first novel appeared in 1993 under the pen name of Janelle Jamison, and the rest is history. She has over twenty-three titles with the **Heartsong Presents** book club and stories in six separate anthologies from Barbour, including the best-selling *Alaska*. From Bethany House Publishing, Tracie has several historical series, as well as a variety of women's fiction titles.

Voted favorite author for 1995, 1996, and 1997 by the **Heartsong Presents** readership, Tracie enjoys the pleasure of spinning stories for readers and thanks God for the imagination He's given. "I find myself blessed to be able to work at a job I love. I get to travel, study history, spin yarns, spend time with my family, and hopefully glorify God. I can't imagine a more perfect arrangement."

Tracie also does acquisitions work for Barbour Publishing and teaches workshops at a variety of conferences, giving workshops on inspirational romance, historical research, and anything else that offers assistance to fellow writers.

This collection of stories come from her early years of writing romance for **Heartsong Presents**.

See Tracie on the Internet at http://members.aol.com/tjpbooks/

Chapter 1

I desire to see her," the tall man stated with an air of one used to his commands being met. His scowl deepened as he awaited an answer.

Duke Geoffrey Pemberton looked sternly at the speaker. It was difficult for him to take orders, much more so from one who was a score of years his junior. Still, the duke of Gavenshire, His Grace Richard DuBonnet, was no ordinary man, and the orders he gave were nearly the same as if they'd come from King Henry himself.

"Surely it would be a waste of Your Grace's time. She is everything your proxy must have told you. I assure you, I speak for my daughter when I say she will go into this marriage with dignity, respect, and honor," Pemberton said in a much controlled manner and added, "Remember, Sire, 'twas your choice to send a proxy to the betrothal ceremony."

Richard brought both fists down on the table. He was weary of dealing with the older man. Weary from the greed and unpleasant cruelties he'd witnessed in things Duke Pemberton said and did.

"Don't question me," Richard said firmly. His breeding and background had given him the skills to easily fight and defeat opponents, but he recognized that the art of diplomacy was wasted on one such as Pemberton. "I want to see her now!" he exclaimed without room for argument.

Pemberton bit back a retort and called for his daughter's chambermaid. The terrified girl appeared, cringing as the duke bellowed out the order that his daughter was to be brought at once to the great hall.

The maid curtsied to both men and, gathering her skirts, lit up the stairs as though a roaring fire chased her.

Richard eased back into the nearest chair. Cupping his hand against the neatly trimmed beard he wore, Richard's green eyes never left his host.

The man was ruthless and cruel and it showed in his dark eyes. Richard had been forewarned, not only by his men, but by the king's messengers as well. Pemberton had a reputation for a quick temper and heavy hand, which led Richard to wonder about the daughter who would soon be his wife.

Just then the frightened maid returned to curtsey again at her scowling master. "My lady is indisposed at present, Sire. She begs to join you in a moment." The girl cowered, awaiting an angry strike, but Pemberton noted the frown on Richard's face and held back retaliation. Before Richard could speak, Pemberton was up the stairs, disappearing from sight.

"You may go," Richard said softly, and the girl hurried from the room, not even raising her eyes to acknowledge the duke's words.

With brush in hand, Arianne Pemberton sat quickly stroking her long hair. The duke of Gavenshire, her betrothed, sat in the great hall below. She'd never even met him before finding herself suddenly engaged. What manner of man would send a proxy for his betrothal ceremonies and leave his bride-to-be wondering at the sight and condition of the man she would vow to take to her side for life?

She hummed nervously to herself, then stopped with a frown. Her father, only moments ago, had sent the maid to fetch her. She had sent the maid back to decline, and no doubt her father would be furious. *But I have to dress my hair,* Arianne thought. *It would have been most inappropriate to have been introduced to the duke with my head bare.*

In spite of her attempts to convince herself she'd made the right decision, the one thing that kept coming back to her was the cruelty she'd known at her father's hand. He wouldn't like her defiance, just as he hadn't cared about her feelings toward the upcoming marriage. She didn't want the wedding, but he did. That put them at odds.

Arianne continued to run the brush through her hair, even while she considered the consequences of her actions. Her father was a ruthless man who ruled all around him with a mixture of injustice and self-servitude. He would not take lightly Arianne's delay.

Arianne's door slammed abruptly open, causing her to drop her brush.

"Get thee below at once!" her father raged. He gave her no chance to stand, but reached out and yanked the girl to her feet and out the door.

Below in the great hall, Richard heard the commotion. Pemberton appeared at the top of the stairs, dragging behind a shapely young woman.

With hip-length auburn hair flying out behind her, Lady Arianne Pemberton was dragged down the steps and landed in an unceremonious heap at her father's feet.

"Here," her father said smugly, "is your bride. Her temper can be a bit much, but the back of your hand will easily settle her disposition."

Richard was on his feet in a heartbeat, and before Arianne could lift her face, he was helping her.

"Your Grace," she whispered and pushed back the wavy bulk of hair that kept her face from his. Dark brown eyes met angry green ones, causing Arianne to instantly realize that her worst fears had come true. She was to marry a man just like her father!

"Milady," Richard spoke softly, delivering her to a nearby chair. Turning abruptly, Richard closed the distance to where the duke stood with a haughty stare of disgust.

Balling his hand into a fist, Richard raised it to within inches of the duke's face. "Never, I repeat, never treat my wife with such ill-respect again or you will feel the consequences of your actions."

Arianne could not suppress a gasp of surprise. No one had ever dared to speak to her father in such a manner. The duke's face flamed red, but he remained silent, further surprising his daughter. He must want this match badly.

With the king's edict that she be wed to the duke of Gavenshire, Arianne couldn't imagine that her father would worry that the marriage wouldn't take place. Perhaps he was simply in awe of the younger man's position with the king. Arianne knew that position and power were the only things of importance to her father and surmised that this must, indeed, be the reason for his good manners.

Completely ignoring the indignant duke, Richard turned to take in the vision of the woman he was slated to spend all of time with. She was everything his men had related and more. They hadn't told him of the way her hair flashed glints of gold amidst the deep auburn mass. No doubt they'd not seen her hair, Richard mused, for it would have been covered with a white linen wimple and mantle.

Arianne grew uncomfortable under the duke's close scrutiny. She'd had no time to plait her hair and cover her head before her father had stormed into her chamber and dragged her to meet her husband-to-be. She was most grateful that she'd dressed carefully in forest green velvet, for while it was simply adorned with a gold and jeweled belt at her waist, it was a becoming color, and Arianne did hope to meet with the duke's approval.

"Milady," Richard said, coming to greet her formally, "I am Richard DuBonnet, duke of Gavenshire." He gave a bit of a bow before taking Arianne's hand in his own and continuing. "And you, of course, are the most lovely Lady Arianne Pemberton."

Arianne wanted to melt into the rush-covered floor. The warmth in his eyes set her heart beating faster, but the gentleness of his touch was as none she'd ever known.

"Your Grace," she whispered, getting to her feet. Even as she curtsied deeply, Richard refused to let go of her hand.

"It would pleasure me greatly, Milady, if you were to call me Richard."

Arianne rose and lifted her face to his. "Richard," she whispered the name, trembling from head to toe.

"And might I call you Arianne?" he questioned. Both of them were oblivious to the older duke, staring on in complete loathing of the gentle exchange.

"But of course, Your—Richard," Arianne corrected herself. She mustn't do anything to anger this powerful man. "You may call me whatever pleases you."

A hint of a smile played at the corners of Richard's lips. "It pleases me to call you my wife," he said boldly. "The king has chosen well for me."

Arianne blushed scarlet and felt her knees grow weak. She couldn't very well reply with her true feelings toward the arrangement. Not with such gallant praise being issued on her behalf. With a quick glance past Richard to where her father stood, Arianne realized instantly that he was displeased.

Richard noticed the exchange at once and led Arianne back to the chair. "Come, we will speak of our marriage," he announced.

Duke Pemberton could no longer remain silent. "I see no need to waste your valuable time, Your Grace. You must have many affairs to oversee. I have already assured you of my daughter's virtue, dowry—"

"Yes, yes. I know all about the business dealings of my betrothal and marriage. What I desire to know now is the heart of your daughter," Richard interrupted with a flash of anger in his eyes.

"But what woman knows her heart on any matter?" Pemberton retorted with a silencing stare directed at his daughter. "Her thoughts are nothing to you or to me. She knows how to tend a household and direct the running of an estate. She is a comely lass and no doubt will give you many fine sons. More than this is unimportant."

Arianne knew better than to cross her father. She was not yet married, and until she came under Richard's complete protection, there was always the possibility that her father would beat her for her remarks. She shuddered, knowing that she still bore lash marks from the last argument she'd had with her father regarding the upcoming marriage.

Richard took the seat beside Arianne and stared thoughtfully at the duke as if he considered his words of value. Then without warning, he turned to her. "What are your thoughts on the matter of our marriage, Arianne?"

Arianne's father seethed noticeably at the disregard of his statement. He flashed a warning to Arianne that told of trouble to come should she say anything to jeopardize her standing in this arrangement.

Arianne bowed her head slightly before speaking. "It is my honor to share vows with you." The words were barely audible.

"You know very little of me," Richard continued gently. "Is there something I might share with you regarding myself that would put to rest any questionable matter in your mind?"

"Nay, Your Grace," she replied, forgetting to call him Richard.

"Is there any matter about yourself that you would like to share with me?" he questioned.

Arianne was shaking noticeably now. On one side stood her father, threatening with his eyes to strip her of her dignity should she say anything outside of his instruction, and on the other side was Richard, who genuinely seemed to care about her feelings.

The room grew uncomfortably silent. The tension between the girl and her father was clear. Richard frowned slightly. He noticed Arianne's trembling and the duke's scowling face. So long as Arianne's father remained within sight, she would no doubt say little or nothing. Without warning, Richard stood and pointed to the door. "Leave us," he commanded the duke.

Pemberton was shocked beyond reason and enraged beyond words. He struggled for the right response, but before he could find any words, Richard called for his men and ordered them to take the duke into the outer room.

Richard knew he was making a great enemy, but he no longer cared. His real concern was for the frightened young woman who sat cringing in terror.

As his men took the duke from the room, Richard called out one final order. "We are not to be disturbed for any reason."

When the door closed behind his men, Richard turned to Arianne and smiled. "Now, Arianne, you must feel free to speak to me honestly."

Arianne's mouth dropped open slightly, and Richard couldn't help but notice her lips. Raising his gaze slightly, he stared into huge brown eyes that reminded him hauntingly of a doe about to be slain.

"I. . .I. . . ," she stammered for words.

Richard sat back down and took her hand in his own. Lifting it to his lips, he gently kissed the back. "Arianne," he whispered, "I can read things in your eyes that are not making their way to your lips. You might as well speak your heart. You aren't going to offend or injure me, I assure you. Now speak to me of this marriage. Are you truly in agreement?" he questioned gently.

Arianne could feel the warmth of his breath against her hand and pulled it back quickly. "I have never been allowed the luxury of speaking openly, Sire—Richard."

"I'm certain you speak the truth," he said with a slight smile. "But your father is no longer a concern to you. You are under my protection and you will leave with me on the 'morrow, so put aside your fears and talk to me. We cannot change what the king has arranged, but we might yet come to a better understanding of it."

Arianne swallowed the lump in her throat. She lifted her delicate face to meet Richard's gentle expression. With the exception of her brother, Devon, she'd never known a man such as Richard. But Devon was hundreds, maybe even thousands of miles away doing the king's bidding, just as she was doing the royal bidding at home.

"I am against marriage to you," she said softly, then tightly shut her eyes and braced herself for his rage.

"I see," he replied without emotion. "Has another captured your affections?"

Arianne's eyes snapped open. "Nay, there is no other," she stated adamantly.

"Then what makes this arrangement so unbearable?"

"I. . .I," she stammered for a moment then drew a deep breath. "I do not love you, Richard."

Richard chuckled.

"You laugh at me?" Arianne quickly questioned.

"Nay, dear lady. I do not laugh at you. Neither do I expect you to love me. Not yet, anyway. We've only just met and this arrangement is new to both of us." Richard paused, getting to his feet. He paced a few steps before continuing.

"Why, in all honesty, I hadn't planned to take a wife, at least not yet. When King Henry suggested this arrangement, however, I knew it would be one that would benefit our families and fulfill his desire to see me properly wed."

Richard's words seemed most sincere and Arianne began to relax. Perhaps the duke was not the kind of man her father was.

Arianne studied Richard for a moment. He was handsome—tall and lean with broad shoulders. His legs were heavily muscled, no doubt from many hours of supporting the chain mail hauberk and chaussures that were customary costume for men of armor. His dark brown hair had been neatly trimmed, as had been his mustache and beard. But most disturbing were his eyes; green eyes so fiery one minute and soft, almost childlike, the next. Arianne truly wished she knew more about the duke of Gavenshire.

"It is a good arrangement for my family," Arianne finally spoke. "I would never do anything to disgrace them. Neither would I do anything to bring the king's wrath upon them. It is my desire to be married to you, just as King Henry wishes."

Richard stopped in his pace and turned. "I don't wish to force an undesirable union upon you, Arianne. The church still presses its people for mutual consent to marriage. I could speak to the king, if it is your wish that we discontinue these arrangements."

"Nay!" Arianne exclaimed, coming up out of her seat. She threw herself at Richard's feet. Her father would kill her for causing the betrothal to be dissolved. Under no circumstances could she appear to be anything but congenial. "Please don't!" There were tears in her eyes. "I beg of you!"

Richard lifted her from the floor and set her down in front of him. "Arianne, you mustn't worry. I understand your circumstances. If you are truly agreed, I want very much for this wedding to take place."

Arianne nodded, unmindful of the tears that streamed down her cheeks. "I am agreed, Sire. I will make you a good wife. I promise."

"I've no doubt about that," Richard stated. He reached up to wipe away the tears on her face. "I simply want you to be happy, as well."

Arianne's heart soared, and the first spark of feeling for her soon-to-be husband was born. "I will be happy, Richard, and in time, I pray it will be God's will that I grow to love you."

Chapter 2

Without a chance for her father to lay a hand to her again, Arianne found herself in a long traveling procession the very next morning. She mused over the events that had led to this day. Everyone had been stunned when the young duke, himself, had arrived to bring the party to his castle. But even more surprising was the way he'd taken control of His Grace, Geoffrey Pemberton. Even Arianne was amazed.

Arianne had never understood what her father expected to gain from her match with the duke of Gavenshire. Of course it bode well to have such a powerful man in one's family lineage, but Arianne also knew that her father was giving up a great portion of estates that adjoined Richard's property. It was part of her dowry, and Arianne was hard pressed to understand how her father would have ever conceded to such an arrangement. The king must have promised him a great deal more than what he stood to lose.

Upon her own fine mare, Arianne enjoyed the passing warmth of the afternoon sun. Soon they would stop for the night, and the next day they would make their way to Gavenshire Castle.

Absorbed in thought, Arianne did not hear the rider approach to join her. Richard held back in silence, taking in the beauty he found before him. She sat regally, he thought, and in truth he had always wondered how a woman could sit so confidently atop a sidesaddle. Arianne, however, seemed not to consider the situation. She was like a child taking in the countryside around her. A look of awe was fixed upon her face.

"Does the ride overtax you, Milady?"

Arianne jerked back on the reins without thought. "My pardon, Sire. You startled me." She released the reins and allowed the horse to proceed. "What was it you asked of me?"

Richard smiled. "I asked if the ride overtaxed you."

"Nay," Arianne replied with a wistful look spreading across her face. "In truth it is something wondrous. I have never known the land outside a half-day's ride from my home. The world is much larger out here."

Richard laughed heartily. "That it is, Arianne."

Arianne fixed her eyes boldly on Richard for a moment, and with her smile deepening added, "There is much that I have to learn." The depths of her brown eyes pulled at Richard's heart.

He leaned forward and in hardly more than a whisper spoke. "It would pleasure me greatly to be your teacher."

Arianne blushed deeply at what could seemingly have been a statement of mixed meaning. Had he thought her a flirt? Before she could speak, one of Richard's men hailed him from the front of the procession and Richard bid her farewell.

That night, it seemed Arianne's eyes had barely closed in sleep before she was being urged awake. Today they would reach Gavenshire, she thought and hastened her steps to get dressed.

She had prepared for this day with great care. Calling the servants her father had allowed her to borrow for the journey, Arianne directed and ordered each one until everything was just as she desired. Too nervous to eat anything, Arianne sent her breakfast away without so much as touching a crumb.

Donning a delicate tunic of pale lavender silk, Arianne nodded her approval and turned to be fitted in the surcoat of samite. The samite blend of wool and silk had been dyed deep purple and trimmed in ermine. Arianne had no desire to appear a pauper before her husband's people.

Within the hour, Arianne's toilette was complete, and she was seated once again on her sidesaddle. She glanced around nervously for Richard and blushed deeply when she met his open stare of approval. With long easy strides, he came to where her mare pranced anxiously.

"Lady Arianne," he said, taking her hand to his lips, "you are the epitome of that which all English women should strive for. Your beauty blinds me to all else."

"Your Grace," she whispered, then corrected herself. "I mean, Richard." She seemed at a loss as to how she should respond to his flattery.

"I trust you slept well," the duke responded before she had a chance to concern herself overmuch.

"Aye," she said with a nod. "Albeit a short rest, 'twas quite refreshing."

"Good," Richard said with a smile. "Then we will be on our way. Gavenshire and her people await their new duchess."

Although Arianne had lived a life of ease compared to many, she was dumbly silent at the vision of Gavenshire Castle. The gray stone walls stood atop the cliffs, rising majestically above the background of the sea's churning waters.

She gasped in awe as they drew ever closer. The spiraling twin towers of the castle seemed to dwarf the village at its feet. Everywhere, brightly colored banners flew in celebration of her marriage to the duke of Gavenshire.

If the castle was not enough, Arianne was absolutely stunned when people lined every inch of the roadway in order to get a look at their soon-to-be duchess.

The crowd cheered, while peasants handed up flowers to her waiting hands. Arianne beamed smiles upon everyone, which prompted even greater response. She was a bit afraid of the sea of people at her side, but Richard had not returned to assist her and so Arianne had to believe that nothing was amiss and that she should enjoy this as her special moment with his people.

Just then, a small girl darted out in front of Arianne's mare, causing the horse to rear. Arianne tightened her grip and leaned into the horse's neck. She soothed the horse into stillness, while the child's mother ran forward to claim her frightened daughter.

"A thousand pardons, Milady. The child meant no harm, she's just excited by the noise and celebration," the woman stated as if fearing for the life of the child she now held. The crowd around them fell silent and waited for their new duchess to act.

Arianne smiled. "Your apology is unwarranted, Madam. I, myself, am quite caught up in the revelry as well."

A cheer went up once again, and Arianne could feel the mare begin to shift in nervous agitation. Soothing the horse with a gentle stroke, Arianne reached down and gave the child a quick pat on the head and moved the horse forward.

Richard observed the incident from where he'd brought his mount to a stop. Arianne was truly a remarkable woman. In one simple act of kindness, she had sealed herself upon the hearts of his people.

The sun broke out from clouds overhead and flashed out across the earth, touching everything in its warmth. Arianne lifted her face for a moment to catch the rays, and as she lowered her eyes, she caught sight of Richard. The look he gave her was so intimate that she quickly looked away. What manner of man was the duke of Gavenshire that he would boldly assess his wife in public?

The days that followed did so with such momentum that Arianne was left breathless at the end of each one. There was her introduction to the castle, which though thorough, left her more puzzled than ever. She comforted herself in the knowledge that exploration and understanding would come later.

The wedding itself, planned by the duke and his household, was more elaborate than Arianne had ever dreamed. The celebrating and festivities would most likely continue for yet another week.

The day of their wedding was perfect. The church at Gavenshire welcomed the duke and his duchess and all who could crowd inside to share in the pledges of matrimony.

Arianne wore her finest clothes. A linen chemise of pale gold with an exquisite tunic of burgundy silk adorned her frame. Over this came a surcoat of dark gold velvet that had been lavishly embroidered and trimmed in fur. At Richard's request, she had left her hair unplaited, a most unusual thing but one that seemed only to enhance her beauty. On her head she wore a veil of gossamer gold that shimmered in the light when she walked. It was held in place by a narrow gold band that glittered from the three stones it held: a diamond, a ruby, and an emerald.

Richard nodded his heartfelt approval as she approached the priest with him. The priest bade them join right hands, and when Arianne touched Richard's large warm hand with her own small trembling one, peace settled over her.

They repeated their vows before God, the church, and their people and waited while the priest expounded on the virtues of religious education, a tranquil home, and a pure marriage bed.

Finally he asked for the ring, which Richard promptly produced. The priest blessed the ring, then handed it back to Richard. Arianne noted that it looked to be a small replica of the band that held her veil in place.

"In the name of the Father," Richard whispered and slipped the ring on Arianne's index finger, "and of the Son," he continued and slipped it to the second finger. "And of the Holy Ghost." He fitted it to the third finger. "With this ring I thee wed."

Arianne thought she might actually faint. The moment was so intense, so intimate, that she could scarcely draw a breath. The ceremony continued, and finally after the nuptial mass, Richard received the kiss of peace from the priest and turned to pass it to his new wife.

Gently, he lifted Arianne's veil and smiled. Her brown eyes were huge in anticipation, melting Richard's heart and resolve. He leaned forward without reaching out to her otherwise and, for the first time, touched his lips to hers. He'd only intended to linger a moment, but it was as if he were held against his will. The kiss deepened until, without thought, Richard had gripped Arianne's shoulders.

A gentle cough by the priest told Richard that the marriage was sealed sufficiently. Sheepishly, Richard pulled back with a half-apologetic, half-frustrated look on his face before taking Arianne's hand. He led her quietly from the church to the waiting crowd. They were heralded by the people with such sincere warmth and joy that Arianne could not keep the tears from her eyes.

"What be this?" Richard questioned, reaching out to touch a single drop against her cheek. "You are not already regretting this union, are you?"

"Nay, Richard," Arianne whispered against his bent head. "I am moved beyond thought at the kindness of your people."

Richard lifted her hand to his lips and gave it a squeeze. "They do love you, Duchess."

If the revelry prior to the ceremony was impressive, then the celebration which followed in the great hall of Gavenshire Castle was extraordinary.

First there were the tables laden with food of every imaginable kind. Huge roasted legs of beef were set before them on gold platters, while baked capons, chickens, and rabbits were arranged on smaller plates. Fruits, vegetables, sweetmeats, and breads filled numerous bowls and platters in a nearly endless display of prosperity.

Arianne sat at Richard's side, sharing with him a common chalice and water bowl. When Arianne inadvertently placed her hand on the goblet at the same time Richard reached for it, the intimacy seemed too much. The warmth of his hand covered hers as he lifted the glass to her lips first and then his own. Those at the table who witnessed the act roared in hearty approval and predicted that many would be the number of sons born to this union.

Arianne grew apprehensive and could not look Richard in the eye. She hadn't wanted this marriage, yet it was impossible to deny that he was kind and gentle with her. She thought of the night to come and nearly grimaced while taking a mouthful of roasted boar. She had always hoped that she could give herself in marriage to a man whom she cared for, nay, loved. It wasn't uncommon that people sought that affection, but in a world where the destiny of one usually correlated to the desires of others, Arianne knew that she'd been most fortunate to end up married to a man such as Richard DuBonnet. She could only pray that love would come.

The festivities continued with jongleurs playing lively songs upon their lutes and viols. A man with a tabor played, while another man sang the words of a love song written on behalf of Arianne. He sang of her beauty and virtue, while most of the hall fell silent in awe.

Arianne herself was moved to tears, but she quickly held them in check. She had never felt such warmth and caring from anyone in her life.

Soon the tables were moved aside and dancing took place. The people's merriment for the day was evident in the whirling and clapping that accompanied the dance. Arianne found herself passed among Richard's knights and one after the other whirled, lifted, and paraded her across the floor with great flourish. She caught sight of her father and Richard only once, but it was enough of a glimpse to tell her that Richard was unhappy with the older man.

Finally the revelry grew somber again and the tables were set with supper. The priest blessed the meal and the house, then placed his hands upon Richard and Arianne and blessed their union once again. He added a blessing for the nuptial bed before releasing them to the feast, causing Arianne to blush deeply.

Arianne found eating impossible. She picked at a piece of chicken unmercifully until Richard finally put his hand upon hers and stilled her attack.

"I have a gift for you," he said softly. Richard turned and motioned to an older woman. Arianne lifted her face to find a radiant smile and soft gray eyes.

"This is Matilda," Richard said. "She will be your lady's maid." Without a word being spoken, Arianne immediately liked the woman. Something in her countenance bespoke loyalty and friendship, maybe even the motherly love that Arianne had been robbed of at an early age.

"Matilda," Arianne tried the name. "I am pleased to have your care."

"As am I, to care for you, Milady," Matilda replied.

Before anything else was said, Richard leaned toward the two women. "Arianne, Matilda will take you to my. . .our chamber. Perhaps you will feel better away from this crowd. I will join you later."

Arianne nodded without meeting Richard's eyes. Matilda was to prepare her for her wedding bed as was the custom of the bride's mother. Gently rising, Arianne followed Matilda from the room amidst the roars and calls of some of the heartier knights. Richard's men intended that he be embarrassed, but he only frowned, knowing the likely uneasiness it caused Arianne.

Upstairs, Arianne permitted Matilda's service, while the woman spoke of the castle and Richard.

"I've know him since he was in swaddling, Milady," Matilda said. She gently removed the heavy belt and surcoat from Arianne. "He is a good master and never a kinder one was born."

Arianne smiled at the woman's obvious devotion. "What of his family?" she questioned. "I've met no one who lays claim to his blood."

Matilda frowned momentarily. "His Grace doesn't allow anyone to speak of them, but I knew them well. I cared for his mother."

Arianne waited while Matilda finished removing the tunic and chemise. She accepted a soft shift of pale cream silk before speaking again to Matilda.

"Is there bad blood between Richard and his family, Matilda?"

"Nay, Mistress. 'Tis no small matter to deal with either, and I would not betray my master by speaking of it." Matilda's words were firm, but she sought to ease Arianne's fearful stare by continuing with stories of Richard as a boy.

Arianne allowed the woman to direct her to a chair, where Matilda brushed her hair until each coppery lock seemed to blaze under the soft glow of candlelight. When the task was completed, Matilda stoked the fire in the hearth and built it up until it was a cheerful blaze. Then she extinguished the candles and took her leave.

Arianne drew her legs up to her chest and tucked the silken garment around her feet. She finally allowed herself to gaze around the room, taking in first the fire, then the shadowy forms of clothing chests, and finally the huge bed that she was to share with her husband.

The bed, half again as long as a man's height was nearly as wide across. Overhead the massive wood canopy was decorated with intricate carvings and rich velvet curtains. It was no pauper's bed, to be sure.

Just then the door opened and against the dim light of the hallway, Richard's well-muscled frame stood fast. He stared at his wife. A more heavenly vision he could not imagine, but even from across the room he could see that she trembled. He slowly closed the door and set the bar in place.

"You are beautiful, Arianne," he whispered, coming to the fireplace. "I am a most blessed man."

Arianne lifted her eyes, meeting the passionate look of her husband. Words stuck in her throat. What should she say? What could she?

Richard wished nothing more than to dispel the fear in her eyes. Fear that he knew held deep root in her heart.

"I was sorry that your brother couldn't attend the wedding," he said, taking a seat on the bed opposite where she sat. "I know very little about you," he continued. "I would be most honored if you would speak to me about your youth."

Arianne relaxed a bit. Richard seemed content to sit apart from her, and his words made her realize that he had no intention of rushing the night.

"My mother died when I was but six years old," Arianne finally spoke. "I remember only little things about her because I was quickly taken off to a convent where I was schooled and held until my father's instruction. My brother, Devon, would visit me often there. We are very close," she said with a sadness to her voice that Richard wished he could cast out.

"My father returned me home when my brother, Devon, was preparing to ride with the king's men. We shared only a few short months before Devon left, and I have not seen him since. That was five years ago."

"And in all that time he's not returned home?" Richard questioned.

"He and my father are at odds," Arianne whispered. "It seems my father finds a rival in everything."

"Aye," Richard murmured, "I can vouch for that."

"I pray my father has not overly grieved you," Arianne replied.

Richard shook his head and reached out a hand to touch her. Arianne instantly recoiled into the chair. She regretted the action, but could do nothing to take it back.

Richard saw the fear return to her eyes and sighed. "Arianne, I'm no monster. I will not beat and abuse you as others must have done. You have nothing to fear from me."

Arianne tried to steady her nerves. Her heart raced at a murderous pace and she found that fear gripped her throat.

Richard got up and pulled Arianne to her feet. "I will not press you to consummate this marriage," he said firmly. "In fact, I will not seal this arrangement until there is no longer fear in your eyes and heart toward me."

Arianne felt the warmth of his touch spread down her arms. "I will not deny you," she whispered.

"Yea, but I will deny myself," Richard replied. "I have but one request in return."

"Name it, Sire."

"That you share my bed upon my honor that I will not touch you," he replied. Then with eyes twinkling and a slight smile upon his lips, he corrected himself. "Nay, I would hold you, but demand nothing more."

Arianne nodded slowly, still amazed that he would do such a thing for her.

She cast her glance from Richard's face to the bed and back again when a horrible thought gripped her mind.

"The virginal sheets," she whispered.

"The what? What are you talking about, Arianne?"

"The virginal sheets." Her voice trembled. "Without them, I'll be shamed and so will you."

Richard stared blankly for a moment and then recalled the barbaric custom of a bride's proof of virtue. He grimaced slightly. "I'm sorry, Milady. I forgot." Then turning to the bed, he yanked down the coverlets and pointed. "Lie down."

Arianne steadied her nerves and straightened her shoulders. *This is it*, she thought, and even though Richard had promised to wait, she quietly obeyed his command.

She closed her eyes as she reclined on the cold sheets. With her fists clenched at her sides and jaws tight, Arianne waited.

Richard stared down at her shapely form with more compassion for her fear than he'd ever known for anyone. "Open your eyes, Arianne," he said after several moments.

Arianne forced herself to look at Richard. In her eyes was the look of a trapped animal, and Richard longed to end her suffering and ease her fears.

"Now, get up," he whispered and extended a hand to help her. Arianne was stunned but nevertheless scooted quickly from the bed to stand beside her husband.

With one fluid motion, Richard drew a jeweled ceremonial dagger from his belt and slashed his forearm with a small stroke.

Arianne gasped aloud at the crimson stain that appeared on Richard's arm. He never took his eyes from her face as he waited calmly for the blood to pool. Then walking to where Arianne had lain, he sprinkled his blood over the sheet.

"There," he said with a sheepish grin. "The virginal sheets."

Arianne stood open-mouthed, staring at her husband. "Why did you do this thing? Why did you shed your own blood?"

Richard sobered. "So you wouldn't have to."

Arianne's heart pounded within her. If she had never cared for this man before, she now felt a deep respect and admiration for him.

"You make this sacrifice for me—to keep me from shame?" Arianne questioned. Richard again smiled. "Too gallant, Milady?"

"No," Arianne said, shaking her head slowly. "Amazing—for you scarce know me and I do not love you."

"People didn't love our Lord Jesus, either, but He gave His blood to save them," Richard said, his green eyes darkening.

Still not knowing what to think, Arianne found her eyes upon his bleeding arm. Tenderly, she placed her hand upon Richard. "Come," she whispered. "I will care for you."

Chapter 3

The next weeks were some of the happiest Arianne had ever known. She was constantly amazed at Richard's devotion to her, all the while honoring his promise to leave her chaste.

He took time to teach her things about his home, while continuing to see to the duties that demanded his attention. She learned that he was twenty-five and held a great friendship with the king that had been firmly in place since Richard's childhood.

She also learned what had caused her father to warm so quickly to her marriage when Richard told her of a young widow who would soon be wed to her father. The arrangement would bring both wealth and property to her father. Arianne had no doubt he cared little for the huge settlement of land he'd had to sacrifice to Richard in her dowry in order to seal the arrangement. The only thing Richard ever denied her was information about his family. Whenever she questioned him concerning his parents or whether he had siblings, Richard artfully changed the subject.

They spent their days as was fitting to their station. Arianne learned the ways of the castle and found that she thrived on its running. She was quick to settle disputes between servants and relished shopping trips that allowed her to pick from among the finest furnishings to make her castle a more pleasant home.

Richard admired her abilities, and when he found her adding figures easily in her inventory of their larder supplies, he gave her a huge purse with which to run the household in full. It eased the burden of his steward and endeared Richard to Arianne's heart.

Still, at night the old fears returned and the dread of what she did not understand. Arianne fought to sort through her confused heart and still could not tell Richard truthfully that she loved him. Until then, she felt certain that the wall of apprehension would remain firmly in place between them.

Even so, she climbed into his bed each night and curled up to the warmth he offered. He spoke softly of his days at court and his accomplishments. He shared brief details of his early childhood and asked Arianne questions that sorely strained the memories she'd buried away for so long.

"Your father seems a most difficult man. Was he always so foul tempered?" Richard questioned one night.

Arianne stiffened in his arms. "Aye." The simple word sounded painful.

21

Richard began to rub her arm until he felt her relax a bit. "Tell me," he whispered.

Arianne hesitantly opened her mind to the memories. Cautiously, she picked her way amidst the anguish and fear to pull out just the right words to share. "My mother never loved him and he never loved her. It was an arranged marriage to benefit their families. My mother, although she would never speak an ill word of my father, was lonely and heartbroken during her life with him. She bore him two children: my brother, Devon, and myself, and died trying to bear a third. My mother's maid told me of her death and how not even upon her final breath did my father speak any word of love to her."

"And that is why it is most important to you," Richard stated simply.

"It must be," Arianne replied as though the thought were new to her. "Yea, 'tis the reason."

Richard ran his fingers through her long wavy hair and sighed. "It is easier to understand why you hold such fear in this arrangement."

"It is?" Arianne barely whispered the question.

"You long to find the love in marriage that your mother never had. You've most carefully and completely buried your heart away to protect it from the possibility that you, too, will know the feeling of being in a loveless marriage."

"I suppose what you say is most reasonable. She died so young, yet even as she lived, my mother was a broken woman. She never knew the love of her husband, only his lust. In many ways it was most merciful that she left this earth," Arianne reasoned, "and her pain."

Richard lifted her hand to his lips and lovingly kissed each finger. "Then you will never know her pain, my sweet wife, for I already love you."

Arianne's eyes widened at his declaration. Never before had Richard mentioned love. But even as her heart told her to tread lightly, her mind reminded her of the various times Richard's actions had already spoken of his heart's true feelings.

"It is true," Richard said with a smile. "I lost my heart to you when you threw yourself at my feet and begged me to marry you."

"I did not beg," Arianne said in mock horror. "I merely insisted you keep the bargain." Her lips curled ever so slightly at the corners.

Richard laughed and held her hand to his heart. "I would never have broken that bargain," he whispered. "Nay, even if the king himself had bid me do otherwise."

Arianne could feel the rapid beat of his heart beneath her hand. Without thought, she leaned her ear to his broad chest and listened to the steady pounding.

"It beats only for you, my Arianne," Richard said, gently stroking her hair. Before long they were both asleep, but only after Richard had spent a great deal of time in silent prayer. He longed for her heart to be healed of its pain and for her fears to be cast aside. He prayed for the day Arianne would come to him without fear in her heart.

It was on these intimate nights of long, private conversation that Richard pinned his hopes. He saw Arianne warm a little more each day to his company and began taking advantage of that warming to press her a little bit further. On many occasions he'd held her hand while they strolled the grounds, and in several daring moments he'd kissed her and found her very close to receptive. It became increasingly important to him that his wife come to love him.

⟳✷⟳

"Let us ride the estate this morning," Richard suggested after they'd shared breakfast one morning.

"I'd like that very much," Arianne answered. It had been a long time since she'd ridden.

"Good," he said, pulling her along with him. "I'd like it very much, as well." His smile was boyish, and his eyes danced merrily as though they were two children stealing away from the eyes of their parents.

With Arianne secured on her sidesaddle, Richard mounted and pointed the way. "There is a path along the waterfront and I would show it to you today."

"Lead on, Your Grace," she said in a teasing tone. She often forgot to call him Richard, and at times it became quite a joke between them.

Richard pressed his horse forward, and Arianne followed at a quick pace behind him until he slowed his mount and allowed the mare to catch up. They rode in silence, each enjoying the warmth of the sun and the view of the ocean that stretched out before them. They rode for over an hour before the land began to slowly slope downward toward the sea.

Arianne thrilled to the sound of the ocean upon the rocks. The power of each swell as the water pounded toward the shoreline captivated her in a way she'd not expected. It lulled her senses, and she found herself forgetting all that had gone before.

Richard, too, seemed to find the water refreshing. He spoke very little, occasionally pointing out some feature or fascination before leading them forward. Neither one saw the rain clouds that moved in and darkened the sky before it was too late to escape the downpour.

The rain came in torrents, saturating everything in sight. When thunder began to crack overhead, Richard sought shelter among the cliffs. "I know this land well. The cliffs will yield much in the way of protection," he reasoned with Arianne. She fought to stay seated, while each crash of thunder threatened to spill her from her saddle.

Eventually, Richard found the opening he was looking for. He dismounted and pulled the horses along a slight incline and then under the shelter of a rocky archway. Securing the horses, he reached up and pulled Arianne's drenched body

23

from the saddle. "Come," he said above the storm and pulled Arianne farther up the cliff side.

Arianne's heavy surcoat threatened to trip her as its velvet absorbed the torrential rain. Richard finally noticed her struggles and easily lifted her into his arms and carried her to the small cave.

Once inside the shelter, Arianne realized she'd wrapped her arms tightly around Richard's neck, while burying her face against his chest. She felt most reluctant to let go and so for several moments just relished the feel of his arms around her. The storm raged outside and Arianne trembled in fear from the noise.

"You are safe, Milady," Richard whispered against her ear. His warm breath caused her heart to pound harder.

Arianne forced herself to ease her hold. She felt Richard's hesitation to put her down and held her breath slightly in anticipation of what he would do.

Richard battled with his heart, mind, and soul as he held his wife. What he wanted to do was kiss her soundly and hold her. He could feel her shaking and wondered if it was the cold or her own fears that caused her to tremble. Gently, he lowered her to the ground, then bid her to sit with him on the floor of the cave where he opened his arms to hold her.

Arianne didn't hesitate to move against him. She was freezing and frightened, and time had proven Richard worthy of his promise. She had nothing to fear from this man, she reminded herself and snuggled down against him.

The storm continued with no sign of letting up, and with each crash of thunder, Arianne buried her head against Richard's chest and prayed that it would soon be over.

Without thought, Richard reached down and cupped her chin in his hand, lifting her face to meet his. He felt such joy at her obvious comfort in him that he couldn't resist pressing his advantage. Slowly, with painstaking effort to keep from frightening her, Richard lowered his lips in a gentle, searching kiss. Arianne's response was accepting, prompting Richard to deepen the kiss.

When he raised his mouth from hers, Arianne's cheeks were flushed red. "My sweet Arianne," he whispered before kissing her again.

Arianne felt confused by his actions. His kisses were pleasant enough and his touch comforting, but she longed to know for sure that she loved him and, as of yet, her heart could not confirm that matter. Frightened that her response might prompt a more intimate reaction, Arianne suddenly pushed away.

"I," she gasped slightly, trying to speak clearly, "I'm sorry, I can't." She started to move away, but found her gown caught beneath Richard's long legs.

"Don't be afraid, Arianne. I'll not harm you. I gave you my word. Now sit here with me and I will tell you more stories about my childhood."

Arianne immediately felt at ease. Richard had a way about him, and she doubted anyone could feel uncomfortable once he sought to assuage their fears. She allowed him to pull her close once again and waited for his story to begin.

"When I was quite young," Richard told her, "I was most fortunate to foster in the care of a godly man. As was the habit of fostering, I went from my parents' home at an early age and learned how to become a man worthy of knighthood.

"This man had been to the Holy Lands and told me such tales as I could scarce believe. He told me about writings that were set upon scrolls from the time of our Lord Jesus and how they told of His life. I was determined from that moment forward to one day have a closer look at those scrolls. I set out to find a way to journey to Jerusalem."

Arianne listened in fascination at the story Richard shared.

"When my guardian learned of my desire, he took me some twenty miles to a monastery, where I was allowed to study their copies of the written Scriptures. It was then that my heart was filled and my eyes opened to the truth of God. Our Lord Jesus Christ came to earth as a babe to give us life everlasting through His blood. I thought to myself what a wonderful gift this was, and the good friars of the church were amazed at my enthusiasm.

"I stayed with them for several months and studied all that they would teach. My heart craved an understanding of God, and it would not be satisfied until I had read every written Word. I spent hours in prayer, which the friars found fascinating. They naturally assumed that I would put myself into the service of the church, but it wasn't the direction I felt God's voice loudest. In fact, the church itself worried me most grievously."

Arianne sat up with a questioning look. "The church?" she questioned.

"Aye," Richard replied with a nod. "The church, it would seem, had somehow added many things that I did not see within the written Word of God. It appeared to me that man had taken upon himself to correct God's oversight."

"Your Grace!" Arianne exclaimed and crossed herself quickly. "What heresy do you speak?"

Richard smiled, knowing that Arianne had been raised in a convent where the church's ways were stressed as divine. " 'Tis no heresy I make, but a simple declaration of insight. The church would have you believe that it is the salvation of mankind, but 'tis our Lord Jesus Christ who holds that position."

"You could be hanged for heresy or burned alive!" Arianne exclaimed with a shudder.

"I do not generally share these words with those who would see me hanged or burned," he offered with a smile. "It is only my desire to share a deep and gratifying love of our God with you, sweet Arianne."

Arianne seemed to find reason in his words. She settled back against him and pressed a question. "Would you see the church dissolved?"

"Nay," Richard answered. "I would see it remade. I would see the Scriptures offered to all mankind and not only to a few pious priests. I would see that men and women of all rank and status would come to understand not only the fear of God as our judge, but the love of God for His children."

"It sounds quite wondrous," Arianne remarked. She realized that Richard's words of God had touched a deep chord within her. This man was nothing like her father. Duke Pemberton also saw the church as a problem, but for reasons of greed and personal gratification, not because the souls of a nation went tended without the truth.

Richard smiled at her sudden acceptance. Most would find his words beyond consideration, but Arianne actually found them worthy of contemplation.

"Have you a heart for the truth, Arianne?" Richard questioned softly, pushing her back enough to see her face.

"Aye," she whispered, thinking not only of God's truth, but of the truth her heart might show her about Richard.

"When we return to the castle, I will show you something most precious to me," Richard stated confidently. " 'Tis a copy of the Gospel of St. John. And a more wondrous book of wisdom you will not find."

Arianne seemed surprised that Richard's personal possessions would include a rare copy of the Scriptures. "I would be most honored to view them," she said honestly. "And, perhaps you could share more about your views of God."

Richard's heart soared. He felt more confident than ever that Arianne was the proper mate for him. Now if he could only allay her fears and teach her to trust him in full.

"What of your parents?" Arianne suddenly asked. "Do they share your views on God and the church?"

Richard frowned. "Nay, they are dead." It was the first time he had spoken of them, and Arianne was taken aback by the words.

"I did not know. Has it been long?" she asked softly.

Richard shook off the question as though he'd already said too much. "Look, the storm has abated. Let's press homeward and get you dry and warm," he said, pulling her to her feet. Arianne grimaced at his evasiveness, wondering again why he wouldn't speak of his family.

They stepped out of the cave and moved slowly down the slippery pathway to where the horses stood. Looking out across the sea, they were rewarded with a priceless display of colors.

"A rainbow," Arianne said, pointing to the sky.

"God's promise," Richard whispered against her ear. "It always fills me with renewed hope." The previous discomfort was forgotten.

Arianne lifted her face to Richard's and wondered at the man she had married. There was so much more to Richard DuBonnet, duke of Gavenshire, than met the eye. And so many unanswered questions.

26

Richard, feeling her eyes upon him, dropped his gaze to the warm brown eyes that beheld him. He turned her in his arms and held her close. "Ah, sweet Arianne—my Arianne," he whispered before kissing her.

Arianne no longer battled her worries. She slipped her arms around Richard's neck and returned his kiss. The moment passed much too quickly for both of them, and when Richard pulled away, Arianne could barely make out his words.

"Much renewed hope," he whispered and helped her into the saddle.

Chapter 4

U pon their return to the castle, Richard and Arianne were immediately set upon by several of the knights. Richard learned that an emissary of the king had called him to bring a good number of his men to lend protection as their entourage crossed Richard's vast open lands.

Richard brooded over the message, even while ordering his men into preparation for the trip. He didn't feel comfortable leaving the castle with so few men to defend it, but comforted himself with the thought that he had no known enemies who might lay siege to his home. Times were peaceful, and his people were content. Still, the summons did not set well with him, and his mood grew uncharacteristically harsh and somber.

Arianne, too, grew somber. She knew the time would come when Richard would be called away from home, but when she learned that his absence might stretch into weeks, she became more fearful than ever. In Richard's absence, she would be in charge of the castle, and all of its problems would be hers to solve with the aid of his chamberlain and steward.

She chided herself for her misgivings, reminding herself that this was the very work she'd been trained to do most of her young life. Still, Arianne knew the task before her was a great one, and she was struggling to acquaint herself with the people whom Richard so trusted and admired.

She recognized the help she would have in Douglas and Dwayne Mont Gomeri, brothers who were Richard's highest confidants. As his chamberlain and steward, they would remain behind to offer their services to Arianne in the running of the castle and its estates.

While it was indeed rare that Richard would travel without Douglas at his side to manage his affairs, the duke felt it in the best interests of all whom he loved that his chamberlain remain behind to support the new duchess. The brothers would also tend to the men left behind and the townspeople, should problems arise, but Arianne would command a place of great responsibility.

Upon reflection, Arianne was suddenly grateful to have spent so many hours in the company of Douglas and Dwayne. They dined daily with Richard and Arianne, along with several trusted knights who comprised an inner circle from which Richard drew wisdom and advice. Because of this, Arianne felt quite comfortable taking matters to them whenever Richard was unavailable.

Nevertheless, Arianne was only becoming used to Richard's presence in her life. The thought of lonely nights without his stories and shared confidences made her heart ache. She couldn't identify this new emotion. Dare she believe it was love?

It took less than a day for Richard to prepare his men, and Arianne waited for the inevitable good-bye. She sat in their chamber, quietly working on her sewing and wondering when he would come to her.

Then suddenly, as if answering her question, loud shouting could be heard in the hall below. Richard had been a relentless force to be reckoned with, and everyone in the household was near exhaustion in the wake of his black mood. The old apprehensions threatened to dispel Arianne's calm, and even though she felt certain that Richard's heart held love for her, she was powerless to keep the fear from her eyes. When he ranted at his men, he reminded her of her father. How could she ever convince him that she wasn't afraid, when indeed she was? Richard would never have believed her had she lied and told him otherwise, for always he said her eyes betrayed her heart.

Starting when the voices suddenly sounded in the hallway outside her chamber, Arianne pricked her finger on the needle and had to put aside her work. She sat like a little girl, sucking on her wounded finger, when Richard blasted through the door.

"It is time," he nearly bellowed, his mind still in the mode of dealing with his men. He crossed the room with heavy-footed strides and threw open one of the clothing chests. The wooden lid banged heavily against the footboard of the bed, but Richard was oblivious.

Arianne, however, cringed at the loudness. He reminded her of her father when he shouted and banged things about. She suddenly wished she could be anywhere else but dealing with this raging man who would command an army to protect the king.

Richard suddenly stopped to contemplate his silent wife. As if reading her thoughts, he stepped forward to where she sat.

"You needn't fear me, Milady," Richard stated firmly. "I am not your father. Now come, I would seek my pleasure upon those sweet lips before my journey takes me far from your side." His boyish grin was all that eased the tone of his words.

Arianne sat trembling and wondered if she could even rise to her feet. "I'm sorry, Your Grace," she whispered and forgot about her sore finger. She lowered her eyes to keep Richard from seeing the tears that formed there. Were they tears of fear, frustration, or of coming loneliness?

"I've given you no reason to fear me," Richard said in complete exasperation before adding, "and stop calling me Your Grace. My name is Richard!"

"Aye," Arianne replied, jumping at his agitated voice.

"And stop jumping every time I speak, and look at me when I talk to you," Richard demanded. The dread of leaving his home had worn his patience quite thin.

Arianne raised her face to meet his. The tears in her eyes threatened to spill at any moment, and Richard's heart softened.

"I'm only a man, Arianne. Look at me. No monstrous form stands here prepared to devour you, and I haven't killed anyone in days!"

Arianne straightened a bit and looked Richard in the eye, catching the humor in his voice and the hint of a smile.

Before she could prevent it, a nervous giggle escaped her lips. Richard smiled broadly, quite pleased with himself. *At least she has a sense of humor*, he thought.

"That's better," he said. "Now come and give me a long kiss. I said I'd leave you chaste for a spell, but I did not say I wouldn't work hard to shorten that span of time."

He was her Richard again, and Arianne threw herself willingly into his open arms. "I wish you didn't have to go," she cried softly.

"You will miss me then?" he asked good-naturedly.

Arianne pulled away. "Of course, I will miss you. You are like no other man I've known. You give so much and expect so little in return."

"Oh, sweet Arianne, I expect a great deal in return." He chuckled softly. "It's just that I am a man whose patience to obtain that which he desires outweighs all else. I'm glad you will miss me, for I shan't sleep a single night without your name upon my lips and the thought of your softness upon my mind."

"Will it truly be so very long?" she questioned hesitantly. Her brown eyes framed by dark, wet lashes grew wider in fear.

"Don't be afraid. Remember, God is by your side, my sweet wife. You must leave my safety and yours in the hands of One who can better deal with it," Richard said, tracing the soft angle of her jaw. "Now, I would have that kiss."

When their lips met, Arianne wished that he might never pull away. In her heart was a sudden foreboding of separation that threatened to strangle the very breath from her. What would become of her if Richard fell to some assassin's sword?

She clung desperately to his neck, knowing that she might be hurting him in her urgency, but so uncertain of her emotions that she could not do otherwise.

Richard sensed all her worries and fears and chose the kiss instead of words to ease his wife's tormented mind. He kissed her purposefully, with a tenderness that seemed so right, so necessary, that it held Richard in awe as well. As he lingered, feeling the tension of her arms give way to trembling, he knew that Arianne cared for him, and it gave him all the drive and passion that he needed to go forth and do his king's bidding.

He pulled away, but not before her tears mingled with the sweat on his face. Would he ever dry those eyes once and for all, he wondered. So much pain was mirrored in their depths, and Richard knew it was only the tiniest portion of what existed inside her heart.

"Be strong, Arianne," he whispered and gently wiped her cheeks. "Be strong and know that God is at your side. I'll be back before you know it, and all will be well."

Arianne nodded and offered the faintest hint of a smile before Richard turned away. He retrieved a bag of coins from the open chest, then without a single glance back, walked from the room and Arianne's sight.

∽◈⤳

In the days that followed, Matilda was Arianne's only real comfort. She spent a good portion of each day with Arianne and often played the comforting mother that Arianne so desperately needed. Many times they took to Arianne's private solarium, the room just off her bed chamber, and spoke for hours of life at Gavenshire and Richard's childhood.

"I don't understand," Arianne said one morning. "Why won't Richard speak of his family?"

"It pains him, Milady," Matilda said, offering nothing more.

"Aye, but he expects me to tell him of my woes," Arianne reasoned.

"But thou art his wife," Matilda replied. "And he is your husband and master. If 'tis a matter for you to understand, it must be His Grace that shares the story."

"You cared for his mother," Arianne continued. "Tell me of her. Was she beautiful? Was she kind? What did she like to do? Where did she come from?"

Matilda sighed. It was from bittersweet memories that she conjured the image of Richard's mother, Lady Evelyn. "She was like a breath of spring," Matilda finally said. "She was all that nobility and gentlefolk could hope to embrace and," the hesitancy was clear in the older woman's voice, "she loved her family with a love that blinded her to all else. She saw only good in people, and because there was only good within her own heart, she presumed others were the same."

"And Richard's father?" Arianne braved the question, hoping Matilda would continue.

"Richard's father was a good man. Highly admired by the king, he was often found in his court. His death was mourned by many," Matilda responded. " 'Twas his close friendship with His Highness that caused Richard to be taken under King Henry's personal care."

Arianne wanted to press for more, but something in Matilda's reply told her that they'd gone as far as the older woman would allow. "Thank you for telling me about them," Arianne whispered. "It's important that I know of them to better know my husband."

It was a start, Arianne reasoned. It was more than she'd known before, and it gave her hope that she might yet learn the full story of the people her husband kept so well hidden away.

Life moved at a painfully slow pace for Arianne. She oversaw her tasks in the castle with skill and strength born of youth, but her heart was not in it and her mind was always far from her home.

Nightly, she climbed into bed and ached for the familiar warmth of her husband. She thought for hours of how they would talk of things so seemingly trivial, yet in memory, they served to give her insight into Richard's needs and desires.

He had once told her of his love for soaking in a hot bath after working hard upon the training fields. Arianne had determined then that she would see to this need and be sure that hot water always waited in their chamber when he returned at day's end.

Then, too, he'd told her of his dislikes. He despised cold food and greasy meat. He hated injustice and mock humility and found even a slightly arrogant man better than one who cowered in feigned subjection. Wool tunics chafed his neck, and he'd stubbornly clung to the same saddle for his warhorse since he'd first acquired the mount. All these things recounted themselves in Arianne's memory.

"I will line his wool tunics with silk," she mused while closing her eyes in sleep. "I will begin tomorrow, and perhaps by the time I've finished, Richard will be home." It offered slight comfort to tell herself this, but Arianne had to have something to look forward to.

⤇

After nearly two weeks had passed, a messenger came to Gavenshire Castle bearing tidings from Richard. The messenger sought out the new duchess to assure her of her husband's safety and left nearly as quickly, taking back with him two of the newly lined tunics and Arianne's fondest wishes for his speedy return.

The incident had both comforted and tormented Arianne. To ease her pain, she arranged to take a long ride. Sir Dwayne accompanied her and, much to Arianne's relief, seemed to understand that she didn't wish to talk.

They rode silently across the land. Only when Arianne reined her mare to a halt, high above the restless sea, did she speak. "He did not say when he would return?"

"Nay, Milady, he did not," her companion replied.

"And what think ye on the matter, Sir Dwayne?"

"I cannot truly say, Milady," the man spoke honestly, then added with a grin, "however, knowing how His Grace feels about his wife, I would say he will make haste in returning once the king has released him to do so."

Arianne smiled and nodded. "Richard may be a patient man, but that has never been one of my virtues. Let us return to the castle and see to the noon meal."

Sir Dwayne nodded and followed Arianne as she urged the mare into a trot. He admired this woman as he had no other, save his mother. She was intelligent and quick with solutions whenever crisis arose, but she was also kind and compassionate, and he felt certain she was responsible for the happiness he'd seen in

Richard's eyes. Happiness that, though haunted by an untold bitter past, seemed strong enough to dispel the ugly wounds and knit together peace and healing.

Arianne never looked back as she pushed the mare home. She'd come to love her new home, Richard's home, and for reasons beyond her comprehension, Arianne found it necessary to return quickly. Perhaps Richard had returned, she dared to hope. With that in mind she gave the mare full freedom to stretch into a jarring gallop, mindless of Sir Dwayne's surprise.

She came rapidly upon the castle and immediately spied the congregation of mounted men that stood at the gatehouse. "Richard has returned!" she called over her shoulder. Still she didn't slow, even though she thought her riding companion called back to her. She ran the mare the full length of the way and only reined back when she reached the men.

Arianne immediately felt a sense of confusion. She was still so unfamiliar with Richard's men that she couldn't find a single face that she could place with a name. Jumping from her horse, Arianne lost track of Sir Dwayne as she pushed through the crowd.

"Where is my husband?" she questioned one man who stood at the gatehouse entrance. He said nothing but pointed through the gateway.

Arianne wondered silently where Sir Dwayne was and turned to see if she could glimpse him when she walked into the solid wall of an armored man.

"Ho, Wench," he said and grabbed her arm tightly. He immediately noted the richness of her garments and the ring that marked her left hand.

Arianne twisted her body to pull away from the painful grip but found it impossible to break his hold.

"I demand that you unhand me," Arianne spat defiantly. "Sir Dwayne!" she called, but silence was her only answer.

The man who held her laughed in a low, quiet way that caused the skin on Arianne's arms to crawl. She couldn't see his face for the armor he wore, but it wouldn't matter if she could. These men were strangers, and she'd managed to place herself in the middle of them.

Lifting her chin and fixing her brown eyes on the man's covered face, Arianne was determined to show no fear.

"Who are you, and why do you handle me so?" she finally questioned.

The man suddenly released her, but Arianne knew better than to move. She was pressed in by a dozen mounted men and Sir Dwayne was nowhere to be found. She waited silently while the man reached up to take the helmet from his head.

Hard and determined eyes stared back at her, and a cruel smile played upon the lips of her captor. "You must be the duchess of Gavenshire," he said in a tone akin to sarcasm.

"I am," Arianne replied, standing her ground. "What business have you here?"

The man looked away laughing, then in a flash turned angry eyes back to appraise Arianne. "You must satisfy the duke greatly," he said in a guttural way that made Arianne feel sick. "I must say I am most pleased at this turn of events."

"I'm sure I do not understand," Arianne replied. She could feel her determination to be strong crumbling into the terror she'd known so much of her life. "I ask you again, what business have you here?"

Without warning, the man's mailed hand flashed out to strike her across the face. The blow sent Arianne sprawling to the ground, where she sat trying to focus her eyes and rid her mind of the threatening darkness.

"You will not take that tone with me," the man sneered. "I'm not in the habit of answering for my actions to stupid women."

The words infuriated Arianne. How dare he call her stupid; but then hadn't she been just that? It was her choice to ride right up into the midst of them, offering herself over as if she were glad to see them. Slowly, she got to her feet to face the man once again. She said nothing, but her angry brown eyes spoke more than words ever could. The man actually seemed taken aback, but only for a moment.

"I will answer your question, but only because it pleases me to do so. I am here today to take you as my hostage until your husband returns so that I might seek my revenge and end his worthless life."

Arianne sank to her knees, her head still aching and ringing with the words of her husband's obvious enemy. He planned to kill Richard, and he planned to use her in order to accomplish it!

Chapter 5

Arianne knew nothing except that she was being lifted up by two of the nearby men. She was half-dragged, half-carried through the gatehouse and into the open bailey outside the castle proper. The men who'd been left behind to defend the keep and its people drew swords and any other available weapon and stepped forward.

At the sight of the armed men, the leader raised his hand and called a halt to the thirty or so men who followed him. A half circle of Gavenshire protectors stood between the men and the castle, making their presence and intentions well known.

The enemy leader, helmet in hand, lowered his chain-mailed arm and spoke. "I am Lord Tancred," he announced. "I claim this castle for my own and its people as well. You may shed your blood here today or you may hand over your weapons in peace. Either way, you will be my prisoners until the return of your duke."

There was a murmur of voices through the crowd, but not one man offered to lower his weapons. Arianne stood proudly straight between her captors at the sight of her people. They were loyal to her and Richard and they would not bend easily.

Douglas Mont Gomeri stepped forward, sword drawn and ready to strike. He moved within ten feet of the man called Tancred before stopping. "I am the chamberlain of this castle and in His Grace's absence, I am the protector of Her Grace and these people. We will not yield our arms to you."

"That is a pity," Tancred said and rubbed his mailed hand over his helmet, contemplating the man before him. "For you see, my foolish man, we have already captured the duchess and her guard."

At this Arianne was pushed forward to fall in the dirt at Tancred's feet. Before she could move, Tancred dropped his helmet and pulled his own sword in one fluid motion. Grabbing a handful of Arianne's hair, Tancred yanked her to her knees and held the sword to her throat. He returned his gaze to the young knight before him with an evil grin.

"Perhaps," Tancred said in a low hush, "you would like to reconsider your position."

"Nay, Sir Douglas, he knows he cannot kill me and have Richard, too!" Arianne exclaimed. "He will not harm me." Arianne's self-confidence was quickly lost when Tancred's heavy hand slammed across her face. This time Arianne felt her body go limp as blackness covered her eyes.

⤳

"Milady," Matilda whispered overhead. A cool cloth was brought against her face as consciousness returned to Arianne DuBonnet.

"Matilda!" Arianne gasped and struggled to sit up.

"Nay, Milady. Do not move. You took quite a blow and should rest," Matilda said firmly.

"Then it is all true," Arianne stated in a resigned tone. "I had prayed it was but a nightmare, and now I awaken to find that it is cruelly true."

"I am sorry, Milady." Matilda had tears in her eyes. She rinsed the rag in the basin before applying it once again to Arianne's bruised face.

"What are we to do now, I wonder?" Arianne didn't expect Matilda to reply, but the older woman had no other choice.

"He is waiting," the maid said solemnly. "He demanded that you be brought to him the minute you regained your wits."

"What of our people?" Arianne questioned suddenly, remembering Sir Douglas's bold stand.

"They laid down their arms when he threatened to hurt you. He told Sir Douglas that he wouldn't kill you, but he would torture you until he yielded. No knight could allow such a thing to happen."

"Oh, Matilda," Arianne cried, "this is all my fault. If I hadn't put myself right in their midst, this wouldn't have happened."

"You cannot blame yourself," Matilda said softly. "No one expected this to happen. No one thought he would come."

Arianne caught a note of something in Matilda's voice. "No one thought he would come," she whispered. "Who is he?"

Just then the door slammed open and an armed man entered the room. "My master is awaiting Her Grace," he said gruffly. "I am to bring her to the great hall."

Matilda stood between the man and Arianne, trying for all she was worth to make her barely five-foot-high frame look menacing. "Milady is injured. Surely your master can wait!"

"Out of my way, Woman," the man said, pushing Matilda to one side. He reached down and pulled Arianne to her feet with a snarled growl.

Arianne's head reeled from the action. She felt herself sway and might have fallen except for the strong arm that steadied her and pulled her forward.

They moved down the hall and then to the stone stairs that would take them to the floor below. Arianne looked around her as if contemplating her escape. Very little had changed except for the presence of Tancred's men. She held her hand against the side of her face where the throbbing hurt most. It caused her mind to drift unwillingly to her youth and the heavy-handedness of her father.

The man at her side seemed not to notice or to care that she was in pain. He was doing his master's bidding.

Tancred sat discussing some matter with two of his men when the knight entered the room with Arianne. The men seemed anxious to be about their orders and barely acknowledged the fact that she had joined them. Tancred noted her entrance, however, and Arianne found herself forgetting about her bruised face.

For a moment she paused, noticing that Tancred had taken the coif of chain mail from his head, giving her a better view of him. He had dark, unruly hair and piercing eyes that seemed to change color even as he lifted them in greeting. There was a lifetime of anger in the eyes that met hers, and with haughty determination, Arianne met their stare straight on.

The man at her side pushed her into a chair, where Arianne made herself straighten with as much poise and dignity as she could muster. She would not back down from this man, cowering as though she were a chambermaid. Nay! She was the duchess of Gavenshire, and her position demanded that she act accordingly. To do otherwise would betray her people's trust.

She waited in silence for Tancred to speak, wondering who this man was and why he had come to kill Richard. If only she'd had a few more moments alone with Matilda. Matilda seemed to know exactly who he was; perhaps she even knew why he hated them so much. At the first possible opportunity, she would have to seek out Matilda and learn whatever she knew.

Tancred dismissed the man who'd accompanied Arianne, but he ignored Arianne. He leaned back against the chair she'd often seen Richard in and scowled at the wall across the room.

Arianne fought the urge to squirm uncomfortably. Perhaps that was what he wanted, she thought and doubled her efforts to remain regal and still. Finally, when Arianne thought she could take no more, Tancred turned to her.

"When is your husband to return?"

"I do not know," Arianne replied honestly. For once she was glad that she didn't know Richard's plans.

"I see," Tancred said and returned to a thoughtful mode before speaking again.

"Mayhap," Tancred began, "you think this a sport. If that is your thought, Madam, I assure you there is no game in this. I am here to take back what is rightfully mine and to avenge my name. Your husband's blood is the only thing that will do that."

"Nay!" Arianne exclaimed and jumped to her feet without thought. "You will not take him!"

Tancred laughed viciously and got to his feet. "You must love him a great deal," he replied in a sarcastic tone. Nevertheless, his words struck a chord in Arianne's heart.

"Given Richard's softness toward the lovely things of this world, I imagine that he, too, cares greatly for you. He yearns to be home like a wounded man longs to be rid of pain. He will make his way home quickly," Tancred continued.

"My husband has already been gone a fortnight," Arianne answered. "I don't expect him to be released from his service any time soon. Why not retreat with your men before he returns? Perhaps you will be no worse for this confrontation."

Tancred snarled and stepped so close to Arianne that she could smell the sourness of his breath. "Milady, you will afford me the respect I am due. You will address me as Lord Tancred and you will serve me as master. It is my right. You are spoils of war!"

"I serve only the risen Lord and my husband," Arianne stated angrily. "I call no man Lord and will certainly not do so for the likes of you!"

Tancred slapped her, but it wasn't anywhere near the blow that had come from his mail-covered hand. "Silence, Wench! You need to learn some manners."

Arianne faced him with tears stinging her eyes. She was determined to stand her ground. "Even an animal learns more from kindness than abuse," she braved.

Tancred stepped back. His expression showed his surprise at her change of tactics. Shrugging it off, he continued as though she'd never spoken. "I care not for your devotion to God or man. I have taken this castle in an act of war and by the rights of that capture, you are mine to do with as I choose. It is not my fault that your husband is a fool. He left a handful of bedraggled knights and peasants to defend a castle and keep. He must pay the price as would any other fool. He forfeits that which was once his."

"He will return," Arianne said suddenly, her heart speaking ahead of her mind. "But he is no fool to march into this castle to dance from a gibbet for your pleasure."

"Perhaps not," Tancred replied. "But I care not either way. I have you, and from what I know of your duke, he will die before he sees one hair on your head harmed."

Arianne began to tremble. "Who are you, and how is it that you know my husband?"

Tancred opened his mouth to speak, then abruptly closed it again. He went back to the table and took his seat. To Arianne, he looked completely burdened by the task before him.

"Who are you?" Arianne pressed, coming to stand on the opposite side of the table.

"It is of no concern to you."

"You plan to murder my husband and me. Do I not have a right to address my executioner?" Arianne asked.

He looked at her for a moment before a wicked grin spread across his face. "I have no plan to kill you, Milady."

Arianne grimaced at the picture in her mind. "If you kill my husband and dare to lay a hand on me," Arianne barely whispered, "I will see to it myself."

"What? A devoted woman of God such as yourself would brave the fires of hell and take her own life?" Tancred questioned with a sardonic laugh.

"Am I not already standing amidst the flames as we speak?" she inquired, pushing her hair away from her face.

"Touché, Milady." For a moment Arianne saw a glimmer of something other than the hatred in Tancred's eyes. But just as quickly, the harshness returned. "It is true, you have no say in the matter. Once your husband clears my name, the king himself will demand his head and I will in turn be given these lands and your fair hand, if I so choose."

"Never!" Arianne spat the word and turned to go.

"Stay where you are! I did not give you leave."

Arianne turned. The rage in her eyes was nearly enough to silence her enemy, but the wildness of her appearance only enhanced her beauty.

"You will yield to my demands." Tancred's words were firm, leaving Arianne little doubt that he would press the issue if she did not remain silent.

"Richard will be warned," she finally said. "Someone will find a way to ride to him and warn him of your presence. My husband will not be fooled into returning empty-handed."

"He will also not be foolish enough to risk that which he no doubt prizes most," Tancred replied. "You forget, my dear duchess. I hold his castle and folk, but most of all, I hold you. That fact alone will drive him quite mad with worry and muddy his thinking."

Arianne began to shake. She clutched her hands together tightly to keep Tancred from seeing the effect his words had. Fearfully, she realized Tancred was probably right. Richard did love her, given his patience and gentleness regarding their marriage bed. He would no doubt be determined to protect her and free her, just as Tancred said.

Chapter 6

Arianne paced the confines of her bed chamber, fretting over how she might get word to Richard. The fear that Tancred would see her husband dead brought tears to her eyes and a tightness to her breast. Somehow she must save her husband!

The narrow window seemed to beckon her, and Arianne momentarily halted her pacing and went to view the situation from the opening. Nothing seemed amiss. There were men in the bailey below, some with their hauberks of chain mail clothing their bodies, others with simple leather tunics and woolen surcoats. It was really no different from when Richard's knights were in control, she thought.

People moved more quietly, Arianne noticed. Women seemed to go out of their way to keep from coming in contact with Tancred's men, and Arianne was certain the reason was the men's lack of respect and chivalry. Gavenshire's people were to be treated as spoils of war, hadn't Tancred said as much? No one was safe—nor would they be until Richard was reinstated.

A light knock at her chamber door brought Arianne whirling on her heel. "Who goes there?" she called.

" 'Tis I, Milady," Matilda replied and Arianne quickly went to lift the bar from the door.

Arianne ushered Matilda into the room, then replaced the bar before questioning her maid. "How goes it below?"

"I cannot bear to think that His Grace will be trapped by this group of uncouth ruffians, Milady. They fight amongst themselves nearly as much as they would war with our people," Matilda replied.

Arianne forgot all about asking Matilda if she knew who Tancred was and what he wanted when another knock, this one loud and demanding, struck upon her door.

"You are to take supper below with Lord Tancred," a man's gruff voice called from the other side.

Arianne rolled her eyes and Matilda openly quaked at the command. "Very well, tell Tancred I will be there shortly," Arianne replied, refusing to call the man her lord.

Matilda reached out to take hold of Arianne's arm. "You must be careful, Milady. He is evil and cares not for the welfare of you or your people."

Arianne's mind was preoccupied, however, and she barely heard the words.

"Help me dress, Matilda. I daren't keep him waiting."

As Matilda helped her into a clean linen tunic of pale green, Arianne's mind already raced with how she could get a messenger to Richard. "Tell me, Matilda, what have they done with Richard's men? Where are Sir Douglas and Sir Dwayne?"

"I'm afraid they've all been locked in the west tower, Milady. It's heavily guarded and no one is allowed near, not even to give them food," Matilda answered and brought out a dark green samite surcoat to go over the tunic.

Arianne frowned at this news. "Someone has to ride and warn Richard," she thought aloud.

"Yes, Milady, but who can go?" Matilda questioned. She brought one of Arianne's jeweled belts and secured it around her hips before retrieving slippers from one of the chests.

"I will learn what I can while I sup with Tancred. I don't know how, but one way or another, someone will leave this castle tonight and take warning to my husband!"

Arianne walked gingerly down the stone stairway. She moved as silently as possible, hoping that it might be her good fortune to overhear Tancred or his men as they discussed their plans. Her stomach growled loudly at the rich aroma of meat as it roasted on spits in the kitchen. Arianne realized she'd not eaten since morning, but with the soreness of her bruised jaw, she wondered if chewing would be possible.

She entered the great hall hesitantly for all was silent except for the rustling movements of servants. It was a far cry from when Richard was in charge. With Richard, the hall was full of hungry men and others who had come at his welcome to eat. How she missed him! How she feared for him!

Moving to the table, Arianne realized that the room was not as empty as she'd hoped. Tancred sat before the fireplace, deep in thought as if contemplating the fate of the world. Her foot caught on something, making a sudden sound. Tancred sprang to his feet, hand on the hilt of his sword and eyes narrowing dangerously. Seeing it was only her, Tancred relaxed his grip and gave a mocking bow.

"Your Grace, it is good of you to honor me with your presence." His words were slightly slurred, leaving Arianne little doubt that he'd had a great deal to drink before her arrival.

She nodded but did nothing more until he held out a chair and commanded her to sit. Moving in lithe silence, Arianne did as she was bid and grimaced when he took the seat beside her.

"We will speak of your husband," he said, and then, as if noticing the discoloration on her face for the first time, he frowned. "You will choose your words carefully so that this is not necessary again," he said, pointing to her jaw.

" 'Twas not necessary the first time," Arianne stated with a fixed stare of hostility. "You are surely in command here. You are larger than me, more powerful, and you have a great many men to afford you aid should it be necessary to vanquish your foe. Surely one woman, such as myself, offers no real resistance to a great knight such as yourself."

"True," Tancred replied, motioning a servant forward. The boy placed a platter of roast before the man and started to leave. "Halt, Serf!" Tancred called. "Bring more wine and be quick about it!"

Arianne watched the poor boy bow quickly before running from the room. His name was Gabe, she remembered, and he had always been most congenial in his work. Funny that it should cross her mind just now. Perhaps, Arianne thought, he could be the one to get a message to Richard. It was worth considering.

When the boy returned with the wine, Tancred took it from him and poured himself a generous amount. When he reached for Arianne's goblet, she placed her hand over it.

"Nay," she spoke hesitantly. "I do not wish it."

Tancred shrugged, but Gabe paled at her protest. Arianne wished she could ease the boy's fears, but it would be necessary to ease her own before she would be of any help to others.

"I would like water, Gabe," she continued.

"Aye, Milady," he replied. "I'll bring a pitcher fresh from the well." Gabe waited momentarily to receive Tancred's nod of approval.

Tancred looked first at Arianne's fixed expression and then to the boy. "Do as your lady bids," he replied and went about serving himself a huge piece of beef.

Arianne waited patiently while Tancred served himself and then, almost as an afterthought, sliced a piece of beef from his own trencher and put it on hers.

"Thank you," she replied softly.

Tancred took the acceptance of the food as a serious accomplishment and continued to fill Arianne's plate with a variety of foods after serving himself.

Gabe brought the water and Tancred dismissed him, while Arianne timidly tried to chew the meat. It was difficult, but not impossible, and her hunger was all the encouragement she needed. That and the thought that she needed to stay healthy and strong for Richard.

"You are a beautiful woman, Duchess," Tancred murmured over the rim of his goblet.

Arianne's head snapped up with a look of astonishment. What game would he play now?

As if reading her mind, Tancred reached out and snatched the head covering she wore and tossed it to the floor. Arianne's copper hair was bound in a single thick braid, which seemed to intrigue Tancred even more.

"Unbind your hair," he commanded and waited while Arianne slowly reached up to unfasten the cord that held it. She ran her fingers through the mass until the braid was unwound, then returned Tancred's stare with blazing eyes.

"Might I sup now?" she questioned with more sarcasm than she'd intended. Her tone served its purpose and broke Tancred's spell.

"By my leave," he smirked. "Eat all that you will. It will not change anything, nor will it keep you from my attentions."

"Very well, Sire," Arianne replied with an overexaggerated sigh and returned her attention to the meal. She felt her hand trembling as she lifted a piece of bread to her mouth and could only pray that he did not see it. She did not wish to appear weak and vulnerable to him.

The meal continued in relative silence. From time to time, Tancred would roar out an order to Gabe for a refilling of his wine cup, but other than that, he seemed content or at least tolerant to let Arianne eat in peace.

Arianne knew when she finished eating that it was a signal of sorts for Tancred to speak. She put her napkin upon the table, folded her hands in her lap, and waited for what would come.

Tancred studied her from drunken eyes. His rage toward Richard seemed muted against her beauty, and for a moment he thought of nothing but the woman beside him.

"The property of this land gives much to warm my heart," he slurred. He reached out a hand and touched the long sleeve of Arianne's tunic.

Reflexively, she jerked her arm away and gasped. "Do not touch me! For all you think you own, I belong to Richard." She regretted her harsh response, fearing another strike would be her punishment, but Tancred's laughter was all that came.

"You belong to an absent duke, eh? A man who had not the wit about him to leave his lady better guarded. Nay, Milady. You belong to me, and a more pleasant arrangement I cannot imagine."

Arianne felt her heart leap with fear. Her own safety had been far from her mind in her worries for Richard. Now a terrible thought filled her mind. What if Tancred forced himself upon her and stole her virtue before Richard and she could consummate their marriage? The thought sickened her.

"I belong to my husband," Arianne stressed. "I am his wife in the eyes of God, the church, and these people. Would you impose your will upon holy bonds?"

"I would and I do," Tancred said, taking yet another deep draw of the wine.

"Is nothing holy to you then?" Arianne questioned.

"Holy? Pray tell what should I find holy, Madam?" Tancred asked, getting to his feet. He pushed the chair back abruptly, sending it backward against the floor. He staggered back a pace, steadied himself, then glared leeringly at Arianne. "Marriage vows or naught, I made but one vow—for revenge."

"Why do you hate my husband so?"

Tancred seemed taken aback by this line of questioning. He grew thoughtful, and Arianne fervently prayed that God would somehow deliver her from the lustful hands of the man before her.

"Your husband," he spoke, twisting his lips into a cruel smile, "cost me everything that was rightfully mine. He poisoned the mind of the king and the people against me, and he must pay."

"My husband would not do that without reason," Arianne replied in defense of Richard. "He is a good man, kind and virtuous, and I would not hear him defamed in his own hall."

"Ugh! Good? Kind? Virtuous? Nay, Milady." Tancred staggered forward and slammed his hands to the table. The very ground around her seemed to shake, and Arianne felt her heart in her throat.

Tancred moved closer to her and reached out to hold a coppery lock. "Nay, those are the words of a loving wife—a maiden in her youth besot with her husband. True love is a rare commodity in this world. Pity you waste yours on one such as Richard DuBonnet."

Tancred's words hit harder than any slap. Arianne sucked her breath in noticeably at the statement of love. Did she love Richard? Was this the proof she'd searched her heart for? Looking deep inside, Arianne felt a warmth spread throughout her body.

Yes! Arianne nearly jumped from her seat. Yes, she loved Richard! It seemed so understandably clear. Her fears for him, the way she missed him and longed for his companionship. It had nothing to do with the lust that she saw in Tancred's eyes and it had nothing to do with the fear that her mother had lived with every day of her married life. She loved Richard with a pure and free love that held no fear or contempt.

Tancred had no idea what thoughts raced through Arianne's head. He saw only the grace and beauty of the woman beside him. He longed for more than the brief touch of her silken hair.

With Arianne's thoughts on Richard, she missed the look of determination in Tancred's eyes. She was stunned when he yanked her up from her seat and tried to kiss her.

Arianne brought her foot down hard on his, but her slippers were no match for his booted feet. She pushed him away and was surprised when her small effort actually caused him to stumble backward.

"Please, God," she prayed aloud. "Please be the protector and companion that Richard says You are and protect me from this man!" Her eyes were lifted upward for only a moment, but when she lowered them, she found her prayers already answered. Tancred continued to stagger backward until he met the wall. From there, he slowly slid down until he landed with a thud on the floor.

"A waste," he murmured and passed out from the drink.

Arianne breathed a prayer of thanksgiving even as she bolted from the room and ran up the stairs.

Chapter 7

Reaching her chamber door, Arianne started at the sound of footsteps behind her. Turning, she let her breath out in a sigh of relief. "Matilda! Hurry, we must make plans."

"I feared for your safety, Milady. Are you well?" Matilda hurried into the room behind Arianne.

"Aye, but not for long. 'Twas only the hand of God that kept me from sharing Tancred's bed this night. I cannot risk such a thing again. I will escape the castle and warn Richard myself," Arianne announced.

Matilda nodded. "I can help," she whispered. "Let me fetch less noticeable garments from my room. They will be a bit big for you, but with a belt they should do well enough." Arianne nodded and paced nervously during Matilda's absence.

"Dear God," she prayed, "I don't even know the land well enough to find my way, much less do I know where Richard might be. Help me, God. Please help me again."

Matilda returned breathless and thrust forward the simple garments. "These will do," she said and helped Arianne to doff her richer wardrobe.

Arianne pulled the thin linen tunic over her head. It was a dark gray color and had seen many washings. The woolen surcoat was nothing more than a shapeless shift of dark blue. She pulled it over her head and with Matilda's help tied a corded belt around her waist.

"We must hide your hair, Milady, for there is no other with such a mane. Come, I will plait it down the back and we will secure it beneath a mantle. I have a dark cloak that will hide you well in the shadows. Now, have you sturdy boots?"

Arianne nodded at Matilda's words and pointed to the chest at the far side of the room. She sat obediently while Matilda dressed her hair and then pulled the boots on while Matilda retrieved the cloak.

Peering down the hallway, the women cautiously moved toward the stairs. Matilda put her hand out and stopped Arianne suddenly. "Nay, let us use the back stairs. They lead straight into the kitchen, and from there I can get you to the tunnels below."

"The tunnels?" Arianne said in shocked, but grateful surprise.

Matilda nodded and pulled her lady along the dimly lit hall. They descended the stairs cautiously, and when they reached the kitchen, Matilda held

Arianne back while she went alone to make certain the room was clear of any of Tancred's men.

"Hurry, Milady," Matilda urged and pulled Arianne into the kitchen. "I will get you food and water. Stay over there in the shadows, and I will take you below in a moment." Arianne moved quickly as Matilda had instructed. It didn't matter that her servant was issuing orders. All that mattered was that she loved Richard and had to find him before he forfeited his life in Tancred's snare.

Matilda brought a small pack designed from one of the tablecloths and filled with provisions. She took one last glance around the room before slipping into the buttery where the wine was kept. Here she revealed a small trap door behind a stack of kegs. "We'll need the torch, Milady," Matilda said with a slight motion of her head to the wall.

Arianne pulled the torch from its place and handed it to the woman. "I suppose this is the best way," she whispered apprehensively.

" 'Tis the only way to escape unnoticed," Matilda replied and started down the ladder that would take them to the tunnels. "When I reach the bottom," she whispered back to Arianne, "throw down the pack and come quickly. Remember to pull the door shut over your head."

Arianne moved quickly and quietly and soon joined her maid in the damp, dank maze beneath the castle foundations. Matilda took hold of Arianne's arm after handing her back the pack of food, then holding the torch high, she moved down the narrow corridor. After they'd gone quite a ways, Matilda stopped for them to catch their breath.

"I must tell you how to leave this place," Matilda said after resting a moment. "We can speak freely here for no one will hear us. Richard will return from the east and so you must go in that direction once you are free of the castle. This tunnel will lead to the cliff walls over the sea. You must move down toward the beach, but not too far. You will have to work your way along the cliff wall until you reach a place where their heights are half of what they are from this place. This will be the sign you are looking for. Here you will climb upward to the top. It will not be easy, Milady."

"I will manage it," Arianne stated firmly. "God will be my helper."

"Aye, that He will," Matilda replied with a weak smile. "I can see you share Richard's heart toward a merciful God who stays at our sides."

"At first, I wasn't certain what to think about it all," Arianne mused. "Truth be told, it seemed to be heresy and I told Richard so. I had been raised to believe that the church held the only true way. But, these weeks without my husband have given me much time to consider his words. I believe that God would have us worship Him and not a religion. I might be burned at the stake for such words, but it is my heart toward the matter."

"You have a good heart, Lady Arianne," Matilda responded with such love that Arianne reflexively leaned forward and embraced the woman.

"Thank you for befriending me, Matilda. I know not what I would have done without your kindness. Now, quickly tell me what I must do after I leave the cliffs."

"There is a woods near the place where you will emerge. Take your cover there. The forest runs the length of the road for several miles and it will provide you protection from Tancred's men. The road will be the one upon which Richard will return. Rest assured that you will hear his men from the woods and you can approach him before he is endangered," Matilda answered.

"What if I move beyond the trees?" Arianne asked. "What then?"

"The land beyond the trees is hilly and open meadowland. You won't find much in the way of hiding places there. It might be best if you wait for Richard to come to you. The woods are a good ways from the castle and will give him ample time to prepare for attack. All that will matter to him is your safety. After that, he will do what he must."

"Very well. Now how do I reach the opening of this tunnel?"

"You will continue down this way," Matilda motioned with the torch. "Always stay to the right of any fork and you will soon be to the end of it." Matilda turned from Arianne for a moment and raised the torch higher. Spying what she needed, Matilda left Arianne's side and retrieved an unlit torch. Setting the second piece ablaze, Matilda handed it to Arianne. "Be certain to extinguish it before you leave the tunnel. It would be a beacon to the guards as they keep watch upon the land."

Arianne nodded, tucked the food pack down the inside of the woolen garment, and took the torch. "Kneel with me, Matilda, and we will pray."

"Surely that is the very best we can do," Matilda remarked and joined Arianne on the dirt floor.

The women offered their silent prayers, then quickly got back to their feet. "God's speed, Lady Arianne."

Arianne nodded and moved quickly down the corridor. She was a woman with a mission and that mission would save the life of her husband and his men. No matter the cost to herself, she had to find Richard and warn him. Then another thought passed through her mind as she edged down the inky blackness.

"I have to tell him that I love him," Arianne breathed aloud. "Most merciful Father, let me tell him that I love him."

The tunnel soon opened out on the cliffs, just as Matilda had told her it would. It was well concealed, however, with a huge boulder that hid the opening from appearing too conspicuous. Arianne put out the torch in the soft sandy dirt and waited a moment while her eyes adjusted to the dark.

She swallowed back her fears and moved out of the tunnel until she stood on the cliff side. Below, the water was stilled in black oblivion. Above, the moon shone dimly in a crescent sliver that would offer little light to direct her steps. Arianne moved cautiously down the rock wall as Matilda had instructed her.

It was imperative that Arianne make the forest under the cover of darkness. She would work at it all night if necessary. She felt her tender hands being torn by the sharp rocks and more than once felt her skirt catch and tear. Her courage was quickly leaving her as she drew ever closer to the water, but just then the rocks evened out and presented a path of sorts.

Arianne moved more quickly along the flattened path, but held herself back from speed, knowing that she was uncertain of each step. Hours passed before the cliff walls lowered themselves as Matilda had promised they would. Arianne gauged the heights to be half those at the castle and, summoning up the last of her determination, she began the climb to the cliff tops.

The rocks bit at her hands and knees as she inched her way upward. Silently, Arianne issued petitions to God for guidance and surefootedness, but always she kept moving—love mingled with concern motivating her forward.

At the top, Arianne stretched out her body and lay flat on the ground. She could see very little in the darkness but knew from Matilda's instructions that the shadowy blackness to her left was the woods.

After catching her breath, Arianne struggled to her feet and took off in a slow run for the trees. She slowed her step when she put her foot in a hole and nearly fell. Knowing that she could just as easily have broken a leg or twisted her ankle, Arianne tried to be more careful.

The trees loomed just ahead, and as she grew nearer, Arianne felt truly afraid. What if some wild beast awaited her in the darkness? What if she lost her way and moved in circles? She remembered Matilda's words. The forest ran along the road. She must stay close to the forest edge and keep the skies overhead in sight. When dawn came, she would move farther into the protection of the trees.

Keeping all of this in mind, Arianne worked for hours in the darkness. She stopped after a time, pulled the pack from her dress, and opened it. She quickly quenched her thirst and ate a piece of bread. When she started to rewrap the contents, her hand fell upon something long and cold. Feeling it gingerly, Arianne realized it was a knife. She took it gratefully and tucked it into her belt. Now, at least, she had some form of protection.

The pack was hurriedly replaced inside her gown before Arianne moved out. Cold dampness permeated her bones, and Arianne ached from the demands of her journey. Never before had she been required to endure anything so difficult, and she was certain that had it been a mission of less importance, she would have given up.

The moon had moved far to the western skies when Arianne realized that she couldn't take another step. She managed to move deeper into the trees, knowing that she would soon collapse in exhaustion. Feeling her way in the darkness, Arianne found a clump of bushes, rolled herself beneath them, and succumbed to her body's demands. Her last waking thoughts were of Richard. Her last words were whispered prayers for his safety.

Chapter 8

Arianne came awake slowly, forgetting for a moment where she was and why. She stretched out her cramped limbs and wondered why her hands hurt so much. Then the pungent smells of dirt and decaying vegetation arrested her senses, and Arianne snapped instantly awake.

She tried to focus on her surroundings and found that she was well hidden beneath a huge mass of leafy brush. She listened, straining against the silence for any sound that would reveal a threat, either two-footed or four-legged, but nothing came.

Pushing out from her hiding place, Arianne wanted to cry aloud at the soreness of her body. She rubbed her aching legs with her cut and bruised hands before trying to stand. Finally, she felt her muscles limber some and got to her feet.

Cautiously, Arianne looked and listened in all directions. She found herself shrouded in a misty fog, yet easily recognized where the forest edge led to the roadway and chided herself for not having gone farther before seeking her comforts in sleep. God must truly have watched over her, Arianne mused, realizing that it wouldn't have been that difficult to spot her had a patrol been on the forest's edge.

She crept through the vegetation, trying to keep her steps noiseless. The task, however, was quickly proving impossible, as her feet crunched lightly with every move. Arianne sighed and kept moving. It was the only choice she had.

After traveling for only a matter of minutes, Arianne froze at the sound of voices. She fell to her hands and knees and tried to hide herself in the underbrush of the woods.

Three men moved just outside the forest's perimeter. They were heavily armed, each sporting full chain mail hauberks and mail coifs that covered their heads. At their sides were sheathed broad swords, and mail chaussures protected their muscular legs.

Arianne's heart pounded so loudly that she was certain the men could hear its beat. She bit the back of her hand to keep from crying out in fear. Only after the men had passed and moved on a good distance did she emerge.

With Tancred's men already searching for her, Arianne doubted she would find Richard in time. She hurried, nearly running through the trees in the opposite direction of the three men. She cast a quick backward glance from beneath her hood and, when she turned, ran smack into the center of a broad, chain-mailed chest.

Huge arms encircled her, and Arianne realized she was caught. Fighting for all she was worth, Arianne began to kick and slap the man who held her. If Tancred thought she'd come back to him easily, he was a mistaken fool.

"What is this—a wood nymph perhaps?" The man laughed at her efforts and wrapped her tightly in her own cloak to still her actions. Arianne took advantage of the man's bare hands and lowered her teeth into the tender flesh of his thumb.

"Ahh!" the man cried out as Arianne's teeth found their mark. "You feisty vixen, I'll fix you for that." He pushed Arianne to the forest floor, then pulled his sword and put his foot upon her shoulder to still her.

Arianne cringed back into the folds of her hood. Would he slay her here and now before Tancred had a chance to do it himself? Instead of bringing the sword upon her, the man cut into her cloak and tore a long strip from the edge. He used it as a gag, which he forced around Arianne's mouth in spite of her protests. He then tore other pieces of material and bound her hands and feet. With this done, he resheathed his sword and with little effort lifted Arianne over his shoulder.

Arianne's mind was frantic. She had failed Richard in her mission and she had failed herself. Now he might never know of her love. She couldn't keep the deluge of tears from falling. As the massive bulk of a man carried her from the forest, Arianne sobbed loudly, nearly wailing by the time the soldier brought her to his camp.

The man seemed not to notice her condition. He was oblivious to her tears, and Arianne was just as glad. She had no desire to evoke sympathy from her husband's enemy. Let them deal with her harshly, she thought, for it made her anger keen and her desire to fight just that much stronger.

"What have you there, George?" a man called out. Arianne couldn't see the man, but apparently he thought it great sport to tease her captor. "Seems you always did have a way with the ladies."

"This baggage is no lady," George replied and Arianne squirmed angrily at his statement. "She bit me and slapped me and would have split my skull had I handed her an axe."

The other man laughed furiously.

"Is she from the castle?" another man questioned. This one Arianne could see from the knees down. He moved forward and lifted back her hood to reveal his helmeted face.

"Aye, she must be," George responded. "Do you know her?"

"Nay," the man replied. "But he will. Best put her in the master's tent and it will be revealed soon enough."

Arianne struggled against this news, and George gave her a firm whack across her backside. "Settle it down there, Wench. I've no desire to be crippled by your flailing."

51

Arianne ceased her struggles, but her mind raced furiously. *I must escape these men,* she thought. *I must find Richard!*

George did as he was bid and took her to a nearby tent, where he dumped her unceremoniously upon a pallet. Arianne turned questioning brown eyes upward, wondering if he would untie her. She raised her hands to emphasize her stare.

"Nay," George said and shook his head. "I'll not be turning you loose upon the men. They are needed to fight the enemy and I'll not have you wounding them before battle."

Arianne struggled against her bonds and muttered beneath the gag that he was an ill-mannered oaf, but the man laughed and walked out of the tent.

With the soldier out of her sights, Arianne tried in earnest to free herself. She thought of the knife tucked inside her belt and tried to reach it, but found it was useless. She raised her hands to pull at the gag but discovered George had secured it too tightly and it wouldn't budge.

Refusing to give up, Arianne worked at the cloth until her wrists were nearly bleeding. She was tired and in pain by the time she gave in and rested from her efforts. Against her will, Arianne fell asleep and dreamed of running through the night mist to warn her beloved of a deadly enemy.

The sound of voices brought Arianne awake. She shook her head to clear her muddled mind and tried to focus on the muffled sound of men in conversation.

Her heart pounded harder as the voices grew louder.

"I assure you, Sire, 'twas no small feat to bring the wench in," the voice of the one called George sounded out and Arianne cringed.

The reply was too low to give Arianne understanding, but George laughed heartily at whatever comment was made. "I'd much rather feel the taste of his steel than another bite from that sly vixen. I wish you better luck in the handling of her."

Arianne began to tremble at the words. Was she to be handed over to Tancred in this manner? Was she to meet her enemy bound and gagged without even the slightest hope of preserving her purity and life?

Dear God, she prayed, blinking back tears, *help me!*

The men were directly outside the tent, and against the shadows of early evening, Arianne could make out their movements in silhouette. The heavier of the two men was no doubt George. Arianne easily remembered that barrel-like frame. The other man still wore his helmet.

"Bring us food," the man told George. Again, Arianne struggled to make out the words that the helmet so effectively muffled. *It could be Tancred,* she thought, *but why would he risk leaving the protection of the castle?*

A mailed hand reached out to pull back the tent flap, and Arianne involuntarily sunk deeper into the folds of her cape. The man entered the tent carrying a single light, which he placed on the ground opposite Arianne.

The dim glow only added to the ominous presence of the soldier. Shadows rose up from his form to make the man look like a towering sentinel. Arianne scooted away in horror, bringing his full attention to her. Pulling off his scabbard, the man gently placed his sword on the ground beside the light.

Next he reached up and pulled the helmet from his head, but Arianne still couldn't make out his features. She wasn't sure she wanted to.

The man looked down at her for a moment and Arianne found herself holding her breath. What torture would he use on her first?

The man stepped toward her. Arianne couldn't suppress a cry. She pushed back with her feet and found herself against the tent wall, unable to go any farther. His hand came down, and Arianne struggled valiantly against him. Finally, the man had both her shoulders gripped in his hands.

Arianne paused only to give him a sense of false security. Reaching to his side, he pulled out a dagger and Arianne feared she would faint. Her ragged breath came quicker and her heart raced in fear as the hand was lowered to her face. She closed her eyes tightly to squeeze out the sight of her own death.

With one quick snap, the gag was broken and Arianne began to realize he did not intend to slay her. At least not yet. The man replaced the dagger and reached forward again to push back the cloak and learn the identity of his captive.

Arianne braced herself to see her captor's face, but what she saw was barely visible. The chain mail coif and the dirt smudged against his face made it impossible to tell if it was Tancred. He pushed the hood all the way off her head and gasped at the sight of her copper hair.

The roar emitted from the man was not what Arianne had expected. It was like that of a wild beast injured in a trap or a battle cry in the stillness of the night. She pushed her bound hands at the man, swinging them back and forth like a club.

"Leave me be, you cur! My husband will have your head for this!" Arianne screamed against the man's chest. She continued her tirade even as the man sought to still her.

"Cut my bonds and give me a knife. We'll see how courageous you are against an armed enemy. I won't allow you to harm my husband without killing me first. I'll warn him of your deceit, and nothing short of death will see me do otherwise!"

Arianne had no idea where her strength was coming from. The man kept hushing her, reaching out almost as if to comfort her, but Arianne knew that couldn't be possible. She felt renewed vigor when she managed to set the man off his feet. Escape was impossible, so she assailed him with praise of Richard.

"You and all the armies of the world could not defeat my husband. You may have caught us unawares, but Richard will know. He will come and cut out your heart for this!" Arianne suddenly stopped when she realized the man was laughing.

The sound of his strangely familiar laughter seemed to frighten her more than his overwhelming presence had.

Turning away, his amusement lingering in the air, the man untied his coif and pulled the mail from his head. Then turning back to face her, Arianne thought her eyes were playing tricks on her.

"Richard!" she gasped and nearly fell back against the pallet.

"The very same, Milady," he chuckled. "The one whom the world's armies could not defeat."

Arianne felt the realization of safety coursing through her veins. Richard reached forward and cut the bonds from her hands and feet. Shock numbed her mind, and Arianne did nothing for a moment but stare in mute surprise.

"Are you injured, Arianne?" Richard questioned, reaching out to touch her hand. He took her fingers in his mailed hand and noticed the cuts and dried blood. He frowned, feeling an anger beyond all that he'd known before.

"What other suffering have you endured?" he questioned, praying that God had been merciful to his young wife.

Dropping her hands, Richard reached for the light and brought it closer. When it shone full upon her face, Richard could see the dark bruise on her jaw. With an anguished cry, he ripped off his mail gloves and took Arianne's face in his hands.

"What has he done to you?"

Chapter 9

The agony in his voice was enough to reach through Arianne's shock. "Oh, Richard!" she cried and threw herself into her husband's arms. "I thought they'd captured me again. I thought I'd never get a chance to warn you."

Richard crushed her against his hauberk. "I feared you were dead. A rider came to warn us. The last thing he'd seen was you at the end of Tancred's sword."

Arianne kissed his face and felt the wetness there. His tears mingled with her own as she assaulted his face with kiss after kiss. "I prayed I'd find you in time," she whispered between kisses. "I had to find you and warn you. I had to tell you—"

"It doesn't matter now," Richard whispered. He was surprised at his wife's response, but knew she'd endured a great deal at the hand of his enemy.

"Yes," Arianne said and pushed away from her husband's steely chest. "Yes, it does matter. I feared I'd die before I could tell you the most important thing of all."

"Then tell me, sweet Arianne. Tell me and relieve your worried mind," he replied.

"I love you, Richard," she said and waited for his response.

Her dark eyes pierced his heart as they confirmed the words that her mouth spoke. "Are you certain?" he questioned hesitantly. "You've been through a great deal and—"

Arianne put her finger to his lips. "I love you and I desire nothing more than for you to know the depths of that love and the warmth of hope it gives me."

Richard pulled her gently into his arms and cradled her against him. For a moment there were no words he could speak. It was certainly not the ideal surrounding that he'd hoped, nay, dreamed, they'd share when she declared her love for him. But the words were just as tender, just as wondrous.

"I love you, Arianne," he whispered. "I thank God you found safety in His care and were able to bring this news to me. Still, there is an enemy upon us and I must see him defeated."

"Who is he, Richard? Why does he hate you so?"

"What did he tell you?" Richard questioned. Arianne slipped from his arms to study her husband.

"He said very little," she replied softly. "He told me he sought revenge for wrong done him by you. He told me little more than to say I was spoils of war, as was my home. He planned to use me to capture you. That was when I realized I could not send a messenger, but instead, must come to find you myself."

Richard grimaced. "Tancred is a problem from my past. One that I must rid myself of once and for all."

"Who is he and what has happened between you that such hatred cries for blood?" Arianne asked, placing her hand upon Richard's arm.

"It isn't important," he shrugged.

"Not important?" she whispered. "This man holds your home and people and you plan to end his life, but it is not important?"

Richard looked at her for a moment, then, shaking his head, got to his feet and began to remove the hauberk. "I cannot tell you."

"I'm not a child, Richard. Why can you not tell me?" Arianne questioned more sharply than she'd intended.

"It is a thing between men," he replied in a curt tone that told Arianne the matter was closed. She refused, however, to be put off.

"Nay, Your Grace," she stated in a formal tone. " 'Tis not a matter between only men. That man would have put himself in your place, not only before your people, but in my bed."

Richard whirled around, jaws clenched and eyes blazing. "You think I do not know what he is capable of?" The anger was apparent in his voice, and Arianne wished she'd not pressed the issue. Perhaps it was better that she not know the details of their war.

Richard struggled to rid himself of the chain mail, but it caught. He raged for a moment at it, before stalking from the tent without so much as a backward glance.

Tears flowed down Arianne's face and her throat ached painfully. She longed for a cool drink and something to eat, but the longing in her heart was stronger yet.

"I have driven him away," she whispered to herself. "I came here to declare my love and I have driven him from me as if he were the enemy."

She fell back against the pallet and sobbed quietly. This was not what she had hoped for.

I should never have demanded that he tell me of this thing between him and Tancred, she thought. *I should have learned from our brief time together that when Richard doesn't wish to speak of a thing, he stands firm in his resolve to remain silent.*

When her tears abated, Arianne resolved not to question Richard on any matter again. She reasoned that men often found it necessary to shield their women from the harmful, ugly things of the world. Why should she expect any different from a gentle, kind man like Richard? Hadn't he already shown her every concern?

Gathering her strength, Arianne sat up and wiped her eyes. If Richard returned, she decided, she would be nothing but the dutiful, respectful wife he deserved.

In time, Richard did return. With him came a very humble George. The man brought a tray with food and drink and placed them near Arianne. Richard, with a lighthearted voice, spoke as if nothing had disturbed him from their earlier conversation.

"Sir George, I would have you meet your duchess," he said in the amused way that Arianne had come to love.

George, with a solemn look of humility, bowed before Arianne. "Your Grace," he began, "I am most sorry for my behavior. I had no way of knowing that it was you. I'm most deeply regretful."

Arianne smiled and took pity on the man. "How is your thumb, George?" she asked gently.

The man raised his head with a sheepish smile. His cheeks were stained red in embarrassment. " 'Tis nothing of any matter and certainly less than what I deserved," he replied.

Arianne nodded. " 'Tis well for you that my knife was out of reach, for I had full intention of slaying whatever dragon barred my way from escape."

"For certain!" Richard exclaimed. "Why, she delivered me some well-placed blows while still bound from your dealings."

At this they laughed and the matter was behind them. Arianne took the opportunity to quench her thirst, while George turned to leave. At the tent flap, he paused.

"I will happily guard your life with my own, Milady," he spoke. "From this day forward, as long as I have breath in my body, I will see to your safety." He walked from the tent then, and Arianne couldn't help but be touched by the display of chivalry.

"You have a champion, Milady," Richard said, coming to sit beside her on the pallet. "I dare say, by morning's light you will find George's lance and colors firmly planted outside your tent."

Arianne smiled and reached out to touch her husband's arm. "I desire but you for my champion," she whispered.

Richard's smile warmed her, and Arianne noticed that he'd washed during his absence from her. She wished she could have done the same, knowing that she must be covered in filth.

"What are your thoughts now, Madam?" Richard said, noting the change in her expression.

Arianne laughed and reached for a piece of cheese. " 'Twas nothing overly endearing," she replied. "I was wishing for a bath and a clean set of clothing."

Richard chuckled. "I think we can arrange both. I was gifted by the king with many trinkets, one of which was a lovely gown for you. I will have George fetch some water while I retrieve it, but only if you promise to finish this food."

"You needn't bribe me to do that, Your Grace," Arianne stated in mock formality. "I am quite famished and only sought an excuse to keep this tray all to myself."

Richard laughed and got to his feet. "Very well. I will see to your comforts while you gorge yourself."

An hour later, Arianne felt like a new person. She was no longer cold and hungry, nor dirty and poorly clothed. The tunic and surcoat gifted her by the king was indeed a richer garment than she'd ever worn. Pity, she thought, that it should be wasted in the middle of a fog-filled forest.

She whirled in girlish style and watched the material fall into place. The tunic was the softest blue silk, while the sleeveless surcoat was deep crimson, lavishly embroidered with gold and silver thread. Giggling in delight, Arianne hurried to finish her toilette.

Richard had even thought to find her a comb, and Arianne sat untangling the waist-length bulk of copper hair when he returned.

"You put all other women to shame," he said, coming to her side.

Arianne glanced up with her heart in her eyes. "The king was most gracious to send such a rich gift," she replied.

"I thanked him most heartily in your absence," Richard answered. "I also thanked him for arranging our marriage. I told him it was a most satisfying arrangement to me."

Arianne blushed, thinking that the arrangement surely hadn't been as satisfying as Richard would have liked. She concentrated on her hair and refused to look her husband in the eye for fear he would understand her thoughts.

"Come," Richard said and pulled Arianne abruptly to her feet. "I would show you off."

"But my hair—"

"Is beautiful just the way it is," Richard insisted.

Outside the tent, Arianne was surprised to find a small encampment of men. Richard's tent had been set aside from the others, just far enough to afford a margin of privacy, yet close enough to defend. Arianne noticed how calm the men were. They seemed oblivious to the danger that awaited them.

When they looked up to catch sight of her, Arianne was delighted to suddenly find herself in the midst of their pampering attention. It reminded her of her wedding night when she was handed in dance from one knight to another. She learned their names and accepted their attentions, all the while noticing the gleam of pride in Richard's eyes. When Richard finally led her back to the tent, a firmly planted lance decorated the entrance flap.

"George's?" she asked, looking up to catch Richard's smile.

"Aye," he said with a nod and pushed back the canvas for Arianne to enter.

Arianne moved ahead of her husband, then turned to stop when he entered the tent. She wanted to say so much, yet words failed her. All she could do was stare at the man she'd come to love more dearly than life.

Finally, the silence grew uncomfortable and Arianne forced herself to speak. "I am sorry for the harshness between us earlier," she began. "I know there is much that I should leave to your care."

"It matters naught," Richard whispered and stepped forward to embrace his wife. "God kept you safe from harm and for that I praise Him. I know not how you escaped Gavenshire, but God must surely have directed your steps."

"He did indeed," Arianne nodded. "Matilda took me through the tunnels and then told me how to climb the cliffs and where to hide. She told me the road you would return by and then returned to the castle to face them in my absence."

"She has always served my family well," Richard remarked.

Arianne thought to question Richard further on this comment, but realizing his family was another of the subjects he desired not to speak of, Arianne instead took his hand.

With a questioning look on his face, Richard followed his wife to the pallet. The warmth of her hand in his was spreading like a fire up his arm.

"You have been most patient with me, Richard, but I would have this thing settled between us," Arianne spoke in a barely audible whisper. "I would not have another take that which belongs to you."

Richard reached out and smoothed back a copper curl from Arianne's shoulder. He thought his heart might burst from the wonder of the moment.

"I don't know what to say," he replied rather sheepishly. The moment he'd waited for since first making his vows to God and this woman seemed somehow lost in the fog of his mind.

"Then say nothing," Arianne said, putting her arms around his neck. "It is enough that you know I love you. It is enough that I know you love me. Whatever else comes from this," she paused, meeting his eyes, "is that which God intended and no man will put asunder."

Richard lowered his lips tenderly to hers and forgot about everything but the woman in his arms. Gone were the images of war and the horrors of battle. On the morrow, he would ride to meet his foe, but tonight he would find peace in the arms of his wife. Little else mattered.

Chapter 10

Arianne stretched slowly and then snuggled down into the warmth of the pallet she had shared with Richard. Images from the night passed through her mind in dreamlike wonder. How very precious the union God had given to man and woman through marriage. The love and tenderness she'd known throughout her weeks of marriage were only heightened by becoming Richard's wife in full.

Arianne thanked God silently for the love He'd bestowed upon her. Daily, it was becoming just as Richard had said: God was a personal friend to each and every one of His children. Richard had translated the Latin Scriptures to quote to her from the Gospel of St. John saying, "If anyone loves me, he will keep my word, and my Father will love him, and we will come to him, and will make our abode with him."

Arianne had pondered those words with great interest. God was offering the very best to His children. He would abide with them, not as a judge or condemner, but as a friend.

Arianne found that friendship a precious thing, and while she had been raised to respect and fear God through the church, she was only coming to know what it was to truly love and trust Him. All of this had been awakened in her spirit because of Richard.

As Arianne came fully awake, she opened her eyes and turned to study her husband. When she found the area next to her empty, she bolted upright and stared at the barren tent.

"Richard?" she whispered, knowing full well that no one would answer her.

She pulled on her clothes quickly, realizing while she did that Richard's armor and gear were gone. Without bothering to comb her hair, Arianne hurried barefooted from the tent to find her husband.

Instead of finding Richard, Arianne found a sober-faced George and two of the men who'd been with him on patrol when he'd taken Arianne captive. All of the men seemed thoroughly embarrassed.

Arianne glanced around and saw that all signs of Richard's other men had been removed. Gone were the tents and horses. Gone were the smiling faces and the warm campfires.

"Where is my husband?" she asked George.

George stammered and refused to look her in the eye. He shifted nervously from one foot to the other, not at all in knightly fashion.

"George?" She took another step forward. "Where is Richard?"

"Gone, Milady," George finally replied.

Arianne heard one of the other men's sharp intake of breath, while George seemed to take a side step, uncertain what Arianne's response would be.

"When will he return?" Arianne questioned, still not realizing the truth of the matter.

"There is no way to tell, Your Grace," George responded and quickly added, "I have food so you might break the fast. 'Tis cold, but nourishing."

Arianne managed to nod and followed to where George indicated she should sit. "Where has Richard gone that you have no inkling of when he will return? And, why did he not awaken me and bid me good day?"

George realized he would have to tell Arianne the truth. "He's gone to Guyenshire, Milady. He did not wish to worry you overmuch with his departure. He bid me tell you that he will see you soon and that he—well he wanted me to say that. . ." George stammered into silence.

Arianne bit back her anger and frustration. "He wanted you to say what, George?"

"That he loves you, Milady."

"Oh," Arianne replied and lowered her head. How could Richard leave her like that? Especially after all that had passed between them in the night. It was as if he couldn't trust her to have faith in him to do the right thing. But then again, hadn't she questioned him most vigorously in his dealings with Tancred?

"I'm sorry 'tis such a shock, but His Grace thought it best," George stated sympathetically.

"I'm no child to be sheltered from the truth," Arianne remarked.

"No, of course not, Your Grace," George quickly proclaimed.

"I don't wish to be treated as an addle-brained woman, either," Arianne declared, raising her darkened eyes to George.

"Never!" George stated indignantly. "Milady wounds me most grievously to declare such a possibility."

Arianne looked intently at the massive man and finally softened her glowering stare. "I apologize, Sir George. I know that you are only doing the duke's bidding. I am, well. . ." She paused, trying to come up with the right words. "I am distressed that my husband would leave without a proper good-bye."

"Mayhap it would have burdened his mind in battle," George offered without thinking.

Arianne grimaced, knowing that George was probably right. At the thought of Richard in battle, her anger faded. "Will they fight today?" She whispered the question.

George shrugged his shoulders. " 'Tis a possibility, but who can say. Perhaps the enemy will give in without resistance when they see the duke's forces."

Arianne tried to reassure herself on those words, but she knew the depth of hatred between the men. She especially remembered the overwhelming desire for revenge in Tancred's voice.

"Gavenshire Castle is more than capable of keeping out unwelcome intruders," Arianne said. "Tancred will see my husband and his men as most unwelcome."

"Yea, 'tis true," George admitted. "Still, your husband has the advantage of knowing the estate more intimately. He will have a few tricks to show that man, if I know His Grace."

"Do you know this man who holds the castle? Do you have any knowledge of Tancred?" Arianne questioned.

George looked thoughtful, then shook his head. "Nay, I'm sorry, Milady. In all our time at Gavenshire, I've never known your husband to have a single enemy. I'm afraid I know nothing more than I am told."

Arianne nodded her head. "It would seem we share that fate, Sir George."

They fell silent and one of the men who lingered in the background thought it a good time to bring Arianne's food and drink. She thanked him and took the offered meal, but her stomach was disinterested. Richard was in danger. How could she eat?

The day wore on in oppressive slowness. Each minute seemed to last hours and each hour was more like a day. Arianne tried in vain to learn more from Richard's men. She wanted to know how Richard would proceed once Tancred refused to open the gates to allow him entry into the castle. The men were of no help. They either wouldn't tell her or didn't know. Either way, it left Arianne more fretful than before.

She paced the small perimeter of their camp, glancing up from time to time to meet the eyes of one of her guardians. They were sympathetic eyes, but also they betrayed an eagerness to be doing something more than playing protector to their duchess. And try though they might, Richard's men could not hide their looks of worry.

Arianne finally pled a headache and retired for a rest. A fine, misty rain had started to fall and she was grateful for the shelter of the tent. Without chairs or furniture of any kind, Arianne took herself back to the pallet and stretched out.

Laying there, she could almost feel the comfort of Richard's arms around her. Why hadn't he said good-bye? At least if she could have told him—

The thought broke away from her mind. What was there that she could have said? She'd already given him the words he'd longed to hear. She'd declared her love for him. Never had any man seemed to find such contentment in a simple statement, but then Arianne knew that Richard understood the price at which her trust and love had come. No, there was nothing left for her to say, but perhaps it was more that she longed to hear reassurance from his lips. Reassurance that everything would be all right and that Tancred would soon be defeated.

"Oh, Richard." The moan escaped her lips, and tears formed in her eyes.

"Father in heaven," she prayed, knowing that no other comfort would be found, "You alone know my heart, and though I am but a mere woman, I have need to know that You are with my beloved Richard. He speaks Your name with the utmost of love and respect. His lips declare Your wonders, and praises are offered up from his heart to Your throne. Now, Father, Richard must face the enemy, perhaps to do battle with a man who would see him dead. I ask, although I am unworthy to make such a plea, that You would shroud him with protection and keep him from harm. Please deliver my husband from Tancred's hand and see this matter between them settled."

Arianne fell silent and wiped the tears from her eyes. Staring upward, she was consumed by the stillness that came to her heart. There came a peace so certain and complete that it nearly took her breath away. Clutching her hand to her breast, Arianne closed her eyes and smiled. *Yes, this is of God.*

❧

When Arianne awoke, she felt refreshed and at ease. Richard was still at a task that she'd give 'most anything to see avoided, but she knew for certain that God was at Richard's side.

She got up and went in search of George, who in spite of the rain and the threat of enemy soldiers, had managed to cook a rabbit over a small fire. Arianne sat with the men, trying to converse with them about the countryside and weather. She prattled on about unimportant matters, hoping to show them that her heart was confident about Richard's fate.

It was the boredom that was setting them all on edge. As soon as the meal was cooked, one of the other men allowed the fire to die out, leaving nothing but a blackened spot where the warmth had once risen. Arianne felt the gloom of the overcast day threaten to dispel her peaceful spirit. Doubts wormed their way into her mind, but her heart held fast to a newly discovered faith in God.

She sympathized with the men as they took turns pacing the camp. With the skies growing darker and the imminent coming of night, one man was posted as guard, while the others prepared to sleep. Knowing there would be little, if any, light once the sun set, Arianne bid them good night and reclaimed the confines of her tent.

There was nothing to do but wait. Wait in the darkness, in the unbearable silence, and wonder at the outcome of her husband's campaign against Tancred.

Giving her mind over to her own curiosity, Arianne tried to remember everything she knew about Tancred. She wanted to know who this man was and why he hated her husband. It was more than a simple problem between them. Arianne knew from the look in Tancred's eyes and the tone of his voice that his conflict reached deep into his very soul. What had Richard been a part of that had caused such intense bitterness?

Matilda seemed to know who Tancred was, but Arianne hadn't been able to get her to speak in any detail. George and his companions didn't seem to understand what the conflict was about, so they were of little help. The only real understanding would come from one of two people: Tancred or Richard. And neither of them seemed inclined to tell Arianne what their war was about.

Chapter 11

Something akin to desperation gripped Arianne's heart at the sound of scuffling and hushed whispers outside her tent.

"Who's there?" she whispered in a shaky voice.

"Milady, 'tis I, George."

Arianne tried to force her voice to steady. "What news have ye that cannot keep until the morn?"

" 'Tis most urgent that we flee this place, Your Grace," George whispered from outside the tent. "The enemy is nearly upon us."

Arianne's heart pounded. The image of Tancred swam before her eyes, causing a convulsive shiver. She got quickly to her feet and rushed headlong between the tent flaps.

"Have you news of Richard?" she asked with a pleading voice.

"Nay, Milady. There is no word. Take my hand and I'll lead you." He reached out in the darkness to offer his hand. Groping against the blackness, Arianne took hold of his arm. "Come, the horses are waiting."

Caring little for her own safety, Arianne allowed George to lead her through the darkness. Her mind forced images of heinous battlefields to mind. Would the blood shed there be that of her husband? *Dear God,* she prayed, *he must be safe. Keep Richard safe.*

They neared the horses, hearing their soft, nervous snorts and hoofed pawing of the earth. Arianne didn't utter a word when George lifted her to the saddle of his mighty warhorse, coming up with the same action behind her. She knew there was no dainty sidesaddle for convention's sake. She knew, too, that it would have been most uncomfortable, if not impossible, for her to ride astride in the gown she wore. Had Sir George been her love, it might have seemed daringly romantic, but George was not her love and the moment was only wrought with anxiety.

"Forgive me, Milady," George whispered from behind his now secured helmet.

"Forgive you?" Arianne asked in near-hushed reverence. "Forgive you for championing me and saving my frail life?" George didn't reply, but Arianne noticed that he seemed to sit a bit taller against her back.

They moved out quietly, pressing deeper into the forest in hopes of eluding the enemy. The man posted to patrol had spotted at least ten riders not far from the camp. It would be only a matter of time before they discovered the location and raided the surrounding woods.

Arianne shuddered at the thought of being once again under Tancred's control. She knew his rage and anger. What would he do after she had so completely outfoxed him? Better to pray that it did not become a possibility, Arianne surmised, for she couldn't dare to hope he would allow such a thing to go unpunished.

Rain had begun to fall again, soaking the little band as it filtered down through the trees. Arianne pitied the men who wore their mail hauberks and plated helmets. The water would make such clothing sheer misery. Arianne, herself, fared little better in the heavy, royal surcoat. Her hair, plastered down against her face, seemed more like a strangling rag than the crowning glory Richard so highly regarded. But hair would dry and so would clothing. Arianne wondered about her husband's condition. Spilled blood would not be remedied as easily as the drying of a garment.

With a heavy sigh, Arianne felt tears flood her eyes. She was quite grateful for the cover of darkness. She didn't wish to alarm her husband's men with foolish fears. Still, she knew they, too, were anxious to know the fate of their comrades.

∼

Richard DuBonnet, duke of Gavenshire, watched his castle and home from the seclusion of the nearby forest. He saw the torches that flickered boldly in the thin-slitted, first-floor windows. Windows too narrow for a man to pass through, even if they weren't barred with metal grilling. They could have been shuttered from inside the castle as well, but no doubt Tancred had put them there to mock any impending attack. He was making it clear that Richard and his men posed no real threat.

Glancing up, Richard counted a dozen or more men as they stood watch on the rampart walkway of the castle's gray stone battlements. They were unconcerned at the force Richard might bring with him. They knew full well that Gavenshire could withstand any onslaught from outside its walls.

Richard smiled to himself. What Tancred didn't expect was an assault from within. Yet, that was just what Richard planned to give him. Richard's father had once told him that a mighty castle, like a mighty man, could never be defeated from the forces outside it. With planning and prudence, both could sustain considerable exterior damage.

Yet a man and his castle were vulnerable from attacks within. A man could not ignore the attacks on spirit or heart without paying a high price. A man was almost always defeated in the realm of his mind, spirit, and heart before he gave in to an outside force. A castle was the same. If the enemy could get inside and weaken the defenses, open the doors and gates, it would only be a matter of time until the prize could be won.

Richard would divert Tancred's attentions away from the one place he would be most vulnerable. Tancred would spend so much time concentrating on the enemy outside, he would forget to keep watch from within.

Richard moved back to join his men. His mind passed quickly from thoughts of the impending battle and, instead, took him back to the pleasant times he'd known with Arianne. How he loved her! Their few weeks of married life had been the foundation for a solid friendship. Their moments together the night before left Richard only more certain that God's hand wanted to bring good to both of them from the arrangement.

Richard was lighter of heart to know that he would not have to attack the castle with Arianne inside. It was hard enough to wonder how many good friends would perish in the fight without having to fear that Tancred would use Arianne as the pawn he had first intended her to be. He was greatly relieved to know she was safe in the hands of his own men, miles from harm.

∽

Arianne sat rigidly straight in front of George. She ached from the position but knew she must leave George free to maneuver. She also wished that there be no appearance of impropriety to shame her or Richard. George had sworn his loyalty to guard her, but Arianne knew there was a delicate balance between her position and his. She would not be the one to create mishap between them.

Her thoughts turned once more to Richard. She worried that he might be hurt or worse. She couldn't bring herself to think that something might be horribly wrong. She couldn't bear to imagine that Tancred might have already killed him. *No,* she reassured her heart, *God is Richard's guardian. No man will come between that.*

The rain clouds moved on and allowed the slight moon to shine out overhead. Darkness had been good cover for escape, but Arianne was glad for a little light. The forest had seemed so impenetrable, so foreboding. Now she could make out the trees as they stood silhouetted against the sky. Arianne was nearly lulled into believing that they would get away unscathed, when suddenly, they were surrounded by men.

"Halt or be slain," a man cried out from behind his helmet.

"Who demands this of us?" George countered.

"I am Sir Gilbert de Meré, and I act on the orders of Lord Tancred. I have been sent to retrieve the duchess of Gavenshire and take her to his lordship."

"I will not go!" Arianne exclaimed. She would have jumped from the horse, but George's hand shot out around her.

"Nay," he whispered against her ear. Arianne froze in position. She had no idea what George would do next, but she was determined not to interfere.

"If you do not yield peaceably to us, Milady," the man spoke again, "I will be forced to kill these good men and take you anyway."

Arianne blanched and swallowed hard. She had not thought of the grave danger to Richard's men. Her men. Men who had sworn to protect and keep her with their lives.

As if reading her mind, George answered slowly. "We are pledged to guard the duchess with our lives. She is worth more than many hundred more. What are we three, that we should not give all that we possess to see her well kept?"

"You are dead men," Sir Gilbert replied. "Even now I see your bones rotting on the floor of this forest."

"Nay!" Arianne shouted. "It will not be so!" Turning to face George, she could barely make out the glow of his eyes from behind the helmet. "I cannot allow your blood to be shed. I will go with them."

"A noble cause, indeed," Gilbert declared as he moved his horse forward.

Arianne heard the sound of swords as they were pulled from their scabbards. The ringing held a deadly tone to her ears.

"I beg you," she stated to all who would listen. "Let there be no blood shed on my account. I will go to Tancred and beg his mercy. He daren't kill me, for he would have no power over Richard."

"Will you yield, sir knight?" the man questioned.

"Nay," George replied.

Arianne put her hand out against the sword George held in his hand. "I command, as your duchess, that you lay aside your arms. Sir George, you will obey me in this." Then in a tone heard only by George, Arianne whispered, "Please."

It seemed forever before George and his companions put down their swords. Arianne knew that it went against every code of honor they had been raised with. She was surprised that her word was heeded. Perhaps George reasoned that a better opportunity would arise in which he might defeat the enemy. Perhaps he knew it was hopeless to expect victory at this time.

Gilbert de Meré moved alongside George's warhorse and pulled Arianne roughly against him. "You are prisoners of my master," he stated. "You will be taken to Gavenshire to await your fate." With that he touched his heels to the horse's flanks and moved out ahead with Arianne held tightly against him.

On the hard ride back to Gavenshire, Arianne gave thought to throwing herself from the horse. She reasoned that even if she could break the iron hold of the man who held her, the fall would most likely kill her and leave Richard with even more hatred for Tancred. No, it was better to face the future.

As the outline of the castle came into view, Arianne bit her lower lip to keep from crying. Where was Richard? Was he already within the castle or did he wait to strike? Would he see her now and grow careless in his fear for her safety?

Gilbert urged his mount forward and cried out for admittance at the castle gatehouse. They were quickly surrounded and escorted inside the walls. Arianne tried not to show fear. She was aware that her people watched her, and she'd not give them reason to believe she was unworthy of their trust.

The mighty oak doors of the keep opened, and with only the benefit of torch light, Arianne knew that the man in the shadows was Tancred. Gilbert halted his horse and threw Arianne to the ground.

She landed hard against her hip at Tancred's feet. Rubbing her bruised side, she dared not look up for fear he would strike her.

"Ah, Lady Arianne," Tancred said the words sarcastically. "You do me honor with your return. Come, let us speak together." He nearly growled the last few words before yanking her to her feet by her hair.

Arianne fought back tears of pain. Her rain-drenched hair made a good hold for Tancred as he dragged her into the castle.

Arianne stumbled and fell twice, but without pausing to allow her to regain her footing, Tancred hauled her up the stone stairs to the second floor.

"I should break your scrawny neck," Tancred raged as he threw her into her bed chamber. "I don't know how you escaped or who helped you, but neither matters. You were a fool to believe yourself capable of warning your husband."

Arianne paled, but remained perfectly still. Her hip was bruised to the point of distraction, yet she remained fixed to the place where Tancred had put her.

"When your husband does return, you will be the only weapon I need," Tancred said with a wicked smile. Arianne's face betrayed her fear. "But worry not, Milady," Tancred said, moving to the door. "I will take you for my wife when he lies dead upon this floor."

With that he slammed the heavy chamber door behind him, and Arianne heard him instruct a man to stand guard outside it. She wanted to collapse into tears, but she managed to hold them back. Getting to her feet, she moved mechanically to rid herself of the soggy garments she wore. There was no fire in the hearth, but at least she could dry off and take refuge in her bed.

"But what if he returns?" Arianne thought aloud. She hurried to don a linen tunic. *I am helpless to keep him from me,* Arianne reasoned. *I am helpless, but God is mighty and fully capable of protecting me from Tancred.*

"Father," Arianne prayed, falling on her knees and wincing at the pain in her hip, "watch over me and keep me from Tancred's plan. Protect Richard and allow him victory over this evil man. Amen."

Chapter 12

A rianne awoke nearly a half hour before the rosy glow of dawn would grace the English countryside. There was an uncomfortable silence all around her. Throwing back the covers, she leaped from bed and ran to the window.

She looked long and hard against the early morning darkness. Something had disturbed her sleep, but what? The blackness would give up none of its secrets, and feeling that nothing else could be done, Arianne stoked up the fire in her hearth and prepared to go back to bed.

Just as the coals were stirred into life, Arianne heard a trumpeting call from outside the castle. Grabbing one of the furs from the bed, Arianne pulled it around her shoulders and returned cautiously to the window.

"I have come in the name of His Grace, the duke of Gavenshire," the man announced. "Yield the castle or meet your fate this day!"

The men on the rampart walkways laughed as though the man had said something most amusing. Looking down into the open bailey, Arianne was surprised when a small entourage of armored men appeared with torches in hand. Tancred was in their midst, barking out orders and seeing to it that each man took his post.

Tancred paused in the procession and cast an upward glance as if he knew he'd find Arianne in the window overhead. He offered her the briefest salute to let her know that he was aware of her vigil, then proceeded to the gatehouse.

Arianne waited for what seemed an eternity. Nothing was said and no one seemed at all eager to reply to the herald's challenge.

Finally, Tancred's voice sounded out against the silence. "Since your master is too cowardly to appear before me himself, I will address his herald and the challenge he lays forth."

Arianne held her breath. Tancred was hoping to bait Richard with the insult. Sending a herald was the commonplace thing to do and Tancred well knew it, as did the men who listened. But there was something more in Tancred's tone that made everyone take note.

"You may tell your master," Tancred called out again, "that I refuse to yield this castle. I challenge him to present himself and yield to me his titles, his land, and his people." The words chilled Arianne. She backed away from the window.

Richard's herald acknowledged Tancred's challenge and offered only one

70

other thing. "The duke bids you take note that this castle is surrounded by some of the finest of the king's armies. The king himself demands you yield this land."

Tancred's hearty laughter was hardly what anyone had expected. "King? What king? I have no king, or has he forgotten that he exiled me from this land? You may tell your duke to come and take this castle if he can, for I will never yield what I am entitled to."

✒

Richard never heard the exchange of words that took place between his herald and Tancred. He counted on the fact that all attention would be drawn to the gatehouse and the surrounding walls. While the main thrust of his men, aided by many of King Henry's finest soldiers, presented a formidable force to Tancred's eye, Richard would take his most trusted and capable men through the tunnels beneath the castle. They would infiltrate Tancred's stronghold, even while he observed the forces outside the castle walls.

Halting his men, Richard raised the torch in his hand. "You know what to do. I will proceed alone, and when the appointed time comes, you will follow. The fate of Gavenshire rests on our shoulders. We will have a moment of prayer."

One by one his knights crossed themselves and knelt in the dirt of the tunnel floor. Richard knelt. "Father, we lift up our task to You. We are but humble servants and seek Your blessing to right that which has been wronged. Go with us into battle, even as you did King David of the Bible, and deliver the enemy into our hands. As You will it."

The knights murmured agreements and got to their feet. Richard turned to the ladder that would allow him to infiltrate Tancred's stronghold.

"God's speed, Your Grace," the man nearest him offered. Richard nodded and took himself up.

✒

Arianne knew better than to let Tancred catch her unawares. She quickly pulled on a burgundy wool surcoat over her linen tunic, then plaited her hair and covered it with a linen headpiece.

She looked regal in her attire, but it gave Arianne little pleasure. The castle was under siege by her husband. The enemy held her hostage, and everyone's fate seemed to rest in the balance of a mysterious hatred of two noblemen. Arianne shivered, still feeling the cold in her bones. She went to a large chest and drew on a fur-lined mantle, looking much as though she were ready for an early morning walk.

The loud pounding at her door caused Arianne to take a step backward. "Unbar this door, Lady Arianne, or I shall have my men render it to kindling."

Taking a deep breath, Arianne stepped forward and removed the plank. Scarcely had she done this when Tancred burst through the door. He halted for a moment at the sight of Arianne in her stately dress. She was changed considerably from the rain-drenched wretch he'd seen the night before.

Lifting her chin defiantly, Arianne met his stare. "What seek ye here?" she questioned. "Your battle awaits you below. 'Tis unseemly that you would dally your precious moments of planning in the company of a woman."

Tancred laughed in her face. "I do so appreciate a woman of high spirit. Still it is well that you learn your place. I have not yet settled with you for your disappearance from my protection."

"Protection, bah!" Arianne spat the words. "You, Sire, have brought me more harm in the few moments we've shared than I've known in all the years of my life. You beat me, press your attentions upon me, and imprison me in my home. You afford me no protection, merely grief and grave reservation."

Tancred stepped forward with a leering smile. "You would surely change your mind should I relinquish my protection and turn you over to my men."

"I fear nothing that you or your men can do. I have the protection of my God and He will see you defeated this day," Arianne replied confidently.

Tancred drew back his hand and slapped her. It wasn't the fierce blow he'd dealt her before, but it was enough to bring tears to her eyes. Nevertheless, Arianne stood fast. "You seem to make it a habit of beating defenseless women."

Tancred clenched his hands into fists, uncertain how to deal with the woman who stood before him. He was used to people cowering before him, and he had certainly never met with the resistance this young woman offered. Choosing his words to break her spirit, Tancred finally answered her.

"Your cowardly husband will taste my steel this day. Bards will create songs that will tell of our battle and how I avenged my name with his blood on my sword." Tancred's eyes seemed to glow in consideration of this accomplishment.

"My husband is no coward," Arianne said softly. "If you have issue with him, why not sit down to a table and discuss it as reasonable men? Why does such hatred between you demand blood?"

Tancred seemed taken aback by her words. " 'Tis no affair for a woman," he muttered.

"So I am told by both you and my husband," Arianne replied without thinking.

"So you did see him?" Tancred more stated than questioned. Arianne felt her stomach churn. What had she done?

"What know ye of his plans?" He stepped forward and grasped Arianne by the shoulders. "How does he plan to attack first?"

"I know nothing," she answered, fear edging her voice notably.

"You lie!" Tancred exclaimed, shaking her vigorously. The rage in his eyes exploded across his face. "Tell me what he plans or I shall beat you most mercilessly."

"A dead man would find that task most difficult," a voice sounded behind

Tancred, followed by the slamming of the chamber door. Both Arianne and Tancred looked up to find the armored man standing, legs slightly apart, sword drawn.

"Richard!" Arianne gasped, as Tancred whirled around, pulling a dagger from his belt. He dragged Arianne across the room, distancing himself from Richard, with the knife at her throat.

"Take one step and I will cut her," Tancred said in a low, menacing voice.

Richard halted, knowing the man would do just as he said. He paled at the sight of the knife at his young wife's throat. Why was she here? He had thought she'd be safely away from this matter, not plunged into the very heart of it. His calm reserve faded. The fear in Arianne's eyes blanked out all reasoning in his mind.

"Leave her be," Richard spoke in a halting voice. "Your war is with me."

"My war is with all that you hold dear. Your title, your lands, your wife. You were responsible for my losses. Now all that you possess will be mine and you will be dead."

"Nay!" Arianne cried out, struggling in spite of the dagger.

"It would seem," Tancred said, pushing the blade firmly against Arianne's throat to still her, "that your lady is quite devoted to you. Pity. No doubt, however, I will be able to change that once she is my duchess."

Richard's eyes narrowed in a hateful stare and Arianne felt her breath catch. He took a step forward, the sword still raised. "You will not kill her," Richard stated evenly. "You will not, because it would leave you defenseless."

"I did not say I would kill her, dear Richard," Tancred venomously declared. "I will, however, cause her great pain and suffering while you watch." Tancred drew the blade along Arianne's perfect face. "Scars upon such beauty would be a shame." He edged her cheek lightly with the knife, while Arianne fought to control her weak legs.

Richard could stand no more. "Do not harm her. I will give up my arms."

Arianne began to sob. "No, please don't give in to him, Richard. He will kill you."

Tancred laughed as Richard placed his sword on the floor. "It will give me great pleasure to tell the world how a woman caused your demise. Now throw down your dagger as well."

Richard did as he was instructed while Arianne continued to cry. "Move to the bed," Tancred instructed, still holding Arianne against himself.

Richard moved slowly back, while Tancred advanced until he took possession of Richard's weapons. His hand still held Arianne's arm possessively, causing Richard to grimace.

"You are a weakling, Richard," Tancred stated.

"I yielded to protect the lady's well-being. You hide behind her skirts and deny me the chance at a fair fight. I wonder now, just which of us is the weakling?"

Richard's words seemed to strike their mark.

Tancred growled and pushed Arianne from him. "I've never denied you a fair fight. You ran from it at every opportunity, until you convinced the king to exile me. Now I have the advantage and you cry foul."

Arianne was getting to her feet, tears blinding her eyes. If only she hadn't been taken hostage again, Richard would not be compromised. This was all her fault.

While the men stared at each other in silence, Arianne considered rushing Tancred. She glanced first at Richard, then turned her attention to Tancred and back again to her husband. As if reading her mind, Richard shook his head.

"You needn't concern yourself, Arianne. God is with us in righteousness and truth. Tancred knows neither and fears not God or His people." Arianne's stare was fixed on her husband. His words seemed to soothe her pain-filled heart. Tancred saw the effect but said nothing while Richard continued. "God will always deal with wickedness and He will always prevail. You believe in His power, Arianne. Never forget that God is not mocked by any man."

Arianne nodded slowly and even Tancred seemed a bit taken aback by this declaration.

"I love you as no man has ever loved another," Richard said with a sad, sweet smile upon his lips. "Tancred cannot change that, nor can he understand it."

"I love you, Richard," Arianne said, taking a halting step forward. "I will give my life to preserve yours."

"Nay, Love," Richard replied, shaking his head. " 'Tis not necessary."

"Enough of this," Tancred interrupted. "You will be taken to the dungeon or cellars or tower, it matters not. You will be held until I am able to send word to King Henry. When I am redeemed, your life will be forfeited and all that is yours will be mine as it was always meant to be. Including this fair child." Tancred stepped toward Arianne, but she darted away from his touch and pressed against the wall.

"I will die first," she spat at the man.

Tancred halted.

"Arianne," Richard called, and the look on his face was most grievous, "you must live. 'Tis not of God to take your life. He will preserve and keep you. Remember the way in which you came to me. God always provides a means, be it at the hand of a king or that of a maidservant."

Arianne stared in confusion at her husband. She opened her mouth to question him, as Tancred moved to the door to call his men. Richard shook his head and gave her one last smile. "Remember," he whispered.

Arianne could neither do nor say anything more. Tancred's men rushed into the room and took the willing Richard in hand. Tancred moved close enough to Richard that they were nearly eye to eye.

"Harm her and answer to God," Richard said in a whisper.

Tancred's eyes narrowed slightly. "I have never answered to God."

Chapter 13

Arianne opened her chamber door only enough to see that Tancred had left a man to stand guard. Silently she closed the door and began to pace the room.

"What did he mean?" Arianne whispered aloud. "What was Richard trying to say?"

She puzzled over his words throughout the day. At noon one of the servants brought her a tray of food and drink, but no one was allowed to come within, and Arianne was not allowed to venture out.

She looked out across the fields to the cliff-edged shores. Men were taking up position in a variety of places, but Arianne couldn't tell whether they were Richard's men or Tancred's. The surcoats of both armies were so similar that Arianne thought she might go mad trying to determine which was foe and which was friend.

Twice she tried to busy her hands by spinning wool on her distaff, but both times she made a matted mess and finally gave up the task. With a heavy sigh, Arianne fell back against her chair and stared up at the ceiling.

"Remember the way in which you came to me. God always provides a means, be it at the hand of a king or that of a maidservant," Richard had said. What did it mean and how could it help him now?

"I came to him through the king's edict," Arianne reasoned to the cobwebs overhead. "I came to him from my father's house. I came to him as part of a bargain, a settlement of the governing powers. I . . ." Again she sighed. It was no use. Nothing made sense.

She longed to go to the castle chapel and pray. She knew Richard believed that a person could pray anywhere, at any time, and for the most part, she, too, believed this was true. But the sanctuary of the chapel always made her feel closer to God. Maybe it was the extravagant stained-glass window that graced the east wall, or maybe it was the fact that there, one could shut out all other influences and turn solely to God. Whatever it was, Arianne longed for its comfort.

"Now look what you've gone and done!" A woman's shrieking voice sounded from the other side of Arianne's door.

Quickly, Arianne took herself across the room, pulling her mantle tight as though it might muffle her movement. The door creaked softly, as Arianne opened it only an inch. She studied the sight before her, unable to clearly see what was happening.

"Old crone! You nearly scalded me with that slop!" the guard raged.

Arianne opened the door a bit more and could see that the woman in the hall arguing with the guard was Matilda.

" 'Twas not my fault you were born blind," she countered, noting Arianne's presence with the slightest grin on her face.

"Clean up this mess, Woman!" the guard roared. "My master will not find it as humorous as you seem to. Be glad I am not given to beating women."

"Beat me?" Matilda yelled back and began screeching and crying with her eyes lifted heavenward. "Help me, oh Lord," she cried out, "for the man surely means to kill me."

Arianne knew that Matilda was staging the distraction for her benefit, but she also knew there was truth in Matilda's prayer. She hastened to ease through the chamber door and secured it behind her, all the while watching the guard as he sought to settle Matilda's ranting.

"I said I would not beat you, old crone," the man muttered over and over. "Just clean up the mess and be gone." He rolled his eyes, completely baffled by the sniveling woman who now threw herself at his feet.

"You are kind, Sire," Matilda moaned her exaggerated gratitude. "Thank you for sparing my worthless life. I will do your bidding and see that this floor is cleaned. Please, I beg you, do not tell the master of this for I fear my life would be forfeited."

The man scowled, but Arianne could see from her hiding place in the shadows near the kitchen stairs that Matilda would not be harmed by the oaf.

Arianne hurried to the kitchen below, grateful that everyone moved in such hurried steps that they seemed to take little notice of one who moved with decided slowness and secrecy. She waited in the buttery, knowing that Matilda would think to look for her there.

The minutes seemed to linger, and Arianne thought more than once she'd been discovered. But to her relief, she was safe for the moment and Matilda was soon to join her with news of Richard and the siege.

"Milady," Matilda said, embracing Arianne as though they were mother and daughter instead of servant and duchess. "I feared for your life. Is it well with ye?"

"Oh, Matilda," Arianne moaned against the older woman's shoulder, "Tancred has made Richard his prisoner and I don't know where they've taken him."

"Hush, Child," Matilda soothed, "for I know of this deed as well as where they have taken your husband."

Arianne's head snapped up. "Where is he? We must free him."

"We could not do it alone, for at least two men guard him, possibly more," Matilda whispered.

"But we must help him," Arianne pleaded. "There must be a way for us to free him from his plight."

"I know of no way," Matilda said sadly. "I knew that I could detain the guard while you slipped from your room, but there would be no such distraction for the men who guard your husband. Unless you have some other thought on the matter."

"Richard was adamant that I remember something," Arianne said with a frown upon her face. "But I know naught of what he spoke."

"What did he say?"

Arianne thought for a moment. "He told me to remember the way in which I came to him. For the life of me I can't imagine what he means. I came to him by order of the King of England. What can I make of that?"

"Did he say nothing else?" Matilda asked earnestly.

"Only that God always provides a means, be it at the hand of a king or that of a maidservant," Arianne replied. "I came to Richard by the hand of the king, that much is true."

Matilda stared thoughtfully for a moment and then a smile began to line her face. "Ye also came to him by the hand of a maidservant," she whispered, "when I led you to the tunnels below."

Arianne's breath caught in her throat. "The tunnels! Richard must want me to go back to the tunnels. Where are they keeping him, Matilda? Can we get to him through the tunnels?" Arianne was already moving to the trap door.

"Nay, they've put him in the cellar. There is no passage to that place from the tunnels, but Richard gained entrance to the castle through the tunnels and he would not have traveled alone. His men must await him below, Milady. Richard must desire that you tell them of his plight and take refuge there until this matter is settled."

Arianne suddenly felt hope born anew. "If Richard's men are below, they will know exactly what to do. Come help me move this door and I will go to them. We both will go!"

The women moved gingerly down the ladder, noting with satisfaction that a lighted torch offered the slightest glow from the passages below. Matilda pulled the trap door closed as she hurried to follow her mistress. She was greatly relieved to leave the conflicts overhead for the sanctuary of the tunnels.

Arianne's feet had scarcely touched the damp ground when she was surrounded by men.

"Your Grace," one of the men said coming forward. "We thought you were safely away with Sir George."

"I was captured, as were the duke's men," Arianne said and quickly added, "They have also taken my husband prisoner. He bade me find you." Another man hurried to aid Matilda down the remaining steps of the ladder.

"Where have they taken your husband, Milady?"

Arianne looked around her at the eager faces. These men were Richard's most loyal or he would not have brought them with him to the tunnels. "He has been taken to the cellar and I know naught of the place, but my maid does." Arianne motioned to Matilda.

"We know of the cellars," the man replied. "We have been given tasks by His Grace. Your appearance here with this grave news gives us cause to seek them out with haste. You will remain here in the safety of the tunnels, Milady, while we venture forth and see to our duties."

Arianne nodded. "Will you return and, give me word of my husband?"

The man's anxious eyes scanned her face, and with a slight nod, he motioned his men to the ladder. The women could do nothing but watch as the men disappeared. Fear bound their hearts with steel bands. Perhaps Tancred had learned of the trap door and even now awaited Richard's men.

Arianne shuddered and Matilda took it for chills. "Come, Milady. We will seek a warmer place."

With a heavy heart, Arianne followed the older woman deeper into the maze. She couldn't help thinking of Richard and the suffering he would be enduring at Tancred's hands. *Because of me, Richard walked right into the trap.* Just as Tancred had hoped, Arianne had been the only bait necessary to capture the young duke.

Arianne also remembered the painful expression on Richard's face as he watched and waited while Tancred put the knife to her throat.

"Why?" she exclaimed without realizing that she spoke aloud.

"Why what, Milady?" Matilda asked, suddenly turning to stop.

"Why did I have to be the reason he was taken?" Her voice betrayed her emotions and broke with a sob. "Why did God allow me to be retaken by Tancred's men? I don't understand. It's only caused more suffering and now my husband is prisoner and this man will most likely seek to end his life."

Matilda grimaced and turned away from Arianne as though an unpleasant thought had come to mind.

"What is it, Matilda? What do you know that I do not?"

" 'Tis nothing but speculation, Lady Arianne. I would not overburden your mind with such matters. Here," Matilda motioned, "this will be a good place to await the men."

Arianne would not be silenced with her maid's excuse. "Matilda, I must know what is going on. Do you have any knowledge of this battle between Tancred and Richard?"

"Aye, Milady," Matilda replied in a weary voice. She allowed herself to sit before seeing to her lady's needs—a most unusual thing for a servant devoted to her job. "I know that the man blames the duke for lost title and lands. I know, too, that he blames Richard for King Henry's decision to exile him from England."

"But why, Matilda?" Arianne asked, taking a seat in the dirt beside her maid. "Why did the king exile Tancred?"

"That, I cannot say," Matilda replied.

"Cannot or will not?" Arianne questioned.

A rustling sound in the passageway caused both women to start. Matilda put a finger to her lips, grateful to silence the younger woman's questions. She felt a growing fear that she would have to explain to Arianne the matter of affairs between Richard and Tancred, and to do so would mean to break an ancient promise to the young duke. No, she decided, she mustn't be the one to break that oath.

Chapter 14

The women waited in the damp darkness for what seemed an eternity. Arianne, with her questioning mind, grew restless and prayed that the time would pass quickly and allow Richard's men complete victory. Matilda, restless for her own reasons, also prayed. She prayed for a way to stay true to her promises, while providing Arianne the comfort and protection she deemed a part of her duties.

When both women were convinced that the sounds had been nothing more than rats in the passages, Matilda was the first to speak.

"Milady," she began hesitantly and in a low whisper. "It is my desire to keep a promise to the duke. It is a promise that I have held since he was a young man. This thing between him and Sir Tancred must be revealed by him alone. I cannot break my oath, no matter how much I would like to do so."

Arianne's eyes betrayed their curiosity, but she nodded in agreement. "I will not question you again," Arianne said soberly, "but only if you can assure me that in your keeping of this promise, Richard's life will not be further jeopardized."

"Nay, Milady," Matilda replied. "His life will not be further jeopardized by my keeping of this oath. Both the duke and Tancred have knowledge of my understanding and what lies between them. 'Tis nothing that will cause either one to be aided or hindered."

"Very well," Arianne said, "then I must be content until my husband feels the matter is important enough to share with me. In the meantime, there is the matter of freeing Richard."

"But, Milady, you heard the duke's men. We should remain here and keep safely out of sight. Richard would be most grieved if you were to be taken again and all because you sought to free him from his confines."

"That is unquestionably true," the young duchess answered. She considered the situation for only a moment before continuing. "However, I cannot sit here in the safety of the tunnels and know that he is suffering, maybe even being beaten or starved. I cannot and will not, and that is something you and my husband must understand."

"Yes, Milady," Matilda said with a slight smile. "I feel the same. What have ye in mind that two women could lay their hands to?"

Arianne smiled. "I have not yet considered that matter. Perhaps if we pray on it, the heavenly Father will put it upon our minds and show us the way."

"That is most wise, Milady."

Both women fell silent, and only the clasping of their hands together broke the deep concentration of their prayers. Arianne pleaded for her husband's life and freedom and begged God to show her how she might once again do something helpful to her love.

Hours passed in the silent meditation of the women, and in the end it was Arianne's concern for whether or not Richard was being fed that opened the window of opportunity for the escape plan.

"He won't be able to maintain his strength if they do not feed him," Arianne said with her hands at the side of her head. Her temples throbbed from the worry in her heart. Richard had promised her that God would win out over evil, but the moment seemed so hopeless.

"Perhaps that is our answer," Matilda said with sudden encouragement. "I can pass throughout the castle as one of the servants and no one will question my actions because, of course, a servant would not be moving about without being directed by those in authority. I can go to the cellars with food for Richard and perhaps when the guards open the cellar door, he could escape."

"It has possibilities," Arianne said with a nod. "But there is too much that could happen. The guards might not allow Richard any food. They might keep it for themselves. Then, too, Richard would need a weapon against armed men, and we can't simply place one upon the tray."

"True," Matilda replied. They seemed once again to come to an impasse.

Arianne sat silently considering the situation, while Matilda got to her feet and paced the floor in front of her.

"The guards wouldn't want the food," Matilda suddenly said, "if it were nothing more than slop."

"I don't believe I understand. Richard would not desire slop, either."

Matilda smiled at the duchess and nodded. "But it would be just the kind of torment Sir Tancred would be capable of. I could tell the guards that it was all that Richard was to be allowed. If I make a stinking mess of the whole mixture, I don't believe any man would come near the tray. I have herbs and all manner of thing that can make it most unappealing. I would have to be allowed to deliver it because the men would want no part of it."

Arianne jumped to her feet. "But perhaps they wouldn't allow Richard to have it, either."

"Of course, they would," Matilda said with her hands on her waist. "It would give them great pleasure to see Richard eating something so utterly disgusting."

"Those men being Tancred's, I suppose you are right."

"I know I am," Matilda replied confidently.

"But what of a weapon?" Arianne questioned. "Richard must have a sword or he will not be able to control the men who guard him."

"That does pose a bit of a problem," Matilda agreed.

"What if you were to hide it in your skirts?" Arianne suddenly asked. She could well imagine the possibility in her mind.

"A man's sword would extend below my limbs," Matilda said, all the while motioning to her short legs.

"A sword would be too long," Arianne acknowledged, "but a dagger or short sword could be hung from your waist, beneath your tunic. It would have to be done so in such a way that it would be easy and quick to free for use, but concealed well enough that the guards wouldn't notice."

"I think I can do that," the older woman said thoughtfully. "I could also pull a cloth around my waist like the cooks do. It would add concealment."

"Where can we get a dagger for Richard?" Arianne questioned. "We can't very well walk into the hall and ask Tancred for one."

"That is true," Matilda responded with great thoughtfulness. "Most of the men guard well their weapons, however, if I can get to one of Richard's men, I am certain he will assist us in the effort to free the duke."

"Then we must be about it," Arianne said, starting down the tunnel.

Matilda's hand fell upon her arm. "Nay, Milady. You cannot go above. 'Twould be most unwise; the men would easily recognize you."

Arianne knew that Matilda spoke truth, but she hated being left behind to do nothing. As if reading her mind, Matilda gave her a reassuring pat on the arm. "You must keep our prayerful petition before God. Knowing Richard as I do, I am certain that it is the very thing he is about, right this minute. You will stand as one in prayerful agreement before God."

Arianne immediately felt peace descend upon her troubled spirit. *Yes, it would be just like Richard to be quoting the Scriptures he'd memorized and praying for God's guidance through his misery.*

"I will stay," Arianne agreed reluctantly. "But you must promise to return to me as soon as you can and let me know that all is well."

"I promise, Milady. I will do all in my power, through His power," Matilda said pointing upward, "to free Richard from Tancred's hold."

Matilda crept through the kitchens, pulling along with her the things that she needed. She sent a whispered word here and there among trusted servants and easily concocted a hideous porridge of rotten meat and garbage.

The already potent smell was enhanced by the addition of several unknown ingredients, which Matilda cautiously threw in when no one was watching. Then, just in case Tancred's men were stupid or desperate enough to want to eat the odorous mess, Matilda added enough sleeping herbs to lay out even the heartiest soul in a long, deep sleep.

Just as she finished this task, Matilda was surprised to find one of Richard's men, Sir Bryant, dressed in the clothes of a peasant and standing at her side.

"I have the dagger you need," he whispered.

"Leave it in the buttery," Matilda replied. When she glanced up to see that the man had heard her, he was already gone.

"I will return for this in a moment," Matilda told one of the cooks. "See that no one touches it." The woman nodded and took the ladle from Matilda.

Matilda slipped through the buttery door and closed it behind her. Sir Bryant waited for her in the shadows behind several kegs of drink.

"Tell me your plan, for we must do what we can to aid in freeing our duke."

Matilda shared their plans with the young knight and waited, half expecting some rebuke or condemnation. She was gratified when none came. Instead, Sir Bryant seemed to understand that this way was best.

"I will not be far away. I will have several of Richard's best men with me and we will await word from you. Here is the weapon. Have you a way to conceal it?"

"I hadn't the chance to consider it," Matilda admitted.

Sir Bryant thought for a moment, then noticing some rope beside one of the kegs, cut off a section and came to Matilda. "This should serve the purpose. Perhaps if you tie it around your waist tight enough that the hilt will not pass through without assistance, it will remain concealed."

Matilda took the rope and motioned the young knight to afford her some privacy while she worked to secure the dagger. Once she'd let her skirts fall back into place, she asked Sir Bryant to determine her success.

"Walk to the door and back," he ordered and Matilda quickly did as he bid.

She felt the steel slide back and forth against her leg, but with a slower step, Matilda felt certain it was not perceivable, and Sir Bryant pronounced the matter settled.

Matilda moved with great slowness as she approached the passageway to the cellar. She knew that her noises would be easily distinguished in the silence of the hall, so she began an ancient singsong tune to announce her approach.

As she came upon the guards, they were ready and waiting for her. One man advanced with his sword drawn, but then the stench of the concoction met his nose. Wrinkling his face into a grimace, the man quickly stepped back.

"What have ye there, old crone? 'Tis surely nothing fit for man."

"Fit only for one man," Matilda said with a haggard laugh. "Lord Tancred," she bit her tongue to keep from taking back the title, "bid me bring this slop to the duke. He's to have naught but this for his meals."

The other man stepped forward and peered into the bowl. "What is it? It smells like death itself."

"Most probably is," Matilda played along. "Would ye care to serve him?"

Both men took a step back at this. "I won't touch that vile mixture," the first man said, while the other just shook his head.

Matilda raised an eyebrow and suddenly thought of how to buy herself more time with Richard. "I can't be leaving the bowl and tray with the prisoner. Must I take his plight upon myself and wait in that hole while he eats his fill?"

" 'Twould seem your only choice," the second guard replied. " 'Tis all he's fit for anyway. The company of old women and pig's slop. Take it to him with our finest regards for his dining."

Matilda screwed up her face to show her feigned distaste with the matter, and when the men only laughed at her circumstances, Matilda knew she'd won. Now she'd have enough time to loosen the dagger and give Richard a weapon.

The men moved to the cellar door and removed the plank that held it in place. The first man called out as the second man stood ready for action.

"It seems our master is not so hard-hearted," the man spoke into the room. "Lord Tancred has sent supper to Your Grace." At that he pushed Matilda through the door and slammed it shut behind her. Only the tiniest bit of light filtered in from the slit of a single window, high in the wall.

"Your Grace? Are ye here? 'Tis Matilda." She waited a moment while her eyes adjusted to the darkness.

A sound came from her right and Matilda turned slightly with the tray in hand.

"Matilda? Why has Tancred sent you to me?" Richard asked from the darkness.

"He did not send me," Matilda whispered the reply. "Lady Arianne and I thought of this."

"Arianne? What of my wife? Is she safe? Has he hurt her again?" His voice grew louder as he neared Matilda. Then his tone changed from concern to disgust. "What is that stench?" Richard asked, coming to stand beside her.

Matilda laughed softly. " 'Tis part of our plan and, yes, your lady is safe."

"What plan?" Richard questioned.

"We thought to free you from your prison, Sire. If you will but hold this wretched brew, I will release the weapon I've brought you from beneath my skirts."

"You managed to get a weapon in here? Did not the guards search you?" Richard asked in complete amazement.

"They would not come close enough to your supper, Sire. It seems they do not have a strong stomach for such matters." She gave the tray to Richard and in spite of the dim light, Matilda turned her back to her duke and raised her skirts cautiously to free the dagger.

"Where is Arianne?" Richard whispered while waiting for Matilda to complete her task.

"She is back in the tunnels," Matilda replied, turning to hold out the dagger. "Compliments of Sir Bryant, who will be waiting just down the passageway with several of your other knights."

Matilda couldn't see his face, but she sensed Richard had a renewal of hope and strength. He took the dagger in one hand while still holding the tray in the other.

"Now what, might I ask, is your plan for getting out of here?" Richard's amusement and admiration were revealed in his tone.

Matilda took back the tray and moved toward the door. "Just follow me, Sire. I plan to douse the ambitious flames of those two pups with the stench from this tray. That should give you enough time to come through the doorway, although I'm afraid your eyes will have quite an adjustment, even in the dim light of the passageway."

"I'll manage," Richard replied. "You simply lead on."

Matilda approached the door and gave her best performance yet. "Open this door. I'll not spend another moment in here. His Grace is unreceptive to your master's gift and this stench is likely to do me harm."

Matilda and Richard both heard the rattling sound of the bar being moved. If the men were lined up as they had been when she'd entered the cellar room, Matilda would have a clear path to cover them both in the horrid concoction.

When the door opened, Matilda lost little time. She moved forward at such a pace that neither guard was prepared for the moment when she feigned a misstep and plunged the tray forward to cover them both.

"Ahhh!" the closest man cried, jumping back. The door slammed hard against the stone wall.

"Mindless crone!" the other yelled and actually dropped his sword in the attempt to rid his hauberk of the mess.

This was all the encouragement Richard needed. He rushed from the room with the dagger poised for battle, while Matilda conveniently stood with both of her feet on the discarded sword.

The entire matter took only a heartbeat, and by the hand of God and the duke of Gavenshire, both men were thrown into the cellar room and Richard was free!

Chapter 15

W hat is the meaning of this?" Tancred asked the surprised guard. They stood outside Arianne's empty bed chamber, each man as puzzled as the other.

"Mayhap there is a secret passageway," the guard offered. "A way that no one but the duke and his duchess is familiar with."

"Nay," Tancred said, shaking his head. "I see no sign of that." He entered the room, however, and began to run his hand along the smooth stone wall. "Nevertheless, the wench is not here and once again she has bested me. This does not bode well with me. I will give a sizable reward to the man who finds her and brings her to me." The guard nodded and waited for dismissal. "Well?" Tancred questioned. "What are you waiting for?"

The man quickly departed the company of his sour leader. He had no desire to bear the brunt of the man's ire. It was bad enough that the woman had disappeared under his watch.

Tancred stared at the room a moment longer, then took himself to the window and looked out at the gathering of Richard's army. As the hours passed, the numbers grew. Tancred understood that Richard hoped he would be intimidated by the mass. It would seem that King Henry, feeling securely delivered to London, had spared a good many of his own men to aid Richard.

" 'Tis amusing to think Henry knows I am here. He thought to deny me my title and country, but I will show him how mistaken he was on the matter. Henry and Richard, together, haven't the power to drive me from England forever," Tancred mused.

Turning from the window, he scowled at the empty room. He was quite perplexed with the young duchess Richard had taken as wife. She was no woman of tender means, of that she'd proved more than once. She was intriguing, Tancred thought, and would make him a good wife after Richard was disgraced and dead.

The sound of the herald's trumpet rang out, catching Tancred's attention. Richard was locked in the cellars, and Tancred felt it to be the proper time to relay this information to his enemy's men. Defeat would be swift without their leader.

Quickly, Tancred made his way through the castle, across the bailey, to the gatehouse. Along the way he noticed several of his men thoroughly searching the yards. Word must have spread quickly regarding his reward for Arianne. He smiled to himself. It would only be a matter of time and she would be under his control once again.

"What has the herald to say?" Tancred questioned the men who kept watch. His dark scowling face caused even the bravest men to step back.

"They claim the castle for the duke and bid us open the gate. If we will not yield, they are prepared to begin the assault."

"Let them," Tancred laughed. "We have their duke in the cellar below the castle. I doubt they will be so anxious to begin their assault when news of this is given."

The surrounding men joined in their leader's laughter, while Tancred took himself up to the battlements.

Many of Richard's men sat atop their mighty warhorses, while others stood amassed on the ground. Their numbers were impressive; even Tancred couldn't deny this. He'd never anticipated this turn of events, having been confident that he could take Richard and the castle by surprise.

Taking a position of authority, hands on his hips and feet slightly apart, Tancred addressed the enemy. "It is well you know that I have taken the duke as my prisoner. I also have his fair wife and many of his men confined within these walls. Their execution will begin immediately if your numbers are not taken from this place."

"The duke gave us orders," one of Richard's knights said, urging his horse forward a bit. "We will not disgrace him by giving up our position at the sound of your idle threats. He may well lie dead at this moment, but we will do as we were bid."

"This castle can withstand your assault," Tancred declared, yet in the back of his mind came the thought that he still had no idea how Richard had managed to gain entry through the castle walls. His men were everywhere and guards were posted all along the walkways. There was virtually no way that Richard could have made his way into the castle unseen, yet that appeared to be exactly what had happened.

Tancred's men seemed to wait for instruction, watching their leader as if puzzled about what they would do next. Tancred clenched his jaw until it ached. He couldn't very well kill Richard until he had a full confession of guilt to present to the king. Even then, it might be necessary to have Richard publicly declare his guilt, and for that reason Tancred desperately needed Arianne.

"If you attack, I will kill the duke!" Tancred declared loudly.

"He will have to catch me in order to do so," Richard called from the south wall. He was surrounded by several of his men, and in the bailey below, the sound of swords at work was already ringing out to capture Tancred's attention.

Richard's men cheered from outside the walls, while Tancred drew his sword and struck a commanding pose.

"You have but a handful of men inside the walls," he announced. "My men still outnumber yours and," Tancred said, hoping that Richard was not knowledgeable of the fact that Arianne was missing, "I have your wife."

"You have nothing," Richard countered. "My wife is safely hidden. Yield to me, Tancred, and I will be merciful."

Tancred laughed. "Never! It is because of your lies to the king that I must clear my name."

Richard seemed unmoved by the words. He remained silent with a fixed stare, which caused Tancred to grow uneasy. Without another word, Tancred took himself below and ordered his men to clear the bailey of Richard's soldiers.

When Tancred emerged from the gatehouse, Richard was gone from the rampart walkway and his men were making easy task of defeating their enemy. Motioning to several of his men, Tancred avoided the open grounds and made his way back to the castle. He had to find Arianne. She was his only hope of keeping Richard at bay.

"Has she been found?" Tancred asked the man who'd earlier guarded her chamber.

"Nay, Sire," he replied. "We are sorely vexed by her disappearance, as well as the other strange happenings within these walls."

"What speak ye of?" Tancred asked.

"Half of the men cannot be found," the man answered.

"Half?"

"Well, very nearly that. I searched for my brother and our cousin, but they are nowhere to be found. When I questioned some of the other men, we totaled the numbers to equal nearly half of those who entered in with us."

"That's impossible!" Tancred declared.

"I wish it were, Sire," the man said apologetically. " 'Twould seem a power greater than ours stands at Richard's side."

"Bah, you prattle like a woman," Tancred said and left the man to figure out what he should do next.

Tancred moved down the shadowy corridor, fearfully watching for any sign of Richard. Should he find Richard before locating Arianne, he knew his life would be forfeited. A noise in the passage to his right caught Tancred's attention, and he cautiously followed the sound.

A small woman scurried in the shelter of the dimly lit hallway. She cast a wary glance over her shoulder before hurrying down the back stairs.

Tancred followed her, immediately recognizing the woman. *Matilda!* He knew the woman well and was confident that if anyone knew where the duchess of Gavenshire had taken refuge, it would be Matilda. With a hand on his scabbard to silence any noise, Tancred moved down the stairs.

He'd barely put a foot to the bottom step when he saw the edge of Matilda's cloak disappearing around the corner. Boldly, he stepped into the kitchens, fully expecting to confront the old woman, but he was once again vexed when all he caught sight of was the overflow of her cloak as she passed from the room.

Hastening his steps, Tancred entered the buttery just as Matilda had pulled the trap door open.

"Halt!" he demanded and stepped fully into the room.

Matilda let the door drop with a resounding thud. She could only stare at the man before her.

"You were going to your duchess, were you not?" he asked, casually leaning against the wall. Matilda refused to speak and Tancred shrugged. "It is of no matter to me whether you speak or not. I know that is where you were going, and you will take me with you."

"Nay," Matilda said, shaking her head. "I will not hand her over to you."

"I believe you will," Tancred said, slowly coming forward. "If you do not, I will slay you here and go below to find her. Don't be a fool, Matilda. Pull up that door and take yourself below."

Matilda moved in hesitant, jerky motions. She didn't know what else to do, fearing for her own life as well as Arianne's.

Before she could give her mind a chance to form a plan, they were in the tunnels. Tancred stared in appreciation of this discovery. "So this is how Richard gained entry into the castle," he muttered.

Matilda turned to run, but Tancred quickly caught her. "Where is she?"

"I'm not certain, Sire," Matilda replied. "You know full well that the duchess has a mind of her own. She may not even be here."

"It is a chance we will take," Tancred replied, eyes narrowing slightly. "Take me to where you last saw her."

Matilda shook her head, raising her voice to protest. "I will not do it. Slay me now, but I will not betray my duke or his wife."

"Matilda!" Arianne's voice called out from down a long corridor. "Matilda, is that you?"

"Answer her," Tancred said with a sneer. "Answer your duchess." He drew his sword slowly so that it didn't make a single sound.

"Aye, Milady," Matilda said. Tears came to her eyes before she let out a scream. "Run, Your Grace. Lord Tancred is here."

Arianne realized too late the trap that Tancred had set for her. She appeared not ten feet from where he stood.

Tancred saw immediately that Arianne intended to run. "Don't move or I will kill the old woman," he commanded.

Arianne froze in place. Tancred stepped forward and took Arianne in hand. Turning to Matilda, he spoke. "You will go find Duke Richard and bring him here. Tell him to come alone because if anyone, even you, shows your face in this tunnel, I will put a great misery upon this woman."

Matilda cast a glance from Arianne to Tancred and back to her duchess. Arianne knew that she awaited her approval, but how could she give it?

"I would suggest, Milady," Tancred said, tightening his grip, "that you release your servant to action. Otherwise, I will be forced into a most unpleasant task."

"Go ahead, Matilda, but only as protection for yourself. Tell Richard I will gladly give my life to spare his own. Once I am dead, Tancred will have no power over him."

Matilda hurried away, feeling much like a coward at leaving Arianne to Tancred's mercies.

When the trap door sounded in place, Arianne turned her glance to the man who held her. "At every moment I have been in your company," she began, "there is always the anger and resentment you bear upon yourself. It is almost as if it were an armor that encases you, but I perceive something else."

Tancred's expression seemed to soften. His brow rose curiously. "Pray tell, Madam, what is it you perceive?"

"Pain," Arianne whispered, surprising them both.

Tancred's eyes narrowed again, but before he could speak, Arianne continued. "I see pain and emptiness. Perhaps desperation and even loneliness."

"You perceive what has never existed."

"Do I?" she asked hesitantly. The iron band of his hand upon her arm tightened.

"Aye, Milady. You give me weaknesses better suited to your husband."

"My husband is a good man. He is fair and just; kind and gentle. But more than this," Arianne said, lifting her chin confidently, "he is a man whose faith is firmly rooted in God. Know ye of that peace?"

"God is for old men and addle-brained women," Tancred replied. "I have no time for a God who allows honest men to be usurped, while evil ones go unpunished."

Arianne sensed that she'd somehow struck a chord. "God's ways are often a mystery, but in time He reveals them to us."

"Through the collection plate of the church? Nay, mayhap God's revelations come through Rome and the papal displays of regality and authority. Better yet, King Henry—there is a man after God's own heart!"

"Nay, Tancred. God need not rely upon a sovereign or a pope. It is true He uses emissaries and heralds, just as you or Richard might, but He comes to men and women as a Father and loves them."

Tancred dropped his hand as though Arianne's arm had grown white hot. "Cease this!" he ordered. "You know only what a woman's heart tells you. You can't begin to understand what a man must do."

Arianne rubbed her arm, but didn't try to move away from Tancred. She sensed that Tancred was fighting a battle of much greater proportions than his dispute with Richard.

"I might be ignorant of the affairs of men," Arianne said, her eyes gently sweeping Tancred's face, "but I believe God knows. I don't know why you were exiled or why you and my husband are at war, but God does and He is righteous. If injustice has been done, He will right it."

"But injustice hasn't been done, has it?" The voice belonged to Richard, and Tancred jumped in surprise before taking Arianne in hand once again.

"So we finally come face to face. Nothing to stand in the way. No armies, no men—" Tancred's words were cut off.

"Not face to face," Richard interrupted. "You hide behind the skirts of my wife."

Chapter 16

Tancred slowly, methodically offered a smile. "I do not trust you. You betrayed me to the king."

"I turned over evidence of a murderer's identity."

"You turned over false documentation and the sworn statements of my enemies!" Tancred countered.

"You forget," Richard said in a deadly tone. "I saw you myself." Arianne frowned. She struggled to understand the embittered war of words that raged around her.

"You saw nothing!" Tancred shouted.

"I saw you murder my father!" Richard cried out, stepping forward.

"Our father!" Tancred countered, pulling Arianne in front of him as a warning against Richard's advancement. "And I did not kill him!"

"Nay," Richard growled. "Never let it be said that we shared common parents."

"You are brothers!" Arianne gasped suddenly.

"Aye, but only because I cannot change the past," Richard replied bitterly.

Tancred threw his arm across Arianne and pulled her hard against him. He raised his sword to point at Richard's heart. "I came back to clear my name," he said in a low, even tone. "You caused me to lose my title and lands. You took lands and wealth that should have come to me, and you are responsible for sending me from my home."

"You were guilty of murder. Be grateful you were allowed to live at all," Richard declared.

"I had no part in the murder," Tancred raged. "I told you that then and I say it again."

Richard's face darkened in a rage that Arianne had never before witnessed. Forced as she was, between the two angry men, she felt her knees weaken. Had Tancred not had a good grip on her, Arianne would have sunk to the floor.

"Father thought you a man of honor, but even after the deed is long past done, you cannot admit to your guilt and shame. Your blackened heart may cry out for revenge, but your soul is in need of absolution."

"My soul cries for justice," Tancred replied. "My soul cries for the years of loss and separation from all that I loved."

"Loved? What know ye of love?" Richard inquired venomously. "The mother who taught you love at her breast then bore your sword into her heart. What love could you have been capable of?"

"I should kill you for saying such a thing," Tancred spat. "Speak not of her again; better that we should have both died the day she perished."

The words surprised Richard and his face betrayed the fact. Arianne watched as her husband struggled with his brother's declaration.

"Were it not for Henry's mercy, you would be dead, for I desired it so," Richard finally spoke.

"The mercy of Henry?" Tancred questioned sarcastically. "Spare me words of your merciful king. The man branded me a murderer, though he had no proof. I still wear his merciful scars."

"I saw you with your hand upon the knife that had been plunged into our father's back. Our mother was not yet dead in her own blood, two paces away," Richard replied coldly.

Arianne shuddered at the image he drew. Richard could not have been more than fifteen when he had witnessed that awful atrocity.

"I found them that way," Tancred said defensively. "I heard her screams, but I was too late."

Richard stared in disbelief at his brother. "You truly expect me to believe that?"

"Perhaps he speaks the truth," Arianne whispered. She wished she'd remained silent when Richard threw her a glaring stare. His eyes clearly silenced her, and Arianne hung her head in sorrow.

"See there!" Tancred jumped at this new opportunity. "Even your wife sees the possibility. You were so blinded by your hatred of me that you could not imagine I was telling the truth."

"And just what is the truth?" Richard's voice held no hint of interest.

"Just as I have told you. I did not kill our parents." Tancred's words were no longer venomous, and Arianne sensed that the tone was nearly pleading. "I've been convinced all these years that you were the one responsible for our father and mother's death. You were conveniently there when you should have been miles away. You were the one who successfully mounted a campaign against me, in spite of your youth and inexperience, and successfully saw me stripped of my title and lands."

"You were not content with the lands you'd obtained through Henry's graciousness," Richard countered. "You wanted our father's land as well. Don't seek to ease your conscience with wild tales of my guilt. I had no hand in our parents' deaths."

"I'm past caring what explanations you might offer," Tancred said, shifting his weight nervously. "I demand that you accept responsibility for the entire matter. I demand that you send a messenger to Henry and proclaim your own guilt, for there can surely be no other who was responsible."

"You were found guilty of the crime, do you forget that?"

"I had no part in their deaths! I want my name cleared of the murders, and I want my title and lands back."

"Never!" The word reverberated throughout the tunnel.

"I will hold your sweet wife captive until the messenger returns with a full pardon. Henry, by your own admission, is quite fond of you. Perhaps he will consider that you were a wayward youth and show you mercy." Tancred's words were riddled with sarcasm. "Should King Henry refuse your admission of guilt, we will prepare a request for an audience with him in which you will openly declare, in person, my innocence and your guilt. Otherwise, I will be forced to end not only your life, but hers."

Arianne lifted her eyes to meet her husband's. Tancred brought the sword against her neck. The cold metal caused Arianne to shudder, but no more so than the look of black hatred in her husband's eyes.

"This is not her battle," Richard said slowly, never taking his eyes from Arianne. At the fear he saw there, he softened a bit. "She has endured much because of our bitterness. The least you can do is fight me man to man."

Tancred laughed bitterly. "The time for that has passed. I cannot trust you to keep your word and you will not trust me for mine."

Richard stepped back with a sigh. "What is it that you would have of me?"

"I've already told you. I want to be pardoned. I want to be reinstated in my rightful place. I want. . ." Tancred's voice fell silent for a moment. He lowered the sword from Arianne's neck. "I want to come home."

The first spark of sympathy was born in Arianne's heart for the man who held her. There was such longing in those few words.

"You will not gain your home by force, Sir Tancred," Arianne said quietly. "Nor will you find relief from the bitterness that haunts you by blaming your brother for something he did not do."

Arianne's words stunned both men. Taking advantage of their silence, she continued. "The murder of my husband will not undo the murder of your parents. King Henry is a just man. Perhaps something could be done to convince him that the charges of murder were placed upon you falsely."

"There was nothing false about them," Richard spat, causing Arianne to jump ever so slightly.

"Richard," she whispered and turned tender eyes to plead with her husband, "Tancred had no reason to risk his life and return here if he is guilty. However, if he is innocent, no price would be too dear to pay in order to see his name cleared of such heinous charges."

"So you believe him?" Richard questioned.

Behind her, Tancred said nothing.

Arianne reached a hand out to Richard's arm, but Tancred pulled her back, fearing that Richard would snatch her away.

Arianne shook her head. "I don't know if he lies, but I do know that I would do most anything to keep him from harming you." There were tears in her eyes, and Richard felt his anger fading.

"And I would do anything to keep him from harming you," Richard countered.

Tancred resented the exchange that left him feeling more alienated than before. "Enough!" he said, pulling Arianne several feet with him. "I grow uncomfortable with this scene. Will you help me of your own free will, Richard, or must I force you?"

Richard glanced hesitantly from Arianne to Tancred. He faced his brother and for the first time honestly wondered if Tancred was telling the truth about their parents' deaths. Arianne's words gave him much to consider.

"Nay," Richard finally answered. "I cannot lie to help you. I will not admit to something I had no part in, even if you have been wrongly accused."

"Not even to save her life?" Tancred asked, nodding at Arianne.

"I cannot sin one sin to cover another," Richard replied. The pain in his face was as evident as the fear in his wife's.

"You would not tell a lie to ensure that this fair lady's life be spared?"

Richard stared deeply into Arianne's eyes, and Arianne lost her fear. God was her strength and the source of hope that she prayed for. Richard had taught her that, and because of his strong convictions, he wouldn't, nay, he couldn't, cast those beliefs aside, not even for her.

She nodded ever so slightly, telling Richard with her eyes that she understood.

"I'm sorry, Tancred," Richard spoke sincerely. "I cannot break a vow to God or tell a lie, even in order to save Arianne's life. I would gladly trade my own for hers, however, and beseech you to let her go."

Arianne watched brother confront brother, wondering which would back down first. She had no doubt that Richard was completely devoted to his faith in God. Tancred, too, was devoted, but to an entirely different cause. A cause that Arianne couldn't hope to understand.

"I can see that you are going to be most difficult to deal with." Tancred finally spoke, and his words were edged with controlled anger.

"Henry would never believe that I, of my own free will, came forward to clear your name. He knows about this attack. Some of his own elite guard accompanied me to take back my castle. No matter what I say or do, Henry will know that I do only that which has been imposed upon me."

Arianne felt the heaviness of her husband's heart. The longing to free her was revealed in his eyes, and she silently prayed that God would give him direction so that the matter could be concluded without bloodshed.

"So you will not help me?" Tancred questioned slowly.

Richard shook his head. "Nay, I cannot."

"Even if it means the life of your duchess?" It was as though Tancred couldn't believe Richard would actually walk away from a chivalrous fight to defend the honor and life of one he loved.

"I did not say I would not fight for her," Richard replied, his eyes narrowing as deep furrows lined his brow. "I will give my life for hers. Let her go and face me as a man."

"I control you through her," Tancred replied, toying with the edge of the blade he held.

"Then kill her," Richard said in a cold, almost indifferent voice. "For one who declares himself incapable of murder, you certainly hide behind its threats often enough. Mercifully slay her now and be done with it."

Arianne's mouth dropped open. She stared at Richard in horror, wondering what he was about. Tancred was so shocked that he pricked his finger on the blade before drawing Arianne tightly to his side.

"What's the matter?" Richard asked his brother. "Haven't ye the stomach for the task?"

"I have no desire to slay her," Tancred replied. "I am no cold-blooded killer."

"Then let her go," Richard insisted.

"Will you assure me safe passage from this place if I do?"

Richard's face contorted in anger. "Why should I?" His words were low and even as he fought to control his rage.

"I will go back into my exile," Tancred answered. "I will seek out another way to clear my name."

"You mean that you will plot my death in another manner, don't you?"

Arianne could remain silent no longer. "Please," she said, lifting her eyes to meet her husband's. "Let him go and be done with this."

"He deserves to pay for the attack on my home and people. Not to mention that he has laid his hand upon you, causing great harm. Nay, he will not go free."

"But Richard," Arianne's voice was filled with pleading, "he will not give himself over. Without spilling his blood and taking his life, your brother will continue this stalemate."

"Then I will end this now," Richard said, raising his own sword.

"Nay, Richard," Arianne cried out, completely ignoring the blade that Tancred held. "His soul is not safe from the fires of eternal damnation. Would you have his blood on your head, when by mercy you could let him live to accept salvation through our Lord Jesus?" By the look on Richard's face, Arianne knew her words had hit their mark.

Tancred was at a loss to understand the battle of wills that raged inside his brother. He only knew that Richard's wife seemed desirous to save his life.

"You would be no better than those who murdered our parents," Tancred offered.

Richard looked at his brother, then sheathed his sword. "I thought you believed me the culprit of that deed."

"Nay," Tancred replied with a laugh, knowing he had the upper hand. "I never thought one so soft-hearted could be capable of using a knife for much more than threats."

Richard's hand went back to the hilt of his sword, but Arianne shook her head. "He provokes you, Husband. Be not concerned with his tongue, but remember his soul."

Richard was amazed at Arianne's calm. She had learned so well his love of God and desire that all mankind would come to be saved that there was no doubt who would win this hand.

Tancred, too, sensed the control Arianne's words had upon her husband. What troubled him was the effect those soft-spoken words had upon his own heart and mind. He had to distance himself from her gentle concern. There was no room for it in this fight.

"Will you let me rejoin my ship?" Tancred finally asked.

Richard stepped back a pace. "Aye."

"And you will give me your oath on the Code of Nobles that you will do nothing to hinder me from passing from your estates?"

"I give you my word. You may leave to return to your exile," Richard promised. "Release Arianne and I will guide you through the tunnels to your ship."

Tancred shook his head, not trusting his brother. "Nay, Arianne knows the way, for obviously this is the means by which she escaped me before. She will guide me to the ship so that no harm will befall me."

Richard's clenched fists were clear signs of his displeasure, but before he could open his mouth, Arianne lifted her hand.

"I will show him the way, Richard. God will not see me suffer at his hands anymore. Put into practice that faith that so strengthens those around you." Her words were peaceful balm on the wounds of Richard's heart. God was in charge of the matter, as Arianne so simply had reminded him.

It went against everything he'd ever known, but Richard backed away and, making a sweeping bow, gave his brother what he demanded. "Arianne will lead you. I will arrange for your men to be at the ship, but mark my words, dear brother, my men will be there also." Then almost as an afterthought, Richard added, "As will I."

Tancred offered his brother a mocking salute. "I will see you at the ship then."

Richard nodded and met Arianne's eyes. "I will come for you, my sweet Arianne. Fear naught, for God is your protector and keeper."

Arianne nodded, feeling complete peace in the matter. God would see her through this, and nothing Tancred could do or say would change how fully she had come to understand her heavenly Father's power. God was in control of the matter, she reasoned. Therefore, Tancred had no power over her life.

"Come along," Arianne bid Tancred. If they didn't move out, she feared, Richard might change his mind.

Chapter 17

The harsh dampness of the tunnels made Arianne shiver. She longed to pull the torch closer to her body for warmth, but Tancred seemed unconcerned with her plight and hurried her forward.

Nearing the tunnel opening, Arianne could hear the crashing waves on the rocks below like a great churning caldron. She wondered if the beach would be covered and if they would have to climb the rocks. Silently, she offered a prayer for strength, knowing that of her own accord she could never make it.

"We are nearly outside," Arianne whispered to the man beside her.

"Aye, I hear the sea," replied Tancred.

"It must be difficult to leave again."

"I beg your pardon?"

Arianne swallowed hard. Had she the bravery to continue this conversation? "I was only saying that it must be painful to leave your home again."

"Gavenshire is not my home. It was awarded to my brother after his faithful service to Henry. My lands were well to the south," Tancred replied with uncharacteristic softness.

"Does my husband also control those?"

"Nay, he didn't want them, so Henry took them," Tancred answered. Light from the tunnel opening guided their steps. "Hurry thy pace that we may reach my ship before Richard."

"Richard will have little trouble getting there ahead of us," Arianne replied. "We still have to climb down to the beach, or if the water is too high, we must climb up the cliff side. 'Twill be no easy matter for me, I assure you."

"You'll have plenty of time to rest once we're aboard my ship."

Arianne stopped dead in her tracks. Tancred was quite serious. "You mean to take me after giving Richard your word that you would leave me unharmed?"

"I don't intend to harm you," Tancred replied softly. He looked at Arianne with new eyes. "I am most sorry for the way I've treated you in the past, but it was necessary to take control. You must believe me. I will see my name cleared, and I will use whatever means I must in order to do just that."

"But you cannot hope to take me!" exclaimed Arianne. "Richard will never allow it."

"My brother loves you more than life," Tancred said, putting out the torch in the sandy soil of the tunnel floor. "I can count on that."

Arianne said nothing more. Tancred pulled her out into the sunlight and surveyed the scene.

"There is adequate clearance for us to take to the shore. We will be quick enough, and my ship is no more than a half a league around the bend. Come along, Milady."

Arianne's mind mulled over Tancred's plan even as he assisted her down the rocky path. She was amazed at the change in his attitude toward her. Perhaps the words she'd spoken had made him think about his plight. Perhaps no one had ever cared to defend him before.

"Sir Tancred," Arianne said, fighting with the skirt of her gown, "I do not fear you any longer."

The words seemed a bold declaration under the circumstances, but Tancred was not offended. He glanced over his shoulder at her with a smile so similar to Richard's that Arianne was stunned.

"It is well that you do not," Tancred replied. "I have no need for more enemies. I perceive that you see something of value in this exiled hide of mine. I do, however, require that you replace what once was fear with a healthy respect for my will. I am not a puppet to be played with, Milady, and in spite of my brother's pliability, you will not find me a character to be dallied with."

"You have much to overcome, Sire," Arianne replied thoughtfully. "I must believe that you were reared to fear God as Richard was. I must further believe from the stories my husband has told that you, too, must have listened to stories at your mother's knee."

"Speak not of my mother," Tancred said in a warning tone. "I will not hear of it."

"She must have loved you greatly," Arianne dared to continue. "I have heard Matilda speak of her."

"Enough!" Tancred said harshly and yanked Arianne's arm.

Arianne remained silent while they worked their way down to the beach. Tancred handed her down onto the shore without comment and pulled her in lengthy strides along the water's edge.

Arianne was gasping for breath by the time they reached the place where Tancred's ship was anchored. On the beach, a small boat with six men awaited Tancred's arrival.

Tightening his grip on Arianne, Tancred moved forward. In a flash, Richard stepped out from behind the rocks and, with him, over a dozen of his own men.

"Halt there!" he called to Tancred. "Release my wife and take to your ship."

Tancred took two more steps then stopped, pulling Arianne to his side. "I'm taking her with me. She will be my guarantee of safety from Henry and from your wrath."

"Try to take her and you will know more of my wrath than you had ever thought possible." Richard's words held a deadly tone.

Arianne's heart pounded at the scene unfolding before her. If she could not do something to assuage the tempers of these men, she could well be a widow by nightfall.

"I beg of you, Tancred," she whispered then turned to her husband. "Please, Richard, let this thing be at peace between you. Your brother knows naught of God and His mercy. You are God's witness to that mercy and love. If you do not show forth the light of God's truth, how will Tancred come to know it?"

"I am not his salvation," Richard replied, his eyes never leaving Tancred's stony face.

" 'Tis true you are not his salvation, but you have knowledge of the way to that salvation that has been forsaken or forgotten by your brother."

Richard's face was etched in pain. The truth of Arianne's words affected him in a way he couldn't explain. For so many years he had carried blind hatred for the man before him, certain that Tancred had been responsible for the deaths of their parents. But maybe Arianne was right. Perhaps Tancred had no responsibility in the murders. Maybe it was time to let go of his hatred.

"King Henry has etched in the walls of his palaces words that are most eloquent and true," Richard murmured. Tancred and Arianne waited in silence for him to continue. "It reads, 'He who does not give what he has will not get what he wants.' I must give up my hatred in order to find the peace that I desire."

"Will you let me pass?" Tancred asked. His grip tightened on Arianne, causing her to wince painfully.

"Not with my wife. You may leave and I freely give you your men and ship, but you will never leave English soil with Arianne. She is my wife and will remain here with me," Richard stated firmly.

Arianne held her breath, wondering what Tancred's reply would be. Without a word, Tancred pulled Arianne with him as he began to edge around Richard.

"I am no fool, dear brother. You could easily send your men to cut me down. With Arianne, I will have my assurance that you will behave in a gentlemanly manner and honor your word."

"You will not take her," Richard restated, and the sound of his sword being freed from the scabbard rang clear for all ears.

Tancred stopped as Richard raised his sword, but it was Arianne who stunned them both into silence. With a strength she'd not known she possessed, Arianne wrenched herself free from Tancred's grip and threw herself between Tancred and Richard.

"You will be no better than him," Arianne whispered desperately to her husband. "You cannot murder him, for his soul will haunt you for all eternity. You will always know that he died without God's forgiveness and that had you been merciful, Tancred might have lived to accept God."

The tip of Richard's sword pointed to Arianne's breast. Dumbfounded at her words, he didn't know how to respond.

Tancred, too, stood frozen in place. He was mesmerized by the young woman who so gallantly defended his right to live. He was troubled by her words of God's forgiveness, but he couldn't bring himself to betray the longing they stirred within.

"Please," Arianne begged, as the wind tore at her copper hair. Several strands fell across the raised blade, bringing Richard back to his senses.

"Go," Richard told his brother, lowering the sword slowly.

Tancred reached out for Arianne, but before Richard could move, Arianne turned to face her brother-in-law.

"Nay, Tancred," she whispered. "I will not go with you freely, and you will not force me. There is something of value within you; something yet redeemable and good. You are harsh and troubled, and there is much that you must confess before God, but you have my forgiveness for the evil you have done me. Let that be your starting place. Remember Henry's words with respect for their value, even if you cannot respect the man."

Tancred stared at Arianne and saw compassion in her eyes. It was the first time in many years that he had experienced such sincerity and generosity of spirit. He quickly stepped back as though being too near her caused him greater pain. Lifting his face to meet Richard's, he saw that Arianne's words had also humbled his brother.

Arianne moved into Richard's waiting arms. She relished the warmth and safety found there and sighed with relief as he pulled her close.

"And what of you, Brother?" Tancred suddenly found his tongue. "Have I your forgiveness as well?"

"Do you seek it?" Richard questioned without sarcasm.

Tancred was taken aback only for a moment. Richard's forgiveness was something he desired almost more than the reinstatement of his land and title. How could he have been so blinded by fury and hatred to have expected his brother to lie, even give his life up, in order to free him from exile?

"I came here to seek my freedom," Tancred answered and the sadness in his voice was not lost on the young couple before him. "I know naught of the peace you know in God. Mayhap in time it will be shown to me in the same manner it has been revealed to you. Mayhap I will lay to rest the demons from the past." He paused and shook his head. "I know naught what manner of woman you have married, Brother, but she is like none I have ever known. Do not consider her lightly, for there are few like her."

Richard smiled down at the woman in his arms. "Aye," he whispered, "I know it well."

Tancred turned to leave and then, remembering his brother's question, paused. "I did not slay our parents. Perhaps my negligence of them somehow aided in the deed, but not because I chose it to be so. I did not kill them."

Richard sobered and nodded. "I believe you." Deep peace filled his heart as Richard realized he meant the words in full.

"Then will you give me your forgiveness?" Tancred questioned.

"Aye," Richard replied. "You are free from my hatred. I desire nothing more than you live out your days in peace and in the true understanding of God's love." Then Richard added, "Will you forgive me?"

Tancred said nothing for several moments. He saw a truly great man in his brother, and it was difficult for him to realize that had things been different, they might have stood side by side.

"Aye," Tancred said. "You have my forgiveness." Without another word, he turned and waded into the water. There was no fear that Richard would have him murdered or waylaid en route to his exile. After a brief salute, Tancred climbed into the boat and never looked back.

Chapter 18

That night, Arianne sat deep in thought beside the hearth in their bed chamber. Staring into the fire, she wondered at the differences between Richard and his brother. What drove men to such contrasts? A noise behind her caused Arianne to look up only to find Richard's intense green eyes watching her.

"You creep more silently than the night itself," Arianne mused, then felt a warm blush edge her cheeks. Suddenly she felt very shy. The look on Richard's face stirred her heart and quickened her breath.

Richard crossed the room and pulled his wife against him. "I've missed you more dearly than anything else these walls could offer." He lowered his face to her hair and breathed in the unmistakable scent of Arianne's favorite soap. The long coppery curls wrapped around his fingers as he plunged his hands into the bulk. "You are perfection on earth," he sighed.

Arianne lifted her face from his chest with a mischievous grin. "I was thinking much the same of you," she admitted, causing Richard to chuckle.

"'Tis most grateful I am to have married a cunning, intelligent woman. Milady, you are a most precious jewel to me, and as long as I live, I will love no other."

Arianne reached up her hand to touch the neatly trimmed beard. "My heart's true love," she whispered.

Her brown eyes held the promise of a life of love, and in their reflection Richard found all that he had ever longed for. Gently, as though afraid the spell would be broken, Richard lowered his lips to Arianne's and kissed her with all the longing that had been denied them both. With his world once again at peace, Richard intended to concentrate on the fact that he and Arianne were yet newly wed.

Weeks blended into months, and Arianne knew a peace and contentment that was like nothing she'd ever imagined possible. Life with Richard was so much more than the routine tasks of the day. She never failed to be warmed by the glint in his eyes when he lifted his gaze from the company of his men to take note of her when she entered a room. Nor could she begin to understand the wonder of lying in his arms at night, feeling the rhythmic beat of his heart against her hand as it lay in casual possession of Richard's chest.

Forgotten were the days of her father's brutality and rage, for in Richard's care,

Arianne knew nothing more than the firm correction in his voice when she erred and the loving approval of his smile when she caused him great pride in something new she'd learned. There were still unanswered questions about his parents' deaths, but Arianne's only unfulfilled desire was to see her brother, Devon.

"Arianne!" Richard called from the great hall. "Arianne!"

Arianne rose from her work in the solarium and went in search of her husband. Matilda met her in the hall with a smile broader than the river that flowed nearby.

"Your Grace," she said with a light curtsey. "The duke will be most pleased to see you."

"And what has he to show me this time?" Arianne questioned with teasing in her voice. "The last time he arrived home with this much excitement, he brought me news that the king intended to receive us as guests. Pray tell, what could top that?"

Matilda smiled knowingly but said nothing as she hurried Arianne to the stone stairway. Arianne knew better than to question her maid, for when Matilda wanted to keep something to herself, she did so quite well.

Arianne lifted her skirts ever so slightly and in a most unladylike fashion hurried her descent. She hadn't reached the final step, however, before Richard reached out and lifted her into the air. Swinging her round and round until Arianne begged him to put her down, Richard couldn't contain his joy.

"What have you done this time?" Arianne asked with a grin.

"I have brought you a gift, Milady," he replied, taking her hand in his own. "And I believe it will meet wholeheartedly with your approval."

" 'Most everything you do meets with my approval," replied Arianne.

Richard raised an eyebrow and stopped in midstep. "Only 'most everything?"

"Well, there was that problem with the puppies you brought into our bed chamber," Arianne laughed, remembering an incident several days past.

"Who knew they could move so fast!" Richard said in his defense. "Besides, I caught them all again, didn't I?"

"True," Arianne nodded, trying to be serious, "but not before they'd tracked mud all over the room and threatened to raise the roof with their yipping and howls."

"Well, this time there will be no tracking of mud and no yipping or howling," Richard promised, pulling Arianne along with him once again.

"We shall see," she mused with a wifely air.

Entering the great hall, Arianne could see that nothing looked amiss. She glanced up curiously to catch her husband's eye, but Richard refused to give away his secret.

"Sit here," he commanded lovingly and assisted Arianne into a chair. "Now close your eyes."

Arianne's brow wrinkled ever so slightly and a smile played at the edge of her lips. "The last time you told me to do that—" Her words were cut off, however, when Richard insisted she be obedient.

"Hurry, now, or you'll spoil everything."

Arianne shook her head in mock exasperation, but nevertheless closed her eyes.

"Are they closed tight?" Richard asked her.

"Yes," she replied. "They are closed as tight as I can close them. Now will you please tell me what's going on."

"In a minute. I've almost got it ready," Richard answered.

"Remember your promise," teased Arianne while she waited in her self-imposed darkness.

"What promise was that, my dear?"

"No mud, no yipping, no howls," she said, laughing in spite of her struggle to remain serious.

"I promise," came a voice that did not belong to her husband. "You will get no such scene from me."

Arianne's heart skipped a beat. Her eyes flashed open wide to greet the vaguely familiar face of her brother. "Devon!" she cried and threw herself into his waiting arms.

"You are an enchanting sight for such weary eyes," Devon said, squeezing Arianne tightly. "We've been separated far too long."

"I can't believe you are truly here," Arianne replied and stepped back to search the room for Richard. He was leaning against the table with his arms folded against his chest and a broad grin on his face.

"I told you it would meet with your approval."

"Richard, you are indeed a wonder. However did you find him, and whatever possessed you to bring him here?" Arianne asked, returning her gaze to Devon.

"You spoke of him so often, I thought he might as well be here in body, as well as spirit. Henry had him in service elsewhere, but then Henry has always had a soft spot in his heart for me." Richard seemed quite pleased with himself, and Arianne broke away from Devon's side to embrace her husband.

"You are a man of many talents, Duke DuBonnet," she murmured against his ear before placing a light kiss upon his cheek.

Richard pulled her close, winking at Devon over her shoulder. "I knew this would make up for the puppies." He grinned.

Devon and Arianne both laughed at this. "I will never bring up the subject of the puppies again," Arianne promised. Her heart was overflowing with the love and happiness she felt at that moment. "How long can you stay, Devon?" she questioned, knowing that she might not like the answer.

"That depends on you," Devon replied with a knowing glance at Richard.

"On me?" Arianne's confusion was clear.

"Aye," Devon said with a nod. "How long will you have me?"

Arianne moved to her brother, pulling Richard along with her. "I'd have you here forever," she answered and looped her free arm through Devon's.

"That might be pressing it, my love." Richard's voice held a tone of teasing. "Why not just until King Henry rewards him with lands of his own for the service he's so faithfully given?"

Arianne could not have looked more pleased. "Truly?" she asked. "Truly, Henry is going to bestow a title upon him?"

" 'Tis true enough," Richard replied. "But, until then, Devon is our guest and—"

Devon interrupted, "And your most humble servant, Milady."

"Nay," Arianne said, shaking her head. "Never that. Just a long lost soul who has finally come home to those who love him." The pleasure on her face was clear. "And, for that I truly thank God, King Henry, and my most tenderhearted husband."

Later that evening, Arianne sought out Richard in their bed chamber. He had just finished with his bath and was donning one of the lined tunics she'd made for him.

"These have worked like a wonder," he commented. "I don't think I've ever had a chance to thank you properly for the thoughtfulness of your work."

Arianne smiled. "It was a task I took to with a glad heart, for I knew it would be well received."

"Aye, that it has. I see that Devon, too, has been well received."

"Oh, most assuredly. Richard, I cannot tell you what it means to me to have him here. I have missed him sorely and look forward to rekindling our friendship. Already he has shared many great stories of his adventures."

"What of your father?" Richard asked softly. "Has he given you word of him?"

"Nay," Arianne replied and walked away to the window. "But, neither have I asked. 'Tis a difficult matter. I am glad my father is not alone, and I pray his new wife makes him happy. I hold him no malice. I simply wish to forget the sorrow."

"No doubt your mother's passing grieved him in a way that left him unable to deal with his children properly," Richard said from behind her.

"Mayhap he grieved that she never loved him," Arianne replied without turning. "He always knew, and in spite of the fact that he never told her, I believe my father loved my mother."

"Hopefully things will be different this time. Devon tells me your stepmother will bear him a child."

Arianne turned and stared at her husband in surprise. "Is this true?"

"Aye," Richard said. He sat down on the edge of the bed and awaited Arianne's response to the news.

"When?" she questioned so softly that Richard nearly missed the word.

"Devon tells me the babe should be born after Hocktide at the end of Easter."

Arianne completely surprised Richard as a mischievous grin spread across her face. "Good," she said, folding her arms against her body. "I shall beat her by a fortnight, at least."

Richard stared dumbly for a moment, not fully understanding the news his wife had just shared.

Arianne continued before he could question her. "Matilda tells me we should expect to become parents in the spring." Anticipation and joy radiated from Arianne's countenance.

Richard shook his head as if trying to awaken from a dream. "Parents?" he questioned, coming to his feet. "You're going to give me a child? How long have you known?"

Arianne giggled like a little girl with a secret. "I've only just learned this myself, Your Grace. But you will admit, 'tis a surprise that ranks at least as high as puppies."

At this Richard's laughter filled the chamber. He lifted Arianne in his arms and hugged her tightly. "Madam, it most assuredly surpasses all my other surprises. I am most pleased at this news. God has given me all that a man could want and then doubled it. My joy truly knows no bounds."

Arianne sighed against the warmth of her husband. "I feel the same, and had I not been forced by the king into marriage with you, I would never have known what a truly remarkable man you are. And had you been any less remarkable, I would never have known what true love was about. You have given me much, Richard. A child, a home, a loving companion for life, but even more: You opened my eyes to the love of God. A love that reigns here," she whispered and placed his hand over her heart, "because one man heard the soft call of His master's voice above the roar of men's."

"Sweet Arianne," Richard murmured, lifting his hand to cup her chin. "In the stillness of His love, we will heed His call together. All of our lives we will face the future knowing that He has seen what is to come and walks the path beside us. There will be no kingdom divided or heart destroyed, so long as we keep our steps with Him."

Alas My Love

To Dr. Doug Iliff, physician extraordinaire and good friend. With thanks for his time, trouble, and good sense of humor when I call up with those pesky questions.

Chapter 1

Helena Talbot held back a strangled cry as the whip came down again. Her tender skin, marred with bleeding welts, bore yet another strike. Would it never end?

Stripped to her lightest linen tunic, Helena received the punishment of her defiance without a word of protest. Twenty years old, without mother or father in this world, Helena faced her stepbrother's demands and temper.

"Will you go?" Roger Talbot questioned, and again Helena shook her head.

He grimaced and raised the whip, while Helena steadied herself as best she could. Her strength had given out hours ago, so she stood on sheer determination alone. She longed for the dizziness to overtake her and put her mind from the whip's biting edge. Even death would be a welcome relief.

"Your refusal has caused this grief," he said firmly but with a hint of gentleness to his tone. "I find no pleasure in punishment." Helena believed it to be true. At one time, she and Roger had been the closest of friends.

"I. . .I cannot." Helena wanted so very much to sound brave, but in truth her words were barely audible. Through fading consciousness, she knew his displeasure. Poor man. If not for his sister Maude, Roger would never have forced the situation. Maude's jealousy had tainted Roger's love. For over twenty years, Maude had loudly protested the interference of Helena's mother, Eleanor, and then of Helena herself. With Eleanor only days in the grave and the words of her funeral service still ringing in Helena's ears, Roger found no way to ignore Maude's demands.

"Give her over to the church," Maude had told him in a hushed whisper while Helena cried over her mother's still body. "Send her with haste."

They believed me too grieved to understand, Helena thought. Even then she'd known this would be a bitter battle to the end.

A chill, damp wind blew across the newly plowed fields. The rich aroma of dirt assailed Helena's meager senses. Home! At least the only home she'd ever known. Now with her beloved mother and stepfather both dead, no one was left who cared for her. No one except perhaps Tanny. Images from the past flooded her mind to offer comfort.

Helena, oblivious to Roger's consternation, slumped against the whipping post. As she did, she could feel the braided hemp bite into her wrists. How long had she been there? First Roger had made her stand for hours, bound to the post

111

and exposed to the elements. After that, he'd deprived her of food and drink, all in hopes that she would acquiesce to his will.

Helena knew, however, that she had a most special circumstance. It was because of this circumstance that Helena remained strong in her resolve, refusing to give even the slightest consideration to her stepbrother and stepsister's plans. Helena smiled to herself, even in her half-conscious state. Her mother, Eleanor, had been second-cousin to the queen. Not only had they been related, but they had also been the dearest friends. Because of this, King Henry III would not hear the demands of Roger Talbot to force a marriage upon his young stepsister. The king had instead listened to his wife and Eleanor in their pleading to allow Helena to marry, not as customary in an arranged affair, but for love.

And Helena had loved. With all her heart she had loved a man who barely knew of her existence. She didn't blame him, though. When last he'd seen her, she had been a mere child of nine, but her love for him was eternal.

"Tanny," she breathed the name, not realizing she'd done so aloud.

"What say you?" Roger stepped forward anxiously. "I demand you speak to me."

Helena's head bobbed and swayed in rhythm with the wind. She barely heard Roger's words. She tried to move, but the fire in her back caused her to gasp for breath before surrendering to the black oblivion her mind offered. Her fading thoughts were of her beloved. Tanny!

"Helena!" Roger rushed forward, afraid that he'd dealt her one blow too many. How many times had he hit her? Five? Six? He reached out for her crumpled form and lifted her upward in order to release her bonds from the overhead hook. God alone would be his refuge if Henry learned of this matter.

"Helena," he spoke once more, this time against her ear. Roger had no way of knowing whether she heard him.

Cursing, he called for help. "Take her to her room," he said to two men who waited nearby. Then turning to Helena's maid, Sarah, he added, "Make her comfortable and cleanse the wounds."

The woman nodded her reddened face. "Aye, Milord. 'Tis my duty."

Helena writhed and moaned as Sarah gently rubbed salve into her wounds. *Thanks be to the Creator,* Sarah thought, *the cuts were not deep.* Still it grieved her and tears rolled down her weathered cheeks.

Sarah, still crying in soft sobs, dressed the wounds as best she could. Her poor lamb did not deserve the heavy hand of her stepbrother.

"Hush now, my little one." Sarah sprinkled a concoction of herbs over the worst of the cuts and offered what consolation she could. "No one will hurt you now."

"Tanny," Helena whispered. "I, I want Tanny."

Sarah struggled to make out the words, but knew without a doubt that Helena was speaking of her one true love.

"Just rest, Milady. 'Tis sure that your love will come one day. Just rest." Sarah spoke the words even if she didn't believe them. She prayed they would comfort the young woman and give her peace of mind.

In her strange state of dreams, Helena saw the face of the man she'd loved. Gentle, dark eyes teased her with winks, and a laughing face crowded out the memory of the burning pain in her back. She imagined her beloved returning from the sea. His longing would match her own and she would rush to his side and proclaim her love. She would write a song for him, she thought through the haze of her sleep. Yes, she would write him a love song.

For as long as she could remember, Helena had been devoted to music. She wrote songs and sang them, always finding a closeness with God when she did so. She devoted most of her music to the goodness and wonder of God and His creation. But some songs, little snippets really, were devoted to more emotional and personal matters. She'd written half a dozen songs to declare her love to a man who thought her only capable of child's play.

Smiling to herself now, Helena imagined the days when they were all together; a time when her stepfather had been alive and Tanny had fostered in their home. She had been but a tiny child then, still under her nurse's care.

"What a frightful sight you are!" It was Tanny's voice she heard, just as clearly as if it had been yesterday. She had been playing in the barn and was covered in a variety of things, some most disagreeable and odorous. Roger and Tanny had found her and knew that her nursemaid would beat her for disobeying and visiting with the animals.

"You've been to the mews as well," Roger had said, picking bird feathers from her hair. The young men agreed to clean her up and keep the nurse from learning of her actions. And that was when Helena had lost her heart. Sitting on Tanny's lap while he used a wet cloth to wipe her face, she had stared into his kind eyes and fallen in love.

A sound at the door brought Helena awake and surprisingly clearheaded. Maude and Roger entered the room, heavy in discussion on the matter of Helena's beating. Helena pretended to sleep, but watched cautiously from barely opened eyes. No sense in letting them nag her just yet.

"You've softened in your old age," Maude said to Roger. "She hardly looks worse for the ordeal."

He stared at her a moment in disbelief. "Did you not see the marks?" He waved a hand over Helena. "Henry will have me swinging from a gibbet."

His frown deepened and he moved away to the window where Helena couldn't see him. "I did as you bade me, Maude. I starved the child and forced her to endure more punishment than our father would have dealt out to a wayward villein."

"Our father was a weakling when it came to Helena. He pampered and spoiled her at every turn." Maude's gray eyes narrowed. "Have ye our father's heart?"

"Our father had no heart for unjust affairs and neither do I. I would hardly call this a pampering."

Helena wanted to cheer Roger's retort. Maude always bullied him, and Helena hated the way he allowed her to dominate their home.

"You have endured Helena's childish demands that she be allowed to choose her own husband, but honestly, Roger." Maude paused to emphasize the emotion of the moment. "She is a woman of a full score. What man would take her now?"

Roger laughed aloud. "Helena could have any suitor she wanted. 'Tis this that grieves you most, me thinks." Helena almost giggled at this and quickly moaned and coughed to disguise her reaction.

Roger came to her bedside, but Maude remained where she stood. "Helena? Can you hear me?" Helena let out another moan, but refused to offer anything more.

Let him think I'm nearly dead, she thought. *Then maybe the fear of what he's done will sink in and he'll stand up to Maude.*

Maude gave Roger no time to consider the matter, however. "Even the king cannot expect you to continue responsibility for one so wayward."

"The king will expect me to heed his wishes."

"But she is past marriageable age," Maude protested, coming within Helena's view.

"So are you, my dear sister. Or have you forgotten you hold seven years in addition to Helena's twenty? Age has not stopped you from looking for another husband."

Maude grimaced. "But I am a widow. My status is more favorable for a union."

Roger sighed. "I have done what you asked of me. I beat the child and still she refused."

"Then have her taken away," Maude said menacingly. "Have her taken away tonight before she regains enough strength to object."

Helena felt her breath catch. Would Roger actually listen to Maude and do as she suggested? If that happened, what hope would there ever be of finding Tanny or of him finding her?

"And bear the wrath of King Henry? When he learns of this, I will be lucky to retain my life, much less my title." Helena felt Roger's hand upon her forehead. He smoothed back her hair, and Helena couldn't resist feeling some pity for him.

Maude viewed the entire matter disdainfully. She clucked her tongue. "Poor brother. The responsibilities put upon your shoulders are too great. I shall ease your burden and make the arrangements myself. She will be removed tonight."

"I am lord of this manor and you are but my sister. Bide thy tongue carefully, or it will be you who makes the journey to the abbey." With that he turned and stomped out of the room, while Maude stared after him.

"Think to threaten me, will you? Ha!" Maude stated to no one in particular. She let her gaze travel to Helena. "Precious Helena. Exalted child. You had but to crook your finger at anyone, be it man, woman, or child, and they would quickly come to do your bidding." Helena's body trembled. Maude's tone was so menacing and hate-filled. Would she go so far as to see Helena permanently removed from her life?

"You are just like your mother," Maude said, her face contorted in rage. "The best of everything came to you both, even though I was here first. You stole my place and took my father's love."

Helena moaned and pretended to be struggling to wake up. She hoped Maude would see this and decide to leave before her stepsister became conscious, but it was not to be.

"Poor Helena. Do your injuries cause you pain? I pray they do. I pray you find the same pain I did. The same pain you and your perfect mother dealt me as a child of seven. I was sent away," she muttered, still staring down at Helena's pale form. "They sent me away to foster in a convent, while you remained to nibble at my father's heart until there was naught left for me. Now I will send you away and there will be no one to mourn your passing."

"Maude!" It was Roger calling from the hall below. "Maude!"

"We will settle this matter yet," Maude whispered and withdrew from the room to leave Helena trembling and afraid.

It was as if the angry words had taken what little strength Helena had. "What am I to do, Lord?" Her whispered voice was little more than a croak.

In the hall, Maude paced out a pattern on the rush-covered floor. Fresh herbs had been mixed in with the rushes just that morning, but the damp, stale odor of the closed-up manor hung thick in the air. It only served to add to Maude's restlessness. She had come at her brother's demanding calls, but found instead that he'd been distracted by a groomsman who needed his advice regarding the saddle sores of one of his cherished horses.

"I wait to do Roger's bidding, while he concerns himself with dung heaps and festering wounds," she muttered. Then as if speaking his name could suddenly conjure his form, Roger crashed through the door. It had started to rain and he was soaked from the exposure.

"Prepare me hot ale," he said to a waiting servant. The man nodded and hurried away to do his master's bidding. After the servant disappeared behind the screens that divided the kitchen from the great hall, Roger finally acknowledged Maude.

" 'Twill be a beastly night," he remarked, casting his drenched garde-corp to a peg beside the door. Freed of this outer coat, Roger found his remaining clothes to be fairly dry.

Maude motioned him to the far side of the room as tables were brought out and set up in preparation for the supper meal. Maude spoke in a low, hushed tone. "I can arrange for Helena to be taken from this house and delivered to the convent.

You are the final authority, of course," she said to placate him.

"You would send her out in this storm?" Roger questioned.

"Nay, 'tis unnecessary to endanger the horses," Maude replied. She knew the lives of his horses were of the utmost concern to her brother.

Maude noticed Roger's uneasy frown. "Fret not, brother dear," she said in feigned sympathy, "the life of a nun is quite good. Our sister will be well cared for and work only six of a day's hours. And those hours will be spent in choir practice—singing as she so loves to do. With a voice such as Helena has been given, surely she will be happy with her life there."

" 'Tis not her choice," Roger spoke absentmindedly.

Maude could see that he was not giving her his total attention. "Helena should have no choice. No other woman would, but because of Lady Eleanor's constant nagging—"

"Now you insult the dead?" Roger interrupted. He paused only long enough to retrieve the drink offered him by a young boy. " 'Twas my understanding," he said, pausing to draw deeply from the tankard, "that we put Lady Eleanor to rest. Must you constantly bring her back?"

Maude scowled. "Indeed not. I seek to dismiss her presence once and for all. 'Tis you, Milord, who keeps her walking the rooms of this pitiful manor. Send Helena away and bury them both."

Roger frowned into his cup. "King Henry will still question Helena's disappearance. With Eleanor gone, no doubt the queen would call for Helena to attend her in court. Would that not suffice?"

"Never!" Maude's screech caused a young woman to drop several empty mugs. The girl hastened to retrieve the still-clattering mess, while Maude lowered her voice. "Never. Helena would punish us both for what has happened. No, send her away with instructions to all that she has taken a vow of silence. Even the king will not question her choice of mourning."

"I will consider it," Roger said. The inviting aroma of beef stew, mutton pies, and roast pigeon caused him to wave away Maude's protests. "First we will sup; then we will reason out the matter of Helena."

Maude nodded, following Roger to the table. Neither one of them saw Helena's crumpled form at the top of the stairs. With barely enough strength to crawl back to her bed, Helena realized she had to make plans and make them quickly.

"Oh God, help me," she moaned, throwing herself across the narrow bed. The fiery reminders of her brother's handiwork pierced her and caused her to cry aloud. "God, where are You?"

Chapter 2

Heavy fog blotted out the scenery surrounding the manor and left an eerie silence to engulf the land. The dampness permeated everything, including the clothes and cloak that Helena had been dressed in for her journey.

Without resistance, Helena had allowed the transfer of her body to a makeshift litter. She feigned great weakness and exhaustion, while Roger ordered a blanket to be placed over her body. Only Sarah knew that her wounds were quickly healing and that the cloudiness had left her thinking. It was Helena's plan to give them no reason to think her capable of escape.

Helena observed as Roger slipped a coin into the hand of the man that waited near her litter. "Understand this, no longer is harm going to come to her. I will, myself, contact the abbess to learn of her well-being."

"As you wish it, Milord," the man replied, revealing a gap where two teeth were missing.

Maude looked on in bored indifference. Helena knew that her stepsister's only concern was that they'd be on their way before Helena regained strength and offered a fight. With deep sadness, Helena closed her eyes.

"Let them be off," Maude finally said.

Helena narrowly opened her eyes to see Roger glance at Maude briefly before nodding. "Aye. Be gone then." The man gave a curt bow, then motioned his comrade to lead his horse forward.

"I'll await your return," Roger called after the man. "See no harm comes to the horse."

Helena waited to open her eyes full until the stranger who walked at her feet moved forward to speak with his comrade. They were oblivious to her, and for this, Helena rejoiced. Jostling along on the litter, Helena contemplated the situation and wondered when opportunity would lend itself to her escape.

She could not let either the men who accompanied her or Roger know where she had gone. Roger would expect her destination to be London and so it would be. But Helena was smart enough to realize that the direct routes would have to be avoided. She could neither take to the road nor seek out help from other travelers. No, it would be necessary to travel under cover of darkness and stick to the fields and forests. So long as she continued south, all would eventually be well.

As she prayed for guidance, Helena remembered the comfort of bedtime prayers when she'd been a small child. The dark frightened her as little else did, and her mother was good to stay by her side and pray away the gloom. *Oh, Mother,* she thought, wiping out the tears in her eyes, *I'm glad you cannot see me now.*

When the morning sun rose high enough to burn off the fog, Helena remained unmoving and silent. Feigning sleep, she opened her eyes only on occasion to see her surroundings. They were traveling south, and from her brother's directions, Helena knew that the longer she stayed with the men, the closer she'd come to London. However, she also worried about her safety with these coarse, unkempt ruffians. They laughed loudly as they talked together and, from time to time, discussed the crude pleasures they would seek once they'd earned the rest of their pay.

Helena shuddered as she realized she had no protector. Why her clothes alone could be resold for more than these two could earn in a month. Was there no one who could know her fate should they decide to do her harm? But even as fear stirred her blood, a small voice inside told her that God was her protector as He had always been. Remembering this came as a comfort and Helena relaxed. God was her protector. It was enough.

She let them believe her asleep until they came to a halt for the night. Only then did she moan out a request for a drink of water.

"Be it well with ye then?" one of the men asked her.

"I hurt," she managed to whisper. It wasn't a lie.

"Aye," was all he said before seeing to the horse.

After the horse was tethered and cared for, the man who'd spoken to Roger brought Helena a chunk of bread and cheese. He said nothing to her, but left the food at her fingertips and took himself off to tend the fire his companion had built.

Helena struggled to sit up. She pulled her cloak tight and ate part of the food given to her. With a watchful eye, she tucked the remaining bread under the surcoat and inside her tunic. She felt strangely at peace with the arrangement. She would watch and pray for the perfect moment to escape, and when she did, she would have food to take along for her journey.

Overhead, the stars were clear and brilliant. They sparkled like diamonds. Helena studied them for a moment and thought of her love. Perhaps wherever he was, he, too, was looking at the stars and thinking of her. Shaking her head sadly, Helena knew it wasn't so. Tanny didn't know she existed. At least not as a woman. No, the Helena he knew existed only as a scrawny tomboyish child.

" 'Tis of no matter," Helena whispered to the starry night. "I hold enough love for us both."

In time, Helena felt herself grow stronger, but for the sake of her companion as she continued to feign weakness. Waiting and watching, Helena's patience was rewarded when the opportunity to escape presented itself to her.

" 'Tis less than a half-day journey," one of the men stated. They were watering the horse and contemplating whether or not to set up camp.

"I say we push on," the other replied. "The abbey will offer us shelter. Better to keep going and spend the night, even a small portion of it, under a roof than out here in the cold."

"It bodes well with me. We can be there before morning and enjoy a hot meal with our rest."

Helena felt her heart skip a beat. The time had come. She didn't know exactly where they were, but she knew they were well away from Roger and Maude. She contented herself with this while contemplating what to do next.

There were woods on either side of the road that would afford her cover during her escape. There was also the blessing of a cloudless night and moonlight to guide her way. The only real problem was escaping the notice of her companions, but that came soon enough.

With the horse slowly plodding along, the first man spoke up. "I say we go to London after the deed is done and our pay is in hand. We can buy our comforts there and gamble for even more."

"London's not fer me. Ye forget I be a marked man there. I say we sail to Normandy. Me sister be there and we could hold up a spell with her."

"Normandy? I'll have no part of Normandy!" They argued on, their voices rising ever higher with the flaring of their tempers.

Knowing that the debate would block out any noise of her escape, Helena rolled from the litter and lay in silence at the edge of the road. A heady scent of the land rushed up to assail her senses. No doubt the soft dirt would ruin her fine burgundy velvet, but no matter. If she could escape to London, there would always be the opportunity for more velvet.

Helena's breathing quickened as she waited for what seemed an eternity, certain that at any given moment the horse would be halted and the men would come back for her. If they came back, she would simply pretend to be asleep and let them assume that she'd rolled off the litter by mistake.

She squeezed her eyes shut tightly, almost as if in doing so she could make herself invisible. They just had to keep going without her, she thought. This was her only hope. When the noisy argument faded into the distance, Helena realized they were unaware of her absence.

Gingerly sitting up, Helena untangled herself from the blanket that had covered her on the litter. She was grateful for the additional warmth as the night chill seemed to penetrate her bones. *Thanks be to God,* she thought, *that the winter was mild and spring has come early.*

Standing came with more difficulty. She had only been on her feet for short periods of time in the past days. Those times had come only out of necessity to relieve herself, and they were brief and nontaxing. Now, however, she faced the need not only to walk a great distance, but to do so quickly. Stretching her limbs, she began to have doubts.

"O God," she whispered to the starry sky overhead, "please be with me. I beg Ye, Lord Father, give me the strength to make this journey." She felt better just in knowing that she would not travel alone.

By the end of her third day and night, Helena was far less confident. She had long since run out of food, and the only water she had was that which she found along the way. Her back, though mostly healed, was stiff and sore, and at times the scabs would rub against the rough material of her tunic.

"I must keep going," she told herself aloud. "Roger's men will find me and I cannot let that be. I must get to London. I must find Tanny." She remembered her beloved with his dark eyes and tender words. What kindnesses he had shown to Helena as a child were indelibly fixed in her memories.

Skirting a nearby village, Helena walked across the ridges and furrows of a newly plowed field. Exhaustion washed over her like waves claiming a shore. Dropping to her knees, she felt despair claim her. *This is hopeless,* she thought. *I can't go on.*

❧

John Tancred DuBonnet stared at the timber framework of the wattle and daub hovel. The wind outside shook it fiercely, and any moment he expected it to give into the force and collapse.

"So fall down upon me," Tancred said, emotion thick in his voice. "At least then my suffering would be done."

He knew deep despair, and the single-room hut with its open floor hearth did nothing to ease his miseries. With something akin to apathy, Tancred reached down to tend the fire. *Why bother,* he thought, *to resurrect a dying flame that offered little warmth and no real comfort?*

Sheltered away from the rest of the world, Tancred faced yet another year of exile from his beloved England. The home he'd once known was long since removed from his grasp, as were his family and friends. Sitting down to the poorly contrived trestle table, he absentmindedly toyed with a wooden bowl of cold pea soup and longed for home.

It had been eleven years since he'd been falsely accused of the murder of his parents. King Henry III of England had listened to the impassioned testimony of Richard, Tancred's younger brother. Richard had found Tancred standing over the bodies of their dead parents, knife in hand, the blood still wet upon the blade.

"Murderer!" Richard had shouted accusingly.

Tancred had pleaded his case, begged for understanding, then listened as his accusers found him guilty. He should rightly have been sentenced to death, but Richard had intervened. Even hatred for his brother could not bring the tenderhearted Richard to support his brother's hanging. He had, instead, encouraged Henry to be merciful. Some mercy!

"Condemned for a deed I had no part of," Tancred muttered. Tancred remembered the blind hatred he had once felt for his brother—hatred that had led him to action. Only last fall, he'd stormed Richard's home in Gavenshire, taken Richard's wife hostage, and later confronted the man who'd been responsible for his painful years of poverty. All for nothing. Tancred's exile continued.

Pushing the dish away, Tancred knew his misery had grown to a level he could no longer abide. Death would be sweet relief from the agony of facing another day. Yet, there was something that kept him from taking his own life. Something planted there in the deepest part of his heart by Richard's wife, Arianne.

"Would that the woman had kept her mouth closed," Tancred moaned, putting his head in his hands. For several minutes he did nothing, then lifting his face again, he stared upward to the hole in the thatched roof where the hearth smoke escaped into the stormy night.

"How can it be that God could care for me?" he questioned. "He leaves me here rejected of man and despised by all. And for what?" Tancred's voice rose accusingly. "For a crime I have not committed. Where be the justice in this?"

Just then a knock sounded. Tancred gazed at the door in disbelief. " 'Twould be madness to be out on this night," he announced, yet got to his feet.

Pulling the door open and feeling the wind and rain pelt his face in sheer fury, Tancred noted the battered pilgrim who stared back.

"Enter, soul," he shouted and pulled the man within the questionable comforts of the hut. Tancred wrestled the door back in place, then turned to study his visitor.

The man was at least a score of years older than Tancred's thirty-one. His stooped shoulders gave evidence to his many hours spent over a writing table, and his ink-stained fingers confirmed his occupation of scribe.

"My thanks to you," the man panted with a broad grin. " 'Tis no night for casual strolls in the countryside."

Tancred nodded but did not smile. "What seek ye here?"

"Shelter, if thou wilt have me," the man replied, pushing back rain-drenched white hair.

"You are welcome to what hospitality this hovel affords. I have but the floor to sleep upon and precious little else to offer."

The man smiled. " 'Tis enough."

"Very well," Tancred stated with a shrug. "Be welcomed."

The man pulled off his heavy wool cloak, revealing a large sack beneath it. "I cannot impose without sharing my own good fortune," the man said, placing the wet cloak on the empty peg beside the door.

Tancred eyed the bag with some interest but said nothing. The pilgrim smiled broadly as he opened the sack and brought out a loaf of bread. He handed it to Tancred and returned to rummage for something else.

"There is more," he said with joy in his voice. "I passed supper with a wealthy merchantman and he bade me take this for my journey." He drew out a grease-stained cloth and opened it to reveal a portion of mutton.

Tancred felt his stomach rumble. How long had it been since he'd enjoyed a fine piece of meat such as this?

"I do not require this of you," he finally told the smiling man. "You are welcome here without need to share such a treasure."

" 'Tis my joy to share with you," the man stated. "I am Artimas, and the Lord is my keeper. He gives to me generously, and I in turn give to those He sends my way. Let us sup together and enjoy this feast, for on the morrow, the Lord will surely supply again."

Tancred shook his head in wonder at the man. "You have great faith indeed to wander from place to place with little more than the cloak. It is always true that God provides for your hunger?"

Artimas smiled. "Do I look underfed, my friend?"

This time Tancred did smile, for the man was rather stocky and bore the look of one who was never late to the noon meal. "You do not," Tancred finally replied.

"Then let my appearance be evidence of God's goodness. Come, we can warm this meat and reason together."

Tancred could only stare after the man as he made himself comfortable by the hearth fire. Was this some divine intervention to keep him from giving in to his despair? Surely God cared little for whether he continued to hope for redemption. Yet if not by God's hand, then from where else could Artimas have come? This hovel was well off the main roadway and of little concern to anyone for miles around.

Tancred moved to join the man at the fire. "How came ye by this way?"

"I was led," Artimas replied simply.

"Led? By whom?"

Artimas glanced upward. "By He who always leads me."

Tancred couldn't accept the deliberate confidence of the man before him. "And why would God bring you here?" he asked gruffly.

Artimas patted the beaten dirt floor. "You might best answer that question yourself."

It was some hours past their first meeting when Artimas looked up from across the fire and questioned, "So ye stand accused of something ye did not do?"

"Aye," Tancred replied with a dark scowl marring his features. "The blood of my parents is upon my head. I did not kill them, but all of England believes it so, mayhaps even all the world."

Artimas smiled indulgently. "I have seen a fair piece of this world in the last few years and I have yet to hear your name mentioned amidst the crowds."

Tancred's face relaxed and for a moment he fell silent. "I seek the true killer," he finally said in a reserved manner.

"Ah," Artimas said with a grin, "to free your name and see justice served."

"Partly." The scowl had returned and the deep brooding in his eyes was now intensified with bitter hatred.

"Only partly?" puzzled Artimas. "For what other purpose would you desire this madman be captured?"

Tancred met Artimas's gaze. "Revenge," he stated softly, then with more clarity repeated the word. "Revenge!"

Chapter 3

Helena awoke to find a plump, young woman lingering at her bedside. She focused her eyes and realized the woman was smiling at her.

"There ye be," the woman said as if Helena had accomplished some wondrous feat. "We were beginning to fret."

"Where am I?" The stiffness in her body caused Helena to cry out in pain.

"There, there," the woman said, easing Helena back to the straw mattress. " 'Tis no good your trying to move about. Rest is what you need."

"Who are you?"

The woman smiled. "I might ask you the same thing. I am Mary. My husband, Felix, found you in the field as he prepared to sow seed. He brought you to me and I have cared for you."

"Thank you, Mary," Helena murmured, gingerly stretching her limbs. "What is this place?"

" 'Tis Gavenshire." Mary's voice betrayed her surprise. "The castle lies yonder."

"I'm not familiar with it. Is it near York?"

"Not so near. Closer to Brid."

"Brid?" Helena questioned.

Mary shook her head at the strange young woman in her bed. "Ye know naught of it? How did you come to be upon these lands?"

Helena frowned. Memory served her faithfully, but a reminder of her brother's henchmen gave her reason to remain quiet. "I know naught," she finally replied. In truth, she knew naught of Gavenshire.

"You have no memory of the journey?"

Helena did not answer. She watched Mary grow increasingly uncomfortable. The silence hung heavy between them for several moments before Mary finally cleared her throat and asked, "What. . .what is your name?"

"Helena. That much I remember." Helena hoped it would ease the furrowed brow of her caretaker.

" 'Tis something," Mary said, trying to force a smile. "I will bring you broth to warm your bones. Mayhaps with food, your memory will return."

"Mayhaps."

Helena watched as Mary bustled around the one-room house. The accommodations were poor and such that Helena instantly felt guilty for the trouble she was causing. Silently appraising Mary's meager surroundings, Helena knew that anything the other woman offered would be a sacrifice. Despite the pain, Helena forced herself to sit up.

"There's no need to put yourself out on my account," Helena stated. The drab little house seemed to grow smaller by the minute.

" 'Tis no bother, Milady," Mary said, clearly acknowledging that she accepted Helena as her superior.

Helena said nothing about this. She watched as Mary put more peat on the fire before bringing her a wooden bowl filled with steaming broth.

"This will see you right," Mary said with a meager smile. "I am sorry 'tis not more."

Helena sampled the soup. " 'Tis fine broth—the best I've ever known."

In spite of her concern, Mary beamed at the compliment.

"Thank you, Milady." She quickly went back to the fire and stoked it with a poker.

Straightening up and looking again at Helena, Mary spoke.

"Ye are gentle born, of that there is no doubting."

Helena swallowed hard and nodded. "I suppose 'tis true enough. The evidence is upon my body." She waved a free hand over her surcoat of velvet.

"Aye, that and the way you talk. Mayhaps someone at the castle knows of you." She left it at that and bustled over to the only other piece of furniture in the house, the herb-laden table.

Mary's plump frame did nothing to slow her down. Helena watched the woman dart around the room and decided to leave well enough alone. If she showed fear or objection at Mary's suggestion, it would no doubt give her further concern. Besides, Helena reasoned, no one at the castle would know her because she had never heard of Gavenshire.

Helena relaxed, drank the soup, and watched Mary at work. She was an earthy creature with a dark brown braid that hung down her back. Her coarse wool kirtle of woad blue did little to make her more attractive, yet there was kindness about Mary that made Helena feel like the shoddy one.

Mary glanced up from where she ground herbs. "Feeling better?"

"A little, thank you. I am certain that your fine care has given me health." Helena finished the broth and started to get up.

Mary rushed to her side. "Nay, stay and rest. My husband will return shortly and we will send word to the castle for your care."

Helena eased back against the straw-filled mattress with a sigh. She glanced across the room to the only window and noted the fading light. There was nothing to do but wait for Mary's husband.

Soon enough the sound of someone nearing the hovel caused Mary to perk up and cock her head. " 'Tis Felix," she confirmed for Helena's benefit, then went to open the door and greet her husband.

Helena watched as a large filthy man in a ragged wool tunic entered the door frame. The man had huge hands, which quickly wrapped themselves around Mary's stout waist.

"Wife," Felix said with a grin, " 'tis the face of an angel ye have."

He gave her a quick kiss on the lips.

"Go on with ye." Mary's mock protest was given with a smile.

Felix noted that Helena was awake and dropped his hold on Mary. "So ye have come around."

Helena nodded. "Mary tells me that you found me in the fields. I am most grateful for your care and hospitality."

Felix noted Helena's refined manner of speech with an arching of his brow and a questioning glance at his wife. Helena saved Mary the trouble of explanation.

"My name is Helena, although I can scarce offer more than this. Your wife suggested that someone from the castle might best assist me. I would be grateful if you would send word on my behalf."

Felix nodded. "Were you traveling alone?"

"I—it seems so." Helena hated being caught up in the deception, but she feared reprisal from Roger more than the consequence of her actions.

"Ye have no memory of it?"

"I—I'm confused." Helena sat up and threw her legs over the edge of the bed. "If it is too much trouble to send word, I can attempt the journey myself."

"Nay, I could not let you," Felix replied firmly. "I will find the bailiff and ask him to settle the matter."

"Thank you, Felix." Helena's voice rang sincere even if her heart questioned the sanity of her actions.

Felix was to only have been gone for a matter of minutes, but instead was gone for nearly half of the hour. Mary began to fret, and Helena worried that she'd somehow caused the man grief. When he did finally reappear, he came with a stranger by his side.

"Milady," the man said, stepping forward to offer his hand to Helena. "I am Devon Pemberton. I am the estate steward for the duke of Gavenshire."

Helena allowed him to help her to her feet and then she curtsied. "Sire, I am Helena."

Devon Pemberton was a tall, handsome man, and Helena found him most reassuring with his warm smile and bright eyes. He eyed her over from head to toe and back again before speaking. "Felix tells me you have no memory of your kin or home. Is this true?"

"My travels have exhausted me, I fear. I remember only a little of the trip, but nothing of the travelers. I'm certain I know naught of the names of those who went with me." Helena comforted herself in the fact that this was no lie.

" 'Tis no matter. You are welcome at the castle, and we will search to find your family on the morrow. Be ye well enough to walk, or shall I send a cart for you?"

"I can walk," Helena said hesitantly. She avoided his searching eyes for fear she would break down in her charade. "I would like to see these people rewarded," she quickly added. "They have been most kind in caring for me and have shared their meager foods with me as well."

Devon nodded. "It will be done. Felix, come with me to the castle and I will issue you food."

Felix and Mary both gasped in surprise and exclaimed in unison, "The castle!"

" 'Tis not necessary, Sire," Felix protested. "We gave nothing more than the good Lord would have asked of us."

Devon smiled and took firm hold of Helena's arm. "A kindness, nevertheless, and one worthy of repayment. Come."

Helena felt the strength in Devon's hand as he pulled her forward. She was deeply aware of his presence. *He is a powerful man,* she thought. He was determined and self-assured, and the very nearness of him gave her cause to think about her beloved Tanny. Would he be as tall as this man? Would his hair be soft and brown like this?

Tanny had dark hair, she reminded herself. Rich brown hair the color of newly plowed dirt and eyes so dark they were nearly black. She could almost see him in Devon's place, and her heart skipped a beat. *Where are you, my love? Why am I not upon your arm instead of this man's?*

In the soft blue and purple haze of twilight, Gavenshire Castle rose beyond the village. The town was closing down for the night, and the soft glow of firelight illuminated the windows of the houses as they passed by. Helena felt a chill and gave an involuntary shudder.

"Are you cold, Milady?" Devon inquired.

The silhouette of his face in the fading light caused Helena to tremble more. Fear was gnawing at her like a hound to a bone.

"Aye," she whispered, unable to offer any other explanation.

Devon removed his own cloak and placed it around her shoulders. "This should keep you warm enough."

Helena snuggled down in the warmth, grateful that Devon could not see the blush that crossed her face.

Gavenshire Castle was a grand affair, Helena decided. She reviewed the bailey as they crossed to the outer stairs and noted the large number of men who guarded the grounds. Torches had been placed strategically to offer light and, in their glow, Helena could make out stables and mews where the falcons were kept.

Devon's ever-present hand upon her cloaked arm made Helena painfully aware of her inability to escape. There was no reason to fear, she reminded herself. But her thought were not all convincing.

She turned at the stairs to find Felix's face awash in wonder.

" 'Tis a fine place, is it not?" she questioned, and Felix smiled broadly.

"To be sure, Milady. To be sure. I must remember every detail and tell my Mary." Devon smiled at the exchange and assisted Helena up the stone stairs.

The castle was fairly quiet, even though the evening meal was in progress. Supper was not as much of an affair as was the noon meal. Many people simply took their food to their own chamber and spent the evening in retired silence or quiet conversation.

"Would you care to dine, Helena?" Devon questioned.

"Nay." She was not anxious to be made the center of attention.

Sensing this, Devon led her to a small room off the great hall. "Wait here while I see to Felix. I will find the duke and announce your arrival."

~

Helena watched as Felix padded off in dumbfounded silence behind Devon. She then allowed herself to survey her surroundings, noting the red and blue woolen hangings that draped the walls. Seeing the way they ruffled in particular spots, Helena had little doubt they blocked out the draft and helped to keep the room warm.

The chamber looked to be a private solar of some type. Perhaps it was a place where the duke received guests privately. At this thought, Helena felt herself weaken. She sank down in the nearest chair and wondered as to what type of man the duke of Gavenshire might be. Would he find it acceptable to take in a young woman with no memory and little more than gentle speech and velvet clothing to prove her right at hospitality in his home?

It was several minutes before Devon returned. With him came a rugged-looking man whose brown beard made him look to be the senior of Devon. On his arm was a woman who was great with child. Helena instantly rose to her feet and smoothed out her skirt.

"May I present the duke and duchess of Gavenshire," Devon announced.

"Your Grace," she said, curtseying first to the man and then again to his wife.

"I am Arianne," the woman said, taking Helena's hand. "Devon is my brother, and he tells me that you are to be our guest. I am glad to receive you, for there is a definite shortage of women in this castle."

"Don't I know that," Devon said with a laugh.

"Don't mind him." The duchess instantly put Helena at ease. "Are you hungry or would you prefer I show you to your room so you might rest?"

"Please, Milady," Helena replied, "do not put yourself out on my behalf. I would not wish to overtax you. 'Tis you who should rest and care for yourself."

The duke laughed. "If you can get my wife to heed your counsel, you may have a permanent home here." Then extending Helena a broad smile, he added, "I am Richard. I will bear up with no formalities between friends. Why don't you sit and tell us how you came to be here?"

Helena swallowed hard. She had allowed the villeins to believe a lie, as had the estate steward, and now she was to lie to a duke and his wife. The moment was too much for her and nearly before Devon could catch her and break her fall, Helena fainted dead away.

Chapter 4

Helena was treated with the utmost care, and the question of her arrival to Gavenshire did not again become an issue. She could only imagine that Devon had shared her situation with the duke and duchess and that they had all agreed the trauma to be too great for her to bear.

Whatever the reason, Helena was glad for the reprieve. She was quickly welcomed into the inner circle of the duchess, becoming fast friends with Arianne, as well as with an older woman named Matilda, who acted as the duchess's closest confidante and friend. Helena soon relaxed in the unconditional friendship offered her.

"You look quite fetching, Milady," Devon offered, taking the seat beside hers at the noon meal.

Helena felt shy next to this man. She'd had so little experience with men, having stayed so close to the protection of her mother. Devon was obviously interested in her, and whether it was simply as a means of solving the mystery about her or because he was attracted to her, Helena was uncertain.

"Thank you, Sire," she whispered and turned her attention to her other side, where Richard seated Arianne. The duchess was laughing about something, and Helena instantly felt a pang of envy for the happiness that emanated from her face.

She watched as the duke leaned down to whisper something in Arianne's ear and caught the look of deep love in his eyes. *Oh to be loved like that,* she thought. Turning away, almost embarrassed for having intruded, Helena caught Devon's smile of knowing.

" 'Tis truly a great love affair," he whispered in her ear.

Just then the noise of the hall faded as a grave-looking man rushed to the duke's side.

"What is it, Douglas?" Richard questioned.

"There is news, Your Grace," Douglas Mont Gomeri, chamberlain to the duke, announced.

"Pray tell?"

Douglas glanced to Arianne, then beckoned Richard to join him outside.

"Nay, Douglas," Arianne stated with a fierce shake of her head. "Share your news here."

Douglas looked at Richard, who questioningly nodded. "I fear 'tis Her Grace's father and stepmother. A fever has taken them."

Arianne dropped her chalice. "They are dead?"

"Aye."

Helena watched as the color drained from Arianne's face. She heard the swift intake of breath from the man beside her and remembered that Devon and Arianne were siblings. She turned to offer her condolences and noted the shocked expression on Devon's face. Little more was said, however, as the duchess doubled over in pain and gasped her husband's name.

" 'Tis the babe," she whispered.

Richard immediately pulled her from the chair and lifted her into his arms. "Douglas, get the midwife. Helena, find Matilda and send her to our chamber."

Helena nodded, watching as the duke carried his weeping wife to the stairs. Devon sat motionless, and Helena wished she could offer some comfort. Not knowing anything she could say, she placed her hand upon his arm, met his gaze with her sympathetic one, and went in search of Matilda.

Richard paced nervously in the great hall. With sidelong glances at the stone stairs that led to the upper level and the lying-in chamber where Arianne lay, he prayed fervently for his wife's safe delivery. Helena sat in silence. She no longer envied the duchess.

She knew full well that pregnancy and childbirth were frightening times for women. Should a child struggle in finding its way into the world, there was little that could be done to assist it. She knew Richard took some comfort in the fact that Matilda was assisting the midwife. Matilda had waited upon his own mother, and Richard trusted her to be honest with him about his wife's condition.

Still, it had been some time since she'd come to tell them any news, and Arianne had been confined to the room throughout the night. Now with daybreak upon them, Richard found exhaustion overtaking his weary mind.

"Dear God," he prayed aloud, "please ease her pain and deliver her safely of our child. Give life to the seed that You caused to grow from our love. 'Tis a selfish man I am, Lord," Richard continued, "but I plead for their lives and beg forgiveness for my concern."

Helena's heart ached for the man. He was clearly worried sick for his wife, and the helplessness of the matter left him frustrated and ill tempered.

"Your Grace would do well to rest," Helena said softly.

"Aye," Devon offered, coming into the room. "You will need your rest to show off that fine babe. 'Twould be a pity should the child have more strength than his father."

Richard tried to laugh, but it came out little more than a huff, and foreboding crept over the hall.

Matilda appeared nearly an hour later, shaking her head. " 'Tis time it takes for these little ones to come into the world. God's timing is best."

"You will let me know as soon as something happens?" Richard asked, already knowing the answer.

"Aye, you know I will." Matilda then turned to Helena. "Her Grace would like it if you would bear this with her."

Helena's face registered surprise. "Arianne has asked for me?"

"Aye. 'Tis certain enough she would prefer her husband," Matilda said with a grin, "but the midwife will have none of that. Come."

Helena looked at Richard, who nodded. " 'Twill ease my mind to know you are with her."

"Very well."

Taking a chair by the fireplace, Richard watched them go and knew that his heart went with them. He thought only to rest his eyes a moment and await word of Arianne. A storm had brewed up off the coast, and the howling wind outside made him feel even more tired. The damp chill of the room caused him to pull his chair closer to the flickering fire. He would just sit a moment and pray. Instead, he fell into a much-needed sleep and dreamed not of Arianne, but of his brother.

Helena patted Arianne's hand supportively, knowing little else she could do. She was honored that the duchess had asked for her, but she found the entire scene quite foreign and frightening.

"Milady," Matilda said to the laboring Arianne, "I've placed jasper in the four corners of the room. 'Tis a good stone to bring about the quick delivery of a child."

Arianne felt the contraction ease and relaxed against her pillow, while the midwife, an ancient woman dressed all in black, rubbed a soothing ointment on her distended abdomen.

"Aye," the midwife said with a nod. "Jasper will quicken the birth." Then turning to Matilda, she questioned, "Did ye open all of the doors and drawers within the castle?"

"Aye," Matilda responded quickly. "The cupboards and larder doors as well."

" 'Tis good," the midwife stated, then glanced at Arianne as she felt the tightening of another contraction. " 'Twill beckon the child out."

Matilda nodded at Arianne and Helena's questioning glances. The midwife gently kneaded the duchess's stomach and asked, "What of the knots? Be there any yet untied?"

"Nay," Matilda answered confidently. "I have overseen it myself. 'Tis sure that all knots in this castle have been undone."

The midwife nodded. " 'Twill keep the cord from knotting about the child's neck," she told Arianne.

Arianne's misery and pain left her little time to consider the traditional forms of midwifery. She knew there was a knife placed beneath her mattress to cut the pain of delivery. Not that it was helping. She'd also seen Matilda sprinkle special herbs about the room, knowing that they were to give off pleasant scents and coax the baby to come with haste. But in truth, this baby was already coming in haste. It was at least a month early by Matilda's calculations, but the shock of her father's death had been too much.

"I'm glad you are here," Arianne told Helena. "I feel as though we've become as sisters these past few days. I pray I have not asked too much of you."

"Never, Milady." Helena again patted the duchess's hand. "I am your faithful servant."

"Nay." Arianne's eyes were bright with pain. "You are now a most cherished friend."

∽

Helena had just reported Arianne's progress to a sleepy Richard, when Douglas Mont Gomeri entered room. "Your Grace, there is a messenger from the king."

Richard came instantly awake, noticing for the first time the brilliance of sunlight that flooded in from the open windows. The silence left in the passing of the storm was nearly deafening. "What be the hour?" he questioned and glanced again to the stairway.

"It is coming upon noon," Douglas replied. "Has the duchess—"

"Nay. Helena has just told me it will still be some time. Show the messenger in." His voice betrayed his concern.

Douglas nodded and returned with a weary-looking man. He wore the colors of King Henry, as well as the markings. Richard acknowledged the man with his eyes, but said nothing. The man, in return, gave a deep bow and produced a wax-sealed parchment.

Richard took the message eagerly and noted that preparations were being made in the hall for dinner. "Will you take the noon meal with us?" he questioned, while breaking the seal.

"I would be most humbly grateful," the man replied.

Richard motioned to Douglas. "My chamberlain will see to your needs. Douglas, please show this man where he may wash."

Douglas led the man away while Richard scanned the words on the paper. There was joy in his heart as he realized that Henry had agreed to pardon Tancred DuBonnet.

"I pray it is not more bad news," Helena said, feeling a faint despair wash over her.

"On the contrary. 'Tis good news." Richard beckoned Helena to sit and then read, "Upon your word and oath that your brother has been falsely accused and because of the grave injustice done him, I do hereby pardon—" Richard's words fell away. "The king has pardoned my brother!"

Helena could only nod. She had little idea as to what the duke's brother needed pardoning for by the king, but such a matter was indeed cause for celebration. "Congratulations, Your Grace," she announced, getting to her feet. "I must return to Arianne. I will come again when there is word."

Richard barely heard Helena's words. Tancred would be pardoned!

❦

"The babe is nearly born, Milady," Matilda said soothingly to Arianne. "Just a wee bit longer and you will know such joy that pain will be forgotten."

Arianne doubted that Matilda spoke the truth, but she gave a final push to appease the midwife's demands. Suddenly it was done. The child was being pulled from her body and the pain was taken with it.

The midwife quickly tied the cord and cut it at four fingers' length from its belly. The slightly blue-skinned baby soon colored to a hardy pinkish-red as its lusty cries filled the chamber.

" 'Tis a son, Milady," Matilda announced proudly, and Arianne wept for joy.

Helena could only stare in dumbfounded silence. What a wondrous event she had just witnessed. Never in her life had she imagined such a thing.

The midwife quickly took the baby to wash him in a readied tub of water. She rigorously rubbed his tiny body with salt, then took honey and rubbed it on his gums and tongue to give him an appetite. Helena left Arianne's side to watch on in amazement as the tiny infant protested such treatment.

" 'Tis a fine son, Your Grace," the midwife called over her shoulder as she bound the baby tightly in a fine linen cloth. His swaddling kept him completely immobilized, but did not interfere with his hearty cries.

"You must take him to Richard," Arianne stated. Helena looked up, wondering to whom she was speaking.

Matilda was weeping tears of joy and nodded to Helena. "He'll be most happy to see you with this news."

"You want me to take the baby to Richard?" Helena's obvious surprise amused Arianne. The midwife placed the bundled infant in Helena's arms before she could refuse. "But what if I stumble? I've not cared for a child before."

"Neither have I," Arianne replied. "Go, take him to his father. You will do well, of this I am certain."

Richard had heard the cries of his son. With little thought to the king's message, he had let the parchment fall to the floor in wonder of the new sounds.

He held his breath, closed his eyes, and thanked God for the child who cried so fiercely. Opening his eyes, he again found the room suddenly filled with people. Douglas came to his side, staring in wonderment at the staircase. Behind them, voices were murmuring with approval and speculation.

" 'Tis a boy for sure, Your Grace," one of the knights called out.

"No other could cry with such a voice," another assured.

In a few moments, a wide-eyed Helena appeared on the stairs, a tiny white mummy in her arms. The cries grew louder as she approached, for the baby was decidedly unhappy with his new surroundings.

"Her Grace," Helena said with obvious pride in her voice, "has been delivered of a son."

A hearty cry of congratulations and approval filled the air. The word was quickly spread throughout the castle and into the surrounding village. The duke had an heir.

"What of Arianne?" Richard questioned anxiously.

"She is well, Sire, and quite pleased."

Richard looked down into the face of the crying babe. Without thought, he retrieved the baby from Helena's arms and studied him closely. The infant calmed under his father's scrutiny and Richard smiled.

" 'Tis a fine son, indeed," he said to no one in particular. Then noticing the shock of burnt red hair, Richard's smile grew broader. "And he bares the mark of his mother, I see." Those in the room drew near to catch sight of the baby.

" 'Tis time I thank your mother," Richard whispered to the child.

Helena followed Richard to the lying-in chamber, where in keeping with tradition, all of the castle's finest treasures had been laid out on display. No treasure there, however, caught the duke's eye save Arianne.

She was lying back against the pillows, eyes closed and copper hair spilling out over the coverlet. The midwife was removing her things from the bedside and glanced in surprise at Richard's early entry into the room.

"You should place the babe in his cradle," she motioned to the darkened corner of the room, "where his eyes cannot be harmed by the light."

He scarcely heard her for Arianne's eyes snapped open at the words and fixed on Richard. She noted the pride in his eyes and the pleasure that seemed to radiate from his face.

"A gift, my husband. A gift from the Lord above and from our love," she whispered tenderly.

"A most perfect gift," Richard replied and drew close to the bed. He placed the small boy at her side and watched as his son turned his face and rooted.

" 'Tis hunger that causes his search," the midwife said, realizing that Richard was not going to heed her suggestion for placing the child in his cradle.

Arianne lovingly guided the baby's mouth to her breast, then started in surprise when he took hold and began to feed. Richard laughed at her expression, then placed a kiss upon her forehead.

"Love has a most unique way of surprising us, does it not, sweet Arianne?"

"Indeed," she whispered sleepily.

Helena silently backed out of the room, feeling much the intruder in this very private moment. She was filled with wonder and thanksgiving. "Oh, God," she said, closing the door to her own chamber, "what a remarkable thing You have done."

Gone were all thoughts of Roger and Maude. Gone were the concerns of being sent to the abbey and never finding Tanny. No, Helena reasoned, a God who would create such a wonderful marvel as this could surely handle the simple reunion of two people.

Chapter 5

Roger was not happy at the news of Helena's disappearance. His anger at the men who bore him the tidings was evident.

"Imbeciles!" he shouted. "I gave you a small task and you could not even see it to completion."

The men begged his forgiveness, pleading their innocence, but Roger silenced them with his raised fist. "Get out of my sight," he growled. The men quickly took their leave, and only Maude's laughter remained to prick at Roger's conscience.

"So she outwitted them, did she?" Maude could not help but take the issue further. "What will you do, brother dear, when our sister shows herself to the queen?"

"London is a far piece from these lands," Roger said, barely controlling his rage. "Helena could never make the journey. No doubt some other destination is on her mind."

"Would that you should believe it!" Maude declared. "I know well our little sister. She will see to it that you are punished for her treatment."

"Me?" Roger questioned accusingly. "Me? What of yourself, or have you forgotten your part in this matter?"

Maude shrugged indifferently and seated herself before the fire. She was mindless of the servants who rummaged about the house and completely unconcerned with Roger's tantrum.

"Helena is gone. Let it be. If she is found, you simply tell them she has gone mad because of her mother's death."

"What of the lash marks upon her back?"

Maude smiled in a twisted manner. "Flesh knits and Helena will heal. I doubt it will leave overmuch of a mark. Besides, you can always plead innocence and declare it the handiwork of someone she met on the road. Better yet, go to Henry first and weep before him with a heavy brother's heart. Tell him your precious little sister has fled and you fear for her safety."

Roger seemed to relax a bit at this. Maude was perhaps right. Appearing before the king in a fit of brotherly concern would offer his feelings for all to see. Should Helena appear to say otherwise, it would remain his word against hers, and now that the Lady Eleanor was dead, Helena's word would surely hold less weight.

"You fret over nothing," Maude assured Roger. "Concern yourself instead with a more worthy matter."

"That being?" Roger questioned, staring down at the immaculately groomed woman.

Maude toyed with the keys that hung from her girdle. "I am of a mind to marry," she stated without fanfare.

"This is not news to me," Roger replied. "Nor is it a worthy matter."

Maude laughed haughtily. " 'Tis worthy enough. I desire to better my standing. Our good neighbor to the south suddenly finds himself a widower, and I seek to remedy that matter."

"Have you given him time to even bury his wife?" Roger asked angrily.

Maude stuck her nose in the air and refused to comment, making Roger laugh. "I see my point has hit its mark. There is time enough to concern yourself with such a thing. I must decide what is to be done in regards to Helena."

"I thought it was decided," said Maude with a look of reproach. "Take yourself with haste to His Majesty's fortress and tell of our deep sorrow. Our sweet little sister has run away."

∽

Working over her needlework while the duchess nursed her son, Helena commented without thought, "You are my first true friend."

Arianne noted the sorrow in her voice. "There is no one else?"

"No."

"Mayhaps it is only that your memory fails you in this matter," the duchess suggested carefully. She was already suspicious of Helena's artful dodge regarding her family.

Helena winced and cast her gaze to the fire. "Mayhaps."

"Still," Arianne continued, feeling deeply grieved for the young woman's obvious pain, "you have a friend in me, and I would like very much for you to stay on here for as long as you like. You may be my lady-in-waiting, if it pleases you."

Helena's heart swelled with gratitude and joy. "I would be honored."

Arianne smiled. "We are quite isolated here, but the city is ever growing and drawing more people. The duke is seeking a charter for the town and that will enable us to have a yearly fair, instead of making the journey to Scarborough or York.

"I have no other lady-in-waiting, and Matilda has been my only friend and companion these long months. The duties of my home require much of me, and you could do much to help me."

"I know naught what capacity I might assist you in," Helena responded, "but I am most humbly your servant."

"Nay," Arianne said with a shake of her head. "Never that. You will be my friend. Perhaps you would find pleasure in helping me with the babe?"

"To be certain, Milady. I would find caring for your son an honor." Helena bubbled the words. "I have never been around children. I was the youngest in my family." The sudden realization of what she'd said hit Helena hard.

The intake of her breath was not lost on Arianne. "See there, a bit of your memory returns. Mayhaps it will not be long before you remember in full."

Helena knew that Arianne was being graciously generous. She offered a weak smile and nodded at the duchess's words.

"Perhaps the first place we should start," Arianne continued, "is in moving you to the chamber nearest my own. Then, too, we shall need to fit you for clothing. I presume you have little else with you?"

"Nay," Helena confirmed with a frown.

"I have fine seamstresses here and can work a stitch quite well myself. We'll have you clothed in no time. What colors do you favor?"

Helena felt her throat tighten. To admit a favorite would be to offer up yet another proof of her memory. "I. . .I am," she stammered, "uncertain."

"Of course," Arianne nodded, then appraised the girl carefully.

Helena self-consciously allowed the scrutiny. She was dressed simply, yet the velvet cloth bore the evidence of her status. She remembered having lost her head covering in the woods one night, and no one, not even Matilda, had offered her a replacement. This thought caused Helena to put her hands to her bare head, sending her needlework clattering to the floor.

"You have lovely hair," Arianne said, noting the long blond braid that hung down Helena's back. "My own, as you can see, is frightfully unsettling."

Helena shook her head. " 'Tis not true, Milady. It is a fine shade. It reminds me of late autumn sunsets when the sun is like a fiery red ball on the horizon. I find it most beautiful."

"Mayhaps, but I am no courtly English beauty." The baby was now sleeping, and Arianne ran a finger against his cheek. "Hair of gold and eyes of blue are what the women of England long to display. Alas, I cannot even boast the eyes, for mine are brown. Yea, you are the very image of refined womanhood, Helena."

Helena blushed at the praise and nervously she sought to occupy herself. "May I put him in the cradle for you?" She motioned to the baby and Arianne offered him up.

"I think crimson would do you justice. Yea, and golden yellows and silvery blues to match your eyes. I'll have the cloth brought to you and you can choose from the bounty of our storerooms."

"You are too generous, Milady," Helena said, fighting to keep the tears from her eyes. She put the baby in his cradle, then turned to face the duchess.

Arianne patted the bed and Helena sat down beside her. "It pleases me to do this." Arianne put her hand upon Helena's shoulder. "I am truthfully glad for your company. Richard is often about his work and sometimes the loneliness does not bode well for me."

"But there are things," Helena finally said, knowing that she couldn't go on lying to Arianne, "things which you do not know about me."

Arianne smiled. "When you are ready, you will speak of them. Until then, I am content to wait. Please know this, however." Her eyes were soft and full of concern. "You are safe here, and no harm will come to you. My husband is a powerful man and good friends with King Henry. If you have fears, Helena, lay them to rest. We are happy to be your protectors with God's help."

Just then the door opened, and Richard entered with Devon at his side. "Am I interrupting?"

"Nay, but the babe is sleeping, so please do not address us as though you were barking orders to your men."

Richard eyed his wife with a grin. "I wouldn't dream of it, Your Grace." Devon chuckled from behind, while Richard gave a sweeping bow.

"Why have you come then?" Arianne questioned in mock annoyance.

Richard straightened. "Devon has agreed to bring my brother home to England. I pray it meets with your approval."

"It does, indeed."

Helena glanced up to find Devon looking at her. His gaze only made her long for Tanny, and she quickly looked away to check on the baby.

"When do you leave?" Arianne was questioning.

"With the tide," Devon answered and crossed the room to peer over Helena's shoulder at the baby. "Has he a name?"

"Of course he has a name. Richard, have you not shared with the castle your own child's name?"

"I have been a bit preoccupied, Milady."

"His name is Timothy," Helena said matter-of-factly and took her seat to begin sewing once again.

"Timothy is a good name," Devon replied. "I'm envious of you, Richard. A fine home, a good wife, albeit that she has a sharp tongue at times, and a perfect son."

"You'll no doubt be following suit quite rapidly. You are now duke of Pemberton, do not forget."

The words were no sooner out of Richard's mouth than he regretted having said them. Arianne's face sobered immediately. While she had no great love for the iron-fisted man who'd been her father, she still mourned his passing.

"I'm sorry, Arianne," Richard said, taking her hand. "Forgive me."

" 'Tis naught to forgive. Your words are true enough. Devon, will you soon settle down and take a wife?"

"I would be most happy to do just that, should the proper young woman present herself. Mayhaps the king will arrange a marriage for me. You seemed to have benefited greatly from such an arrangement."

Arianne smiled, the grief of the moment passing. "Indeed, I have benefited."

Helena looked up at this exchange. She had never known arranged marriages to be anything but pure misery for those involved. How often she had heard her mother discuss the unhappy unions of her friends.

Devon noted her expression and smiled. "I do not believe our guest finds truth in this matter. Mayhaps she suffered from such an arrangement."

"Nay, not I," Helena answered too quickly. Three pairs of eyes turned to gaze in surprise at her, and Helena colored crimson under the close scrutiny.

Several moments passed before Richard broke the uneasy silence. "It is settled then. Devon will go to Bruges and we will expect you back by Easter."

"By Easter, eh?" Devon turned from Helena with hands on hips. "I take it you will allow no complication upon the sea to slow down my trip."

Richard laughed. "None. 'Twould be most unacceptable. I will have to give the matter over to God and beg His blessings on it. I would enjoy celebrating the resurrection of our Lord with my family. All of my family."

" 'Tis settled then," Devon stated, and after briefly bowing to Helena, he touched his lips to Arianne's forehead and bid them good-bye.

"Thank you, Devon." Richard's words were clearly heartfelt and his eyes were filled with gratitude. " 'Tis a good brother you have, Milady." Richard lifted Arianne's slender fingers to his lips. "Goodness must be a family virtue," he grinned before placing a lingering kiss on the back of her hand. Helena enjoyed the tender exchange.

Timothy took that moment to let loose a cry, causing Arianne to chuckle. "Let us hope 'tis a virtue that extends to the generations."

Chapter 6

"Can it not wait?" Arianne questioned, following Richard into their bed-chamber.

Helena had been caring for Timothy and got up to leave, but Richard waved her back down. "You needn't go."

"Nay," Arianne replied sarcastically, "because the duke is going instead." Helena raised questioning eyes. She'd never been in the middle of one of Arianne and Richard's squabbles, but in a castle there were few secrets.

"You would like for me to tell the king it is an inconvenient time to do his bidding?" Richard questioned with a smirking grin.

Arianne rolled her eyes. " 'Tis unfair. Henry knows you have a new son. 'Tis not fitting to draw you away just now."

"Bah!" Richard said, slapping a leather tunic on top of the clothes and slamming down the lid. "The matters of state wait not for one such as Timothy. He is but one small child in the eyes of his king. Perhaps the king has need of me in ways that will affect many such as Timothy."

Helena tried to occupy herself with her needlework. It was hopelessly snagged, however, and she could only pull at the threads in a desperate attempt to free them.

"I will miss you."

Helena thought Arianne sounded close to tears. She silently wished she could slip from the room, but the duke had already instructed her to stay.

Without considering Helena's presence, Richard crossed to Arianne and pulled her in his arms. "My heart will long for you every moment of my day. Each beat will be for you alone and each breath I breathe will whisper your name." He tilted her tearful face to his and gazed deeply into her eyes. His lips were only inches from hers, the warmth of her breath was upon his face, and her tears now fell against his fingers. "Ah, sweet Arianne." His words were nearly a moan. Slowly, with all the longing and passion that had followed him through the final months of Arianne's confinement, Richard kissed her. Arianne returned the kiss, also uncaring that Helena sat only a few feet away.

"Come below and see me off. Helena, bring Timothy and come, too."

Helena nodded and quickly retrieved the baby, grateful to be done with the emotional farewell scene.

In the bailey, Richard's men were restless to be on their way. They waited

141

patiently while final instructions were issued and additional precautions were made against strangers approaching the castle. Hadn't it been an overtrust of this peaceful existence, Richard had told them that had caused Arianne to fall into danger when Tancred had stormed the castle?

Helena was rosy-cheeked and filled with emotion at the love she watched transpire between Arianne and her husband. *Such love only comes to a person once,* she thought as Richard bent from his horse to offer Arianne a final kiss. It was more than she could bear, and she looked away.

Clutching Timothy tightly to her bosom, Helena could not fill the ache that grew there. The most immense ocean could not fill the void that left its mark so deeply engraved upon her heart.

"Have courage, Wife," Richard was calling, causing Helena to lift her head again. "When I return, I will bring your brother and mine as well. God will it to be so!"

"Aye," Arianne said with an earnest face. "God will it to be so!"

"You will have all that you need. Seek out Sir Dwayne in any matter that you cannot resolve." Richard's words were said in the same authoritative manner he used with his men, and Helena knew all moments of tenderness between duke and duchess had passed.

"God go with you, Richard," Arianne said in parting.

"And with you, Milady."

The little band watched until all riders had passed through the gatehouse and into the village. Arianne brushed away tears and noted that Helena seemed close to them herself.

"We must surely be a sight," she contended, and Helena nodded in agreement. "Come," Arianne said, taking Timothy into her arms, "let us partake of something warm to fill the chill within." But Helena knew that no refreshment would find its mark and ease what ailed them.

They climbed the stone steps to the great hall, and Arianne motioned Matilda to her side.

"We seek refreshment against the dampness and chill. Would you bring it to my solar?" Arianne requested.

"Of course, Milady," Matilda said with the slightest nod.

Arianne noted two servants squabbling in the corner of the room and, without thought, handed Timothy to Helena and motioned her to the stairs. "Wait for me in my chamber," she bade. "I will see to this matter."

Helena was grateful for the reprieve. She lovingly took Timothy in hand and carefully made her way upstairs. Noting Timothy's growing agitation, Helena realized it had been some time since he'd received a changing.

Placing the babe in his cradle, Helena drew water from the ever-filled hearth pot. She tested it to make certain it was neither too hot nor too cold, then poured it into a basin and added rose oil. Her final act before retrieving the squalling Timothy was to pull out new swaddling and a fine linen drying cloth from a nearby chest. This was a procedure she repeated every three hours during the day.

Without giving thought to what she was doing, Helena began to sing a song of love. It was the first time she'd lifted her voice in song since her mother had died. Now, for a reason beyond her understanding, Helena not only desired to sing, she found that her heart demanded she do so.

The lyrical notes filled the room and joined with Timothy's cries, which immediately ceased.

"Come see, come see the tiny babe," Helena sang. "Lullay, lullay, the tiny babe. Before you now, this blessed day, Lullay, lullay, the tiny babe." It was a song from her childhood in celebration of the Christ Mass.

The silky soprano tones seemed to mesmerize Timothy as Helena unwound his swaddling bands and gently placed him in the bath. She felt her heart swell for the child whom she'd come to love as dearly as her own.

The aching that had so totally held her captive only moments before seemed somehow eased in this simple task and song. Helena washed the tiny infant, then dried him with the linen cloth and rubbed more rose oil onto his body. She carefully rewrapped him in the swaddling bands, for it was well known that until the babe was old enough to sit, this would prevent his limbs from twisting. Still, she couldn't help but like it best Timothy was free of the binding and his soft baby fingers would wave upward to her face.

"You must await your mother," she whispered to the expectant child who even now rooted against her for satisfaction. Timothy knew full well this routine, and his mother's breast always followed his bath.

Arianne entered the room none too early. "I see you have already bathed him."

"Aye," Helena said with a warm smile. " 'Tis your face he cries for now."

Arianne chuckled softly as she took the baby. "Mayhaps not so much my face, eh?" She quickly settled down to the task at hand and watched as Helena pulled back the woolen wall-hanging that hid the garderobe door.

" 'Tis certain with all the rose water we dispose of here," Helena mused, "you surely have the most fragrant latrine in all the castle." She retrieved the small basin of water and emptied it into the dark hole.

"No doubt," Arianne said with a laugh. " 'Twould be a finer service still to bathe the entire castle in such sweetness."

Helena replaced the basin and dropped the cloth back into place. Just then Matilda entered the room with a tray containing two steaming cups and thick slices of warm bread.

"Ah," Arianne whispered, "our refreshment."

Timothy was nearly asleep at her breast, and Helena quickly prepared his cradle before taking the offered mug from Matilda.

"Join us," Arianne said, placing Timothy in his bed.

"I cannot, Milady," Matilda responded. "There is much that needs my care."

Arianne nodded and took the tray. "Thank you, Matilda." She waited until Matilda had closed the door behind her, then turned conspiratorially to Helena. "She thinks I know naught of her birthday. 'Tis but two days from now and I have a fine warm surcoat and tunic for her gift."

"She will be pleased," Helena said, taking the chair beside Arianne's.

"I think so." Arianne put the tray on the table beside her chair and offered Helena a slice of bread. They shared the silence of the room in nibbled bites and satisfying drink.

Helena was the first to turn from their feast. She picked up her sewing, a small embroidered gown that Timothy would wear when he outgrew swaddling.

"You have a most unusual stitch there," Arianne said, leaning over to note the piece.

"My mother taught me this," Helena said proudly. "When I sat at her knee and listened to gentle instruction, I thought there surely must be no other place so perfect."

Arianne said nothing of Helena's pleasant memory. "My own mother died when I was young," she noted instead. "I was taught to sew at the convent where my father sent me. It was a good life, but none that I would have called perfect."

Helena felt a sadness wash over her. "The loss of a mother is not one easily borne by the child, at any age."

"Nay," agreed Arianne. " 'Tis surely not."

Days later, Matilda was indeed proud to show off her new gift. She embarrassed at the fanfare Arianne made of her day, and when the duchess suggested Matilda take a quiet day of repose, the woman could only gasp.

"But my duties. . . ," Matilda began to protest.

"Can wait," Arianne stated firmly. Just then the lyrical notes of Helena's nursery songs filtered down to reach their ears. Casting a glance at the stairway, Arianne shook her head. " 'Tis a voice like no other. Oft I have heard her sing long into the night, and it comforts me greatly in Richard's absence."

"Aye," Matilda agreed. "Many say she is instructed by the angels."

❧

In the solar, Helena composed a new love song for her beloved. She hummed the notes of the melody, picking and choosing each carefully, discarding those whose tones were too harsh or dour. The music always came first—notes of melodies that raced inside her head and would scarce let her rest before she'd fully composed them into song.

Timothy stared up with watchful blue eyes from his cradle. So long as Helena sang, it mattered little to him what the meaning of the words were.

"If my beloved were a king," Helena put to the melody she'd just completed. She tested the words against the notes and decided they worked well. It was to be the song she'd promised Tanny when Roger's whip had lain her ill.

"If my beloved were a king," she whispered and sighed. "Oh, Tanny, you are a king. King of my heart." Dropping to her knees, Helena prayed, "Most Holy Father, You alone know where my beloved lays his wearied head. You alone see his sorrows and his needs. Go with him and send my love along. I miss him so." She felt the wetness upon her cheeks. How long would it be? How long before she saw him again?

Several nights later, Helena anxiously paced her room. There was such a restless spirit within her. She had spent hours in the castle chapel listening to the gentle words of Father Gies as he prayed for her to have the peace of God. Each morning during services, she had prayed fervently for such a peace to ease her longings, and of yet, no peace had come.

Without thought, Helena lifted her voice in a church song of Scripture. The Latin words were heavy compared to the Anglo-French she more often used for song, but the words encouraged her heart.

"*Sine fide impossible est placere Deo,*" she sang in earnest. *Without faith it is impossible to please God.*

"Oh Father," she whispered, "my faith comes so hard these dark lonely nights. I listen to sounds of life within the castle and know that no life stirs within my own walls. Nay, only the empty ramblings of a faithless woman. Yet, without faith, I cannot please Thee."

"Helena?" Arianne's soft voice called from outside her door. Wiping her tears with the back of her linen robe, Helena opened the door to her duchess.

"I heard you singing," Arianne said simply. "I am about to nurse Timothy. Come sing for me."

Helena followed her into the hall, grateful for the reprieve from her lonely walls. Arianne settled down on the bed and took Timothy to her side. "It seems so dark sometimes," she said faintly as Helena took a seat on the end of the mammoth bed. The high wooden canopy created shadows against the dying firelight's glow.

"Aye," Helena whispered. "Quite dark."

Arianne reached out her hand to Helena. "Tell me of your home. Tell me of the family you have left behind."

Helena's fingers had barely touched Arianne's hand, but the words spoken caused her to jerk back as if stung. "I cannot."

Arianne pulled Timothy closer and sighed. "I do not hold you in contempt for your choice. I feel strongly that you remember full well your past and all that remains there for you."

"I cannot," Helena replied again, her voice a sob.

"Helena, I will not judge you harshly."

"I know," the sorrow-filled young woman replied. "I judge myself and the lack of faith within me."

"Then judge no more," Arianne replied. " 'Tis God's job and His alone."

Helena lifted her eyes to meet Arianne's. "I remember it all," she admitted, "but 'tis nothing worth sharing with gentlefolk." Then more adamantly, Helena continued. "I love this life. Please do not send me away."

"Send you away?" Arianne gasped. "I would rather lose my arm than lose your friendship. You are welcomed here for all time, Helena. Know that here and now."

"Thank you, Milady." Helena felt a world of weight eased off her shoulders. "My love of God is deep, and for all these many years, I have felt its return in only the love of my mother. Now, I see differently. I see His love in you."

" 'Tis but a reflection of that which shines in you, Helena. He has not forsaken you. Be at peace and know He cares."

Chapter 7

Tancred DuBonnet leaned against the rail of the ship and stared at the filmy image of English shoreline. Home! It had come at last. After eleven years, he was going home.

"I wonder," Devon began, coming up from behind him, "if you will find it changed."

Tancred smiled weakly. "Perhaps yea, perhaps nay. The true point is that England will find me changed."

"For the better or the worse!" Devon questioned seriously. He knew all about the rough treatment his sister had suffered at Tancred's hand.

Tancred continued to stare across the waters. A light, salty mist assailed him, leaving droplets on his bearded face. "Would you have asked that but a short time ago, I might have answered strongly in the latter. I was a most bitter man."

Devon pushed back his cloak and adjusted the sword at his side. The cold steel felt good against his hand, and were this man still considered his enemy, he'd find little difficulty in challenging him to fight to the death. Thoughts of Arianne being beaten by this bitter man caused Devon to turn narrowed eyes on his companion.

"And now?" Devon's voice was low and formidable.

Tancred never broke his gaze. "Now, I am not so bitter. Perhaps now I am more thoughtful and filled with reasoning."

"Reasoning? Reasoning for what, pray tell?"

Tancred raised an eyebrow as if casually considering the matter. His camlet garde-corp, woven of the finest camel hair in Cyprus, offered him cherished warmth. It also reminded him of the giver. Artimas.

"I met a man not long ago. A pilgrim philosopher on his journey to Paris. A man of more difference and provocative thought I have ne'er met."

"A man of philosophy?" Devon asked in a tone of disbelief.

"And what heresy did he preach or did you contemplate angels and how many existed on pin-tops?"

Tancred laughed and turned to the younger man. "Nay, but my thoughts were much the same as yours, even though I had no concern of heresy. I had long ago presumed my soul unsaveable. That was, until I met your sister."

Devon's face tightened. "Yes, you were most uncharitable to her as I have learned."

Tancred nodded thoughtfully. " 'Tis true and nothing of pride for me. I

147

acted out of spite and hate and have no other excuse to offer. I posted my sincerest regret to the woman and begged her forgiveness. Richard's scribe penned me a fine letter in her name, releasing me from the debt."

" 'Tis like Arianne to put aside a difference so easily. Still, I have not her ease of reconciliation."

Tancred said nothing for a moment. "Mayhaps I should seek your forgiveness as well," he paused, meeting Devon's eyes, "for the offense you still carry in her name."

Devon was clearly convicted by Tancred's words. He swallowed hard, released the sword that he'd toyed with throughout the conversation, and looked away. "Mayhaps, I should seek yours."

"Then we are in agreement," Tancred said and returned his gaze to follow Devon's. England's shoreline drew ever closer.

"Was it your philosopher who changed your heart?" Devon questioned in a voice barely audible.

"Nay," Tancred replied. " 'Twas God. Artimas only assisted in pointing out the finer details."

"Such as?"

"So much was muddled in my thinking. The church had done nothing to aid me when I was accused of my parents' murder and exiled, although I had beseeched Rome on many occasions. I worked for over ten years, putting together all my worldly goods. This, in order to see my brother brought to justice for something I knew in my heart he was incapable of having done.

"I knew I hadn't killed our father and mother, but Richard was the only other person close at hand. I tried to imagine him capable of the act, but knew full well it was impossible. But I came anyway and was defeated by him, as you well know. But the defeat came in so many ways far deeper than the obvious."

Tancred grew silent for a moment in memory. "Arianne prayed for me. She told me so. She told me that she saw a remnant of good left over from the past. It gave her hope that I could be changed. She pleaded with my brother for my worthless life, for she knew my soul was condemned."

Devon smiled. He could well imagine his sister's meddling. "She has a tender heart."

"Aye," Tancred responded softly. "Would that all men could know the love of one such as she."

Devon nodded. "She is more dear to me than life itself."

"Arianne's words haunted me these last months. I knew I was without hope. I could not bear to share my heart, even with the priest, for fear of hearing confirmation that I was completely unsaveable."

"And did your philosopher see the error of your thought?"

The ship pitched against the waves and both men gripped the railing for support. Tancred could nearly smell the English soil, and all that was in him cried for the sights of home.

"Artimas," he said, fixing his eyes on the landed horizon, "told me of his own teacher. A man of great intellect. His name is Thomas Aquinas. Artimas was on his way to meet with his master when he took his comfort with me." Tancred chuckled in memory. "Of course there was plainly little of comfort in that hovel you found me in, but Artimas made it seem unimportant.

"He asked me of my life, and I laughed at the man. I truly had no will to live and plainly told him so."

"And what did he say?"

"He told me that the will was the single strongest source of motivation to all the other powers of the soul."

"Meaning exactly what?" Devon asked, now fully curious of this man's philosophy.

"That without will, nothing can be done." Devon nodded in understanding, but waited for Tancred to continue. "Artimas believes that faith is the one thing that gives power to the will."

"And where does faith find birth when a man has no desire to live?"

Tancred smiled. "Through action and reason. Faith and reason are dependent upon each other. Aquinas teaches that reason without faith is meaningless, but then so, too, is faith without reason. Faith is that substance that causes a man to say, 'Yea, I will believe even though it is impossible,' while reason finds a way to make the impossible happen."

"Spoken like a true philosopher!" Devon declared.

"In the second century after the death and resurrection of Christ, people heard St. Justin proclaim that God had given philosophy to the Greeks even as He had given his Law to the Jewish people. I believe philosophy is not without merit."

"But what of the argument that you can either be a philosopher or a Christian? If Christianity contains the truth, then all else must surely not contain it. I've always been given over to the thought that it is not our place to join them together, but to choose one or the other," Devon said with honest interest in the matter.

Tancred nodded. "I've heard it said as well. People fear that to question and reason that which causes them difficulty might in fact nullify their faith, and faith is most necessary to please God. The Scriptures make this clear."

"*Sine fide impossibile est placere Deo*—without faith it is impossible to please God," Devon remembered from his childhood training.

"Exactly. But man, being man, questions things quite naturally. To reason a matter seems a logical choice until another comes along and declares you a heretic for having no faith."

"A twisted matter to be sure."

"Alas," Tancred said with a look of peace so clear upon his face that Devon could not doubt the truth of his statement. " 'Tis more important that God has given peace to my soul."

Devon nodded, knowing that peace for himself. "Aye. 'Tis indeed most beneficial."

⚈

In a small, unpretentious room, Richard found himself face to face with his king. Henry, in his surcoat of green and gold, entered the room and waived off the cleric who dogged his every step.

"I have no need of you here, Man. Await me in the outer room," the king spoke, and the man quickly responded to his command.

"Richard!" Henry said with a heartiness he reserved for family. " 'Tis good you are with us. There is a matter that I believe you will find much to your liking."

"You have always treated me generously," Richard replied.

"And you have served me faithfully. Therefore, I have brought you here this day to inform you of a particular matter. I am granting workers and monies to see an expansion of your harbor. You will soon have a fine place to receive goods and trade of all manner."

Richard stared in surprise. "I had no idea. I sought but a charter to give our town a fair each year. I had little reason to hope such a thing as this could be within my grasp."

Henry smiled benevolently upon the man who had once held residency with his own family after the death of his parents. " 'Tis a generous act, for a good man."

"I am most humbly honored."

"There is yet another matter," the king said, pleased with the announcement he was about to make. "I have had word that your brother's ship safely entered our harbor yesterday. He and your wife's brother are making their way north to Gavenshire. I release you to join them."

Richard's face revealed his anticipation and pleasure at the news. "What of your men and the harbor plans?"

"I will send them north within a fortnight. Give it no further concern for the time," Henry replied, then lowered his voice as if to imply secrecy. "Richard, I know you seek the murderer of your father and mother. You have my leave to bring that person to justice. I pray you are successful, only make certain of the facts. A man's life is now eleven years gone, and all because we rushed to judgment. I regret that deeply and beg God's forgiveness."

"I, too," Richard admitted to the pious king he so admired. " 'Tis a lesson I'll not soon forget."

"Aye," Henry answered, nodding. His face seemed to change from the sobriety, however, in a flash. "Then be off with you, Man. They have a lead on you by more than a day's ride."

Richard bowed, and then the matter of Helena came to mind.

"Sire, there is a matter that I feel should be aired."

"Pray tell?"

"I have taken a young woman into the protection and care of my castle. Her name is Helena, but she claims memory of nothing more. She is gentle born and clearly a lady."

"I see," Henry said, thoughtfully stroking his chin. "No one knows of her origins?"

"Nay," Richard replied. "I sent out riders and they returned without a single word to encourage us. Helena says very little, but she is a kind and hearty soul. I gave her leave to remain with us, but thought you should be made aware of the matter. There is always the possibility that someone may seek her out, and should they begin their search here, you will already be aware of the circumstance."

"I will bear it in mind."

⁂

The sound of riders caused Devon and Tancred to come to their feet. A heavy fog had just begun to cloud over the land, and what the darkness did not blot out, the misty whiteness did.

"Who goes there?" Devon called out, his hand on the hilt of his sword.

"His Grace, the duke of Gavenshire," came the call. A look of relief crossed Devon's face and he released the sword. Tancred, also armed, did likewise and stood with a sobering glance in the direction of the voices.

"Richard?" Devon called.

"Aye, 'tis me," Richard replied, riding into the soft glow of their campfire light. He drew his horse up and dismounted. Throwing the reins to his squire, Richard stepped forward with a determined stare and met his brother's gaze.

"Henry told me you had arrived. I found it most gratifying to spend the day in yon saddle in order to reach you by nightfall."

"Gratifying is not a word that comes to mind," Tancred replied in jest, "when thinking of a hard ride to London on a beast such as that."

Richard laughed tensely. " 'Tis good to see you again."

"Better circumstances than our last meeting, eh?" Tancred's dark eyes were lit with amusement, yet there was hesitation in his manner. Would his brother truly forgive him and honor this new peace between them? Everyone seemed to watch and wait for Richard's reply.

"Aye, the matter is clearly a more pleasant one." Then with a smile, Richard stepped forward a pace and opened his arms.

"I pray it is well with thee."

Tancred hesitated for a moment, then embraced his brother. There were tears on his cheeks, and Tancred was grateful the darkness covered his embarrassment. Yet when he pulled away, he noted there were tears in Richard's eyes as well.

"We have much to discuss," Richard said in a voice none too steady.

"Aye," Tancred replied. "Eleven years' worth."

Chapter 8

Helena watched Arianne and Matilda, almost as if she were detached from the life around her. The more she kept up her deception and refused to speak of her past, the worse she felt. Now the Easter season was upon them and great preparations were underway for the celebration that would come.

The castle took on a rumbling of excitement. Servants worked a little harder and faster, while knights, clerics, and clergy anticipated the fine feasts and parties that would follow the unveiling of the cross on Easter Sunday.

But, Helena reminded herself, Easter Sunday was still several days away and there was much to be done. She tried to keep her hands busy at the tasks Arianne had assigned her, but her heart wasn't in the work. She watched Timothy, cradled at her side without a care in the world. He stared up at her with dark blue eyes as if to say, "My life and yours be not that different." Helena thought it true, whether Timothy was actually considering such a weighty matter or not.

The parish priest had stated that Easter was a matter of faith. Faith that the stone would be rolled away. Faith that the Savior would rise from the dead. Faith that in such an action, death would be defeated and all the wrongs in the world righted. But Helena felt her faith wane. It had been so long since she'd had any reason to believe that her wrongs would be righted.

There was a commotion in the kitchen, and Helena couldn't resist smiling at the way Arianne quickly settled the dispute. Arianne was quite competent, and Helena greatly admired her. Admired and was jealous of her, which Helena had sought forgiveness for on more than one occasion. It wasn't that she would wish any other life for the duchess. Nay, it was that she longed with all her heart to have a joy and happiness similar to that which Arianne called her life.

Oh, Tanny, she thought. *Would that you could take me as wife and dispel my longing and anguish. What would be the price I would pay for your return, for a single day, even an hour, to sit by your side?* Tears came unbidden to her eyes, and Helena lowered her head so that no one could see her cry.

"Oh, Father," she whispered, "I fear I cannot bear up under this burden any longer. 'Tis more than I am able to conquer." Timothy seemed to think she was talking to him and gave a gurgling sound.

Helena smiled and lifted the babe to see the activity that bustled around him. "See there, young sire," she said softly, "your mother, the duchess, is planning quite a celebration."

Arianne glanced across the room to see Helena holding Timothy. She smiled and came to extend her hands out to take her son. "What mischief are you about, my Timothy?" she questioned in amusement.

"I told him you were preparing a feast," Helena offered. "He seemed quite interested."

"No doubt," Arianne said with a laugh. "In a few years he'll race with the other boys and tilt at the quintain. Soon enough he'll go off to foster with others and my time with him will be greatly diminished."

"But you'll have other children," Helena reminded her.

"Yea, but I'm thinking the first is something different. The first born gives you cause to think and remember the sheer wonder of God." She looked down at her son with such love that Helena had to lower her gaze. It hurt too much to be so near what she needed and yet know that it could not belong to her.

Why God? she wondered silently. *Why must my heart belong to one who is so very far away; one who knows not whether I come or go? One who may very well be dead.* This last thought caused Helena to shudder. If Tanny were dead, she would have no reason to go on.

"God is good, is He not?" Arianne offered softly, not knowing the gloomy thoughts of her friend.

Helena had barely heard the words and took a moment as if to translate their meaning. "Yes, He is good," she finally replied. *But not always swift,* she added to herself.

It was hoped that Richard would be home by Easter, but when Good Friday arrived and the duke was still absent, Arianne tried to make the best of it.

Throughout Lent, the observations of the season had been met with enthusiasm. The castle chapel, as well as the church in the village, found its sanctuary hung with veiling to shroud the cross and holy relics. Good Friday presented a memorial to that day when Christ had gone willingly to the cross to offer salvation to all mankind.

Leaving one of the other chambermaids to care for Timothy, Arianne and Helena led the castle procession in the "creeping to the cross."

The women bowed low and walked slowly in reverent memory of the crucifixion. Helena couldn't hold back her tears. She was deeply moved at the sacrifice her Lord had made, but so, too, was she in deep sorrow for the loss in her heart. Somehow their combination was appropriate, and she instantly felt that God would have her leave her heartache on the church steps with the cross.

Approaching the now unveiled cross, Helena rose up only slightly and kissed it, declaring to God as she did so that just as they would bury the cross until Easter Sunday, so Helena would give over her anguish to be buried as well. At least this had been her heart's desire.

If the duchess thought it strange that her lady-in-waiting sobbed openly at the symbol of Christ's sacrifice, she did not say so. Instead, as they left the steps to allow the others to come forward, Arianne simply placed her arm around Helena's shoulders.

They watched from the side as the ceremony concluded. The priest took the cross and wrapped it tenderly in white silk and placed it in a prepared sepulcher set deep inside the church wall. With this done, a veil was set over the opening, candles were set to surround the tomb, and each candle was lit as a prayer was recited.

The time that followed the ceremony was one of reflection and sobriety. The castle was strangely quiet, and even the servants worked in hushed effort. It was as though the entire community held its breath in anticipation.

Helena found it strangely comforting. She went about her duties, seeing to Timothy's needs when Arianne was busy with other tasks and writing songs in her head when moments of inspiration came upon her.

On Easter Eve, the candles surrounding the sepulcher were extinguished. A single candle, the great Paschal candle, was lit as an all-night vigil of the clergy began. Arianne watched with Helena, deeply disappointed that Richard had not yet returned. Helena felt her lady's sorrow and reached out a hand to reassure the duchess.

They walked back to the castle in silence, a procession of knights and their families following behind. Many parted at the castle gatehouse for their own homes, while unmarried knights took refuge in the barracks provided for them within the castle walls.

To Helena it seemed as though a great shroud had been placed upon them. The silence fell heavy in an almost smothering way. Each sound seemed magnified against the stillness; each footstep rustling against the rushes upon the floor echoed loudly within the dark, damp halls. It was a hallowed time.

Matilda handed Arianne a cresset lamp with oil. Without being told, she lit the wick and nodded, as though words would somehow have been a blasphemy of the moment. Arianne, bearing the lamp, went upstairs with Helena following closely behind her. They parted at Helena's room, Arianne placing a silent kiss upon her cheek.

"Let us pray that Richard returns soon and," she added almost as an afterthought, "that Devon will return and bring Richard's brother home."

Helena nodded and sought the refuge of her room. The fire burned low, and Helena knew it would only be a matter of time before the castle curfew or "cover fire" would be upon them and the watchman would make his rounds to stoke up the hearth fires for the night.

Feeling the cold and damp penetrate her skin, she readied herself for bed. A song came to her lips, and only when she began to sing did Helena realize it was a requiem. The mournful words flooded the room, while the haunting melody seemed to drip down from the walls and flood the stones below.

With slow, almost practiced steps, Helena went to the bed and knelt on the turned-back covers. Reaching up, she loosed the ties that held back the canopy curtains surrounding the bed and closed them around her.

Heavy brocade snuffed out the light from the hearth. It was like burying herself in the sepulcher, Helena thought. She pulled the covers high to her chin and settled upon the satin-covered pillow. Then with a will of its own, her mouth opened and again the eerie strains of mourning filled the night's silence.

∽

Arianne stood at the window of her bedroom. While the priests kept vigil in the church, she kept her own for Richard's return. Silently, she brushed her copper hair and with each stroke thought of her husband's absence and the longing she felt for his return. Had it only been weeks? It truly felt as though a lifetime had passed since she'd last felt his arms around her or heard his boyish laughter ringing in the halls.

Putting the brush aside, Arianne hugged her arms to her body and looked out upon the darkened lands.

"Oh, Richard," she whispered. Just then, Helena's sad voice came through in a muffled song.

Arianne strained to hear the words, but couldn't make them out. She thought of how blessed Helena was. The voice of an angel, Matilda had said, and Arianne thought perhaps even angels would behold Helena's voice in awe.

But tonight was different, Arianne thought. Usually Helena's songs were light, lyrical, and joyful. This was music for the dead, and Arianne knew that it came from deep within Helena's own heart. Was she wishing that she were dead?

"Dear Father," Arianne prayed in earnest, "go to her and give her peace." Then glancing out again to a world that would offer no hope of her husband's return, Arianne pleaded for the same comfort for herself.

"Bring him home, Lord," she begged. "Bring Richard home soon and with him Devon and Tancred, as well."

Timothy began to fuss, and Arianne went to the cradle and tenderly took him in hand. Taking him with her to the bed, Arianne settled down to nurse him. She took great comfort in this action. Somehow with Timothy beside her, she felt Richard's presence. Her cheeks flushed warm at the thought of Timothy's life coming out of her love for Richard. What wonders God had wrought and how inconceivable His ways, Arianne thought.

Just then Helena's singing ended and somehow its absence made the silence seem overwhelming. Arianne cuddled Timothy closer and nuzzled his soft head with her lips.

"Dear Father," she whispered, "let this night pass quickly."

Chapter 9

Helena awoke and pushed back the bed curtains, just as the morning sun was streaking the horizon with pale, rose-colored light. Taking the fur that had been placed upon her bed for added warmth, Helena wrapped it tightly around her and stood in the open window.

As each inch of darkness yielded to the light, Helena felt a small corner of her heart yield as well. It was easier to be brave in the light, she mused. Staring out across the newly plowed fields to the forest of trees in the distance, Helena wondered how much longer she would be able to stay at Gavenshire.

"Oh, Father," she whispered in a moan, leaning heavily against the stone that framed the window opening. There was little else to say, for in her heart she had no words. Words seemed inadequate. What more could she ask of God?

From the village and bailey below her came sounds of the morning. Cocks crowed and hushed voices rose to sounds of merriment and laughter. It was Easter, and today they would celebrate the resurrection of Christ. Helena smiled sadly. She had tried so hard to bury her suffering, yet daily it seemed to come back to life with a will of its own. *What strange creatures we must seem to God,* she thought.

It wasn't long before a young girl appeared at Helena's door to help her dress for morning services. Helena felt extremely privileged as she donned a tunic of the finest pale pink silk. It felt soft and cold against her body, but Helena relished it. The neckline had been embroidered by her own hand with tiny flower buds and ivy twining. Next came a surcoat of amber velvet. Helena had never known anything so regal in all of her life.

"You look grand, Milady," the girl said boldly. And indeed she was right in saying so.

Helena waited patiently while the girl dressed her hair and secured a thin white wimple to cover her head and neck. She was bringing Helena her slippers when Arianne knocked on the door.

"Good Easter morn," she announced, sweeping into the room.

She was resplendent in her sendal tunic of cream and surcoat of dark green velvet. The sendal material made a rustling sound, causing Arianne to smile. "My finery will no doubt announce me in church."

Helena laughed and curtsied. "You are truly a pleasure to behold your grace. Would that your husband could be here."

156

"Aye," Arianne sighed. "I prayed it might be so." Her words seemed sad, but still she smiled. "The day is not yet out. Perhaps Richard will arrive after church."

"Let us hope so," Helena replied.

They made their way to the bailey below with a crowd of others following and gathering around them. Easter was quite a celebration for the people. The villeins would be given time off to enjoy a rest from their labors, knights would test their skills against each other in mock joust, and nobility would survey all from amidst the revelry and deem it good.

Helena had been a part of Easter celebrations before, but never anything so grand and glorious. They made their way to the church, finding smiling faces and happy greetings wherever they went.

"I truly love this," Arianne stated as they walked. "I have enjoyed our own castle chapel, but the church in town allows me to be amidst all the people. I feel as though I've always belonged here."

Helena grimaced, but did not allow Arianne to see her pain. The words only served to remind her that she did not belong here or anywhere and that only by Arianne's kindness had she been allowed to stay. What would happen when the duke returned? Perhaps he would insist Helena reveal her identity and go home. What would she do then?

The pealing of the church bells brought Helena out of her stupor. It was impossible to be lost in such gloomy thought with such glorious sounds all around her. It made Helena want to sing, and in spite of her resolve to be quiet, she began to hum to herself. If Arianne heard, she said nothing. She was too busy laughing and greeting the people around her.

"Richard told me that the priest has arranged to present the *Quem quaeritis,*" Arianne said in a whisper to Helena. "It will come at the end of the mass."

"I have heard of this but never seen it," Helena replied as they walked up the steps of the church and were greeted by the priest.

Ushered inside by two of Richard's most trusted men, Arianne and Helena stood upon the straw-covered floor and awaited the procession on the priests and choirboys. With a song of celebration, they entered the church. Helena watched in complete captivation as the cross was brought out from the mock sepulcher and laid upon the altar.

At this, they knelt in the straw and bowed their heads as the priest offered up a Latin prayer. The service progressed in a series of prayers, songs, and ceremony. At the end of the service, the priest stepped behind a screen and then reappeared with three other men for the *Quem quaeritis,* a reenactment of the resurrection story.

One priest, dressed in white vestments and holding a palm in his hand, represented the angel at the tomb. *"Quem quaeritis in sepulchro?"* he questioned. "Whom do you seek in the sepulcher?"

The others, representing the three Marys, answered in unison, "Jesus of Nazareth."

Helena's breath caught. It was a moving play, and in her mind, she could very nearly imagine it was all real and happening for the first time. "Whom do you seek?" a voice seemed to question within her soul.

Tears came to her eyes. For all of her life, she had been raised in the beliefs and understandings of the church. She had never once questioned the existence of God or of His Son Jesus Christ. She practiced with the utmost reverence the requirements of her faith, yet in all that time she could not say in honesty that it had been God whom she sought.

"He is not here, He has risen," the angel-priest was announcing.

With this, the three Marys turned to the choir and replied, "Hallelujah, the Lord is risen today!" Then, the choir joined in a chorus of praise.

The angel-priest moved to where the cross had been placed in the wall. He lifted the veil that now covered the opening and said, "Come, see the place."

The Marys crossed to peer inside, while two men representing the apostles Peter and John appeared from behind the screen. John was in white and holding a palm, while Peter was dressed in red and carrying keys.

John reached the sepulcher first, but Peter reached inside. He pulled out the gravecloth in which the cross had been wrapped on Good Friday. "He is not here."

"He is risen as he said," the angel-priest announced.

Helena felt the tears flow down her cheeks. "*Quem quaeritis?* Whom do you seek?" She thought of Tanny and the love that might have been given to the hope that she would one day find him. "Whom do you seek?"

She watched the play continue with the exit of two of the Marys. The third, dressed in red and representing Mary Magdalene, stood weeping. For some reason, this made Helena cry all the more.

"Woman, why weepest thou? Whom seekest thou?"

The voice went straight to Helena's heart. She knew that God had been with her through all the years of anguish and lonely heartache. Now, it seemed as though this simple trooping of the resurrection story had brought a realization to Helena's soul. God wanted her to seek Him, Him alone. Not Tanny and not a home or place where she'd feel safe. God wanted her to seek only Him.

"They have taken my Lord," the man playing Mary stated in a sobbing voice.

The miracle unfolded, and the man playing Jesus revealed himself to Mary, much as God was revealing Himself to Helena as she stood and beheld the story.

"Rabboni," Mary said, falling to the ground. "My master."

"Rabboni," Helena whispered, knowing in her heart that God had truly taken control of her life.

The performance ended with a glorious hymn sung by the choir. "*Te Deum*

Laudamus—We praise Thee, God." Overhead, the bell pealed in celebratory announcement. "He is risen. He is not here."

Helena left the church a converted woman much, she imagined, as Mary must have left the garden. Just the knowledge that she was no longer bound to her fears gave Helena the first real happiness she'd known since her beloved had gone away.

All around the revelry was evident. There was dancing and singing, feasting and gifting. The tenants of the land brought eggs in payment to the castle, while in return Arianne had planned a great feast for all the people.

Arianne acted as hostess with Helena never leaving her side except to take baby Timothy upstairs in order to remove him from the noise of the castle bailey. Helena knew that Arianne scanned the horizon constantly for some sign of her husband, and when evening was approaching, the call that she had waited for finally came.

"The duke approaches!" one of the battlement guards called out.

"The duke!" Murmurs ran through the crowd, and people stopped their feasting to line the entryway into the castle.

Arianne glanced around for Helena and then remembered that she'd gone to take Timothy for his changing. "Matilda!" she said, beckoning the woman from the crowd. "Run, get Helena and Timothy. I would present him to his father and show Richard how much he has grown." Matilda quickly went in search of Helena, while Arianne rushed forward to greet her husband.

Three horsemen appeared in front of the procession, and Arianne instantly recognized each rider. Richard rode slightly to the front, with Devon and Tancred bringing up the rear.

"Richard!" she shouted and hurried to his side.

Richard dismounted in a leap and pulled her into his arms. "I have missed you sorely, sweet wife," he whispered and kissed her boldly in front of everyone.

Cheers below went up from the crowd, and Helena could only wonder at what matter had stirred them this time. There had been such cheering and shouting all day, and at times, Helena had worried that the babe's ears would be harmed from such noise. Nestling Timothy against her tightly, Helena moved through the happy people.

She knew from Matilda that the duke had returned, and no doubt his people were simply celebrating that fact. As the crowd parted for her, however, she found herself only a few feet away from the embracing couple and instantly flushed at the scene.

Arianne pulled back and saw her. "Richard, come see your son. He has grown wondrously since you last saw him."

Richard smiled at Helena, who was now trembling. "Your Grace," she said, as Richard reached out and took the baby.

"You are looking much better than the last time I saw you," Richard said with a smile.

Helena nodded but refused to meet his eyes. Would he send her away? Again, peace washed over her, and Helena realized it didn't matter. Lifting her gaze, she smiled.

"Much better," Richard said, then smiled down at his son. "And you truly have grown."

Helena noted the two men who were dismounting but gave them little thought until Arianne went to embrace each one of them. They had their backs to her, but Helena could see the smile of pleasure and something akin to relief in Arianne's eyes.

Richard handed Timothy back to Helena and pulled her forward. "You must meet my brother," he said firmly.

"It has been a long time," Arianne was telling one of the men. "I am glad you have returned."

Helena thought little of the matter, but when her eyes lifted to meet the man whom Richard introduced, she was stunned silent.

"Helena, this is my brother, John Tancred DuBonnet."

Helena's eyes were drawn to Tancred's against her will. "Tanny," she murmured so softly that no one understood her. Her arms began to shake, and she thought for a moment she might drop Timothy. Arianne noted her state and quickly took the baby from her.

"Helena, is it well with you?" Arianne whispered against her ear. But Helena only stared dumbfounded at the man before her.

"Milady," Tancred said, with a slight bow. He was mesmerized by the huge blue eyes that refused to break their hold on him. She was clearly the most beautiful creature he'd ever beheld.

"Helena?" Richard said, noting the whiteness of her face. "Are you ill?"

"Mayhaps she's just taken in by the charming faces of these men," Arianne teased lightly. She was truly worried about her lady-in-waiting, but refused to cause Helena any further embarrassment. "Helena needs to attend to Timothy's bath. Come, no doubt my son will seek his feeding as well."

Helena allowed herself to be led away by Arianne, but still she said nothing. How could it be so? Tanny, her own beloved Tanny, had come to her. Still, he knew her naught. She had been but a child when last they'd met, and now she was a grown woman. Should she go to him and reveal herself? Yet in revealing herself, she would also betray her true identity.

"Have you not heard me?" Arianne questioned with a gentle nudge.

"I am sorry," Helena whispered. "I am just a bit spent from the celebration. It has been a most taxing day."

Arianne nodded. "I asked you if there was something you wanted to tell me.

Has the past somehow caught up with you?"

Helena looked panicked as her gaze met that of the concerned duchess. "May we speak of it another time?" Her voice was soft and pleading.

Arianned nodded. "Of course. Would you prefer I take care of Timothy's bath?"

"Aye," Helena replied. "I would like to lie down."

"Then do so and know that when you feel better, I will be here for you." Arianne reached out a hand to touch Helena's slender arm. "Don't be afraid, Helena. You have a home here for as long as you want one. No one will put you from Gavenshire."

Somehow she knows, Helena thought to herself. Somehow the duchess had understood a portion of her fear. *But what will the duchess of Gavenshire have to say when the entire truth is revealed?* Helena wondered.

Closing her chamber door behind her, Helena leaned heavily against the wood. He was here! Her heart quickened, and she crossed to the window, anxious to catch some sight of him in the bailey below. Darkness and shadows refused to offer up anything, however, and Helena felt cheated.

"Tanny, it is I," she said softly in the silence of her room. " 'Tis your Helena, whose heart has ever been and evermore shall be yours and yours alone."

Chapter 10

Roger Talbot paced anxiously while awaiting his appointment with the king. It wouldn't be easy to explain Helena's disappearance, but if he handled the matter carefully, he was certain he could be convincing.

"The king will see you now," a pious chamberlain announced.

Roger entered a room where the king sat in conversation with two other men. The chamberlain made the introduction, and Roger waited to be acknowledged. In time the king motioned Roger forward.

"You have requested an audience with me?" Henry questioned.

"Yea, Your Majesty." Roger choked back bile. His nerves were raw, and this matter did not bode well with him.

"Then be at it, Man. What matter did you wish to discuss?"

" 'Tis my sister, Helena. As you will recall, her mother, Eleanor, was cousin to the queen."

"Aye, I remember it, Man. I remember it well. What do you seek?"

"I seek my sister. Helena disappeared from our home and I have not found her, though we have searched the land far and wide." Roger hoped he sounded convincingly worried.

"Helena?" The king spoke her name and instantly the memory of Richard DuBonnet entered his mind. "I believe I know where your sister is."

"You do?" Roger swallowed hard. Had Helena somehow managed to venture to London without his knowledge?

"Yes, yes," Henry nodded enthusiastically. "She is at Gavenshire. Duke DuBonnet mentioned the presence of a young woman named Helena. She has only been with him a short time and claimed no memory of her family or home."

"DuBonnet?" Roger questioned. He felt his stomach lurch again.

"Aye, Richard DuBonnet, duke of Gavenshire. You know of the place, do you not?"

"Aye," Roger replied between clenched teeth. "I know it." The DuBonnets had long been known to him, especially Richard's brother, Tancred. "I will seek her out immediately."

"By my leave," the king said, dismissing Roger Talbot as though there was nothing more that interested him about the man.

Roger seethed at the thought of his sister under the care of a DuBonnet. Tancred DuBonnet, once his most trusted friend, had dishonored Maude and refused to marry her. A scandal of outrageous proportions had been narrowly averted only when an aging earl had agreed to make Maude his wife.

He had thought himself well rid of DuBonnets when Tancred had been convicted of killing his parents. Roger remembered with great satisfaction the day he had learned of Tancred's sentence. Would that it could have been his death rather than his exile.

With his mind made up, Roger called a messenger to him and paid the man well to take word to Maude. There was no point in putting off his journey to Gavenshire, and he had little desire to confront Maude before doing battle with Tancred's brother. Mounting his horse, Roger grimaced and took the reins in hand. "Once again the DuBonnets cause me grief. This time I shall put an end to it."

≈∂≈

The days of Easter celebration passed in a mixture of bliss and pain for Helena. She watched with dedicated interest as Tancred moved about the castle. From behind carefully guarded eyes, Helena kept track of his every move.

From the first break of dawn and morning services, Helena's eyes seldom failed to keep Tancred in their view. When they partook of the meals, Helena tried to react in a calm and collected way, but knowing that Tancred sat on the other side of Richard made her nervous and testy. How much longer could she stand being so near him and not confide in him who she was?

It no longer worried her that she would be sent from Gavenshire. Now what concerned her was that Tancred would not return her love. Her beloved Tanny had left her childhood days as a strapping young man of twenty. Now he was a brooding man of thirty-one years with a mission to find the true murderers of his parents.

Obviously, Helena realized, he had no time or inclination for romance. She thought of the hours she'd spent dreaming of the day they'd meet again. Now that day had come and gone, and it was nothing of what she'd dreamed about.

As they sat at supper one evening, the revelry of festivities in the village still going on in celebration, Helena picked at her food and listened to the conversation around her.

"What a difference this life must be from the one you spent the past eleven years," Richard said to Tancred.

"Aye. The food is much better, the housing much drier, and the company preferable to any that I knew abroad."

Arianne leaned forward. "Devon tells me of your philosopher Artimas. He sounds like a wonderful man. I would very much like to meet him one day."

"He was, indeed, a great man, dear sister. I found the seeds you tenderly planted in my heart grew under his careful watering."

Helena felt a twinge of jealousy rear within her heart. "Pray tell, what seeds

163

does he speak of, Your Grace?"

Arianne smiled. "I but saw the potential in Tancred that he could not see for himself. I told him of his value in the eyes of God. Artimas apparently found a way to cultivate that meager planting."

" 'Twas far from meager," Tancred said. His eyes were reflective of the deep emotion he felt. "I felt hopelessness such as I beg never to feel again, but even in the darkest moment, Arianne's word of love gave me cause to hope."

"Hope is often all that keeps us going," Helena said softly, her eyes lowered to her trencher.

"Faith," Arianne added. "Faith is hope at work."

"Very good, Sister," Tancred said with a smile.

∽

Later that night, Tancred stood in the quiet of his chamber, undressing for bed. He thought back over the last few days, but his mind could not let go of Helena. He saw her everywhere, even when he slept. It was as though he knew her, and yet there was nothing of recollection in his mind.

"She watches me with the eyes of a hawk," he thought aloud. Yet lovelier eyes of crystal blue Tancred was sure he'd never seen. She was a most fetching woman, and he decided on the morrow he would speak to Arianne about her.

"No need for the woman to haunt my every step. At least not without my reasoning out why." He drew the bed curtains and closed his eyes in sleep. As was true for every night since having been introduced to Helena, Tancred fell asleep with the soft, tender features of her face on his mind.

"Is your husband already among his men?" Tancred asked Arianne the next morning as she sat in the counting room. A long ledger lay before her on the table.

"Aye, he's already gone. You might find him in the stables."

"What of Helena and Matilda?"

"They are upstairs with Timothy. Why do you ask?" Arianne put aside her quill and stared up at her brother-in-law.

Tancred closed the door behind him and pulled up a chair. "I have some questions to ask of you."

"I see. Pray tell, on what matter?"

"Helena."

Arianne smiled. "So she has vexed you as you have her."

"I have vexed her? How so?"

"I am uncertain that I should say. Be it simple enough to conclude she finds you most appealing to her sense. Why, my own brother, Devon, found her fascinating and paid her many compliments, but she saw him naught. She never questioned me about him, either."

"And she questioned you about me?" Tancred's dark eyes pierced Arianne.

He leaned forward, intent on her every word.

"Aye." Arianne's voice was soft and her eyes danced with amusement. "She has scarce discussed anything else."

Tancred smiled in spite of himself. "And why not?" he teased. "Am I not worthy of discussion?"

"Oh, prideful man," Arianne said with mock disdain, "thy pathway leads to destruction."

Tancred laughed aloud. "Never mind that. Tell me what she has asked of you."

Arianne grew thoughtful. "She asked me about your arrival here last year. She asked if the things we had heard about you were true."

"What things?" Tancred's eyes narrowed.

Arianne grew uncomfortable and involuntarily her hand went to her face—to the cheek Tancred had so sorely bruised when he'd hit her in anger.

"Oh, that," he replied before she could speak. The sorrow in his eyes matched that in his voice.

"I told her you were beside yourself in hopelessness. I told her you were desperate and that you saw all that you loved taken beyond your grasp." Arianne paused and reached out to touch Tancred's arm. "I told her there was a void in you that could not be filled, and she told me that this was something she could understand."

"You are most gracious, Arianne. I do not deserve your kindness."

She smiled and squeezed his arm. "I have such happiness with Richard and Timothy. God took me from a frightful existence and no earthly love, save that of my brother, and gave me an abundance. My advice to you, Sir Tancred, is that you grasp firmly what is held within your reach. Helena is besot with you, and I believe she considers herself in love with you."

"Did she say that?"

"Nay. She didn't have to." Arianne took her quill back in hand. "Sometimes the heart speaks most loudly when the mouth says nothing at all."

Tancred took Arianne's words with him, and they only served to double his determination to seek out the alluring Helena and learn the truth from her. He had spent so much time in conference with Arianne that he was certain Helena would no longer be in the rooms with Timothy. Where she might be was a mystery to him, but experience had shown him that Helena would no doubt find him.

Coming down the outer castle stairs, Tancred could not believe his good fortune when he spied Helena planting herbs in the castle garden. He watched her for a moment, knowing that she was unaware of his presence.

There was something strangely familiar about her, and yet Tancred knew he had no recollection to their ever meeting. Perhaps that was what he should ask her first, but then again, mayhaps that would only serve to scare her off.

She was singing softly and the sound rose up to greet him in a pleasant way.

Arianne had said that Helena had the voice of an angel, Tancred remembered. It was one night after dinner when someone had mentioned hearing singing in the castle.

He couldn't make out the words, but her voice haunted him and he felt almost mesmerized by the melody. He came down the steps quietly still studying her form as she dug at little spots of dirt and patted seed into the ground.

He was standing directly behind her, and it wasn't until Helena noticed his shadow on the ground that she started and turned to face him.

"I–I. . ." She couldn't form the words.

"Lady Helena," Tancred said, reaching his hand down to draw her up. "I wondered if we might talk."

"Talk?" She was shaking and refused to take the offered hand. *I can't let him touch me,* she thought. *He'll feel how I tremble and he'll know what I'm thinking.*

Tancred was unconcerned at her aloofness. He reached out and pulled her to her feet. "Aye, talk. Come along, there is a bench over here."

Helena felt him draw her along, and all the while her mind could scarcely take it in. This was Tanny. This was no dream, but a living, breathing man—the man she'd pledged to love for as long as she lived.

"Here," he said, allowing Helena to take a seat. For a moment he stood towering over her, arms crossed against his leather tunic. He looked much like a father about to scold his child, and when that image filtered through to his senses, he softened and took the seat beside her.

"You have been much on my mind of late," he began. "I wonder why that is?"

Helena couldn't answer. Her throat felt constricted and her tongue too big for her mouth. Swallowing hard, she wavered between fainting and gasping for air.

"You are a comely maid, and I find that your beauty is most appealing. However, I am not used to such attention, and I feel I must ask why you have sought me out?"

"Sought you out?" Helena questioned, finally finding her voice. "But, Sire, you brought me here. 'Twas your idea to talk."

"Yes, yes. But, what else could I do? You watch my every move. You peer down even from your bedchamber to watch me upon the training field. I know, for I have seen you there."

Helena paled, then blushed. "Aye, I have watched you."

"For what purpose, if I might ask?"

"I–I do not. . . ," she stammered, then tried to get to her feet, but his hand shot out to take hold of her.

"Nay, do not leave. Answer my question."

Helena could bear it no longer. The sight and scent of him, the feel of his ironlike grip upon her wrist, even the very breath he breathed called out to be taken into account.

"Why do you watch me?" he asked softly.

"Because I love you," she declared, and the words so shocked Tancred that he dropped his hold. "Because I love you now and always have and forever will." She hurried from the bailey, running up the stairs and vanishing out of sight while Tancred sat with open mouth.

"She loves me? But she knows naught of me," Tancred said, staring at the stone stairs. What did she mean by it? The words came back to haunt him. *Because I love you now and always have.* Did he know her? He searched his memory for some woman named Helena and gave up without a face to set it in place.

"Helena," he murmured, and the word wrapped itself as a band around his heart.

Chapter 11

Richard was soaked in sweat from the sword fights he'd endured with his men on the training field. He was aching in several muscles, which told him he'd let himself get soft. He shook his head ruefully and determined that he would begin practicing daily. Plunging his head in the water trough, he didn't hear the first call from his sentry that a rider approached.

Richard took an offered towel from his squire and dried his face.

"Will you see the man?" the squire asked his master, knowing full well Richard had not heard the sentry's announcement.

"What man?"

"A rider has been announced." The squire motioned to the sentry on the battlement overhead.

"A single rider?" Richard questioned. The sentry confirmed this. "Admit him."

The lone horseman rode into the castle and was soon surrounded by several of Richard's knights. One held the man's horse while the stranger dismounted. Richard strode forward to meet him.

"I am the duke of Gavenshire. How might I help you?"

The man was clearly amazed at being greeted by the duke himself; nevertheless it was hostility that sounded in his voice and not surprise. "I am Sir Roger Talbot, and you have my sister."

Richard stared at the man for a moment. "I do not believe I understand."

Roger's anger surfaced more boldly, and several of the knights moved to stand beside their duke. "You have Helena!"

Richard studied the man for a moment. "There abides here a young woman named Helena; that much is true. You claim she is your sister?"

"Aye, that she is. King Henry told me himself that she was here. I've come to take her back."

"I see. Why don't you come inside with me and we will speak to Helena on the matter."

"Helena has no voice in this. She will do as I tell her." Roger was livid. His face was purplish-red, and veins in his neck were engorged.

Richard narrowed his eyes. "Helena is under my protection, and I say we speak to her on the matter."

Roger gritted his teeth and realized the duke would not be bullied by him.

"Very well," he muttered.

Richard motioned him to follow and called for one of the castle maids to seek out Arianne and Helena. The girl went quickly upstairs to the bedchambers while Richard took Roger to his private receiving room just off the great hall.

"Perhaps we will be more comfortable here. Will you not have a seat?"

"No." Roger's voice was clipped and cold.

"Have I offended you in some way?" Richard asked, his eyes narrowing. "You barge into my home and make demands and do so with the utmost rudeness. What is there between us that merits such action?"

Roger remembered Tancred's dalliance with his sister Maude and frowned. "Your brother was John Tancred DuBonnet, was he not?"

"He still is. What is it to you?"

"He fostered in my home when we were boys. He played false with my sister, Maude, and nearly ruined her, and you ask me what there is between us that merits my anger?"

"I suppose I was too young or too busy with my own fostering to worry overmuch about Tancred's deeds. Still, the past is no call for bad manners. You and I have no quarrel, so why not be civil?"

Roger eyed Richard suspiciously for a moment, then nodded. "Very well. We will be civil. I have come to take my sister home. She ran away many weeks ago, and I have been quite worried for her safety."

"I see. May I inquire as to why she ran away?"

" 'Tis a family matter. The girl's mother passed away not long before, and she could scarce deal with her grief."

Just then Arianne entered the room in conversation with Helena. The two women did not look up until they were well within the room, and when Helena spied her brother, she stopped dead in her tracks.

"Helena!" Roger stated, taking a step forward.

Helena moved back a step, and Richard noted the fear in her eyes. Interceding, he introduced Arianne. "May I present the duchess of Gavenshire." Then turning to his wife, he added, "Arianne, this is Helena's brother, Sir Roger Talbot."

"I am pleased to meet you," Arianne said, but realized Roger's eyes were on Helena. Arianne tried to draw Roger into conversation. "We have very much enjoyed your sister's company and would be happy if you, too, would consider yourself welcomed here."

"Helena, I've come to take you home." Roger stepped forward, rudely ignoring Arianne's statement.

Helena shook her head fiercely. "No! I am not going anywhere. The duke and duchess have opened their home to me, and I would very much like to remain here for a time."

"You are coming home," Roger stated flatly and stepped forward to take Helena in hand.

Helena did the only thing she could. She turned and ran for the door, counting on the fact that she knew the castle and Roger did not. She also planned on Richard intervening and calling his men. What she did not plan on was running into the broad, iron chest of Tancred DuBonnet.

Helena was shaking so hard that even Tancred could not mistake the trembling. He looked down at her and found frightened horror in her eyes.

"Helena, what is it?"

"Let her go, DuBonnet," Roger's voice called from behind his sister. Turning to Richard, Roger's eyes blazed. "What would Henry say if he knew you harbored a fugitive? This man is supposed to be in exile for the murder of your parents."

"Henry pardoned Tancred weeks ago. I have the writ upstairs. He is innocent of the murders."

Roger snorted. "I remember the day the king said otherwise. I do not believe him innocent nor pardoned."

"It matters little to me what you think," Tancred replied dryly. His arms engulfed Helena's small frame.

"Unhand her!"

Tancred kept a firm grip on Helena and pulled her closer. Looking past her, he met the eyes of his onetime friend, Roger Talbot.

"What is she to you, Talbot?"

"Fool, she is my stepsister, Helena. Remember? She's the one who used to pester you when you dallied with my sister, Maude." Roger moved forward, but this time Richard put himself between them.

Tancred stared down in wonder at the woman in his arms. "This is that little squirt of a girl we pulled out of one scrape and then another?"

Helena was still shaking as she lifted tear-filled eyes to meet his softened expression. "Oh, Tanny," she whispered in a near-mournful tone.

"But you were just a baby," he said, still staring in disbelief. That little girl from his past was the young woman who so fiercely declared her love to him in the bailey only yesterday. It was impossible to comprehend.

"Babies grow up, Tancred. Now unhand my sister and—"

"No!" Helena raged and pushed Tancred away. "I won't go with you. Not now, not ever!" She ran from the room, leaving Tancred to stare after her and Roger to yell a stream of curses.

Helena was grateful for the festivities that still occupied the attention of most of the town. No one paid any attention to her as she ran from the protection of the castle and made her way out across the land.

Tears blinded her eyes, and her heart pounded against the reminder that her brother and Tancred had faced each other for the first time in eleven years. She knew of the past between them. She knew, too, of Maude and the lies that had passed between her and Roger regarding Tancred.

It was all too much.

Fleeing to the sanctuary of the forest, Helena collapsed into a heap on the ground and cried until she felt her heart would break. How could Tanny ever love her now—now that he knew who she was? He hated her brother and her brother hated him. How unfair it all was!

"Oh, God," she cried and hugged her knees to her breast. "Oh, God, 'tis not the way I would have it be. I love him so that I scarce can start my day without my first thoughts being of him." She buried her face against her knees. "Oh, God."

She pleaded for solace and begged for understanding, and still all she could see was the raging eyes of her brother and his determination to take her from Gavenshire. Now that he knew about Tancred, he would no doubt force the issue.

Strong arms lifted her upward, and without looking, Helena knew it was Tancred. She let him hold her while she cried uncontrollably. This would probably be the only time she'd ever feel his arms around her. She wanted to remember the comfort he offered and the way it felt to bury her face against his chest.

Tancred sat down on a fallen log and held the sobbing woman close. She was beautiful, and he could not deny the feelings she had stirred in him in her adoration throughout the week. Yet now, for reasons beyond his ability to consider, her feelings were quite precious to him. In his memories, Helena was but a child. A little girl with torn tunics from her antics and a dirt-smudged face that begged to be washed. Who was this woman who had replaced the child?

Gradually her sobs subsided, and Helena felt strengthened by Tancred's presence. Drying her face on the edge of her surcoat, she looked up at him with reddened eyes.

"I remember a time when you had fallen from the rafters in the stables," Tancred began. "You were no more than eight years and you cut your knee. Remember?" Helena nodded. "I remember holding you like this and telling you that big girls should not handle their miseries in such a fashion." His grin broadened to a smile. "I suppose the same advice would work in this situation as well."

Helena reached up her hand to touch Tancred's trimmed brown beard. She searched his eyes for some confirmation of his returned feelings.

"I have loved you since I was a child, Tanny. I cannot be untrue to my heart. When you spent so much time among us, I couldn't help but fall in love."

"But you were a child, a little girl," Tancred said softly, still not trusting the declaration.

Helena wasn't offended by his words. "Cannot a child love?"

Tancred smiled down at her. "Apparently so."

Helena nodded. "I watched Maude treat you badly. I knew she had her numerous suitors, but for a little girl of nine, there was no real understanding for the game she played. I knew, however, for I'd watched her in the stable with others, that you did nothing to steal her virtue. I hated her for setting Roger against you, but my mother told me it was a matter that had to be resolved among adults. She would not allow me to go to Roger nor to defame my stepsister."

"Your stepsister was looking to make herself a wealthy match. 'Twas not my desire to become a husband." He added with a chuckle, "At least not then."

Helena boldly threw her arms around Tancred's neck, surprising them both. "I love you. 'Tis real enough and true enough and whether you ever love me or not, it will remain just as it is and always has been."

She sobered, but kept her hold on Tancred. "I know my brother will never approve of my feelings. He hates you and has often said as much. He believes you killed your parents, but I do not. I have always known it would have been impossible for you, for your heart is rich with love and goodness.

"When they told me of the accusations, I defended you and raged at them for their pettiness. I told Roger, even though I was only nine, that he owed you his loyalties. I reminded him that he had once exchanged signet rings in bonds of friendship. I insisted that he was wrong—that everyone was wrong. I knew that you were incapable of such a disgusting act." The absolute certainty in her voice was evidence of her convictions.

Tancred stared at her with sheer gratitude in his eyes. "You are the only one who believed me innocent, and you were just a child." In his mind, she was still a child, yet the reality of the woman he held made it difficult to hold those memories in place.

"But I am no longer a child."

"I am most certain of that," Tancred stated, running his hand down her arm. "Most certain."

"And my brother seeks to put me away now that my mother is dead. Maude is jealous of me and cannot bear for me to be in the same house. They plan to put me in a convent and intend to see me remain there for life."

It was Tancred's turn to surprise them both by throwing his head back and laughing. Helena stared at him, not speaking or even blinking.

"Forgive me, Love, but I can think of many far better things to do with you."

"Pray tell?" Helena eyed him suspiciously, a hint of a smile on her lips.

Tancred stood up and placed Helena on the log. "For now, suffice it to say that I am quite intrigued by your devotion. I no longer find a child before me, but a grown woman—a very beautiful grown woman."

"And what will you do with me?" Helena asked innocently.

"Well, 'tis certain my thoughts do not include a nunnery."

Chapter 12

"Come." Tancred pulled Helena to her feet. "Let us go reason with your brother."

"There is no reasoning with that one."

Tancred put Helena's hand upon his arm. "Perhaps not, then again maybe there is. We've dealt him a double blow this day. First he finds you after many weeks and then he finds me not far behind. Now that he has had time to simmer, perhaps he will listen."

They walked out into the clearing and Tancred paused. "I have known days past when your brother was a reasonable man. I trust God can give him the ability to deal evenhandedly with this, Helena."

"Roger cares naught for fairness or evenhanded dealings. He cares for Roger." She paused and let her gaze go to the open meadow where men and women laughed and cheered the children in three-legged races. "I fear him, Tanny." She couldn't help but shudder. "He hated me, mayhaps not as much as Maude, but nevertheless I was a thorn in his side. Henry would not allow him to force my hand in marriage and that angered him greatly. He could neither touch the dowry left me by my mother, nor could he benefit from a wealthy arranged union."

"You have never married?" Tancred asked in disbelief. "But you must be at least. . ." The image of Helena as a little girl faded more and more.

"I am twenty," Helena said with a frown. "And no, I could not marry when my heart belonged to you."

Tancred shook his head. "All those years spent in my miserable exile and you were here across the sea."

"I would gladly have shared your exile, Tanny. Most gladly."

Her eyes pierced his heart in the warmth of their sincerity. Her love caused him to feel strong in a way he'd not felt in years. Uncertain of what he might do should they tarry any longer, Tancred led her forward and motioned at the castle in the distance.

"My brother and I will not allow you to be taken. Roger will have little to say in the matter when Henry learns of this. But tell me, why did you refuse to tell us your story?"

Helena lowered her head in shame. "I could not admit to being Lady Helena Talbot. Richard would no doubt have sent word to Roger and in turn my brother would have retrieved me. I could not bear the thought of another beating at his hand. Nor could I agree to his terms in regards to the abbey."

Tancred stopped abruptly. "He beat you?"

"Aye. 'Twas the reason I ran. While he was just boisterous and raging, I could handle him and Maude as well. But Maude convinced him to starve me and then put me to shame at the whipping post. I bear those lash marks even now."

Tancred's eyes narrowed in rage. "He will answer for it with marks of his own."

"Nay, Tanny," Helena begged, her hand firmly gripping his arm. " 'Twould resolve nothing. I am reconciled to the matter and know that Roger would never have acted as he did, if not for Maude."

She held him in her pleading gaze and finally Tancred nodded. "Very well, but I pledge to you that it will not happen again."

Helena smiled. "Thank you. You have always seen fit to rescue me from one bad situation or another. Many was the beating I avoided as a child because you and Roger interceded. Now I can only pray that the good Father in heaven will intercede on my behalf today."

" 'Tis my way of thinking He already has."

Roger was not happy to see his stepsister enter the castle on Tancred DuBonnet's arm. He began his tirade on the bailey lawn, but Richard prevailed and suggested they return to the privacy of his chambers. Begrudgingly, Roger agreed and followed Tancred and Helena inside.

Tancred seated Helena near the fire and stood behind her in a protective fashion. He gave Roger little doubt in the menacing stare he offered that he would and could protect Helena from further attack.

Richard took his seat and motioned to Roger. "Be seated, Talbot, and let us speak as gentleborn folk."

"There is nothing gentleborn in that man's manner," Talbot said, refusing to sit. "I demand you release Helena to my care and stay out of this matter."

Helena surprised them all by speaking up. "I will not go with you, Roger. As nearly as I can understand it, you sought to send me to the convent in order to appease Maude. Her desire was that I be put from the house and now I am. So where lies the problem?" Unafraid, her gaze met his.

"Maude's desires are not the only ones to be considered here. I would see you well cared for. You refuse to take a husband and I—"

"I did not refuse to take any husband. I simply refused the ones you offered. You know my heart on the matter."

Roger clenched his fists. "You would throw yourself at this cur's heels? The very man who soiled your stepsister and nearly caused her complete disgrace."

"Ha! Maude caused her own disgrace," Helena declared. "You forget, I was a child then."

"What has that to do with it?"

"Much. I was able to slip into the shadows unobserved. I watched the things my stepsister played at. 'Twas not this good man who stole your sister's virtue, and this I know full well."

Roger stared at her in surprise. "What do you mean?"

Helena folded her hands and glanced up at Tancred. "Tanny never played false with her. He refused her advances, and so our dear sister sought revenge upon him. She set your mind against him, though he was not the one to be the cause of your grief."

Roger sat down and stared in silence for several moments as if trying to decide if Helena spoke the truth. He looked at Tancred, the man who had been like a brother to him. Was it possible that Maude's interference had separated him from the dearest friend he'd ever known?

"I had just received my title and lands," Tancred said, breaking the silence. "It was a most attractive package to your sister, and when she learned of it, her pursuit ensued. I'd simply have no part of it, for I did not love her."

It was too much to concede and Roger, instead, changed the subject. "Maude is not the only issue here. What of the murder? You were convicted by your brother's own testimony." He turned to Richard. "Was this not true?"

" 'Twas a mistake and one I deeply regret, for it cost my brother eleven years of his life."

"But there were witnesses to the act," Roger protested. "I know because I paid special attention to the details of the matter."

"They were false witnesses," Richard stated. "Obviously the true murderer paid them well to sing their song. Tancred and I intend to learn the truth of the matter."

"I do not believe you," Roger said, still clearly shaken by Helena's declaration.

Tancred stepped from behind Helena's chair. "It matters little what you believe. 'Twas a time, however, when your loyalty would have remained with me. I believe the poisoning of your mind can be traced back to Maude's hard heart. If you are honest with yourself, you will agree."

" 'Tis true, Roger." Helena's voice was soft and tender. "You once rode with this man at your side. How many times did you conspire with him to keep me out of trouble? How many times did you take the full punishment when our father learned of the matter?" Roger said nothing and Helena continued. "Maude met Tancred one afternoon in the mews. She didn't realize I was there, and she began her tirade before I could take my leave."

Helena lifted her face to smile at Tancred. "Tanny knew naught that I was there watching him work. 'Twas my fondest pleasure, just to be near him. Maude came into the mews and began to weave her spell. She flattered and played at his pride until I was certain Tanny would do most anything she asked. Of course, I was enraged, knowing that only the night before she'd been with the neighboring earl's son.

"Maude pleaded her love to him and begged him to reject her naught. She concocted stories of her miseries. Her mistake came in the fact that Tanny already knew of her dalliances."

"How could he know? Did you tell him these things and, if so, why should he believe a child?" asked Roger.

"I said nothing to him. My mother would not allow me to become a part of the matter."

"I was no fool, Roger." Tancred spoke in his own defense. "Neither were you, and if you think back on the matter, you will know the fact of this."

For several moments nothing was said. Helena felt sorrow for Roger as he reconciled himself to the truth. She could see his eyes soften for just a moment before he hardened himself again.

"It still does not excuse your actions. You refused to even defend yourself to me," Roger finally stated.

"I should not have needed to defend myself to a friend."

Again, Roger was taken aback. "Perhaps, but just because Henry absolves you of murder does not mean I do. I see no proof of your innocence."

"I intend to find it," Tancred replied. "Until then, my clear conscience is all the proof I need—that and your sister's fierce loyalty." He put his hand on Helena's shoulder.

Helena cherished the touch. She could scarcely believe that he stood at her side. Better yet, that he had not rejected her love. *Oh God*, she prayed, *please lay these matters to rest.*

Just then Arianne entered the room with Timothy. " 'Tis the supper time and I know my own hunger is great. Come to the table and resolve these issues on the morrow."

Richard went to her and took Timothy in his arms. "I believe my wife is the only one with any sense. Talbot, a room has been prepared for you. Will you stay?"

Roger got to his feet and nodded. "Aye, for this is not yet concluded, and my sister and I must talk."

Helena felt her peace dwindle. What would Roger do to force his hand in the matter? She decided then and there to not allow Roger to speak with her alone. Tancred could not follow her everywhere, and when his back was turned, Roger very well might steal her away. She was so lost in thought that she did not realize that everyone but Tancred had left the room.

"Is it well with you, Helena?"

She looked up to find his brow furrowed in a worried expression. Forcing a smile, she nodded and accepted his hand. "It has been a most taxing day."

"And a most revealing one." He smiled at her upturned face. Then surprising them both, he leaned down and placed a brief kiss upon her forehead.

"Aye," Helena murmured, her cheeks blushing scarlet.

When darkness fell upon Gavenshire, Arianne and Helena took Timothy and retired to their chamber. Helena could hear voices in the great hall as she closed her door. Would they take matters into their own hands and refuse to consider her will in the affair? She felt frightened for a moment, and then the words from the Easter sermon came back to her. *Whom do you seek?* Forcing her will to come under control, Helena realized that seeking out God first was harder than she'd believed. Still, by placing herself in God's hands, Helena knew peace.

Letting contentment replace her fear, she doffed her garments and slid into bed. Thoughts of Tancred's kiss played on her mind. She touched her finder to her forehead and frowned. Was it only a brotherly kiss? The more she considered it, the more it seemed to be the kiss of an adult to a child. Chiding herself for questioning Tancred's motives, Helena smiled.

Without further contemplation, she lifted her voice in a song of praise to God. The joyful melody filled the silence of her chamber and warmed the room with hope. For the first time in years, she snuggled down into the cover of her bed and knew a deep, heartfelt serenity. Tanny was home. It made her song just that much sweeter.

In his chamber, Tancred heard the lyrical voice and strained to catch the words. Who was it that sang with such purity and joy? He opened his door for a moment and cocked his head into the hall. Just then the watchman was making his way to stoke up the fires.

"Who is it that sings?" Tancred asked the man.

" 'Tis the Lady Helena. Her voice is like no other."

Tancred nodded and closed the door with a smile on his face. Helena was a woman like none he'd ever known. It was a pleasant surprise to find her springing up from his past, yet it was a wonder to replace the image of Roger's little sister with that of the warm, shapely woman Helena had become.

Preparing for bed, Tancred remembered the way she'd defended him, nor could he put from his mind the way she'd cried in his arms and declared her love for him.

" 'Tis certainly more than I expected," he said to the empty room. Then a thought of Artimas came to mind. The man had told Tancred in complete assurance that God's planning was always best and never out of time.

"If I'd remained here with my land and title," Tancred mused, "I no doubt would have married and fathered many children by now. Helena was but a child and not yet even fostered. I would never have looked to her for companionship." Somehow the idea of this gave Tancred a start. He suddenly realized just how unwelcome this thought was.

Getting into bed, Tancred smiled. "She loves me." He closed his eyes, extremely satisfied. "Someone loves me."

Chapter 13

M ilady, he's asked to see you again," Helena's young maid told her. Helena shook her head. "I cannot." She looked at the girl with sympathy. Sending her off to meet Roger's disappointment and anger wasn't an easy decision. "Tell him he can talk to me later when I am with Her Grace and young Timothy."

"Aye, Milady." The girl curtsied and finished helping Helena into a samite surcoat of yellow. The shade did her pale complexion justice, and the gold threads that had been embroidered at the neckline brought out the gold of her hair. Smoothing down the richness of the wool and silk-blended gown, Helena felt the knotting of her stomach as the church bell began to peal. It was time for church and no doubt Roger would seek to accompany her. It wouldn't matter that he couldn't speak to her at that moment. He would simply take charge and make his presence known.

Hastening her maid, Helena pulled on the pale yellow wimple and tucked all but a few wily strands of plaited blond hair beneath its covering. She wondered at her predicament when a light knock sounded on the door.

"Helena, 'tis Arianne."

The maid quickly opened the door for the duchess and took her leave. Arianne entered the room with Timothy in hand. "I thought you might like some company."

"To be sure, Milady." Helena nervously slipped her feet into matching yellow slippers and stood to face Arianne. "Thank you," she whispered.

Arianne put a hand upon Helena's arm. "Richard has assured me that you will not be forced to leave this place. Your brother has much to answer for, and we will not allow him to harm you."

Gratitude flashed into Helena's eyes. "But he is my guardian."

Arianne nodded. "Aye, but Richard has Henry's ear, and before you are given over against your will, we will see it brought before him."

Helena took a deep breath. "I do not wish to be left alone with Roger. Please."

"Of course. I will see to it that one of us accompanies you at all times."

"Thank you, Arianne. I owe you much and can never hope to repay it."

Arianne smiled slyly. "I have but one question for you."

"Ask it." Helena's curiosity was peaked. What could the duchess possibly want to know? All of her secrets were in the open. Her mind raced to consider what the duchess might want to ask.

"Are you truly in love with Tancred?"

Helena's mouth dropped open and quickly she struggled to conceal her surprise. Arianne's face was lit with amusement and even Timothy cooed as though delighted by the aspect of Helena's answer.

"I think you just answered my question," Arianne said with a grin. "I am most gratified at this turn of events. Tancred needs a good woman at his side. A strong woman—one who can soften his roughness and strengthen him where he is weak."

"Tanny is not weak," Helena said firmly. "He is the strongest man I have ever known. He has endured so very much and yet survives to tell of it. I greatly admire him, and yes, I love him. I have since I was a small child."

"Good." Arianne shifted Timothy and took Helena by the elbow. "Then we must work hard to see you two brought together."

" 'Tis no matter of hard work, Your Grace," Tancred stated from the doorway. He stood there with arms crossed, leaning against the stone wall as though he had been there for some time.

Helena blushed and refused to meet his eyes. She was confused that after all of these years of loving him, she should suddenly feel shy.

"Ah, so you are in agreement." Arianne reached out to hand Helena over to Tancred. "That saves me much time and trouble."

Tancred grinned at his sister-in-law. His dark eyes met hers. "Would that Helena have saved all of us the time and trouble. Do you know she cared for me since she was a child?"

"So she says."

"Do not talk as though I were not here," Helena protested, raising her head to meet Arianne and Tancred's amused faces.

"I see your sudden case of vapors has passed," Tancred said and took firm hold of Helena's arm. "Come along, you two. The priest will have vapors if we keep him waiting."

After church there was a warming breakfast with thick bowls of porridge and a special treat. Matilda had overseen the making of a special sweet bread. The delicacy was laden with almonds and raisins, and everyone at the table agreed it was a delightful surprise.

Roger had tried twice to corner Helena, once as she was coming out of the chapel and the second time as she was being seated for breakfast. Both times, either Tancred or Arianne had interceded and prevented Roger from whisking his sister away for the private discussion Helena so dreaded.

At the table, Helena found herself carefully positioned between Arianne and Devon, just as she had been since her arrival. On Devon's other side sat Roger with a scowl on his face that clearly stated his frustration. Helena glanced his way only once and shuddered at the expression she met. Arianne, noticing the problem, gave Helena's hand a reassuring pat.

Relaxing a bit at this gesture of support, Helena knew that she was truly safe. Arianne was a wise and thoughtful woman, and Richard was completely devoted to her and heeded her suggestions. Helena knew, too, that Tancred would intercede in a heartbeat, should Roger distress her with more than a glance.

Thank You, Father, she prayed silently. *Thank You for the protection and comfort I have found among these people.* Lifting her head, Helena smiled. She felt sated with reassurance, and even Roger's sour face could not distract her from feeling secure.

～

"I keep thinking there is something that I have overlooked," Tancred said, running his hands through his dark hair. "I have relived the night of the murders over and over until I'm nearly certain that I am there again."

"Aye, as have I." Richard's tone held only sadness. They had agreed to come together and discuss the matter of their parents' death, but now Tancred was uncertain it would do any good.

"I was excited about returning home after spending much time in London," Richard continued. "It seemed I had been gone an eternity, and I was anxious to greet our mother and know her gentleness once again."

"How came you to return home?"

"It came as a surprise, actually," Richard replied. "I was working upon the training field when a messenger arrived explaining that the king desired an audience with me. I went to Henry, and he told me that our parents had requested I return home to attend some matter. He did not say what that matter might be."

"But you arrived at the manor only moments after I did?"

"Aye, and the rest you know full well."

Tancred nodded. "I was settling down for the night on my own estate. It was still a wonder to me that I was titled and in control of such a large piece of land." Just then Helena's voice could be heard. She was singing to Timothy, and Tancred couldn't resist pausing to listen.

"I had just put the business of Roger's sister, Maude, to rest. At least so much as I could. Maude was outraged that I could walk away from her. She was so certain that she could dupe me into marriage, and when it didn't work, she destroyed my friendship with Roger." Sadness overtook Tancred's features and softened him in a way that Richard had never seen. There were tears in his eyes when Tancred continued. "I loved him as dearly as I did you. He was a brother to me in every way. We grew up together, trained and fought together, laughed and sought entertainment together. Never was there a better friend than Roger."

" 'Tis a pity that a woman should destroy that bond."

"Aye, but one very hard and embittered woman. Maude only sought to better herself and she cared naught for whom it destroyed in the meantime. But that aside, I go back to that night and remember it early on to have passed in relative peace."

Helena's singing comforted Tancred as he recalled the latter parts of that tragic evening. The parts that offered no peace. His face grew rigid. "There came a man with a message bearing our father's seal."

"Who was this man?" Richard asked .

"I knew him naught," Tancred replied. "He was there but a moment and then gone. Before I could even break the wax, he had slipped into the shadows of the night and disappeared. I thought little of it. I presumed the letter was but our father's suggestion for resolution in a matter I had with my villeins. I took the message to the fireside and at my leisure broke the seal and read it."

"And that message called you to the manor?"

Tancred began to pace restlessly, while Richard shifted in his chair and stretched his legs. Tancred could see the message only too clearly in his mind. The words still haunted him.

"It read, 'Your assistance is needed immediately. There is grave danger this night for us.' Of course, I readied my horse and went to them."

"You are certain the message came from our father?"

"Aye," Tancred said rather indignantly. "I recognized his seal, it belonged to no other."

Richard raised his hand as if to calm Tancred's growing agitation. "I simply wanted you to be sure in your mind. It might be something that would help us learn the truth."

"It bore his seal. The same that is upon the ring we three wore. There was no mistaking it."

"Very well," Richard replied, and his soft-spoken voice seemed to calm Tancred immediately. "Pray tell, what happened then?"

Tancred finally took a chair opposite his brother at the hearthside. He stared into the flames, remembering the fire of another night. "I rode to the manor and found the barn set ablaze. The villeins were already working to put out the flames. I searched for Father, but was unable to find him. One of the men told me he was in the manor house, but I could not believe that our father would allow others to do all of the work. He loved his land and his people and would have served at their side."

"This is true," Richard agree.

"I went to the water trough and he was not there. I searched the faces on the way to the manor and realized neither he nor our mother was among those who watched and waited." Tancred continued to stare into the fire. His mind had transported him back in time. Back to the night when his world was suddenly destroyed.

"The smoke was thick and putrid. It smelled of burnt animals and manure. It seemed a hopeless cause, but the villeins did manage to keep the fire from spreading, which was, itself, a miracle. I believed the matter to be what Father had referenced in his message. I continued my search for him and finally went into the manor house.

"It was dark inside. No fires burned in the hearth and no candles or lamps were lit to offer light. The eerie glow of the barn's fire was all that directed my steps. I called out to Father, but no one answered. I heard something at the far end of the hall. It was nothing more than a scurried scratching sound, like a rat upon the floor. It was too dark to know what the source of it was, so I went back outside and found a torch."

"You saw no one in the house?" Richard asked skeptically.

Tancred shook his head. His soul writhed in agony, pierced with the regret that if he had stayed to investigate the noise or perhaps come directly into the house upon his arrival, their parents might still be alive. "I heard voices upon my return. Muffled voices, barely audible, but nevertheless there. I called out again, but no one answered. With the torch in hand, I lit some candles and checked out the hall. There was no one. No house servants, no one at all. I knew something must be terribly wrong, and that sense of foreboding followed me through the house.

"I had come to the screens that divided the kitchen area from the hall when I saw something out of the corner of my eye. A booted foot. I came closer and saw the blood. Then the truth of the matter was clear. Our parents were there, together, dead."

His voice fell flat. "They had both been stabbed several times, and the knife was still plunged there in Father's back. I drew it out—"

"That's when I arrived," Richard stated. The memory of that night was only too clear in his mind. "I came upon you just as you had drawn it out."

"It truly must have presented a grisly picture. I cannot fault you for what your eyes must have demanded to be true."

"But I can fault myself for my lack of faith in you. I was greatly humbled by Helena's bold declaration of your innocence. She spoke with Arianne and me not long ago, and to hear her tell the tale, there was never a doubt in her mind that you might have performed the deed."

Tancred smiled, his look haunted with a bitter sweetness. "I was redeemable only in the eyes of a child."

Richard closed his eyes, and Tancred saw that he fought for control of his emotions. There were tears in the duke's eyes when he opened them to face his brother. "I wish to God most earnestly that I would never have arrived to stand as your accuser. How I have prayed a thousand times that I could take back that single night."

" 'Tis no sense in living with regret of that night," Tancred said, meeting his brother's pain-filled gaze. "The matter is no longer between us. We need to combine our forces and seek out the true murderer."

"Aye," Richard said with a nod. "I have tried these long months to find the men who bore you false witness."

"And?"

"They are of no help to us, Tancred. They are dead."

"Dead?"

"Aye. Shortly after the trial was completed and you were sent into exile, both men met with untimely deaths. Both died in their beds from what their families can remember. But after eleven years. . ."

"It will not be easy to learn anything after all this time, but there must be something that will open the door for us. Even a small thing that can prove the matter in one direction or another."

"We must pray it will be so," Richard said with confidence. "God in heaven would not allow this injustice to continue. I know not what reasons He has for this matter, but I trust He will guide us to a solution."

"May it be so, Brother," Tancred replied. "May the truth be known to us both."

Chapter 14

Tancred was greatly impressed by Richard's newest addition to the castle. His weapons storeroom was not large, but it was well stocked. Tancred admired the collection of swords, battle axes, and flails.

"With the town growing larger and stronger, there may not be so much to fear," Richard remarked, "but we'll be ready nevertheless."

"The tunnels you have below the castle are invaluable to you also," Tancred reminded his brother.

Richard smiled. When Tancred had taken over Gavenshire in hopes of clearing his name, Richard had used the tunnels to gain access to the castle. "Aye, the tunnels are most beneficial."

"You've done well here, Brother." Tancred could appreciate the hard work and fortune spent upon the fine arsenal.

"The men have trained throughout the winter, and I believe they'd almost relish the chance to make war upon someone."

Tancred laughed. " 'Tis the way of our kind, I suppose. We make war upon things and conquer."

"I pray we might not find the need to make war just yet," Richard said earnestly. "I've only begun my home and family. I'd not relish the thought of giving up my peaceful life so soon."

"God grant us a long peace and the strength to defeat our enemies when war does come." Tancred's words were still ringing in the room when Devon appeared in the doorway.

"Richard?"

"What is it, Devon?"

"We have a visitor to Gavenshire."

"Another one? Well, let it be so. Spend as much time here as you like, Tancred, and I'll go see to our newest guest."

Tancred nodded and picked up a well-made shield. It was expensively crafted with heraldic work gracing the face with Richard's coat of arms. He paused to trace the lines of the design, but his mind was upstairs on the fair Helena. What was he to do about her? He had nothing at this point to offer her, and so marriage was out of the question. He could not subject her to his shame, and until he cleared his name once and for all, Tancred knew he would not feel comfortable even in paying her court.

With a heavy sigh, he contemplated the matter. He would have to speak to Helena and let her know how he felt, and yet, there was so much he still couldn't understand. Eleven years had passed, and throughout that time, Helena's faith had never wavered. Even when the rest of the world had condemned him as a murderer, Helena had never believed him possible of the feat. How could he now tell her that he could have no part of her until the matter was resolved?

Forgetting the shield, Tancred saw, instead, Helena's sweet face. He wanted nothing more than to go to her and proclaim his love, for if one thing was truly clear in his mind, it was that he held a deep, abiding love for her. It was hard to imagine that he was capable of such a thing after so much had happened to embitter him and harden his heart. But God had released him from that pain, and the sorrow that he'd known deep down in his soul was now only a fleeting memory.

"Ah, Helena," Tancred whispered in the shadowy privacy of the room, "I do love you. First as a tiny girl, flitting about under my feet, and now as the woman you've become."

⚮

"I would like to speak a word with my sister," Roger Talbot said. He stood just inside the common room where Arianne and her maid servants spent time sewing and spinning wool.

Arianne and Helena glanced up together, but neither one said a single word to acknowledge Roger's presence. The women working alongside the duchess cowered back a bit, but Arianne refused to be intimidated.

"I have come some distance, and I refuse to be put off any longer. I looked for your husband, but was unable to locate him. In his absence, I implore you to consider my request," Roger stated, this time a bit less harsh.

Arianne glanced at Helena for only a moment before returning her gaze to Roger. "I do not believe it to be in Helena's best interest."

"Helena's best interest!" Roger bellowed. "What about my best interest? I have lands that need my attention and villeins who are most likely robbing me blind—"

"Then I suggest you return to your land and people," Arianne interjected. "No one is forcing you to stay here." She paused for a moment to make certain her words were heard. "Just as Helena will not be forced to leave."

"She is my sister, and I am her guardian."

Helena lifted her face to meet her brother's angry stare. "I will appeal to King Henry," she stated matter-of-factly. "I have that right. I am kin, and you are not."

Roger paled noticeably at this. "You have caused me nothing but grief."

Arianne's temper got the best of her. "She has caused you grief? How dare you? I have seen the marks upon her back. She certainly did not put them there of her own accord. I wonder, Sir Talbot, who might have lain a whip upon the back of the queen's own relation?"

"I am not proud of the past, neither am I content with the present." Roger paused, as though weighing the situation.

Helena forced herself to watch him. He wanted very much to frighten her because, in her fear, Roger found his power. She shuddered at this thought. Roger's power and Maude's vindictiveness were all too close in her memories. It was the reason she so adamantly pleaded with Arianne for protection. It was the reason she could not allow Roger to corner her alone.

"Your Grace, I beg your indulgence." Roger spoke to Arianne, never taking his eyes from Helena's face. "This is but a family matter. The child is grief-stricken and knows not what she wants or needs. As her guardian, I am obligated to make the best possible choices for her well-being."

"And those choices include a sound lashing when she refuses to do your bidding?"

Helena felt Arianne tense beside her. She'd never seen the duchess truly angry. Timothy started to fuss, so Helena reached down to the floor where he lay and lifted him to her lap.

"This is my bidding," Roger stated angrily, waving his arm to where Helena sat with the baby. "I only wanted her to have a family of her own. She needs a good husband, one who will care for her and give her children."

"And she was to find this in a convent?" Arianne asked sarcastically.

"Nay! The convent was my last alternative. I intended to see her cared for, that is all."

"Then why not allow her to live on with you?"

Helena spoke so softly that at first Arianne and Roger seemed not to have heard her. Handing Timothy to Arianne, Helena got to her feet. Her eyes were blazing.

"I am tired of this constant battle on my behalf, with no consideration to my desire. I sit in this very room, and while I want no part of conversing with you in seclusion where you would take advantage of my weaker nature, I certainly do not wish to be discussed as though I didn't exist.

"If I were to return to the manor with you, would you swear an oath that I would be allowed to choose my own mate? Would you put Maude away from me and refuse to listen to her contrivances against me? Would you forget the foolishness of sending me to a convent? And before you answer, dearest brother, might I remind you that perjury is a mortal sin."

Roger stared blankly at her for a moment. He'd known Helena to speak up from time to time, but never to defend herself with the strength he saw here. Perhaps it was only that the duchess's presence made her brave. Perhaps it was finding DuBonnet and proclaiming her love. Whatever it was, he found it most disturbing.

Helena moved across the room to stand only inches from Roger. She was tired of cowering before him and angry for the way he continued to treat her as though she were nothing more than a serving girl. "Can you swear an oath to any of my requests, Roger?"

Roger shook his head. "I need not swear to you anything. I have a responsibility to you, and whether or not you like it, I am your guardian. It is my right to see you properly wed—"

"I intend to be properly wed," Helena interrupted. "I intend to be a wife and to keep a home and, yes, even to bear many children. But I will do so with the man I love and not with some addle-brained milk sop that you pawn me off on."

She snatched off her wimple and tossed it to the floor, where she stepped on it roughly. "I'm nothing more than this cloth to you. Something to be trampled beneath your feet, for your good pleasure and will. I refuse to be that any longer, Roger Talbot. I will not be commanded by you or your sister."

Roger was so taken aback by her actions that he was near to cowering himself. He stared in surprise at Helena as though seeing her for the first time.

Helena turned from him to face Arianne. "I most humbly apologize for my overzealous manner. My stepbrother has greatly vexed me for some time. It amazes me that one as refined as Roger can act so completely void of intelligence. He has no loyalty and no honor."

Just then a commotion arose from the door where a young serf was urgently trying to precede an overdressed woman into the room.

"I'm sorry, Your Grace," he apologized. "The duke bid her wait in the hall, but she heard the voices and—"

"I refuse to be put off any longer," Maude announced, pushing past the boy. "Roger, tell him to leave me alone and be gone."

The boy looked to Arianne for his instruction. "The matter is no longer your concern," Arianne told him. "Bid my husband to join us."

"Aye, Your Grace," he said and gave a brief bow.

"Helena, precious little sister," Maude said, reaching out to offer a kiss of greeting.

Helena pulled back and her eyes narrowed. "Don't touch me."

Maude was notably shocked, and Roger laughed out loud. "It seems our little sister has found her voice useful for more than singing. She was just informing me of her demands."

"Demands? From her guardian?" Maude said in a snide tone that immediately set Arianne on her feet.

"This is my home, and I would know who you are. Surely you forget yourself." Holding Timothy close, she eyed Maude sternly and waited for the older woman to speak.

"I am Lady Maude Talbot. I was wife to Lord Ricbod before he died in poverty and disgrace. As sister to Roger and, of course, Helena," Maude said with contempt in her eyes, "I reclaimed my family's name."

"Very well, Lady Talbot, I am the duchess of Gavenshire," Arianne stated and did not offer to lessen the formality by giving her first name.

Maude's eyes widened for just a moment before she regained her composure and curtsied. "Your Grace." The words were muttered, but nevertheless, the title was offered.

"I am quite unused to people refusing to keep my husband's orders. This was a private conversation, and I would keep it that way."

Maude realized her opponent and changed tactics. "I beg your pardon, Your Grace."

Helena recognized Maude's plan immediately. "She begs no one for anything. She is not to be trusted, Arianne."

Maude stepped forward with her hand raised as if to slap Helena, but a firm hold on her wrist stopped any forward motion. "What in the—" She stopped in midsentence as she realized who held her. "Tancred DuBonnet. But you can't be here," Maude said, completely aghast. "The king—the king, he found you guilty of murder and exiled you."

"Aye, and that same king set me free with pardon." He released Maude's hand and went to stand beside Helena. "I suppose you have come out of deep concern for your stepsister."

Helena felt her spirits soar at the evident support that Tancred was offering her. She stepped a bit closer to her beloved Tanny and felt his arm slip around her in a protective manner.

Maude nearly blanched. "How dare you touch her?"

"He dares because I will it so," Helena declared.

Richard entered the room, with Devon not far behind. "I thought I gave you instructions to await my return." He gazed hard at Maude. It was the first time Helena had ever seen her shrink back from any man.

"I heard the voices and knew it to be my family. You must forgive me, Your Graces, but my worry for my sister was greater than my fear of reprisal. I do beg your pardons." Maude's voice was as smooth as polished silver.

Helena snorted. "Hah! She has been my misery these twenty long years. The only thing you fear, Maude, is missing out on a good fight."

Maude looked at Roger for support. "Are you going to let her talk to me that way?"

"What would you suggest I do? Challenge the men of Gavenshire to a fight? Swords at dawn? Be reasonable, Woman, Helena has the upper hand here, and so long as the good duke intercedes on her behalf, we have naught a say about it."

Roger came up alongside Maude and stared past the woman to Tancred. "As for this man, our sister fancies him to be her true love." No one missed the sarcasm in Roger's voice. "She has worshipped him since she was a swaddling, or so it would be told."

"You cannot mean it," Maude said, turning to see if her brother was serious.

"Oh, but I do. Fair Helena intends to marry the fool."

Helena blushed crimson and would have turned away from Tancred to bury her hands in her face, but he held her tight and answered the assault. " 'Tis my understanding that she has the king's blessing to choose her mate. A man would be a fool, indeed, were he to reject the devotions of one so innocent and pure." He reached across to caress Helena's cheek.

"You are not married yet," Roger said, his voice low and menacing. "Unhand her and treat her with more respect."

"Respect such as you would offer?"

"Stop it!" Helena exclaimed.

"Yes," Richard said, interceding. "I would see this matter concluded. Lady Talbot, you are welcome to stay. I have ordered a room to be prepared for you. If you desire, I will have one of my people show you there."

Maude looked at Roger for a moment and then at Helena. "I would be happy to take my comfort here."

"Very well." Richard motioned to one of the women. "Take Lady Talbot to her room. As for you," Richard turned to address Roger, "I will keep peace in my home. Should that not be possible with you or your sister within the walls of this castle, then you will be asked to leave."

Sometime later, Maude stood looking out her chamber window. She was seething with rage and jealousy. She hadn't missed the loving way Tancred had rushed to Helena's defense, nor had she missed the devotion and admiration in Helena's eyes. It was surprise enough to find Helena had survived her ordeal and taken refuge with the duke of Gavenshire, but this was too much.

Tancred DuBonnet was in England. Not only in England, but here. How wonderful he looked, Maude mused. He was only better after all these years, and now, with the king's pardon, he would no doubt be reinstated with the title and lands.

"And that little baggage thinks she can snatch him away from me," Maude said venomously. "Methinks there will be no wedded bliss for you, dear stepsister. Tancred DuBonnet rejected me once. He dare not do it a second time."

Chapter 15

Tancred felt sweat run down the middle of his back as he hoisted the sword overhead. The leather tunic was newly made and not very supple, and because of this, his movements were far less fluid than he would have liked.

"You fight like a woman," Roger said smugly. He had been observing the knights in training and found it to be a most disturbing display. His own men were far from being trained as well, and even Tancred, with his years in exile, fought better than many of Roger's most trusted people.

"Then hoist up your skirts and enter the fray," Tancred replied, meeting the sword of his opponent with a dull thudding ring.

"How dare you!" Roger's face reddened as several idle men guffawed and snickered. He glared at them sharply, but to no avail. These men knew he was of little threat to their well-being.

Tancred waved his hand to call off the mock battle and approached Roger. "You have no war with me, Talbot. Be gone from this place so we can work in peace."

Roger drew his own sword with one fluid motion and pointed it at Tancred's chest. "I most certainly have a war with you. You have dallied with my sister's affections."

"Helena told you the truth about Maude."

"I speak not of Maude, but of Helena, herself. You speak of her devotion and love amidst the castle's audience, yet you have no possible hope of ever returning her love."

"Why say ye this?"

"Because you are nothing, Tancred DuBonnet. You have but a name and not even that, for it bears the tainted blood of your parents. Therefore you are without even that honor. What will you offer my sister? Oh, true enough she has a fine dowry, but it does not include land, and what is a man without land and honor?"

Tancred grimaced at the words. Were they not the same ones he'd focused on throughout the night? "I need you not to explain my plight, Sir Talbot. But Helena's heart is tender, and I will not see her broken by your anger."

"Tell me naught of your concern, DuBonnet. Pick up your sword and let us clear this matter once and for all."

Tancred stared blankly at his old friend. "You wish to fight me?"

"Aye, that I do and to the death!" The words were hissed out between clenched teeth. One of the young squires went running to the great hall, but otherwise no one moved.

"I do not wish to fight you, for in spite of the wrong you have done me, you are like a brother to me. Had I said that only months ago, it would have meant little. I would have fought Richard to the death over the anguish and bitterness my soul carried into exile. Now, however, my soul is at peace with God, and therefore, I am at peace with man."

"That may well be," Roger said, raising the sword to strike, "but I am not at peace with you." He brought down the sword hard, causing Tancred to reflexively ward off the blow with his own sword. It was a simple enough way for a fight to begin.

The clanging of metal against metal rang throughout the bailey. Men moved out of the way and surrounded the two fighting knights, but instead of the usual cheering and betting that went on in most disputes, the audience was as silent as a spider spinning a web.

"I see you won't die easy!" Roger called out after deflecting Tancred's thrust.

"I seek peace with you, not blood!"

Roger swung around and pulled the sword across in a great arcing sweep. Tancred fell back a step, regained his balance, and deftly managed to ward off the attack.

"I seek revenge!" Roger bellowed against the blows.

"You seek it for a thing that never happened! You know the truth!"

Inside the castle, Helena was just descending the stone stairs when the squire appeared, proclaiming the battle on the castle grounds.

" 'Tis a fight between His Grace's brother and Sir Talbot!" the boy exclaimed.

Helena's hand went to her throat, and several men who sat below in the great hall scurried for the door. She, too, had intended to follow, but her foot no sooner reached the floor when Maude appeared from nowhere.

"And where do you think that you are going?" She took hold of Helena painfully hard. "We need to talk, little sister."

Helena's surprise was so great that she could do nothing but allow Maude to pull her into the privacy of the duke's receiving room.

"What is the meaning of this?" Helena finally found her voice. Jerking away from the talonlike hands of her stepsister, Helena refused to let Maude have the advantage. "Be gone from me. I have matters that do not concern you."

"Pray tell? If you mean the matter of Tancred and Roger doing battle, then it is you who have no place in the matter. They are fighting over me."

Helena laughed. "So say you. I believe it to be otherwise, and I will go to Tanny and offer my encouragement."

Maude screeched at her with hands raised and nails bared. "You insufferable ingrate. Roger has given you everything, and you scorn him." She stopped just short of tearing at Helena's face.

Helena backed away. "I have known nothing but misery at your hands and Roger's. I wish only to be left alone."

"That is no longer possible for you. You have cost me too much and now you must pay the price."

"I have cost you?" Helena's stunned tone did not bode well with her stepsister.

"Aye, and do not deny it. You have grieved me in every way, but especially where that man is concerned."

"Tancred?"

"Aye, your beloved Tanny." Maude's face contorted in disgust. "You, a mere child. How old could you have been? Eight? Nine? Surely, not old enough to know the truth of love, yet here you stand proclaiming for the world your undying devotion to a man you scarcely know. He is a deceiver, and I would be less than a loving sister to not guide you away from his cruelty."

"He is not a deceiver!"

Maude laughed loud and harshly. "So you say. I have the painful memories to haunt me. I have the broken promises—"

"You have nothing!" Helena countered in anger. "I was there. I saw you throw yourself at him, begging for him to save you from the misery of your love-less home. I wanted to retch at the way you played him for a fool, pleading your purity and innocence, pledging your virginal love. Hah! I saw what you did, night after night. Playing many a man false, offering of yourself whatever it took to get some trinket or bauble that you took a fancy to."

"How dare you!"

"I dare because it is the truth!"

Maude's face turned reddish-purple, and her eyes were narrow slits that stared evilly back at Helena. Her voice dropped to a deadly softness. "You have always come between me and my suitors. You think I could forget that? I will see you dead before you marry Tancred DuBonnet. Do you understand me?"

"You speak idle," Helena said, turning to leave.

"Do I?" Maude called, making no move to stop her. "I still have the bottle of poison I used to rid myself of your mother." Helena froze in place. She turned to see the wickedly satisfied smile on Maude's face. "That's right, I killed her. What of it?"

"I will tell my brother. I will tell the duke of Gavenshire and King Henry as well!" Helena declared. There were tears in her eyes as she thought of her mother dying painfully at Maude's hand. "Murderer!"

"Call me what you like, but you will say naught to Roger or anyone else."

"And how do you intend to stop me?" Helena questioned. She was trembling in fear, but prayed silently that Maude would not see how she'd upset her.

"If you do anything to imply my responsibility in Eleanor's death, I will see to it that Tancred dies most painfully."

"He may already lie dead by Roger's hand, for all I know. You're evil, Maude, and I will have no more part in this." Helena opened the door and quickly made her way across the hall.

Maude was immediately at her heels, whispering in a hissing tone that could not be understood. "Should you seek our brother's ear on this matter, it will cost Tancred's life."

Helena paused to look at Maude. There was no doubt of her seriousness. *What should I do?* Helena wondered. *What can I do?*

"Aye, I will do the deed," Maude replied. "But if you keep your mouth closed, return home with Roger, and leave me to rekindle the flames of passion that once existed between Tancred and myself, then I will let him live. Otherwise. . ."

Helena looked away from Maude and contemplated the words. "He may well lie dead at this moment."

"Roger will not kill him. There is nothing more than a misunderstanding between them. I've been most fortunate that it's lasted eleven years. I cannot hope for it to bear through even another day. Nay, your problems do not lie with Roger."

Helena heard her name being called, and soon a young woman came through the castle's outer door. "Come, Lady Helena, Her Grace has sent me to fetch you."

Helena turned to leave, but Maude was at her heel again. "Remember what I said."

Helena said nothing. Instead, she hoisted her skirts and ran most unladylike down the stairs to the bailey. She followed the messenger at a run, and when she came upon the scene of Tancred and Roger's fight, she wanted to die a thousand deaths. Roger had Tancred on the ground, his sword poised at the hollow of Tancred's neck, ready for the kill.

Just as Helena opened her mouth to scream, Roger burst out laughing and Tancred joined in. Helena was stunned. She wanted to sink to her knees from shock, but Arianne quickly came to her side and extended her arm.

"Remember that time when we were boys," Roger said, laughing so hard he could barely stand up. "You and I were staging a battle for my father. He was so impressed with our abilities and entered the fray himself. It wasn't long before he had both of us pinned to the ground in just this manner."

"I remember it well," Tancred replied, his laughter joining Roger's. "He said, 'Will you yield?' and instead of answering, you made a face at him."

"Aye, and it so surprised him to see his honorable son, in training to become a knight, with tongue waggling from side to side and eyes rolling in circles that he was taken unaware when you pushed him backward. He landed with a mighty thud, as I recall." Tancred remembered the moment with great pleasure.

Roger sobered for a moment, then slipped his sword into the scabbard and extended his arm to Tancred. "I have wronged you greatly. Never have I once truly believed you capable of killing your parents, yet I allowed you to bear the shame alone. I did nothing to defend you."

Tancred took the offered hand and got to his feet. " 'Tis a matter for the past."

"Only if you place it there," Roger said quite seriously, "for I still carry the wrongfulness of it here." He placed his hand over his heart.

"You have my forgiveness, Friend," Tancred replied. His dark eyes softened. "Have I yours?"

"Aye, that and much more!" Roger exclaimed and embraced Tancred heartily.

Helena watched the reunion as if in a dream. Only moments before she had learned that Maude was responsible for the death of her cherished mother. Now Roger and Tancred were embracing with all possible joy, and it was quickly becoming too much for Helena.

" 'Tis wondrous the way that God works in our lives," Arianne whispered in Helena's ear.

Helena turned and found Maude approaching her. A low moan escaped her lips, and Arianne turned to see what the problem might be. "Come with me to the solar," Arianne suggested. " 'Tis time for Timothy's feeding."

Helena could only nod and allow Arianne to lead her toward the castle. She knew that with Arianne present, Maude would say nothing, and because of this, Helena felt a false sense of security. It was a security that was quickly snatched from her, however, when Helena met Maude's hateful stare. Her eyes burned into Helena and it was more than she could bear. Without warning to Arianne, Helena fainted dead away.

"Helena?" She heard her name being called. The voice was soft and muffled. The blackness that held her spellbound was lifting, and Helena could barely make out Tancred's face overhead.

"Helena, wake up," he commanded, and she fought hard to be obedient.

"Oh, Tanny," she whispered, reaching out to touch his face. "What happened?"

"I was to ask you the same thing. Do you not remember?"

She gave him a gentle, sleepy smile, but then the memory of Maude's threatening words came back to haunt her, and Helena abruptly pulled back her hand and tried to turn away.

"What is this?" Tancred questioned, taking hold of her shoulders.

Arianne was at her side in a moment. "What is it, Helena? What is wrong?"

Helena moaned and shook her head from side to side. She couldn't speak to either one of them. She mustn't give Maude any reason to harm yet another person. Hot tears formed in her eyes and threatened to spill.

"Please go," she finally said.

"Go?" Tancred questioned, turning her to face him. His eyes were so full of tender concern that Helena wanted nothing more than to throw herself into his arms. Instead, she forced herself to push against him.

"Yes! Go! I don't want you here!" The tears poured down her cheeks as she turned away. She wasn't quick enough to avoid seeing the hurt in his eyes. Burying her face in her hands, Helena sobbed.

Tancred looked up at Arianne, who stared thoughtfully at the young woman. With a shrug, she motioned Tancred to the door. "I have a feeling there is much we do not know. Do not be too quick to judge her in this matter. Something is amiss, and I will seek to find out what it might be. Until then, please do not lose hope."

Tancred glanced from his sister-in-law to the sobbing woman across the room. "But I know not what I've done."

" 'Tis my strong suspicion," Arianne said, with a note of anger in her voice, "that you've done nothing to bring this about." She touched his arm reassuringly. "Give us time, Tancred. Secrets have a way of coming out."

Chapter 16

In the shadowy glow of firelight, Roger, Richard, and Tancred sat discussing the death of the DuBonnets. Tancred's mind was still confused by Helena's outburst. What did she mean by pushing him away? And, too, why did she look so frightened?

"Our parents had no enemies." Richard was staring, and Tancred forced himself to pay attention. "Our mother was the local healer, with a loving hand and calm word for anyone who sought it. Our father was a fair man who allowed his villeins to earn their freedom and generously bestowed gifts upon them throughout the year. I know of no one who sought to do them harm."

Roger agreed. "I knew your parents well. They were highly regarded, even in the lake lands up north."

"So then, if not an enemy of our parents," Richard paused, looking at his brother, "then maybe one of yours?"

Tancred laughed, but there was no humor in the sound. "You could have picked from a dozen or more who would have seen me dead. But, I would not have expected a single one of them to seek their revenge in that manner. Nay, the men who would have seen me dead would have aced me themselves. My enemies were a noisy lot who had little difficulty in making themselves well known."

"But perhaps there was one," Richard suggested. "All it would take would be one."

Tancred gave it concentrated thought while staring hard into the dying fire. "There were many who envied my position and lands. It mattered little that I had earned the right to those things—jealousy would not allow some to let the matter rest."

"Perhaps one of them felt Henry had unjustly rewarded you. Mayhaps they were angry enough to seek revenge, but knowing they could not get to you in person, they sought to settle the score in another fashion."

"It is possible," Tancred admitted.

"Think, Brother. Is there not some face that comes to mind? Some name that can traverse the years to utter itself to you?"

Tancred shook his head. He stared at Roger for a moment. "Is there anyone you can think of?"

"Nay," Roger said without second thought. "I know of no one."

Moments later, Roger dismissed himself to go to bed. He was fretful and restless from the hours of conversation. He knew, too, that if he had to spend another moment contemplating the death of Tancred and Richard's parents, he very well might say things he would later regret. He stepped into the darkened great hall and let out his breath.

He only knew one person who hated Tancred enough to see him suffer to the extent he had. Maude.

"But how?" he whispered.

Maude would never have been capable of such a feat on her own, and besides, she would have been only six and ten—a tender age with romantic notions and marriage on her mind. He laughed aloud at his own foolishness. Nay, there was no point in looking to Maude for the deed. True, she had hated Tancred for spurning her love, but she quickly got over it as Roger recalled to mind.

He made his way up the torch-lit stairs, still chuckling to himself. He no sooner reached the top when Helena appeared in her night robe.

"Why be ye here, Girl?" Roger asked. "Is it well with you?"

"I. . .came. . .to. . .to seek you out," Helena said, her teeth chattering more from nerves than from the cold stones beneath her feet.

"You did not wish to talk to me privately, remember?" His voice was soft and gentle.

"I remember, but now I find I must. Please hear me out." She was shaking, and Roger motioned to her open door.

"Go back to bed. We can talk on the morrow."

"Nay!" she exclaimed a bit louder than she'd intended. "It must be done now."

"Then speak before you catch your death. If this is about Tancred, you waste words with me. I have ended my war with him, and we are at peace with each other."

Helena nodded. "I know and I am glad. Tancred was always faithful to your friendship, and he was wronged deeply by you."

"I know." Roger's eyes softened, and he suddenly saw Helena as the devoted woman she really was. "You never lost faith in him, did you?"

"I knew him incapable of hurting anyone purposefully." Helena wanted very much to end this part of the conversation. It only made what she had to say that much more difficult. "But that is in the past."

"Then what do you want of me?"

"I want to go home." The words were stated simply and echoed in the near-empty hall.

"You what?" Roger stared at her in utter amazement. "I could not have heard you correctly."

"You did," Helena replied, refusing to lower her face. "I have to go home. The sooner, the better. Please, Roger. 'Tis the reason you came here for me."

"Aye, 'tis true enough, but what of Tancred? What of your love for him?"

"It hasn't changed, but there are many problems that need to be overcome. I was only a child when Tancred left England."

"But you are no child now, neither does he see you as a child. I know the heart of men, and I know that man better than most. He cares deeply for you, Helena. If this is a matter of him not having a title or lands of his own—"

"His title, or lack of one, does not matter," Helena interrupted indignantly. "I care little for such things. I would live in a hovel with him were I only able to be his wife."

"Then why leave? The duke has bid you stay as long as you desire. Tancred and His Grace hope to resolve the death of their parents, but that may take some time. I no longer object to you marrying Tancred."

Helena put her hands to her head as if to stop the pounding against her temples. "Cease!" she demanded. "I cannot bear this much longer. I want to go home. It matters not why. Will you take me on the morrow?" She dropped her hands and reached out to Roger with pleading in her eyes. "Please."

Roger nodded. "If that is your desire."

" 'Tis not a matter of desire," Helena whispered, desperately close to tears. " 'Tis what must be done."

Roger stepped forward to put an arm around Helena, but before he could do so, Maude's voice sounded from behind them.

"Yea, 'tis what must be done."

Helena drew closer to Roger. She glanced up to find him frowning, then dropped her gaze to the floor. There was no way she could explain it to him. Maude knew full well the reasoning behind her sudden declaration to return home, but Helena knew she'd say nothing.

"What causes you to skulk about the halls like a rat in feeding? Are you feasting upon our private words, Maude?" Roger demanded.

"Some privacy," Maude retorted and drew closer. "I heard you to my room."

"Still, it was not your concern." Roger's mind went back to his earlier suspicions about his sister. Somehow, seeing her made his thoughts take a bit more validity. Roger's arm went protectively around Helena's shoulders. For once, he was not going to allow Maude to bully the younger woman.

"I heard her say she wants to go home. I believe this most beneficial to all concerned. With the facts before us and Tancred cleared of wrongdoings, I desire to resume our friendship. I can scarce do that with the child in my way, now can I?"

Roger laughed. "Tancred would not notice you if Helena were removed to the Holy Lands."

"How caustic your words are, dear brother," Maude said, straining to control her temper. She glared down at Helena and hated her even more. "Yours is but a childish fascination. What existed between Tancred and myself is something far more real."

Helena said nothing. She could not very well defend herself and plead with Roger to keep his word and return her to his estate. Maude's murderous threats continued to haunt her. Maude would no doubt poison Tancred's drink or food if Helena refused to leave Gavenshire.

"Mayhaps she is right, Roger. Either way, I will be ready in the morning." Helena eased herself away from Roger and stepped toward her bedchamber door. Her heart was sickened at the thought of giving her beloved Tanny over to Maude. "Please, put the matter to rest," she whispered before hurrying into her room and securing the door. Once there, Helena gave into heart-wrenching sobs that did not cease until well into the night.

Morning came too soon for Helena. She had tossed about the large bed throughout the night and had found no peace. How could she leave him when she'd only just found him? How could she allow him to believe that she no longer cared, when her heart was near to bursting for all the love she felt for him?

Getting up and washing her face, Helena no longer cared what happened. She knew that Roger was a changed man, and for that she was grateful. She had seen the softening in his eyes and known in his voice a gentleness that had been missing for eleven years. He would not hit her again. In fact, he would probably hurry to see Maude married off, even to Tancred, and allow Helena to stay at home and care for him until he found a wife. After that, Helena sighed, after that she would go to the convent. What purpose would there be to fight that move if Tanny were already married and beyond her grasp?

Without waiting for assistance, Helena found the burgundy surcoat she'd worn on her arrival to Gavenshire. It was patched and stained, a poor companion to the grand and beautiful things Arianne had made for her, but it belonged to Helena and she would leave with nothing more. Pulling it on in the dim light of dawn, Helena could scarcely keep from crying anew.

When she stepped into the hall, Helena half expected Maude to be waiting. When she found that Maude was nowhere in sight, relief washed over her. It would be hard enough to leave without having to face Maude again. Helena's most fervent prayer was that she could somehow escape speaking with Tancred, as well.

"What would I say?" she muttered to herself. How could she declare her love one day and callously take it back the next? He would see her as deceitful and wicked, and there would be nothing Helena could say to keep him from such opinions. His anger, even hatred, might make her departure easier, Helena thought. But then, she truly doubted that anything would help.

She came upon Roger, who was talking with a stunned-faced Arianne. Richard was at her side and looked up first to spy Helena.

Arianne turned and, recognizing Helena, rushed to her side. "Is it true that you asked your brother to take you home?"

"Aye," Helena whispered. " 'Tis what I desire, Your Grace. He did not force me into this."

"But you told me only yesterday—"

Helena held up her hand. "I know, but 'tis different now."

The chapel bell began to peal, calling the castle to services, and Helena relished the excuse to hasten away before anyone could question her further.

Tancred came upon his brother and a teary-eyed Arianne. He was so taken aback by Arianne's tears, that he instantly scowled. "Is something amiss?" he asked Richard.

"Aye, 'tis a matter most disturbing," Richard replied in a hushed tone as they walked on toward the chapel.

"Why does she weep?" he asked, leaning in close to his brother's bearded face.

"Helena told us she's leaving with Roger. They plan to depart after we break the fast."

"What?" Tancred's voice rose and Arianne's head shot up.

" 'Tis true enough. She claims Talbot has not forced the matter, but that it is her desire to go." Arianne's words were hardly more than whispers.

"I don't believe it," Tancred stated. "I cannot believe she'd leave without word to me."

Richard shrugged. "Perhaps you are the only one who can learn the truth."

"I will learn the truth," Tancred replied between clenched teeth. "I swear it."

Tancred saw Helena flee the chapel as soon as the service was over. He stalked after her with determined steps and never noticed the look of dissatisfaction on Maude's face at his actions. Helena could not leave him now. He loved her, and though he could not declare it and ask for her hand in marriage, he was determined that she know the extent of his feelings. He would insist she wait for him. Wait at least until the matter of his parents' death was cleared. Then, if need be, he'd beg Richard for a home at Gavenshire and take Helena as his wife.

Reaching back to childhood instincts, Helena fled to the mews where the hooded falcons were kept. She had loved to venture to just such a place as a child and now it offered her a comfort of sorts. She leaned hard against the far-end wall and buried her face in her hands. Would the tears never dry up? She had cried bucketfuls in the night, and her face was red and her eyes swollen from the tirade. But still, she cried.

"Oh, Tanny," she moaned his name softly through her sobs. "Tanny."

"I am here," he said softly. Startled, she looked up and saw that he had followed her into the mews.

"No," she said and cried all that much harder. She couldn't look at him or the truth might come from her lips. She couldn't let him know her fear or the circumstances that drove her away.

Tancred pulled her shaking form against his body and held her firmly.

Helena pushed away from him, but he'd have no part of it and drew her that much tighter against him.

"Why are you leaving me?" He whispered the question against her ear

Words refused to form. Helena fell limp against him and cried. She drenched his chest with tears until the surcoat was wet and uncomfortable against her cheek. Tancred waited patiently, stroking her face gently.

"Why are you leaving me?"

Chapter 17

Roger was desperate to find Helena. He'd seen her fearful glances at Maude and could well imagine that the older woman had threatened and browbeaten the younger into submission. Why had he tolerated it all those years? Helena had never been anything but joy to him. Sadly enough, a joy he had denied himself when his heart had hardened against Tancred.

Following the path he'd seen her take, Roger came into the mews and found Tancred holding the weeping Helena.

"Is she ill?" he questioned.

"I am uncertain as to what ails her. I found her here weeping, calling my name, and yet she refuses to speak to me."

"Helena, stop up the flow and speak to me," Roger demanded.

Helena lifted her face and turned her red, swollen eyes to meet Roger's gaze. She drew a ragged breath but still could not speak. Shaking her head dispiritedly, she buried her face in her hands.

"What is this about?" Roger asked more gently. "Please tell me. I promise I am not the man I was before. I will listen and understand."

"I cannot speak of it," Helena managed to croak out between sobs.

"Pray tell, why not?" It was Tancred's turn to ask questions. "I have patiently waited for you to put your tears aside and talk to me, and now you say you cannot speak of it? Am I not worthy of an explanation?" Helena looked back to Tancred and knew she was lost.

"Oh, my love," she whispered, "you deserve more than simple words."

"I will happily settle for them alone," Tancred replied with the barest hint of a smile. "Later, however, I might well extract a heavier payment."

Helena shook her head. "I have endangered you. Perhaps you as well, Roger. Please ask nothing more of me. I cannot speak of it!" She pushed away from Tancred and turned to leave, but neither man would hear of it, and each took hold of a slender arm.

"You are no longer a child, Helena." Roger's voice was stern, yet loving. "I insist you bear the truth to me. I will protect you from whatever you fear." Helena looked up and met his gaze.

"As will I," Tancred promised.

She turned from Roger's face to Tancred's. Both men were so hopeful in their desire to help her, but memories of Maude loomed in her mind and spoiled the scene.

"Nay!" Helena shook her head violently. "You cannot take my punishment this time." She ripped away from their hold and put several paces between them before turning. " 'Tis true enough I am no longer a child. In matters such as these, the stakes are much higher and I do not merit a child's punishment. Nay!" She choked back a harsh, near hysterical laugh and held up a hand to Tancred's advancing form. " 'Twill be no simple denial of supper or extra hour of house-cleaning. 'Tis now a matter of life and death and I will not be the one to cause bloodshed."

"What are you saying, Helena?" Tancred's voice was soft, yet demanding. "Whose blood is to shed?" He took another step.

"Never mind." She struggled to calm her nerves.

Tancred again moved forward. "Helena, whose blood?"

"I've said too much."

"Nay, you have said too little. Whose blood is to be shed?" He was only inches away from her now.

"Yours!" Helena exclaimed, then put her hand to her mouth. Her eyes grew wide with shock at the word she'd spoken. There was no taking it back, and she knew Roger and Tancred well enough to know that this simple announcement would not go unquestioned.

Roger saved her the moment of dilemma. "Maude." He stated the simple word, knowing full well that his guess was accurate.

Helena dropped her hands and stared in wonder at her stepbrother. "I. . . But how. . . ?" She couldn't answer.

"I thought as much." Roger's eyes narrowed in anger. "You will sit down and tell us all."

"But I cannot," Helena said, shifting her gaze from Roger to the face of her beloved Tanny.

"You will do as you are told," Tancred said, taking the falconer's stool and pulling Helena to his lap. "I believe we used to resolve problems just like this when you were but a child. Shall we play one of our guessing games and learn of your dark secrets?"

Helena was appalled at the amusement in Tancred's voice.

" 'Tis no matter of games. She means to wed you or—"

"Or kill me?" Tancred threw back his head and roared. "She was always one to weave tangled webs. Think not much of it, nor trouble your heart on that one."

"She killed my mother!" Helena exclaimed and tears came again to her eyes.

"What say you?" Roger stepped closer. "Can this be true?"

Helena's trembling shoulders slumped against the security of Tancred's arms. She gave only a brief nod before giving way to her sorrow.

"But how?"

"Poison," Helena finally admitted. "Oh, can you not see? My mother was a thorn in Maude's side. Mother did nothing but offer her love, and Maude cast it aside as though it were tainted. She blamed my mother and me for all of her hurts and miseries." Helena's trembling voice had steadied as she reached her real concern. "She tired of my mother's interference and poisoned her. She'll do the same to all of us, but especially to my," she paused, "to you, Tanny."

He smiled and slipped his warm fingers under her chin. "Maude is no threat to me, except that she divide us apart. I cannot cast off the devotion of one so dear and true in fear that one so evil and false would see me dead."

"Do not trifle with Maude. She is evil, Tanny," Helena said, hoping that the seriousness of the matter would settle upon him.

"Aye, I can vouch for that," Roger agreed.

"You are in as much danger as Tancred," Helena said. "Is it not true that should you die, Maude will take control of the estate? After all, there are no male heirs and not one relative beyond you two who lay claim to your father's blood."

"You are right, and the point is well taken. I had not considered Maude's limitless treachery. The matter is such that we must work together and lay a trap for this beast."

"But how? If I do not leave within the hour, Maude will know that something is amiss."

"I will state that our journey is to be delayed by a day. That should give Tancred and me plenty of time to set our plans into action."

Helena dried her eyes with the back of her well-worn tunic sleeve. "I cannot let you risk your lives. I haven't the heart for such matters, nor the faith."

"What say ye—this great woman of faith, who knew no fear of the years or miles that separated her from the love of her heart? Faith is all that we do have." Tancred stroked her cheek fondly. "Without faith, we are lost."

"Yet let us be up and about putting faith into action," Roger interrupted. "Were you not telling me of your great philosopher and his mind toward reason?" Roger smiled conspiratorially at Tancred.

"Aye, 'tis true enough. Faith and reason. The two walk as friends, hand in hand. Ye cannot be a man of faith without putting that faith to the test. And testing your faith oft pushes a man to great depths of reasoning. Still, 'tis God's reasons and faith in Him that lead us forward."

"I do not understand," Helena said, looking defensively from Tancred to Roger.

"Be of courage, Helena. That is enough of a task for you," Roger reassured. "Tancred and I can manage Maude."

Roger and Helena entered the great hall together. Helena was notably subdued and kept her head down to avoid meeting Maude's stare. Maude was already seated, impatiently awaiting the formal announcement that she'd anticipated since the night before, while Arianne and Richard shared intimate conversation with Tancred.

The priest offered a blessing on the food and the fast was broken with warm bread and porridge. Helena had no stomach for the food. In her mind she kept imagining the death of her mother. Food had been the bearer of Maude's misdeeds, and as she thought of it, Helena choked on her porridge.

Coughing quietly into her linen napkin, Helena felt Arianne's reassuring hand on her arm. She glanced up to meet warm brown eyes that sympathetically assured her that all was well. The slightest smile touched Arianne's lips and then faded as the duchess turned to receive a question from one of the serving boys.

Devon had been called away, so Roger took the seat beside Helena. *How very different a matter of days has made,* she thought. *It was once a terrifying thought to have Roger so near, and yet now Roger offers immense comfort.*

"I am afraid I must plead the duke's indulgence," Roger announced amidst the table conversation.

"By my leave," Richard replied, playing out his part.

Helena realized instantly that Richard and Arianne were well aware of their roles. It was the reason for Arianne's smile and for Richard's calm, deliberate manner. Helena wished she had some of the duke's calm assurance. The butterflies in her stomach refused to settle, even as Roger continued with his announcement.

"With your permission, Sire," he began, "my sister, Lady Helena, and I will be departing for our lands."

"I beg you, no!" Richard said in a voice that hinted surprise. "My wife has come to greatly depend on your sister. Might you reconsider?"

"I wish it could be so, Your Grace, but there is much amiss in my land. Only this morn, I had word of a border dispute. I must return."

"Aye, 'twould be for the sake of your people and land. I see the need, still, could Lady Helena not stay on? We have extended a home to her as long as she desires one."

"Aye," Arianne joined in, turning to Helena. "You are most welcome here. Timothy will scarce know how to fall asleep without your angelic song."

Helena smiled sadly. She was still uncertain of her own part, and for all the lives that hinged on her reactions, she was uncomfortable with the plan. "I must go," was all she managed to say.

Arianne knew the younger woman's distress and hurried to move the conversation on. "I will have Matilda see to your packing."

"Nay," Roger said with raised hand. "My sister has requested that those generous garments be left in your care."

Arianne said nothing more, and Richard picked up the conversation. "You will certainly require provisions, and with two women, you will require an escort."

"I beg Your Graces' indulgence," Maude interjected. "I should plead upon your mercy and ask that I might be allowed to remain behind. I fear I am not up to the long journey and request a few more days of respite."

"Of course," Richard replied after a quick, reassuring glance at his wife. "You are most welcome to stay with us."

"Thank you, Your Grace." Maude bowed her head in feigned humility.

"That still leaves you with Lady Helena's safety in mind," Richard continued.

" 'Tis no problem, Brother," Tancred nearly roared. It was the cue he had waited for. "I would like very much to accompany Sir Roger and Lady Helena. Upon a time, their home was my own. It would give me great pleasure to once again view it. That is, should Sir Roger and his sister be in agreement with this idea."

" 'Twould be my delight," Roger exclaimed as though hearing the idea for the firs time. "I pledge you shelter and comfort for as long as you desire."

Maude's head snapped up at this new development. Helena noted her disgust but continued quietly picking at a piece of bread, while Roger and Tancred played out the scene.

"By my brother's leave, I could take several of his men and accompany you," Tancred announced.

"It would be greatly appreciated," Roger replied, and both he and Tancred turned to Richard for confirmation.

"A splendid idea!" Richard's words were given in such positive affirmation that Helena nearly laughed aloud. She barely controlled the smile that played at her lips, but when her gaze fell upon Maude's pinched expression, Helena instantly sobered.

" 'Tis settled then," Tancred said after taking a long drink from his mug. "I will prepare as soon as we adjourn."

"Nay," Richard said thoughtfully. "I would ask that you spend yet another night in my care. I have need for my men until the morrow. Would another day matter, Sir Roger?"

Roger looked down at Helena. "Would the morrow be soon enough, my sister?"

Helena nodded nervously. She was twisting the dark burgundy velvet of her surcoat. "Whatever His Grace wills."

Roger added his confirmation. "We are your humble servants."

Everyone at the duke's table could clearly see Maude's irritation. She tore at her bread and crashed her cup around as though she were trying to stave off vermin.

Conversation carried them through the rest of the meal, and though nothing more was said of the Talbot departure, Helena was certain that Maude contemplated her revenge. Helena knew that her stepsister would find a way to blame her for these developments. Of course, in this case, she would have reason to do so, but Helena would give her no satisfaction in knowing that.

When breakfast was completed, Roger helped Helena from her chair and

Richard did the same for Arianne. Servants hurried around the room to clean up the mess, while everyone else flooded into the various parts of the castle and grounds to begin their day.

The duke immediately caught Roger's attention, leaving Helena momentarily wondering what she should do with herself.

"Please say you will come and sing for Timothy," Arianne said, with a hopeful smile.

"Of course, Your Grace," Helena replied. " 'Twould be my honor."

"I shall miss your voice when you are gone from this place." Arianne's words were genuine and heartfelt. "I have enjoyed not only your songs, but the words we have shared in conversation. I have no sister, and so I have but glimpsed the delights of one through our friendship."

"Sisterly delights are overly credited," Maude said in a haughty tone from across the table. " 'Tis well enough to share company as grown women, but as children," she paused with a meaningful glare at her stepsister, "the matter can be quite different."

Arianne gave a brief lyrical laugh. "I would well imagine it to be so. I was not without sibling. My brother, Devon, was my fondest companion, at least while I was at home."

"Then he must know well how little sisters can play cruel jokes and spy out from their lairs. 'Tis mostly mischief and mean-spirited games that young ones have to offer."

"I cannot call you false, Lady Talbot," Tancred interrupted, "but neither can I imagine either Lady Helena or the duchess as mean-spirited. 'Twould be impossible for a cruel word to pass from either of those sweet mouths."

Helena wanted to laugh, but the sight of Maude clenching her velvet surcoat in her balled fists kept her from uttering a peep. Instead she allowed Arianne to take hold of her arm and lead her from the room.

At the stairs, Arianne paused and turned to find Maude scowling. "You are welcome to come with us, Lady Talbot."

But Maude had already sent a serving girl to retrieve her cloak and shook her head to reject the offer. "I am afraid I require a bit of fresh air. My condition is not so that I would feel comfortable with the child."

"Very well," Arianne replied sweetly. "But surely you will come and see your nephew, Tancred?" Helena stared at Arianne's suggestion, and Maude turned red in anger. There would be no way for her to take back the declined invitation should Tancred accept.

"I would be most honored to hear Lady Helena sing. Seeing my nephew would be a fond way to pass the hour, as well." Tancred joined them at the stairs. He offered his arm to Arianne, who simply shook her head and nodded to Helena.

"I would not presume to interfere," she said with a grin.

"Nor would I presume to contradict the duchess of the land," Tancred said, flashing a charming smile at his sister-in-law.

Helena felt it was wrong to goad Maude, but a part of her delighted in the obvious attention. Arianne had made it perfectly acceptable for her and Tanny to spend time together, and Helena was not going to do a simple thing to discourage it. She turned to Tancred from the gray stone step above him. From here they were nearly eye level with each other, and Helena found the moment quite moving. Tancred put out his hand, and Helena touched her fingertips to his. For a moment neither one did anything more. It was as if the rest of the world had completely forsaken them.

Tancred's harsh face softened as his dark eyes drank their fill of Helena. She felt a blush warm her cheek and her heart beat faster. How she loved this man! Melodies welled up from within her soul, and Helena felt as though she might burst into song at any moment.

"And what will you sing for us, sweet Helena?" Tancred breathed the question in a hushed whisper, almost as if he had read her mind.

Helena smiled and spoke in an almost seductive way. "Mayhaps I shall sing a long song." Her eyes twinkled mischievously. "But only if I am so inspired."

Tancred stared at her quite blank-faced, but his eyes sparkled in amusement. "Of course. Let us pray it is so."

They hurried up the stairs together, neither one noticing the cloaked form that stood in the shadows below. Maude's brooding glare followed them from behind the hood of her cape.

"I warned you, Helena," she murmured, but there was no one to hear her, nor to understand the danger Maude had come to represent.

Chapter 18

In the duchess's private solar, they gathered with Timothy. The baby cooed and gurgled his approval of the new company, and when Arianne handed him to Tancred, Helena laughed aloud at the expression on his face.

"He will not break," Arianne said with a smirk, while Tancred held Timothy stiffly. The look on his face said it all. "Do not tell me the great fearless lord of the land who came last year to best my husband now trembles before his son?"

Helena giggled, then cupped her hand to her mouth at Tancred's look of mock disgust.

"I thought you loyal to me," he said sternly, then softened the words with a wink.

"To find another as loyal as this one," Arianne said, taking a seat, "would be quite impossible." She watched her brother-in-law in his discomfort. "By my leave, Tancred, please sit down."

He did so in a manner that caused him to move as little as possible from the waist up. Helena could not refrain from laughing out loud.

"I heard that snickering and will deal with it later."

"Forget not, I am under the duke's protection," Helena said in a singsong voice. "Harm me and deal with him."

"Aye," Arianne acknowledged conspiratorially. "My husband would be far from tolerant."

"Cease your prattle!" Tancred said in a voice louder than he'd intended. This sudden sternness caused Timothy to pucker his face. Tears filled the baby's eyes, and soon he was wailing loud enough to bring down the walls.

Helena reached out and took the baby when Arianne sat back and watched in amused anticipation. Tancred was relieved to be rid of the squalling infant. He had little experience with babies. The frailty and tininess of them only served to make him feel cumbersome and awkward. Helena, he noted, was quite at ease with her charge. She began to sing to him with such love and gentleness that the infant instantly calmed.

"I will surely miss her ways with Timothy," Arianne said softly. "She has been a wonder and pleasure to have in our care."

"I can see why," Tancred said with a smile. He could well see in his mind's eye a home of his own and Helena singing to his son or daughter. What man wouldn't count himself blessed to make that vision an actuality?

Helena stopped singing and smiled over her shoulder. "He is the pleasure. I have been healed of my mother's passing while caring for this one."

"I never thought of it being a benefit to you," Arianne confessed. "I was so pleased to have your companionship that I began to fear 'twas selfishness on my part."

"Never fear it to be so." Helena brought Timothy back, and before Tancred could protest, she placed the baby in his arms. "I love children and I want an estate filled with them, or," she paused, "even a hovelful. It matters naught, so long as they are loved and made to feel wanted. The place, the wealth, the manner of life, none of it be as important as love."

"Love will not fill an empty belly," Tancred said, meeting her meaningful gaze. He was well aware of what she was saying to him.

"Perhaps not, but love will sustain a person through all forms of torture and heartache. I know this full well and will listen to no other on the matter."

Arianne grinned at her brother-in-law, who was now relaxing a bit with Timothy. "It would seem you are bested in this matter. I suggest a compromise."

"And what might that be?" asked Tancred with a grin.

"Marry the wench," Arianne said in a low-bred manner.

Helena blushed at Arianne's boldness, while Tancred sobered considerably. " 'Tis not a matter that I may yet address."

Helena said nothing. Perhaps Tanny had no interest in ever marrying her. Would he do the one thing Roger had accused him of with Maude? Would he dally with her feelings and leave her to face life with a broken heart? Nay, that could never be.

Arianne was the one who spoke, and again the conversation played itself out as though Helena were absent from the room. "Pray tell, why not? Is her love not true enough?" the duchess questioned with the slightest hint of sarcasm in her voice.

"You know very well that is not the case."

"Then what? She has offered you a life of devotion. Should it seem so strange that you might take her hand in marriage?"

Tancred's voice took on a tone that warned the women he was not pleased with the turn of this conversation. " 'Tis not a matter we should attend to at this time."

Timothy again found his uncle's voice overbearing and began to cry. Arianne took this as the perfect reason to excuse herself and got to her feet. "My son is hungry. I will take him to my chamber where we might rest. Feel free to reason this out together." Her words were spoken as a hopeful suggestion.

"There is little here that may be discussed," Tancred replied, handing the baby to Arianne. "I will, however, endeavor to clear what you have muddied." He wasn't truly angry at Arianne, and he relayed that fact with his eyes. The matter did need to be addressed, in spite of his desire to avoid it.

Helena watched as Arianne took Timothy and left the room. Her heart was in her throat, and she wanted to avoid Tancred's eyes as he got to his feet and crossed the room to where she stood.

"I am sorry if I have distressed you," he began. " 'Tis not my desire to do you harm." He fell silent, wondering how his words would be received. "I have wanted to speak with you on this matter. Come, sit down and I will try to explain."

Helena allowed him to take her hand in his. It was warm and comforting to feel his large fingers close around her smaller ones. She wanted so badly to throw herself into his arms and plead with him to flee with her before Maude could do more harm, but somehow she knew the words to come had little to do with Maude.

Sitting, Tancred stared at her for a moment. Helena met his stare uneasily, and she fought to keep tears from forming in her eyes.

"Helena, might I be forthright with you?"

"Of course," she replied, fear creeping in to sour her tone.

Tancred eased back against the chair and chose his words. "I am a pardoned man, that much is true. The king realized that I am not the one to blame for my parents' death, but the matter is not resolved." Helena nodded so he would continue. "The fact is," Tancred paused and looked at her intently, "until my name is truly cleared, I cannot even call it my own. It still bears the blood of those I loved."

"Tanny, you know it matters naught to me." Her voice was soft. "I don't care what the whole of England thinks, I love you and always will."

"But it matters to me!" Tancred bellowed. He frowned intently at his manner. "I beg your forgiveness, but I am not a man of gentleness."

Helena smiled, and though she wanted to avoid anything he might perceive as confrontational, she shook her head. "You are wrong, my love. You are a very gentle man. Tanny, the past has left its mark on both of us, but it needn't bury us as well."

"I have nothing to offer anyone, much less a wife. I cannot put my burden upon the shoulders of another. Especially one such as you."

"And what do you mean by that remark, Sire?" She was clearly offended.

Tancred got to his feet and paced a few steps before turning back to face her. "You are a delicate blossom and should be cherished and preserved for all that is lovely and truly good in this life. I cannot give you those things, Helena. I cannot even give you my name, because I have no name. I have but the letters that form a word, and that word stands for nothing but pain and betrayal. Until I learn of the true murderer's identity, I don't even have my name to share."

"Bah! Purely talk of a man. Why say you this? Is a name so much more important than what dwells within your heart? Is God not the source of your light and life? Is that to be perceived as nothing?"

"Nay, of course not," Tancred's voice sounded in frustration. "Listen to me, Helena. You pledge life and love to a person you know nothing about. I've given this much thought and believe that you have fallen in devotion of a man who no longer exists."

Helena took a deep breath. "You cannot return my love and so you look to put my love away from you? Is that your game?" Her heart was aching at the mere thought of such a thing.

Tancred stared at her in confusion. He seemed to be trying to sort through the words. "You doubt I could care for you?"

"It seems you doubt I could live with such caring." Helena stood and crossed to Tancred. She did not reach out to touch him or even to offer him her hand. "You misjudge me, Sir. I am more durable than you can imagine. I leave you, however, to your decisions and choices. I cannot be false to myself. I cannot pledge ignorance of my heart. Be it well with you or not, I am offering my love and life."

She walked away from him, leaving Tancred stunned. How could he explain to her what he felt, knowing that he must ask her to wait—perhaps forever?

Helena passed into the hall and lost her bravado. All of her courageousness was but an act, and here, alone, she could admit to herself that the outcome of their meeting left her frightened.

Helena slipped into bed early. She hadn't bothered to go down for supper, and when her chambermaid appeared with a tray of food, she'd sent the girl away without sampling a single morsel. Arianne had pleaded an audience with her, but Helena had begged her understanding and sent her away.

Her heart was heavy with grief and worry. How could Tancred consider letting her go away from him? Had he not proclaimed his joy at their finding each other again?

The wind picked up outside and made a howling sound against the window. The restless waters of the sea crashed against the rocky cliffs just beyond the castle estate and left little doubt in Helena's mind that a storm was brewing.

With the first flash of lightning, Helena steadied herself for the crashing response of thunder. When it came, she nearly missed the light-handed knocking upon her bedchamber door. She thought to ignore the sound, but decided against it. No, best to answer it and make her excuses. Pulling on her robe, Helena opened the door to reveal a young boy.

"I bear a message for you, Lady Talbot." He gave a brief bow and handed her the rolled parchment.

Staring down at the parchment as though it was something foreign in design, Helena immediately recognized the DuBonnet signet in the wax. "Thank you," she told the boy and quietly closed the door behind her. What DuBonnet would be writing her a note? Was not parchment plenty precious? Could not any one of them simply come to her door?

Tanny, she thought. She broke the seal and quickly read the contents.

Meet me in the west tower. Hurry.

There was no signature, but her heart told her the letter must be from Tancred. She glanced down at her robe and wondered if she should take the time to dress. There was no doubt precious little time, yet to appear in public without some proper form of attire was unthinkable. She quickly grabbed the surcoat she'd worn earlier and shed herself of her night clothes.

There was lighting enough to make her way unhindered through the castle. Helena felt her heart pounding in anticipation.

Tanny wanted to talk to her!

Perhaps he had reconsidered the matter and had a change of heart. Then again, mayhaps his heart was decided in a way she would not like. Maybe he had decided to go away and leave her.

With trembling hand, she reached out for the tower door and pushed it open. The spiraling stone stairs bore no evidence of life. Even the rats in their constant vigil for food had neglected this part of the castle.

With nothing but the lighted torches on the wall to guide her steps, Helena began her ascent. "Tanny?" She whispered his name into the shadowy confines, but no reply came.

The first level revealed only storage. There were wooden crates with unknown goods and stacks of materials on top of unneeded tables. In the corners of the room, spectral figures rose up and proved to be nothing more than rolled wall hangings. Helena shivered nevertheless. It was an unpleasant place to be, and she longed to find Tancred to ease her worried mind.

Progressing up the stairs, she squealed in fright when a fat mouse crossed her thin-slippered foot. The noise she made echoed in her ears.

"Tanny?" she called out a little louder this time, but still heard no reply.

With one hand on her skirts and the other against the wall to balance her, Helena again trembled. The dampness of the cold stone seemed foreboding. Perhaps she should turn back.

A noise from above caught her attention. Quickly passing the unused rooms of the second level, Helena made her way cautiously to the third-floor room. She knew from here there were ladders that would reach the highest castle battlements.

With her right hand constantly feeling the way, Helena remembered that the stairs had been spiraled to allow defenders coming from the top to use their right-handed swords, while the attackers would be at a disadvantage with the wall at their right. After all, it was well known that only the truly evil were able to fight left-handed.

The third floor revealed a door slightly ajar and light coming from within. Helena reached to push the heavy wooden door open. "Tancred, are you here?"

She stepped inside and searched the room with her eyes. The ladder to the roof stood in one corner, while the circular room otherwise bore no sign of life save the lighted torch.

The door slammed shut behind her with a resounding thud. Helena jumped and turned to find Maude staring at her with a malicious smile.

"So you got my message."

"Yours? I thought Tanny sent it." Helena backed up against the wall at Maude's advancing form. "What do you want?"

"I want a great deal, and with you in my life, I cannot have it." Maude stopped several paces away and looked Helena over from head to toe. "I cannot see what the fuss is about. 'Tis true you are comely, but not overmuch. Your hair is fine yellow, but your eyes are too pale."

Helena touched her unbraided hair. It hung in ringlets around her shoulders and down to her waist. There had been no time to dress it before coming to the clandestine meeting.

Maude continued taking inventory of Helena's appearance. "I cannot see that your figure is any more shapely than mine. Nor are you more graceful or capable." Maude seemed to genuinely puzzle over the younger woman's merits. When she turned slightly away, Helena ran for the door and managed to pull it open, but Maude saw her movement, reached over, and slammed her hard against the stone wall.

"You certainly are not as intelligent as I."

"Maude, what is it that you want? I did what you told me. I told Roger to take me home, and he is doing so in the morn."

"Cease! I will not listen to your lies. Tancred is also going with you. What spell did you weave to capture his heart? Is it the same one you used to wile away my father's love?"

Helena blinked and swallowed hard. "I never strove to put distance between you and Father."

"Do not call him that! You have no right. He was not your father. Your mother came into our house with you heavy in her belly. You were not my father's child, but the orphan of my father's friend."

" 'Tis true enough that my father died upon the battlefield, but your father loved him dearly and saw my mother's need. With your own mother long dead and mine without hope, they formed an agreement and joined their estates. What possible fault can you find in that?"

"Dear Helena," Maude stated sarcastically. "Sweet, precious Helena. My father strutted about the house as proud as a peacock on the day you were born. What think you of my lot when that hour came? I was but seven years and had, until that time, held my father's heart in full. Even Roger loved me best, and I knew much kindness from the people upon our lands."

"That needn't have stopped on my account. You brought sorrow upon yourself with your bitterness and anger. You treated my mother badly, and your father could scarce stand to see her grieved."

"Do I not know this for myself? I oft wonder if my father did not love your mother long before their union."

Helena shrugged. "Mayhaps, but what can we make of that now? My father and yours were closer than brothers. Neither had kit nor kin beyond the offspring they were to give life to. It bonded them in a way that could not be severed. It seems natural that our mothers might also have been close. It matters naught."

"It matters!" Maude screeched. "You took away from me the only things that did matter. Every suitor—"

" 'Tis not true!" Helena interrupted. "I but lost my heart to Tanny, no other."

" 'Tis true indeed. You batted your eyes and flashed your smiles at the men, until even though you were but a child, my own courters were asking Roger about your betrothal arrangements."

"But I had no part in that," Helena protested. "I was but a friendly child. I simply enjoyed the company of people. I sought not to destroy your marriage plans."

" 'Tis unimportant now." Maude stepped closer, and Helena slid against the wall, away from the door and her hopes for freedom. "You have the eye of the one man I want. Tancred DuBonnet is mine. He has always been mine, and I will bear no other becoming wife to him."

"Surely you jest," Helena said, suddenly feeling bold. "Tanny loves me. I know that he does."

"Mayhaps," Maude said, bringing a dagger up to Helena's face. "But will he love a corpse?"

"You mean to kill me?" Helena questioned, suddenly realizing just how serious this matter was.

"You stand between me and happiness," Maude replied. "I have but to rid myself of your existence in order to obtain that which I desire."

"And you believe Tancred would ever find it possible to love you? He knows how you played him false when we were younger. He saw your ways. Would he now look aside and wed the murderer of his own true love?"

"Cease this prattle! You have no claim on a love falsely taken. You stole his heart. It rightly belongs to me. You are a witch and have cast a spell over my beloved. I have but to put an end to your life in order to break the spell and have Tancred for myself!"

Chapter 19

Tancred found Richard in his counting room, reviewing the ledgers left him by Arianne and his steward.

"If this is a bad time. . ."

"Nay," Richard said, motioning Tancred forward. "I am finished. You can see the candle is burned nearly down. What is on your mind? Have you thought of something more concerning our parents?"

"Nay," Tancred said, taking a seat. "I have come on another matter." Just then thunder rumbled loudly.

Richard raised an eyebrow. "Roger and Helena?"

"More simply, Helena."

Richard grinned and stroked his beard thoughtfully. Arianne had told him of the two lovers and their devotion for one another. She had also told him of Tancred's worry regarding the matter. "My wife mentioned your interest."

Tancred smiled. "She would. There is not much that escapes that woman. She mystifies me at times and often reminds me of our mother."

"Aye," Richard stated in surprise. "I had not thought on it, but you are right. She's been wife to me for nearly a year, and every day I learn something new about her. But you did not come here to speak of Arianne. What of Helena?"

It was Tancred's turn to look thoughtful. "I have been pardoned by Henry, but nothing was said of returning my land or title."

"True. I never thought of it that way, but I suppose it is a grave concern of yours."

"Of course it is a concern. 'Tis not that I am not most happy to be pardoned of a crime I did not commit, but what is to become of me henceforth? I do not, in fact, even have full use of my name. It bears the stain of blood from the trial and consequent punishment that I endured. Many know the name of Tancred DuBonnet and believe that man to have been a murderer."

"I think I understand," Richard replied, suddenly seeing his brother's dilemma. "You love Helena, but cannot offer her your name in marriage because you feel you have no name."

"Leastwise not one I would share with such a tender heart."

Richard nodded. " 'Tis a difficult matter, but surely not one that is without hope. We will go to Henry and inquire of him about your land and titles. If you are reinstated those things, then people far and wide will know of your redemption."

"Aye, but that may well take years. I do not wish to lose Helena in this matter. I have come to ask a favor."

"Name it. I owe you that much."

Tancred shook his head. "Nay, there is no obligation here. Please hear me out. I seek only to ask for a home here at Gavenshire. At least until we can learn of my chances with Henry."

"But you have no need to ask that. I have already given you that. You need never feel obligated to me for a roof overhead and food in your belly. I denied you. . ." Richard help up his hand to stop Tancred from speaking. "Nay, 'tis truth enough and I beg you hear me out. I denied you a home and your name because of my blind fury and desire for revenge. Tancred, I know I have your forgiveness, but I do this to offer you my heart. My home is yours."

"Thank you," Tancred said and hesitated for a moment before continuing. "But, what if Henry refuses to give me back my land?"

"Then I will bestow land upon you myself. 'Tis my right. This lot and more have been given to me through Henry and my marriage to Arianne. I will see you reinstated one way or another."

"I am happy to work at your side and do the service of a knight," Tancred said. "I will be idly kept."

"I knew it would be so with you," Richard said with a grin. "You may come to regret those words."

"Nay, I think not. Still, there is another favor."

"Pray continue." Richard was now genuinely curious.

"I would like to beg a place for Helena as well. You see, I intend to take her as my wife. That is, if she will still have me. I was a bit brusque with her earlier this day."

Richard laughed and shook his head. "There is no doubting she will have you. She's defied her stepbrother and sister, and were Henry not sympathetic with his wife and Helena's mother, Helena would no doubt have challenged the king of England as well. I could very nearly envy the devotion you have in that woman."

Tancred nodded with a sober look of awe. " 'Tis a wondrous thing, indeed. I have no mind for it. The love I feel for her is a newborn thing compared. I loved her as a little sister when I fostered in her home. I've dried her tears and played games with her, protected her from her overbearing nursemaid, but all in all, it was nothing.

"Through my years of misery I did not call her face to mind. If I had, 'twould have been the face of a child that filled my vision. Still, it is easy to give her my heart now."

"And why so?"

Tancred's face went momentarily blank, almost as if Richard's words were incomprehensible to him. "Why so? Because she fills me. My heart beats because she bids it do so. I cannot see the future without seeing her in it as well."

Richard laughed and pounded the table with his fists. "A love match! How rare, indeed! You are blessed, Brother, and why not? You have suffered through much, and now God gives you back in full measure, just as He did Job. Have no fear, I believe your lands and title will be returned by and by."

Tancred smiled. "Would that I might have your confidence."

"Where is that faith you boast, Brother?"

" 'Tis here," Tancred said, thumping his fist against his chest. "But he is still a timid fellow."

"Then let him be bold. I give you and Helena my pledge. Gavenshire shall be your home until you desire it no more. Even then, I shall never close its doors to you and yours. Marry her quickly and be assured that even in your death, she will know my protection."

"Thank you, Richard." Tancred stood, and Richard did so as well. "I will go and speak with her on the matter. Roger has already given me his word on it. If Henry will but agree. . ."

"Never fear, I've a feeling Henry desires to right this wrong as much as I do. Henry will give you all that you ask."

Tancred left the room with a purpose. He would seek out Helena, even though the hour was late, and ask her to marry him. He would pledge his love and life and promise to make her a new home. Taking the steps two at a time, he felt his heart lighten in a way he'd never known. Helena was his. For the moment, it was enough.

The door to Helena's room was ajar, something Tancred had not expected to find. He pushed it open full and walked inside, fearful that something might have happened.

On the grate, a fire burned brightly, and on the rumpled covers of the bed, Helena's linen robe lay discarded. Wherever she was, Helena had apparently been drawn from her bed to be there. Perhaps, Tancred thought, Arianne had need of her service. It was possible that Timothy had been inconsolable and Helena had been fetched to sing. Still, there was no sound on the air, and always before Helena's voice had drifted through the halls to warm his blood.

He glanced around the room again, hoping to see something that might tell him where she'd gone. It was then that he spied the letter. Near the door, on the floor, a pale flicker of firelight shone on the single page. Tancred bent and retrieved it.

Immediately his eye fell on the wax signet. His signet. His and Richard's. He opened the page and read. Helena was beckoned to the west tower, but by whom? Taking the parchment, he went below to confront Richard and, instead, met him on the stairs.

"Did you write this?" Tancred questioned, thrusting the parchment forward. Richard strained to see it in the dim light. "Nay, 'tis not my writing."

"But 'tis our seal. I found this in Helena's room. She is not there."

"I did not send it, and I presume you did not."

"Nay, I did not," Tancred reaffirmed.

"We should go to the west tower and find her. This would seem an unsavory matter," Richard said, keeping his voice a husky whisper. "But who would have our signet ring to seal the wax?"

"Roger Talbot has a ring such as ours. I gave it to him eleven years ago." Tancred was getting an uncomfortable feeling in the pit of his stomach.

"Is it possible that Talbot would endanger Helena?"

"I pray not, but what else might this mean?" Tancred asked. Then glancing behind him, Tancred asked another question. "Where is Roger's room?"

"There," Richard pointed. "The room to the left of the stairs."

Tancred crossed the distance quickly and pounded upon the door. A sleepy-eyed Roger appeared, wearing nothing more than a linen chausses.

"What are you about, Tancred?"

Tancred motioned Richard to bring the note. "Did you write this?"

Roger pulled the parchment close to the wall torch. "Nay, 'tis not my writing."

"It bears my seal and none save Richard and you have ever worn that ring, with exception of our father." Tancred's voice was edged in anger.

Roger eyed him for a moment before handing the note back. "It pains me to admit this, but I lost that ring only three days after you gave it to me. 'Twas among my things one day and the next it was gone. I searched but never found it again. Besides, why would I send you a note to meet me in the west tower? I have no reckoning of this place. I would not know the rooms or the way to them."

" 'Twas not written to me," Tancred said, stuffing the note into his tunic.

"Then who?"

"I found it in Helena's room, and she is gone."

Roger didn't bother to ask for more information. He dressed quickly and, while pulling on his boots, a desperate thought came to him.

"Maude wrote that letter," he announced suddenly.

"What?" Richard and Tancred asked in unison.

"I believe that letter to be Maude's handwriting. She could well have stolen that signet those many years ago. She was determined to have you for herself, mayhaps she thought to use the ring to bear witness against you. Perhaps she intended to give it over to the king and declare it a symbol of your pledge. For whatever purpose," he said getting to his feet, "I believe it is Maude's writing."

Tancred paled. "Then Helena is in grave danger."

"Why say you this?" Richard asked, now the only one who did not perceive the circumstance for what it was.

"Because the same hand wrote and sealed the letter that took me to our parents the night they died."

Richard and Tancred exchanged a look and then glanced to Roger. "Maude!" the men said in unison, and Richard motioned them out the door.

"The tower is this way."

Chapter 20

For all of my life, I have lived in your shadow," Maude spat hatefully. "You were always there to make my days unbearable, and when I could stand it no longer, I married a man I did not love. All, I might add, in order to escape the presence of you and your mother."

"Maude be reasonable. Mother held naught but kindness in her heart for you, and I was a child of ten years when you married. I had naught to do with that choice or decision."

"I wanted DuBonnet!"

"I had naught to do with that, either. My love for him was not returned. Certainly the love of a grown man could not be given to a child. If Tanny had loved me, he could have asked for my hand. We could have been betrothed—others were at ages younger than mine. You speak false if you say I had anything to do with keeping Tancred from seeking your hand. He didn't know I existed."

Maude help up the dagger. Her face contorted in rage. "You spoke out against me! You told him I was unworthy of his love."

"Lies!" Helena's anger matched that of her stepsister. "I would have, but my mother would not allow it. She said 'twas a matter for adults to decide. 'Tis true enough that I wanted to keep you from Tanny, but I said nothing!"

"Then 'twas Eleanor."

"Nay! My mother would not have done such a thing. She would have happily seen you married off. What was it to her but to be rid of your sour face in her home?" Helena knew the feelings were more her own than those of her departed mother.

"It was my home first! You were intruders. You, who came into my house and stole all that would be mine. I dealt with Eleanor for her treachery, just as I dealt with Tancred. Now, I will deal with you."

Helena's eyes widened. "Tancred? Have you slain him already?" Her voice betrayed the anguish.

Maude laughed dementedly. "Nay, not until a priest joins us in marriage. I am not stupid."

Relief flooded Helena's face. "Then what speak you of having dealt with Tancred?"

Maude's face relaxed and a smile formed upon her lips. "Revenge has always been my closest companion. When others would not do my bidding, revenge served me well. Just as I make Tancred pay for rejecting my affections, so I will make you pay for stealing his love from me."

"I do not understand. How did you avenge yourself against Tancred?" The cold of the stone wall was seeping into Helena's body, but still she did not move.

"When Tancred would have no part of me, I decided 'twas only fair to exact a punishment." Maude toyed with the dagger, then waved her arms. Before she could speak, a noise sounded outside the open door and drew her attention. With a quick glance at Helena, Maude turned to investigate the noise.

Helena hurried to the roof ladder and might have made an escape, but her surcoat tripped her up and the ripping sound of material, along with Helena's headlong fall, quickly brought Maude back into the room.

"You cannot hope to defy me in this. The rats may make merry in the tower, but you will die this night."

Helena picked herself up and tried to hold the torn garment together. Her blond hair was wildly askew and her breathing came in panting gulps. "How," she gasped, "how did you avenge yourself? I would know that much before I die."

Maude smirked at the younger woman. "He kept from me what I loved most, so I took from him what he loved most."

Realization suddenly dawned on Helena. "His parents!"

"Aye, his precious father and mother." Maude's eyes gleamed at the memory. "I sent him a message, much the same as I did for you this night." She moved the dagger to her left hand, and it was then that it occurred to Helena that Maude was right-handed.

So much for the left-handed being the only truly evil. Helena's thoughts were interrupted as Maude retrieved something from the pouch of her belt. Holding it up, Helena saw that it was a ring. " 'Tis the DuBonnet signet. The same I took from Roger's room and kept with me unto this day. A simple thing, yet it yielded a way to trap the man who would not be trapped."

"You sent for Tanny and called him to his parents' home, but how. . . ?" Helena's voice faltered. She couldn't say the words.

"How did I arrange for them to be killed? 'Tis what you are asking, is it not?" Helena nodded and shuddered. "Aye."

"I could not very well kill them myself. So I took coin and paid it to be done. I arranged it carefully so that when Tancred arrived upon his homelands, it would be a signal to those who lay in wait. The deed was done, and just as I had planned, Tancred arrived first upon the scene. 'Twas luck, plain and simple, that Richard arrived shortly behind to find the knife in his brother's hand." Maude slipped the ring on her finder and shifted the knife.

"But what of the witnesses?" Helena questioned, again backing up to feel the wall behind her.

"They were paid and later poisoned to keep them from telling their tales.

The real murderer did not live long enough to be dealt with by me. He was killed the next day fighting over another man's wife. So you see," Maude stepped forward in determined steps, "you are the only one who lives to tell my story."

"They will find me," Helena murmured.

"Perhaps, but not for a long while. Especially not if I play the details out properly. I will go to Roger and tell him that you were desperate to leave the castle. I will tell that you could no longer bear your misery here. He will look upon the road for you. No one will seek you here."

"But I left your letter in my room," Helena said, grasping at the slim hope Maude would falter.

"I will simply retrieve it when the deed is done here. No one will be the wiser."

"Roger knows," Helena finally admitted. She had to make Maude see reason.

"Pray tell, what does Roger know?"

"I told him that you were forcing me away from Tancred. Tanny knows, as well, and he will never be yours after this." Helena drew a deep breath and continued—afraid that if she stopped for long, Maude would refuse to hear her out.

"Tanny found me crying, and Roger insisted I tell the truth. He and Tanny waited with me until I explained it in detail. I told them you were forcing me away. I told them I had no desire to leave, but that you wanted Tancred for your own.

"They assured me you would be no threat to them. Roger planned this entire matter and arranged it so that you would stumble upon your own words. He knew it was your plan to remain here at Gavenshire, so he and Tancred agreed that Tanny would accompany us. When you had played out your game here and returned to the manor, Tancred was to accompany me back to Gavenshire at the request of the duchess."

Maude's lip curled. "You are more deceiving and wicked than I gave you credit for. It matters naught! For this as well you will die!" She came at Helena with the knife, but just as her arm came down, someone pulled Maude backward. With a muffled thud, Maude hit the floor with her attacker. She quickly rolled away and found Roger springing to his feet. Tancred and Richard rushed to Helena's side.

"You have caused enough pain, Maude," Roger stated, while Maude struggled to her feet. "You have lied and forced your will upon innocent people. Now I personally will see you before the king to admit your guilt in the killing of the DuBonnets and Lady Eleanor."

"Never!" Maude steadied herself and held tightly to the knife. "I will not be made the fool. You played me false, Brother, and you," she said looking hard at Tancred, who stood in front of a shaking Helena, "you played me a fool. You made me believe there was hope when there was none. You toyed with my affection and left me behind to suffer when it suited your purpose."

"The only hope you saw for a union between us," Tancred replied, "was one you conjured in your evil mind. I had no love for you and would never have thought to offer you my name."

Roger ignored Maude for a moment and stepped toward Helena. "Are you injured?" he questioned.

"Nay, my gown suffered more than I." Helena looked up at her stepbrother with gratitude. " 'Twould have been much worse had you a slower pace."

"You have Tancred to thank for my pace. He awoke me and brought this matter to light."

Helena turned her eyes to her beloved. "Oh, Tanny," she whispered. Her heart pounded all the harder at the passionate emotion she saw in his eyes. "My dying gratitude to you, my love. It would seem that once again you have rescued me from trouble."

Tancred smiled down at her with pure pleasure. "Seems I am ever called upon to perform such tasks. 'Twould be only fitting that I make proper arrangements to keep you under my guard on a more permanent basis."

Helena raised a brow in question, but Tancred had no chance to reply before Maude let out a scream. All four turned to find her on her feet, dagger in hand, and face contorted in rage.

"He is mine! No other shall have him!" She rushed forward to stab at Tancred, but Roger easily deflected her blows and sent the knife clattering across the stone floor.

" 'Tis ended, Maude. You have spilled enough blood. Must I spill yours to still your hatred?" Roger growled.

Maude refused to cower, but her voice took on a frail air. "But I love him. I have always loved him. He was to be my husband and—"

"I was never to be your husband, Maude. I never loved you and never will. You have no hope of a marriage with me. Not then, not now, not ever."

Maude lowered her head in complete dejection, and Roger exhaled a sigh of relief. "I am truly sorry for my sister's behavior, Your Grace. I would never have endangered your family had I known what Maude was fully capable of."

Richard shook his head. "There is no need for apologies, Talbot. You had no way of knowing."

"She murdered your parents," Helena said, stepping from behind Tancred to face Richard.

"Aye, we heard her confession." Richard's voice betrayed his sorrow. "At least it is put to rest."

"I am so sorry," Helena murmured, tears forming in her eyes.

Tancred put his arm around her and pulled her close. " 'Tis no longer a matter for consideration. 'Tis finished."

"At least it will be when—" Roger's words were interrupted by Maude's sudden bolt to the door.

"I will not hang for this," she screeched and raced down the stairs. Before anyone could move, a terrible scream rang out, followed by a thud, and then ominous silence.

"Come," Richard said to Roger. "Tancred, you keep Lady Helena here."

"Aye," Tancred replied, feeling Helena trembling beneath his hold.

Helena gripped Tancred tightly and buried her face against his chest. It was all so ugly and heinous. How could any of them bear up against Maude's violence?

She wanted to say something. Anything. What words would show Tancred how much she grieved for him, for his loss? Nothing she said would bring his parents back. Just as there were no words that could bring back her mother. All three were dead because of one person's selfishness and twisted cruelty.

Tancred was smoothing her hair, and Helena relaxed against the rhythmic strokes. He was so strong, and he'd borne so very much. Helena knew she would always love him. Even if he could never offer her marriage, Helena would go on loving him from afar.

Roger returned to the tower room with a grim set to his face. "She is dead."

"Dead?" Helena choked out the word.

"Aye, she broke her neck in the fall. Her days of inflicting pain and suffering are finished."

Helena looked at Tancred and then to Roger, wondering what it all meant. What would happen now? Could they prove Maude was responsible for the killings and free Tancred from further humiliation?

Richard entered the room just then, and Helena noted that his expression was one more of relief than sorrow. "We will bury your sister and then go to the king." Roger nodded and Tancred only tightened his grip on Helena. Richard continued. "I've instructed my men to remove Lady Talbot and see her to the priest. I will beg him to take pity on her and offer her a proper burial."

"You mentioned the king," Helena said, pushing back her long blond hair.

"Aye," Richard said solemnly. "We will go, your brother, mine, and myself. We will give Henry the facts of the matter and allow him to determine what is to take place from this moment forward. If you will excuse me, I must go speak with the priest."

"I will go along, as well," Roger offered.

When they were both gone, Tancred released his tightened grip on Helena and held her at arm's length. "You are truly unharmed?"

Helena nodded. She sheepishly held up the torn edge of her surcoat. "This is the worst of it."

"It is well. It vexed me sorely to imagine you had come here, thinking as you must that I beckoned you, only to be injured at Maude's hand."

Helena nodded. "How did you find us so quickly? I had not but come a short while before you entered."

"I had come to speak with you and found you gone. The letter was upon the floor."

"I must have dropped it in my haste."

"When I saw it, I could only imagine that someone meant to trick you. I knew I had not written it, yet it bore my signet. I thought I recognized the writing, and after learning that Richard was innocent of it as well, I presumed it must have come from Roger."

"You thought Roger had played us false and planned to harm me again?"

"That did cross my mind." He studied her hard for a moment, his eyes seeming to drink her in with an unyielding sobriety. "I feared that moment as I have never feared anything done to me."

Helena smiled and lowered her head. " 'Twould seem you might care a bit for me. I am glad."

Tancred pulled her close, causing Helena to raise her gaze to meet his. His finger lightly stroked her cheek. "A bit? You think I might only care a bit?"

Helena's smile broadened. "I cannot guess more, Sire. 'Twould be a dangerous assumption on my part. There has been little more to prove such hope."

"Then let this be your proof," he said and lowered his lips to meet hers in a passionate kiss.

Chapter 21

It was most trying to be left behind, but Helena and Arianne found themselves once again in that position.

"'Tis the lot of women," Arianne sighed when the second week had come and gone with no word from Richard.

Helena tried not to look too downcast as she nodded. "'Tis well there is much work to be about." She looked down at the tunic she was stitching and realized she would have to pluck out the thread on a good portion of the seam she'd just made. "Yet I cannot keep my hands and mind working together on this matter." She held up the material sadly.

Arianne laughed. "I know how it is." She held up her own piece, a linen coif for Richard. "This has borne my frustrations poorly."

"Will the king believe them?" Helena asked softly. She let the tunic fall to her lap.

"I believe so. There is really no doubt in my mind." Arianne's words were not simply given to encourage; they were heartfelt.

"Do you believe Henry will restore Tancred's property and title?"

"That is a matter I have no head for. Richard believes it so, however, and he is scarce wrong when it comes to his beloved king."

Helena nodded and got to her feet. "I'm going to the chapel. It would seem I feel best when on my knees."

Arianne put her sewing aside, checked on the sleeping Timothy, and joined Helena at the door. "Matilda and I have been praying as well. God will do what is best. Never forget this."

"I won't."

Helena went below and walked somberly to the chapel. She spent a great deal of time there in prayer, and when she entered the room, she immediately felt strengthened.

The chapel was empty; no other sole had come to pray, and the priest was in the village attending to matters there. Helena was glad for the solitude. She loved to look up at the stained glass of the chapel window and think.

Richard had surprised Arianne at Christmas with the window of deep scarlet, blue, and yellow. It was the likeness of an empty tomb, with a cross overhead. Richard said it reminded him that Christ's story did not end at the cross, but began anew. The empty tomb, he had told her one evening in reflection, was one of the most hopeful symbols of all. It was there to remind us that we are resurrected in Christ, that just as He rolled the stone aside and walked away from death's grip, we, too, could do the same in Him.

Kneeling in the rushes before the altar, Helena prayed for some time, asking blessings upon those she loved. She asked that God would grant the king wisdom and mercy in dealing with Tancred and added selfishly her desire that He make Tancred her husband soon.

She was startled when someone knelt in the rushes beside her and opened her eyes to find Tancred.

"Tanny?"

He reached out to take her hand and kissed it lightly. "Your prayers have brought me home."

"In more ways than one this is true," she replied. "Would you pray with me now?"

"Aye, it would be most fitting." They bowed their heads, and after several moments of silent communion with God, Tancred pulled Helena to her feet. "Come. We must talk."

Pausing outside the chapel, Helena casually let her gaze travel the length of Tancred. Disheveled a bit from an obviously fast-paced ride, Tancred's hair begged her touch and Helena could not resist.

"Do I meet with milady's approval?" he asked, grinning.

"Aye, very much so. You could stand a bit of grooming, but otherwise I find you perfect."

"Nay, it will never be so, but I am glad to find you satisfied with me."

"Pray tell, why?" She looked at him with little-girl innocence.

Tancred's grin turned roguish. "I could say, but I'd much rather show you." He pulled her into his arms and kissed her lips soundly.

Helena wrapped her arms around his neck, totally forgetting where they were. Her heart pounded from joy and passion, and she sighed a deep, throaty sigh when his lips traveled boldly from her mouth to the side of her face and then just below her ear.

"I most enjoy this talk," she teased.

"You are a hard vision to put from my mind," Tancred whispered between kisses.

"No more so than you," Helena countered. "Remember I held your face for eleven years in my heart."

"And glad I am that you did." The spell was broken, and Tancred set her away from him just a bit. "Which reminds me."

"I know," Helena grinned. "We must talk."

"Aye, and quickly."

Tancred led her out beyond the castle walls. The brilliance of spring grass and wildflowers set a lively mood that infected Helena. Beyond the castle, a calm, blue sea awaited their review, while gulls flew overhead, searching for bits of food.

To Helena, it was as if spring had come all at once. " 'Tis so beautiful!" she exclaimed and strayed from Tancred's side to do an animated jig. She hummed a song to herself and laughed when Tancred pulled her back to him and held her fast.

"You have not yet asked what happened with Henry."

"True." She sobered a bit. "Mayhaps you will tell me now?"

Tancred reached up and pulled the linen wimple from her head. "Pesky things. I rather fancy the way your hair was spilled out that night in the tower." He toyed with the wisps of blond hair that had come loose from her braid.

" 'Tis pesky when a man would undress a maiden's hair without the right to do so," Helena said snidely. "If I had a champion, he would be called to defend me just now."

Tancred chuckled and tossed the wimple aside. "You have a champion in me, Milady." He bowed low before her, making Helena giggle.

"I would rather have you for a husband," she stated boldly.

Tancred rose and shook his head. "It would seem that you and Henry agree on the matter."

"Oh, Tanny! Did the king give us permission to marry?"

"Aye."

He seemed quite pleased with himself, and Helena couldn't help laughing. "Tell me all!"

Tancred put his hand about her waist and walked toward the cliff edge with Helena snugly beside him. "Henry listened to all we had to say and made a full record of Maude's treachery. He was most satisfied that the matter was ended."

"Did he restore your lands?" Helena asked hesitantly lest she sound greedy.

"Nay," Tancred said softly in a reflective manner.

Helena frowned and looked up to catch his eyes looking out across the vastness of the sea. She squeezed his hand. "Alas, my love, 'tis of no matter. It will be well with us so long as we have each other. I care naught for the land or the titles, only for you."

Tancred gazed down upon her with such deeply felt love that Helena had to look away. "He could not restore my lands for they were given to the church and made into a monastery. He did, however, give me lands not far from these. I will not make a beggar's wife of you, my dear."

Helena gasped. "Lands here?"

"Aye, within a two-day journey of Gavenshire. We will join Richard's land on one side, while Devon's estate joins them on the other."

"How wonderful!" She hugged him tightly and was not surprised when his arms wrapped around her and held her fast.

"Marry me, Helena," he whispered.

Helena melted against him. "Aye," she murmured. It was the culmination of a lifetime of dreaming.

Pulling away, Helena turned her back to Tancred and stared out across the sea. "These waters once separated us, and for many years I cursed them and mourned my loss. But the same waters brought you back again, and I curse them no more."

Tancred pulled her back against him, nestling his face against her shoulder. "I pledge you that no one shall separate us again. There may come a day when I am summoned to do the king's work or attend to matters of my own, but here in my heart, we shall ever be one. I love you, Helena. I vow always to love you."

Helena felt tears upon her cheeks and wiped them away with her hand before turning to face her beloved Tanny. Her heart nearly burst at the sight of him. She opened her mouth to speak, but instead a song came to her lips. Tanny's song:

> If my beloved were a king,
>   I couldst not love him more.
> Were he a jester to make men laugh,
>   My love I would implore.
> But, alas, my love is but a man,
>   Of heart and soul so free.
> And I couldst no more break my vow,
>   Than break the heart in me.

If Only

Prologue

England, 1349

The bubonic plague has wrecked havoc upon all of Europe. In England, over one-third of the population is dead or dying from the dread disease. In its wake, the plague has left entire families dead, whole villages burned, and vital records of both destroyed for all time. This dark, macabre age would haunt generations to come.

As people mourned their losses, an anguished cry rose from the depths of their souls. . .if only. If only we knew what caused this grave disease. If only we could save the lives waning before us. If only we had not sinned and caused such devastation to be rained down upon us. If only. . .

Chapter 1

Mary Elizabeth Beckett crouched behind the kitchen screen in hopes her father would not spy her out. *'Twould be a pity to miss out on this,* she thought.

Guy Beckett, oblivious to his daughter's whereabouts, directed his two colleagues into the house. He motioned them past the kitchen to the small, dark corner room. Here, Guy Beckett performed his experiments and looked for the elusive answers to questions that vexed him regarding the human body and medicine.

"Be careful with it," he instructed the men. They carried a large trunk of considerable weight and only grunted a reply of acknowledgment.

Mary's excitement urged her to peek out from the screen as the men cautiously made their way into the secluded room. A dull thud told her that the trunk had reached its destination.

"You are sure no one saw you?" Guy questioned his friends.

"We are as much at risk as you," stated one. Mary knew this man to be a fellow physician of her father's.

"Aye, 'twould not bode well for us to be caught with this baggage in hand," the other, a stranger to Mary, said with a wave of his hand over the trunk.

When the door closed, Mary sprang up with a lightning step from her hiding place and hurried up into the loft. Her room was directly over her father's workshop, and for many years she had peered down to watch his actions. *He will not mind,* she thought, certain that her father knew full well of her observations. And why not? Mary worked hard at his side and loved healing the sick as much as he did. He would only see this curiosity as one more part of her training.

Gently, so that she would not disturb the procedures in the room below, Mary lifted the knothole in her plank floor and eased down to place her eye against the opening.

"He's quite a puny fellow," her father was saying.

She watched as the three men laid out the body on her father's work table. Her heart raced in the realization that her father was about to perform a much forbidden dissection.

"He was from the prison. Died just this morning," the other physician was saying. Mary waited for some further comment about the cadaver, but none came.

"What news do you bring from Paris?" her father asked his friend.

"The news is much the same as it is here. The Italian Fever has nearly emptied the halls of our great university. Many of your old acquaintances are gone, ravaged by the terrible disease. 'Tis sheer madness, and the horror of it is enough to make me risk the church's disapproval and—"

"And death," the third man added. "Whether it comes by the hand of the church or this destructive disease—'tis certain one or the other will claim us."

Guy Beckett nodded. "They think to frighten us with reproaches of hell for the single action of seeking to know the human body better."

"I have seen the likes of hell," the man replied. " 'Tis in France. Marseilles is deserted. So many lives were lost last year, there were scarcely enough left to bury the dead. Nearly all those who remain have suffered one malady or another."

" 'Tis rapidly turning that way here in England," Guy stated with deep sorrow. "As the weather has warmed, more and more cases are evident, and yet by what means? We have so little knowledge regarding this matter, and clearly there is nothing in the handful of books available to me."

"Feel not at loss for this. There is nothing in Paris either. We have concluded, however, 'tis most likely a planetary conjunction. In the year of our Lord 1345, March the twentieth to be exact, the planets of Saturn, Mars, and Jupiter were aligned. 'Tis well documented."

"I heard our good colleague Dr. Dupré speak of this. He believed it to have corrupted the atmosphere," Guy replied.

"Aye, but alas our friend has also succumbed to this plague," his friend added.

Mary ached for her father. He had tried so hard to save the villagers from this sickness, and now he had lost another good friend. There seemed to be no reason for the illness. It struck young and old, rich or poor. It mattered not who you were. The plaguing fever with its horrible blackening marks came just the same.

"You will take down what we find here," Mary's father stated. She saw him reach across the table with one of his ledgers. There was no way of knowing to whom he had just directed his order, but Mary presumed it to be the unknown third man.

Since she had been a child, Mary had worked alongside her father to learn about illnesses and healing. Her father had studied at the University of Paris and was quite knowledgeable in the field of medicine. Many came to seek his advice, and often the scene that set itself below her was repeated with other friends and fellow learners. He had a great craving for knowledge, especially the knowledge to save human lives. It was a passion for her father. It was a passion for Mary, as well.

"See here," her father's muffled voice stated from behind a birdlike mask. Physicians had taken to wearing the masks when working on the truly ill. Because of this they were often called beak doctors. "The buobon area shows the engorged nodes."

Mary remembered from her Greek studies that buobon meant groin.

Frustrated that she couldn't view this part of the dead man's body, Mary concentrated on the man's neck and upper torso, noting the swollen glands there as well. It was certainly the bubonic plague, she surmised, although only physicians called it so.

She wondered how rapidly the disease had claimed its victim. Some people went to bed perfectly healthy one night and never woke up again. Others lingered for days and died in bizarre, frenzied terror. Mary shuddered and tried to concentrate on her father's voice. She had to learn as much as she could or she would be no help to the people around her.

Her father was just making a long incision in the man's abdomen when a loud ruckus broke out in the night. Angry shouts filtered up to her room, causing Mary to spring to her feet and dart to her window. Easing the shutter back, she peered into the dark.

"Come out, Beckett. Yer doin' the devil's work. 'Tis an unholy thing, and we mean to be no part of it!" Mary recognized the voice of the village butcher.

Another voice joined the first. "You cursed us all, and now our children be dyin' from the fever. God has cursed us because of you!"

"No," Mary moaned and leaned back from the window. What would happen if the villagers stormed the house and found the cadaver? They blamed her father for not having the answers to the disease, which claimed more lives daily. They eyed him suspiciously because neither he nor his daughter had fallen ill from the plague. Now they formed an angry mob, and there would be no reasoning with them.

Mary hurried downstairs to warn her father, but he was already approaching the door. "Get thee to safety, Child," he whispered and motioned her away from the door.

"I will not see you harmed," she cried and felt the rough hands of the stranger move her away from her father.

"We will go with him," the man assured her, and Mary could only nod and allow it to happen.

The three men went outside to meet the crowd, while Mary wondered what possible good she could do. Voices raised in anger. The hatred startled her, but not more than the people's despair. From the background came a wailing of women who no doubt had lost more loved ones than they could bear, and Mary felt their heartache as fiercely as if it were her own. Had she not nursed their sick children? Had she not seen them die one after the other?

The sound of rocks being thrown at the house sobered Mary. What was she to do? What could she do?

Hurrying from the front room, Mary made her way to her father's workshop. She pulled out a large traveling bag and began to fill it with bottles of medicinal herbs and instruments. The crude assortment was limited, but important, and

Mary could not let it fall into the wrong hands. Neither, she thought, could she allow her father's years of hard work to fade away. If the very worst were to happen this night, she would be the only hope of keeping her father's studies alive. She pulled open the cupboard where her father kept his journals and hurriedly gathered them.

The noise outside grew louder. Calls for killing the trio struck terror in Mary's heart. Suddenly she knew there was no hope of ever seeing her father again. She crammed the journals into the bag, added whatever else looked useful, and hoisted the bag to her shoulders.

Escaping the madness was all she could think of, but when Mary moved toward the door, her gaze fell upon the face of the dead man. He was younger than she'd thought him to be. How sad that he should die so horribly. Without thought as to why she did it, Mary reached down and pulled a linen cloth over the body. Somehow she felt comforted by this simple act. Somehow it seemed the only normal thing to do in the midst of such chaos.

Taking her cloak, Mary slipped out the back door. She could still hear her father trying to reason with his neighbors and thought for a moment that she might go to his aid.

" 'Tis a natural fear you have, but anger will not heal your children. You must return to your homes and allow me to come and bring you medicines."

"Your medicine may well be the death of us," a woman cried. "My child lived and breathed before you and your witch of a daughter came to my house with your precious potions."

At that comment, Mary realized she would be less than welcome should she appear at her father's side. She raged within at the thought that these people, once friends, could be so blind in their superstitions. *If only they could see the truth,* she thought sadly.

Forcing herself into the dark cover of the forest, Mary watched the scene play itself out. "Witch, indeed," she muttered. "Just because I find no value in the babblings of the priest and work to learn healing alongside my father, they think me a witch."

As if having heard Mary's thoughts, another woman screeched through the noise. "Ye be indentured to the devil, hisself. I have seen with my own eyes."

"What say you to that?" the butcher shouted to Guy Beckett.

"I am innocent of such a charge, as are my good colleagues and daughter. I seek to learn of the human body in order to heal it. Nothing more. Nothing less."

" 'Tis a heretic, he is," the woman yelled. "He mutilates the flesh of the dead!"

"Heretic! Heretic!" the cry went up from the masses.

They stormed the house, taking Guy and the other two men with them. Mary noted that the third man was only moved from his place after several villagers took hold of him.

There was no sense in lingering, Mary knew. She slipped deeper into the woods and made her way to the top of the hillside, where she hoped she could somehow view the fate of her father and home. The mob would find the cadaver, and the priest himself would see the house burned to the ground. No reasoning, no amount of pleading could bring her father back from certain death.

Struggling with the bag, she wiped away tears and pushed forward. She had just made the top of the hill when the house erupted into flames.

"No!" she cried, clutching the bag to her breast. Her cloak caught the wind and billowed out behind her. " 'Tis not fair, God!" She shook her fist to the sky. "You have never been for me or him! Now he is dead. Is that Your price? You have taken him from me, and now I am alone. Where comes the justice or good in that?"

The villagers were chanting and raging at the burning house. It was more than Mary could bear to witness, and without a second glance over her shoulder, she pushed on into the night and the sheltering haven of thick English forest.

The moon was well into the western skies when Mary stopped running. Pain wove its way through her body, making breathing almost impossible. Everything hurt, but she wanted it to. The numbness in her heart threatened to consume her body. She wanted to hurt, wanted to feel anything rather than lose herself in emptiness.

Mary fell upon the ground and cried in agony. Nothing had prepared her for the death of her father. Nothing she'd experienced in the wake of the plague had terrified her as did this night.

What should she do? Where could she go? Most of her father's friends were in Paris, and she had no coin to make her way there. Her mother, long dead in child-bearing, had no kin, and other than her father's mother, a woman he despised for her religious rhetoric, she had no one.

Feeling her breathing steady, Mary forced herself to sit. She could see nothing but black empty spaces and knew she was a great distance from the next village.

"I dare not go anywhere I am known," she muttered aloud. "If they know me not to be dead, they will simply seek to finish the job."

She clutched the bag close to her and scoffed at her own foolishness. " 'Tis a sorry pilgrim I am," she mused. No food, no coin. Only a bag filled with herbal remedies, useless instruments, and her father's medical journals.

"Your grandmother sought her beliefs, and I sought mine," Mary remembered her father saying. "She believed her God could produce miracles just like that." He had snapped his fingers before Mary's eyes.

"But why do we never journey to see her?"

Her father had shrugged his shoulders. "Most likely she would not have us. I scoffed at her God and chose a more valid means of study. Science. When I left for the university, she was greatly disappointed in me."

"Then she forbade you to come home?" Mary had questioned.

"Nay, I forbade myself."

The memory faded, leaving Mary more lonely than ever. She had only one choice. She would go north and seek out her grandmother. All she remembered was that Lady Beckett lived near York. Surely that small knowledge would be enough to help Mary find her. Then a terrible thought crossed Mary's mind. Her father had not been a young man. Surely his own mother would be dead by now, if not by old age, then from the plague fever.

" 'Tis the only choice I have," Mary reasoned. "I cannot go back. I must go forward. Mayhap my grandmother will welcome me."

Clouds gathered overhead and blocked out the little bit of moonlight. Foreboding overtook Mary, causing her to draw her knees to her chest with the bag lodged awkwardly between. She pulled the cloak tight as if to ward off the uneasy sensations.

" 'Tis sorry I am, Father. I know you'd not want me going to Grandmother's home. I have naught but this and can see no other way. Please do not be angry with me."

She rocked back and forth, tenderly stroking the bag, feeling the presence of her father in his last earthly possessions. Somehow she would find the strength to go on. Somehow she would take her father's work forward and use his understanding to help others.

Succumbing to her misery, Mary slumped to the ground and rolled into a ball around the bag. She had to go on for the sake of the only man she had ever loved. If only she could make it to her grandmother's home, all would certainly be well.

Chapter 2

Sir Peter Donne had always been popular among the ladies and gambling houses. He'd known his fair share of time with both and never missed a chance to grab the best life had to offer. From the unruly brown curls that met the collar of his tunic to the well-trimmed mustache and beard, Peter Donne was all man and all charm.

He was a head taller than most men, and his shoulders were broad and thick with muscle. He'd spent his years since turning ten and five in service to King Edward III of England, and now after seven years of such devotion to king and country, Peter had come home.

But 'twas a changed England to which the man returned, and in like, 'twas a changed man who returned to England. Gone was the cocky youth who had charmed and lied his way across Europe. Gone, too, was the wit and roguish behavior. Peter had seen too much death and too many horrors.

Stepping onto the dock, he glanced around him and noted the faces colored by fear and anguish. It was the same wherever he went. Most of Europe had seen thousands dead from the dreaded plague, and now he could see that the same was true of England. Already he smelled the stench of death. Where would it end?

Part of him wanted nothing more than to get back on the ship and sail away. But where could one sail to escape the terror of everyday life? No, his allegiance to Edward demanded that he stay. Besides, running away from a fight had never been Peter's style.

He pressed on, passing the scant crew of dock workers and fishmongers. Most seemed to eye him with relative disinterest, but occasionally a surprised man would look up to see the regal king's man in his short tunic of braided leather over dark wool and hose. His well-muscled legs betrayed his athletic prowess, and no one who observed him doubted that there was still a good fight left in Peter Donne. But more than that, Peter represented health and prosperity—something many folks only dreamed of these days.

Moving away from the docks, he wound his way through the narrow city streets. Here between the shops and alleyways, people moved with single-minded purpose. Some held posy bouquets to ward off the smell, while others simply used rags to cover their mouths and noses. Peter grimaced at the stench, but did neither. It had been the same in France.

The same stricken look had crossed the channel to mar the faces of the

English as well. Crying could be heard in the streets and, as Peter moved deeper into the populated sections of town, he found the sight he'd most dreaded to see. The plague dead themselves lay in wait upon the curb for the body collectors to bury them en masse.

Such scenes had stolen Peter's youth from him. This horror of everyday life caused him to consider each waking moment with question and sleep away each night in unspoken terror.

He forced himself to ignore the dead. He could do naught for them, and the smell, so overpowering even without the added discomfort of seeing the corpses, caused Peter to hasten his step. But where could he go? There was no place to avoid this confrontation. Even the houses were marked with crucifixes and the words, "Lord have mercy on us."

A filthy beggar woman approached Peter and cried out, "Alms, for food. Alms, Sire, please."

Peter eyed her cautiously. He'd thought her quite old when she'd first approached him, but as she stretched her hand out to his face, he realized she wasn't much older than he was. He reached into a small bag on his belt and produced a coin. It wasn't much, but the woman blessed him for it and offered him a charm to keep him from the plague. It was little more than a rotten piece of cloth, but she swore it had been blessed by the archbishop and that it would keep him from evil.

Peter nodded and hastened away from the woman. When he'd crossed the alleyway and was well out of sight, he tossed the material to the cobblestone street and tried to forget the pain-stricken look in the woman's eyes.

"Lookin' for a warm bed, Luv?" a voice called from a nearby doorway.

Peter looked up to find another haggard woman. This one also sought to make a coin, but not in the manner of the first. "Nay, 'tis no rest for the likes of me," he said, trying to sound good-natured. The woman shrugged her shoulders and let him pass without further comment.

Where had all the beauty gone? he wondered. Were there no charming ladies in velvets and satins to feast his eyes upon? And if there were, would he find any comfort in their presence? Once such diversion would have been uppermost in his mind, but now 'twas a distant memory of another time. . .another man.

Peter picked up his pace. At this rate his squire and armor would precede him to the king. Reaching King Edward suddenly became Peter's focus. He'd summoned Peter from France and beckoned him to make haste. The matter troubled Peter, but he would not share his concerns with his squire or any of their other traveling companions. If Edward sought him for a task, Peter would take the duty on with honor and be true to his knights' calling. Still, Peter knew he had little heart for any task. How could he give himself over to any job when the issue of his own mortality refused to be pushed aside? *Will duty and honor mourn me when I am dead and gone?* Peter wondered. Had he wasted his life upon the battlefield, fighting against a people who had never wronged him?

So many things had been clear before this confounded sickness had taken the world captive. At one time, Peter had known what he wanted from life. *Now,* he thought with a harsh laugh, *I have no thought for life because death consumes my time.* Staring with hard, cold eyes at the madness around him, Peter realized that death was consuming much more than time.

Arriving at the palace, Peter was confronted by King Edward's chamberlain. "His majesty refuses to be disturbed by anyone," the short, squat man told Peter.

"Is he ill?"

"Certainly not!" The man seemed surprised by Peter's question.

Patience had never served well at Peter's side. "What then is to be my task?"

"His Majesty wishes you to go out upon the land. You will take this," the man handed Peter a thin parcel, "to the abbey outside of York. I will give you the name of the abbott and a letter of introduction."

"For this I returned to England?" Peter's surprise was clear. "Have you no other errand boys?"

"Aye, but His Majesty called for you." The chamberlain was indignant at Peter's questioning. "His Majesty requires a greater service of you. You are to take account of the devastation upon the land. As you pass on your way to York, the king desires that you make a written account. In each monastery and town you will seek out those in authority and learn the numbers of their dead."

"Am I to go alone?"

"Aye, there are scarcely enough in service here to send you with an army." The chamberlain took advantage of his station and pressed the issue. "You are to move swiftly and be not hindered by even so much as your squire."

"But I have need of my squire," Peter protested. Things were definitely not going the way he'd hoped.

"The king has need of him here. You are to be given a swift horse, provisions for the journey, and this." The man dropped a small bag of coins upon the table. "There is enough money here to meet any need you may have."

"Money?" Peter laughed at this strange turn of events. While money still held its power, it meant so little in the face of sickness. It could not buy a cure. With so many already dead, the fields went untended and food was fast becoming scarce. For those who had something to eat, no amount of coin could entice it away. One could not eat silver and gold.

The chamberlain had clearly reached the limits of his tolerance. "I will inform His Majesty that you are well on your way."

Peter locked eyes with the man for a moment. He saw both fear and longing within the older man's gaze. *How alike we are*, Peter thought. Both of them were questioning the sense of this trip, but neither could speak on the matter and neither had a choice about whether it would take place.

Peter picked up the bag, added it to his belt, and nodded. "The journey should prove tedious, nevertheless I will endeavor to fulfill my duties. Give the king my word of honor on the matter."

Peter happily left the city, not because of the task before him, but because of his desire to escape the sights that lay before his eyes. The city that had once nurtured him now smothered him and drained his strength. He knew the roads would be congested with pilgrims and other travelers, but on horseback he could move faster than most and soon he would leave all of them behind. Perhaps the open countryside would relieve him of the growing burden in his heart.

But the burden only grew as Peter stared into the faces of his fellow travelers. They all seemed to ask each other, "Why am I here? And to where should I go?"

Peter had contemplated like questions for many miles. His youth made him eager to work, but he'd grown weary of killing and destroying. Where man left off dispensing death, the plague had pushed ahead. The sickness had spread from Italy to France and now to England. There was little hope of escaping its effects, yet the people on the road were proof enough of the desire to try.

Peter slowed his mount to a trot and noted another band of travelers ahead on the road. They all wanted to forget what lay in the city, but where could any of them go to erase those memories? There were so many questions. If only there were answers.

The first night of his journey found Peter taking refuge in a rundown ale house. The proprietor showed him to a sectioned-off room and pointed to a straw-filled mattress. Exhaustion so claimed him that Peter completely ignored the stench of previous use and fell into a deep sleep.

The next night found him better off, barely making it in time to pass through the Trumpington Gate into Cambridge. People eyed him suspiciously but moved out of his way.

He reined back on the horse in front of the Red Boar Inn. It looked to be a decent enough place to stay. Peter paid a young boy to care for his horse and offered him another coin if he had the horse waiting for him at dawn's first light. The boy, a filthy child who looked as though he slept his nights in the stable as well, happily complied.

Peter grabbed his things and hurried inside the inn. His body ached from the long hours upon the trail and his stomach growled in protest at the aroma of stew and fresh bread.

"Be needin' a room, Milord?" the innkeeper asked.

"First a meal, then a room," Peter replied, running a hand through his sweat-soaked hair. "Perhaps a bath?"

"For coin, me wife can fill a kettle for ye, but we have no tub."

"I will pay extra for a tub." The words surprised the proprietor, as well as Peter. He'd not thought about a bath until that moment, but now the idea consumed him. He tossed a coin to the innkeeper, and immediately the man became devoted to Peter's needs.

"Ye can count on me to see to it, Milord. Let it ne're be said the Red Boar could not care for its own." He turned from Peter to call out, "Josiah!"

A boy of about twelve appeared in the doorway. "Aye, Father?"

"Take the tub to the room at the top of the stairs. Then see to it that ye fill it with hot water. Leave two bucketfuls besides." The boy nodded and hurried to do his father's bidding.

"No tub, eh?" Peter said with a hint of a smile. He'd learned early on that things were seldom what they appeared.

" 'Tis not often requested," the innkeeper said with a shrug. "I forget its existence at times."

From the smell of the man, Peter knew he spoke the truth. "I want food brought to the room. Here." He tossed the man another coin and watched as his eyes grew large. It was twice the price he'd thought to ask. "Later, I will desire to speak with you privately."

"As ye wish, Milord." The man hurried to show Peter to the room and nearly knocked his son down when the boy rushed through the doorway.

Water sloshed out from the buckets, but was quickly soaked up by the dry plank boards of the floor. Deep cracks from years of wear seemed to suck up the liquid as though it were a thirsty dog lapping water. Peter tossed his provisions bag to the small bed and began to remove his clothes. After two more trips, the boy had sufficiently filled the tub and Peter waved him away when he returned with two more buckets of steaming water.

" 'Tis enough, leave them and go."

The boy dropped the buckets beside the tub and hurried out of the room. He'd no sooner gone, however, when a knock came upon the door, and Peter, wearing only his woolen hose, opened it to find the innkeeper.

"Me missus sent these, Milord." The man held up a linen towel and sliver of soap.

"Thank your good woman for me," Peter said with only a hint of irritation in his voice. He turned to close the door, but the man held out his hand.

"I have yer food, as well." He reached down to the floor and brought up a tray.

Peter's stomach growled loudly at the sight of the thick stew, bread, and drink. "Again, my thanks." This time the man did nothing to stop him from closing the door.

Peter put the tray beside the tub, grabbed a chunk of the bread, and dipped it into the bowl. With one hand he filled his mouth and with the other he discarded his hose. Steam from the bath beckoned him, and with one fluid movement, Peter immersed himself in the water, still chewing the stew-soaked bread.

He lost track of time. Soaking in the tub seemed to ease away the memories of the past few weeks. It had been a great many weeks since he'd enjoyed a hot bath and a real bed. With the penetrating heat soothing his tired muscles, Peter began to forget about the outside world and concentrated only on his food and bath. Perhaps there were still some pleasures in life.

Hours later, the innkeeper returned and, with Peter's nod of approval, commanded his son to remove the tub and empty tray.

"Ye wished to speak with me?" The man seemed nervous, and Peter couldn't help but smile.

"That I did, my good man. I am about the king's business."

At this the man's eyes nearly bugged out of his head. "The king himself? 'Tis a fine day when this sorry lot keeps company with one of the king's own men."

Peter nodded. " 'Tis my hope you will aid me in my duties."

"Anything."

"I will be traveling about the town tomorrow. 'Tis the king's desire that I account for the dead and the number of sick among your town. I will need a guide, perhaps your son. What was his name?"

"Josiah, Milord, and he would be happy to assist ye. Why he knows this town like the rats themselves."

"Good. I must go to the churches."

"There be thirteen parish churches," the man responded with genuine eagerness. "Ye'll hear that for yerself in the morn. The bells will ring morrow-Mass, and such a ruckus could wake the dead."

Peter nodded. The man no doubt had forgotten that Peter, under service to the king, would have heard just such a ruckus in London and any other number of cities before coming to Cambridge.

"I can send Josiah in the morning."

Peter dug into the bag on his belt and produced another coin. "Take this for your trouble. The boy will be with me throughout the day."

"Aye!" the man exclaimed with a bow. "Will ye hang your shield upon our door?"

Peter knew it was customary for persons of importance to place some symbol of their arrival outside the inn door. He, however, had little interest in announcing his presence and shook his head. "Nay, 'twill not serve either of us for good. I leave on the morrow after making my inquiries."

"Ye cannot hope to do it all in one day. Mayhap another night here. . ."

"Nay. I will leave on the morrow. Speak naught of this to anyone."

Peter showed the older man out and fell across the bed without even bothering to undress.

Chapter 3

M ary hesitated at the sight of a small band of travelers. She longed for human companionship, yet she feared recognition. What if one of the villagers traveled among those she joined? With a sigh, she stared down from her hillside perch and contemplated what she should do.

"Ho! There on the hill."

Mary's head snapped up, realizing that one of the men below was addressing her. Slowly she got to her feet. It seemed her decision had been made for her.

" 'Er ye going north?" the man asked.

Mary slowly made her way down the slippery, dew-coated hillside before answering. "Aye, I am bound for York." She looked the sorry lot over, counting five in the group. One, the only woman, was evidently heavy with child.

"Ye can join up with our band," the man offered. "We be bound for the north as well. We seek the Lady of the Moors."

"Who?"

"Have ye not heard of her?" Mary shook her head and clutched her bag close. The man seemed genuinely surprised at this. He scratched his filthy chin and smiled. He was missing several teeth. "Well, 'tis no matter. Yer welcome to travel with us."

Mary eyed the group more closely. The four men were filthy, and the woman was no better. They had evidently traveled for some time by the looks of their ragged shoes. Then again, Mary realized, those were most likely the only shoes these people had known for some time. How strange she must look to them. She wore new shoes and a warm woolen cloak, which had cost her father a tidy sum.

"My father is dead," she offered, seeing them stare at her in unspoken questions. "I would greatly appreciate traveling with you. I can make myself useful, as well."

"How so?" the leader of the group questioned.

Mary pulled the bag out. "I am a healer. I will act as midwife to this fine woman when her time comes."

"Ye be a healer?" one of the other men questioned.

"Aye, 'tis true enough. My father was a great man of medicine. I learned at his side."

The band looked at her for a moment as if trying to decide if she spoke the truth or not. Finally the leader broke into another smile. " 'Twill be a pleasure then to have ye join us. To be sure, this woman will have need of ye. Her husband died a fortnight past." Mary gave the woman what she hoped was a sympathetic look. "Her name is Grace. This here be Ralph." The man pointed to a younger version of himself. "He is my son. And this be Edward and Galdren of Bristol. They are brothers."

"And who are you?" Mary questioned.

"I am James of Southhampton."

"I am Mary," she offered, refusing to add anything else.

The man glanced heavenward. "We'd best be off. The day is passing fast."

Mary traveled in silence, wondering at the devotion her companions felt for the mystical Lady of the Moors. They spoke of her with such reverence that Mary was hard pressed to not question them about this woman's existence. She sounded more the stuff of legends and fireside stories than a flesh-and-blood person.

For the most part, however, Mary simply kept her thoughts to herself, believing that her silence would serve her best. She was now a great distance from home, with nearly a week having passed since the night of her father's death. It was certain that these people would have no knowledge of her. After all, they were from cities well removed from her village, and none had so much as raised an eyebrow in question of her.

The hardest thing for Mary remained the uncertainty of where she was to go. Should she be unable to find her grandmother, what hope would there be? Her skills at healing would not keep her fed, for there were doctors throughout England. Men, well respected and some not so well thought of, were stingy with their practice. A woman would not find a welcome in the business of medicine. She could present herself as a midwife or herbalist, but her claim to anything more would be ignored.

" 'Er you alone in this world?" Grace asked her. They traveled side by side, Mary keeping pace with Grace's slow, lumbering strides. The men were well ahead of them, and it suited both women quite well.

"Aye," Mary replied. "I have a grandmother, but she may be dead by now."

Grace nodded. "I have no one." She ran her hand over her swollen belly. "No one but the child."

"When is the child's time?" Mary questioned.

"Soon," Grace replied, her brows knitting together in worry. " 'Twas my hope to reach the moor country before delivering."

"You needn't fear," Mary said, trying to offer reassurance. "I have delivered many a child into the world."

"You? But ye look to be a child yerself."

Mary wanted to laugh. She did not feel like a child. Fear, exhaustion, sorrow, and anguish had joined to age her at least ten years.

"My father was a physician. He was a great man, and I worked at his side." Mary's wistful tone betrayed her pain. "I wanted to learn to heal, but of course," she glanced around as though sharing some great secret, "as a woman, it will never be allowed."

"Aye," Grace nodded. "I cannot boast such knowledge. I be a simple woman. My husband died of the fever, and a more hideous death I have yet to witness. He was a weaver by trade, and we knew a good life." Grace's eyes misted over, and Mary felt the compelling urge to reach out and pat her arm. Something inside, however, kept her from offering the comfort.

"This be our firstborn," Grace continued. Her tone took on a new air, one of love and bittersweet joy. " 'Tis all I have now of my Gabe. I pray 'tis a boy with red hair like his father."

Mary smiled sadly, and this time she did reach out to touch Grace. "I am certain 'twill be a fine son or daughter, no matter which."

Grace sniffed back tears and said nothing more.

That night while sharing a meager supper of roasted hare, Mary listened to the tales woven by James regarding the Lady of the Moors. The group evidently thought the Lady a saint or angel in human form, and their praise of her was unrelenting.

" 'Tis said she speaks directly with God."

Mary scoffed at James's words. "Would not the church consider that heresy?"

James pushed back his greasy black hair and considered Mary's statement. "The Lady is no heretic. She may well be a saint."

"Mayhap she is a heavenly visitor," Edward offered.

"Aye, God Hisself may have put her here to help in our time of need. Mayhap she has been blessed with special power."

Mary shook her head. "I doubt seriously that this woman is capable of the great miracles on which you base your journey. 'Tis possible the woman does not even exist. You know this country runs full into its cups with stories and legends of old. Mayhap this great Lady of the Moors is yet another example."

"Nay!" James said adamantly. "She performs miracles. I have heard it told with my own ears."

"Yet you have never witnessed the same, have you?"

Mary's words seemed not to discourage the determined man. " 'Tis of no matter what I have or haven't seen. I have the faith to believe 'tis true. That is enough to make me journey north."

"I suppose each person needs something to believe in," Mary said thoughtfully.

"And what do you believe in, Mistress?"

Mary shook her head. "I wish I knew. I have seen cruelty at the hands of those who spout superstitious rhetoric and religious litany."

"Surely you do not doubt the church," Galdren spoke up.

Mary laughed. "I do not see that the church has kept England from the plague. Nor do I see where God's mercy is evident in the same." Bitterness edged her voice. "I may be burned alive for my doubts, but better to be honest in the face of death than live a lie."

The group stared at her in silence for a moment. Finally Grace put out her hand and spoke. " 'Tis only your great sorrow that causes you to speak thusly. God is still merciful, and though we be an evil people, well deserving of far worse, 'tis He alone who can aid us now."

Mary stared at the woman for several seconds before shaking her head. "I cannot believe God merciful in the face of this terror. Have you not seen the people? Have you not heard their cries and known their fears? You lost your husband to the plague—did he not writhe in the horror of it? Did you not stare into his eyes and see death itself stare back?"

Mary knew her words were cruel, but she couldn't seem to stop their flow. "All of you are hypocrites to call God merciful. If He cared so much, would He not at least spare the children? But, no, they are harder hit yet by the sickness and they suffer, too, from the loss of their parents. They are left behind to starve to death, when no one lives to care for them." Mary got to her feet. "I see no mercy. Seek your Lady of the Moors if you must, but fault me not for my disbelief."

She walked away from the group seething in her misery. How could they so calmly speak of God and His mercy? How could they put faith in One who had done nothing to prove Himself worthy of faith?

"Mary." It was Grace. "Mary, I know ye are hurting and 'tis sorry I am that your loss so consumes ye."

Mary turned to face the woman. Set against the distant glow of the campfire, she couldn't see Grace's features, but knew the kindness in her voice. "I am sorry for letting my temper better me."

"I know," Grace said, taking another step forward. "Mary, I have a favor to ask and I know I have no right."

"What is it?"

"Yer words caused me to think, and I fear for my child. If I should die, there is no one who will tend to its needs. Mary, would ye take the babe and see it cared for? I could not bear to leave this world knowing that my own would suffer as those ye described."

Mary instantly felt guilty for her outburst. *Poor Grace. 'Twas bad enough to be with child at a time of such great suffering and horror, but I have doubled her burden by painting a picture of hopelessness for the future, as well.*

"Grace, you will not die. I had no right to put such fear in your heart."

" 'Tis not a fear for me. I feel confident of my heavenly home, but the earthly one in which my babe might have to live is a frightful thought. For without a single soul to watch over him, he will die a painful death."

Mary could no longer bear the woman's worried tone. "I do not believe anything will happen to you, but if it eases your mind, I will care for the child if you should die."

"Thank you, Mary." Grace's words came out with a sob. "I thank God ye have come."

Mary shook her head and watched the woman struggle back down to the camp. *She thanks God for me? What absurdity, for I have done nothing but strain her mind and worry her heart. How could she thank God for one such as I?*

❧

Peter was mortified at the mounting number of deaths he recorded in his ledger. He had seen death upon the battlefield and watched good friends die within arm's reach, but this disease was something he could not understand. At least a known enemy could be faced and dealt with, but this enemy crept in unannounced and there seemed no way of defense.

He made his way alone, detesting the sights and sounds that assailed him, realizing with each and every step that death might well await him at the next turn.

The sun, high overhead, beat down on him, causing great beads of sweat to roll down his face. The leather cotehardie clung to the under tunic, making his chest feel bound and uncomfortable. Urging his horse into a brief gallop, Peter relished the breeze it created and ignored the pounding ache the jostling ride created in his head.

He approached the village of Byrnbough and reined back his horse to find that there was no village. Not in the true sense. Many of the buildings were nothing more than charred remains, while the houses and shops that stood bore no sign of life. An eerie feeling settled over Peter as he nudged the horse forward. He stared in complete disbelief at the ghostly sight.

Where were the people? Where were the shopkeepers? Did none remain to greet the day?

The horse whinnied nervously, sensing the destruction and oddity around him. Peter gave his mount a reassuring pat, wishing silently that he might find some reassurance for himself. The small village had once been home to some two hundred souls, but now only emptiness and silence held residence.

Peter brought the horse to a halt at the small church in the center of the village. There seemed to be some notice tacked to the door, and Peter quickly dismounted and tethered his horse in order to take a look.

"To those souls who may pass this way, know now on this day that the village of Byrnbough is no more. May God have mercy on our souls." Peter read the note twice to make certain he understood. Had the plague claimed the entire village?

He scouted the remains and found nothing but graves and deserted homes.

Returning to his horse, Peter took out his ledger and wrote down that the entirety of Byrnbough had been either deserted or given over to the plague.

Pressing on, he found the scenario repeated twice more in smaller villages. The reality of it all caused him to feel light-headed. He, a knight of the king, a man who'd done battle in Crecy but three years past, was nearly undone by the deafening silence of forsaken towns.

Death seemed to stretch its bony fingers closer at every stop. Each time, Peter sensed his own life ebbing away. What madness was this? He had gone nearly two days without a single soul to talk to. Would he find nothing but the same ahead of him?

He prepared to leave the latest scene of devastation when a sound reached his ears. It seemed to be the cry of a child. Peter maneuvered his horse to the alleyway but lost the sound. Retracing his steps, he secured his horse and went on foot.

He stopped, listened, and heard the sound again. Yes, he truly had heard the crying. It wasn't madness, he told himself. Peter picked his way through the streets, making note of the discarded items. A churn, a broken chair, several tubs, and empty casks were among the debris. It looked as though the owners had fled in haste without concern for their meager possessions.

Rounding the place where the butcher's shop had once known business, Peter spied the child. He was no more than seven or eight. Sprawled out across the body of a woman, the boy wept inconsolably and didn't even notice Peter until he was upon him.

"Son." Peter murmured the word, gently touching the boy's shoulder.

The child jumped to his feet in fear. He stood guard over the woman and refused to move, in spite of Peter's obvious interest in whether the woman lived or died.

"Is this your mother?" Peter questioned. "Is she sick?"

The boy's body jerked from sobbing, and his eyes were swollen from hours of crying.

"Son, I want to help you. I will not hurt her. I am a knight of the king, and I give you my pledge."

The boy seemed to take note of this. "She went to heaven," the child finally said and stepped back.

Peter saw no sign of blackened marks or swollen glands and wondered what had taken the young woman's life. "Was she sick for a long time?"

"No," the boy said, fighting back his tears and wiping his nose on his ragged sleeve. "She just fell down and never woke up."

"Was she your mother?" Peter asked gently, reaching out to touch the boy's shoulder again. This time he didn't resist.

"Aye," the boy said, before giving into his tears. "I want her to come back."

Peter felt strangely moved at the child's declaration. Had he not lost his own mother at an early age? He had never been allowed to give much thought to her passing, remembering his father's severity regarding Peter's childish tears. His father had been an advisor to the king, and he'd wanted no sissy for a child. Peter remembered a harsh reprimand and promise of punishment if he should so much as shed a single tear at her funeral mass.

Without thought to what he did, Peter scooped up the child into his arms and nestled the boy against his chest. The boy did not resist, but instead seemed to cling to Peter as though he were the last soul remaining on earth.

Peter had no idea how long he stood there. He stroked the boy's fine golden hair and spoke words he couldn't remember until the boy was finally sleeping and silent. What now? Peter wondered. What should he do with the child? He certainly couldn't leave him behind, and yet where could he find help for him in the midst of the sickness? No one would have the time or inclination to care for a small boy such as this one.

Spying a wagon filled with straw, Peter gently placed the sleeping child there and went in search of a shovel. He planned to bury the woman before the child awoke, then perhaps he could decide what was to be done.

With each shovelful of dirt, Peter thought of the woman he buried and wondered by what means she had died. There was no mark upon her body or swollen bulges at the neck. Peter was by no means indiscreet enough to uncover her body and examine it in full. He had no medical training, and it seemed most indecent to even wonder at the matter. She was dead, and that was enough.

He finished tossing the last bit of dirt on the mound and then wondered at the lack of a priest to offer some service. Not knowing what else to do, Peter lifted his eyes heavenward and spoke. "Jehovah God, though I have not been a man who has spoken Your name oft, I have no other choice but to give this woman over to Your care. Have mercy on her soul."

When he looked down, Peter saw that the boy had joined him.

"Will God take care of my mother?" he asked soberly.

"Aye," Peter replied, uncertain whether he believed it or not. He smiled at the child. "What is your name?"

"Gideon," the boy replied.

"Well, Gideon, it looks like you will travel with me now. Have you anything to take along the journey?"

The boy shook his head but looked up with hopeful eyes. "You will not leave me here?"

"Nay, Gideon. I will not leave you." At the look of relief on the child's face, Peter suddenly knew that no matter the cost, he would not allow this child to be parted from him. Perhaps it was the fact he himself had been orphaned at an early age. Perhaps it was nothing more than honor and the vows of his knighthood.

Whatever the cause might be, Peter knew his feelings were foreign to him, and while they troubled him deeply, they also provided a sense of strange comfort in a world gone mad.

"Come." He took the boy by the hand and led him back to where the horse stood. "We must ride hard if we are to keep the light of day. There is a place not far where we will seek shelter." Peter hoisted Gideon up with him onto the horse's back.

"I never rode a horse before," Gideon admitted.

"You will find it the very best way to travel," Peter answered with a smile.

Just as the sun dipped down below the horizon, Peter and Gideon arrived at the monastery. It seemed unnaturally quiet, and Peter presumed that it must be a time for prayers.

He lowered Gideon to the ground, dismounted, and rang the bell at the gate.

It wasn't long before a pale-faced monk appeared. He shuffled forward, looking gaunt and sickly. "God be with thee, Soul. What seektest thou?"

"A place to rest for the boy and myself. Perhaps a meal."

"This place is consumed with the fever," the man replied. "Ye cannot stay here."

"The plague has been our constant companion. Better to die here with the blessings of the good Lord than to meet our fate upon the roadway, eh?"

The monk shrugged and opened the gate. "Ye have been warned, but so be the will of the Lord God. Enter and know peace."

Later, with Gideon nestled snugly against him, Peter thought back on the words of the monk. The man had spoken of the will of God. *What might that be?* Peter wondered. He had spent long hours in church, made vows in the name of the Lord, and pledged upon the relics of long dead saints, but these actions had been cause for little thought in his heart.

Gideon moaned in his sleep, and soon little sobbing cries came in his restless slumber. Peter nudged the boy until he opened his watery eyes.

" 'Tis only a bad dream," he told Gideon. "You are safe here."

"My mother is gone," Gideon replied sleepily.

"Aye," Peter replied. "But I am with you."

"You will not go?"

Peter smiled at the groggy boy. "Nay, I will not go."

Chapter 4

Morning brought no hope. Peter, with Gideon ever at his side, found that most of the monks were consumed in various stages of the dreaded fever. The abbott himself lay near death, writhing and crying out in his misery.

"Have you food?" Peter asked the man who had admitted them the night before.

"There are stores of grain behind the bake house," the man replied. "If you seek a meal, I will show you the kitchen."

"Have all of your brothers fallen ill?" Peter questioned while they walked. He felt Gideon take hold of his hand, but said nothing. He squeezed the boy's fingers reassuringly and looked to the monk for an answer.

"Most have taken to their beds. Even now there are dead awaiting burial."

"Why is this?" Peter asked.

"No one has the strength to dig the graves," the monk replied sadly.

Peter nodded. "I will dig your graves. After we eat, you will show me what is to be done."

The monk seemed relieved at this declaration. "God has truly sent you. I will remember you in my prayers this day."

Digging graves became a consuming task. Peter toiled throughout the day, seeing no end in sight. The stench made him ill, but he forced his hands to continue turning the spadefuls of dirt. Gideon brought him water to drink, and when the sun appeared high overhead, a monk appeared with hard bread and cheese.

"The abbott has died," the man stated simply and turned to walk away. He'd barely taken two steps when he collapsed to the ground.

Peter jumped up out of the hole and ran to the man. "He still lives, Gideon," he said, noting the anguish in the boy's eyes. Lifting the monk in his arms, Peter told Gideon to collect their food and go to the kitchen. "I will come there when I have seen this good man put to bed."

"You will not leave me?" Gideon asked, his voice quivering.

"Nay, Gideon. I gave you my word. I will not leave you."

Peter found two monks in the infirmary who had not yet succumbed to the fever. He delivered their dying brother to them with great remorse. "He has been good to me. I would know his name."

"He is Brother Francis," the man nearest Peter answered. "I am Brother Jude," he added.

"I am Peter. Sir Peter Donne, upon the king's business. I have been charged with assessing the extent of the fever and delivering into the hands of the abbott near York a package from His Majesty, King Edward."

"We are honored to share our humble home with you, Sire," Brother Jude said somberly. "As you may well see, however, we are most compromised by this grave circumstance."

"Aye. I know it full well. I have this past morn buried many of your dead."

"Alas, we may but bless them and sew them into graveclothes," the monk said sadly. " 'Tis no time for proper mass or tribute."

"Brother Francis had just told me of the abbott's death."

"Yea, but I fear we are too weak to even ring the bells. Surely God has turned His face, this day, from the sight of His children."

The days that followed passed much the same. Peter relieved his burial duties with short trips into the fields to hunt for meat. Gideon, ever fearful of desertion, watched Peter leave on these trips and would not touch a bit of food or even speak until his companion returned.

On the fourth day, Gideon awoke to a strange burning heat. He sat up in bed and realized that Peter still slept at his side. Reaching out a hand, Gideon found Peter hot to the touch.

"Peter," Gideon said, shaking the knight. "Peter, wake up."

The only sign of life came in the form of a moan. Gideon began to cry. "You said you would stay," he sobbed and fell against Peter's still form. "You said you would not go."

❈

"Push hard, Grace," Mary instructed. "The babe is nearly here." Mary knew the woman was exhausted. More than ten hours had passed since her labor had begun, and Mary feared for Grace's life and that of the child.

"I cannot do it, Mary," Grace panted, then let out a scream. "I cannot."

Mary silently contemplated the situation. There was naught that she could do, but let nature run its course. The babe's head was showing, but Grace had no energy to expel the child. She vaguely remembered her father speaking of a delivery where the woman had died, being too small to pass the child into life. He had then cut a larger opening and pulled the baby forth, allowing the child to live.

"Grace, you must listen to me. The babe cannot be born without your help."

Grace barely opened her eyes, and when she did, they were filled with pain. "Remember your promise, Mary. Remember your promise."

"Grace, you will not die. I will not let you die!" Mary's voice rose anxiously. "I will get one of the men to help. They can push the child from on top, while you push from within."

Grace did not argue, and Mary took that as a sign of compliance. She saw that the men were congregated some twenty yards away, uneasy with the childbirth and Grace's screaming.

"James!" Mary called and moved across the open ground. "I need your assistance."

James separated from the group and met Mary halfway. "What be ye needin'?"

"You must help me with Grace. I need your strength to push the child out. Grace is not faring well, and I fear for her life and that of the babe."

James nodded and followed Mary to where Grace lay strangely still. "We be too late, Mistress. She has already departed."

Mary looked down at Grace. "Nay!" she cried and threw herself down. "You cannot die, Grace."

"She is gone," the man said, crossing himself. "May God have mercy on her soul and on that of the wee one."

"Nay!" Mary reached into her father's bag and pulled out a knife. "I will not let it be so."

James stared in horror and fascination as Mary did what her father had once described and pulled the baby from Grace's body. For a moment, Mary feared she'd waited too long. The tiny baby girl lay blue and lifeless in Mary's hands. Quickly, Mary cleared the child's mouth and began vigorously rubbing the baby with a warm, wet cloth.

It started only as a tiny squeak, but then a mewing cry could be heard. Before long a lusty wail bellowed out from the baby, and Mary smiled satisfactorily at James. "She lives!"

"Yea, but the mother is no more. Mayhap it would have been better for the child to have stayed with her, for who will now care for it?"

"I will," Mary announced firmly. "I made Grace a promise."

"Yea, but the sickness is all around us. 'Twould be best for ye to leave the wee one here with its mother. Ye have no milk to give it nourishment and surely no nurse can be found upon the road."

"I made a promise to Grace. I will not break my vow."

James stepped forward and knelt down beside Mary and the baby. "The child will die—if not from hunger, then from the fever. The little ones are too weak to fight it." His soft words pierced her heart.

"I will find her food," Mary declared, wiping the eyes of the infant. "I will care for her, James. I must. I gave my word."

They buried Grace near the place where she'd died. James pounded a crudely formed cross upon her grave, while the other men placed stones upon the dirt to discourage interest from the wild animals of the region.

Mary stood to one side, cuddling the baby. She had fed her a bit of honeywater, which seemed to satisfy the child for the time, but silently Mary wondered what she could do in the future. James had spoken correctly. The plague had a penchant for killing off the weak. And infant mortality itself held high numbers without the aid of epidemic sickness.

"Are ye ready?" James asked Mary softly.

"Aye, let us go." Mary reached down to pick up her father's bag, but James took it from her.

"Ye have the wee one to carry. I will take this for ye."

Just days before, Mary would have fought to the death anyone who would have tried to take her father's bag. The thought of even being parted momentarily from it had caused Mary to never allow it from her sight, but now things were different. The bag was, after all, not a living, breathing thing. It held precious memories and pieces of helpful, useful things, but it wasn't flesh and blood—unlike the child she cradled against her.

"Thank you," she whispered and followed James to where the others waited.

It was nearly dark when they spotted the monastery and completely black when they approached the open gate. A single black cloth fluttered against the post, causing all but Mary to shy away. The baby now awoke, whimpered, and cried for food.

" 'Tis the sickness," James announced, and the others nodded in agreement.

"I must find milk for the child," Mary said. She looked at the others who clearly would have no part of the monastery.

"We will travel on," James told her.

"Nay, I will stay here. Surely even a small monastery will have a goat or cow. I must feed the child."

"I will not risk my life on account of that baby," Edward stated. "I choose to go ahead."

"Aye," the others replied in unison.

"Very well, go. I chose to stay, and so we must part company here." Mary reached out and took her bag from James.

"God be with ye, Mary," James said softly. Even now the others were walking away from the gate. "I have come to care for ye. Are ye certain ye will not come ahead with us? You could leave the child here, for surely the monks will see to it."

Mary thought she'd misunderstood James's words. "Ye care for me?"

The darkness hid his face from her, but Mary heard the nervous cough he gave before continuing to speak. "I do. Will ye not leave the child and come north with us?"

Mary could scarce believe her ears. She'd never had a man declare his interest in her, and it was a most disturbing moment for her. Finally, her senses returned and she realized that James had no interest in her keeping the baby.

"I made Grace a promise," Mary murmured. "I cannot go with you." Her voice sounded neither regretful nor sorrowful.

"I suppose I understand. A man's life is only as good as his word. A woman must feel likewise. Good life to ye, Mary," he said and was gone.

Mary stood for a moment longer before ringing the bell at the gate. When no one appeared to answer her call, Mary pushed the gate open wider and stepped into the yard.

A strange silence rose to meet her, not unlike that of deserted villages she had known on her trek with James and Grace. Were they all dead? Was no one left alive to help her?

She crossed the yard and went into the first building she came to. "Is anyone here?" she called out. Nothing.

Pressing forward, she passed from one room into another and realized herself to be in a small chapel. Candles surrounding a crucifix burned on the altar, illuminating the room in a haunting mixture of shadows and golden light. At least someone lived to light them, Mary reasoned.

The baby cried in misery, and Mary knew that her first goal must be to find nourishment for the child. Exiting the building, she hastily walked to the next and found it locked. Moving on, she finally entered what appeared to be the kitchen. Placing her bag on the table, Mary went in search of food for herself and the child. There was bread—hard with age but edible—and a pot containing some type of soup. The fire beneath it was barely kindled, so Mary placed the baby on the stone floor beside her and stoked the fire into a hearty blaze.

"Are you an angel?"

The voice so startled Mary that she grabbed the baby and jumped to her feet. Spying the small boy in the doorway, she let out a sigh.

"I am called Gideon. Are you an angel?"

"Nay," Mary replied. "I am Mary Beckett." The baby screamed out in misery and Mary tried to shush her with a crust of the ancient bread. "Suck on this, little one. 'Twill not help much, but I am looking for what will."

"Why is your baby crying?" Gideon asked.

"She is hungry, and I have no milk. Do you know if there is a goat or cow that might feed her?"

Gideon looked thoughtful for a moment, then his eyes grew wide. "I have a friend. His name is Peter, and he is very sick. If you come help him, I will find food for the baby."

Mary looked down doubtfully. " 'Tis no game we play, Gideon. This child has scarce had a meal since her entry into the world."

"Please come. He promised he would never go away, but he is sick. Please. I will find food for the baby." Gideon's pleading was too much for Mary.

"Very well," she sighed. "Take me to your friend."

Mary took up her bag and followed the boy down a long, arched corridor.

The unsettling silence clung to every stone, and Mary found herself almost wishing she had followed James.

"Help me. Help me."

The voice called from the room at Mary's right. "Wait, Gideon," she called and stuck her head inside the room to see what the problem was.

It appeared to be an infirmary of sorts. Several beds were placed side by side, and in each one, a man lay in some stage of illness.

"Help me," the voice came again, and Mary went to the man who called out. "What can I do for you?"

"Water, please," the man cried out. "Water, please."

Mary spied a bucket and ladle near the door. Placing the baby on an empty bed, she went to bring water to the man. Gideon frowned disapprovingly but said nothing.

"Are all of you ill with the fever?" Mary questioned.

"Aye. We are most nearly all dead." The man drank only a small amount, with most of that dribbling down his chin and onto his linen gown.

Mary thought to instruct Gideon to assist her, but the boy was gone. With a sigh, Mary felt the man's forehead and noted the swelling under his ears.

" 'Tis the plague," she murmured to no one in particular. "Of that I am certain." There was nothing she could do but make them comfortable and watch them die. Hadn't she done as much in her own village?

Stoking up the fire and lighting several more candles, Mary wondered if there were others in the monastery who still lived. She turned to quiet the baby when Gideon appeared at the door, leading a small female goat.

The goat bleated in protest, but Gideon jerked the cord and came forward. "I found milk for the baby, now please come help Peter."

Chapter 5

Mary sat Gideon in one corner and gave him the baby to hold. "I must milk the goat," she said. "You will sit here and hold her. She will most likely cry, but hold her close and do not drop her."

Gideon nodded at the awesome responsibility. Mary smiled at his sober face. "You are a good lad, Gideon."

Next, she took up the goat and after searching the kitchen for a bucket, tethered the nanny to a table leg and began to milk her. When enough milk covered the bottom of the bucket, Mary took it up and poured it into a small wooden bowl. She had no idea whatsoever how to actually get the milk into the baby. She rummaged in her father's bag but found nothing that would aid her.

Hearing the baby cry inconsolably, Mary took up a small piece of linen cloth from her bag and dipped it in the milk. She held it up and watched as the milk dripped from the cloth. It just might work. She took the bowl and cloth and went to where Gideon fussed and talked to the angry baby.

"Here," Mary said, putting the bowl down and taking up the baby. "Let's see if this works." She dipped the cloth again in the milk, then put it on the baby's lips.

The baby cried all the harder and milk oozed down her cheeks and neck. Mary, not to be outdone, took hold of the infant's face very gently and forced the cloth into her mouth. The baby began to suck and, to both Mary and Gideon's relief, instantly quieted. Mary repeated the process with the cloth until the baby had fallen asleep. With great satisfaction, Mary smiled at Gideon, and he smiled back.

"Now will you come take care of Peter?"

"Aye, Gideon. Take me to your friend."

"He didn't wake," Gideon said sorrowfully. "He has been sleeping for a long time."

Mary nodded and positioned Gideon in a corner on the floor and handed the sleeping baby to him. "Hold her carefully, like I showed you."

Gideon possessively took hold of the child. "I like her. What do you call her?"

Mary suddenly realized that the baby had no name. "I do not have a name for her yet. Would you like to think on one while I tend your friend?" Gideon nodded enthusiastically.

Mary picked up her bag and went to Peter's bedside. She wasn't prepared for what she found there. In spite of his illness, Peter's face had lost none of its rugged charm. His beard was a bit overgrown, which rather added to his appearance, but it was his long dark lashes against tanned, weathered cheeks that drew Mary's attention. She instantly wondered what color his eyes might be.

She sat down beside him and ran a finger lightly along his face. It was hot, as she knew it would be. She checked his neck for swelling and found none. A good sign, she told herself.

"Gideon, how many days has Peter had the fever?" she asked, looking over her shoulder.

Gideon shrugged. "I do not know."

"But you think it has been several days?"

"I went to sleep four times," Gideon answered.

"Four times? Did you wait for it to get dark or did you nap during the day as well?"

"No, I waited for the dark. I went with the monks. They showed me how to put the wet cloth on Peter's head."

Mary looked around and spied the bowl of water and cloth. "You must have done a good job, Gideon. Where are the monks now?"

Gideon shrugged again. "Most are sick, but there be some in the building by the well."

Mary felt a sense of relief. Perhaps others were still alive. Turning her attention back to Peter, Mary checked his breathing and heartbeat. If it had been at least four days since he'd fallen ill, then surely it wasn't the plague. Mary had seen time and again the dreaded swelling of the nodes, and blackened marks appeared by the third day.

"He is not sick like the others," she told Gideon. "I will watch him and care for him, but you will have to help me."

"I can help," Gideon assured her. "I will take care of Anne."

Mary looked at him. "Anne?"

"That is the name I picked for the baby."

"Why Anne?"

"My mother's name was Anne," the boy said, and his eyes filled with tears. "She lives in heaven with God."

"What of your father?" questioned Mary, reaching out to take the baby from the boy.

"He died afore I was born."

"I am most sincerely sorry for that. He would be proud of what a fine young man you've grown up to be," Mary said, putting a hand on Gideon's cheek. "Weep no more, Gideon. Anne and I have need of you."

"You will call her Anne?"

"Aye, it is a fine name for her," Mary replied. "Will you help me make her a bed?"

"I know the perfect bed for her," Gideon said, jumping to his feet. He ran from the room and was gone only a matter of minutes before he returned with an empty wooden box. "The monks used this for bringing in vegetables from the garden."

Mary smiled. " 'Tis a perfect size. We must knock out the dirt and pad it with blankets."

"I can do it," Gideon said in an authoritative eight-year-old voice. He paused for a moment. "What are you called?"

"I am Mary."

"Like the mother of Jesus?"

Gideon's words surprised her. "I suppose 'tis true enough."

"My mother said Jesus came as a baby to the world. Do you think He was little like Anne?"

Mary did not know how to respond. She'd pushed aside thoughts of church and God for so very long. She had not been trained up in the way other children were. She knew various parts of church teaching, including the arrival of Christ to the world, but other knowledge was limited. "All babies," she finally said, "are born little."

Gideon nodded, satisfied with the answer. He went to work on Anne's little bed, leaving Mary in dumbfounded silence. *Why should it bother me?* Mary wondered. *I have lived these many years without concern about such matters. Father always said to place my trust in the real things of this world.* Mary looked down to the face of the sleeping baby. So tiny and frail, helplessly dependent upon someone bigger and stronger for the things of life. *Are we like that?* Mary wondered. *Be we frail beings who need an omnipotent God to watch over us? Or is it as Father said, we are creatures of our own making?*

Gideon soon returned with the box. It was prepared quite sufficiently. Even Mary agreed that she could not have done a better job. Gideon beamed with pride, while Anne slept contentedly in the vegetable box.

"I am going to see who else I might help," Mary told Gideon. "We will need to find supplies for the baby. Swaddling cloth to wrap her tightly so that she doesn't hurt herself by flailing her arms and legs and some other way to feed her."

"I can feed her like you showed me," Gideon reaffirmed.

"Aye, but there may yet be a better way. I will search it out. Will you stay here with Anne and Peter?" Mary questioned, glancing back at the form of the sleeping man.

"Aye," Gideon said, sitting down determinedly by the box. "I will watch over them, just like God watches over us."

Mary shook her head. "Why do you say that Gideon?"

He looked at her with a genuinely puzzled expression. "Say what?"

"That God watches over us. Have the monks here taught you to say it or perhaps your mother before she died?"

Gideon still looked at her in surprise. "Aye, they say it, too, but I know God is here."

Mary was intrigued. "How is this, Gideon?" She held her breath, awaiting the boy's response.

"Because He said He would be," Gideon replied without doubt. "In the Great Book, God said He would always be with us."

"The Great Book? You mean the collection of Scriptures the church uses?"

Gideon nodded enthusiastically. "I saw a bit of it. Brother Michael showed me. I cannot read the words, but my mother said that believing them was more important than just reading them."

"When did your mother tell you these things?" Mary could barely form the words. Gideon's faith filled her with a longing she could scarce understand.

Gideon's lips puckered a bit. " 'Twas when the people were dying. She told me not to be afraid. We belong to God and He promised He would be with us." The little boy took great comfort in the words and repeated them. "He promised."

Mary felt a trembling within. She left the room without another word and hurried to the kitchen. What manner of child was Gideon that he should shake her beliefs to the very core of her reasoning? *He is but a boy with a childlike grasp of decades of church rhetoric. His words mean little in the face of those of a great man such as my father,* she reasoned. *He repeats what he finds comfort in. Nothing more.*

Going to the hearth, Mary sampled the soup that warmed there. The weak broth of rabbit gave Mary an insatiable appetite. She found another bowl and filled it with soup, managing to capture a few of the elusive pieces of meat.

Drinking it while she stood near the fire, Mary could not let go the words of Gideon's faith. "He promised He would be with us," the boy had said in complete devotion to a God he had never seen. A God who had taken his beloved mother and many others before his young eyes.

How can you love a God such as this? Mary wondered. She finished the soup and thought of taking up another portion. Perhaps there were those who were too ill to feed themselves, she thought. *Best I go about the place first, and see for myself if there are any to be cared for.*

In her search, Mary found seven dead monks and another dozen ill with the fever. Two of those who were sick seemed actually to be recovering from their ills. Mary saw to it that they had nourishment and promised to figure a way to remove them to a room away from the others.

Giving this new challenge some thought, she returned to find Gideon faithfully sleeping beside Anne. He had made a pallet of straw and blanket for himself upon the hard stone floor. Mary checked Peter and found him cooler, but still he slept undisturbed by her touch. *Who is this man?* she wondered. *What caused him to travel this way?* She sat beside him and lifted his hand in hers. It was a strong hand, calloused and large, with long slender fingers. Somehow it comforted her to hold it in her own for a moment.

"Wake up, Peter," she murmured against his fingers, not even realizing that she'd brought his hand to her lips. "Wake up that I might at least know the color of your eyes."

The man stirred, moaning an incoherent word. Mary dropped his hand as though she'd been caught doing something wrong. How foolish. She got up from the bed and tucked his arm at his side. She turned to check on Anne and only then did she notice that Gideon had prepared a pallet for her beside him. It was small, but she recognized it as a most welcome sight.

Seeing that she could do no more good for the night, Mary gratefully sought the refuge of the blanket and straw. With a sigh, she shivered and pulled the blanket closer.

Gideon rolled over and opened sleepy eyes for only a moment. "I said my prayers," he murmured, snuggling close, then fell back to sleep.

Mary looked at the sleeping boy for a long time. His peaceful face troubled her. In the face of horror and adversity, this small boy seemed confident of something she could not begin to reason for herself. This was not church litany or papal discourse. This was faith in its purest and simplest form.

Chapter 6

Upon exploration, Mary found ten small rooms within the main building. Further investigation revealed a bake house, malt house, infirmary, dovecote, two chapels, and several storage buildings. And behind all of these were gardens, now desperately in need of care, and a great field left untended.

"Where are the people?" Mary asked one of the recovering monks. She knew that most monasteries were run just as castle lands. Instead of a great duke or earl, the abbott served as landlord to his tenants.

"Most are dead. The others have gone away in fear. When the abbott fell ill, they feared the curse of God was upon them and fled."

"And what do you believe, Brother James? Is the curse of God upon us?" Mary asked with intent interest.

The poor man seemed weary from just such contemplation. "I am of the mind that God allows His children to endure certain conflict for the purpose of strengthening and refining the good and destroying or redeeming the bad. Perhaps a great sickness is the only way in which God may attract the attention of some more stubborn souls."

"But if He be God, why should He stoop to the practices of man?"

The monk eyed her suspiciously. "Ye are not of a faith in His omniscience? Ye, a mere woman, would question the actions of God?"

Mary shrugged. "I daren't believe I deserve to be burned as a heretic, but blind obedience unto the church was not my father's way. I suppose now that he is dead, I am of an open mind for such matters. After all, my father's science did not keep him alive."

The monk nodded. "Nor could it. There is none save our God who has the ability to breathe life into flesh."

Mary thought on the words long after she'd left Brother James to sleep.

⤜⤝

Throughout the days that followed, Mary fell into an endless routine. Had it not been for Gideon, she would never have been able to accomplish much of anything. He proved to be quite capable at a number of tasks. He could milk the goat and feed the baby. He helped with the laundry of swaddling, which Anne seemed quite happy to keep dirty for them, and always he was devoted to Peter.

"Is he your kin?" Mary asked Gideon.

"Nay, he found me by my mother. He put her in the dirt and brought me here.

He promised he would not leave me." Gideon spoke the words with a furtive glimpse at Peter's still form.

"Rather like God, eh, Gideon?"

Gideon smiled and nodded. "Aye."

"Yet Peter is silent and his sickness keeps him from reaching out to you. Is God silent, too?" Surely it was unfair to expect an answer to such a question, but Mary posed it nonetheless.

"Sometimes God has to rest," Gideon said brightly. "I heard it said so. On the seventh day, God rested."

But there was no rest for Mary. She made litters to pull corpses to the grave-yard and had no heart to mourn the passing of so many. Exhaustion became her constant companion, and fear and bitterness followed shortly behind. *If Ye be resting, God,* she thought silently, *then perhaps it is time You were awakened.* But instead, Mary felt something inside of her awaken—longing and desire to believe in something more than the death and dying around her. If only she could find the truth. If only she could know for sure whether God truly cared.

Toward the close of evening on the fourth day, Mary felt completely done in. She poured soup into a bowl, fully intending to eat it herself, then for a reason unbeknownst to her, she took up a spoon and went to the room where Peter lay sleeping.

Anne slept happily in her box, and Gideon was seeing to the chore of giving water to those who could still drink. Taking the soup, Mary sat beside Peter. Somehow she had known that he would open his eyes, and when he did, she found herself gazing deep into their warm brown depths.

"I have brought you broth," she said softly. " 'Tis time you were up and about."

Peter smiled and tried in vain to reach up to touch Mary's face. "Be ye an angel?"

Mary laughed. "Gideon has already asked that question. Nay, I am no angel."

Peter closed his eyes as if contemplating her declaration. "Who are you?"

"I am Mary," she replied, then remembering Gideon's reaction to her name, she hastened to add, "Mary Elizabeth Beckett."

" 'Tis a beautiful name," he whispered hoarsely.

"Open your eyes, Peter," she said sternly. "You must take nourishment, and this broth will see you stronger."

Peter opened his eyes again. "How be it that you know my name?"

"Gideon told it to me." She placed the bowl upon the floor and propped Peter up as best she could. Retrieving the soup, she brought the spoon to Peter's lips. "Open," she commanded.

Peter allowed her to feed him without protest. By the time she'd given him most of the bowl, he seemed to have better color. His mind also seemed clearer, and he desired to talk.

"How came you here?" he questioned.

"I journey north to find my grandmother. I traveled with a band of pilgrims, and when I could not go on with them, they left me here at the monastery."

Peter suddenly seemed to remember the place. "I came here with Gideon. Where is the boy?" he asked, glancing about the room.

"He is helping me by giving water to the sick. I find I cannot be everywhere at once, and there are only two who seem to be recovering from the fever."

"The great fever?"

"Aye, the plague fever," Mary admitted. "Most of the brothers are dead, as well as the abbot."

Peter nodded. "I buried quite a few."

"I have replenished the supply," Mary commented. "I have not the strength to dig the graves, but the bodies are removed to help keep down the smell of the place."

Peter seemed all at once frightened. His eyes sought hers, and his breathing quickened. "Have I the fever?" he asked. Despair rang clear in his voice.

"Nay," Mary replied and instinctively reached out to put her hand against his bearded cheek. "Fear not. You have been ill with yet another cause. I am uncertain, but believe it to be nothing more serious than you have already known. I believe you will heal now."

Peter remained still against her touch. "How come ye by this knowledge?"

"I am a healer. My father was a doctor. He had trained at the university in Paris. I learned at his side, and though it is unacceptable for me to become a practicing physician, I am capable at my duties."

Peter nodded. " 'Tis evident." His dark eyes held hers captive. " 'Tis in your touch."

Realizing that her hand caressed Peter's face, Mary pulled away as though burned. She felt her face grow hot in embarrassment. Peter seemed not to notice, however, as he had closed his eyes. Mary thought perhaps he had gone to sleep and got up to leave.

"Please do not go," he called without opening his eyes. " 'Tis most cowardly for a knight of the king, but I fear this time of sickness."

Mary stared down at his still form for a moment, then eased back down to the small space at his side. " 'Tis not cowardly," she said softly.

Peter opened his eyes, and again, Mary noted the despair. "I fear because I do not know the truth."

Mary felt her heart skip a beat. Had she not longed to know the truth, herself? Had she not pondered the reasoning of her faith, or lack of one, with this same desire in mind?

"The truth?" she questioned weakly.

Peter nodded. "I have known great wealth and power. I have served the king and been amply rewarded for my service. I have known many pleasures in this life, and yet, being here," he paused and glanced around the room, "they mean nothing."

Mary smiled. "I, too, have known comfort and possessions. My father kept me well before his death."

"And now you are alone?"

"I know naught," Mary replied softly. Her eyes welled with tears. Peter reached up and wiped at them as they ran down her cheeks. He nodded, understanding her pain.

"I know naught, either."

"Ye have no family?" she questioned, feeling uncomfortable with Peter's ministering.

"Nay, only God and king, and I am uncertain about God."

Mary nodded. "I suppose I can understand that well enough. Sickness causes a person to wonder upon his faith."

"Or lack of one," Peter added.

Mary trembled, for he had spoken her very heart into words. " 'Tis fearful to face so much death and be uncertain," she finally allowed herself to say.

"Aye, Mary Elizabeth, 'tis most fearful. I have seen much death. Death upon the battlefields at Crecy. Death in the towns and villages where no soul remains to speak of the past. Too much death to ignore, yet I have no reasoning for such matters."

Mary smiled. "One of the monks suggested this is the only way in which God may attract the attention of more stubborn souls. Of this, I am certain to be one, but 'twould be more to my liking had God chosen another plan."

Peter tried to laugh but seemed to lack the strength. "I have been called worse than stubborn."

"That you are still here is proof enough of that," Mary teased.

" 'Tis fear that keeps me here."

"How be this?"

Peter drew a heavy breath. "I fear dying without knowing God in truth. I have ignored much. Mayhap 'tis time I opened my eyes."

Mary nodded solemnly. "Perhaps you are right."

❦

The demands upon Mary continued. The sick grew sicker, and most died, leaving Mary to dispose of the bodies and work in desperation to keep down the stench. Those who were sick watched their comrades writhe in the telltale agony of painful terror. The system was affected in so many distinct ways that Mary could very nearly calculate the time of death for each person, well ahead of their appointment. First, the headache, weakness, and chills. Then the pulse became rapid, the speech slurred, and extreme fatigue sent the victim seeking the refuge of a bed. Of course, by that time the fever had gradually risen, and swelling of the nodes beneath the neck and in the groin were evident by the third day. From that point it was generally only another day or two at most. Mary knew that panic would strike each person. Her father said it was because the fever had literally baked the brain's ability to reason. Whatever the cause, people died in abject horror, smelling the smell of their own death, watching their flesh turn black with hemorrhaging blotches and festering wounds.

The real mystery came in those who actually recovered and in others still who died almost the same day they began to show symptoms of the illness. Mary could not hope to figure it out. All she could do was treat the ill as best she could and pray she did not succumb to the disease herself.

❧

Several days later, Peter gingerly swung his legs over the side of the bed and tested his strength by trying to stand. Gideon watched in silence, waiting to see if his dear friend would need his help.

Peter looked up with a sheepish smile. "At least I am on my feet."

Gideon nodded. "Mary will be pleased."

Peter's smile broadened. "You think it so?"

"Aye," Gideon said, coming to his side. "She is very kind."

"Aye, that she is," Peter said, remembering the black-haired beauty. Now that he was well on the road to recovery, Mary came less often to his room. She had even moved herself and Gideon to another room in order to afford Peter peace and quiet. The move had not met with his approval, but Peter had said nothing to stop her.

"She be pretty, too," Gideon said, pulling Peter from his thoughts.

"Has she vexed your heart, young sir?" Peter questioned, easing back down to the edge of the bed.

Gideon laughed. "I want to marry her. I think she is wonderful."

Peter looked at the boy with a stunned expression. "Gideon, you are too young for such thoughts."

"Then I will let you marry her. She needs someone to help her with the baby."

"Baby?"

"Baby Anne," Gideon said, as though Peter should already know this. "Mary let me name her." As if on cue, Anne began to cry from the room next door. "I have to go help her now," Gideon said and hurried out of the room.

Peter sat and stared at the open door for several moments. He had not known that Mary had a child. She had said nothing of it. In fact, she had told him she was alone. Or would be so if she found her grandmother to be dead.

He scratched the uncomfortable growth of beard. For some time he'd worn his beard in the manner of Edward—a sort of homage. Then, too, when he'd first grown it, Peter had thought it made him look more like a man than a boy. Now it just seemed cumbersome and irritating. Shaving, he decided, would be his first adventure for the day. He thought about asking Mary to assist him, but instantly discarded the thought. She was already working too hard. He'd seen her as she passed in the hall or when she'd come to check on his own progress. She had dark circles under her eyes. Beautiful eyes, Peter remembered, that were very near the shade of wild violets.

Anne's cries subsided and Peter wondered about the child. Was Mary's husband dead from the plague? She was far too beautiful to be left alone to wander the countryside, he decided. All manner of ill could befall her. He would speak to her later that night and suggest that she wait until he was back on his feet. *Then,* he thought, *I can provide her an escort and get to know her better.*

~

Mary startled at the sound of the abbey bell ringing. She hurried to the front gate and found a band of pilgrims. They were all filthy, some sick, and all starving. Two small children, wearing nothing but rags, peered out from behind their mother's swaying form. Mary blanched, for the woman already showed signs of swelling at the neck.

"We have the fever here," Mary announced, "but I see it is your companion as well. Come. I will tend you as best I can."

"We are humbly your servants," a man murmured before collapsing to the ground.

"Bring him," Mary said to two other men. She motioned the rest of the group to follow. "We have beds and some food. I will do what I can and take in return any help you feel strong enough to give."

Day blended into night, and Mary was not even sure where the hours had passed. Two pilgrims died within hours of their arrival. It seemed strange that they showed no signs of the plague, and Mary decided they must have died from sheer exhaustion and starvation. Three more with swelled nodes and fever-ridden bodies succumbed to the disease near dawn, and Mary could only add their bodies to the growing pile in the cemetery. It was a complete wonder that they had journeyed with the others. Sheer determination must have kept them on the road.

The mother with her two small children most worried Mary. She wanted very much for the woman to survive. She reminded Mary of Grace, and for that reason alone, Mary devoted herself to seeing the woman well. Two pairs of large, round eyes followed Mary's every move as she worked to ease the woman's suffering. The children were so tiny and frail that Mary worried perhaps they too were sick. A cursory check of their bodies, however, relieved her mind of such worries. Though they were dirty and ill-kept, they showed no signs of illness.

Mary heard the cock crow and, with a hand to her aching back, crossed the room wearily to look out the window. The rosy pink dawn did little to lift her spirits. *Another night of death,* she thought to herself. *Another day of death.*

The faint cry of Anne brought Mary to the realization that she'd had very little to do with the baby since finding Gideon such a willing helpmate. Checking the children and their mother once more, Mary made her way down the hall. *I have to take care of Anne,* she thought. *The baby needs me now. Anne needs me.*

Mary kept pushing these thoughts through her head, hopeful that if she focused her attention on them, she could stay awake and alert. Sleep pulled at her senses and dulled her mind with dizziness. Reaching out to the stone wall, Mary steadied herself for a moment before pushing on. She'd had nothing to eat since the previous morning and little sleep since she'd arrived at the monastery.

Anne's crying grew louder, and Mary fought hard to make her legs work. She was so very tired. It seemed as though she could not walk more than a step or two without succumbing to her exhaustion. Leaning heavily against the wall, Mary saw the room spin uncontrollably. *I cannot be sick,* she thought. A sinking feeling of despair filled her heart. *I cannot give in to this. Anne needs me, Gideon needs me. Peter. . .*

She felt herself falling. "Peter," she whispered the name as strong arms reached out to catch her.

"Mary!"

"You are here," she said weakly. "I simply said your name and you appeared."

Peter's worried expression softened and a hint of a smile played at his lips. " 'Tis my lot, Milady. Rescuing fair maids who have no one else to champion them." He lifted her easily into his arms. "You must rest now, Mary."

Mary nodded and allowed her head to fall back against his chest. How good it felt to rest. How good it felt to be held and cared for.

Mary was asleep before Peter could get her to a bed. He worried that she suffered from more than exhaustion, but seeing no sign of fever or swelling, he relaxed a bit.

She is beautiful, he thought, sweeping back ebony ringlets from her face. Her wild dark hair, tied simply at the nape of her neck, gave her a gypsy look. Peter could not tear himself away from her. Instead, he held her hand for a moment and wondered at the woman who had so selflessly cared for everyone else. Who was she? She dressed simply enough, but the cloak upon her bed revealed quality in its design, and the shoes upon her feet were nearly new.

The daughter of a physician, he remembered and wondered why she had introduced herself thusly, when she was obviously a wife or perhaps widow and mother besides.

"Who are you, little Mary?" he whispered, before laying her hand gently across her waist. "And why have ye vexed me so sorely?"

Chapter 7

Peter used his newfound strength to assist the monks in caring for their own. With Mary completely succumbed to exhaustion, Peter found filling her shoes an endless chore. He checked the abbey rooms for more dead and grimaced at the ever-present stench. When had he last breathed clean air? Air, sweet with the smell of wildflowers and new grass.

Coming upon the room where Mary had placed the woman and her children, Peter was greeted with the sobbing cries of the little ones. They couldn't be any older than two or three years, he surmised. Stepping closer, he found they had no fear of him but were simply mourning the loss of their mother.

"How is it," he murmured, closing the dead woman's eyes, "that ye know of her passing?"

The child who looked to be the oldest crawled across his mother's body and touched Peter's hand. "Eat."

Peter smiled and lifted the child into his arms. "So you are hungry." These words seemed to cause the other child to cry even harder. Scooping up the younger child, Peter carried them both to the kitchen and sat them on the floor.

"Play here, while I find you a bit of bread," he said softly.

Searching out the cupboards, Peter realized there was little food to feed the waifs. Mary had been the only one well enough to cook, and she certainly would have had little time to bake bread. Just as he feared there'd be nothing to satisfy their hunger, Peter happened upon a cupboard with several wheels of cheese.

"Ah, this will work nicely."

He tore two chunks and handed them to the children. With an appetite that stunned Peter, the children gobbled the cheese in moments and held up their hands for more. Hungry himself, Peter broke off several more pieces and picked up the children.

"We will go to where Gideon is," he told the two. "You will like Gideon. He is like you, only bigger. 'Tis of no matter though. Gideon has a big heart and will see you fed."

Peter went to the room where he'd left Mary sleeping soundly. He wanted to stay near her, yet worried that the noise would disturb her.

" 'Tis little chance of that," he mused, and the children looked at him strangely. It would take a great deal of noise to penetrate Mary's exhaustion.

"Gideon," he called softly. There was no response.

Putting the children again on the floor, Peter handed them some cheese and went to search out Gideon. He remembered Mary saying that they'd taken the room next door, so Peter went there first and found Gideon feeding Anne.

"What have ye there, Boy?" Peter questioned, seeing that Gideon held what looked to be a leather bag at Anne's tiny mouth.

" 'Tis what Mary uses to feed Anne. She cut a tiny hole here," Gideon said, pulling the bag away from Anne.

Peter realized it was some type of coin purse. A single piece of leather had been folded in half and sewn up at the side, giving it a bit of squaring at the bottom. It was here where Mary had made the hole. As Anne began to fuss, Gideon popped the piece back into her mouth, and Peter had to laugh at the ingenious makeshift nipple.

"It works well," he said, ruffling Gideon's hair lightly. "I imagine some food in your belly would work well, too." Gideon nodded and Peter retrieved a chunk of cheese from inside his cotchardie.

"I cannot eat it and feed Anne."

"Mayhap, I could feed the babe," Peter said, uncertain even as he did so that this was a wise move on his part.

"Ye must hold her just like this," Gideon replied, evidently happy to be rid his burden. He pulled the bag away long enough for the exchange.

Peter sat rigidly on the bedside. Anne stared up at him with trusting blue eyes, wide and searching. She seemed mesmerized by Peter's face and for a moment forgot her lack of milk.

"Then ye hold the bag like this, else the milk will spill out," Gideon instructed.

Peter smiled when the baby latched onto the sack without further prompting. He held both just as Gideon had instructed. It was not the chore he'd feared. In fact, the baby stirred something deep within his heart.

"Will Mary die?" Gideon asked, taking Peter by surprise.

"I think not," he answered as evenly as possible. He prayed it would not be so.

"Good, I like her, and I do not wish for her to die." Gideon ate at his breakfast for a few moments before adding. "Will you marry her?"

Peter chuckled. "What a question! I know her naught, and she scarcely knows me. We both have our duties to see to and such a thing as marriage requires great consideration."

"I hope you will marry her," Gideon said with insistence. "Then you will be my father, and she will be my new mother."

Peter looked at the boy for a moment and said nothing. Gideon could not possibly know how his words affected Peter's heart. Peter was uncertain of their impact himself. Something in this waif and the others as well had caused him to consider all that was missing in his life. A wife and children had never been of interest to him. Living life one day to the next, answering only to his king, that was the life Peter Donne had chosen. He'd stolen many a kiss and taken up many a bet, but always without commitment or concern for what the morrow would bring. Now, however, something had happened within him. Something different, deeper, and more personal than anything else he'd known.

Mortality was a frightful thing to consider. Especially one's own mortality. Peter had faced death and held it back at arm's length, but now, his own existence seemed worthless and frail. He had little to show for his exploits and no one to care.

"Can I see Mary?"

Gideon's voice brought Peter back to reality. "I think we will both go see her," he said, finding Anne asleep with little trickles of milk seeping out from the corners of her tiny lips. "Take this bag and do with it whatever you do. I will put Anne in her bed, and we will take her with us."

"The box is her bed," Gideon instructed.

Peter acknowledged his words by placing Anne gently in the wooden box. He smiled when she gave a satisfied sigh, fluttering her eyes open for a moment before closing them again in sleep.

Lifting the box, Peter told Gideon, "Bring your things. We will all stay in one room. That way we can keep an eye on Mary and you may help me with the other children."

"Others?" Gideon questioned.

"Two more," Peter replied. "Their mother died like yours. Will you be a brother to them so that they will not be afraid?"

Gideon's face lit up. "Aye and Anne will be their sister."

"That's a good boy."

Peter felt a sense of relief when he entered Mary's room and found the children sleeping soundly on the pile of straw Gideon had once used.

"What are they called?" Gideon asked.

"I know naught," Peter replied and placed Anne's box near where they slept. "They are quite young. Mayhap we will have to name them."

"I named Anne," Gideon said with a smile of accomplishment.

"Mayhap you could think on two more names. I believe this one to be a boy child, but I do not know for certain. The other is a complete mystery, but I am certain given the needs of very small children, we will learn soon enough."

Gideon wrinkled his nose. "Babies make messes in their clothes."

Peter laughed out loud, then glanced at Mary, fearful he'd disturbed her sleep. "I must go about the abbey and see to fixing us something more substantial to eat. I must also see to the others. Will you be able to tend to all of this?"

Gideon's chest puffed up a bit as he threw back his shoulders. "I will take care of everyone."

"Thank you, Sire," Peter said, giving a slight bow. "You will make a fine knight one day."

Peter hunted and killed two scrawny hares. They weren't much, he surmised, but they'd go well with the cabbage he'd located in the garden. He cleaned the animals and put them to boil with the cabbage in a huge black caldron before going to check on the sick.

Peter carried out the dead, nearly succumbing to the stench and losing his breakfast. Besides the children's mother, there were four additional monks who'd died in the night. Looking at the pile of bodies in various stages of decay, Peter could only imagine digging a very large hole and making a mass grave. There was no other way to handle the circumstance. There were simply too many bodies for him to dig individual graves for each one.

He set himself to the task and by late afternoon had managed to dig a good-sized pit. *'Tis not large enough,* he thought and decided to put off the burial until he could make it bigger. *What is one more day?* he reasoned.

Sweat soaked and dirt encrusted, he went to the kitchen and checked on the soup. The appetizing aroma wafted up to assail his senses. How very good it smelled. Peter thought that nothing he'd ever eaten tasted quite as good as this poor soup. After filling his bowl twice, Peter took down additional bowls and poured soup into each one. Hesitating, he ladled up one for Mary, uncertain as to whether she'd be able to eat.

Leaving these to cool, Peter took two more bowls to the recovering monks. Brother James and Brother Daniel were the only two men who seemed to be getting any stronger. Both were awake, but just barely able to sit, when Peter brought them the meal.

" 'Tis poor fare," Peter told them with a smile. "I am not well trained in the kitchen."

The men smiled weakly and Brother James shrugged. " 'Tis good simply to be able to partake. God's blessing on you for this meal."

Peter nodded and went back to the kitchen. He felt strange when reflecting upon the monk's blessing. Many had been the time when Peter had been blessed in pomp and ceremony, always dressed in elaborate fare, with hearty feasts and celebrations to follow. Such blessings seemed commonplace, almost insignificant. But Brother James's sincere blessing had been one of personal interest in Peter. *God's blessing,* he remembered thoughtfully. Lifting his eyes heavenward for just a moment, Peter contemplated just what that might entail.

Still deep in thought, Peter put the cooled soup on a tray and journeyed down the hall. Now he would check on Mary and the children. Something in his heart seemed to push him to hurry. A feeling of anticipation flooded his thoughts, and with a startling realization, Peter knew he looked forward to spending time with Mary and the children.

Gideon had the two new children preoccupied with a game he'd created out of counting straw. Anne slept peacefully, as did Mary, so Peter joined the children and offered them the soup.

" 'Tis good," Gideon said. He took another long, deep drink from the bowl and smiled. The other two children did the same, and Peter noted that no sound of discontent came from either of them.

"Come and I will tell you a story," Peter said, beckoning the youngsters forward. They placed their empty bowls on the floor and scooted in closer while Peter began a tale of knightly bravery.

"On a great steed," he told them, "the king rode into battle."

"I rode on Peter's horse," Gideon told the little ones.

"Me ride," the boy said, holding his arms out to Peter.

Peter laughed. "I will be your steed," he said and motioned to Gideon. "Place him on my back, and I will ride him about the room."

Gideon thought this great fun and put the boy on Peter's back. Laughter bubbled up from the boy as Peter pranced about. It took only moments for the second child to insist on a turn. Peter obliged them both and even Gideon had a turn. They fell down laughing, Peter found himself attacked by the other two children, and soon a free-for-all of tickling and wrestling sent up peals of giggling to fill the room.

Mary awakened to the sound of laughter and thought how very good it seemed. For a moment she lay perfectly still, just taking it in and loving the very essence of it. Slowly, so as not to disturb the source, she rolled to her side and peered at the pile of wiggling bodies.

Peter Donne lay in the center of the pile, and Mary wanted to laugh out loud at the scene. Besides Gideon, the two children she'd seen with their mother were jumping up and down on the stately knight. Raising her head up on her elbow, Mary couldn't prevent her hair from spilling down over the side of the bed. *What a fright I must look,* she thought, but put the matter away from her mind. The pleasure of the children's game was much more heartening to consider.

"It seems most every time I turn around," Mary said, bringing all eyes to her, "the number of children is doubling."

"Mary!" Gideon cried with a shout of pure joy. "You are not dead! Peter said you would not die."

Mary smiled at Gideon, then turned her gaze on Peter. His warm brown eyes met hers with an intensity that nearly caused her to look away.

"Is it well with you?" he questioned, shaking off children and getting to his feet.

"I feel much rested. How long have I slept?"

"Not nearly as long as you are going to," Peter said firmly. "I have some soup for you, but after that you must sleep some more. I fear our noise has disturbed that slumber."

"Nay," Mary said, sitting up. She started to get up, but Peter shook his head.

"I am quite serious, Milady. You are to remain there for the rest of the day.

I cannot see allowing you to cause yourself illness when there is little you can do that I have not already seen to."

"But the children—" Mary started to protest.

"Are quite well. Anne sleeps and Gideon has shown me how to feed her. Gideon is quite capable of helping me with these little ones, so as you see, we are fine."

"But what of the sick?"

"Brother James and Brother Daniel are recovering nicely. The rest, I fear, will be dead within hours whether you tend them or not. I have done what I could, but they are too ill."

Mary nodded and fell back in resignation. Peter was right. There was little she could do. "What of the children's mother?"

"Dead," Peter said simply.

"I thought it would be so," Mary said softly. She lay in silence, thinking back to her cursory examination of the woman. *I am so limited*, she thought. *There is so very little I can do and even Father's knowledge does not enable me to save them.* She looked thoughtfully at the children, realizing that she would somehow have to care for two more. With a smile, she met Gideon's enthusiastic face and questioned Peter. "How came you by Gideon? He says you found him."

Peter brought the soup and sat down beside Mary. Already Gideon and the other two children were playing. "Here, sit up and drink this. 'Tis soup I made, and though weak, 'tis better than nothing."

Mary again sat up and rested against the stone wall. She tasted the broth and smiled. " 'Tis quite good. You shame yourself by calling it weak. 'Tis most hearty."

Peter chuckled. "I thought it quite good, myself. When one is hungry, truly hungry, even a crust of bread seems like a feast."

"So tell me of Gideon," Mary said between sips of soup.

" 'Tis naught much to tell. I found him weeping over his dead mother, much the same as these young waifs. I knew I could not leave him." Peter stared hard at Mary, causing her heart to skip a beat. "I brought him here, and surely you must know the rest better than I."

"I had scarce stepped foot through the gate when Gideon greeted us and pleaded for me to see to his friend. A more devoted ally surely could never be found."

Peter smiled. "I cannot say why, but I feel obligated to the child."

"He said you would get well, for you had promised to never leave him." Mary could only wonder what such a commitment by Peter might mean to her. Something about him caused her heart to flutter wildly, and the nearness of him made her feel safe and cared for.

"Aye, I promised, and I am a man of my word."

Mary met his eyes hesitantly. She started to speak, but just then Anne began to fuss.

"I will feed her," Gideon said authoritatively. "I must go get milk." He took up the bag and went off in search of the goat.

"Why is it that you do not feed her?" Peter questioned offhandedly.

Mary nearly laughed out loud at the expression that crossed Peter's flushed face when he realized how personal the question was. "Anne is not my child," Mary offered simply. "I helped her into the world, but her mother died. The folk I traveled with would have me leave her to die as well. I chose motherhood over murder."

Peter nodded. "And I chose fatherhood over desertion."

Mary laughed. "What of the other two? Shall we split them?" She asked in jest but saw Peter's face grow sober.

" 'Twould seem unfair—they have come together."

Mary nodded. " 'Twas not a serious question, Peter. I would never dream of separating them. They are a family."

"A family," Peter murmured. " 'Tis a good word."

"Aye," Mary said, feeling her breath catch in her throat. She looked across the room to the two children as they played with the fussing baby. Without thought, she looked back to Peter, whose eyes seemed to reflect all that she was feeling.

"We will not separate them," Peter said firmly.

"Nay," Mary affirmed. "We will not."

Chapter 8

The silent empty halls of the monastery bore no evidence of the peaceful worship that had at one time been resident. Mary drifted through the hallowed chapel, now untended and forgotten like the guests of a wedding once the bride and groom have gone. She counted the days to be nearly twenty since her arrival. By those calculations, Anne was nearly a month old and soon the weather would turn cold and make traveling difficult.

"I thought you were resting," Peter said from the door of the chapel.

"I am," Mary said with a smile.

"The little ones are napping, and you ought to be as well," Peter said, with a slight reprimanding tone to his words.

Mary stared at Peter for a moment and realized that he brought something alive in her. Something that she'd never known in all her years. His gaze met hers, and it seemed to Mary that he could read her thoughts, for his eyes blazed passionately, causing her to tremble.

He stepped forward, and Mary noted his legs beneath the tight-fitting hose were heavily muscled and firm. He wasn't a tall man, no more so than average, she thought, but he carried himself with the air of one acquainted with nobility.

When he stopped only a few paces from her, Mary allowed her eyes to travel up to meet his face. He smiled rather roguishly, causing her to blush.

"You examine me with a physician's eye," he teased.

"Hardly that," Mary said, without thinking. Peter laughed heartily at this, causing her blush to deepen. "I only meant that. . ." She fell silent. How could she explain to him that she had yet to ever feel such heartfelt stirring when contemplating a mere patient?

"You only meant what?" Peter questioned softly.

Mary shook her head. "Mayhap later," she said with a hint of a smile. "Now seems not the time or place."

Peter reached out and took hold of her hand. "Then let us walk and pass both the time and the place. I would know what is in your thoughts, sweet Mary."

Mary allowed him to lead her, but only because his comment had taken her by surprise. *Sweet Mary?* she wondered. *He says my name with such an endearment and acts as though nothing is amiss.*

"Did you hear me?"

Mary jerked up her head, almost afraid to meet his seeking eyes. "I admit I did not."

Peter grinned and opened the door. Passing through, Mary found them to be in the unkempt garden grounds. She realized immediately that Peter intended to continue their conversation when he led her to a small bench and motioned her to sit.

"Now that I might have your attention," he said lightly, "I asked what plans you had for the future."

"Oh," Mary replied, hoping she didn't sound disappointed. "I suppose I have not thought much on it. My goal is still to journey north and seek out my grandmother. However, I felt it only right that I remain to help with the dying and encourage the healing in others."

Peter nodded. "Brother James and Brother Daniel are the only ones left. The abbey is desperately neglected, but what else can they do? There is no one to reap the grain, much less to collect the rents and oversee the land—that is if there were those left to rent and work the lands."

" 'Tis sad to see the devastation. I am tired of death and yet there is no place where it seems not to be." Her voice sounded sad, even in her own ears, so it didn't surprise her when Peter put his hand upon hers. It was a bold move, but the times were such that many proprieties were cast aside for the comfort one might seek.

"Mayhap in the north we will find there is less sickness," he offered softly.

"We?" Mary questioned, unable to keep her voice from revealing the surprise she felt.

"I am about the king's work," Peter answered with a shrug. "My business takes me north, and there is no reason we should not journey together."

Mary relaxed a bit. In her heart she thrilled to this announcement. She knew the journey would be a taxing one with the children, yet it was the separation from Peter that troubled her more than she was ready to admit.

"Brother James has given me a donkey and cart," Mary finally said. "He thought it would be easier to travel with the children that way."

"Aye, he told me this morning. There will also be provisions, for he showed me where to find the foods in storage. 'Twill make the journey much easier, as well."

The silence fell awkwardly between them, and Mary wished she could tell Peter what thoughts were on her heart. But how could she explain them? She scarcely understood them herself. He haunted her every thought, and when she closed her eyes in sleep, it was his face that met her in her dreams.

"We should begin before much longer," Peter told her.

" 'Tis certain we cannot wait or it will turn rainy and be too hard on the children."

"Aye," Peter agreed. "I propose we start on the morrow. What say you to this?"

"Very well," Mary replied, then thought of a matter that had caused her much consideration. "Peter," she began slowly, "what of Gideon? I have a great fondness for him, and he is very helpful to me with the children. I know you have promised to never leave him, but as a knight of the king, can you, in all truth, keep that promise?"

Peter studied her for a moment before answering. "I, too, am quite fond of the boy. He has become a son to me in every aspect. The other little ones, as well, are important and have managed to secure a place here," he said with a hand to his chest. "I have given some thought to the matter, however. Your words are true enough, and it would be unfair to drag the boy to the battlefields, at least not without proper training."

Just then Gideon interrupted them. "Peter! Brother James sent me to fetch you."

Peter glanced from Mary to where Gideon stood in the stone archway. "I will come," he stated, then getting to his feet, offered Mary his hand.

Mary took it hesitantly, knowing the effect of his touch on her being. Refusing to meet his gaze, Mary looked to where Gideon danced around the arch, waiting for Peter.

"Then you do agree to our accompanying you and the children?" Peter questioned, moving toward the archway.

"I am very happy for the protection and companionship," Mary replied. "I am also glad that I may postpone bidding farewell to Gideon."

Peter tightened his hold for a moment, then paused. Mary looked up, wondering why he had stopped. Peter searched her face. Mary shifted uneasily. *What is he looking for?* she wondered. *Have I not offered my approval?*

When Mary blushed under his scrutiny, Peter grinned. "I am glad, too. For I am delighted at the prospects of postponing my farewell to you, sweet Mary." He lifted her hand, kissed it lightly, then left her to join Gideon.

As he walked away, Mary's face broke into a smile. *He must have feelings for me, as well,* she mused. Her smile broadened, and she was glad that Peter had his back to her. She did not notice Gideon's watchful eye, however.

In the kitchen, Mary sampled a thick mutton stew and smiled. It reminded her of days gone by with her father. It surprised her that she'd thought so little of him in the last weeks. True, the work had been merciless in its demands, but her father had been more dear to her than life itself.

"You always loved my stew," she said softly and tasted another spoonful. "You said it stuck to your ribs, and I teased you that your knowledge of anatomy had gone sour." Mary cherished the memory.

Crossing the room, she put bowls on the trestle table and pulled up a long bench that Peter had brought from elsewhere. It worked well to feed the children here, and Mary was grateful for such simplicity. Her final chore while the stew simmered was to milk the goats. Brother James had advised her where others were to be found, and once Mary and Peter understood the extent and needs of the livestock, they became the keepers of the same. There were eight goats, three of which were nursing nannies who always seemed to have plenty of milk to share. Mary happily accepted this, as the other two children were small enough to crave milk, just as Anne did. Gideon had named the boy William, and his younger sister was to be called Sarah. Mary thought them perfect names, and even William and Sarah accepted the change without objection.

"So long as their bellies are filled," Mary said to herself, "it matters little what they are called."

"Who are you talking to?" Gideon asked, stepping into the room and looking around.

Mary startled but recovered her composure. "I was simply thinking aloud, Master Gideon. 'Tis time I milk the goats."

"I can milk them for you," Gideon offered.

"Mayhap we should milk them together," Mary countered. "It will make the work half for each of us."

Gideon agreed to the arrangement and followed Mary into the yard. The small stone building that housed the animals doubled as stables and smith shop. The goats instantly began bleating at the appearance of Mary and Gideon.

"We have become good friends, no?" Mary suggested.

"Aye, this one is my favorite," Gideon said, pointing to the black and white nanny who searched his hand for a treat.

Taking up stools and buckets, Mary and Gideon went to their task in silence. The sound of milk being squeezed out into the wooden buckets made rhythmic music against the stillness. *'Tis comforting*, Mary thought with a sigh of contentment. *These simple tasks and the companionship of a child are more to me than I had imagined them.*

"I saw you smile like that at Peter this morn," Gideon said, startling Mary.

Peter was just passing by when he heard Gideon's comment to Mary. Standing still against the stone frame, he waited to hear what response Mary might give the boy.

"What nonsense are you speaking now, Gideon?" Mary questioned.

"I saw you smile after Peter kissed your hand. Do you love Peter?"

Peter wanted to chuckle at the child's brazen question, but he also wanted to hear Mary's answer. He had seen something in her eyes that gave him reason to believe her feelings for him were every bit as strong as his for her. However, every time they had a moment in which to speak of it, Mary would either change the subject or someone would interrupt them. Peter intended that no one interrupt Mary's reply to the boy.

"What a question!" he heard her say. "I cannot say when I have ever known a child as presumptuous as you."

"What is presum, presum—"

"Presumptuous," Mary filled in. " 'Tis a word that means you asked a very personal question that deserves no answer because. . ." She paused and Peter wondered what she would say. "Because. . .because 'tis none of your concern."

"But it is," Gideon protested. "Peter is going to be my new father, and I told him that I wanted him to marry you so that you could be my new mother and Anne could be my sister. Now William and Sarah can be in our family, too."

"Gideon!" This time, Peter did laugh softly at the shocked tone Mary's voice held.

"You always look at him different like," Gideon said. "And when you smiled this morn, you looked so happy. I think you love him, and I am glad."

"Gideon, stop this minute. Whether I do or not is nothing for me to speak on with you."

Peter was completely intrigued by the conversation. She hadn't once denied the possibility nor indicated an unwillingness to such a matter. Could it be possible she loved him, just as he almost certainly loved her?

"Will you speak to Peter on it?"

Peter heard Gideon voice the question and again nearly laughed out loud. *Good boy,* he thought. *Make it clear that she needs to bring it to me.*

"Nay!" Mary replied in a voice that betrayed her concern. "I will not, and neither will you. Peter has enough to think on, and we will not vex him with such matters."

Peter heard rustling sounds and knew that Mary and Gideon had completed their milking. He moved quietly in the direction of the kitchen, whistling to himself as he did so. *She must have feelings for me,* he decided. *Otherwise she would not have hesitated to deny them to the boy.* His whistling stopped as a smile drew up the corners of his lips. *Ah, sweet Mary,* he thought and felt his heart pound a little harder. *You already vex me with such matters.*

He paused at the door and turned to see Mary and Gideon head up the walk. Gideon struggled with his bucket, and Mary leaned over to retrieve it.

"Might I offer a hand?" Peter questioned, coming toward them as though he were heading out instead of coming in.

Mary blushed and quickly lowered her face. "Not a word, Gideon," Peter heard her whisper.

"Telling secrets, Mary?" Peter questioned, taking the buckets.

Mary looked up and met his stare. "I. . .we were just. . ." She squared her shoulders and brushed past him. "I have to tend the stew."

Peter laughed and followed with the buckets, while Gideon fairly danced through the open door. He was going to enjoy drawing this secret out of Mary's heart.

Chapter 9

Mary smiled back at Gideon with a strong sense of satisfaction. The small, two-wheeled cart made a perfect traveling coach for the children, while Mary found her ease—what little could be had—on the roughly hewn driver's seat. The donkey, a beefy little character with a surprisingly good nature, seemed unburdened by the chore of pulling them. The children were excited and perceived the journey with imaginative enthusiasm. The goat, their new traveling companion, did not think much of his new circumstance. It made Mary chuckle.

" 'Tis better to watch the road before you," Peter said, riding up beside her.

Mary turned back to check the road before lifting violet eyes to meet his glance. She could think of nothing witty to reply and so simply met his gaze and returned her attention to the donkey.

What is it about him? Mary pondered. *Since the first moment he opened his feverish eyes, I have found myself most captivated.* The thought that Peter had somehow captured her wakeful attentions, as well as her nighttime dreams, truly vexed Mary. *Is this love?* she wondered.

"And where do your thoughts lead you today, Mary?"

Peter's voice caused Mary to tighten her hands on the reins.

"To the future, Sire," she answered honestly. Let him make of it what he would, she mused.

"Ah, yes," Peter murmured from above her. Mary refused to look at him again, so Peter continued. "Have you given more thought to these babes and how you will care for them?"

Mary shook her head. "Nay, 'tis a heavy matter for certain. I can only pray my grandmother is still alive and that she is still a wealthy woman."

"And if she is not?"

"Why do you ask me these things?" Mary questioned more harshly than she'd intended. "You know full well that I have naught to offer them. I am alone in this world. Why cause me to continuously ponder the matter?"

"Mayhap because the matter will not ponder itself." His words were gently offered. "I have considered it myself, and it is not a problem easily resolved. Children need food, clothing, warmth, and love. I have little doubt that you can offer them love, but what of anything else? By your own admission you have no home. Therefore, they have no home so long as they live with you."

Mary nodded without looking up. "I know it well."

"I say not these things to grieve thee, Mary. 'Tis simply something to be considered with a clear mind. Out here, away from the crowds and the dying, it seems best to regard these matters at length."

"I will think on them by and by," Mary offered and said nothing more.

Peter scouted the areas alongside the road, all the while keeping the little cart within view. *She is wonderful,* he thought, allowing himself a brief glimpse of Mary. The wind picked up enough to play havoc with her long dark curls. She had tied them at the nape of her neck and Peter was captivated by the way they rolled down her back in blackened waves. Were she a lady of court or of more noble means, no doubt her hair would have been braided and bound, hidden away beneath any number of coverings. He tried to imagine her in the jewel-encrusted robes favored by the queen or in the rich velvet surcoats trimmed in fur, which had been so popular amidst the ladies at court.

Peter shook off the image of finery, however, and concentrated on the woman he saw. She wore a simple surcoat and linen tunic, and Peter thought her more beautiful than all the noble ladies of London.

Just then a noise to his left caught Peter's attention. It sounded like the cries of a child. He reined back on his horse and strained to listen. It was distant but nevertheless very real. Peter waited for Mary to catch up to him before swinging down from his mount and throwing the reins to her.

"I heard a cry. Hold the beast while I go search it out." Peter didn't wait for her approval before taking off in the direction of the cry. Gnarled limbs and briar branches made his passage into the woods difficult. Overhead, huge oaks sheltered the forest floor from the pale yellow light of the sun. The deeper into the woods he went, the darker it grew. Only the moaning sobs kept him pushing forward.

Except for the cries, an eerie silence gripped the forest. It seemed unnatural to Peter, yet was not most of the world in an unnatural state?

Catching his pointed-toed boot against a tangle of vines, Peter nearly fell headlong onto the ground. Righting himself, he paused long enough to determine the direction of the crying before pushing on.

Just as he began to fear he would never locate the source of the cries, Peter found himself standing before a young girl. She was scarcely more than a mite, so tiny and frail, yet Peter judged her to be Gideon's age. She looked up at the stout knight with huge, fearful eyes, and Peter's heart melted.

"Are ye hurt?"

She nodded, but said nothing. Tears still poured down her face, but the sobbing had ceased.

Peter knelt beside her, but the child pushed back and cried out in pain. "Do not fear me," he said, putting a hand out to still her. "I have come to help. Where are you hurt?"

"I fell," she whimpered. "I hurt my leg."

Peter gently lifted back the loose linen of her skirt. The leg in question was swollen and purple just below the child's left knee. "I have a friend with me," he told the girl. "She is a great healer. We will have her look at this." The child still eyed him fearfully. "What is your name?" Peter asked her.

"Gwenny," the girl replied.

"And where be your parents?"

"I do not know. We ran when the bad people came to our house. I got lost, and I could not find my mama."

"How old are you, Gwenny?"

"Almost ten years," she answered, seeming quite proud of this.

Surprise flickered across Peter's face. *Such a tiny thing,* he thought and reached out to lift her. "I am Peter. I will carry you to our wagon. Mary, the woman I spoke of, will tend to your leg." The girl did not resist Peter, and so he continued talking as he walked. "We have other children with us as well. Their parents are dead, however. You are welcome to stay with us. We are going north, and mayhap we will find your people."

Peter emerged from the woods to find Mary restlessly pacing the road. She had tied off the donkey and horse to allow them to graze and waited most impatiently for his return. Peter saw her expression soften the minute she spied his baggage.

"Is she hurt?" Mary questioned.

"Aye, her leg is broken," Peter replied, and the child looked up at him fearfully.

"Will ye cut it off?" she questioned, nearly hysterical.

"Nay," Mary soothed, reaching out to push back matted brown hair from the girl's face. "Do not be afraid. I will look at your leg, and we will figure how to best treat it."

"Her name is Gwenny," Peter said, taking the child to a grassy spot where Mary already knelt in anticipation of the examination.

"And how old are you, Gwenny?" Mary asked, lifting the child's skirt to observe the leg.

"Ten years," the child replied again to the question Peter had already asked.

Peter watched Mary's gentle ministering. She felt the leg tenderly, talking all the while to the frightened child. When at last she was satisfied with her examination, she bade Gwenny to remain still, while she and Peter gathered the things they would need to help her.

Mary motioned Peter away from the child. " 'Tis broken, but I believe we can set it to better heal."

"What can I do?"

"I will need two sturdy sticks. At least as thick as Gideon's arm." Peter nodded. "We will have to pull the leg back into place. Father said a broken bone must always be pulled apart first, then be allowed to go back together. I have not set one by myself, but I have watched it done. I will need your strength to hold the girl while I pull the leg."

"I understand. Let me find your sticks. Do you need anything else?"

"Nay, I have some herbs that will help with the pain, and I will tear strips of cloth from my kirtle to bind the leg." Even as she spoke, Mary lifted her surcoat and ripped a portion of the undercloth away.

Peter noted shapely ankles before the surcoat was dropped back into place. "I will get the wood."

He returned quickly and noted that the children were already stirring in the cart. "You must be very quiet," he told the three oldest. "This little girl has a broken leg, and Mary is going to fix it." Gideon nodded in somber silence, while William and Sarah just stared in curiosity.

"Will these do?" Peter questioned, and Mary reached up to examine the two sticks.

"They are perfect. Can you trim off the ragged points?"

"Certainly, Milady." Peter did as she asked and returned the smoothed sticks.

"Peter will hold your arms, Gwenny. Remember, I told you it would hurt a bit while we pull on your leg, but then I will bind it up and it will not hurt as much."

Gwenny nodded, fear written clearly in her eyes. Peter patted her gently on the head and took up a position behind her. He waited for Mary's direction, fascinated as she nimbly worked with her meager supplies.

She gave Gwenny a piece of twisted cloth. "Bite on this—'twill ease the pain." The child took the cloth hesitantly, and Mary nodded to Peter. Gently, Peter gripped the child around the arms and pulled her back against him. " 'Twill be like a big hug," he whispered in her ear. "Just pretend I am a bear." This made the girl giggle.

"I will pull on the count of two," Mary told Gwenny. She looked to Peter and added. "You must hold her firm until I say otherwise."

"I will do just as you bid, Milady." Peter hoped that Mary saw the tenderness he felt for her. She seemed so strained by the task, almost as though she felt every bit of the child's pain.

"Very well. One. Two." Mary pulled and Peter held the screaming child tight. He actually heard the bone snap into place. Mary released her hold, admonishing Gwenny not to move. It was an unnecessary directive, however, as the child had already fainted from the pain. This only made Mary's task easier, and she smiled up at Peter when she saw him stroking the child's forehead.

" 'Twould seem we have added to our family," she quipped.

Peter started at the suggestion. They truly had become a family, and he liked it very much. How could he just allow Mary and the children to wander out of his life? Even this child seemed precious to his heart. What had become of the fun-loving rogue of his younger years?

" 'Tis set," Mary exclaimed, tying the final piece of cloth in place.

"I'll make her a place in the cart," Peter said, gently easing the child onto the ground. "Will she heal?"

"I believe so," Mary replied. "The break is clean; it did not cut through the skin, and that is good. She is young and seemingly strong, and that, too, is good."

Peter nodded and looked to the wagon, where three sets of eyes peered down at him and Mary. " 'Twould seem we have an audience," he whispered and got to his feet. "We will need a soft place for her to rest," Peter said, coming to the cart. "Gideon, smooth out the straw over there, and I will bring her."

Gideon immediately went to the task just as Anne began to fret and cry. Mary went to Anne, and Peter gently carried Gwenny to the wagon. Placing her in the cart, Peter motioned Gideon to bring Mary's mantle.

"Will you watch over her, Gideon?" Peter questioned man to man. " 'Tis the responsibility of men to care for the women. Gwenny is older than you, but she is more frail and in need of your care. Can you do this thing for Mary and for me?"

Gideon's countenance glowed with pride. "I will care for her, Peter. I will do a good job. You will see."

"I knew I could count on you, Gideon. You will make a fine knight one day."

Their journey north continued, and before they had been gone from the monastery even a week, heavy rains made their labors nearly impossible. More than once they stopped for the night in a nearly deserted town, only to be faced once again with the despair and heartache that accompanied the plague.

Mary did what she could for those who remained behind, but for the most part, people were superstitious and wanted no part of strangers. The most troubling sight to Mary was the deserted children. Some were orphaned by the death of their parents, while others were deserted and left to die because of superstitious nonsense and rhetoric.

"Do you know," Mary said in a voice bordering on rage, "that this baby was left to die because the parents were convinced he had caused the sickness in the village?"

Peter looked down at the infant in Mary's arms. No more than a year old, the chubby boy reached out for a lock of Mary's hair.

"Pray tell, why would they consider such a matter valid?" Peter questioned, taking the child from Mary's trembling arms.

"Because he bears a mark upon his back," she said, with clenched fists at her side. "I cannot believe such superstition would allow a mother to leave her child. This baby is barely walking and certainly could not have been weaned. How could she leave him, Peter?"

Mary knew her temper was out of control, but it no longer mattered. This child was innocent of wrong-doing, yet an entire village marked him as the cause of their woes, simply because he bore a mark that made him different. Tears came to her eyes as she watched the roly-poly baby giggle with glee, while Peter made growling noises against the baby's stomach

It was simply too much to bear. How could there be so much cruelty and stupidity? Unable to stave back the tears, Mary stalked off to a place away from the wagon and the other children. She did not wish them to see her break down.

"Oh, Papa," she moaned, remembering her father's gentle touch and kindness to her when she'd been sad. How she longed for his embrace and tender words of love. He had been her entire life, and now he was gone. Somehow in the face of such ruthlessness, the pain seemed worse than it had before.

Leaning against a towering oak, Mary hugged her arms to her breast. It could not fill the emptiness inside. *Why do You allow such pain, God?* she wondered silently. *If You are truly merciful and all-knowing as the good monks told me, why do You hurt Your children so?*

"Mary?"

She turned her reddened eyes to Peter's gentle voice.

"People are ignorant," he said softly. "They do what they believe they must and know not why such things should be perceived as strange. There must be hope, though. We are here, and we will care for the babe."

"But what of all the others?" Mary questioned. "There must be many more who have been left behind because of nonsense such as markings or superstitious mumblings. Surely even God is not so cruel."

"Nay, I do not believe God to be cruel," Peter said, lifting her chin. "We must have hope, sweet Mary. Surely God Himself has led us to these little ones. Think on that. There is only so much we can do. Only so many we can care for."

Mary felt her heart skip a beat at the loving expression on Peter's face. Without thought, she reached her hand up to touch his cheek. The bristle of his newly formed beard felt foreign, but Mary loved the feel of it and ran her thumb across his jawline.

She heard Peter's quick intake of breath before his hand closed over her wrist and pulled her hand away. "Come sit with me," he said, pulling her along.

"But, the children. . ."

"Gideon has it all under control, and Gwenny is feeding Anne."

Mary felt her raw emotions and wondered with fear if she had somehow offended Peter with her touch. Immediately she sought to apologize as Peter pulled her deeper into the cover of the forest.

"I am sorry for my boldness," she whispered.

"I am not," Peter replied and swept her into his arms.

Mary felt her breath catch as Peter's lips gently touched hers. The kiss left her breathless, and without warning, she crumbled to her knees when Peter released her.

"Mary!" Peter exclaimed, kneeling beside her.

Dark hair tumbled over her shoulder, hiding her face. For once, Mary was glad for her disheveled state. She desired nothing more than to hide her face from Peter. What a wondrous but confusing feeling she held in her heart. How could she dare to face him and try to explain?

"Mary?" he said again, this time much calmer. He turned her face, forcing her to look at him. "Are ye well?"

Mary nodded, her eyes huge in wonderment. "I am."

Peter grinned and Mary felt her face grow hot at his words. " 'Tis your first kiss, am I right?"

" 'Tis no concern of yours, Sire," Mary said, pushing his hand away. She was completely humiliated for reasons beyond her understanding.

Peter stretched beside her, leaning back on his elbows. "I am glad to be the first."

Mary said nothing, trying hard to regain her composure and still her quaking emotions. She looked away from Peter and chose a neutral topic. "I am taking the boy with us."

"But of course."

Mary snapped around to make certain he did not jest with her. "You truly do not mind?"

Peter chuckled. "We have already amassed five. What is one more?"

Mary felt tenderness anew for the rugged knight at her side. She wished she could tell him all that she felt, but it was beyond her to know how to put any of it into words. Getting to her feet, she looked down at Peter, whose passionate eyes still stirred her heart.

Not able to think of anything else, Mary confided, "I am glad you were the first, as well." Then without waiting to see his expression, she hurried back to the wagon and the children.

Peter stared after Mary with a smug smile. More confident than ever of the building emotion she felt for him, he was satisfied that she had been willing to admit pleasure in his kiss. Making his way back to the wagon, Peter was surprised when Gideon approached him with a question.

"When are you going to wed Mary?"

"What a question," Peter said, rumpling the boy's hair. "How can you be so bold?"

Gideon grinned. "We are getting a whole bunch of children," he said with a tone beyond his years. "Would it not be well to get a mother and father, as well?"

Peter shook his head. "Get on with you, Gideon. 'Twould be best we make ready to leave before Mary finds yet another child in need of a family."

They left within an hour, but after a week more on the road, the count of children in the wagon had grown to ten.

"'Tis certain the donkey will pull no more," Peter said, taking William and Sarah up on the horse with him.

"I will walk," Mary said with pleading eyes fixed firmly on Peter's face. "What is one more?" she questioned, mocking his words of a week past.

"One more will do in the beast, that is what. I pray we find that grandmother of yours soon. 'Tis getting truly difficult to feed them all."

Mary smiled. She knew Peter's gruff tone was nothing more than show. She looked back at the wagonful of children. They ranged in age from baby Anne to the ten-year-old Gwenny, who had taken it upon herself to mother all the others. If only they could find her grandmother and a home to shelter them all in. If only. . .

Chapter 10

I t met with the satisfaction of both Peter and Mary when a monastery came into sight. It wasn't just any monastery, however, it was the very one in which Peter was to deliver the king's missive. They were growing ever closer to York, and with its nearness, Peter's confusion grew.

Sitting alone that night in the quiet of the abbott's study, Peter reflected on his journey north and wrote in the journal he'd kept for King Edward. The number of dead had lessened as they moved north, and to Peter's relief, they had found no more children in need of a home.

With a yawn, he rubbed his tired eyes and contemplated what he should next do. He had done as the king bade him, and now he should return to report his findings. But returning to Edward meant leaving Mary. And the children.

"Is it well with you, my son?" the abbott questioned, entering the room.

Peter suppressed another yawn. "I am nearly spent, but otherwise well. I am more relieved yet to find no sickness among your walls."

"Aye, we are most grateful to God for such a blessing."

Peter sat back and looked quizzically at the priest. "Is this illness the hand of God? His punishment upon a faithless people?"

"There are those who say it is. The Egyptians were sent plagues in the time of Moses. Still, these are not the things upon which I personally choose to concentrate. Sickness often does bring a man closer to God, and oft it brings him thoughts of his own limitations and his own death."

Peter nodded. "I confess, 'tis so with me. I lived a life of ease, and even though I lost my family at an early age, I was blessed with comfort and purpose. I have seen much and lived much, but never gave thought for the morrow because it simply did not matter."

The abbott took a seat on the bench beside Peter. " 'Tis not unusual for man to think thusly. The church is always here to guide and offer direction to mankind, but without a repentant heart, there is no salvation."

"This salvation you speak of," Peter said, suddenly realizing he needed to know more, "is it that which saves man from death?"

"Not physical death," the abbott replied. "By God's Holy Scripture, man is instructed that he must die in his flesh, yet a spiritual death will follow for those without the forgiveness of Christ. For what is a man but that which makes up his spirit? The flesh is weak. 'Tis here one day and gone the next. By your own witness you have seen such a thing be true. The soul of man is that which physical death need not touch. The soul of man is that which can be given over to God in obedience to the Scripture and thus a spiritual death may be avoided."

"I have heard this within the walls of great cathedrals," Peter admitted, "yet it seemed unimportant at the time. I went to the battlefield at a young age, and there as an orphan was made squire to Robert d'Artois, a French nobleman who had won great favor with King Edward by pledging his undying support. He taught me much about warfare and fighting. I was with him when he took the city of Vannes. Scarcely a drop of English blood was spilled and even the Countess de Montfort came to offer her congratulations to d'Artois. I remember watching the pomp and ceremony and thinking, 'This is what makes a man great. This is what makes a man's life worth living.'" Peter paused. "A few weeks later, d'Artois was dead by the same men he had once defeated."

"And what thought you then?" questioned the abbott.

Peter smiled ruefully. "I thought that a man's true obligation should be to his own pleasure, for obviously life was quite undeterminable. I went back to England with d'Artois's body. Edward had requested he be buried by the Black Friars in London under great ceremony. I suppose it was then that I gave myself over to self-satisfaction and left behind all notions of the morrow."

The abbott nodded. " 'Tis often the way of man. Dealing with the inevitable truth of our frailty and brief passing upon the earth causes many a man to turn to self-serving pleasure. How think you now? Now that you have witnessed even more death and destruction? Are you more convinced that life is so fleeting that you must give your every moment to selfish ambition?"

Peter shook his head. "I pray there be more."

The abbott smiled. "There is. Let me tell you about the forgiveness of God and life eternal."

❧

Mary stood in a protective pose, almost as if threatened by the presence of the dark-robed men. They had just suggested that the children were the responsibility of the church and that her duty was to turn them over to the care of the monks.

"We have many in the village who would welcome the wee ones," one man argued. "They would be well cared for. What can you offer them upon the road?"

"I will not leave the children behind," Mary stated firmly. "They are as much family to me as any I have been bound to by blood."

"But mistress you have no husband," the man tried to continue without luck.

"I will not hear of it. Should you threaten me, I will simply take them in the night and make my way to my grandmother's estate." Mary hoped the word estate would make it clear that the monks were dealing with more than a pauper.

Peter came into the argument at this point, and Mary hurried to his side, pulling him with her to where the men stood. "They want to take my children," she announced possessively. "They feel it is the place of the church to provide care for the orphans. I will not hear of it. Peter," she said, turning her dark, angry eyes upward, "you will not let them take our children, will you?"

Peter put a supportive arm around Mary's thin shoulders. "Nay, we will not be parted from the children. If you will excuse us," he said to the monks and pulled Mary outside into a courtyard.

"The very nerve of those men. They believe because they are men of the church, they can force their will upon others. I will not hear of it!" She was angry and knew her temper was nothing new to Peter. "They cannot do this thing, Peter!"

"Calm down, Mary. No one is taking the children just yet."

"What do you mean, just yet?"

"I am simply saying that the matter is nowhere near the point of causing panic. You must calm yourself." He dropped his hold on her arm and motioned to a bench. "Sit here and talk to me."

Mary crossed her arms. "I do not feel like talking. I feel like leaving this place."

"Be reasonable, Mary. The children are asleep and it is quite late. I thought you would be sleeping as well."

"I might have been, but for those testy souls within. Imagine those men thinking they could do a better job in caring for the children!"

"But Mary, we have nothing to offer them. Perhaps that is all the monks were thinking. We are not a family in the eyes of the church."

"The church! Who cares what the church thinks?"

" 'Tis heresy you are speaking now. Would you have them burn you at the stake for your lack of faith?"

"What of your own lack of faith?" Mary questioned, casting a sharp look down to where Peter sat.

"Mayhap my faith is not lacking now."

"Oh, so I suppose they have convinced you to see reason in their part," Mary said angrily. She felt tears come to her eyes. Would she have to face this thing alone?

"Do not be afraid," Peter said softly. "I still champion you, sweet Mary."

"I am not afraid!" Mary declared. "I will care for the children, and no one will take them from me. No one!"

Peter seemed weary as he ran a hand through his hair. "Mary, there are ten children. Mayhap giving over some to the monks is not a bad idea. They have families who work the lands here and who would care for the little ones."

Mary shook her head. "I cannot. I love them as though they were my own."

Peter nodded. "As do I. But love should not be a thing that brings harm. Would you love them at the price of their empty bellies?"

"I will care for them," Mary said with a sobbing voice.

Peter got to his feet and reached out for Mary, but she pushed him away. "Touch me not! You could give away my children without so much as a second thought. I will not have any part of you."

"They are as much my children as yours, Mary."

Trembling built up to rage. "Which would you give over, Peter? William and Sarah? Gwenny? Surely even you would have a hard time bidding Gideon farewell." In the brilliant glow of the moonlight, she saw Peter's face fall. In her heart, Mary knew that she would regret her words, but anger pushed her forward. "Mayhap my faith is lacking, Sir Peter, but my love is not easily given, nor is it easily taken back. I will not desert these children to live in hopes of yet another who might one day love them. They are mine surely as I am theirs. No one, not you or the monks or God Himself, will separate me from them."

Chapter 11

Mary ignored Peter and the monks, as well, when all offered to help her in the feeding of the children the next morning. With Anne nestled in her left arm, Mary helped Gwenny to sit comfortably with the marked baby boy they now called Edward.

"I do not wish to solicit your assistance," Mary said coldly to Peter. Turning her back, she muttered under her breath, "You might seek to give one of them away when my back is turned."

If Peter heard the comment, he said nothing. Mary didn't care. Her motherly instincts took over, and she was determined to fight for each and every child as though they truly were her own.

When she had seated herself beside a young girl named Ellen, one of the last to join the band, Mary nodded to the children that they could eat. "Gideon, you help William and Sarah." Gideon nodded but seemed more quiet than usual. Mary feared that he was being affected by her fight with Peter, but there was no honorable way to make peace at this point and so she did nothing to ease the boy's noted concern.

Staring down the table at her little family, Mary felt strongly about her decision to keep them together. After baby Edward, they had added two sisters—Ellen and Matilda, ages nine and eight, respectively. The last two to join the group were boys. Darias, a ten year old, had been left for dead after taking on the plague. Miraculously, however, he had lived, and Peter had found him eating grass for sustenance. Smiling at the boy, Mary watched him eat porridge with a hearty appetite. Six-year-old Robert completed the group and won Mary's heart with his huge blue eyes and happy laughter. How children could laugh in the midst of such tragedy was beyond Mary's ability to reason.

The monks departed the room, but Peter remained behind. Determined to reason with Mary, Peter joined the feasting children, receiving Mary's frown as he did.

"You all look well rested," Peter said, rumpling Darias's hair. "And I see that porridge agrees with you, Master Darias." The boy smiled and nodded.

"Mary, it appears these children could use a bath," Peter said, and moans followed his comment around the table.

"I will see to their needs," Mary snapped.

"I only meant to offer my help. The boys might want to join me at the lake.

'Tis just beyond the dovecotes."

Mary said nothing, and Peter took her silence to be acceptance. He dished himself a bowl of porridge and took up a piece of hard bread before continuing, "We can go after we finish eating. The water will be chilly, but it will do all of us good to bathe. The good brothers of the abbey have even given me a small piece of soap."

"I said I would see to them!"

Peter met Mary's angry stare with his own mounting temper. "I care not for your protests. I am saying this. The boys will come with me to the lake after we break the fast. I will return the soap to you and you may take the girls. I will even carry Gwenny to the water for you."

Mary threw her spoon down. "I am surrounded by willful men."

"Willful men? Take a look at yourself, sweet Mary."

"Do not call me that!" she protested.

"I should not, for 'tis certainly not true this day." Peter noted Gideon's frown and the woeful stares of the others. "I will not argue with you in front of the children."

"Good, then you will not speak with me at all, because my place is with them and I will not be taken from them. Not for bathing exercises or any other cause. Do I make myself clear?"

Peter took in the scene with reserved control. He saw no need to frighten the children. "You make yourself very clear. You are selfish and lack all common sense to make good judgment. Nevertheless, now is not the time to discuss the matter further. I am going hunting, as I promised the friars fresh game under the protective permission of King Edward. We will speak of this later."

He got up and with one last look at Mary to emphasize the seriousness of his words, he turned to leave. At the door he paused, and with a slight smile he added, " 'Tis most glad I am to learn of your flaws before seeking your hand in marriage. I would have been most annoyed to believe you of one character, only to find you a wife of bitter nature." With that he left the room, fully satisfied at the shocked expression on Mary's face.

Mary finished the last of the children's baths before seeing to one for herself. She was filthy and felt as though her skin crawled. It would feel wonderful to be clean again. After instructing Gideon, Darias, and Gwenny to see to the others, Mary took a linen towel and monk's robe and went to the lake. She tried not to think about the kindness of the men she'd so thoroughly offended the night before and again at breakfast. They had seen her limited wardrobe and offered her the robe to wear while her own clothes dried. The gentle-spoken abbott told her that such times made strange demands upon people. He promised to send one of the brothers into the village to seek out clothes for Mary. She had protested such a need but in her heart was thankful for the suggestion. Her own clothes were ragged and torn, and she seriously doubted they would hold up to a good washing.

It was only here, in the privacy of her bath, that Mary allowed herself to think on Peter's words. Had he been serious about seeking her hand in marriage? And what if he was? She scarcely knew the man, and while it was not uncommon for such marriages to take place, Mary had always seen herself as independent of the need to wed.

Still, in her heart, Mary knew she was lost. She cared deeply for this bedraggled knight of the realm. He had a good mind and gentle spirit, and his love for the children was evident. He'd never once lifted a hand to strike any of them, and even when Mary argued with him, he had held his temper in check.

But his words about her character, more than the idea of marriage, bothered her most. Was she a woman of bitter nature? Had the past and the scars transferred to her by an angry, embittered father, left her without a hope of gentleness?

She thought of her recent actions and in the stillness of her meditation realized how childishly she had behaved. Children must have food and shelter, as well as love and protection. *Can I give them what they need?* she wondered. *Or will my pride cost them their lives?*

She finished her tasks, and after leaving the surcoat and tunic to dry upon a bush, Mary returned to the abbey. She felt suddenly shy about facing the men, knowing full well that she'd acted poorly in their presence. But her embarrassment and concern had no time to linger.

"He stepped upon a trap," one of the monks told Mary as she came into the kitchen.

She inquired of the bleeding man now lain out upon the kitchen table. "When did he do this? Is there a doctor among you? The wound should be seared to stop the bleeding."

"We cannot do such a thing," the man responded.

Mary pushed her way through the gathering of brothers and took the man's bleeding foot in hand. "Why are you unable to help him?" she asked of the abbott who had just arrived.

" 'Tis a decree by the Council of Bayeux. In 1300 it was decided that none of the clergy could be given over to any act of surgery, including cautery and incision."

"Bah! What nonsense. The man will die if we do not help him." Mary glanced around the room and spied the linen towel she'd brought from her bath. She had still been drying her hair when the injured man's cries took her attention.

"Bring that cloth," she ordered one of the monks. Ripping a piece from the towel, Mary first tied back her still damp hair. "Now bring me a pan of water from the hearth, and you," she pointed to a young friar, "go fetch my bag." The man nodded and hurried to do as he was told.

Mary searched out the drawers of the nearest cupboard and found a large knife. Giving it over to yet another man, she directed him to put it in the fireplace coals.

Tearing more pieces of cloth, Mary dipped them in the hot water and began to clean the bleeding wound. The man cried out in his misery. "Hold him still," Mary directed, "and give him something to bite down on. This will not be a gentle task."

The abbott nodded to his men, and Mary took a cup and poured water over the gaping wound. The man screamed and fainted dead away, much to Mary's relief. She took up her bag, searched through it for a variety of bottles, and motioned a young monk to assist her. "We will make a paste of these," she said authoritatively. "Mix in a pinch of each and only enough water to make a thick paste. I will sear the flesh and apply this afterward." The man nodded and went to work.

"Bring me the knife," Mary instructed, satisfied that she had cleansed the wound as best she could. The abbott himself brought the knife and, after murmuring a blessing, handed the heated blade to Mary.

"God's grace upon you, Daughter."

Mary nodded, but said nothing more as she placed the blade against the torn, bleeding skin. Several monks quickly left the room at the heinous smell of burning flesh, but Mary noted that the young man worked on at making her paste, seemingly oblivious to the stench.

"Now the paste," she called and the bowl was brought to her. "You did a good job," she told the man in her way of thanks. Smearing the concoction upon the wound, Mary then bound it securely with linen and tied it snug. " 'Tis not to be touched for three days." She eyed each man who remained and received solemn nods.

"You have the touch of healing from God Himself," the abbott said approvingly. " 'Tis unseemly for a woman, but we are most grateful for your skills."

Mary stuffed bottles back into her bag and turned with a smirking expression. "God had naught to do with my healing skills. I learned them at my father's side." The abbott opened his mouth as if to reply, but Mary grabbed her things and stalked out of the room, unconcerned with what he might say.

Throughout the day, Mary contemplated what she might say to set things right with Peter. When nightfall came and he had not returned, Mary began to fear he had deserted them. She nervously paced the kitchen, turning from time to time to the open door. Quick glances across the field left Mary disheartened at their refusal to yield forth Peter.

"Have you supped?" The voice of the abbott sounded from behind her.

Mary turned, and having a contrite heart for her previous actions, she shook her head and moved toward the man. "I must apologize for my words earlier this day. I have not been myself, and I gave no concern for the feelings of others."

"You are forgiven, Daughter. Come sup with me and tell me of your father. He must truly be a fine physician."

"He was," Mary said, nearly wincing with the memory. "He died at the hands of our villagers. They believed him to consort with the devil."

If her words shocked the abbott, he did not respond by so much as raising a bushy white eyebrow. His soft blue eyes bore into her soul, and immediately Mary felt at ease. He brought roasted meat, fresh bread, and drink to the table and waved Mary away when she sought to serve him. He blessed the food, and Mary found that his prayerful words reached deep into her heart.

"How is it that you can be certain He listens?" she questioned the abbott.

"You mean God, of course?"

Mary nodded. "I have not been brought up to have faith in that which I cannot prove or see. Heresy, perhaps, but my teacher is now dead."

"As a physician, your father could often not see the workings of man's flesh. Still, he knew that something caused the heart to beat. Did it cease to exist simply because you could not see it?"

Mary felt the first spark of understanding. "There were evidences of the heart at work. Things are different within a body in which the heart beats and one in which it has stopped."

"So, too, it is with the spirit. Thus the spirit into which God has breathed life is different from the one that knows Him not." The abbott paused and offered her a tender look. "You have endured much and you desire to be at peace." He sliced bread and meat and offered them to her.

"What must I do?" Mary asked, bringing her hands to her head. "I know my way is not right. I have felt it since I first spoke with the mother of baby Anne. She was a good woman who had a strong faith in eternal life. It caused me to think, but many years of my father's anger and disapproval of the church kept me from serious consideration. Then, too, is my desire to work at healing. The church frowns on the science of medicine."

"The church frowns on man putting himself above God. If God chooses to take a soul from this earth, where is it man's place to interfere?"

"But did not Christ, Himself, heal people of afflictions?"

"True enough, and the church has no argument with the physician who seeks to use prayer and the things God has given us in this earth in which to aid healing."

"But does the church believe scientific medicine such as surgery to be the work of the devil? Is it not possible for God to have given man the knowledge of this thing?"

The abbott grew thoughtful for a moment. "Good knowledge comes from God; that much is true—just as evil and chaos are weapons the devil uses. But knowledge in the hands of the wrong person can be used for evil."

" 'Tis God not knowing enough to work His good in spite of these folk? Cannot a man or a woman of good heart, seeking to be in accordance with God, perform simple procedures to aid and assist the hurting and dying?"

"But when a man is appointed to die, he dies," the abbott said firmly.

"Exactly so. My surgery will not interfere with God's predestination of life or death. Is that not true?"

The abbot smiled. "You are a cunning young woman."

Mary sighed. " 'Tis not my desire to be so idly, and yet in my heart I feel the need for a spiritual healing, yet always before when that emptiness made itself known I put it from me."

"And now?"

"Now, I find that I can scarce face the new day without wondering about God and what plan He might have. Will He hear me, Father? After all these years of denial?"

"Do you desire to repent of your sins?"

Mary thought on this for a moment. "I desire to make right whatever is wrong between myself and God. I desire to know that when I pray, He hears me and not only this, but that He cares, as well."

The abbott smiled and closed a big hand over Mary's smaller one. "He hears and He cares, Mary. Repent your sins and ask for His saving grace. Christ Jesus will be your Lord and Saviour, and a home in heaven will be yours forever."

"And in honoring God with my trust, will He punish me for my desire to heal? Will I need to put such concerns aside?"

The abbott shook his head. "I believe your desire to be for good, Mary. God honors all who seek His face and strive to do His will first. If that is where your heart is, God will deal justly with your ambitions."

"Then I will trust Him."

Mary prayed, and immediately a peace such as she had never known descended upon her. She looked up at the abbott with wet eyes, feeling that deep within, she had rid herself of the creature that had once existed.

"God's love is a healing love, Mary. He makes right that which is wrong."

"But there is so much in my life to set right," Mary said honestly. With a sad glance over her shoulder at the empty open door, Mary felt her tears fall anew. "I fear I have wounded with my words."

"Wounds need but a bit of care, no?"

"I drove Peter away with my harshness," she admitted. "Mayhap he will not forgive me for such a fit of temper."

"Were your words unjust?"

"Aye," Mary replied. "I felt he did not understand my love for the children, yet I know it not to be true. He loves them as well, and it would tear at his heart to see a single one of them misplaced."

The abbott nodded, seeming to understand her plight. "You spoke out of fear and not out of trust."

" 'Tis hard to trust," Mary confessed. "But my love bids me to do so."

"Your love for the children?"

"Nay," she answered, wiping at her tears. "My love for Peter."

The old man's face broke into a wide grin. "You have given your heart to that young man?"

"I fear 'tis true enough for all the good it might now do," Mary replied. "We know so little of each other, yet a strong bond grew. I pray I have not destroyed it, for I love Peter with all my heart."

" 'Tis a good thing," Peter's voice called out from the doorway, "for it might help me in winning the king's permission to make you my wife."

Mary jumped to her feet and turned to face him. He was filthy from his hunt and exhaustion could clearly be read in his eyes, but there was joy in them as well.

"Oh, Peter!" she exclaimed, both embarrassed and happy that he'd overheard her confession. "You were gone so long. I had begun to despair of your return. Are you well? Did you have trouble?" She paused with a sudden understanding of his declaration. "Make me your wife?"

Peter laughed out loud, and even the abbott chuckled from behind her. Mary shook her head, fearful that she'd dreamed the entire thing. "Did you truly say—"

"Aye," Peter interrupted, stepping forward to take hold of Mary. She was glad for the clean clothes brought to her by the monks and hoped Peter found them fetching on her as he scrutinized her from head to toe. "The bath seems to suit you well. I do not remember these clothes, but they pale in comparison to your beauty."

"Oh, Peter," she said with a sigh. "I am sorry for my harsh tongue. I drove you away, and it frightened me through and through."

He touched her cheek lightly. " 'Tis forgotten and forgiven."

"But I should make it up to you."

Peter grinned. "You may start by saying yea to my proposal."

Mary felt her pulse quicken. "You were serious then?"

"As serious as a man can possibly be about the woman he loves."

"Loves?" Mary swallowed hard. "You love me?"

"I would not wed you unless I did," he replied somewhat harshly, then softened, pulling her near. "Aye, I love you, sweet Mary, and I want nothing more than to know you better and help you care for that growing brood."

"I love you, Peter," she said with such joy that she thought she might burst into tears anew.

"Is that a yes?"

She nodded, dark hair dancing behind her.

Chapter 12

Gideon peered eagerly into the faces of his conspirators early the next morning. "You have to do this," he said, trying hard to sound older than his eight years. "Mary and Peter will never get married and keep us if we do not help them get back together."

"But what have we do with this?" Gwenny asked, doubting Gideon's reason.

Gideon's glance darted from Darias to Gwenny and then to Matilda and Ellen. Gideon had chosen them to listen to his plan.

"Mary and Peter have been fighting," he begun, and all heads nodded in acknowledgment. "They really love each other, and I think they will be our father and mother, but only if they stop fighting."

"They are adults, and we are but children," Darias chimed in. "We cannot make them marry."

Gideon sighed. "Mayhap we are children, but do not children need parents?"

"Aye," Gwenny replied. "We need them, but we have lost parents before. Why should we think to have parents again?"

"Because I prayed," Gideon answered confidently and looked to each eager face as if to reaffirm his words.

"I have been with Peter since the beginning, when there were no other children," Gideon continued. "That makes me the leader."

"What are your plans?" Darias asked in a way that showed acceptance of Gideon's predetermined position.

"I am going into the woods. I will hide there, and you will tell Peter and Mary that I have gone. Tell them that I was sad because they were fighting. Tell them that I want them to be my mother and father. Tell them 'tis what we all want."

Ellen and Matilda remained silent, but Gwenny was still unconvinced. "You could be eaten alive by some animal," she suggested.

"Nay, 'tis morning and they will be full from eating all night long."

"Would it not be safer to stay here and just tell them we want them to wed and care for us always?" she questioned.

"Nay!" Gideon's exasperation with the group was starting to show. His eight-year-old face took on a worried expression that seemed as grave as his words. "They will not listen right now. They are mad, and when you are mad, you do not listen."

" 'Tis true enough," Darias stated as one who knew. "I cannot listen when I am mad."

"See?" Gideon said, looking to Gwenny. " 'Tis true." He looked nervously around the room to where the others played in silence. "They are too little to be left alone. We must not let the monks take them away."

Gwenny looked defensively to where Anne slept at her feet. "No one will take little Anne away. I will not let them."

"But we are only children, and big folks seldom listen to us."

"So you will run away to the woods," Gwenny began, "and when Mary notices that you are gone, we are to tell her that you were afraid?"

"No," Gideon replied patiently, "tell them together. Make Peter and Mary both come to hear what I told you."

Gwenny and Darias exchanged a glance and then nodded at Gideon. His face lit up as he realized they would do their part in his scheme.

"Now remember, do not tell them until time to eat, else I will not have enough time to hide," Gideon reminded the group.

Gideon had been gone for over an hour when Mary appeared at the door to call the children to the morning meal. Making a routine counting of heads, Mary noted that Gideon was missing from the group. No doubt the boy had made his way to Peter's side.

" 'Tis time for breakfast," Mary announced. Coming to Gwenny's side, she reached down and took Anne. "I will fetch Peter to carry you to the table, Gwenny."

The girl nodded but refused to meet Mary's eyes. Darias, only a few feet away, kept his gaze on the floor and went to retrieve Edward.

"You are most unusually quiet this morning," Mary said cautiously. She looked at each of the somber faces and worried that her fight with Peter had caused them all to fear her. "What is it that vexes you so?"

When no one answered, Mary truly began to worry. Anne cooed softly in her arms, but otherwise even Edward remained still. Looking from one child to the next, Mary felt her breath catch in her throat.

"Has something happened that I should know about?"

Gwenny looked up at Darias and then to Mary. Slowly she nodded her head.

"Tell me then!" Mary commanded a bit louder than she'd intended. "Tell me now."

"We cannot," Gwenny finally spoke. "Peter must be here, too."

"What say you?" Mary questioned, tightening her hold on Anne. The baby began to protest with a screech of indignation. Mary lessened her grip and drew in a deep breath. "Where is Gideon? Has this to do with him?"

"Aye," Gwenny replied. "But he bid us to silence unless you and Peter were both here."

Mary nodded curtly and went in search of Peter.

"Peter! Peter!" she cried his name aloud. Her voice frightened Anne to tears. Trying to hush the child and still call out, Mary gave up and let Anne cry. Where could Peter have gotten off to? Better yet, where had Gideon gotten off to?

'Tis foolishness to worry, Mary told herself. *Gideon is probably just playing a game with us.* But in her heart she knew it wasn't the case. Gideon had taken her fight with Peter most personally. He alone had been her mainstay in the early days when Peter had been so sick. He alone knew how much Mary and Peter had come to care for each other.

"Peter!" She was growing desperate and began to search the yards behind the guest house. Tears formed in her eyes. Gideon had to be all right. He just had to be.

Anne's incessant wailing announced their arrival to the malt house. *Peter just has to be here,* Mary thought and pled with God to make it so.

"Peter!"

The large empty room filled immediately with echoes of the baby's lusty cry. A quick glance confirmed that no one was there.

Mary's tears began to fall in earnest as she continued her search. Her imagination ran wild with images of Gideon lying hurt and defenseless in the woods. The distant sound of the river caused her to shudder with thoughts of the boy's lifeless body washing to shore.

"Peter!" she called out against her sobs. "Peter!"

∽

Peter's skin was nearly blue when he emerged from the river. He'd taken the quiet hours of the morning to slip away from the others and bathe. His mind reflected on the events of the past few days.

He was to marry. He'd actually asked a woman to be his mate. Somehow the idea was not nearly as foreign as he'd imagined it might be. He thought of Mary and her long dark tresses. He imagined the violet eyes and dark sooty lashes. She'd bewitched him with her girlish smiles and gentle touch, and now she was to become his wife. What a wonder!

The responsibility of such a thing was never far from his thoughts. Toweling dry, Peter thought of the multitude of children who now were in his charge. He'd led men upon the battlefield, sometimes to victory and ofttimes to fall back and fight another day, but never had such a task loomed at him with this depth of solemnity. Children needed a great deal of care, and while Mary was quite willing to give herself over to the task, she could not possibly provide for their nourishment and shelter. No, that responsibility would be Peter's, and how could he give himself over to it without lands of his own and a place to call home?

These new thoughts caused him no small amount of concern. Would Edward be willing to give him leave from the battlefield in order to settle an estate of his own? Surely with this blight upon England having claimed so many lives, Edward would see the need to begin again. Peter could benefit not only his newly acquired family, but others as well. Perhaps he could take up established lands and see that crops and livestock once again thrived.

These new thoughts intrigued him. Dressing quickly to ward off the morning chill, Peter had just taken a seat on the ground when he caught the faint sound of someone calling his name. Quickly he pulled on his boots, secured his belt and sword, and gathered up his belongings.

"Peter!" It was Mary. "Peter!" She called again, and he thought he denoted desperation in her tone.

A feeling of dread washed over him. Perhaps someone had fallen ill. Perhaps it was one of the children. Peter quickened his steps and through his mind ran images of the children. Darias with his bowl-style haircut and huge brown eyes. Gwenny, hobbling with the crutches Peter had devised.

"Peter!" The voice tore at his heart.

"I'm here, Mary!" he called, and in his mind he saw each of the children. Ellen and Matilda, such tiny mites with dark blue eyes and pale complexions. Robert, independent for his six years and willfully stubborn. William, Sarah, and the babies Edward and Anne. "Dear God," he panted the prayer, "do not let harm have come to the children."

He ran through the brush, mindless of the branches that beat at him in his passage. He burst into the clearing and saw Mary with Anne bundled against her, rushing across the empty field to him. It was then that Gideon's face came to mind, and somehow Peter knew her news had to do with the blond-haired boy.

When she reached him, Mary collapsed into Peter's arms. Anne objected with her howls and cries, but both adults ignored the baby and clung to each other.

"Gideon?" Peter questioned, and Mary nodded breathlessly.

"The children," she gasped out, trying to regain her breath.

"What of the children? What of Gideon?" Peter had taken a firm grip of her shoulders. His face softened tenderly as he saw the misery in her eyes. " 'Twill be all right, sweet Mary," he whispered.

"He is not with the others," Mary finally managed to say. Anne settled a bit as Mary's voice calmed. "Gwenny told me he wanted us to hear the news together. I believe he has run away."

Peter took Anne in one arm and pulled Mary along with him. "We had best find out what the boy is up to," he said.

"Oh, Peter. I think he is worried about our fight. I saw how he looked when I argued with you, and he has no way to know that we have made up our differences."

"That may well be the case," Peter replied, "but he has no cause to grieve you like this."

Peter's eyes took in the landscape around them. The monastery held an abundant number of hiding places. Beyond the walls of the abbey were forests, field, and the river from which he'd just come. There was no real way of knowing where the small boy might have taken himself off to.

The expression on the faces of the other children told Peter all he needed to know. Gwenny sat quietly playing with Edward, while the other children, seeming to sense the gravity of the situation, sat silently watching and waiting.

"What is this that you must tell us?" Peter asked the children collectively.

Gwenny darted a look to Darias and back again to Peter and Mary. "He has gone away."

Peter felt Mary stiffen at his side. "Did he say where he was to go and why?" Peter questioned.

"He went to the woods," Darias offered. "He thinks it will make you. . ." He fell silent and looked imploringly to Gwenny to finish.

"He feared you would give us over to the monks," Gwenny finally managed. She put Edward down to toddle across the floor in awkward baby steps. "You would not do that, would you?"

"Of course not. What made him think this?" Peter's words were soft as he knelt beside the girl.

"You and Mary were fighting, and it scared him," Gwenny said, then lowered her eyes and added, "It scared me, too."

"But why Gwenny? We would not hurt you."

"Gideon said you and Mary were our only hope of staying together," Gwenny confided. Her eyes were huge and mournful. "He, that is, we, want to stay with you. We have no kin and noplace to go. If you do not wed and take us with you, we will have to stay here."

"I will never leave you here," Mary interjected before Peter could speak. "I could not leave you."

"Nor I," Peter agreed.

"Gideon thought if you saw how much we wanted to stay with you, how strong we felt," Darias finally spoke, "he figured you would keep together and not fight."

Peter chuckled in spite of the somber moment. "I would imagine even together, Mary and I will have our moments of disagreement." Getting up, Peter bent over and lifted Gwenny. "Your breakfast is getting cold. You must eat while Mary and I decide what is to be done."

Darias grabbed Edward, while the other children shuffled up to stand before Mary and Peter. Warm love for the children flooded Peter's soul. They were perfectly helpless without him, and their faces bespoke of such trust that Peter's heart swelled with pride. The urgency to find Gideon surged through him like fire.

Ushering the children to breakfast and leaving them to the ministerings of the monks, Peter motioned Mary outside.

"I am going to go look for Gideon. I do not imagine him to have gotten far." Mary nodded, and worry lined her expression.

Peter reached a hand to her cheek, still amazed at the softness of her skin. Her eyes darkened with emotion at his touch. "Fear not, my love," he said, feeling Mary tremble beneath his touch. "I will find our boy."

Mary sighed. "I know you will."

Peter longed to kiss her, but instead reluctantly released her. "I had best go."

Mary watched him trot off in the direction of the nearest trees. Thick undergrowth and brush kept her eyes from being able to search beyond the first tall oaks.

"Most precious Father," she whispered as Peter disappeared into the woods, "please keep them safe and bring them back to me." The chill autumn wind picked up and stung her cheeks. With a weary glance at the overcast skies, Mary added, "And please hurry."

Chapter 13

Peter saw the signs of Gideon's passage and breathed a sigh of relief. Following the well-laid trail, Peter called out to the boy.

"Gideon! Gideon if you can hear me, please answer!"

Silence greeted him, and the shroudlike cover of the forest's ceiling made Peter pause to listen for any sound. Every breath he drew echoed in the stillness. When the wind picked up, Peter could see the rustling of the treetops, but little else. Here in the deep coverage of the forest it was dark and damp but well protected from the ravages of the wind.

Silently, Peter prayed for guidance before continuing. Prayer and trust in God were things so new to him that Peter often forgot their importance. It seemed odd, he thought, that so many years of knightly service should surround him with religious rhetoric and yet leave not a single mark upon his soul. It took, instead, the devastation of nations by a disease no one understood to even give him cause to think upon God and what might lie beyond this earth.

Pressing forward, Peter followed the beaten-down pathway where twigs had been snapped in two and the undergrowth had been clearly tread upon. The trail was leading him back to the river, and Peter felt a shudder of apprehension run up his spine at the thought of Gideon helplessly trying to master the river's swift current.

"Gideon!" he called out, hurrying his step.

The sound of the river grew louder. The water could have been a soothing sound as it fell against the stones and hurried its way downstream. It could have been had the moment not been so serious.

Peter glanced quickly upstream. The trees thinned out but still lined the banks. Overhead, a heavy gray sky promised rain, and Peter knew he had to hurry.

Downstream seemed more heavily overgrown and looked the most likely place for a small boy to hide. Choosing that direction, Peter was soon rewarded with a small set of footprints in the mud.

"Gideon!"

The water rushed by, blocking out all other sound, and Peter strained his ear for any murmur or noise that might betray the boy's presence. The wind was able to reach him and so, too, the first drops of rain.

There was nothing to do but go forward. Peter could hardly leave the boy to fend for himself. As the rain increased, Peter longed for the comfort of a warm fire and Mary at his side.

With rain making it difficult to see, Peter pulled close the hood of his cloak and fought to make out the trail. Small prints led down to the water's edge, where it appeared to Peter that Gideon had attempted to cross the water. There was no way of knowing what had happened, whether the current had been too swift or the water too cold, but prints led away from the water and down the bank.

Silently thanking God, Peter wiped water from his face and moved ahead. When the muddy prints headed back to the safety of the forest, Peter was again thankful.

"Gideon!" Peter called out when he'd come a short way into the woods.

"Peter? Is that you?" the small, uncertain voice called back.

"Gideon, where are you? Come out this instant!"

Peter glanced quickly around the shadowy haven. In a moment, Gideon emerged from the undergrowth with a sheepish look on his face. Peter could tell from the look of the boy that he feared he might well be in deep trouble.

"Where's Mary?" Gideon asked, looking behind Peter as if he expected to see her standing there.

"She is back at the monastery, where you should be," Peter admonished. "You could not possibly desire she risk her life as you have your own, in order to be here."

Gideon's expression sobered. "I did not want you to go away, Peter."

Peter felt his fear and anxiety melt away. He could not be angry at Gideon, and he opened his arms to the child. Gideon rushed to the knight and clung tightly to his neck when Peter lifted him into the air.

"You promised you would stay with me," Gideon said, pulling away just enough to see Peter's eyes.

"Aye, I promised. And I kept my word. I did not leave, but you, my good sir, did."

"I felt bad you and Mary were fighting. I was afraid you would leave us with the monks and go away," Gideon said with tears in his eyes.

Peter could hardly bear the fear he saw in the child's eyes. "I am a man of my word, Gideon. I told you I would not leave you, and I will not. At least not until I can make a home for you and the others."

"Mary, too?" Gideon asked with a voice that betrayed his fear of the answer.

"Aye, Mary, too. I have asked her to be my wife and she has consented."

"Does that mean she said yes?" Gideon's eyes were hopeful.

Peter laughed aloud. "That it does, my boy. That it does."

"And you will keep all of us with you?"

"Aye, Gideon. I will make a home for all of you and any more that come our way."

The boy squealed his delight and wrapped his arms even tighter around Peter's neck.

"I see this meets with your approval," Peter said, making his way through the trees. "Let us return to the others and show Mary you are safe. You have sorely grieved her heart, and you owe her an apology."

Gideon's joy left him, and he again pulled back from Peter. "I did not mean to make her sad."

"A good man does not set out to mindlessly hurt others. Our womenfolk must be protected and cared for. They are very precious, Gideon, and we have an important job to keep them safe and provide for their needs." Gideon nodded as if he knew exactly what was expected of him. Peter continued. "Women are wondrous creatures, Gideon. They are one of God's very best gifts to the world. They love with the very depths of their hearts, and when that love is taken away, they bear the scars of that wound."

"Is Mary's heart hurt?" Gideon asked with grave concern.

"Aye," Peter replied. "Her heart was near to breaking for your absence. She felt responsible because she had argued with me in front of you."

Gideon lowered his eyes. "I thought I did a good thing, Peter. I did not mean to hurt Mary's heart."

"When you see her, Gideon, you be sure and let her know how you feel."

"Will her heart get better?" he asked hopefully. "If I tell her I am sorry, will that help her not hurt?"

"Aye, Gideon," Peter answered softly. "Aye, it will help a great deal."

∽∾

The rain saturated the ground in torrents, and Mary feared for Peter and Gideon's health. She paced the room, watching and waiting for their return, always a prayer upon her lips for their safety.

The children played quietly, sensing Mary's fear. Even Anne and Edward were silent, having fallen asleep some time back to the steady rhythm of Mary's feet pacing upon the stone floor.

Then, just as she had begun to despair, Peter came through the door with Gideon wrapped tightly beneath his cloak.

"Oh, Gideon! Peter!" she exclaimed and went to take the boy from Peter's arms. She looked him over for any signs of harm, and when she was satisfied that there were none, she hugged him long and hard.

"I was so afraid," she murmured against Gideon's face. "I prayed and prayed, and now here you are safe and sound." She glanced up to see Peter's tender expression. "Oh, thank you, Peter, for finding him. I do not wish to think what life would have been without Gideon." Tears of relief and joy streamed down her face.

Gideon reached out his hand to Mary's face. "Peter said that I hurt your heart when I ran away."

"Aye, Gideon. That you did," Mary replied with a quick, knowing glance at Peter.

"I am sorry, Mary," Gideon said, tears welling up in his eyes. "I only wanted you and Peter to stay together. I only wanted all of us to stay together."

By this time the other children had wandered over to where Mary and Gideon clung to each other. Gwenny was the first to speak.

"Aye, we want to be a family."

"With Peter for our father and you for our mother," Gideon added quickly.

"We do not want to stay with the monks," Darias interjected. "We do not want to leave you."

"You will not leave me," Mary stated firmly. Her voice took on an air of authority. "I will fight to keep you with me. Every single one of you. I love you all so very much. I cannot imagine my life without you in it. If even one of you were gone, it would make an empty place in my heart."

"Then you will be our mother?" Gwenny asked hopefully.

"I will be your mother," Mary confirmed.

"And I will be your father," Peter said, coming to put a hand on Mary's shoulder.

At this, Mary released Gideon and stood to meet Peter's gaze. "We will marry and make a home for all of you."

The children rushed around them with small arms extended to embrace the already embracing couple.

"We are going to be a family," Gideon said happily, putting first one hand in Peter's hand and the other in Mary's.

That night, after all the children were asleep, Peter motioned Mary to follow him. Mary wondered to herself what possible problem they would now have to deal with, but when she closed the door behind her, Peter swept her into his arms and kissed her soundly.

"Peter Donne!" she exclaimed in mock horror. "You have no right to take such liberties."

Peter laughed and pulled her tighter. "I have longed to kiss those cherry lips of yours since you first appeared in the fields this morning."

"It seems like a lifetime ago," Mary said, feeling suddenly flushed. "But," she added shyly, "truth be told, I have hoped for such a kiss as this from you."

"We've a great deal to discuss, my Mary."

Peter's fingers trailed up her arm, spreading warmth wherever they lingered. Mary found it nearly impossible to think.

"I suppose 'tis true enough. We have fingers, I mean, further to go," she said, coughing nervously at her mistake.

"Ah, Mary." Peter moaned her name and released her. "Let us seek out the abbott tonight and wed."

Mary began to tremble anew at this thought, but realized the impossibility of the matter. "You belong to Edward. 'Tis his permission you need to seek."

"I belong to you," he said, leaning forward with a suggestive grin. "And I would have you belong to me for now and all time."

Mary giggled nervously to break the tension of the moment. "You may live to regret such a desire."

"Never!" Peter exclaimed and again pulled her close.

Mary relished the scent of him and the warmth of his sinewy arms as they engulfed her body. "Will the king allow you to wed?" she asked, hesitating to mention anything that might give Peter cause to recant his declaration of love.

"Edward will see the sense in it. I am going to seek him out just as soon as we reach your grandmother's estate. 'Tis not far from here."

Mary jumped back in surprise. "You know of my grandmother?"

Peter smiled. "I questioned the abbot. He knew well of Lady Elizabeth Beckett. She is alive and well on estates just north of this place. 'Tis no more than two days' walk."

"Two days? You knew this and told me naught?"

"Forgive me, but I had much on my mind."

Mary seemed stupefied at the news. "My grandmother is alive."

"She is as far as the abbot knows."

"Can we leave on the morrow?" Mary felt her breath catch in her throat. Her stomach churned nervously.

"Can you be ready on the morrow?" Peter asked teasingly.

"I can be ready now," Mary stated firmly. Then with a glance backward to the closed door, she sighed. "But 'twould be unfair to wake up the children because of my impatience. I can wait until daylight."

Peter's eyes grew dark with passion. He leaned down and placed a long, lingering kiss upon Mary's lips before speaking. "And I can wait for Edward's blessing, although I will not promise to be a patient man about the delay."

Later that evening, Mary lay down to sleep and found her mind on the trip to come. *What manner of woman will she be?* Mary wondered of her grandmother. She'd only heard her father's negative comments regarding Lady Beckett's religious faith. She couldn't remember a single kind word or fond memory of the woman. Always, her father had issued conversation regarding his mother with a bitterness and regret that threatened to swallow him up.

"Oh, Father in heaven," Mary whispered in the inky blackness of her room, "please make a way for my grandmother and me to come together. I am so afraid." She pulled the cover to her chin and trembled.

Grandmother is all I have left, she thought silently, and then a warm memory of Peter's lips upon hers came to mind. Behind this came the vision of ten little faces and their happy, trusting expressions when Mary had pledged herself to be their mother.

"I have made myself accountable for much, have I not?" She breathed the question and gave a heavy sigh. A ripple of fear shot through her as she contemplated the awesome responsibility of caring for the children.

"Dear God," she whispered, "please guide me and let me deal wisely with the children and their needs."

Finally giving in to the exhaustion of the day, Mary slept with visions of the road to come.

The next morning, Mary was overwhelmed by the kindness of the monks and abbott. The men had chosen to provide a more sturdy wagon and an elderly, but agile, mare to pull it. There was plenty of room for everyone, and Mary found herself hugging the abbott without thought.

"Thank you so very much," she said with complete sincerity. "You have given me more than I could have ever imagined."

The abbott smiled. "God's ways are not always imagined or understood. But if we trust and allow Him to work His great wonders, we see that we are well cared for and every needed thing is no farther away than a prayer."

Mary nodded. "Thank you." With Peter's help, she climbed into the wagon and took up the reins.

"Are you ready, Milady?" Peter questioned with a wink.

"I am, good sire."

Peter gave a brief bow and stepped up onto his mount. "Then let us press forth into the future and what awaits us there."

Chapter 14

The Yorkshire countryside had not seen the devastation of the plague in the same way southern England had. There had been cases of the disease, but for the most part it was more isolated and far less consuming.

Mary watched the open country with great interest. She'd never seen the moors, but had heard her father talk much about roaming the hillsides during his youth. Rocky ravines occasionally broke the monotony of the endless gray hills, but trees were few. She tried to imagine it green and flowering, but the bitter wind made those thoughts quickly fade.

With the damp chill of winter upon them and the rains coming more and more often, Mary became gravely concerned for the children. The monks had provided blankets of wool for the trip and they helped greatly to keep the children warm, but Mary knew they needed a home and shelter. *Will Grandmother take us in?* she wondered with a side glance to where Anne slept. The baby was nearing three months of age, and Mary found it hard to accept the changes that had taken place in such a short time.

She looked to the man ahead of her. Peter rode in regal style upon his steed, and Mary's heart quickened at the sight of him. Only a few short months before, she'd not known of Peter Donne, and now, now she was pledging herself to become his wife. Had she made the right choice? Had she agreed only for the protection of the children? The questions haunted her in earnest.

They stopped for the night in a small borough where the only inn had two rooms and both were taken. Peter tried unsuccessfully to barter for the rooms and finally accepted the stable as lodging.

"The innkeeper says there is a fine loft above the livery," Peter told Mary. "The roof is sound and the sweet hay there will make ample beds and keep us warm."

Mary looked at the exhausted children and nodded. "I suppose we have no other choice. We cannot very well press on, only to end up without shelter of any kind."

"I will carry the little ones up. You go ahead with the blankets and make it ready for them."

Mary looked at Peter and noted the weariness in his eyes. "You look as though I should make a place ready for you," Mary teased.

Peter scratched his bearded face and gave a lopsided grin. "I would rather a hot bath and a shave. I grow weary of this beard."

Just then Anne began to cry. Mary knew it was well past her feeding time. As if inspired, Edward, too, began to fuss. "I will care for the babies first. Bring Gwenny up, and she can help me."

When all the children were cared for and sleeping soundly in the hay, Mary asked Peter to watch over them and disappeared from the loft for a short time. When she returned, she brought a pan of hot water and a towel.

" 'Tis no bath," she said with a grin, "but 'twill suffice for me to shave that face of yours."

Peter leaned up from where he'd stretched out. With a quizzical look, he questioned, "You? I should let you shave me?"

Mary's smile broadened. "I shaved my father's face daily. You will prove to be no great challenge after dealing with him." Peter shook his head and dark brown hair fell across his eyes. "A haircut might also be in order," Mary added and motioned Peter to a small milking stool.

"Did you think to bring shears as well?" he quipped and dragged himself to where Mary stood.

"Nay, but I believe there is a pair in the stable below for shearing the sheep. 'Twould be simple enough to pretend you were just one more woolly creature."

Peter laughed and pulled Mary close. "You are a charming nymph, Mary Beckett. How is it that I am fortunate enough after a life of pursuit in kingly courts to manage to convince a woman like you to be my wife?"

Mary pushed him away and pointed to the ground. "We are not wed yet, Sir Donne. Now sit and let me be about my task."

Mary placed a hot, wet towel upon Peter's face and went to retrieve the knife. She thought of Peter's words just moments earlier and couldn't help but ask, "What women pursued you in Edward's court?"

She wasn't certain, but she thought she heard him question her jealousy from beneath the towel's muffling. Stripping the towel from his face, she stared down into his dark eyes and questioned him again. "What of it, Peter?"

He smiled. "Mayhap I should wait until after you have shaved me," he said, noting the knife in her hands.

"Very well," Mary replied and went to work, "but I intend to know."

They sat side by side after Mary had finished. She was pleased with her job, having not nicked Peter's face even once. She had even managed to trim his hair using the same knife with which she'd shaved his face. He looked like a new man, and Mary was very pleased with the results.

"Now tell me of your life before the fever came," she insisted.

Peter's face took on a distinctly distant look. "I grew up around the court of Edward. I was always cared and well provided for. I never knew want with one exception."

"And what was that?"

"Affection." Peter said thoughtfully. "Love."

Mary looked at him earnestly and realized he was quite serious. "But a man such as yourself. . ."

"Had many admirers and pursuers. That much is true," he said, not boasting in the least. "But I had never to wonder at the reason they strived to snag me. Women were plentiful." He paused for a moment as if traveling back to another lifetime. "Beauty was everywhere, and death was not a concern. At least not in the manner of today. There were always battles to fight and such, but the all-consuming fever and death were no concern to us. We were untouched by that which could harm. At least we deemed ourselves to be so."

Mary listened intently and watched Peter's face as he continued. "Velvet-and satin-clad women were everywhere. Gold and silver adorned every single person, and there was no place to set your gaze upon that did not speak of all that was good in life.

"I had my pick of silken-clothed beauties," he remarked, and Mary immediately touched the ragged wool of her own clothing. Suddenly she felt inadequate. She'd grown up with more than most in her village, but she was not affluent enough to boast of silks and satins, dripping with gold trimmings. How could Peter possibly give all of that up for the likes of a physician's daughter? Why, he might very well be given in marriage to a woman of real means and know a title and lands so vast he would always know comfort. What could she possibly offer him?

Mary was so lost in thought, she hadn't realized Peter had stopped talking. He now looked at her with passion-filled brown eyes. Swallowing hard, Mary blinked back tears and forced her worried thoughts to the back of her mind. Peter, however, seemed to know where her imagination had taken her.

"There were none who could compare to you, sweet Mary," he whispered.

Mary forgot herself. "But I have naught to give you. No dowry, no lands, not even a name of well-being." She fidgeted with her skirt before continuing. "I had not thought of all you would give up by marrying me."

Peter chuckled softly. "I would give up treacherous, traitorous hearts. Women who only sought their best advantages. Women who knew naught of love, but everything of greed."

"I do not understand," Mary said in a soft, sad voice.

Peter reached out to still her hand. "Mary, you are so much more than those women. You have come to understand about life and death in a way that they never stop to consider. I have watched you give of yourself until there was naught left to give. I have seen you risk your own life and well-being to care for complete strangers. Your heart is of finer gold than the gowns of those in court. Your thoughts are of purer silver and your eyes are the richest of jewels."

"Peter, be reasonable," Mary said amid his words of poetry. "You are a knight of the king and entitled to much, much more than you will know with me. I have no real silver or gold."

"One need not possess silver and gold in order to love," Peter said, stroking her hand with his thumb. "One need only to possess a heart filled with love. Have ye a heart for me, Mary?"

The stroke of Peter's thumb upon her hand caused a tingling sensation to run up her arm. She lowered her eyes. "Aye, I have a heart for you."

Peter ran his fingers up her arm to Mary's face. Gently, he lifted her chin. Mary saw the expression of boundless love in his eyes and her heart filled with longing.

" 'Tis all we need," he assured her. "My heart is yours and your heart is mine. Naught else matters."

Mary reached her hand to his clean-shaven cheek. "The little ones need clothing and shoes. They need food in their bellies and shelter overhead. You were once the reasonable one of us." She paused with a smile. "Now it would seem that task falls to me."

"Nay," Peter replied. "I am still most reasonable. I know these concerns of yours, and I will provide for them. That, my Mary, is my responsibility. I will not have you fret so. Trust me. Trust me to see to the needs that you speak of."

"Would not a court of silver and gold be of more ease and comfort?" she whispered. "I want only that you would be certain of this union. Mayhap the king will not approve of your desires. Have you considered this matter?"

Peter nodded. "I have. I know my king, and he will hear my reasons, all ten, no, eleven of them."

Mary ran her hand down the side of his face, and Peter quickly captured her hand and kissed her fingers one by one.

"I love you, Peter," she whispered and let him pull her forward for a kiss.

She wrapped her arms around him, letting her hands play with the curls of hair that touched his collar. He kissed her with a tenderness that melted away Mary's concerns. *He loves me*, she thought and reveled in the knowledge. *He loves me more than silver and gold. He loves me more than the women in velvet and silk. He loves me.*

Mary slept soundly after taking her place between Anne and Edward. Peter slept near the loft ladder even though Mary had feared he'd roll off the edge in the night and plunge to severe injury on the stone floor below.

The next morning, the children sensed Mary's anticipation, and when they were once again on the rode to York, Gideon's animation got the best of him.

"Will we live with your grandmother?" he asked in eager fascination.

"It is my hope she will take us in," Mary replied, giving the old mare her head. Peter rode ahead of them as always, and Mary knew the horse would not get far, should she be of a mind to head away from the road.

"I do not know my grandmother, Gideon. My father and I never journeyed to see her. I have heard very little of her, but it is my prayer that she has a kind heart and a generous spirit."

"Will you and Peter marry in York?"

"I cannot say," Mary replied. Her wistful glance to Peter's back was not lost by Gideon's watchful eye.

"I am glad you love Peter. I love him, too, and I am going to ask him if I can call him Papa instead of Peter."

"I think he would like that, Gideon. He loves you a great deal," Mary said and leaned down to whisper. "You will always be very special to him because you were the first."

Gideon's eyes brightened. "He told me I might one day be a knight. I want Peter to be proud of me. I want you to be proud of me, too."

Mary tousled his hair. "I am proud of you, Gideon. You saw things of great importance before either Peter or I could use them for ourselves. You are special to me as well, and I love you very much."

Gideon grew sober for a moment. "I never knew my father, but my mama was always with me. Do you think she would care if I called you mama, now?"

Mary looked away quickly to avoid letting Gideon see the tears that came to her eyes. "I am sure she would only want for you to be happy and loved."

"Then she would be glad I am with you and Peter, Mama." Gideon squeezed closer to Mary and put his hand in hers.

Mary could find no words to express her heart. She lightly squeezed the boy's hand and held it in her lap for a long time.

Spying a band of travelers ahead of them, Peter rode on to catch up with them and learn of their plight.

"We are bound for the Lady of the Moors," a toothless woman crooned. "We have sick and injured among us. Some have not lasted the journey."

"I have a healer with me," Peter said, motioning back to the wagon. "She is quite skilled in a variety of treatments. Perhaps those in your number who are nearing death would best be tended by her."

The old woman nodded. "We have several who are gravely ill."

"Is it the fever?"

"Nay, leastwise not the fever from across the sea. 'Tis another matter."

Peter noted the approaching stream. "I will fetch my lady and see if she can help. Why don't you set up camp over there by the water? We will join you shortly." He reined his horse back and made his way to Mary and the children.

"There is great sickness in their group," he informed Mary. "I thought perhaps with the sun getting so low, we might make camp and you could tend them."

Mary nodded. "But why are they upon the road?"

"They were making a pilgrimage to the Lady of the Moors."

Mary's eyes widened. "I have heard of this woman. She is said to be a great healer and," Mary added with a smile of understanding, "one who talks to God and to whom He listens."

Peter smiled. "Mayhap you two will meet and you can share your secrets."

Mary observed the people ahead as they set out to make camp. "Mayhap."

"I will set our camp away from them," Peter said without waiting for Mary's thought on the matter. "There is no sense in the children becoming ill as well."

"But I may be a long while with the others," Mary said, noting the numbers. There were at least twenty people in the group.

"I will be fine. Gwenny will help with the babies."

"I can help, too," Gideon said suddenly. "I helped first with Anne, remember?"

Peter nodded. "Of course, and I will depend on you to honor your word and give me your best." Gideon beamed.

Peter arranged their camp while Mary gathered her things and left final instructions with the older children. Making her way to the ragged group, she wondered how to best serve their needs.

"I am Mary," she told the toothless woman.

"I am Margaret of Derby. We travel with our sick to the Lady of the Moors."

"I see. Are there those here who I might help?"

The woman nodded and pointed a crooked finger to where a group of people lay upon the ground. "They are not long for the world."

With a prayer in her heart, Mary went quickly to her task.

They were to remain at the camp for three more days. The people who Mary nursed were gravely ill and further travel was deemed impossible. Some of the band of twenty continued north, leaving their fellow travelers behind. Toothless Margaret stayed at Mary's side to help where she could, and more than once the people told Mary she was blessed with healing from God.

Mary smiled, thinking of how she would have found their words offensive at one time. Now she knew comfort from them and wondered if her father could have possibly known the same peace in his heart.

"You are marked by God to be a healer, Child," Margaret told her as Mary mixed a balm.

"My father and grandmother were healers as well," Mary replied. " 'Tis in our family."

The old woman nodded. "Where are ye bound with your brood?"

"North, to my grandmother's estate. She lives outside of York."

" 'Tis our good fortune and the hallowed Father's blessings to have crossed our paths with you and your man. We are too weak to care for ourselves properly, yet your man has seen to our needs for food and fire, while you have cared for our sicknesses."

Mary finished her task and got to her feet. "I am glad God saw fit to cross our paths, Margaret. He always seems to know just when to bring folk together."

"She has the Lady's touch," one man remarked to Margaret. "She should journey to the Lady of the Moors and join her in healing."

"God guides her steps as He does the Lady's. I would think if it be befitting for them to join, He will do the joining."

"I will go ahead and see if I can locate your grandmother's estates," Peter said to an exhausted Mary.

She struggled to keep her eyes open long enough to consume the bowl of stew Peter had placed in her hands.

"Gwenny is able to get about on her leg without too much interference, and Darias, Gideon, and Ellen have promised to see to the others. I should only be gone a few hours, maybe more, but I will be back before nightfall."

"When will you go?" Mary asked in a barely audible voice.

"At daybreak. I will see everyone fed and then be off."

Mary took one more drink of the rich broth and put the bowl down on the ground. "I need to rest," she murmured and stretched out beside the fire. She was sound asleep before Peter could bring a cover to place over her.

Peter watched her for some time and reflected on her concerns for his losses should he marry her. *But what of the gains, sweet Mary?* he thought. She had no means of realizing the value he placed on her.

A memory from another time came to Peter's mind. He could see the rich, jewel-encrusted gown of a newly widowed duchess. It was impossible to remember her name, but Peter well remembered her words.

"You would be an amusement to me," she had whispered against his ear. "I would give you control of my lands, and you would give me whatever I asked for." The purring voice echoed in his ears. There had been others like her as well. Women who were selfish and greedy. Women who sought only to satisfy their own desires.

Peter looked again to Mary. Her lips were slightly parted and her cheeks, though pale, were illuminated by the flickering campfire. Sooty lashes fell against her skin, and ebony hair tumbled down around her shoulders in an alluring curtain.

It will be hard to leave her for London, he thought and made his bed on the opposite side of the fire. He glanced quickly to the wagon where all of the children were sleeping, crowded together for warmth. All was well, and a deep, saturating contentment washed over Peter. God was in His heaven and all was well with the world.

Peter rode out the next morning as promised. He looked back several times and noted the sorrowful expression on Gideon's face.

"Hurry back, Papa!" Gideon called, and Peter's chest tightened in a way he could not explain. The boy had only taken to calling him that in the last few days, and even now, though it sounded foreign to his ears, it seemed quite appropriate in his heart.

With a wave, Peter nudged the horse into a gallop and went north to seek out the home of Lady Elizabeth Beckett. It was a well-known estate not far from York. By his best calculations, Peter knew they were no more than a day away from York, and it seemed natural that Lady Beckett's home would be nearer still.

His plan had been forming slowly, ever since he'd decided to take Mary north under his protection. He would reach the estate first and break the news of Guy Beckett's death. Then he would speak to Lady Beckett of allowing Mary and the children to remain with her while he journeyed to London.

The country was a lonely one with rolling moors and marshy wastes. There, the wind blew straight down from the north and the wetness of it could chill a man in minutes. Peter tightened his grip on the reins and urged the horse to hasten.

The single beaten road made a fork, and remembering the instructions of the monks, Peter chose the left fork and pressed on. Before an hour had passed, he spied the rooftop of a huge stone manor house, and as he drew closer, the gray stone wall protecting the estate came into clear view.

The silent emptiness of the moors was soon behind him, even though the estate was planted firmly in their spaces. The grounds were filled with a multitude of people and activities. Dismounting, Peter led his steed through the clamoring people and made his way to the manor house door.

"Sylvia, take these new ones to the bathhouse and see that they are cleaned up and clothed," a silver-haired woman was saying. The young woman to whom she spoke curtsied lightly and motioned the people to follow her.

The woman turned to enter the house, when Peter spoke. "Are you Lady Beckett?"

The woman stopped and noted Peter for the first time. "I am."

"I am Sir Peter Donne, servant to His Majesty King Edward III."

Elizabeth Beckett, a small woman who greatly resembled her granddaughter in facial appearance, smiled. "And how might I be of service to His Majesty's aid? What ailment do you boast, and how might I see to it?"

Peter looked at her with confusion. "I do not have an ailment. Why do you ask?"

Elizabeth laughed. "Look around you. They all come here for healing. I presumed it must be so with you as well."

Peter did look around him and then the truth dawned on him. "You are the Lady of the Moors."

"I see you have heard the legends. Although I am no legend, and no mystical magic is woven here. Simple prayer and common sense with a pinch of the right herbs and tenderness is all I use."

"And so it is with your granddaughter, Mary," Peter said, waiting to see what reaction might come from the older woman.

Elizabeth gasped and the color drained from her face. "Mary?"

Peter stepped forward to take hold of her arm. "Might I come in and explain?"

She nodded and led him into the house. Here, there was only the movement of servants, and Peter was grateful for the quiet.

Elizabeth motioned to a chair. "Please tell me what you know of my granddaughter."

Peter took a seat beside Lady Beckett. "Your granddaughter is well. She is nearby and making her way here."

"How can this be?"

Peter frowned. "I'm afraid the news is not good. Your son, Guy, is dead."

Elizabeth clutched a hand to her throat. "Dead? Was it the fever?"

"I think it best Mary share her news of that with you. She knows it better, and I would only muddy the tale. There is more, however, that I can share, if you are up to it."

"Please," Elizabeth said in a near frantic tone. "Tell me all."

Peter relayed his first meeting of Mary and led Elizabeth through the tale of their growing entourage. "I left her with ten children and at least that many sick, just south of here."

"Harsh weather is due to set in. We must bring them all here," Elizabeth stated firmly. She was regaining her strength from the shock of Guy's death, Peter deemed.

"I saw the signs myself and feared a rain before I could even return. I will bring them here, but a wagon will be needed for the ill and injured."

"I have one," Elizabeth replied. "I have two in fact and will send one of my best groomsmen to aid you."

Peter got to his feet. "Lady Beckett, I have a strange request of you."

Elizabeth stared up questioningly as though his words had rooted her to her seat. "What is it?"

"I plan to marry your granddaughter as soon as I can journey to London and complete my business with the king. I have no doubt he will allow us to wed once he hears of my great love for her. I ask only that you allow Mary and the children to remain with you until I can prepare a place for them. I have no lands of my own at this time, but many has been the time when the king has promised them to me. I will simply put forth my request that his promise be realized."

Elizabeth got slowly to her feet and held out her hand. She took Peter's large, calloused hand in her own and smiled. "My child, you and Mary are welcome here for all time. The wee ones you are caring for will be welcomed as my own. You see for yourself, this is a place of healing and love. I could not turn away my own flesh. They are welcome here, as are you, for as long as needed."

Peter, with his hand still firmly held by Elizabeth, bowed low to show his respect. "You are a gracious lady," he whispered. "The stories I have heard of you were all true and more."

"Go quickly," Elizabeth said with tears in her eyes. "God go with you and safe journey. I will leave fires burning on the walls in order to guide you here."

Chapter 15

M ary heard the clatter of wagons and somehow knew that Peter was responsible. She saw in the purple twilight that not one, but two wagons were making their way toward the camp and that Peter's horse lazily tagged along behind the first.

When Peter jumped down from the wagon seat, Mary wanted nothing more than to run into his embrace, but at the moment her hands were greasy with ointment and the patient at her side was far more in need of her comfort than she was of Peter's.

Hurrying with her task, Mary felt Peter's presence before he spoke.

"I am nearly finished," she said softly, without bothering to look up.

"I have brought two wagons to transport these folk to your grandmother's estate."

"My grandmother!" Mary said and instantly left her work. "You have seen her? Truly?"

Peter's gaze was warm and loving. "Aye, I have seen her and she is well."

"What of me? Did you tell of me?" Mary asked, her voice betraying an anxious note.

"I did and she was most pleased." Peter reached out to take Mary's hand, but she quickly turned back to her patient.

"My hands are covered with balm. Give me a moment and I will wash them." She finished with the boil-infested man and walked to the water. Peter held out a towel when she stood again and instead of leaving her to dry her hands, he took up the task with a slow, methodic stroke.

"I told her of your father's passing," Peter said, gently rubbing her fingers between the material.

Mary nodded, feeling her pulse quicken from his actions. "I suppose 'twas most difficult for her to accept."

"Aye, she was deeply sorrowed at his passing. I did not tell her how he died. I thought perhaps it best to leave that to you."

Mary said nothing. She could only imagine this woman, her grandmother. What would she say to her when they first met? How could she explain the journey she'd taken and what she'd learned since that terrible night so long ago?

Her hands were more than dry, but still Peter continued rubbing them. Now, however, the towel had been discarded and it was Peter's own warm hands that covered hers.

In the background, Mary could hear the commotion of the sick being loaded into wagons, along with the singsong excitement of the children as they, too, prepared for the journey.

"My hands are dry," she whispered hoarsely, wanting very much to act as though his actions had not affected her.

"Aye," he whispered, still staring deeply into her eyes.

"We should be about our work. There is much to be done if we are to break camp this eve."

"Aye."

Mary felt him draw her close. His arms surrounded her with a circle of strength, and Mary cherished the moment and drew courage from it for the future.

"What is she like?" Mary finally questioned.

"Your grandmother?"

"Aye. What is she like?"

"She is loving and gentle, like you." Peter's whispered words fell against her hair, and Mary couldn't help but sigh.

"And she is well?" Mary forced herself to ask.

"She is. And she looks forward to seeing you."

Mary allowed herself one more moment of Peter's embrace before she pulled away. "Then we'd best be about our way. I saw signs of rain, and the wind bespeaks of cold weather."

" 'Tis the same thing your grandmother told me." He grinned at her. "Come along then. The sooner we get to Lady Beckett's, the sooner I can journey to London and get Edward's blessings on our union."

"You will go so soon?" Panic rose up in Mary. Unbidden tears formed in her eyes. It was only that she was so tired, she told herself. Tired and worried for those in her care. "What of the children? What of me?"

Peter took her hand and kissed it lightly. "Lady Beckett assures me we have a home with her for all time."

"The children as well?"

"Aye, the children as well. You will find your grandmother a most fascinating woman."

Peter was not wrong on that matter. Mary was amazed at the bustle of activity going on in the manor yard so long after night had darkened the skies to black.

They arrived with another group of travelers. One in their band stood ringing the gate bell and beseeching the house to allow them entry.

"What business have ye here?" an older gentleman asked the band of travelers.

"We seek the Lady," the man replied.

"Enter soul," the man said, pulling back the heavy wooden door. He immediately spied Peter and the wagons and motioned them through as well.

"We have expected your return, Sire," the man told Peter. He turned and called to several others, and soon a bevy of people swarmed around the wagons.

"We have rooms in the building yonder," the man told Margaret. "Ye will be cared for by the Lady."

"Be ye speaking of the Lady of the Moors?" Margaret asked anxiously.

Mary was startled at the question and thought to offer Margaret the answer, but before she could speak, the old gatekeeper answered.

"Aye, the Lady is about the manor just now. She prepares for her granddaughter's arrival."

"My grandmother is the Lady of the Moors?" Mary asked no one in particular.

"Did I fail to mention that?" Peter questioned with a mischievous grin.

"Aye, did you leave out much else? Say perhaps that Edward is already taking up residence in the barn?"

Peter laughed out loud, causing the children to wake. "Nay, King Edward is not here, although I wish he were. 'Tis likely to be a cold night, and I would relish a wife at my side to keep me warm."

Mary felt her face grow flush and was grateful for the dim light of torch and campfire. "Your steed should make an ample companion," she teased and jumped down from the wagon. Taking up Anne in her arms, Mary looked to the manor house. "But if you do not mind so very much, Sir Knight, I would like an introduction first."

Peter climbed down from his mount and handed the reins to the gatekeeper. "I will happily make this presentation," he said, taking up Mary by the arm. "Gideon, Darias," he called over his shoulder, "you help the others down and follow us to the house."

Sleepily, the children began to move to the back of the wagon. Gwenny, who was now quite capable on her own, grabbed up Edward and followed after Mary and Peter as quickly as she dared. Like ducks waddling after their mother, the children fell into line. Now wide-eyed and fully alert to the new surroundings, all seemed eager to know of their new home.

In the doorway stood the figure of a woman, and Mary knew it would be her grandmother. Flashes of conversation between her father and herself came to mind. "My mother's love of religion and all its trappings outweighed her love for me." Mary remembered her father's sad voice speaking the words and suddenly she longed for his presence like never before. *If only they could have put their differences aside,* she thought silently. *If only.*

"Lady Beckett, may I present your granddaughter, Mary." Peter's voice feigned formality, but Mary knew he was quite at ease with the circumstances.

Elizabeth Beckett stepped forward and reached out to embrace Mary. She cried openly at the sight of her only granddaughter. "I have dreamed of this day, yet thought I would never live to see it. My heart is filled with such joy, little Mary."

Mary felt her apprehension melt away. "Grandmother," she whispered and buried her face in the aging woman's wimple.

Anne slept through the reunion, but the other children began clamoring about their empty stomachs.

"Come, come," Elizabeth said to the brood. "I have hot meat and bread by the fire. You can eat your fill."

Mary wiped her eyes and looked at Peter as her grandmother led the little ones away to eat. "Thank you, Peter," she said and stretched up on her toes to kiss his cheek.

"Why, Mary," he teased, "what a bold woman you are."

She smiled and shifted Anne in her arms. With a casual glance over her shoulder as she walked away, Mary replied, " 'Tis a pity Edward is not in the barn."

The following dawn brought Mary and Elizabeth together to work on the sick and injured. There was much talk about the Italian fever, and Mary related to her grandmother how Guy Beckett had strived to find a cure.

"The fever has not been so great here in the moor country," Elizabeth told Mary. " 'Tis a colder climate, and I believe less suitable to fevers. We do not suffer over much here, even with winter's cold upon us."

"My father believed a chill could make the fever worse. They would not allow bathing for the people who were exposed to the disease."

Elizabeth finished binding the wound of a young woman and turned to Mary with a gleam in her eye. "I was told you could catch the disease from lustful relations with old women."

Mary giggled. "That, my father did not mention in his journal."

"Journal? Your father kept a journal?"

"Aye, he had many. I brought them with me," Mary said, rewinding a strip of bandage cloth. "I will share them with you."

"Tell me of your father," Elizabeth said, motioning Mary to follow her. "Come, we will sit and share a few quiet moments."

Mary followed her grandmother back into the manor house and up the stairs to her private solar. Pointing to the canopied bed, Elizabeth took a seat at the head. "This will be most comfortable," she said, and Mary quickly agreed.

"Your Peter would not relay the death of your father. How came he to die, Mary?"

Mary was not prepared for this straightforward questioning. "I despise the very memory of it."

"Please tell me," Elizabeth said in a pleading tone. "I must know the truth."

Mary settled back against the post of the canopy. "My father was a good man, although he found religion a grievous thing to bear. He spoke seldom of God or of the church."

" 'Tis the man I remember," Elizabeth said with a sad smile.

"My father was a man of science. He studied long hours with colleges, even braving the church's retribution by performing dissections."

"Do tell!"

" 'Tis true," Mary admitted. "I watched them from a hole in the floor of my room. I believe he knew I watched, for the positioning of the bodies was always such that my modesty would not be compromised. I worked at his side the rest of the time. 'Tis a fond memory for me indeed. He taught me the use of balms and potions, things that would aid the healing of sick and ease the miseries of the dying. I cherished those times with him, for he treated me as an equal and not merely a child."

"Was he a good father?" Elizabeth asked earnestly.

"Aye, I thought him the best," Mary replied. "He cared for me in the best ways possible, and I never wanted for anything. Even at the end. . ." Her mouth suddenly grew dry.

"Please, go on," Elizabeth urged.

"My father had arranged for a dissection. The body of a newly dead prison inmate was to be delivered and evaluated. The man had died from the plague and my father desired to continue his studies of plague victims in order that he might find a way to help those still living."

"What happened?"

"Two men brought the body in a chest, and apparently someone in the village learned of this. The villagers stormed the house, calling my father and his colleagues to account for their sins. When my father went outside to meet them, I hurried to gather as much as I could and sneak out the back. I thought perhaps if the worst happened, I would be able to preserve a small bit of my father's work. At best, I could return the things and no one would be the worse for it."

"But things went badly?" Elizabeth questioned, yet her voice held a tone that told Mary she knew full well the answer.

"Aye. They called my father a consorter of the devil. They called me a witch and his friends were just as evil. They said we had caused the plague upon their village. My father's actions were deemed the reason for their children dying en masse."

"How awful for you, Child." Elizabeth reached out an aged wrinkled hand and patted Mary's trembling one.

"My father had only sought to help them, Grandmother. He did not desire to see them hurt or dying."

"Of course not."

329

"He resented the church's interference. He felt God had abandoned him long ago. He felt that you had chosen God over him, and he could not bear the possibility that I might do the same."

Elizabeth's eyes filled with tears. "I told him 'twas no contest of God and man. God had His place and my child had another. Guy felt that if all my heart did not belong to him, then no fractioned part could, either. I tried to explain that God's love surrounded us and came out through our love for others. I told him 'twas not a matter of him getting a lesser part of his mother's love, but that my love was only possible because God had loved me first."

"I see that now," Mary said softly, "but then, when my father spoke of his loss and the sadness he felt, I could only resent the God that took you away from him."

"Mary, God never took me away from your father. Guy did that. Guy took himself from me in a fit of rebellion and independent will. I never knew your mother and would probably not have heard of your birth had it not been for a kindly friend who journeyed south one year and spoke in person to your father."

"I was afraid to come north to you after his death," Mary admitted after several moments of silence. "I feared that perhaps my father's words had been correct. I feared you would not want me here."

Elizabeth held open her arms, and Mary went into them like a child who had suffered a fall. "Oh, Child," the older woman whispered, "I have wanted you near since I first heard of your birth. I love you and it gives me great pleasure to open my home, as well as my heart, to you."

"I thought I was all alone, but God keeps showing me ways in which I am most surely not."

"I think that He has perhaps given you more than just an aging old woman, am I right?" Elizabeth asked, her tone light and teasing.

Mary, reluctant to pull away, nodded her head against her grandmother's shoulder. "The children need me."

" 'Twas not children I spoke of. What of your young man? What of Peter?"

Mary sat up at this. "What did he say of me to you?"

Elizabeth smiled, and her face grew radiant in her love for Mary. "He asked me to care for you while he journeyed to London. He asked before even bringing you here, just in the fear that I might say no."

"That would have presented a great problem, indeed." Mary's voice was thoughtful. "I had not thought of what a burden it would be upon a man such as Peter."

"Men think differently than women. At least it has been my observation that they do. Your grandfather, God rest his soul, was an even-tempered man with a heart for justice. But let something happen that threatened my well-being, and the man became fierce. Men concern themselves with things such as protection and preservation. Peter's concern is how to provide a home for you and the children. I sensed that more than heard it in the words he spoke. His first duty was to provide for you in whatever manner he could. With my acceptance of you and the children, he is now free to go out and conquer a more permanent arrangement."

Mary nodded absentmindedly. "I kept adding children to our number. I only thought of the love they needed or the fact that they were alone in the world, as was I. I never thought of how to feed them or what I would do to shelter and clothe them. I simply saw them and loved them."

"That is the balance in us, Mary. We show our love in different ways. Men show theirs in one and women in another, yet both are still love and still greatly needed. Children need both a mother and a father to nurture and grow them strong."

"I know that well, for my mother was dead long before I could understand the loss."

Elizabeth nodded. "I did not even know I carried a child when your grandfather was killed. I had these lands and the income that came from them, but I was certain it was all he had left me of himself. How joyful I was to learn of my mistake. Still, I knew it to be hard upon your father to grow up without a man to guide his days. Perhaps if he had known a father's love, he might never have rebelled so completely against God's love."

"I pray he chose the true way before his death," Mary said with a trembling voice.

"He knew full well the truth, Mary. I am sure when he saw his own death coming that he would not allow pride to keep him from God. We must pray it was so and leave it to the mercy of God. There is naught else we can do."

"But I want to see him in heaven," Mary protested. "I cannot imagine my contentment there without him."

Elizabeth tenderly brushed back a strand of ebony hair. "Trust God, Mary. His heaven is filled with joy, and no sorrow can live there. You will not go into His gates with a heavy heart."

Mary lay back against her grandmother and relished the comfort of feminine arms. She had never known a woman's touch. Never known a mother's love. Softly she began to sob for all that she had lost.

"You are home now, Mary. You are home."

Chapter 16

The following morning, Mary stretched leisurely from her bed and wondered at the quietness of her room. Where were the children? Where was Anne with her incessant morning cries for milk? For a moment Mary panicked, and then memory served to remind her she was in her grandmother's house. No doubt Lady Beckett had already seen to the comfort and needs of the children.

"Oh, Father in heaven," Mary began, "I am so blessed. Thank You for bringing us safely to this place. Thank You for my grandmother and her loving heart."

A knock on the door interrupted her prayer. "Come in," she called out and pulled the cover high.

"I feared you might sleep all day," Elizabeth said good-naturedly. "There is an anxious young man in the yard below. He prepares for his journey and would not be happy to leave without sharing a word with you."

Mary felt the color drain from her face. She leaped from the bed and pulled on her only clothes. "He is leaving?" She gasped the words. Dragging a brush through her thick black mane, Mary didn't even bother to braid or tie it back.

If her grandmother answered her, Mary never heard. She was compelled to be at Peter's side and fearful that she would find him already gone from the manor. Without thought for shoes, she hurried down the cold stone steps and out the front door.

Rains had come during the night, leaving everything saturated. Even now the skies threatened to pour again, and Mary shivered against the steady wind that blew down from the north.

"Mary Elizabeth!" her grandmother called from the door.

Turning, Mary saw the old woman hold out her shoes and a thick cloak. "Even without stockings," her grandmother began, "your feet will be happy to accept these."

Begrudgingly, Mary retraced her steps and put the shoes on her feet. Elizabeth wrapped the cloak around Mary and pointed to the barn. "He is in there."

"I wish King Edward were as well," Mary muttered.

Peter stood checking the feet of his horse when Mary entered the barn. She was terrified the feelings they had shared would somehow be dissipated by their arrival at the Beckett estate.

For a moment she said nothing, instead choosing to pull the thick blue wool closer to her body. Her black hair tumbled down in a frenzied veil, leaving her wild and gypsylike in appearance. *There is too much I want to say,* she thought. *Too much I want to share. I know him not and now he is going away and perhaps I will never see him again.*

A lump came to her throat. *You are being a silly child,* she chided herself. But when she looked at the man before her, all Mary could think of was how she longed to keep him from going. *I will not cry and beg him to stay,* she promised. *I will not make this more difficult than it has to be. If he has changed his mind in the light of day, I will not make it impossible for him.*

She had nearly convinced herself to turn around and go, when Peter seemed to sense her presence and turned from the steed.

"Mary! I began to think I would have to drag you from that bed," he said with the laughing voice that Mary had come to appreciate.

He was dressed in a dark green tunic and leather cotehardie. His heavily muscled legs were clad in matching green wool with high knee boots that laced up the middle. His brown hair was carelessly combed, and his face newly shaven. It was all Mary could do to stay in place.

"Grandmother said you wished to tell me good-bye," Mary said, trying to force her voice to sound normal. *I will not cry,* she reminded herself.

"Aye, London calls." Peter said without giving his words much thought. He went back to checking the horse's hooves and added, "Your grandmother has agreed to keep you and the children here."

"Aye, she told me as much," Mary answered. In her mind she thought of velvet-clad ladies with their wily ways and titles. *I am but a physician's daughter. A woman without means or the ability to provide a dowry.* A fleeting thought reminded her that her grandmother was titled and owned the estate upon which she stood. But it wasn't Mary's land and title, and it certainly wasn't about to become hers any time soon. Maybe never.

"I will be back before you know it. I intend to deliver my report and plead our case before the king first thing. Barring any complications, which of course there is always the possibility of, I will return here with Edward's blessing to marry."

Mary barely heard the words. He was really going away. He would return to London and his life at court. He would taste good food upon fine china plates and enjoy the best drink available served in gold and silver goblets. He would sit beside sweet-smelling women in silks and satins. Women who would see his comely face and deem him a fair catch. She bit her lip hard to keep from crying out and begging him to stay.

She hadn't realized that Peter was watching her. Glancing up, she caught his quizzical stare as he leaned against the horse's stall.

"You are very quiet, sweet Mary. Pray tell what is going about in that very busy mind?"

Mary straightened a bit and pushed back her shoulders. Determined to remain emotionless, Mary tried to sound offended. "There are many sick people about me. I cannot very well stand here all day and not consider their needs."

Peter shook his head. "You lie. You are thinking not of the sick."

Mary swallowed hard. "I have much to think on. The children, my grandmother, and. . .and. . ." She could think of nothing else to say.

"And me? And the fact that I am leaving. Are you thinking of my departure and the distance I will place between us?"

Mary wanted to scream her affirmation, but instead she whirled around to leave. *If I stay, I will say something foolish,* she thought. *If I stay, I will cry and I will plead and it will be the most regrettable thing I have ever done.*

"Stop right there, Mary!"

The authoritative manner in which Peter called out, left her little choice but to halt. Wishing she could lose herself in the heavy cloak, Mary held her breath and waited for what Peter would say next. *If I do not look at him, mayhap I will keep myself from tears.*

"Mary, come here."

His voice was compelling, but Mary remained rigidly planted to her spot. She drew a deep breath. So far, so good. Just a few more minutes and he would leave. Just a few more precious seconds of shared time together, and he would ride away from her and take her heart with him.

His touch was her undoing. Peter's hands upon her cloaked shoulders caused Mary to begin shaking so hard it made her teeth chatter.

"Are you cold?" he asked softly, turning her to face him.

"No!" she exclaimed and tried to wrench away.

"But you are trembling," he said sympathetically. "Come, I will see you to the. . ." His words fell away as he lifted her chin with his finger. "You are not cold."

The statement and the look in his eyes told Mary he'd guessed her innermost thoughts. With a knowing smile, he swept her into his arms and kissed her so ardently that Mary's feet left the floor. She could barely steady herself to keep from falling flat when he released her.

"Think you that I could share this affection and leave you without another thought? I might once have been such a cad, but that was before the truth of God was within me."

Mary shook her head. "I know very little of the man you were, or for that matter, the man you are."

"Have my actions not told you of my love? Has the life lived before you not spoken louder than any tale of the past?"

Mary tried hard not to think of the aching in her heart. She tried hard to remember the wonder of his touch only moments before. *If I think on these things, I will fall apart.*

"You are a man of honor, Peter Donne," she finally spoke.

"And I have given you a pledge of love, a promise to marry, and my word that I will return. What more would you have of me?" he asked her seriously.

A sob broke from deep within, and Mary turned to flee his presence. Peter would have none of it, however, and caught her by the cloak and whirled her back around.

"Leave me be," she begged and pushed him away as he took her in his arms. "I cannot bear this one second more."

"Ah, Mary," he whispered against her ear. "Please believe in me."

His pleading tone caused her to stop fighting, and when Mary lifted her gaze to his, she found tears in his eyes.

"Yes," she said softly. Stretching to reach his lips with her own, Mary kissed him with all the love she felt for him inside.

"You are mine, sweet Mary. You are mine, as I am yours."

"Aye," Mary said, believing it to be so. She wiped at her tears with the back of her hand. "I am yours."

Watching her walk away was the hardest thing Peter had yet to do. He had fought battles in France, watched scores of people die from the plague, and journeyed hundreds of miles across nations in the name of his king. But all these challenges paled in the face of this moment. His heart told him he was a fool to leave, yet there was no other choice.

Climbing onto his horse, Peter cast a quick glance at the children who stood anxiously at the gate. Darias and Gideon were trying hard not to cry, while Gwenny sobbed and cradled a distracted Edward much too tightly. The others were somber but at least did not cry, and for this Peter was grateful.

"I will bring you something from London," he promised, and the faces of the little ones seemed brighter.

A steady drizzle had begun, and the longer he lingered, the harder it seemed to rain.

"I will ride hard and return in a fortnight," he called to Mary. He doubted the truth of his words, knowing the roads would be saturated and the passage slow. Should he tell Mary of the possible difficulties and further worry her? Saying nothing more, he waved and gave the horse his head.

∽≫

Christmas Eve arrived, and still Peter had not returned to the Beckett estate. Mary was devastated. Surely something had happened to him. He might even have fallen victim to the plague fever and she would never know that he had died.

Restlessly, she tried to put her fears from her mind and join in the festivities of the season. The huge yule log was brought in and placed in the oversized hearth in her grandmother's dining hall. It would burn for the twelve days of Christmas until Epiphany arrived to mark the coming of the wisemen.

Outside, rain continued to make a daily appearance, leaving the fields standing in puddles of icy cold water. The manorial servants were given these days away from regular work, and an atmosphere of celebration lightened the hearts of even the harshest soul. Elizabeth had seen to the decorations of holly and ivy in the great hall of her manor, while in the kitchen a grand feast was in order to make the celebration even finer.

The children had been given new clothing, a gift from their grandmother Elizabeth, as well as a toy. The boys were happy to play with carved wooden swords, and the girls were given dolls dressed in soft, white gowns.

Mary tried to show a festive spirit. She dressed in the bright red velvet gown her grandmother had chosen for her. She even managed to arrange her hair in a fashionable style and trimmed her hair-covering with bits of holly and ivy. But there was an emptiness in Peter's absence that kept her from true joy.

When the tenants of Elizabeth's estate began to arrive for the annual Christmas feast, Mary dismissed herself to the privacy of her bedroom and prayed. "I know 'tis the celebration of Your Son's birth," she began, tears falling in steady streams from her face, "and I know for the first time what it is to honor this day for that reason. But Father, my heart is sorely vexed and the reason is well known to You. I fear for Peter, Father. I fear that he has fallen ill or, worse yet, has died."

She spoke the words and even then realized that more fearful still was the possibility that Peter had simply decided not to return to York.

Downstairs, Mary could hear the singing and laughter, but her heart would not be comforted. A light knocking caused her to wipe her eyes and take a deep breath.

"Come in," she called.

Gideon appeared to peek his head around the door.

"Why are you here, Mama?" he questioned, and Mary felt a bit of the sting leave her heart.

"I thought to pray a moment." It was completely true, Mary reasoned. No need for Gideon to know her fears.

"You are worried about Papa," the boy said, closing the door behind him. "You should not worry. God goes with him."

"Aye, I know 'tis true," Mary said, realizing that keeping her heart from the boy would be impossible. "Still, it has been so long."

"Grandmother said it had been only a month and that with the heavy rain we should not worry." His face was filled with innocence and love.

Mary knelt, opened her arms, and held the boy against her for a moment. He seemed so grown up in his miniature cotehardie of blue wool. Had not her grandmother spoken just the night before on the faith of children? Children, she had told Mary, were invested with the ability to believe with all their hearts. They trusted their parents, never wondering whether or not they would provide or remain to care for them. God asked that we come to Him as a little child with faith that He would remain true to His Word. How very hard that was, Mary deemed.

"He will come back," Gideon said softly, and leaning up, he kissed her cheek. "You will see. Papa is a man of his word. He promised he would never leave me, and I believe him."

Mary pulled Gideon away for just a moment. Yes, she could see the truth of his words in the warm glow of his eyes. He held no doubt, but then Gideon was a child and he did not know the ways of riches and wanton women.

"You go on below and play the games with your new brothers and sisters. We are a family now, and we should celebrate as one. I will come below in just a moment."

Gideon smiled broadly. "Grandmother said we could have the wastel loaves." He spoke of the traditional game of finding the bean inside a loaf of bread. Whoever found the bean was king for the feast. "I hope I find it."

"And what will you decree as king?"

Gideon looked thoughtful for a moment. "I will call for sweet pies to be served all day."

"Oh, Gideon." Mary laughed and sent the boy on his way.

When Mary came below, the children rushed to her side. The little ones held up their arms to be picked up, while Anne on a blanket in front of the fire was sitting up, grinning at Mary. *How quickly she has grown,* Mary thought.

"She has progressed quickly," Elizabeth said, echoing Mary's thoughts as she crossed to her side. The revelry in the hall nearly drowned out her words. Both women studied Anne for a moment.

"I feel as though she has always been my own," Mary said, laughing at the way the baby tumbled over while studying her own fingers and toes. "Do you think it wise to leave her out of swaddling so soon?"

"Bah!" Elizabeth replied. "I have never cared for the idea of binding children until they are struggling to move about. I think the earlier they do flex those little limbs, the sooner they grow strong and healthy. Do not fear, Mary, Anne is fairly shining with health."

Gwenny came to Mary's side, her limp barely noticeable. "Mary, will you come and share the wastel?"

Mary glanced at the children's eager faces. "Of course. And if I do not win today, then perhaps I will win tomorrow on Christmas."

"There are twelve chances for the twelve days," Darias reminded her.

"And the Three Kings Bread on Epiphany," Grandmother Elizabeth declared. "I always put a coin in that loaf to remind us that the wisemen brought gifts of gold to the Christ child."

"A real coin?" three children chanted in unison. "And we may keep it if we find it?"

"Of course," Elizabeth said, her eyes fairly dancing. "Now you children go and play. Mary and I must check on the sick, but we will be back before you know it."

Taking hold of Mary's arm, Elizabeth led her from the room and out the back of the house. "You seem to be in good spirits when you are with the children."

"I love them so," Mary admitted. "I suppose I never really considered what it would mean to be a mother and care for a child. I was always so busy with Father that I never considered marriage and a family of my own. Father needed me to care for him, and a husband seemed unimportant."

"And now?"

Mary looked at her grandmother, knowing full well the older woman understood her fears and misery in Peter's absence. "Now it is most important. Love is a terrible and awful thing, as it is a wondrously joyful thing. Just when I believe myself to understand the matter, it baffles and confuses me until I am nearly dizzy in my contemplations."

Elizabeth laughed out loud. Pausing outside the door to the sickroom, she reached her hand to Mary's face. " 'Tis always the way with human love. The road is one that not only takes us to the mountain, but plunges us deep into the valley. God's love, however, is the one type of love that never changes. His love is constant, and when human love fails us, His love will continue."

"If only I had the faith of the children," Mary wished.

" 'If only' is a key that opens a door to regret," Elizabeth chided gently. "You cannot spend your life wishing that you had chosen another path. It will not change the first choice and it will not offer comfort on the journey forward. You can spend your life in regrets, Mary Elizabeth, or you can put your best foot forward and trust that you are making choices based on the influence of God's guiding hand."

"Oh, Grandmother, I am so blessed to have you. God was good to bring us together," Mary said, embracing the woman tightly. "If only. . ." She paused and issued a giggle. " 'Tis an easy statement to give." Mary pulled back to see her grandmother's amused face. "I would have said, if only I had been allowed to grow up within your care, how very different things might now be."

"Just remember, Mary, in trading one life for another, we cast away all the good and lovely things we would have known in the first. Would you have traded your father's devotion and the time spent learning at his side?"

"Never!"

"Then mayhap we should trust that the very best has come to pass in each instance."

"Aye," Mary said with sudden understanding. "And more good is yet to come."

Chapter 17

New visitors to Beckett Manor continued to arrive even through the twelve days of Christmas. Epiphany came and went, with Gideon the happy recipient of the "king's coin." He pledged to take everyone into town and buy gifts for all. Mary didn't have the heart to tell him the coin would not stretch quite that far.

It was on the Monday after Epiphany, Plow Monday, as it was called, that Mary found herself warmly dressed and standing in the fields of her grandmother's estates. Today there were contests to see how many furrows each man could plow. Whatever soil he was able to break would be his when true plowing time came at Candlemas in February.

Mary laughed at the sight and joined in with the others to cheer the group of villeins on with their work. It was a festive day and would mark the end of the Christmas celebration. Spying a new set of travelers, Mary left the festivities and made her way to the woman and child at the gate.

"My little one is suffering from a burn," her mother told Mary. "She was scalded by a caldron of water."

Mary gently took the child from her mother and motioned with her head to the place where the sick were kept. "Come with me and we will tend her."

Mary was unprepared for the hideous sight of the child's back and side. The reddened flesh was festering and peeling, and Mary feared that the child would succumb to her wounds.

"I will call the Lady of the Moors to help me," Mary said. "Keep her quiet, and I will return shortly."

Mary went out from the building in search of her grandmother. A wave of nausea at the memory of the child washed over her. How terrible for the poor little waif to bear up under such a burden!

She found Elizabeth handing out pieces of candied fruits to the congregation of children from her estate. "Grandmother, there is a child who is quite gravely ill. Her mother has brought her, and I have her in the sickhouse."

Elizabeth nodded and gave the bag over to one of the servants to finish the task. "What is her condition?"

"She has been hideously burned. The wounds are festering, and I know not if she will live."

Elizabeth nodded and made her way to the sickhouse. Throwing off her cloak, she went to the worried mother and tiny, lifeless girl.

"Mary, bring fresh well water, cold and clear."

Mary did as she was bid, and when she returned, Elizabeth was placing a spoonful of something in the child's mouth. " 'Twill make her sleep, for the treatment will be most painful."

The mother of the child seemed to weaken at the thought, and Mary led her away to sit on a chair outside the room.

"First we will cleanse the burns with water, then with wine," Elizabeth told Mary. "I find greater healing when I wash a very bad wound, such as a burn, with a good stout wine."

The two women worked side by side to master the situation. Elizabeth removed pieces of burnt skin, and when all had been cleansed to her satisfaction, she directed Mary to bring a clean cloth of linen.

"We will soak this in a mixture of rose oil and essence of peony. I will add a bit of poppy oil as well, and we will cover the worst of the burns with the cloth. This should stay moist for three days. We will also need to keep the child resting, so administer a teaspoon of this every mealtime with a cup of broth."

"Will she live?" Mary asked hopefully.

"We will pray it so," Elizabeth said, placing her hand upon the child's brow. "She is such a tiny mite, but she seems quite strong."

They finished with the child and, after instructing the mother, made their way back to the celebration.

" 'Tis hard to see the little ones suffering so," Mary said, absentmindedly.

"We do what we can, Mary, and trust God for the rest."

"It would seem trust is the one thing God is working to teach me most earnestly."

"Has He made progress with you yet?" Elizabeth teased.

"Aye, but 'tis no easy battle."

Realizing she'd left her cloak back in the sickroom, Elizabeth turned back.

Mary put a restraining hand on Elizabeth's arm. "I will fetch it for you, Grandmother. Stay here with your people." She hurried away before her grandmother could stop her. Truth be told, Mary longed for a few quiet moments to pray at the child's bedside.

"There is warm food in the house," Mary instructed the child's mother. "I will wait here a moment with your daughter while you get something to eat." The woman's eyes grew wide as though she could not believe her good fortune. "Go now," Mary urged, "and return here with your plate."

The woman had no sooner left than Mary bowed her head and prayed in earnest for the child. It was the first time Mary had truly given a patient over in prayer. How different it felt from the times when she had only her medicines and father's teachings to rely upon.

" 'Tis in Your hands now, Father," she whispered and noted that the child breathed evenly and without pain.

Turning to leave, Mary clasped her hand to her mouth to keep from crying out. Peter stood in the door not five feet away, resplendently dressed in the garb of court.

"Surely you are not adding another to our number, sweet Mary," he said with a grin.

"Peter!" she gasped his name, and mindless of who might see, she threw herself into his arms and covered his face with kisses. "Oh, Peter!"

His arms went around her waist and held her tightly against him. Mary could scarcely allow herself to believe the moment had finally come. Surely this was just another dream, she told herself and then pulled back to assure herself it was all very real.

"You are truly here," she whispered.

"Aye," he replied softly. "Had you given over to despair of ever seeing me again?"

Mary took on a look of surprise in order to keep from betraying her real feelings. "Of course not!"

Just then, the child's mother returned, and Mary quickly pulled Peter into the manor yard. She was stunned to find an entourage of men being directed by her grandmother to where they could seek shelter. She looked to Peter with a quizzical stare.

"They are mine," he answered her unspoken question. "Edward has sent them to help me establish our lands."

"Our lands?" Mary questioned, but just then Elizabeth called out a greeting.

"Peter, you are answered prayer," she said, embracing him in a motherly fashion.

"As were you for me. I trust Mary has not overstayed her welcome here."

"Never!" Elizabeth declared. "She and the children have been purely a joy. I would keep you all beside me forever."

"Well, you shall nearly have your wish," Peter said, pulling from his cloak a leather satchel. "I have here Edward's permission to marry your granddaughter," he announced with a sly look at Mary's surprised face. "Do not look so surprised, sweet Mary, 'tis the main reason I returned to London."

Before he could continue, Peter found himself surrounded by the children.

"Papa!" Gideon called over and over, and the little ones mimicked him.

"Papa! Papa!" they chanted.

"Nothing has ever sounded sweeter," Peter said, hugging the little bodies close to his. "My, but you look so fine in your new clothes. Were these gifts from Christmas?"

"Yes," Gideon stated excitedly. "Grandmother had them made for us. Did you bring us a present from London?"

"That I did. More than one. First and most important is something I was just telling your grandmother and Mary. King Edward has given permission for Mary and me to wed and care for you as our own children."

Cheers went up from the older children, which in turn caused the younger ones to clap their hands and dance around.

"I told you he would come back, Mama," Gideon said, taking Mary's hand in his own. "I told you."

Mary smiled down at the boy. "Aye, you told me well, Gideon." Glancing up, she noted Peter held a questioning look on his face. "Now what else were you to tell us, Sire?"

Peter held up the satchel. "Edward has given me the adjoining lands to the west of your grandmother's estate. We will be neighbors, Lady Beckett."

"What joy! I have long prayed for this day," Elizabeth said, and tears of happiness fell freely from her eyes. "You must have struggled long to get here. Your men told me of the many perils you faced. Come to the house and warm up and eat. You can tell us everything there."

The children, including Gideon, were already pulling Peter along to the house, chanting their stories of all that had happened in his absence. Arm in arm, Mary followed with Elizabeth.

"Now I will never be without my family," Mary said softly. "You will be near to me, and we can help one another."

"I truly meant it when I said this is answered prayer," Elizabeth replied. "I have long wondered to whom I would leave these lands. I hated to imagine they would simply fall back into the hands of the crown, only to be issued out to those who knew me not."

"Please do not speak of leaving for any reason," Mary admonished. "I want to know your company for a great many years. I have much to make up and much to learn from you."

❦

The children had long been asleep in their beds and the candles and lamps extinguished to shine another day, when Peter and Mary finally found themselves alone.

Sitting before the low-burning fire, Mary reached out to warm her hands, while Peter finished sharpening his knife. She suddenly felt shy and uncomfortable. Stealing sidelong glances, she watched Peter work, still amazed that he was truly here in the same room. Outside the wind howled in a mournful reminder of winter's gripping cold, and Mary shuddered.

"Are you cold?" Peter asked thoughtfully, putting the knife to rest beside the whetstone.

"A little," she answered, wondering what he would think if she told him of her discomfort.

Peter retrieved a heavy wool shawl he'd seen Elizabeth use earlier. "This should help," he said, placing it around her shoulders. His hands lingered to pull her hair free from the shawl, and Mary trembled at his touch.

For several moments, the only sound was that of the wind outside and the tiny pops and crackles of the wood on the grate. Mary fought to steady her nerves, while Peter remained at her back, his hands in her hair.

"So you thought I would not return." It was more statement than question. His voice sounded a little sad, and Mary stiffened, wondering how to respond.

"Why do you say that?" Mary asked hesitantly. She knew full well Gideon's words earlier in the day had prompted such a response, but she was not yet certain how to speak on the matter.

Peter came around to join her on the bench. "My love for you is quite real, Mary." He looked at her with such pleading that Mary had to look away. "You were ever on my mind. You and the children rode with me wherever I went. All I could think of was you."

"I did not mean to fret," Mary finally said. She looked ahead into the fire. " 'Tis simply that I have never loved a man, and I know naught of the ways of such a union." She felt her face grow hot. "We pledged ourselves to marriage without knowing much of each other."

"People are married in that manner quite often. Why, my own mother was pledged to my father at the age of nine. She knew nothing of him. When they were wed, she was but thirteen years old, and still she only knew that he was of a proper house, befitting her station."

"I am certain you speak the truth," Mary replied, "but I am not familiar with such things. I was sheltered away. I cared for my father, cooked and cleaned, sewed, and worked at his side. I knew the love of a father to his daughter, and romantic love seemed a world away and unimportant. Now," she said, reluctantly looking at Peter's tender expression, "I find this love to be a confusing thing."

He reached out his hand. "How be that, sweet Mary?"

Mary put her other hand over his. "I had never known jealousy until my heart belonged to you. Now, all I can imagine is the life you knew before and the women who would take you away."

Peter surprised her by laughing, and Mary pulled her hand away and got to her feet. " 'Tis not funny. How can you laugh when I have shared my heart with you?"

"I am sorry, Mary. I only find it humorous to imagine that any other woman could compel me to leave you."

"How is that so?" Mary stuck out her lower lip in a definite pout. She was not yet ready to concede that his laughter was justified.

"Mary," Peter said, getting to his feet, " 'tis true enough that I have played the rogue and toyed with the affections of many. I have lived a life I am not proud of and have sought God's forgiveness for the harm I have caused. As a knight of the king, I knew wealth and adventure and certainly found myself among a great many beautiful women—"

"See then," Mary interrupted, "I am right to feel this way."

"Nay," he whispered with a finger to her lips. "There is no one between us except that which you place there. If only you will trust me, Mary, I will be the finest of husbands. I will pledge you my devotion, my love, and my loyalty."

Mary seemed to awaken to these words. "Grandmother said that 'if only' was a key to the door of regret. I suppose I see her meaning from my own wishes. I kept telling myself, if only we'd known each other longer or if only I were a lady of means."

"You would not have liked the man I used to be," Peter assured her. "But that man is no longer a concern. I am reborn through God's love and our Saviour's sacrifice. I am grateful that you knew me not when I was younger."

Mary began to feel a wave of peace wash over her. God had given them both rebirth from the old, selfish creatures they once were. "I love you, Peter," she said, reaching out her hand to his face. "That love frightens me a bit, for I know naught of how to be a wife or mother."

Peter pulled her into his arms and sighed. "Your loving heart has already made you capable of both tasks. Now put aside your fear and let trust come to life." He kissed her tenderly, and Mary felt herself giving into the warmth of their embrace. When Peter raised his head, he stared down at her with fiery brown eyes. "We need no longer wish for Edward to be in residence in the barn; he has granted his consent."

Mary smiled impishly. "Did you tell Edward of your ready-made family?"

"I did." Peter joined her teasing air. "He asked if I thought ten was quite enough or should I like to take a few more back with me from London."

"And what did you tell him?"

"I declined, believing that someone else should know the joy that had befallen me. I made it clear that ten was a hearty number and more than enough for a new knight and his lady fair."

"But what of our own children?" She questioned, releasing him in mock concern. "I'd always heard it told children were a sign of a healthy love between a man and woman."

Peter grabbed her around the waist and pulled her back. "Then we will surely double the number," he said with a mischievous wink, "for my love of you is. . ." He kissed her forehead. "Quite. . ." He kissed her nose. "Healthy." He kissed her mouth soundly.

Mary sighed and wrapped her arms around his neck. No longer were there doubts or lingering thoughts of "if only." There were no regrets in the love she felt for this man or in the heavenly love God had given her.

After a long, passionate kiss, Mary weakly pulled away and grinned. "There is a friar in the guest house," she whispered. "He came for the holiday celebration, and Grandmother thought it wise to keep him handy."

Peter caught her hand and pulled her to the door. "And you have kept this to yourself all this time? If only you would have spoken sooner, sweet Mary. If only. . ."

Five Geese Flying

Chapter 1

T he arrangement has been that you would cancel all debts accrued over the last five years," François de la Fontaine reminded his opponent. And indeed, it seemed that the two men were squaring off for a battle rather than arranging a marriage.

Jeanine de la Fontaine watched the entire ordeal from the hearthside, where she continued to spin wool with her distaff until her fingers felt as though they would bleed at any moment. How could her father just give her over to Antoine Colbert? The man was hideous and nearly twice her age. His greasy blond hair hung matted around his balding head, only to be awkwardly accompanied by an equally matted beard. It was as if God had taken the hair from his head to put it on the man's face.

Jeanine shuddered and continued to listen to her father's bartering. Before the night was out, she would be the betrothed of Antoine Colbert, and there was nothing she could do about it.

" 'Tis true enough that I have agreed to such an arrangement in the past," Antoine was saying, "but, I did not chance to imagine the depths to which you would plunge into debt."

"You know well enough, Milord, the River Zwin is filling with silt. It makes trade difficult at best. Two of my finest ships were grounded with entire sections of the hull torn away. It made repairs costly and difficult. Some of the cargo was lost to us, but the remainder should bring a fair price."

"Aye, but what will you do for trade when the river closes altogether? How then will you pay me rent and taxes?"

"I'll trust the Lord God to provide at that turn," Jeanine's father replied.

Antoine Colbert laughed heartily, and Jeanine watched as his rotund, overfed belly shook in maniacal delight. "If the Lord God cared that much, Fontaine, mayhap He should have had the foresight to keep the river from filling in the first place."

"Talk not in such a manner against our Lord," her father answered angrily. "Our house is one that serves Him first. You may own a portion of this village— indeed, you may believe you own me—but I am God's servant."

Jeanine glanced up to make out the tightened features of her father's face.

He was only forty years old, but he looked half again as many years. His face was etched with worry lines that made Jeanine fear for his health. Her mother took this moment of tension to bring drinks and bread to the table. Jeanine watched as her mother gently brushed her father's shoulder while Colbert dug into the refreshments. Margarite de la Fontaine knew how to soothe her husband with a simple touch. Jeanine watched as the anger washed from her father's face.

It appeared to Jeanine that Colbert would see the unity as a threat and maybe even a defeat. His countenance changed as though he were considering exactly how far he could push this family. He cast a glance to Jeanine and caught her watching him before she could look away. Her body shuddered at the thought of marriage, and Colbert grinned wickedly as if reading those thoughts for himself.

Colbert squared his shoulders and looked her father in the eye. "You drive a hard bargain, François, but I will honor my word. After all, what be a man, but that which is his word—eh?"

Jeanine saw her father nod hesitantly. "And you will cancel out the entire five years?"

"Aye," Colbert replied, returning his gaze to Jeanine. "She appears well worth the debt. Her hands are swift to create as she has proven with her woolens. She is sound of mind, which makes the arrangement twice the bargain. I fear the madness of poverty and plague has left many a young woman addlepated. Her skin is not pox marked and scarred. Neither is it of ill pallor. Aye, she will warm my bed well and give me many strong sons. Five years' debt seems a mere pittance."

Jeanine wanted to club the smirking man over the head. He treated her as though she were a brood mare being purchased off the block. If she'd had less love and respect for her father, she might have protested and declared her disgust with the entire arrangement. Her mother and father had married out of arrangement as well, but they had also loved each other and thus found such matters completely acceptable. Their arranged marriage bore little resemblance to the marriage that awaited Jeanine. Antoine Colbert was notorious for his filthy habits and perversions. That her father had found himself helpless against this man sorrowed her deeply. That he found it necessary to give her over in barter to him left her angry and frightened.

"I will have the contracts drawn," Colbert said, pushing back from the table. His chair went tumbling over backward and crashed against the wooden plank floor. "I suggest an immediate union."

Jeanine could stand it no longer. "I beg you, Father, pray give me time to arrange myself for such an alteration in my life. There is much to be done before I can leave your house and become the wife of Monsieur Colbert."

"You are a woman a full score in years," Colbert replied haughtily. "Methinks after twenty years there cannot be much in the way of preparation yet undone. Surely your life has been given over to learning the proper skills to be pleasing to a husband."

Jeanine felt her face flush and was grateful for the nearness of the fire. Perhaps no one would notice in the dim light of the room, but should they see her flushed, 'twould be fitting they blame the warmth of the hearth and not her anger.

"My mother has trained me in the services necessary to the keeping of a household, I assure you." Jeanine folded her hands demurely in her lap and turned a hopeful expression on her father. "Please, Père. I beg you give me but a short time to complete my preparations. I've not yet created a gown in which to be married."

Her father's expression turned tender. "I suggest six weeks from this day would give the child enough time," he said, turning to face Colbert.

The man looked as though he might argue the point, then gave a stiff bow and nodded. "Very well. That will put us well out of the Lenten season. There should be no further cause for delay after that."

Jeanine rose and curtseyed. "You are most gracious, Milord." She barely choked the words out from between clenched teeth. There was nothing gracious about the man. He was an unmitigated boar and a self-centered pig.

Colbert left with the promise that he would return when the contract had been put to paper. The door to the de la Fontaine house was scarcely closed behind him, when Jeanine's father sat down heavily and put his head in his hands.

"Why did you risk bringing his ire down upon this house, ma petite angée?"

"I'm no angel, Father. I could not bear the man's stench, much less the idea of becoming his wife," Jeanine declared. "I cannot see why this arrangement must include me as the solution." She tossed her distaff aside. "I did not want to show disrespect to you in front of him, but how can you expect me to marry him? He's grotesque, and you know his reputation. 'Tis one that suggests much misery and horror."

Her father raised his head and regarded her for a moment. When he answered her, he spoke in a tone of total defeat. "You will do as you are told. 'Tis not my way, but that which must be done, will be done."

She opened her mouth as if to rage at the injustice of it all, but she could see the pain on her father's face. She knew that her beloved père would not have forced her into this marriage had the circumstances not been severe. She left her place by the fire and came to stand beside her father. "Oui. I will do as you say, and 'twill be well with me," she murmured.

Her mother took the seat opposite them and sighed. "I would rather see her betrothed to Madame Luchaire's prized swine." All three laughed.

" 'Tis true enough there is not much difference in girth or smell," Jeanine said.

"I am sorry, Daughter. It seems the only way. Had the trade been better, had the ships not run aground, I might have kept you for our house alone. But there must always come a day of settling accounts. Our Lord God makes that clear. To everyone there comes a season of reckoning. Colbert holds the power to see us all put to debtors' prison and left to rot."

"I understand." And in truth, Jeanine did comprehend the gravity of the situation. The entire town joined together could not have understood her plight any better.

"I have but one request," her father said, reaching out to take her hand. "One prayer."

"What is it?" she asked, looking first to her mother as if to gain the truth in her eyes.

Her mother reached out a hand to lightly touch Jeanine's free hand.

"I ask that you might forgive me," her father said softly. " 'Twas not my desire to come to this end. My own mismanagement and lack of foresight has brought us to this ruin. I ask your forgiveness for bartering you into marriage with Antoine Colbert."

"Forgive me, too." Her mother's eyes were filled with tears. "For we know the kind of man he is, and your father did not accept this arrangement lightly."

Jeanine saw the anguish in their expressions and knelt beside the table to humble herself before them. "I know 'twas not your wish to marry me to Monsieur Colbert. There is nothing to forgive. You had no other choice. The trade is poor, and my brother is long overdue from the sea. You have more worries than my marriage. Rest assured that I will trust God for my existence."

Evening vespers were managed in a spirit of heaviness. Papa prayed for the safe return of his son, Étienne, whose ship the *Crispin* was long overdue. He prayed, too, that God might in some way save his daughter from marriage to Antoine Colbert and, if not, that God might transform Colbert into a man of Christian honor.

Jeanine listened as her father prayed on behalf of each member of his family. She wanted so much to have faith that God would deliver her from this nightmare. She wanted to know peace for her future and to feel hope once again that all would be well. It was true that she was twenty years old and that most women her age were already married and had children. Ofttimes they were widowed. But she had remained in her father's house, quietly keeping faith with her parents, carding and weaving wool, helping in whatever manner her mother desired. She had known real happiness in her life with them, and now she could see that joy slipping away.

Lifting her head while her father continued to pray, Jeanine felt an ache in her heart at the thought of leaving them. Her mother was so fragile, and she longed to remain at her side to continue aiding her. Her well-trained eye told her that Margarite de la Fontaine might not have many more years of health, mayhap even life, and Jeanine longed to keep company with her beloved mother for as long as possible.

Then, too, her father held the very core of her heart. She had been the doted-upon daughter, the youngest child who held favor in her father's eye. Never had he returned from his trade trips abroad, but what he had brought her some special trinket. She knew full well that she held his heart in her hand. If only she could prevent the deeds that were soon to be upon them.

Having concluded their prayers, Jeanine received her parents' blessing and slipped upstairs to the third floor, where her bedroom allowed her the most privacy of any place in the house. Fear gripped her heart, and she longed for someone to shake her awake and declare it all nothing more than a bad dream. Moonlight filtered into her room through the pasty thick glass of her window, drawing her, beckoning her to come stand in the glow. It was impossible to make clear the images outside through the thick glass, but somewhere out there Antoine Colbert was planning her future.

"Why, Father?" she whispered reverently. "Why must this happen? Why must I suffer this fate?"

Chapter 2

As the weeks slipped by, Jeanine became more despondent. She tried to keep busy in order not to dwell upon the inevitability of her marriage, but more often than not, despair was her most obvious companion.

Needing to escape the reminders of her future with Colbert, Jeanine took herself from the house and made her way down the cobblestone road. Her one thought was to seek solace at her grandmother's grave. Grandmère de la Fontaine had died some four years earlier, but the memory of their closeness lived on in Jeanine's heart. Bundling up against the harsh winter cold, Jeanine made her way to the small cemetery where her grandmother had been laid to rest.

The wind whipped mercilessly at her clothes, and casting a quick glance at the skies overhead, Jeanine feared the imminent arrival of yet another storm. Pulling her thin cloak tighter, Jeanine knelt beside the grave and let out a heavy sigh. Her warm breath puffed out against the frigid air, and with it, Jeanine felt her hopes slip away as well.

"I tried hard to be brave, Grandmère," she whispered to the gravestone. " 'Tis not my desire to give my parents reason to be overburdened with grief, but you know how difficult this is for me. To marry that pig, Colbert," she said, from behind clenched teeth, "makes me want to retch."

For all her short years, Jeanine had seen a great many reasons to find marriage to one such as Colbert a dismal prospect. Colbert was a wealthy landowner with a great many properties and investments. He was a staunch supporter of the French king, Charles VI, while most of Bruges, in fact most of Flanders, aligned itself with the English king, Richard II. The situation had been in dispute since William the Conqueror had taken England in 1066, and still the two countries made war over the issue. At last, however, they were enjoying a sort of peace. A de facto truce had begun in 1380 and had somehow managed to linger—mostly because the English were still arguing over Richard's position on the throne. He'd been barely nine years old when King Edward III had died in 1377 and had just reached his majority the year before, in 1389.

There remained in the country an air of constant upheaval because of the torn loyalties. Flanders remained, overall, a supporter of English rule, but because it was only a small province, it appeared futile to hope that it might have the rest of France see things its way.

"Oh, Grandmère, it all seems so hopeless." Jeanine sighed and muttered a phrase she had heard since a child whenever calamity struck: "Dieu m'a fait compagnon à Job." God has made me a companion for Job.

Indeed, that was what Jeanine felt like. Job of the Bible had found himself tested sorely. He had lost most all that he loved and cared about, coming close to the point of death, but only enough to share in the miseries of life. She thought of Latin Scriptures read in the great cathedral and those shared with her in a more common French by her dear friend Dr. Grosz.

Job had sat in the midst of his miseries, lamenting, "What is my strength, that I should hope?"

Jeanine wondered the same. "How can I have hope amid this nightmare?" She looked heavenward. Her conversation with the stone and her grandmother's memory concluded. "Mon Dieu, where is my hope?" Her prayerful question brought little but turmoil to her heart. Her hope should be in God, Himself. But she felt as though He might well have closed a door between them when Antoine Colbert stepped into the room. Perhaps God had arranged a test of faith for her, just as He had allowed Satan to test the faithfulness of Job.

"Please, Lord God, do not test me as Job," Jeanine prayed. "I am not of his strength, and my faith is most weak. You know my heart. It is not my desire that any portion of it might belong to anyone save You. Please hear my cry and deliver me from the hands of mine enemy—Antoine Colbert."

She had barely breathed the prayer when a tiny voice called to her. "Mademoiselle Jeanine."

Getting to her feet, Jeanine immediately recognized a small boy. "Jacques, what are you about that you should trudge through the cold to be at my side?"

"I have a message for you. 'Tis from Dr. Grosz."

Jeanine nodded and took the small slip of paper. "Merci beaucoup!" The boy nodded in acknowledgment of her thanks and hurried back toward the heart of town.

Jeanine unfolded the paper and read the simple words. "Five geese flying." It was their agreed message should Dr. Grosz require Jeanine's assistance. Refolding the paper, she put it into the pocket of her apron and hurried back to her father's house.

For several years, Jeanine had been making her excuses and taking leave of her mother to perform a most unusual service for the poor and destitute. With the help of her aged friend Dr. Grosz, Jeanine had found a passion for medicine and the art of surgery. But such things were clearly illegal for women to participate in. It seemed only fitting, however, that because Dr. Grosz was Jewish and therefore also forbidden to practice medicine in Bruges, the two should conspire to create their own hospital of sorts.

Simon Grosz lived near the docks on the River Zwin, and because his home was really no more than a hovel, he was fairly ignored by those in powerful positions. But Simon meant the world to Jeanine and to the poor, who gladly kept his secret. Jeanine had met him one day walking back from seeing her father's ship off. Her father had planned a northerly route by sea to the harbor of Danzig, and because he would be gone for such a long time, Jeanine had donned her brother Étienne's heavy, more masculine cloak and dared a venture to the docks.

No one had bothered her, and even her father had been startled to find his comely daughter behind the protective covering of her brother's cloak. He had taken her to the privacy of his cabin, chided her sternly for such foolishness, then kissed her soundly and embraced her with much love. She was his favorite, and well she knew it. But it had given her much cause for reflection on her attitude and actions.

"Poor Father," she thought, making her way along the same cobblestone roadway that had taken her to the docks so many years ago. "It isn't his fault that the river is filling with silt. He's a good businessman, but now he will have to find flat-bottomed boats or make his trade routes over land."

Simon's residence loomed up ahead. It looked like any one of a number of ramshackle riverfront buildings. Two stories in total, it was joined on either side by two other places of business. Outside the building, each of the businesses hung rickety signs that announced their professions. Simon's sign was a book, and it was well known to all that he was a copier of written work. But among the poor and poverty-stricken souls who lived and worked along the docks, it was just as well known that the old man was a physician of extraordinary ability.

Jeanine never failed to marvel at how the people protected their dear Dr. Grosz. It was hard to maintain a prejudice against a man who had just saved your child from disease or reset the broken leg of a man who by another physician would have seen it cut away and cauterized in order to be done with it. In spite of their superstitions and fears of religious excommunication, the people kept Dr. Grosz's secret, and hers as well.

Jeanine nodded to a passerby and smiled against the wintry cold as she pushed open the thin wooden door to Simon Grosz's shop. Inside, the front room bore all the signs of being a legitimate copy shop. The copy table stood against the wall where the room's single window allowed light to flood across the writing board. Beside the board a sheet of parchment awaited the quill. There were assorted tools—a razor for scraping, a pumice stone, a narrow ruler for accurate lining of the text, and a boar's tooth for polishing. Jeanine knew that in the drawer of the table there would be quills and ink. Everything necessary to copy a book.

"Bonjour! Bonjour!" Simon greeted her enthusiastically. "I was afraid Jacques would not find you. Twice he returned to me saying, 'She is not at home.' So I think to myself, 'Where could she be on such a day?'"

Jeanine laughed and removed her cloak. "And you knew I would be visiting my grandmère's grave, non?"

"But of course," Simon said, taking her cloak to hang it by the door. "Come. We have a great deal of work to do. I have a young boy who has a fishing hook imbedded near his eye. My own eyes are too blind for such close work, and I knew that you would be just the one to assist me. The boy will not be so frightened when he learns of your gentle touch."

Jeanine nodded and immediately began to unfasten the elaborately embroidered belt that snugly encircled her waist. The very simple lines of her houppeland made it easy to change into her disguise. The gown was utilized by both men and women and hung as a shapeless shift to the floor and boasted overly long, full sleeves. Both men and women wore houppelands, the only difference being the manner in which they were belted or decorated. Men sometimes didn't bother to gird the flowing robe with a belt, but women generally did. It provided the perfect way to decorate and brighten their gown and to show off their tiny waists

Jeanine slipped into the back room to change her very feminine houppeland of pale blue and lavender for a more masculine one of black. She didn't belt the robe, but left the gown to hang, hiding her very feminine figure from view. Her long curly brown hair was tightly braided up and secured under a man's woolen head cap. Simon had ingeniously sewn some of his own course hair along the bottom ridge of the cap, giving Jeanine an even more masculine appearance. She then took mud and ashes and smeared her face and neck until they were amply darkened. This, too, added to her appearing more masculine, and she checked her reflection in the mirror before joining Simon.

"Ah, Dr. Font," he said with a smile. " 'Tis good to have you join me. I have great work for you today."

Jeanine smiled and gave a deep-throated, "By your leave, Monsieur Docteur."

It was only when she was operating as a physician that Jeanine felt truly whole. She had long believed that God had called her to heal people, but the law was clearly against women participating in the healing arts as licensed physicians. Much more, Jeanine enjoyed surgical procedures, which by the admission of even the most knowledgeable man, were in their infancy and scarcely understood. Even the church had come out against surgery as being spiritually depraved. But Jeanine found that when she could help a dying person recover, she had actually allowed herself to be used of God. When she helped to deliver a newborn, she felt the thrill of life in her hands and the glory of God's wondrous power. How could that be wrong?

Of course the lies she found necessary to tell her parents and others were very wrong. She had lived with the weight of such deceit for so long that she hadn't even realized the heavy burden it had become. Jeanine knew it would have been impossible to explain her missions to her parents. They would have feared for her well-being. Having a young maiden in the area of the docks was worry enough, without that young woman performing an illegal act. But the poor people needed her, and it seemed that her lies were justifiable. Surely God understood.

Simon had already seen to cleansing the boy's wounds and also to giving him an herbal balm of mandrake to induce sleep. The boy now slept in perfect silence, unmindful of the procedure that lay ahead. Jeanine took up her instruments and worked cautiously over the small boy for over an hour. She found the fishing hook a great challenge to master. If it had entered an inch to the left, it would have embedded itself deep into the boy's eye. The barbs made it impossible to pull back through the opening. They would catch and embed themselves deeper into the flesh should they be pulled upon. With gentle care, Jeanine finally managed to direct the hook upward. It created yet another wound of exit, but it did far less damage to the tissue beneath the surface of his skin. Blood trickled from the hole, and Jeanine immediately set to cleansing the wound with egg whites, a common help for purification.

The boy's mother watched with horror as the procedure concluded when Jeanine secured a bandage at the side of her son's eye. Wearily, Jeanine straightened up and met the mother's expression.

"He'll be as good as new," Jeanine said with a low gravelly voice. "You must leave the bandage in place, however, and return to me in three days' time."

"Oh, Docteur," the mother said, openly weeping. "It was all my fault. I should never have let him go to the boat with his father. He's too young to be left unattended."

Jeanine smiled sympathetically and patted the woman on the back as she had observed Simon do on many occasions. "Do not fret. The Blessed Father has looked over you this day. Your son will heal. Setting blame will not retrace your steps, nor will it speed his recovery."

The teary-eyed woman nodded. "We are very poor. I have no money with which to pay, but if you have no wife, perhaps I could offer my services to clean or cook. I am a good cook."

"Non," replied Jeanine. "I do my service unto the Lord. He will provide the pay as well."

"Oh, merci! Merci!" She fell to her knees and kissed Jeanine's cloak. The woman was incredibly dirty, and as her tears fell, they caused streaks against her dirt-laden face. "May God bless and keep you all your days," she managed to say.

Jeanine touched her head. "And may He keep you and your family as well."

Jeanine went to wash her hands as Simon helped the woman to collect her sleeping child. There was a deep sense of satisfaction in having given of herself, and to Jeanine, it mattered very little that she couldn't perform her feats of medicinal wonder for all the world to see. She had meant what she'd said. She was working unto the Lord God in heaven. He knew her hands and their work. He had blessed her in ways that she did not yet begin to understand.

"If only You would tell me of this marriage to Antoine Colbert," she whispered, glancing upward. "If only You would show me a means of escape."

"So you have made yet another conquest, Dr. Font," Simon said, entering the room as Jeanine toweled her hands.

"He was so sweet. Did you see his precious little face? He will not suffer overmuch with his new scar. Mayhap it will give the ladies something to fancy when he grows into a fine young man, eh?"

Simon laughed and took a seat behind a sturdy desk. He pulled out several copies of well-worn medical books and motioned Jeanine to take a seat. "I have received an addition to these books," he said conspiratorially. "People think it not odd for a book copier to have medical works. Good thing they do not know I am rapidly going blind and would find copy work quite impossible. But if my eyes would but allow, I would copy this book over many times."

Jeanine nodded. "What new book do you speak of?"

Simon beamed a brilliant smile. "A copy of Mondino de' Luzzi's book of anatomy entitled *Anthania*."

Jeanine nearly squealed with delight as she reached out to take the book in hand. She opened it and skimmed the pages. "It's in French!" she declared, quite delighted, for most medical books were in Latin and difficult for her to read. "Oh, Simon, it's marvelous. What a find."

"Oui," Simon replied. "I thought you might find pleasure in this."

" 'After the muscle, the bones. Now the bones of the chest are many and are not continuous,' " she read from the text. "This is truly wonderful. Just imagine what I can learn from this." Thoughts danced madly in her head.

"Which is precisely why I intend to send it home with you this very day. I have secured for you a false-bottomed basket. That way, should anyone stop you and search your wares, they will find nothing but the simple treasures of a maiden."

Jeanine grinned. "This is a blessing from God."

"What a difference time makes." Simon's face seemed to reflect a memory of something long gone.

"How so?"

The old man gently rubbed his coarse gray beard. "I was thinking back to my time at the university in Montpellier. It was the only university to allow a Jew to study medicine. I was—"

"Docteur! Docteur!" a deep male voice called from the alleyway door.

Jeanine immediately got to her feet and handed the book back to Simon. "I will see what the commotion is about."

She went quickly to the door and opened it to find a trusted friend. "Pierre, what is wrong?" she asked the burly sailor.

"There is a ship come just now to harbor. There are several injured on board, but one man in particular lies close to death."

Jeanine felt her stomach lurch. Her father's ship, the *Crispin*, was long overdue, and Étienne de la Fontaine, her brother, was the ship's captain. "Which ship was it, Pierre?"

"The *Crispin*," he replied, confirming her suspicions.

"Tell them the doctor will be there posthaste." Pierre nodded and was gone, while Jeanine turned back to face Simon. Great turmoil churned in her heart. " 'Tis my father's ship, and my brother sailed her. If I go to the docks, there is a chance they will recognize me."

"But if you do not go, good men may die. Your brother included."

"Oui," Jeanine replied with a heavy sigh. "I will go, and you must pray for me."

"But my friend, I pray always for you," Simon replied.

∽

The commotion surrounding the *Crispin* left Jeanine with a churning sense of fear. Was her brother alive? Was he one of the injured? She moved quickly, trying to take long masculine strides and praying all the time that no one would recognize her as a woman.

"Make way! Make way!" Pierre called when he spotted Dr. Font in the gathering crowd.

The injured men were being moved from the ship and brought down the gangplank as Jeanine approached. She searched each face, feeling both relief that her brother didn't occupy one of the litters and compassion for each man's miseries.

"This man's arm is broken," she growled out and then checked the head wound he'd received. "He's not mortally wounded," she announced, feeling that the skull was firm. She quickly moved on.

The next man suffered a crushed left leg and would most likely require an amputation. The man after that was already dead.

"What happened?" she asked, as a sailor halted in front of her.

"A storm," the man replied as if further explanation was unnecessary.

"A storm?" she questioned.

"Oui. The main mast snapped in two. Three men were swept out to sea amid the waves."

"Where is your captain?" she asked, almost forgetting to lower her voice. She felt desperate to see Étienne. To know that he was well.

"On board. He was unharmed, but he tends the most critically injured man."

She breathed a sigh of relief. Étienne lived! Pushing her way on board, Jeanine came upon her brother and would have flung herself into his arms had her identity not been disguised. He looked weary from his ordeal. Several small cuts and bruises marred his handsome face, but other than that he appeared well.

"Are you injured?"

"Non," he replied. "But this good fellow has suffered mightily." Étienne clearly wanted the focus moved from his own needs.

Jeanine forced herself to look away from her brother. The ashen, unconscious face of the man on the litter, struck her deeply. He was handsome and carried the look of a nobleman, but his temple revealed an ugly bruising that instantly worried Jeanine. Gently she ran her fingers along the lines of his skull. The indentation was obvious when her hand pressed against the temple. "The skull is fractured. He will have to be taken to a place where I might care for him. Come. I will lead the way."

"His name is Victor Pindar," Étienne offered. "He is an Englishman."

Jeanine tried to maintain her masculine attitude. " 'Tis sure he will be a dead man if we do not see him rapidly taken from this ship."

Étienne motioned Pierre and another stocky worker to grab up the litter. "Follow this good doctor. He will instruct you." The men nodded and Jeanine breathed a sigh of relief. Étienne had not recognized her.

Back at Simon's, Jeanine worked feverishly over Victor. His body had sustained multiple injuries, including several broken ribs and two rather nasty gashes along his right thigh. Simon had his own hands busy with the other patients, and no one seemed to question whether he had a right to practice medicine. The dockworkers knew the old man and his young assistant, Dr. Font, and little else mattered. The poor had an inner-working of communication, and word of mouth was quick to spread that Dr. Font and Dr. Grosz could be trusted. It was also understood that for reasons both known and unknown, the doctors were not allowed to practice medicine under the scrutiny of the public eye. Therefore, they were quite cautious about letting anyone know about their good doctors.

Jeanine bathed Victor's head wound, far and away the most serious of his injuries. The discoloration was spreading, and the man refused to regain consciousness, making it quite evident that the brain was hemorrhaging. If she didn't do something quickly, Victor Pindar would die.

"Simon," she whispered. The old man glanced up from where he was stitching the wounds of another man. "This will take us both," she added.

Simon finished his work and came to stand beside her. "He's nearly dead," he said in a tone that suggested she give him over to God.

"Oui, but I think we still might save him."

"The pressure from the blood must be relieved or he will die," Simon said, palpating the depressed temple.

Jeanine knew for herself that too much time was slipping by. "Can we drill into it? Will not the blood then come through the opening and relieve his brain of the pressure? You have oft told me of trephining. Might we try it now?"

"Yes, but it isn't a simple procedure. It is most dangerous, and it could prove to be his death."

Jeanine shook her head. "But this will prove to be his death if we do not at least attempt it."

Simon nodded and went to retrieve his instruments. While he was busily preparing for the dangerous surgery, Jeanine found her hand brushing back the brownish black hair of her patient. She felt a tenderness for the man that she could not explain. Her heart ached with the sight of him damaged and wounded from the storm. She tried to imagine him healthy and vital as he must have been before the accident.

"Dear God, help us to heal this man," Jeanine whispered. What was his name? Étienne had told her, but for some reason it had slipped her mind. Victor, something. Yes, that was it. Victor Pindar. She continued to stroke his hair as though in doing so she might somehow induce him to live.

"Here we are," Simon said, laying out the instruments they would need. "Call Pierre to help, just in case the man wakes up."

Jeanine nodded and went into the alleyway where Pierre was giving water to several of the less critically injured men. "Pierre," she called, "we are going to perform a serious surgery and need your assistance."

The burly man nodded and handed the water bucket to one of his companions. Jeanine led him to the washstand where she thoroughly scrubbed her hands and then motioned Pierre to follow suit.

"First," Simon said, "we must clear away the hair. My eyes are not so good, Dr. Font. You will have to be responsible for this surgery, but I will guide you as you perform."

"Me?" Jeanine found herself squeaking out the word. "You want me to. . ." She couldn't say the words.

"You will do fine. Remember, this is what you have spent so many hours in study for."

"But I've not yet studied this type of surgery," she protested.

"Then you are about to," Simon said with a smile of reassurance.

Carefully they considered the wound and decided how best to continue. They pulled back the thick hair and shaved clean a portion of scalp. This done, Jeanine cut into the soft flesh, and while Simon held back the patch of skin, she took up yet another instrument to saw into the bone of Victor's skull. Carefully, with Simon's constant instruction, she maneuvered artfully until the tiny circle of bone was removed and dark blood began to seep out.

"We will allow the blood to drain, and as it does, our patient may well become conscious. We will have to be careful that he not thrash about."

Jeanine nodded, grateful that Simon and Pierre had already tied Victor securely to the table. Pierre stood alert at the man's side, prepared to restrain the man if necessary.

When Victor showed signs of movement, Simon felt that enough blood had been drained in order to complete their surgery. Together, he and Jeanine worked until only the raw, freshly stitched patch remained to show their work. With any luck, the thickness of his hair would hide the scar.

Victor's moans began before Jeanine had secured the last stitch, but it wasn't until some minutes later that he actually opened his eyes.

"Eleanor." He moaned the name over and over.

"Perhaps his wife," Simon suggested.

Jeanine nodded, feeling sudden disappointment. Of course the man was probably married. He looked to be ten years her senior. He probably had a fine wife and a great many children who were even now wondering where their father might be.

But she didn't want there to be a wife and children. For reasons that she couldn't understand or comprehend, Jeanine wanted Victor Pindar for herself.

Shaking her head at such a ridiculous thought, Jeanine tried to busy herself by collecting the instruments. Why should she think such a thing? She had only just laid eyes on him. There was no telling who he was or what kind of man he had been. Beyond that, Jeanine was in no way available to consider such matters. She was betrothed to another man, a man whose happiness meant settled debts and peace of mind for her father.

With a sad resignation that made her feel aged, Jeanine pushed aside the image of the handsome face and his murmurings for a woman who didn't even know he lay perilously close to death.

Chapter 3

For several days, Jeanine managed to sneak away from her mother's watchful eyes and make her way to Simon's. It was becoming increasingly difficult, however, to come up with a good excuse for her absences, and Jeanine knew it would not be long before she would be hard-pressed to leave for any reason.

Lies mounted on top of lies, and Jeanine felt great sorrow in her deeds. Her mother would be sorely wounded at learning of her daughter's deception, yet even this could not make Jeanine give up her plan. The only real problem was her impending marriage to Antoine Colbert. No matter how Jeanine prayed that her heavenly Father might give her direction and take the responsibility from her, God seemed silent on why she should suffer such a fate.

Securing her disguise in place once again, Jeanine emerged from Simon's back room as Dr. Font. Putting thoughts of her betrothal aside, she hurried to learn the news of her patient. She longed to see Victor and know of his night under Simon's care. Each day seemed to bring only welcomed news. He was much improved—this much she had ascertained for herself in previous days. Nevertheless, she longed to see him. To know that he was healing and that he would recover without any permanent damage.

"Bonjour, Simon," she said in a low husky voice.

"Ah, I knew you would come with the first crowing of the cock," Simon answered with a smile. "I did not hear you come in. I was with our patient."

"How is he?" she asked in a whisper, her gaze darting to the room that housed Victor Pindar.

"He is recovering well. I changed the dressings on his leg wounds and found them healing nicely. His ribs will be bound yet for another week before we test them to see how they are faring."

"And his head?"

"Much improved," Simon answered, preparing to mix a concoction of herbs together. "Why don't you see for yourself?"

Jeanine nodded and slipped quietly into Victor's room.

"You are the doctor, are you not?" the man's voice called weakly to her in English.

Jeanine didn't understand the words very well, but doctor sounded close enough to docteur, that she felt confident of his meaning.

"I am Dr. Font," she said in slowly spoken French. "Do you speak my

364

language?" She came to his bedside and caught sight of his weathered face. His dark eyes beheld her for a moment before closing.

"Oui," he managed behind a grimace of pain.

"You are in pain?" she said, barely remembering to keep her voice low.

"Oui."

"Your head?" she questioned, checking the incision for signs of infection. "You have sustained a bad wound. The mast of my. . ." She paused. She'd nearly said, The mast of my brother's ship. That would never do. She pretended to examine his head first one way and then another, all the while trying to calm her raging heart. "The mast broke and fell upon you. Your skull sustained a heavy blow."

"I don't remember what happened," he said softly.

Jeanine was momentarily mesmerized as he licked his dry, chapped lips. "No, I supposed you might not. 'Tis not unusual. Injuries to the brain are difficult to understand. We do not yet know what makes one man completely lose his senses and another regain his memories when consciousness is lost. There are theories, of course, but that is unimportant to you, non?"

"It is important to me to get a message to England."

Jeanine was once again reminded of the name Eleanor and the possibility that this man belonged to another woman. "A message?" she managed to question gruffly.

"Oui. My sister, Eleanor, resides in Dover with her young son, Marcus. I live there, and I am long overdue. She will be heartsick."

Jeanine let out a long-held breath. Eleanor was his sister. He had no wife. Or did he? "And what of your wife?" she questioned. "Your children? Should we not also send a message to them?"

"There is no wife. No children."

Just then Simon returned with a glass. "I have prepared a potion that will give you relief from your sufferings and aid healing."

"What have you prepared?" Jeanine asked.

"Sweet marjoram to help heal the brain," Simon answered, handing Victor the glass. "Fruit of the mandragora to induce sleep and dull the senses of pain, and fennel to control brain fever."

Jeanine's eyes widened as Victor drank down the smelly brew. "Has he suffered brain fever?"

Simon smiled. "Non. 'Tis certain the fennel is working, eh?"

Jeanine nodded and followed Simon reluctantly from the room. "Will he sleep right away?" she asked, keeping her voice to a bare whisper.

"The medicine is potent. It should work quickly. Why do you ask?"

Jeanine glanced at the still-open door. "He mentioned a sister in England. One to whom a message should be delivered."

"Eleanor?"

Jeanine nodded. "The same. He lives with her in Dover. There is no wife or children, and besides this sister 'tis my thought that he is alone."

" 'Twould seem amiss for us to delay in sending the message," Simon said, eyeing her strangely.

Jeanine felt her face grow hot and was grateful for once to be smeared in ashes and mud. "I just thought to obtain the place where the message should be sent. Surely Dover is so large a town that we would need a more specific address."

Simon smiled and nodded. "Go back to him then. Sit for a time if it brings you comfort." He seemed to understand her longing without Jeanine having to confess her feelings.

" 'Twould seem fitting," she replied and quickly took herself to Victor's bedside before Simon could take back his words.

Victor appeared to hear her enter, for when she approached his bedside, he opened his eyes and looked up in anticipation of what she might next do.

"You did not tell me where I might send word to your sister," she said in a strained, masculine tone.

Victor seemed to consider this for a moment before yawning and closing his eyes. "She is on her estate. The lands belonging once to her dead husband, Lord Bramston."

Jeanine memorized the name and adjusted the pillow on which Victor's head rested somewhat more easily. "Is the draught helping with the pain?"

"I. . .believe 'tis. . .better. . .now." His voice was weak. The medicine was helping him off to sleep.

Jeanine pulled up a chair and sat by the bedside. "I will wait here to make certain you fall asleep," she murmured. "And I will offer up a blessing for you as well." She thought for a moment, then continued. "May the Lord God heal you now. May He see your needs and reach where human hands may not go."

Victor seemed not to hear. For a moment he appeared peaceful, then he reached out to touch her hand. "There is trouble with the buttresses," he whispered. "You must see to them." He turned toward her as if to sit up, winced in pain, and fell back against the mattress, even as Jeanine put a hand to his shoulder to still him. "The cathedral. . .must finish." He moaned. "Transepts. . .uneven."

Jeanine stared at him in wonder. What manner of thing did he speak of? Buttresses and transepts? She leaned closer to better hear him, but just as she did, he lapsed into English and further understanding was completely lost to her. He muttered softly for several minutes before finally settling into a deep sleep. With a sigh, Jeanine touched his brow and a longing grew within her to better know his face—his hands.

Tenderly, she picked up his hand from where it had fallen away from her own. His hands were large, with long slender fingers that appeared well groomed and cared for. She longed to ask her brother about him, but it escaped her how she might bring up the subject. Étienne had spent most of his time assessing the ship's damage, as had her father. When the men had returned at close of day, they were exhausted and surly, completely unwilling to discuss much of anything. Beyond that, for all they knew, Jeanine had never met Victor Pindar. And because his recuperation was spent at Simon's and not in her home, Jeanine might never have reason to express her concern or interest.

After leaving Victor's side to study with Simon, Jeanine felt restlessness overcome her. Her mind refused to remain on her studies, and in spite of the fact that Simon continued in his patient manner, Jeanine could no longer deal with the issues of anatomy.

"I wish I did not have to leave him here," she said, staring longingly at the closed door for the tenth or eleventh time. Then worried that Simon might misunderstand her reasoning, she added, " 'Tis naught to do with your good work, however."

Simon closed his book and leaned back in the chair. "Dr. Font is worried about his patient, eh? Or is it Mademoiselle Jeanine has lost her heart, and Monsieur Pindar holds the secrets to where we might reclaim it."

Jeanine blushed. "I suppose I am being but a twiddle-headed girl. Truly 'tis not what I planned." She sighed and looked Simon in the eye. "He makes me feel. . .well. . .I don't really have words for how I feel."

"Perhaps you are sick," Simon suggested teasingly.

"Heartsick, mayhap." She got up and shook her head. "Medicine has become my life. I have no interest in marrying Antoine Colbert, even though our wedding is but a short time away. 'Twould suit me better to join a nunnery, but then again 'twould be impossible to practice surgery there."

Simon laughed. "As though 'twould not be the same with Monsieur Colbert."

Jeanine frowned. "Forgive me, Jeanine, I did not mean—"

" 'Tis all right. You speak but the truth. How might I fault you for that, dear friend? You are right. 'Twill be most impossible to slip away from Antoine and come here. I will find myself forced to tend only those around me, and surely there will be no practicing of surgery."

The cathedral bells chimed out the hour, causing Jeanine to start. "Oh, my! 'Tis noon already. I must hurry home." She began pulling off her cap. "I will check back later this day if I find a proper excuse for leaving the house."

"Never fear, my dear docteur, I will see to our patient's care. Should I need you—should he worsen, I will send someone for you."

⁓

That night over dinner, Jeanine was pleasantly surprised to find her brother and father in residence. The hour was early and their spirits were light, which led Jeanine to believe that things were going well with the ship's recovery.

"Another day, maybe two," her father announced, "and we should see the completion of the repairs."

" 'Tis good news indeed," her mother said with a smile.

They ate in silence for several minutes, before Jeanine dared ask the question on her mind. "And how is your friend, Étienne?"

Her brother stared dumbly at her for a moment, then smiled. "Oh, you're speaking of Monsieur Pindar, non?"

"Yes," she smiled. "I believe that was his name. Is he well now?"

"To tell you the truth," her brother replied, "I haven't had time to check in on him. I turned him over to the capable hands of a doctor, and that was the last of it. He isn't actually a friend, you know. He simply was a man in need of passage home. I told him I could bring him to Calais, but after that he would have to find passage to England. Of course, the storm put an end to that."

" 'Tis a pity he must suffer without the care of those who love him," Jeanine replied, trying hard to concentrate on her bread and cheese.

To her surprise and relief, her mother took up the conversation. "I quite agree. 'Tis unseemly for you to leave him with strangers. I cannot say that I know what you were thinking when you performed this most uncharitable act."

Étienne seemed genuinely wounded. "I had only the desire to see him put into the care of a doctor. 'Tis my own fault that I've not taken up his cause beyond that."

"You could find Monsieur Pindar," Jeanine encouraged. "Perhaps if he is still ill, he could recuperate here. I would gladly give up my room to help such a man."

Étienne laughed. "No doubt your Monsieur Colbert would bring down this house with his rage if he were to learn that you had taken another man into your room."

Jeanine gasped. "What scandal do you speak? I only meant to imply that I would be happy to help in caring for the man. After all, 'twould be our Christian duty. Would it not?"

"I think Jeanine has a point," her mother replied. "The man is a stranger in our land. He was injured aboard our boat. Now let us do an act of charity and care for him while he recovers. Surely 'twould be fitting."

"I hadn't considered it," Jeanine's father inserted before his son could answer, "but such plans seem quite reasonable. Étienne, why not go fetch the man home this very night?"

"I promise I will," Étienne replied.

Jeanine smiled to herself in satisfaction. Tonight, with providence and God on their side, Victor Pindar would be a patient in her house. Not only her house, her very room! Suddenly things seemed quite different. Here, in her own home, Jeanine could be a woman and care for him as a woman. At Simon's she had found it necessary to maintain her disguise and remain a man. There was no hope of sharing her interest in him if he couldn't even spend time during his recovery to see her as a woman.

"When will you go after him?" Jeanine asked, trying hard not to sound overly interested.

Étienne looked at the expectant faces of his parents and sibling. Grabbing up a piece of bread, he stood. "I suppose I might just as well go now. 'Tis of a certainty I will be without any peace 'til I do.

Jeanine, too, jumped to her feet. "I'll go prepare the room now." She smiled to herself and hummed all the way up the stairs. Victor Pindar was going to be her private patient, and because she would help to heal him in her own home, no one would accuse her falsely for dabbling in medical procedures.

Chapter 4

"H ere are clean linens," Jeanine's mother said, entering the bedroom and placing the stack on a nearby stool.

"I have stripped off the old linens and turned the mattress. 'Tis certain that it would be more comfortable with another stuffing of feathers, but 'twill have to do for now," Jeanine said, staring blankly at the mattress. In her mind's eye she was envisioning Victor in sleep upon her bed. Dreamily, she reached down to smooth out the mattress, then quickly pulled back her hand, suddenly realizing how foolish she might appear to her mother.

Her mother seemed not to notice, however. She was busying herself by taking up the two modest rugs. "I'll take these for a good pounding," she said.

Jeanine nodded and hurried to remake the bed, anxious to have her room in order. After this task was complete, she rushed around to insure that the remaining portions of the room were fit as well. Her small dressing table, cluttered with a variety of herbs and healing balms, as well as various other trinkets, nearly cried for her attention, but Jeanine couldn't take the time to put things in order. Already she heard voices in the main room below, and her heart pounded faster. Could they have already returned?

Hurrying, she unbound her hair and combed through the thick brown ringlets. All of her life she had wanted to curse the curls that naturally formed on her head. Most of the time she wore her hair braided and hidden from view, but she wanted to look feminine and pretty, something she seldom cared about. Running the brush through the waist-long mane, Jeanine smiled to herself. Tonight, Victor would see her for the first time as a woman. Perhaps then he, too, would lose his heart. One final smoothing of the curls, and Jeanine replaced the brush and went in search of her brother and Victor.

The home of François de la Fontaine was a relatively simple four-story structure. The first floor was devoted to his merchandise and business affairs. The second floor was the main floor for the family. It was here that they dined and shared quiet times in front of the fire. The third floor was devoted to bedrooms, while the upper level contained the overflow of the other three floors.

Jeanine made her way down the stairs, struggling to keep her heart from pounding right through her chest. She felt like a giddy schoolgirl and knew it was silly. She chided herself to calm down, but never having ever felt this way about any man, she was almost relieved to experience the feelings. She had despaired of ever falling in love, and now she was certain that with little or no effort, she could be deeply in love with Victor Pindar.

Reaching the final step, Jeanine felt light as a feather and nearly danced across the room to find her family. What she found instead was Antoine Colbert.

"My, my," he said, low and seductively, "but you are bewitching."

Jeanine froze in place. The smile faded from her countenance. "What are you doing here?" she asked.

"I came to see you," he replied and stepped forward.

Jeanine caught a whiff of his stench and grimaced. "My father has not yet returned, but when he does you may keep your company with him."

"Why would I desire to keep his company, when I have a beautiful wife to consider."

"I am not yet your wife, Monsieur," she replied defiantly. Her chin lifted ever so slightly in the air as Colbert frowned.

" 'Tis yet another reason I am come. What say we put an end to the final three weeks of waiting. I would see our marriage take place on the morrow."

"Impossible!" Jeanine exclaimed, feeling sudden revulsion at the thought of Colbert's wishes being adhered to. "My father is even now retrieving a very ill comrade into our home. I will be needed to assist my mother in his care. There is no possible time to plan a wedding at this point. Mayhap," she said, pausing thoughtfully, "we might delay it another fortnight beyond."

"Never," Colbert said, crossing the distance between them. Without warning his pudgy fingers closed over her hands. "You are mine, Mademoiselle, and I will have what I want." He pulled her closer, but Jeanine pushed at him, backing away.

"I do not love you, Monsieur. Surely 'twould be a better marriage to seek a woman whose heart is not set against you."

"I care not where your heart is set," he said. Again he stepped forward, only this time he backed Jeanine against a wall. Letting go of her hands, he gripped her arms tightly. They were nearly the same height, so their gazes met equally as they stood only inches apart. Colbert's thick stomach aided his hands in holding Jeanine in place, and she fought to push him away, sickened at the thought of his touch. Colbert only laughed and breathed heavily against her ear. "I am a wealthy man, my dear. I can see your father put out of business and driven from this place before you can so much as scream."

Jeanine realized that she was treading dangerous water. She thought frantically for how she might soothe the man's anger, without yielding to his demands. "Monsieur, I am but a simple maiden. I have no mind for such matters, but it is my understanding that you and my father have an agreement most binding by the laws of our land. I do not doubt that you are a powerful man."

At this he laughed and pressed his body closer still. "I am a very powerful man."

Jeanine fought to keep her emotions from revealing themselves on her face. She glanced upward, nearly faint from the foul smell of the man's breath. "You surely would not wish for people in the village to say you go back on your word. Breaking faith with my father would not bode well for your reputation."

"My dear Jeanine," he said, his wet lips perilously close to her own mouth, "I intend on breaking faith with no one. I have come, in fact, that the agreement might be completed sooner than expected."

Jeanine easily realized that she had led him in the wrong direction. It was her desire to put an end to their betrothal, not hasten its conclusion. "But monsieur, I do not wish to be a wife to you."

"I care not," he replied quite matter-of-factly. "Your desires and wishes are of little importance. You will be my wife, and you will give me many fine sons." He lowered his mouth to hers, just as Jeanine turned her face. The slobbery wet lips fell only upon her cheek, yet even this made her feel ill. Violently, she twisted against his hold and tried to push him from her.

"You forget yourself, Monsieur!" she declared, but Colbert was ruthless in his pursuit.

Not standing a chance against him, Jeanine thought of screaming as he put his thick hand to her throat. "Be still, or I'll give you a beating you won't forget."

She froze in fear. "You are not my husband. You have no right."

"Ah, but I soon will be, and there is nothing you can do to prevent your fate. Now I demand a kiss, and should you resist, I will remember this day upon our wedding night and exact my revenge quite thoroughly."

Jeanine was at a loss, and Colbert took her silent contemplation as acceptance. He kissed her roughly and ran his hand along her neck and down her shoulder.

"What is this? Monsieur, you forget yourself," Margarite de la Fontaine said as she swept into the room.

Colbert pulled away, his gaze defying Jeanine to say one word against him. "I was overcome by your daughter's beauty," he said, turning to smile at Margarite.

Jeanine's mother looked unconvinced that such an excuse was reasonable for the liberties she'd just witnessed. "Monsieur, she is but a maid. You will frighten her with such bold advances. Please," she paused to motion him to the fire, "come sit here and woo her gently."

Jeanine grimaced behind Colbert's back. She wished with all her heart that she might soundly club the man over the head. Just then he turned and smiled as if reading her thoughts. Jeanine drew in a sharp breath. He reached out his hand to take hold of her arm. "Let us do as your mother bids."

"But, ma mère, have you forgotten? We are expecting a guest. A very ill guest," Jeanine said, straining to pull away.

"Our guest will not require your attention," her mother said in an anxious voice. Her eyes seemed to warn Jeanine not to upset Colbert.

Jeanine suddenly realized the desperation of her plight. She could not further injure Antoine Colbert without her family falling prey to some retribution for her actions. Quietly, she allowed the offensive man to lead her to the bench by the fire.

"Madame de la Fontaine," Colbert began, "you must persuade your husband to shorten the time before our vows. I long to take your daughter to my home—to make her my beloved wife—to see her happy."

Those three things can never coexist, Jeanine thought grimly as he continued his plea.

"I have cared for your daughter from afar, and now that your husband has agreed to the contract of marriage, I see it as foolishness to continue this lengthy waiting period."

Jeanine's mother shrugged. "Monsieur, I cannot speak for my husband. His word is law in our home."

Colbert nodded. "As it should be. I only ask that you might influence him a bit. Perhaps I could even sweeten the pot, say by adding additional funds to be disbursed for your pleasure?"

"Monsieur, you would find your answer only with my husband."

"Oui, but a beautiful woman often holds sway over those caught up in her spell."

"It doesn't seem to be helping me any," Jeanine muttered.

Colbert tightened his hold on her arm and sat down, drawing her with him. Jeanine was caught off balance and nearly landed on his lap. Colbert only chuckled. "See?" he questioned, looking upward to catch her mother's horrified expression. "She already longs to be near me."

Jeanine tried to add distance to the space between them, but Colbert held her fast. "Talk to your husband, Madame. See if he won't see things my way. 'Twould be most beneficial for your family."

Casting her daughter an apologetic look before curtseying, Madame de la Fontaine responded, "I will do as you ask."

Colbert nodded. "Good. Then leave us to make our wedding plans."

Jeanine knew her mother was in no position to argue. The older woman left the room with a look of panic that made Jeanine's heartache only worsen. How dare Colbert come into their home and treat her mother so disrespectfully? But then, the law gave him full right. They were indebted to Colbert, and without his generous offer to resolve their debt, Jeanine had little trouble believing he would see them all thrown into prison.

With her mother gone, Jeanine wondered what he might try next. She dared a glance and found him watching her.

"Milord?"

"It is my opinion that you are the fairest creature in all of Flanders," he said in a near breathless manner. "I find I hunger for you and that my hunger must be satisfied. Think not that you will escape my plans for you. No other will have you, Jeanine de la Fontaine. You will belong to me for all time. Now and always."

Jeanine shuddered. *Dear Lord God,* she prayed, *do not let it be so.*

Chapter 5

Jeanine felt immense relief when Colbert took his leave. He mentioned attending to some affair of state and said it was the only thing that could tear him from her side. She ran for the water bucket after his departure and scrubbed her face and arms where the touch of Colbert left her feeling tainted. It was while doing this that she heard her father and brother struggling up the back stairs.

"Père?" she called, casting a glance over the landing rail.

"Oui," he grunted. He precariously balanced the weight of a litter between his bulky shoulders, while Étienne, standing several steps above his father, was nearly bent in half in order to keep the litter even.

Jeanine dared a glance at the litter, and her breath caught in her throat. Victor Pindar was staring up at her with an expression something between pain and confusion. "I have the room already prepared, Père," Jeanine said.

Again her father grunted, but he said nothing until they had managed to gain entry onto the second floor. "Go, make clear the way," her father ordered, and Jeanine fairly danced to do his bidding.

She called to her mother, announcing the arrival of Monsieur Pindar, then pushed back the door to her room and stood aside as her father and brother carried Victor to her bed. Once they had settled him on top of the clean linens, Jeanine went to work to make him comfortable.

"Are you warm enough, Monsieur?" she asked, bringing yet another thick wool blanket.

"I am fine," Victor managed to say. He lifted his gaze to Étienne. "You are most gracious to see to my needs. I will one day repay this debt."

"Then pay it back to my sister. To tell you honestly, I was much consumed by the damage done my ship. I fear I left you to the care of others without much more than a brief thought," Étienne admitted. "Jeanine pointed out the error of my ways."

Victor turned ever so slightly to catch Jeanine's intent study. "Thank you, Mademoiselle. You were most kind to suggest such care."

Jeanine smiled. " 'Tis our Christian duty to see to our fellow man, n'est-ce pas?"

"Indeed it is so, Daughter," her father stated. "Now, I suspect this young man would be in need of rest."

"And I have brought just the healing balm to bring about such a thing,"

Margarite de la Fontaine said, entering the room. She held out a draught of thick dark liquid.

Victor took the mug, downed the contents, then smiled ever so slightly. " 'Tis not nearly so bitter as that which the good doctor prescribed."

Jeanine laughed at the thought of Simon's concoction. "Medicine was not intended to taste good, but to make one feel good or at least better. Mother has a way with herbs, and no doubt you will be quite satisfied with her abilities."

"No doubt," Victor said, nodding acknowledgment to Madame de la Fontaine.

"Come now, let us leave the man in peace. He should sleep well here tonight," Jeanine's father said. Turning to Victor, he added, "And should you need anything, one of us will be close at hand."

"Oui," Jeanine said, turning to gather up several things. " 'Twill be my place to sleep outside your door. Just call to me for any help you might need. My name is Jeanine."

⁓

What had started out seeming the perfect solution to her problems gave Jeanine little satisfaction. Victor seemed not in the leastwise interested in her ministrations. She cared for him daily, taking an interest in anything that had to do with him. She had even gained the raised eyebrow of her mother by offering to bathe Victor two days after his arrival. That suggestion was quickly dismissed, and instead Madame de la Fontaine attended to that need. Nevertheless, Jeanine maintained hope that somehow she could convince Victor to fall in love with her. Or at least take a marginal interest in her.

Sitting at his bedside on the fourth day of Victor's stay, Jeanine realized that nearly another week had passed, moving her ever closer to becoming Antoine Colbert's wife. She grimaced as she worked her needlepoint. There seemed no hope of escaping the inevitable.

"That color must hurt your eyes," Victor said, rather groggily.

Jeanine's head snapped up to find him watching her. "Why do you say that?"

"You could not imagine the expression on your face," he replied and eased himself up a bit in the bed.

Jeanine dropped her sewing and helped him to sit up against the headboard. She liked the feel of his warm arms against her hands and the way the muscles became hard and firm as he worked to push himself up. He was used to hard work, she decided, and yet he seemed very much to take on the part of the wealthy nobleman. He spoke French in perfect order and seemed most intelligent, yet he didn't take on airs with her or her family.

As she bent over him to pull the pillow into position, Jeanine found that her face was only inches from his. She froze, finding her gaze drawn to his. For a moment, neither one said anything, and Jeanine felt her breath catch in her throat. Victor's dark eyes beheld her with almost amused interest. His face fascinated

Jeanine in a way that she could not explain. It caused her to commit to memory every line and wrinkle, but mostly it caused her heart to beat faster and her palms to grow moist.

"I suppose this is some new manner of care," he finally said. "You are breathing your breath into me, willing over your health to my body, is that it?"

Jeanine startled at such a thought and straightened up quickly. "I. . .I. . .am. . . sorry." She felt her face grow hot with embarrassment. She went quickly to retrieve her sewing and pricked her finger three times before giving up the pretense. When she glanced up, she found Victor still studying her.

"So how is it that you are still in your father's house?" he questioned her finally. "You look old enough to be wed and caring for several babes."

Jeanine felt even more embarrassment over this reference to her age. She toyed with the idea of remaining silent or even of changing the subject, but since this was the most attention Victor had ever offered her, she was eager to answer. "I am very old. I am twenty. But I've been useful to my parents," she replied, not knowing what else to say.

Victor smiled ever so slightly and rubbed his stubbly chin. "Yes, I can well imagine."

He continued to stare at her, and Jeanine, not knowing what else to do, decided to turn the conversation in another direction. "What are transepts?" she asked.

"Where in the world did you hear that term?" he asked, eyeing her oddly.

Jeanine suddenly realized that the only time she'd ever heard the word was while Victor was delirious and under the care of Dr. Font. She felt momentarily frantic to think up an excuse, but none would come. "I don't know," she lied. "I think I heard some men talking one day. I thought to ask my father, but I forgot and thought perhaps you might know."

He continued to study her in silence as if deciding whether she should be privy to such knowledge. His look made her uneasy, and Jeanine instantly dropped her gaze to her handwork.

"A transept is the extended part of a cathedral that crosses and separates the nave from the choir," he finally answered.

"Nave? Choir? You mean the singers?" she asked, forgetting her earlier embarrassment.

He grinned. "Not exactly. 'Tis a term for architects, those builders of cathedrals. The nave is the portion of the building where you stand in worship during the services." Jeanine nodded as if visualizing it in her mind. "The nave usually has robing rooms or chapels on either side of the main room. The choir is that portion at the front of the church and on the other side of the transept, which is nearest the altar. Understand?"

"Yes, thank you. Are you an architect?" she asked boldly. Her need to know more about him outweighed her concern that he might question her intrusion into his privacy.

"Actually, yes." He looked thoughtful for a moment.

"And have you built such a cathedral?" she asked.

"You are most perceptive," he answered, turning slightly and wincing as he did.

"You should not move without help," she offered, starting to get up from her chair. "Your ribs are broken."

He waved her back. " 'Tis unnecessary. I grow stronger every day thanks to the care of your family and my good physicians."

"Yes, I heard from my brother that you were nearly dead when they took you from the ship." Jeanine wondered what if anything he remembered of his ordeal at Simon's.

" 'Twould seem true enough," he answered and relaxed against the headboard of her bed.

Jeanine liked the way his disheveled hair hung down onto his forehead and across his right eye. When he reached up to push it back, she longed to touch it as well. She couldn't resist wondering what it might feel like against her fingers. Unpleasant memories of Antoine Colbert's grease-laden hair made her shudder.

"Are you cold?" Victor suddenly asked.

Jeanine's thoughts were brought back in line. "Nay, I was just imagining how terrible a storm at sea might be." Again she lied, and her conscience began to sorely bother her. She seemed to bring falsehoods into every walk of her life.

"It was a bad storm," Victor agreed. " 'Twas our good fortune that your brother is the seaman he is. He risked his life more than once for his men, and I hold him in the highest regard. Of course some things could not be helped. The waves were fierce and there were several men washed overboard. But your brother did what he could."

Jeanine beamed a smile at this. "Aye, he is a good man. A loving soul who deserves much more than he has. I would like to see him find a good woman to marry. With his infinite patience, he would make a wonderful father."

Victor raised a dark brow as if contemplating whether this might be true. The silence fell awkwardly between them, and Jeanine sought to think of a topic. Then memory served her another reminder, and it seemed the perfect thing. "Do you have a brother?"

"Non," Victor answered. "I have a dear sister and nephew, but no one else. My sister lives in England, and when I am in England, I live with her and her little boy, Marcus."

"What is her name?" Jeanine asked, knowing full well the answer.

"Eleanor. Lady Eleanor Bramston. She has a wonderful estate outside of Dover. Her husband died some time back, and now she keeps the lands for her son."

"Are you close?"

"Aye," Victor said softly. "As close as two people can be."

Jeanine felt an instantaneous envy for the woman. His obvious admiration for his sister made her wish he might feel something half so strong for her. But Victor seemed to show absolutely no interest in her whatsoever. He seemed equally content whether she came to offer him care or her mother came in her stead. It didn't appear to matter who kept him company nor in fact whether he had any company at all.

"I had your father send her word of my recovery," Victor finally added. "I could not bear to think of her fretting over my well-being."

"You are most thoughtful," Jeanine said. "Most men would not consider the feelings of a woman to be worth much."

Victor looked at her as if she had spoken some hideous lie. "A man of honor and valor would," he said flatly, almost as if challenging her to deny it.

She smiled weakly and pretended to pick at her embroidery thread. "Then there is a short supply of such men in Flanders."

Victor chuckled at this. It was apparent he had taken no real offense at her words. "Mayhap you should visit England."

Jeanine looked up and smiled. "Mayhap I should."

❧

In her guise as Dr. Font, Jeanine tried hard to put her mind from Victor and turn to the studies at hand. Finding it nearly impossible to concentrate, Jeanine looked at the words in the book until her vision blurred.

"I am thinking your mind is not entirely with us this day," Simon said, suddenly leaning back in his chair.

Jeanine attempted a smile. "I suppose it isn't."

"And might this have something to do with our patient, Monsieur Pindar?"

"It might." Jeanine lifted her gaze to meet Simon's grandfatherly regard.

"So, our study of humors and apothecary treatments is of little interest in comparison—eh?"

"Non," she said, shaking her head. " 'Tis not a lack of interest, I assure you."

"Very well, then let us continue." Simon pointed to a sketch of the brain. "Tell me of the humors related here."

"Phlegm," Jeanine replied. "This humor is associated with the brain and is represented by water, because it is cold and moist. Treatments are used to either reduce the heat of fevers or to induce the moisture in order to aid the humor."

"Good, and this?"

"Blood, associated with the heart," she nearly sighed the latter word. "It is hot and moist and represented by air." Or Victor Pindar, her own heart told her.

They passed quickly through a recitation of the other two humors—yellow and black bile. Jeanine listened with halfhearted interest as Simon reviewed the information that a good balance of all humors was called eukrasia, while an imbalanced body was said to be in a state of dyskrasia.

"Now let us discuss the remedies at hand that we might use in the treatment of the body," Simon suggested. "What of dill?"

Jeanine frowned and tried to remember everything she could associate with dill. "It is warm and dry with usefulness for relieving a cold and windy stomach. It can be harmful to the kidneys and is best taken with the juice of a lemon."

"Good. And oil of almonds?"

"Warm in the second degree and moist. Helpful for the chest and for coughs. Too much can damage weak intestines, but overall it generates moderate humors and is useful in temperate bodies."

"And ricotta?" Simon pressed her to concentrate.

Jeanine shifted uncomfortably. "Cold and humid. Best obtained from pure milk. Good for fattening up the body." She thought of Victor Pindar and her care of him while with Simon. She remembered testing his broken ribs and finding that there wasn't an ounce of fat to mar his frame. How very unlike Antoine Colbert, who apparently indulged in ricotta at will.

Simon eyed her critically. "You aren't listening."

"I am sorry," she said softly. "My mind is greatly consumed."

"With a certain young man, no doubt."

She felt her face flush. "Why do you say that?"

"Because I know you too well, Dr. Font." Simon closed his apothecary study. "So how is Monsieur Pindar?"

"He is well. Amazingly so. His scalp has healed nicely and there seems to be no bad effect from the trephining." She was eager to discuss Victor, and it showed. Showed so much, in fact, that Simon began to laugh. "What?" Jeanine questioned.

"Methinks this topic is of much greater interest than the others."

Jeanine let out a heavy sigh. "You know me far too well, Simon. How is it that you see through me so readily?"

"You wear your heart on your sleeve, my dear docteur." He gave her a knowing smile. "Yours and monsieur's."

"Would that I could have his heart," she said rather miserably.

"For dissection, no doubt," Simon teased. "A thing that all comely wenches desire."

Jeanine looked up in surprise. She had never heard Simon talk in such a manner and said so.

"But then, I've never needed to deal with you as a lovesick ninny," he said in a rather sympathetic tone. "You have given your heart to this man, non?"

"I'm afraid so," she said, knowing the dejection in her tone would not be missed by her mentor.

"And this is bad?"

"Not in and of itself." She looked away, then eased her elbows onto the table and leaned her face in her hands.

"Then why such an expression on so beautiful a face?"

Jeanine laughed. "Ashes and mud become me, eh?"

"There is beauty that no disguise may hide. But you have not answered my question. Why is there such despair in realizing that you have given your heart to a man?"

" 'Tis not the giving that is of despairing nature," Jeanine admitted. "But I fear that my heart has very much been returned. He could not possibly be less interested in me."

"I find that hard to believe. How could any man reject so lovely a creature?"

Jeanine smiled. "You are kind, Simon, but I'm afraid I had more attention from him as Dr. Font. Although, we did have a nice conversation yesterday morning. 'Twas my hope he might have found favor in me, but I was mistaken."

"And what makes you so certain of this?"

"When I returned later that afternoon, he waved me off and wished to be left to his letter writing. That sister of his is all that he concerns himself with."

Simon reached out and touched her arm. "You must never despair. God has a purpose in this."

"A purpose in breaking my heart?" Jeanine asked quite seriously.

"Perhaps it is not so much breaking that He has in mind, as it is preparation."

Jeanine sat back and shook her head. "No, Victor has no interest in me, whatsoever. And in two weeks I am to marry Antoine Colbert."

"A grave problem, to be sure."

"I am doomed," she said sadly, wishing she could find hope in their conversation.

"You must pray about this and seek God's heart. His eye is upon you and He attendeth all mankind, so think yourself not included if that is your wish, but 'twould be a lie."

Jeanine smiled. "I suppose you are right. I will pray about it and seek His will, but I hope He will answer before two weeks are concluded."

"God has His own timing," Simon assured her. " 'Tis never too late, nor too early. Wait patiently for Him, Jeanine, and He will direct your steps."

Chapter 6

Antoine Colbert shifted uncomfortably on his gouty foot, all the while watching the book copy shop of Simon Grosz. For the last week he'd found Jeanine's daily foray into the dock district a perplexity of grand proportions. Why did she journey to this place, day after day? Better still, why did she spend hours within the rundown walls after her arrival? Unable to put off a personal exploration any longer, Colbert tightened his hold on his purse strings and hobbled painfully across the busy street to the shop.

Entering the darkened room, Colbert called out. "Good day!"

Simon appeared, wiping his hands on a towel. "Greetings, good sir, and how might I assist you?"

This created a moment of confusion for Colbert, who was uncertain what he should ask of the old man. Just as he took a step, however, his gouty foot caused him to nearly fall forward. He grimaced in pain, and Simon seemed to immediately understand.

"Your foot grieves you. Come this way and the doctor will consider it."

"The doctor?" Colbert questioned.

Simon laughed. "Oh, but you thought it to be me. But of course, I am a physician. My eyes, however, are bad. Dr. Font will see to your need."

"Dr. Font," Colbert whispered. He allowed Simon to help him into a chair. Bringing a stool, Simon elevated the man's aching foot and admonished him to remain still. "The doctor is finishing with another patient, but 'tis certain your wait will not be long."

"Very well," Colbert replied.

He sat for some moments contemplating the room in which Simon had left him. It appeared to be some manner of sleeping quarters. Two crudely built beds edged up against one wall, while a counter of weather-beaten wood held a tray of assorted, indistinguishable instruments.

The inner room was dark except for the warming glow that spilled out from the fireplace, and the entire house smelled of something Antoine could not quite place.

"I am told your foot is giving you trouble," a smallish man said, entering the room with a trident-styled candlestick holder. The flames flickered from atop the tapers as the man moved to place it across the room. Pausing beside the tray of instruments, the doctor seemed completely absorbed with his task.

Colbert watched him closely. With the man's back to him, Colbert could distinguish nothing but black robes and a bit of graying black hair at the edge of his cap. The man stood of slight build, but seemed most determined in his duties. Colbert wondered what this man might know of Jeanine and opened his mouth to ask that very question when the man turned and stared at him in surprise. The clattering of the metallic instrument against the wooden floor echoed loudly in the silent room.

Huge brown eyes, eyes that had widened in fear at him on every occasion of greeting, now stared back from the ash-smudged face. Jeanine!

"What are you doing here?" Colbert questioned, rage evident in his tone.

"I. . .I. . . ," she stammered, unable to answer him.

He got to his feet, forgetting his pain, and came to where Jeanine de la Fontaine stood. Dragging the cap from her head, he instantly saw the carefully sewn strip that contained the coarse dark hair. "What game is this?" He studied the cap for several moments as if trying to force the object itself to answer.

"Monsieur Colbert." She barely breathed the name as he dropped the cap and yanked her around to pull at her tightly pinned hair.

"Answer me! What game is this?" The thick braid came free in his hands and the luxurious silken mane begged his touch.

" 'Tis no game," Jeanine said in a whimper. She seemed frozen in place as Colbert ran his fingers through the braid, loosening the tight weave until Jeanine's curly hair spilled out across his open hand.

He turned her again, and this time tightly held her while he shook her most severely. "It looks to be nothing but a game. Why are you here and dressed thusly?"

Simon took this moment to return to the room and stared in stunned disbelief at the scene before him. "What are you about, my good man?" he asked Colbert. "Unhand the good doctor."

" 'Tis no doctor I hold. This is my betrothed. I'm alarmed to find her parading in men's garments and pretending to be a physician. I want to know why, and I want to know now." He tightened his hold. "Answer me or I'll burn this place down around us!" He watched, gloating under the intimidated expressions on the faces of his opponents.

"Monsieur, you are hurting me," Jeanine protested, struggling to free herself.

"I will do more than that if you do not tell me the truth." He could see the fear on her face and felt a certain victory in the way she trembled. He had longed to make her tremble after him in another fashion, but at present this was most gratifying. He thought again of her father's bargain and how within a fortnight she'd be his to control. She'd no doubt fight him then as well, but it would all be for naught. He'd have her as his wife, and he'd take control of her life from that moment on.

"Please, Monsieur!" Jeanine begged.

"She must disguise herself in order to help the poor," Simon offered, but Colbert paid him no attention. He stared into the haunted eyes of the small woman instead.

"I am a physician," Jeanine said. "Please let me go." Her eyes implored him to set her free, but Colbert was greedy for her.

"You practice the art of medicine when you know it is forbidden?" he asked in a low whisper. She nodded very slowly and fearfully. He smiled. "I could have you killed for this. I could have you put before the church and condemned as a witch. You know that, do you not?"

"Please, Monsieur, she is very good to the people around her. They cannot afford another doctor, and so they come to her," Simon offered by way of explanation.

"She is to be my wife!" Colbert growled the declaration and finally dropped his hold. He studied the trembling woman before him. "This is most unacceptable, my dear Jeanine. You have long kept secrets from me, but this is a most delicate matter that must be handled immediately. We will go now and be married. Our elopement is the only answer in order to save face."

"You must be mad!" Jeanine declared and moved back several paces—her gaze locked on his face. "I have no desire to marry you now or ever. 'Tis the truth I've told you at every turn. My practice here is no secret to those who seek my care. The secret comes in that men like yourself refuse me the right to practice openly. I am a good physician."

"Aye, I well imagine that you are. But a physician of what? Broken hearts? What manner of woman have you become, my dear Jeanine?"

"Sir, I protest your implications of her character," Simon inserted. "Mademoiselle de la Fontaine is of impeccable virtue. She is kindhearted and given to sharing the love of God with her people. Fault her not for seeing their pain and suffering and deciding to do something in order to put an end to it. If you would but—"

"Enough!" Colbert shouted, turning to Simon. "And who are you that you should have such a thing go on behind these walls? I own a great deal of property in this town. I am a powerful man. One word from me will see you driven from this village without a single soul to mourn your passing. The ruination of this woman will be upon your shoulders."

" 'Tis untrue," Jeanine said, completely enraged. She went to stand beside her friend. "Simon is a good man, and many would mourn his passing. I, for one, would be quite lost without Simon, and he has done nothing to compromise my reputation."

Colbert yanked his intended away from the side of the strange little man. No doubt he was of foreign birth, which made Colbert even happier to see to his disposal. Foreigners were gradually increasing in numbers around the small town, and Colbert would be quite happy to see them driven out. Never mind that they boosted the otherwise sagging economy of Bruges and had allowed for an expansion. He despised them all. "You are not of our people, are you?" Colbert asked, eyeing Simon suspiciously. The question was nearly an accusation in and of itself. Jeanine tried to place herself between the two men, but Colbert drew her back so sharply that she stumbled and fell.

"No," Simon admitted, grimacing at the rough treatment Colbert inflicted upon Jeanine. "I was born many miles to the east and am of the Hebrew faith."

"A Jew!" Colbert exclaimed. "I should have recognized the stench."

"Antoine!" Jeanine cried, using his given name. She managed to get to her feet and put herself at Colbert's side.

Colbert smiled with an evil leer. " 'Tis the first time you have called me by that name. I like the way it sounds upon your lips. Particularly when it rings with pleadings for my mercy."

Jeanine swallowed hard, and Colbert could tell that she fought with herself against speaking out too quickly. "I am pleading mercy for this man. He is a good man of no consequence to you. I will leave this place, but you needn't punish Simon for something he is not guilty of."

"He is a Jew practicing medicine. The laws of the land make it quite clear this is a punishable offense. His guilt or innocence is for a court to decide. But as for you. . ." Colbert reached out and with one fluid motion rent the black houppeland Jeanine used for her doctoring duties.

Gasping, Jeanine clutched at the garment in spite of the heavy linen chemise that she wore beneath the robe. "How dare you!"

"I dare because you belong to me." He leaned close, enjoying the pleasant scent of her. "You would do well to remember that. Be there a ring on your finger and words made before a priest or not, you are contracted to me, and I will see this thing through in prompt order. But for now, I want you out of that offensive costume and properly clothed immediately. I will not have the town folk see you in your shame."

Jeanine nodded hesitantly and went to the changing room, while Simon stepped forward to issue his own thoughts. "You, Monsieur, must understand. God has blessed Jeanine with the ability to heal the sick. Why should this be of offense to you?"

"It is of offense to me because she is a woman, and she need not soil her hands in such a manner. It offends me because in the eyes of the church and the laws of this good land it is illegal for her to practice such a position. Women are incapable of such complicated thought."

"But she—"

Colbert slapped Simon hard across the face. "Silence, Jew. You have obviously interfered enough in this matter. You have corrupted her, and I will see you put in prison."

"No!" Jeanine declared, coming from the changing room, still trying to secure her belt. "Simon is a good man." Her hair flew out wildly behind her.

Colbert grabbed her by both arms and moved his face to within inches of hers. "I will not brook disobedience, Woman."

"Please do not hurt her," Simon said, coming to put a hand on Colbert's shoulder.

The mere touch enraged Colbert. How dare this sniveling little Jew touch him and defile him in such a way! Dropping his hold on Jeanine, he gave Simon the back of his hand, sending the man sprawling onto the floor. Simon clutched first his face and then his chest as the look of shock changed to one of fierce pain.

"Come along, Mademoiselle," Colbert said, taking Jeanine in hand.

Simon gasped for breath and moaned.

"No," Jeanine said, fighting against Colbert's grasp. "Cannot you see? He is hurt, mayhap even dying. He needs me."

"I care not. The man may rot for all I care." He tightened his hold and pushed her toward the door.

"Please, Antoine, let me see to him."

Colbert pulled her out the door and onto the street. "He is a Jew. If you must care for someone, come care for me, my dear. In but a few short hours you shall have your hands filled with all that you need pay attention to." He laughed mercilessly as she attempted to flee him. It was good to finally have the upper hand where the wench was concerned. She'd put him off for far too long, and now he would have his way. Even her father wouldn't be able to refuse his demands.

Chapter 7

"Jeanine should have been home hours ago," Margarite de la Fontaine said with a definite look of worry. She tried to busy herself with the dried herbs she would use for their dinner, but it was obviously of little help.

Étienne shrugged his shoulders. " 'Tis her way to be out and about the town. Mayhap she has taken herself to the grave of our grandmother. Would you wish that I go in search of her?"

His mother nodded. "Please."

Étienne smiled tolerantly and kissed her on the forehead. "If it gives your mind peace, then so it will be. Please tell my father where I have gone when he comes in from tending the animals."

Again his mother nodded.

Étienne, dressed in a blue tunic and cotehardie that reached just below his red-hose-clad thighs, strode in long easy steps down the main street of Bruges. His little sister was often given over for her fanciful flights, but he could see the worry in his mother's face and would soundly chide Jeanine for her thoughtlessness this time.

He began to whistle a tune, finding it a perfect day to be out. In another fortnight he would be back upon the sea, his first and only love. He had already decided that if the silting of the river was impossible to reverse or control, he would move to Calais or Antwerp and continue with shipping from there. At least in Antwerp, the trade was good and the crossroads of several overland routes passed through the city. Added to this, the River Scheldt showed no signs of silting. Étienne had tried to convince his father to settle his debts and leave Bruges behind, but he knew it would be difficult at best for the man to uproot himself after living a lifetime in the city.

Étienne smiled to himself. His father was a sensible man. There would come an answer to him in one form or another. There always did. And when the answer came to François de la Fontaine, they would join together to see the thing brought into existence. His father was just that way. So, too, was his sister, and Étienne nearly laughed aloud at the thought of Jeanine taking up the banner of moving the family to Antwerp. No doubt she'd have them all packed and ready to board one of the family ships before their father even knew what was happening.

Rounding the corner little more than two blocks from the de la Fontaine home and business, Étienne stopped in his tracks. Gone were the pleasantries of the day. Just ahead, Antoine Colbert approached with Jeanine most attentively clutching his arm.

"And what might the meaning of this be?" Étienne asked, seeing a sudden panic in the eyes of his sister.

"Ah, there is much that you have a right to know," Colbert answered without allowing Jeanine to explain. "But we should do our talking in private. I am now come to do just that. Lead the way, my good man, and I will explain all."

"Étienne, he has some misguided notion—"

"Pay her no attention. The time has come that we can no longer keep our secrets, my sweet," Colbert interrupted, and Étienne watched as the man threw Jeanine a leering grin. "After all, some secrets refuse to be kept, eh?"

"I know not what you speak of," Jeanine declared, but as if remembering they were on the common street, she added, looking at her brother, "Let us go to our father, and I will explain."

Étienne nodded, wondering what possible explanation the couple would offer. If Colbert's implications were of any merit, it could only mean one thing. And to imagine that made Étienne's blood boil within him. The couple lagged behind him, and glancing back, Étienne watched as Colbert whispered into Jeanine's ear. She seemed to pale, then nodded most vigorously in agreement to whatever he had suggested. Étienne knew something must surely be amiss, for he'd never known his sister to comply willingly with anything Colbert suggested. Perhaps she had realized the futility of fighting the contract. Or mayhap—and Étienne found this almost impossible to believe—his sister had gained some manner of feeling for Colbert that differed from the hatred she had always conveyed in the past.

❧

"I'm not entirely certain that I understand," François de la Fontaine said, eyeing his daughter, scrutinizing her for the truth. They were gathered together on the second floor, near to the exact spot where they had finalized the arrangements for the betrothal.

Colbert refused to allow Jeanine to talk. It was under the threat of completely destroying her family and of seeing Simon dead, if he were not already in that state, that Colbert had insisted she remain silent while he explained.

"I know 'tis my own doing," Colbert began, "but in truth, such deception was not my plan from the beginning. Jeanine and I simply forgot ourselves."

Jeanine grimaced and lowered her head. She knew it appeared that she was too burdened with her shame to consider the faces of her family, but in truth she was outraged. How dare he lie to her father?

Then a horrible thought came to her. For years she had lied to her entire family. Telling them that she was out to visit one friend or another while hurrying to hide herself and her identity, all in order to practice medicine. This caused her yet another pain-filled thought. Not only had she lied to her parents, but she had broken the law. Consumed with guilt, Jeanine thought perhaps she was receiving exactly what she deserved.

"These past weeks have been a trying time for the both of us," Colbert said with mock humility. "I'm afraid your daughter has not gone in truth to visit her friends, but rather has made her way every day to meet. . ." He paused as if to force Jeanine's attention.

Her head snapped up to meet his expression. Would he tell them the truth? Would he put Simon's life in jeopardy? Oh, that the earth would open up and swallow her whole. She bit her lower lip and looked away. There was nothing she could do about that which he would say.

Colbert smiled evilly. "Jeanine came to meet me. I'm afraid it is now most imperative that we marry immediately."

Jeanine brought her openmouthed gaze back to his cruel, self-assured expression. He had just implied their intimacy. He hadn't implicated Simon, but he'd ruined her just the same. Her mother began to weep, while her father stared at the couple as if trying to decide the truth of the matter. Surely, Jeanine thought, even if he believed such a thing were true, he would remember her disdain for Colbert and believe him capable of forcing the intimacy between them. But there was no intimacy, Jeanine's mind raged. How dare he imply that she had soiled herself with him? He, whose very countenance sickened her. Confusion filled her mind. How could she manage to refrain from further lies to cover the ones she'd already told.

"Are you telling me that my daughter is with child?" François de la Fontaine asked sternly.

At this Jeanine's mother sobbed and bit at her hand to silence her anguish. Étienne looked at Jeanine with a hard stare of disappointment, while her father continued to meet the haughty look of Antoine Colbert. How could they believe such nonsense was true?

" 'Tis nothing new to this continent," Colbert offered offhandedly. "I still intend to marry the wench. It isn't as though I would desert her while she carries my babe in her belly. I merely thought it prudent to explain and see the wedding concluded on the morrow."

"And what say you for yourself, Daughter?"

Jeanine met the eyes of her father and wanted to die. She longed to cry out in a voice of anguished protest that it was all a lie. Her life, Colbert's declarations, this circumstance. But she worried that Simon, poor Simon with his chest full of pain, would be exposed and put from Bruges or, worse yet, killed. How could she risk his life now? Mayhap he was already dead, but if not, she had to protect him, even at the cost of her own disgrace. Then, too, if she declared Colbert to be the scoundrel that he was, he would call her father's note due immediately and see him ruined.

Finally, with a heavy heart, Jeanine spoke. "You know well my heart, mon père. I have long wished to do that which is right in the eyes of our Lord God. But I have lied." There. She had done it. She had said just enough to leave little doubt in anyone's mind of her guilt. Turning to face Colbert, she refused to react to his smirking grin. "I will marry Monsieur Colbert on the morrow."

There was little else to be said. Her mother cried inconsolably, while her brother shook his head in disgust. Her father, once the light of her life, looked upon her as though she'd suddenly acquired the plague. Nay, with the plague she would have merited his pity and sympathy. His look of disgust mingled with bitter disappointment caused Jeanine's eyes to well with tears. If only she had never lied about her medicinal practices. If only she had long ago explained Simon to her parents and told them openly of her work with the poor.

"I believe the matter has settled itself," Colbert said confidently. "And to show my generosity, especially now that it is proven she is not barren, I will add yet another sum to our agreement."

Jeanine wanted to gag. He was blatantly carrying the lie a heartbreaking distance to insure that her parents not protest the speedy union. Feeling a wave of nausea when Colbert bent close, she had to force herself to keep from pulling away.

"Soon, my dear. Very soon you will be mine," he told her, while her father tried to comfort his wife.

"Monsieur, I would ask you to return in the morning. It is necessary that we have a time to converse among ourselves. I am greatly distressed that you would take advantage of one so innocent as my daughter. I had thought to trust you as a man of your word."

Colbert got to his feet and made a low sweeping bow. "I throw myself upon your mercy, Monsieur, just as you threw yourself upon mine not so long ago." His voice was filled with sardonic overtones.

"Of course," François de la Fontaine said, barely able to form the words. "We will meet again on the morrow."

Colbert shot Jeanine a look of victory and hobbled off toward the stairs. Jeanine thought for a moment about his gout, wondering if he'd sought any real treatment for the problem, when her father's low question roused her thoughts.

"How could you shame this house in such a manner?"

Jeanine was mindless of the question, having spied Victor Pindar as he made his slow, labored descent down the stairs. Her father seemed not to care that the stranger would hear his tirade and Jeanine's shame.

"Answer me!" her father said, pounding his fist against the small wooden table.

"I meant not to shame anyone," Jeanine replied softly. "I had hoped to explain, but it seems the words of another are weighed more heavily than mine."

Victor watched her with an odd expression on his face. She wished only to run from the room or to jump up, declaring her innocence. But nothing she said now was going to change the future. Colbert would see Simon driven from Bruges if she dared to refuse him now. It was also possible that Simon was already dead. She had seen men suffer from the heart pains that had attacked Simon. Of course, without having been allowed to thoroughly examine the man, she had no way of knowing his ailment, but it appeared most grave. She tried to remember his ashen face and pain-filled expression as she faced her family and bore her shame.

"I was unwise to lie," she admitted. "But it was not my intent to bring shame upon this family." Then as if to ease her own conscience, she added, "After all, 'tis your contract, not mine."

Étienne shook his head in disgust. "You have grieved your mother most unforgivably."

"Non," François de la Fontaine said, holding up a hand to stop his son. "All can be forgiven. Your sister's humiliation will soon be quite apparent, and Monsieur Colbert is good to take her in spite of this. At least he has not refused to see after his affair. He could have just as easily left your sister to bear her child alone."

Jeanine found her gaze drawn uncontrollably to the face of Victor Pindar. He watched as though observing a play. His face was unemotionally observant, his expression unreadable. Jeanine felt her heart in her throat. *Oh, Father,* she prayed, *I have lied and I have sinned, but 'tis not the sin they think me capable of. I only sought to help the poor and afflicted.* She longed for escape.

"I cannot believe that you should do this thing after so completely convincing me that Monsieur Colbert was an abomination to you," her father continued. Jeanine started to open her mouth, but her father silenced her. "I am ashamed of you. Look around you and see the pain you have caused. You have broken with the commandments of our Lord. You have told falsehoods and have lain with a man who was not yet your husband. Take yourself from my sight and pray for your salvation."

Her father's harsh reprimand caused tears to stream from Jeanine's eyes. She longed to clear her name, but instead took herself upstairs. She had closed the door to her bedroom before remembering that it was now Victor's room. Victor. The very image of his expression in her memory caused her great pain. He no doubt thought her to be little better than a common dock woman.

"Father, this is most unfair," she whispered the prayer. "I cannot bear such shame. Nor can I face such a future with Monsieur Colbert."

Going to the foot of her bed, Jeanine reached underneath and pulled out a bag. 'Twould be a simple enough matter to slip away in the night. But a destination of protection eluded her. Where could she run that Colbert would not hunt her down and find her? And now that she was publicly shamed, who would receive her? Hearing voices on the stairs, she took the bag and hurried out of the room and up to the fourth floor, where she had made herself a pallet during the time Victor had shared their home. A few of her belongings were arranged there also, and with little thought to their care, Jeanine pushed them into the bag and waited for night to bring sleep upon the house. She wouldn't wait to become the wife of that brute. No matter the cost, she would not marry Antoine Colbert.

Reclining on the pallet, Jeanine prayed fervently for forgiveness. "Oh, Lord God," she began, even as heaviness descended upon her. "I have sinned, and I am sorry. I have made lying a way of life. I have given false witness at every turn whenever it suited my purpose. But I did not think 'twould cause damage. I only sought to do good with my medical skills."

Hot tears trickled from her eyes. "It was wrong to lie, but it was all I felt I could do. To explain to them my interest in medicine seemed hopeless." With that single word spoken aloud, Jeanine instantly thought of her grandmère's gentle guidance. She had always admonished Jeanine that hope could consistently be found in choosing God's way over one's own way.

"I see my error, Lord," Jeanine admitted. "My mother has long taught me to seek forgiveness, but somehow I believed that a sin done for the purpose of a greater good was somehow not a sin at all. Now I see that I was wrong, and yet 'tis too late. The people I love are hurt by my faithlessness, and the one man I might truly love will never be mine because I must either flee this house or marry Antoine Colbert on the morrow.

"Forgive me, Lord God. Please forgive me." And in that instant, Jeanine knew she was forgiven. Not that it undid the wrong that had already been done, but it did ease the burden she had carried around with her.

The silence of the room seemed to wrap itself around her. It drew her into a cocoon of protection, beckoning her to let go of her worries and sleep. Quickly, Jeanine uttered up a prayer for Simon's health and safety. Then just as she began to doze, she prayed that Victor might not believe the worst of her.

Chapter 8

Jeanine awoke with a start. The room was silent and black. She sat up, struggling to clear her groggy mind. For a moment, she remembered Colbert and his actions, and for just as short a moment thought perhaps it had all been part of a bad dream. But upon throwing back her covers, she discovered an unknown bulk at her feet. The bag. It confirmed that her nightmare was quite real.

Getting to her feet, Jeanine had little idea of the hour, but regardless, it was time to go. She lit a single candle, gathered what few things of hers remained, and made her way gingerly down the creaking steps. She paused at the third-floor landing as if to whisper good-bye to her family. Then her eyes fell upon her own bedchamber door. Victor would always believe her guilty of her sins. How she wished that she could assure them all that she had never known Colbert in the manner to which he eluded. How she longed to find favor in her father's eyes one more time. Perhaps in time she would pen them a letter and explain all the details that had led to that moment when Colbert had announced her a woman without virtue.

She started for the stairs, but a sudden thought of articles yet unclaimed came to mind. The closed bedchamber door did little to reassure her that she might collect her things without causing further disgrace to herself or family, but her grandmother's brooch and combs were of immeasurable wealth to her. They were all she had left of her grandmother. All that physically existed, she reminded herself, for indeed, her grandmother had left her a legacy of stories and tales from the days gone by. These would forever stay with Jeanine, even if the combs and brooch were beyond her reach.

She put her bag on the floor and pushed the door open very quietly. Leaving the candle outside and trusting her lifelong memories for her sight into the blackened room, she paused inside the threshold and waited to see if Victor's sleeping form would be disturbed by her entry. He didn't move. Cautiously, she went to the foot of the bed and opened her trunk. It groaned loudly, but was soon forgotten when a hand grabbed her from out of the pitch black void and encircled her wrist. She smothered a scream with her free hand.

"What are you doing?" Victor's voice questioned.

Jeanine panted for air. "I'm. . .sorry. . .if. . .I disturbed you. I had only thought to retrieve something from my trunk."

Victor let her go and went to the hearth, where the dying embers barely gave off enough light to outline his form. He tossed several sticks of wood on the fire, causing the room immediately to grow light, and Jeanine could see clearly that Victor was grimacing in pain.

"Please, go back to bed. You are hurting yourself."

" 'Tis nothing more than these sore ribs," he said, rubbing a hand across his chest.

" 'Tis broken ribs that pain you," Jeanine corrected and motioned him to at-least sit. "Please rest. I'm sorry for the disturbance, but now that I am here, I will get what I came for and be gone."

Victor said nothing, but watched her intently as she rummaged in the trunk. Jeanine tried not to be overly nervous. She found her grandmother's articles, then came upon a thick woolen shawl her mother had made her and took that up as well.

"You are leaving, are you not?"

Victor's question in the heavy silence between them surprised Jeanine so that she found it impossible to hide her expression. "I. . .ah. . .I am preparing myself for my departure. That is true."

"But you aren't departing on the morrow, are you? You are leaving now."

Jeanine thought to lie to him, then decided there had been enough lies from her lips. Had she not spent time already in prayer, begging God's forgiveness for such a thing? She had even thought to confess the truth of her medical practice to her family, then decided it would be easier this way. At least by slipping away in the night, no one need further encounter her. No one else need be hurt by her mistakes.

"Well?" Victor's soft voice warmed her heart.

"Aye."

"But where will you go? Surely your condition will soon begin to show, and then what will you do?"

Jeanine could no longer bear the humiliation. It was bad enough that her father believed her to have joined herself with Colbert, but to allow this wonderful man whom she'd totally lost her heart to, to believe such a thing made her quite ill.

"I have no reason to fear, Monsieur. I am not with child, nor have I ever been given to Monsieur Colbert in that manner."

"But he told your father—"

"I know," she said, sadly. " 'Tis a matter I cannot explain."

Victor got up from the bed and came to sit on the very end by the trunk. He studied her thoroughly for a moment before speaking. "You speak the truth—of this I'm certain."

Jeanine laughed bitterly. "For once. I fear my lies have caused this entire matter. I have learned a cruel lesson about covering one's actions with falsehoods."

"But you did not defend yourself against those lies."

"I could not then, nor can I now. There is much that I cannot say on the matter, but suffice it to be that I am taking care of the problem in my own fashion."

"By running away?"

She looked up into his eyes and lost herself for a moment. Why couldn't he have loved her? As quickly as that thought came to mind, Jeanine pushed it aside. What good would it have done if he had? Her father had signed a contract with Monsieur Colbert. It would matter very little whether Victor cared for her or not. The agreement was most binding. It was this thought that caused Jeanine to sink to her knees.

"What will happen to my father?" she questioned softly.

Victor's expression betrayed his confusion. "What do you mean?"

"After I am gone."

"So you are intent upon leaving?"

"I have to. I despise Colbert. He has pursued me at every turn and has ruined my reputation before my family, all in order to have his own way. I cannot remain here to become his wife."

"I see," Victor replied and seemed to consider the situation. "I take it your father owes the man quite heavily?"

"Aye. The river silt has caused his shipping trade to be greatly reduced. He borrowed money and had hoped to make enough to pay Colbert back upon my brother's return, but alas that is not to be the case. The ship upon which you were injured required all extra monies in order to see it repaired. Soon the river trade here will be dead, and then Bruges will be dependent upon flat-bottomed boats or land routes. My brother has even talked of moving to Calais or Antwerp, but I'm certain my father would never hear of it for himself. Colbert offered to take me in trade. No woman of reputable means would have the man, and he needs heirs to secure his fortune for the future. The women who could be bought are not the type he would present as a wife, and those of purer means would not take a vow with him for any price."

"You included."

"Aye. I worry, though. I know my father has signed an agreement with Colbert. I worry over what will happen to him. Have you any thought on the matter?"

Victor shook his head. "No. I suppose 'tis a matter for the courts and Colbert to decide."

"Then no doubt they will see him sent to prison. Oh, why must this be so?" she said, wearily. It mattered little that she was on the point of breaking down completely. Victor had already seen her humiliated before her family. What did it matter that he saw her like this now?

"Mayhap they will only see you as a frightened bride and hold off on action for a time while they decide what has become of you," Victor offered.

"Mayhap. If only I had the money to give over that my father might pay his debts. Surely then, the court would dissolve the papers." Suddenly she felt inspired. "Monsieur, you are a man of means, are you not?"

Victor smiled. "I have been called that. Why?"

"I am not certain what these things might bring in sale, but would it be possible that you could purchase them, perhaps for your sister?" She held up her grandmother's things. "They are mine, so fear not that I have stolen them from the family coffers. My grandmother left them to me upon her death."

Victor took the combs and brooch and held them up against the firelight. "They are quite fine. The combs are ivory, and they look to be trimmed in gold and rubies."

"Aye. It was a gift from my grandfather who was well propertied and in good stead with the king."

"And this brooch is of course quite valuable," Victor admitted.

"My grandmother said it was nearly one hundred years old. The gems are sapphires and rubies. I had thought to offer it to my father some time back, but I knew he'd never hear of it. Oh, Monsieur, take pity on me now. Could you please find it in your heart to purchase these and give my father the money that he might pay off Monsieur Colbert?"

Victor considered the brooch for another moment before his hand closed around it. "Consider it done."

Jeanine let out a heavy sigh. "You are most kind. I will not forget you." If only he knew the degree to which that was true. She would forever remember his ruggedly handsome face, the long noble nose, and thick black brows. She would ever think on the full lips and dark eyes that haunted her dreams.

With that much settled, Jeanine got to her feet and took up the shawl. "I am sorry I woke you, but not sorry that you have shared this time with me. It has comforted me greatly to know that at least one soul in this world knows the truth."

"But what of the truth?" Victor questioned. "Is there no one else to defend you in this matter? What of the time you spent away from your father's house?"

Jeanine smiled and shook her head. "It is of no importance now." She thought of Simon and his fierce defense of her. " 'Tis enough that you know."

"But where will you go?"

"I have some friends in the country," she said, suddenly realizing that this could well be her answer. She remembered the poor family who had arrived in Bruges not long ago with a severe intestinal disorder. They were en route to the home of the woman's parents and had assured her, upon their recovery and departure from Bruges, that should she ever need anything, she had only to come to them. She knew roughly the area to which they had departed and now it seemed a logical choice.

"But how will you—"

Jeanine held out her hand to stop his questions. "It is unimportant, and if you knew where I was to go, you would have to tell them truthfully when they asked. I cannot have them following after me to force my hand. I pray you understand."

Victor got to his feet. "I do, but I cannot help but worry after your welfare."

"I go with God," she replied. "For once, with a clear conscience that no more lies will come between us."

She turned to leave, but Victor's warm hand closed over her arm. "At least let me offer you this," he said, handing her a small dagger. "There is great harm in the country—wild animals, highwaymen. Take this for protection."

Jeanine felt deeply touched that he should so worry about her. "Thank you. Your sister is a most fortunate woman." For a moment, Jeanine was perilously close to admitting her love for Victor. Looking into his dark, sympathetic eyes, she could almost believe he might return her feelings.

But just as she thought she might lose control, Victor broke the spell by sitting back down. He clutched at his side and offered her a lopsided smile. "I am impatient to be made whole."

Jeanine nodded, then without thought she offered a blessing. The same blessing she had murmured over him as Dr. Font. "May the Lord God heal you now. May He see your needs and reach where human hands may not go."

Victor's expression changed to one of perplexity. It was as if he remembered her words from long ago. Jeanine held her breath and swallowed back the urge to explain. She turned instead and hurried to the door. "Please do not forget your promise to see to my father. I could not go in peace if I knew he would suffer even more."

Victor, lost in contemplation of a memory that would not come, nodded. "He will suffer the loss whether I give him money to settle his debt or not. He will suffer from your absence, but rest assured, I will see to your wishes. I owe this family my life, and on it, I pledge to see the matter taken care of."

Jeanine nodded and slipped from the room. She picked up the bag and placed the dagger inside, again touched by Victor's gesture. She stared longingly for a moment at the closed doors of her parents' and brother's rooms. Picking up the candle, she whispered her good-byes and made her way down to the first floor. Glancing around, she tried to imagine a life without the familiarity of all she had known the past twenty years. Every nook, every scratch and mark upon the wall suddenly seemed precious. Blowing out the candle, she sighed again. She couldn't look back, she told herself. Elsewise, she might never find the courage to go forward.

Pulling her cloak on, Jeanine closed the shop door and made her way around the side of the house. She had barely gone ten steps when a thick hairy arm closed around her neck. Screaming loudly, Jeanine remembered little else as the pressure increased and cut off her air supply.

Chapter 9

Victor had just managed to ease himself back into bed when a scream that could only belong to Jeanine rent the silence of the night. With strength he didn't know himself capable of, Victor flew to the window and tried to make out the images in the street below. Between the clouded window and the dim light of the half-moon, Victor could only see two nondescript figures scuffling in the street at the edge of the property.

Jeanine!

It had to be her, and furthermore, it had to be Colbert or one of his men Victor made his way down the stairs, the jostling giving him new degrees of pain. He knew he was much recovered, but the nagging soreness from his leg wounds coupled with the dull ache from his head and chest made him very much aware that he was in no condition to fight for the honor of any woman.

He finally made the last step and crossed the darkened shop of the first floor to open the outer door and peer into the now-empty street. Surely he hadn't imagined the whole thing. He stepped out and looked up and down the street, hoping for some indication of where the girl might have gotten off to. But there was nothing. For a moment, Victor even questioned whether their entire conversation had been a dream. Then, as if to confirm the events of the night, Victor spied Jeanine's bag.

He walked cautiously to the place where the bag had been discarded, and with an eye turned ever upward to the street around him, he bent to retrieve the article. Still there was no sound or sight of Jeanine. Feeling exhaustion wash over him, Victor made his way back into the house. He would have to wake up one of the family, and because he knew Étienne better than the others, it would fall to Jeanine's brother to make the decision on what was to be done.

Dragging himself back up the stairs, Victor recalled the frightened expression on Jeanine's face as she had struggled to explain her situation. She had taken on the humiliation Colbert had placed upon her, and for what? What was it that caused her to allow everyone to believe such a lie about her? Clearly, it had caused her much pain and grief, or she'd never have found the need to explain herself to a complete stranger.

Knocking lightly upon Étienne's door, Victor was surprised at how quickly the thing was opened. It was almost as if Étienne had awaited his approach.

"Victor? What is it?"

"I fear I've come with bad news. Might you hear me out?"

"But, of course," Étienne said, sweeping a hand to motion Victor into his room. "Please sit. Even by my fire's light I can see you are quite spent."

"Thank you." Victor took a seat on the crude boot stool at the end of Étienne's bed. "I'm afraid Jeanine has gone. In fact, has been taken."

"What?"

Victor drew a deep breath, relieved that the pain had lessened in his chest. "She came to my room a few moments ago in order to retrieve some of her things."

Étienne frowned. "I am sorry she disturbed your rest."

"Not at all," Victor said, taking in the look of disgust upon the man's face. "Monsieur, I know we have little between us to call us friends, but I would like to be that to you and your family."

Étienne's expression changed to one of acceptance. "I find that most agreeable. Would that better circumstances might have thrown us together."

"Indeed," Victor said, then hurried to continue. "Your sister is innocent of the things that Colbert accused her of. I know this because she confessed it to me but a few moments ago."

"Confessed what?"

"She has never lain with Colbert. She despises the man, but there is some power over her that he has maintained in order to gain her compliance with his wishes."

"I had wondered at such a thing myself," Étienne admitted. "I saw him whisper to her on the streets, and while she nodded her agreement, she looked most disturbed at such tidings. Still, when she did not defend herself to our father, I assumed the worst."

"Aye, and we can only imagine why. The man is a brute and a beast as far as I can see. He has nothing to offer."

"Nothing, but the cancellation of our debt." Étienne's hand brushed back a wayward lock of hair. "Forgive me. I should not have made mention of that. 'Tis a family matter and naught for you to consider."

"But the matter has been given over to my consideration this very night. Your sister, indeed, has already bargained for the solution."

"She is the solution. Father saw no other way but to allow Colbert his request, nay, his demand that she marry him. Father would rather have rotted in debtor's prison than to allow Jeanine to become Colbert's wife had it only been himself that needed considering. But my mother's health is poor, and she would never have survived the conflict."

Victor nodded. "Jeanine knew this and knew, too, that by running away she would only bring Colbert's punishment down upon her family. She knew he would call the debt due in full, which is why she made a request of me."

Étienne seemed not to hear him. "She actually ran away? I cannot believe she would put Father in this position."

Victor wanted to explain about the brooch and combs, but he knew that precious time was slipping away from them. "She didn't have a chance to run far," he interjected. "I heard a scream, and saw two people struggling in the street below. It was impossible to see who it was, but I'm certain Colbert probably staked men around the house fearing that Jeanine would run, as she did indeed decide to do."

"Colbert has taken her?" Étienne began, yanking on his clothes. "The man should be horsewhipped for the things he's done to her already."

Victor nodded. "She is innocent of any wrongdoing, of this I am certain. There is no telling what lies have been told in the past, and for what reason, but I feel confident that the words given me by your sister this night were true." The memory of her blessing came back to haunt him. He knew beyond a doubt that he'd heard the words given before, but he couldn't clearly remember where or when they'd been said.

Étienne pulled on his boots and stood. "I should wake up our father and see what is to be done."

"Please, before you do, let me say this. I owe you my life—indeed I owe your entire family my life and well-being. Let me return the service by arranging with Colbert to see this debt cleared. I am a man of means, and besides that, your sister—"

"No, Monsieur," Étienne said, refusing to hear Victor out. "My father is a proud man. He would not hear of it. The kindnesses we have offered have been out of true Christian charity. Our Lord God admonishes us to care for one another as He has cared for us. Have you not heard the priest say that the Scriptures tell us if a man asks for your coat, give him your cloak also?"

"I have heard those words spoken," Victor replied, "which gives me standards for my desire to help you in return. Though I am not a strong man of God, I do desire to do right in the eyes of our heavenly Father. I may yet be the world's most terrible sinner, but I would seek to bless this family by whatever means are available to me."

Étienne smiled. "You have no need to pay a debt that is not rightly yours."

"And neither did our Savior, yet He bore our sins to a cross and died for us there that we might have eternal life."

"You are a difficult man," Étienne said, his grin even broader.

"I have been called that and more," Victor declared, matching the younger man's smile. "Now will you take me to Colbert that I might attempt to see this thing resolved?"

"But what of your injuries, Man? You can barely sit a chair, much less a horse."

"I will manage," Victor promised. "I'm made of stronger stuff than you give me credit for. See now?" he asked, pulling back his dark hair. "Even now the wound on my head heals quickly. My ribs, though sorely abused, are not incapable of keeping me upright, and the wounds on my legs are still nicely bound in the bandages created by your dear mother. I lack only a steed and the direction of the man I seek. Will you be my guide?"

Étienne considered the matter for a moment. "It is nearly dawn. A visit to the estate of Colbert would not be out of line. Especially given that you are certain he has my sister within his walls."

Victor smiled. "Good. Then let us be at it." He continued smiling even as he forced himself to stand. *Dear God,* he prayed, *give me the strength of which I boast, that I might help save this poor woman from her fate.*

"You dress, and I'll go ready the horses," Étienne suggested. "We have several miles to cover, so dress warmly."

Victor nodded. "What of your father and mother?"

"I'm fairly certain Father will hear the commotion and be up and about before we leave, but if not, I'll explain it later. Right now, Jeanine needs us."

"Yes," Victor said, a warmth spreading through his body like a flame. For all his reasoning, he could not set aside the desire to protect her.

≪≫

Jeanine could not see the face of her assailant, but in her heart she knew that the man was most likely a flunky of Colbert's. Having mercifully lost consciousness when assaulted, Jeanine had not awakened again until the rhythmic pounding of the horse's hooves against the roadway had jarred her senses. She tried to turn to see the man, but he roughly forced her back against him as his arm tightened its already painful hold on her. She slammed back against the thick, barrellike chest and struggled only briefly before the man threatened her.

"Settle yourself, or I'll see you bound and gagged and thrown over the back of this beast."

She stopped fighting, realizing the futility of her struggles, and instead took careful consideration of her surroundings. Light was just beginning to touch the distant horizon, and the sky was ever so gradually putting aside its blackness in favor of a rich indigo hue. Except for soreness in her throat and the man at her back, Jeanine might have enjoyed such a setting. But there was no enjoyment to be found in this perilous ride.

The horse continued at a full gallop for many miles until the man finally slowed him to a trot. They were well away from the town proper, and Jeanine had little doubt that the estate that loomed up at them in the distance was none other than the home of Monsieur Antoine Colbert. She grimaced and tried not to think of what he would do to her. He would of course be furious that she had attempted to run away, but he had also obviously known she would try such a thing or he'd never have kept a man at her father's house.

Then again, what if this man was not paid by Colbert? But of course, he must be, she reasoned with herself. Who else would care whether I came or went?

"Where are you taking me?" she finally decided to ask.

"There," the man replied.

Jeanine thought to ask him to explain, but she decided against it. The man had been brutal enough, and her throat still ached from the stranglehold he'd put on her. If indeed Antoine Colbert awaited her, she would simply explain that Victor now had the money to pay off her father's debt and suggest he call upon the man before the ceremony of marriage be further considered. She was certain that money would mean more to him than a wedding to her. After all, the church insisted that both parties consent to marriage, and no worthy priest would consider performing a ceremony without her approval.

Still, Colbert had ways to hurt her that Jeanine hesitated to think about. There was Simon, but of course, for all she knew, he might be dead. She had hoped to see him before she'd left Bruges. She longed to know his state of health, and now that she had no choice but to go with her kidnapper and face whatever fate awaited her, Jeanine felt more desperate than ever to assure herself that Simon lived.

They rode through an open gateway and past stone walls that appeared to be the dividing defense of the land. Jeanine could see more clearly now as the molten orange of the sun cleared the newly grassed meadowland. Spring had come upon them without her notice. The countryside smelled of freshness and the promise of things to come. The man behind her was not quite so sweet of scent. He smelled as though he made his bed in the stables, and if he worked for Colbert, it probably was exactly where he slept.

The man reined back on the horse and halted at the heavy stone stairs that led upward to the front door of the estate. There were two towers on either side of the huge manor house that gave it the appearance of having tried hard to look like a castle fortress. While the building was of native stone and designed in the most modern architectural styling, it looked like nothing more than a prison to Jeanine. In her heart, she knew that was exactly what the estate would be for her.

Her captor forced her from the horse and, after binding her hands tightly behind her, dragged her up the stairs and into the house. She was surprised that no one came to greet them. She was especially surprised to find Colbert absent when she arrived at what was obviously the great common hall of the house.

"Here," the man said, shoving her to the right. "Up those stairs."

The open doorway revealed a spiral of stone steps that led up into an impenetrable darkness. "But we need a light," Jeanine protested. "I cannot see."

The man grunted and pushed her against the steps. Having no way to catch herself, Jeanine turned just in time to bear the weight of her fall on her left shoulder and hip. She struggled to regain a sitting position while the man apparently went after a torch. He returned just as she managed to steady herself against the tower wall and was contemplating how she might make her escape.

"Does this light make your ladyship happy?" The man's sarcastic tone and grimacing face left little doubt in Jeanine's mind that he cared nothing for her well-being. He was taller than her by a foot and appeared to be a giant of a man—thickly muscled and quite powerful. His nose, strangely bent to one side, suggested he'd seen more than one good fight in his lifetime, and that thought coupled with the fact that the man stood leering at her in a most distasteful manner caused Jeanine to become quite docile. She couldn't very well fight this man. Especially not bound as she was.

"Thank you," she forced herself to say, just before he yanked her to her feet with one of his beefy hands.

"Go on," he ordered.

They trudged up the stairs, Jeanine stumbling on the hem of her gown more than once. Each time the man seemed quite happy to put a hand on her. He laughed menacingly as she struggled to push him away, and Jeanine knew it was no use to further irritate him. Who knew what the man might do to her? Mayhap Colbert had even given the man free hand with her. She cringed at this thought and was about to offer up a prayer for safety when the stairway opened upon a room and the man shoved her inside.

She fell, this time face forward onto a cot. Grateful for the small amount of cushioning afforded her by the straw mattress, Jeanine hurried to turn and face her captor, but he'd have none of that. Putting his knee to the small of her back, he pushed her down.

"Stay there while I untie you," he ordered.

Jeanine swallowed hard, wishing silently that she might have a cup of water to quench her parched and aching throat. She felt tears welling up, and the fight to keep them from spilling over only made her throat feel worse.

"There," the man said.

Before Jeanine could turn over, the door to the room was pulled shut. Sitting up quickly, Jeanine realized that she was alone. There was the sound of a bar being lowered across the door outside, and she had little doubt that he'd just locked her into the room. It didn't matter. She was greatly relieved, at least momentarily, that he had gone and left her alone.

Spying a narrow slit of a window, Jeanine rushed over to stare outside at the lighted landscape. She was grateful for the cool air that rushed in against her face. Pressing her cheek against the smooth stone wall, she sighed and struggled to steady her nerves.

"Oh, Father God," she prayed aloud. "What is to become of me now? Will Antoine have his way? Am I to become his unwilling bride?" She let loose hot tears and sobbed into the sleeve of her houppeland. "Where are you, God? Am I to be as Job, stripped of all that I care for? Left to suffer alone?"

But she wasn't alone, she reminded herself, and neither had Job been. God was with her now, even as He had always been. Her actions had caused this thing to happen. She had no one to blame but herself. Sinking to the floor, she cried in earnest.

Chapter 10

Jeanine heard the door bar being lifted and knew that the time to confront her captor had come. She had not yet been told that this was the estate of Antoine Colbert, but she was certain that it could be no other. Trembling, she awaited the same lumbering giant who had taken her there the night before. The man motioned from the doorway, almost as if hesitant to come too close to her. He refused to smile or even acknowledge her with more than the single grunt and motion of his hand that indicated she should come with him.

Jeanine drew a deep breath and prayed for strength to face whatever came. She knew that only the hand of God would deliver her from a despairing fate. Step by step, she retraced her way to the ground floor, and when she emerged and came into the great room, she could see that Antoine Colbert did indeed await her.

"So you thought to escape our plans, eh?" he asked her and motioned her to take a seat at the table where food had been placed in order to break the fast. "We will eat and talk of this matter while my man goes to fetch the priest."

Jeanine shook her head, even though her stomach growled loudly in protest. "I will not share a table nor any other thing—be it name or bed—with you."

Colbert laughed. "If you choose not to eat then you punish only yourself. If you choose to refuse me, then it will be up to my own cunning to persuade you otherwise."

"I do not love you, Monsieur Colbert," Jeanine stated frankly and came to the place where he now seated himself behind a huge platter of food. "I cannot marry a man for whom I have little regard, much less love."

"It takes not love, nor regard, to impregnate a woman," Colbert said crudely. "I need sons, Woman! Not romantic platitudes and flowery words."

"Therein lies the difference between us, Sir," Jeanine said, tilting her chin upward in defiance. "I require love. I cannot give myself in marriage to a man I despise."

"What? The good little Christian admits to despising her fellowman."

Jeanine felt her defenses go up like dry kindling to a spark. "I despise what you stand for, Sir. I despise that you treat people like so much trash to be swept away. I despise that you have wronged and grieved my family."

"Wait there, Wench. 'Twas not I who broke with our agreement," Colbert said, roast duckling midway to his mouth. He waved the drumstick like a scepter.

"You were the one running away. You take up offense for the purported wrongs done you and your family, yet you lied to those very people in order to take yourself to the docks to play physician to the poor. Yea, and you lied to them as well, for they thought their good doctor was a man, not a scrap of a young woman."

Jeanine had no argument for him. She was guilty as charged and would have succeeded at her plans had Colbert not had the foresight to stop her. "I might once have been guilty of deception. That much I cannot deny. But those days are over. I have made a pledge to God that I will not lie. That is why, even for the sake of my family, I will not lie to God or the priest and make a pledge to you."

"We will be married, whether you lie or not," he said, finding her declaration of little interest.

"You are ruining the lives of good, gentle people, and that does not bode well with me. My mother is heartsick. My father is filled with desperation. How can it be that you can find such joy in their defeat?"

"Because I am who I am. You can make all your pretty speeches about despising my actions and not me, but the truth is, my dear lady, my actions are a representation of who I am. I am heartless and bold. I am aggressive and self-centered, and I care not one whit what you think of me in that matter. I see you as a woman of health and ability. I see you as the vessel to carry my children and to nurture them when they are come to this earth. I do not need your love or admiration or even your honesty, but by my word, I will have your obedience and fear."

"So I am to be nothing more than your trained dog, Monsieur?"

Colbert laughed and tore off a chunk of the meat with his yellowed teeth. Grease ran down his beard. Speaking with his mouth full, he said, "Would that you might be as obedient as my hounds. You will come to understand your place in time, but for now sit and await the priest. Eat or eat not. It matters little to me."

Jeanine watched him as he shoved more food into his mouth and washed it down with who knew what from a silver goblet. She wanted to protest the game being played out between them, but silently went to the seat he had indicated her to take and waited what he would say. But before Colbert could clear his mouth, a servant appeared at the table.

"Sir, there have come visitors."

"Visitors? Here?" Colbert asked indignantly. "When no man was bid?" He seemed not to remember the open practice of offering hospitality to passing pilgrims.

"Aye, Milord. Two men, but neither will speak to me their name."

Colbert considered this news for a moment, then waved the drumstick again in the air. "Bring them in, and we shall see what it is they are about."

The servant bowed briefly and hurried from the room. Jeanine could tell by the look on the smaller man's face that he'd been most grateful to have reason to leave. No doubt he, too, had been witness to Colbert's temper, Jeanine thought.

"So you are to have visitors for your wedding day," Colbert said by way of conversation.

"I have already told you, I cannot marry you. I do not love you, and I have already arranged for my father's debt to be paid." Jeanine suddenly regained her strength and continued in a hurried fashion before the strangers could appear. "You have but to consult Monsieur Pindar, who is even now in residence in my father's house. He has the money to pay the debt and annul the contract."

Colbert laughed. "But I have no desire to annul any contract, and thus it remains legally binding. You are very foolish to think that this is an issue of money alone."

"But you said—"

"I said nothing that would indicate that I offered this contract solely based on your father's hefty debt. True enough, he owed me, but I've already made clear my first concern."

Jeanine shuddered. "An heir?"

"Aye," the man replied and speared a huge piece of pickled fish. Slopping the fish across the table to his platter, Colbert appeared to have lost interest in all else but food.

"Good morning, Monsieur," Étienne called out as he and Victor entered the room.

Jeanine felt a surge of elation and relief course through her at the sight of them. *Thank You, heavenly Father,* she prayed silently and awaited her brother's demands that she be returned to the house of de la Fontaine.

"Ah, Monsieur de la Fontaine," Colbert replied. "Have you come to watch your sister take her vows in marriage?"

"No, I have come to put an end to such a farce. 'Twould hardly be fitting, given that she bears no child of yours and has never encouraged that such a union take place."

"So she told you of my little deception, eh? Well, 'tis of no matter. I intend to marry her this day or see your father thrown in debtor's prison along with his beloved wife. Oh, and of course you would join them now that you are partners with your father."

"And if I tell you that I have come to settle the debt?" Étienne questioned.

Jeanine's heart surged with hope. She got up from her chair and would have crossed to Étienne and Victor, but Colbert denied her such action.

"Sit!" he demanded, then motioned to two of his men who had lounged quietly in the shadows of the hall. "My men will help you back to your chair if need be."

"I do protest," Jeanine declared. "I have already told you that I will not marry you this day. You cannot keep me prisoner here."

"Oh, can't I?" Colbert asked, pushing back from his seat. He nodded toward her brother and Victor. "They are little match for my men. Do you doubt that I could see them both killed for trespassing before the sun crosses the sky?"

Jeanine felt herself grow light-headed. "You would kill innocent men because I do not love you?"

"I would kill any man who stands in the way of that which belongs to me."

"She does not belong to you, Colbert," Victor stated matter-of-factly.

"Oh, and you believe she belongs to you?" Colbert asked.

Jeanine lowered her gaze to keep from betraying her feelings, but it was too late. She heard Colbert laugh menacingly.

"I have come to pay the debt owed by the family of François de la Fontaine," Victor announced, ignoring Colbert's comments.

Jeanine's head snapped up to meet Victor's gaze. He had come to her rescue. He had heard her screams and had known that Colbert was responsible for her disappearance, and he had come for her.

"I will not negotiate the terms with you, Monsieur. You are not of the family."

"No, but I am a friend, and I owe this man my life."

" 'Tis of no concern to me. Surely you can understand that a man in my position has need of an heir. I desire this woman bear that heir, and because I own her father's notes, she will do as she is told."

"Will you also demand her firstborn be a son?" Victor asked sarcastically.

Jeanine could see that he was in pain. She could read it in his expression and wanted only to go to him.

"I will demand what I will, and you will have no part in it."

Victor shrugged. "I'm willing to double whatever is owed on the contract."

Jeanine gasped, her hand going to her throat where she clutched the fine linen of her gown. Her heart overflowed with love for Victor. Not only had he risked his life for her, but he was willing to give over his funds for her rescue. What more could she have desired of him, save love?

"Double, you say?" Colbert dropped the meat in his hand and stared at Victor for a moment, then turned his attention to Jeanine. "You would pay double to prevent our marriage?"

"As I said, I owe this man my life. His family has been good to see to my care, and I feel I must return the kindness."

"It must also help that she is obviously in love with you," Colbert said flatly.

Jeanine turned sharply to meet Colbert's intense gaze. The moment she saw his eyes, she knew that it would be impossible to deny the truth. However he had figured out her heart on the matter, Colbert would now use her feelings to destroy her. Suddenly she felt very afraid for Victor. What if Colbert decided to challenge him to some kind of duel? What if he called his men to simply throw Victor into the dungeon or the tower?

"You are merely trying to devise a means by which you can drive up your price," Étienne protested. "Your plan is foolishness. My sister barely knows this man. Now be reasonable and listen to what we propose."

"No, I believe I have found something far more interesting to focus on," Colbert said, getting to his feet. He wiped his greasy fingers on his coat and walked in a contemplative fashion toward Jeanine. He had grasped his pudgy hands together behind his back and was even now staring up at the ceiling as if to learn something important from the timbers there. Coming to stand in front of Jeanine, he paused and lowered his gaze. "You have declared this day that you do not love me. Perhaps you would care to enlighten this group as to whom you do love?"

Jeanine felt her face flush with heat. Her knees began to shake, and where Colbert had found it impossible to intimidate her before, now faced with having to admit her love for Victor, Jeanine thought she might actually faint.

"Well, my dear?" Colbert asked, pressing closer. "Care to offer up some of those romantic platitudes we discussed only moments before your brother's arrival?"

"Leave her be, Colbert," Étienne announced, coming forward to where they stood. Victor came along behind him as if uncertain what might next take place. Jeanine found it impossible to look either one of them in the eye.

"Your sister has proven in the recent past to be capable of deceit. She has, but this morning, declared herself to be finished with lies. She has made a pledge before God," Colbert said in a sardonic manner. He walked a pace or two away, then turned to eye Jeanine again. "So you understand, she has given her word to the God of heaven and earth, and to lie now would mean certainly that her soul would be forever condemned."

"What are you getting at, Colbert?" Étienne questioned.

Jeanine had begun to get a sick feeling in her stomach. Her instincts told her exactly what Colbert's motives were in this line of discussion. He intended to see her humiliated before Victor and her brother, and he didn't care at what price it came.

"Good sirs," he said, turning to Étienne and Victor. "I would very graciously consider your proposal of doubling my payment, on one condition."

Étienne looked at Victor quizzically before answering. "What is the condition?"

Colbert threw a look of wicked delight at Jeanine. His smug assurance was more than she could bear. She knew without him speaking the words that he would ask her to bare her heart before them now.

"If your sister can deny that she holds love for this man, then I will accept your payment and cancel the contract of marriage."

All eyes turned to Jeanine. She swallowed hard and lowered her head. "But of course, I love all mankind," she said, barely above a whisper.

"Ah, but that is not what I speak of," Colbert replied. "For I see even now a spark of passion between you and Monsieur Pindar."

"This is utterly ridiculous," Étienne said, shifting uncomfortably.

"Is it? If that be the case then I will be a wealthy man, non?" Colbert took hold of Jeanine's arm. "Tell them true, my dear. Do you or do you not fancy yourself in love with this man? Remember now, you have vowed to God from this day forward nevermore to lie."

The silence was unbearable. Jeanine lifted her face to meet Victor's confused expression. Her brother seemed annoyed and anxious to be done with the entire matter, but by the look on Victor's face, Jeanine could tell that even now he was coming to understand that Colbert's suggestion was not totally unfounded.

Oh, Father, Jeanine prayed, *how can I admit to this thing without totally humiliating myself?* She took a deep breath.

"Well, Milady?" Colbert pressed.

Jeanine nodded. "Oui," she said with heavy resignation. "I love him."

Étienne stopped shifting and stared at her in dumbfounded silence. Jeanine couldn't even bring herself to look at Victor. She couldn't bear it if she found abhorrence or disgust in his expression.

"So, there you have it, gentleman. My betrothed has fallen in love with another and has been unfaithful to our contract. I could have her put away, perhaps even stoned for adultery."

"I have done nothing wrong, Monsieur!" Jeanine declared, no longer caring about her bruised emotions. "I have never played you false. I have never loved you, nor have I approved of this arrangement. I only agreed for the sake of my father's debt, but now it can be paid otherwise, and you have no right to force me into a loveless marriage."

Colbert laughed menacingly. "You are very wrong, Milady. I have full right to you and to our marriage. But it grieves me to know that you are in love with this man. Mayhap I should call him out, here and now, and be done with it. 'Tis unseemly that I should go forward into our marriage with another man sharing love with my wife."

"He doesn't feel anything for me," Jeanine protested. "The feelings are all on my part."

"I find that impossible to believe." Colbert turned on the stunned men. "After all, he is here offering his funds to save you from my clutches."

Jeanine opened her mouth to offer some weak argument but was saved from further disgrace when Colbert's servant appeared.

"Sir," the man said nervously, "the priest has come."

Chapter 11

By all means, send him in," Colbert said, wiping his hands against his rotund belly. The cotehardie he wore was of crimson velvet and did nothing to hide the stains.

Jeanine fled his presence and threw herself into her brother's arms. "You cannot let him do this. I swear I'll throw myself off the tower before becoming his wife."

Étienne wrapped a protective arm around her shoulder. "You heard her, Colbert. She prefers death to sharing your name."

"I'll put a guard on her, rest assured. Your precious sister will not meet with any untimely fate."

Jeanine searched her brother's face, praying to find an answer in the depths of his eyes—finding nothing there but hopelessness and anger. She fell silent as the priest came into the room. His pious nod was the only acknowledgment he gave her.

To her surprise, before either Colbert or the priest could speak, Victor posed a question. "Good father, is it not the wishes of the church to see both parties agreeable in the marriage union?"

The priest turned and nodded. "But of course. Marriage is ordained by God as a most holy union. Both man and woman must agree to the arrangement."

Victor smiled smugly at Colbert. Jeanine watched him issue a silent challenge and felt hope surge within her. Clutching Étienne's hand, she turned to face the priest.

"I must beg your pardon then, Father," she said without hesitation. "I do not wish to marry."

The priest shook his head and turned to Colbert. "Are you the one who has sent for me this day?"

"I am," Colbert responded, his eyes black with hate.

"And were you aware that the woman was not in agreement with marriage?"

"I was and am even now aware," Colbert admitted. Then to Jeanine's utter surprise, he added, "But 'tis hardly a wedding I am suggesting between myself and this witch."

"What say you, Man?" Étienne growled out the question. He put Jeanine aside and stepped forward as if challenged. "You had better explain yourself."

"You both heard me," Colbert replied.

Jeanine cast a helpless look at the priest, then without thinking, turned to look into Victor's dark eyes. He seemed to consider her for a moment, then smiled ever so slightly, leaving Jeanine's heart aflutter. Would the circumstance have been different, she might have offered an explanation and declared that her love for him was pure and true, but instead she found Colbert's enraged voice interrupting her thoughts.

"See, even now she is trying to cast her spells upon this good man."

"I am doing nothing of the kind," Jeanine responded in anger. "I am no witch, and I protest your accusations."

"Sir, by what means do you accuse this young woman?" the priest questioned quite seriously.

"I have witnessed her actions myself," Colbert replied. "Ask her yourself. Ask her to deny that she has concocted potions for the purpose of producing effects on the bodies of her victims."

The priest turned. "What say you of this?"

"He has twisted the truth, Milord." She looked to her brother for support, but Étienne and Victor both looked at her with questioning expressions.

"Mayhap we might sit," said the priest. "My journey here was much hurried and tiresome."

"Oh, but of course," Colbert said, the picture of congeniality. "We were just breaking the fast, perhaps you would care to join in?"

"Nay," the priest declined. "I wish for this most heinous accusation to be addressed."

Colbert led them to a small solarium off the great hall and waited until all parties were seated before shutting the door with a loud thud. Jeanine jumped at the noise and felt all gazes once again settle on her.

The priest scrutinized her with his pale blue eyes, as if weighing by mere sight the value of Colbert's words. "Are you in the habit of practicing witchcraft?" he asked quite frankly.

"Non, Father. I am not." Jeanine glanced to where Colbert had seated himself.

"Monsieur, would you please explain your proof?"

Colbert passed a brief smile upon Jeanine before answering. "This woman was to be my wife. Her father signed the marriage contract with me some weeks past. It was my belief that she was pure of heart and godly in her practices. She was known to attend church and to honor her parents, and I believed her of good quality. However," he paused, looking first to Jeanine and then to Étienne and Victor, "there came a suggestion to me that my intended might be less than honorable."

"How so?" asked the priest.

"She was seen to be loitering about the docks. This happened not once, but many times, often on a daily basis."

"And what were her actions while upon the docks?"

Colbert sneered. "She did not stay upon the docks. She took herself to a book copy shop owned by a Jew named Simon Grosz."

Jeanine shifted uncomfortably and tried to concentrate on the dark blue linen of her gown. How could she explain to the priest that it was only her desire to heal the sick that sent her to Simon? No matter what she said, she'd be condemning herself in the eyes of the church. She had consorted with a Jew and practiced medicine. Not only that, she had performed surgery, and it was well known that such things were widely opposed in the church. Jeanine scarcely thought of anything else, however, as Colbert launched into the matter of her love for Victor Pindar.

The priest raised his hand for Colbert's silence. "The things you have shared are in no way proofs to me of this woman's participation in the black arts. Have you something more compelling?"

Colbert nodded. "Indeed I have. The book copy shop Mademoiselle de la Fontaine frequented was only a cover for her practices. The old man, Monsieur Grosz, was nearly blind and could not possibly have operated a copy shop with any competency."

"And it was while here that you believe she was practicing witchcraft?"

"I know it to be. I followed her there and found that in her spell-casting, she had taken on the form of a man. She was dressed completely in black and her hair had taken on the course, gray-black texture of the old Jew. Her face was blackened and she moved about the room preparing all manner of potion in preparation for her spells."

"Is this true?" the priest asked Jeanine.

"Father, the circumstances hold some basis of truth, but not in the manner for which Monsieur Colbert would have you believe. I was merely seeking to help Simon—Monsieur Grosz—"

"So you admit to consorting with the Jew?"

Jeanine felt a deep sense of frustration from his interruption. "Simon and I became friends. He did not seek to turn me from my faith in God."

The priest appeared quite vexed about this and looked to Colbert for help. "Can this Jew be summoned?"

"Nay," Colbert replied, eyeing Jeanine for her response. "He is dead. She killed him."

"Nay!" Jeanine declared, jumping to her feet. " 'Tis untrue!"

"She found me in the room and was greatly distressed. Her spell was broken, and I was able to see clearly that she was but a woman in men's clothing. I opposed her, and she argued with me most bitterly. She threatened my life, and when I laughed at her, she began to chant her incantations. The Jew got in the way, however, as he feared I might strike her away. When she threw the spell, it was the Jew and not myself who bore the effects."

The priest's eyes narrowed and his expression changed to one of obvious distaste. "And what were those effects?"

"He immediately clutched his chest and fell over dead. 'Twould have been my fate had the old man not got in the way."

"I see. And what say you for yourself, young woman?" the priest questioned coolly. Gone was any attempt at cordiality.

"I did not cast a spell. Simon's heart attacked him because he was worried about me. Monsieur Colbert was most unkind and treated me quite roughly. Simon was only attempting to protect me."

"No doubt he practiced her black art, as well," Colbert replied.

Throughout the entire interrogation, Jeanine had noted her brother's looks of confusion and disbelief, as well as Victor's seemingly intense study of each person in the room. She wanted to scream that they should all just go away and leave her to her humiliation, but it was not to be.

"Given the circumstances and the evidence," the priest said, getting to his feet, "it is my suggestion that the young woman be held where she cannot harm anyone else. Give her over to a room that has been blessed and strip it of all articles. Put nothing more than a pallet of straw upon the floor and a blanket to ward off the chill. Bring her meals on a flat board and give her nothing but water to drink."

Colbert nodded enthusiastically, but Étienne had finally reached his limit of silence. "Hold there, Father," he said, rising to meet the priest face-to-face. "This woman is my sister, and I have never known her to consort with demons or cast spells. She is well known in the community as a God-fearing soul, and she is generous with her time for those who need her."

"As much as I would like to believe you," the priest replied, "I have seen the likes before. Ofttimes we believe ourselves to have knowledge of a person, only to be astonished by their true natures."

"I will grant you that people are many times not who they appear to be, but this case is different."

The priest held up his hand. "We will save her defense for her trial before the council of the church."

"What!" Jeanine exclaimed. Now she, too, was on her feet. "But I have done nothing."

"Nothing save kill a man," Colbert reminded his audience.

"You will be held here on the estate of Monsieur Colbert," the priest stated firmly. "I will arrange for the council, and your trial date will be set. Until that time you are to be held without any visitation from others lest you cast your spells upon them and seduce them to aid you in your circumstance."

"But I am innocent!" Jeanine felt herself growing ill at the thought of weeks, mayhap even months under Colbert's heartless keep.

"That is for the church to decide," the priest replied without emotion. "Until that time, you will abide by this decree or face excommunication." He turned to Étienne and Victor. "That would also go for any man who aids her in an attempt to avoid trial."

Jeanine saw Victor's eyes darken and his jaw grow tense. She wondered if it was the pain of his ribs or anger that caused such reaction. She had little time to contemplate it, however, as Colbert motioned for his men to take Jeanine in hand.

"Remove her to the tower."

"First allow me to bless the room."

Colbert bowed to the priest. "But, of course. Come, I will lead the way while my men stand guard over the woman."

Colbert and the priest took their leave, and Jeanine found herself staring after them in disbelief. How could her life have become so completely topsy-turvy?

"Jeanine," Étienne whispered, reaching out to touch her arm. "I will find help. I will figure out what must be done."

Victor slowly stood, and Jeanine caught her breath as his expression warmed. "We will work together," he assured her.

She wanted very much to say something, anything that might ease the embarrassment of her declaration of love, but for the life of her there seemed nothing of sense to be told. If she tried to justify her feelings, it would only serve to dig her deeper into the grave she'd already prepared for herself. Tears formed in her eyes and streamed down her face. She tried hard to ignore Colbert's burly guards as Étienne took her into his arms and comforted her.

"Hush, sweet sister," he whispered. "All will be well. You will see."

"I see only the hopelessness of this situation. Oh, what have I done?"

"That, I suppose, is yet to be discovered. Tell me in truth, what cause did you have to go to the old man's shop every day?"

Jeanine choked back her sobs. "I was working as a doctor, nothing more—nothing less. Simon had trained me in the ways of medicine. I only wanted to help the poor. They have so little, and when they fall ill, they cannot afford the care of a physician. I only wanted to help them." Her body shook fiercely with sorrow.

"Jeanine?" Victor spoke her name soft and sweet.

Raising up from where she'd buried her face against Étienne's tunic, she met his sympathetic gaze. "Oui?"

"Do not despair. God is with you."

Jeanine sniffed back tears. "I am sorry to have made you a part of this." She wanted to ensure his freedom from further entanglements with her cause.

To her surprise, he grinned and raised her hand to his lips. "I have no regret of it. It gives me much to consider."

Jeanine lowered her gaze and fought the pounding of her heart. His lips were warm on her hand and the very thought that those lips might one day touch her own, caused her to momentarily forget her problems.

"Listen to me, Jeanine," Étienne said, breaking the spell. "We will go back to town and seek out help."

"Please, please find out what happened to Simon," she begged.

"Of course," Étienne promised. "He might well aid us in this case."

"I pray it is so, but only if he can be kept from harm. He is a Jew—that much is true. And he was practicing medicine illegally, just as I did. But he is no demonic soul. He believes in God, albeit, he rejects Christ as his Savior."

"I will find the old man and talk to him. Try to be strong. We have very little control over Colbert or the priest's actions. You will be cared for, but if Colbert so much as lays a finger on you, I will personally see to his death."

"As will I," Victor promised.

"Thank you, both," Jeanine said, just as Colbert and the priest reentered the room.

"It is completed," Colbert announced.

"I ask you, Father," Étienne commented, as Colbert took Jeanine in hand, "what protection does my sister have against this man's unwelcome advances?" Colbert reddened and his grip tightened on Jeanine's arm. Étienne continued, "She is a maid, innocent and pure, whether Colbert chooses to believe such or not. I have heard of this man's reputation, and I fear for my sister."

The priest looked from Étienne to Colbert and Jeanine. Then, as if seeing the man's concern as valid, he nodded. "Monsieur Colbert, I charge you in the name of the Father, Son, and Holy Spirit, that no harm either physical or spiritual might come upon this woman. She must be tried before the council. If she is a witch, it will be up to the church to determine her fate. If she is found innocent, then she must be allowed to return to her life, unharmed and unknowledgeable of the ways of the world. Will you assure me on threat of excommunication that you will see to this woman's safety?"

Colbert grimaced then forced a laugh. "I would not dream of touching the witch on fear of my soul."

The priest was satisfied, and Jeanine knew there was nothing else Étienne could demand. She caught one final glance from Victor and an assuring nod from her brother before being led from the room and back to the cold stone stairs of the tower.

"You thought to have victory over me," Colbert whispered in her ear as they ascended the steps together, "but 'tis I who have the victory."

"You are wrong, Monsieur," Jeanine said, pausing long enough to meet Colbert's cold stare. "The victory will be God's and God's alone. He will not tolerate your lies against one of His own. I have learned my lesson about speaking the truth, but you have yet to learn yours."

Chapter 12

Nearly a month had passed, with only the briefest of messages sent by Colbert to Jeanine's family. Learning the fate of their daughter, François and Margarite de la Fontaine had appealed to Colbert for mercy, but he had made it quite clear that the matter was out of his hands. They had paid a visit to the cathedral only to discover that their own priest was reluctant to interfere until the church formally resolved the conflict.

Étienne had gone back to the shop where Simon had cared for Victor, but the old man was gone and the shop was closed up tight. After asking neighboring establishments about the old man's whereabouts, Étienne was no better off. Simon had seemingly disappeared into thin air.

Victor found the waiting almost more vexing than anyone else and for reasons that came as a total surprise to himself. As his wounds healed and he spent his time in recuperative rest, he couldn't stop thinking back to Jeanine's declaration of love. He always smiled as he remembered her embarrassment and shy regard for him. How odd that the maid had fallen in love with him.

As the days slipped by, Victor's contemplation led him to startling discoveries, and as he realized the full implication of his thoughts, he couldn't bring himself to believe his conclusion. Cornering Jeanine's brother late one night, he shared his theory.

" 'Twould seem you have much on your mind to keep you from rest," Étienne said, as Victor joined him in front of the common room fireplace.

"I would not wish to awaken your parents, but my thoughts are such that sleep is quite impossible," Victor responded in a hushed voice. "I've been thinking about Jeanine."

"Ah," Étienne replied and poked the fire. "Her words of love, I suppose."

Victor grinned. "Well, there is always that to turn my head. What of your sister's declaration? Have you ever known her to speak thusly?"

"You mean to declare herself in love?"

"Aye."

"Hmmm, let me think back. There was that one time when Pierre lived next door. He was dark-eyed, just as you are. Perhaps that is the attraction," Étienne teased.

"And she was in love with him?" Victor asked, not liking that such conversation made him feel tense.

"Oh, that she was. She was always after his attentions." Victor sat in glum silence, and Étienne roared with amusement. "Of course, she was only six at the time."

Victor caught the look of knowing on Étienne's face and shrugged. "I suppose it is hard to help myself from feeling something for her. She looked so forlorn standing there. To imagine Colbert having the nerve to accuse her of witchcraft."

"Oui, but she had gone to Simon's in order to illegally practice medicine."

"Which is truly where my thoughts are leading me this night," Victor admitted.

"How so?"

Victor hunched his shoulders and leaned his elbows on his knees. "Jeanine is the one who cared for me. She is most likely the one who performed the surgery on me."

Étienne looked at him in stunned silence. Victor knew that his words were preposterous. It was hard enough to imagine that he had survived the ordeals of brain surgery, but to suggest that a slip of woman like Jeanine had taken the instruments in hand to complete the task was almost more than he could allow himself to believe.

"I know what you are thinking, because I've thought it myself," Victor admitted. "She is but a woman, petite and weak, but you yourself heard Colbert's evidence. He stated that Simon Grosz had such weak eyesight that he could not possibly perform the tasks of book copying. How much less would he be able to perform surgery?"

"I suppose you have a point worth noting," Étienne agreed. "But Jeanine?"

Victor laughed. "I can believe almost anything possible of that woman. She could not have surprised me more with her declaration of love. To tell me she saved my life as well seems most fitting."

"But surgery? To actually cut into a man's flesh and bone?"

Victor nodded. "And then to care for him in the guise of a male physician, all in order to see to my needs. 'Twould be then, most likely, that her feelings developed for me."

"For all the good it does either of you now," Étienne said, reminding Victor instantly of their plight.

"Aye, 'tis a difficult situation at best. I've given over long hours to prayer, but the answers seem slow in coming. I have one hope, besides my faith," Victor added.

"And what might that be?"

Victor eased back in the chair. "I have posted a letter to the king."

"You what?" Étienne's voice rose in surprise.

"I have overseen the creation of several buildings for the king. Two cathedrals and a summer estate, to name a few. I've held his favor for some time, as well as that of England's king. I've sent a post to him, as well, through my sister."

"You could not surprise me more had you told me you'd journeyed to Rome to plead Jeanine's case before the pope," Étienne admitted.

"If I thought it would do any good, I'd gladly go there. I can't help but feel responsible for this situation. Perhaps if your sister hadn't fallen in love with me, she might have married Colbert without a fuss or fight."

"Then you do not know my sister very well," Étienne responded.

"No, but I'd like to," Victor said with a sad smile.

"Truly?" Étienne watched him carefully as if searching for some telltale sign that he lied.

"Truly. I have to admit, I came to enjoy her companionship while she cared for me. Now, just thinking of her stuck in that place with Colbert. . ." He fell silent, anger evident in his expression.

"What goes on here?" François de la Fontaine asked, coming sleepily into the room. "I thought I heard voices."

"Oui, and I'm sorry we woke you," Étienne said. "We were just discussing Jeanine."

"And what else would we talk about these days? I can scarce work for thinking of her. My poor, poor child." Monsieur de la Fontaine sat down heavily and put his head in his hands.

"I've come up with a plan to steal her away from Colbert," Victor said, surprising both father and son.

"You might as well not try," Étienne said, before his father could respond. "Colbert guards that place like a fortress. He will have her under bar and lock, no doubt. He has quite an army of men, and you must remember he owns most everything your eye can take in."

"I care naught for what he owns. I weary of awaiting the church's decision of when they might come and listen to her case. I am angry that an entire moon has cycled itself in full while a young woman's life hangs in the balance."

Jeanine's father looked up and eyed Victor carefully. "You speak as one who cares."

"I do care. I care more than I had believed myself capable of. I feel responsible, too, for it is of my opinion that much of this might never have happened if I had never entered your house."

"Hardly that!" his host exclaimed. "You have done nothing but attempt to rescue us from despair and certain doom. If you must fault anyone, fault me for signing the marriage contract. I felt foolishly that there was no other way. I did not trust God to provide, and this is my punishment."

"I think you're both wrong," Étienne replied. "This is evidence of Colbert's corruption. 'Tis nothing of our fault, either implied or imagined. Colbert is evil and heartless, and he has begun this thing—but I will see it finished.".

"As will I," Victor promised.

"You mustn't try to take Jeanine from the tower," her father admonished. "The Lord, Himself, knows that if I thought it would work, I would try it, but we would need an army stronger than any I can imagine. No, we must appeal to the church council and pray God intervenes on Jeanine's behalf."

"It would be most helpful to find what became of Simon Grosz," Victor said, with a yawn. "I believe on the morrow I will go in search of him again. After all, it has been a fortnight since we talked to the dock folk. Mayhap someone has heard of something since our time there."

"I'll go with you, if you like," Étienne offered.

"Non, you have enough that demands your attention. I will search, and if I find something, I will consult you both."

In his room later that night, Victor was more than a little aware of Jeanine's presence. The bedroom had been hers for who knew how long, and even now the fresh scent of her lavender soap could sometimes be caught in the air.

Victor tried hard not to think of her fearful expression as Colbert led her away. Thinking about that scene made him want to go for a horse and journey posthaste to Colbert's estate. Growing frustration nagged at him, and in spite of the late hour, Victor wondered seriously if sleep would ever be his companion that night.

He went to the dresser where Jeanine had many of her concoctions and herbs. He smiled as he imagined her studying the effects of each and what their medicinal values might be. He picked up one bottle and tried to imagine what the leafy green object was inside. That was when he spied the slip of paper beneath the bottle. Picking it up, Victor opened it to find the words, Five Geese Flying. He noted the script was feathery and disjointed, as if the hand that held the quill had been feeble and shaky. Had Simon Grosz been the author of the message? If so, what did the message signify?

Tucking the slip of paper inside his tunic, Victor vowed that on the morrow he would find Simon, dead or alive. Victor would seek to set into motion the future of the young woman who so fearfully admitted her love for him.

Victor paused outside the ramshackle shop front that identified Simon Grosz's residence and book copy shop. Unlike two weeks earlier when the place had born no sign of life, today the door was very much open, as were the windows. Stepping up to the portal, Victor knocked loudly and announced himself.

"Bonjour, is anyone here?" Victor made the decision to step inside and call again. "Bonjour?"

"Bonjour, Monsieur," Simon said, coming slowly from the back room. "Ah,

Monsieur Pindar, is it not?"

"Oui," Victor replied. " 'Tis I."

"I had thought perhaps we would not meet again," Simon replied. "Please, come inside and sit with me. How are you feeling?" The old man tottered a bit as he led the way to a small table where two chairs awaited their attention.

"I might ask the same of you. It was my understanding that you had fallen ill. As for myself, I am well. Thanks be to you, God, and Jeanine de la Fontaine."

"Do you know of her? How is she?" Simon's face was grief-stricken. "I have thought of her constantly and asked blessings on her. A horrible man, Antoine Colbert, took her from me some time back. I could not help her, and now I fear—"

"The news is not good. Colbert has accused her of witchcraft," Victor admitted.

"But I thought he wished to share matrimony with her."

"He did, but Mademoiselle Jeanine had other thoughts."

"I know that well," Simon replied, then lowered his face and smiled. "She did not have love for Monsieur Colbert. Her heart was otherwise engaged."

"Oui. I know it well."

"So she told you?"

Victor grinned. "It was not in the setting she would have liked, but yes. To my great shame, I must admit that Colbert ascertained her heart before I did."

"I suppose that did not brook well with the man," Simon said, the amusement in his voice quite evident.

"Non, it did not. I believe that is why he decided to accuse her of witchcraft. He had already sent for the priest to marry them, and when I pointed out, with the priest as witness, that the church required both parties to agree to marriage, Colbert changed his story. He told the priest he no longer desired to marry Jeanine, but that he had sent for him to accuse her before the church of witchcraft. He cited the day he found her here posing as a doctor."

Simon looked surprised. "You know of her work?"

"Oui. I know, too, that she is the one responsible for this," he said and pulled back earth-black hair.

Simon leaned forward to take in the trephining scar. "It has healed well."

"She is the one who performed the surgery, is she not?"

Simon nodded. "I told her what to do, and she saved your life. Blood was pooling against the brain, and it left you unconscious. 'Twould have killed you had we not opened up your head and relieved the pressure."

Victor smiled. "She has gotten into my head in more than one way."

Simon chuckled. "Jeanine has a way of doing that. 'Tis certain the girl has a gift, and I only sought to help her use it. True, it is against our laws, and I have probably jeopardized her life by my foolishness. I only longed to pass on that which I knew and to help her realize her desires to help others."

"You did the right thing, Simon. Elsewise, I'd be long departed from this earth." Victor pulled the slip of paper from his tunic and handed it over to Simon. "I found this in her room last night. What meaning has it?"

Simon looked at the words and nodded. "Five geese flying was a code we agreed upon. It was my message for her to come to the docks for emergencies. Otherwise, she slipped down here whenever she could, and we would study and improve her knowledge."

"But why five geese flying?"

" 'Tis from Jeanine's own stories of childhood. Her grandmother was a storyteller, and before she died she had imparted many tales of spiritual value. Her grandmother told Jeanine of the geese and how five geese flew overhead the day she met Jeanine's grandfather. Five geese also were seen from her window the day she gave birth to Jeanine's father. She believed it a sign of hope and love. It seemed fitting for the calling of a physician to aid in the healing of his, or her, in this case, beloved people."

Simon smiled as Victor tried to put all the pieces together. "But there were other reasons for the attachment to such matters," he continued.

"Jeanine's grandmother reminded her of how the geese would fly south in the autumn. With the winter and the burial of all that seemed alive, she would admonish Jeanine to search her heart and soul for that which should be left as dead. Hurtful feelings, ugly words said without thought, the kind of things that were best left buried with the coming winter snows."

Victor nodded his understanding, and Simon continued. "Then, too, with the return of the geese and the coming of spring and summer, Jeanine was encouraged to open her heart to new growth. Her grandmother told her to seek out God's direction for her life and to know the renewing of the spirit that only He could give."

"Jeanine's grandmother sounds to be a very wise woman," Victor said softly.

"When she left this world," Simon added, "she left a deep void in Jeanine's heart." He shrugged. "But who knows, mayhap you will fill that void, eh?"

"Mayhap," Victor replied, deep in thought. "Mayhap. But first, we must find a way to free her from Colbert's plans. He would see her burned at the stake rather than give her over to me. I have tried to come up with a plan for her defense, but it seems that I am lacking direction in that area."

"Jeanine would say that the direction we seek is only a prayer away."

Victor eyed the old man with a knowing nod. "Oui, she would say exactly that."

"Then we must honor her and listen to just that suggestion, non?"

"You are very right, my dear fellow. I allowed myself to grow discouraged and to take my eyes from the hope that I have in God. But no more. I will be in touch," Victor said, getting to his feet. "Please send word to me at Monsieur de la Fontaine's residence should you need me. The previously arranged code will work as well for me as it did Jeanine."

Simon laughed and followed Victor out of the shop. "Mayhap our little goose will do her own flying soon."

"I pray it will be so," Victor told the old man.

Chapter 13

Jeanine found herself brought before the church council and, to her surprise, a gathering board of university physicians. The two groups seemed to be unlikely companions, but for the purpose of stamping out witchcraft they appeared willing to tolerate each other. They were seated at a long table at the head of the great hall.

The physicians took up the left side of the table. They seemed almost bored and annoyed by the summons that had brought them to Flanders. On the right side of the table were the clergy. Two scribes, clerks to the bishop, sat side by side, and in the center sat the bishop, himself. He was by far the most foreboding of the group. He stared at her stern-faced and dark-eyed, and his expression was one of complete intolerance.

Jeanine, herself, had been made to stand in the center of the room. She was allowed to bathe and wear a clean gown, which her mother had brought to her that morning, and her hair had been braided and a plain simple cap of white linen had been placed upon her head. She knew she must look ridiculously small before the mighty assembly of men, but she bit back her fear and bolstered her determination. She would face the truth nose to nose, and whether these men found value in her work or not, she would refuse to lie in order to ease her discomfort.

"We will now hear the case of Jeanine de la Fontaine," the bishop said, glancing down at the parchment in front of him.

Jeanine glanced around, comforted marginally by the presence of her family, but deeply wounded by Victor's absence. She tried to offer her mother a smile, but found it impossible. She had only to look into the anguished faces of her parents for tears to form in her eyes. Étienne appeared stalwart and true, but his brow was wrinkled in worry. Jeanine turned back to face her accusers. It was infinitely easier to face her enemies than her loved ones. What did she care if she disappointed those folk who wished her nothing but ill? But to see the sorrow and fear in the eyes of her family was more than she could bear.

"Who accuses this woman of heresy and witchcraft?" the bishop asked impatiently.

Jeanine turned to meet the scowling gaze of Antoine Colbert. For the last month she had endured his advances and lewd suggestions, all the while reminding him of the priest's threat of excommunication. Colbert cared very little about the church and whether or not he found acceptance in the eyes of Rome, but he did care about his businesses and landholdings. He knew that to anger the church would mean certain financial doom.

"I accuse her," Colbert said, struggling against his rotund midsection to stand.

"Your name, Sir?" the bishop asked by way of meeting the formalities. His clerks were busy dipping their quills and noting all details of the conversation.

"I am Antoine Colbert."

"Monsieur Colbert, do you hereby give charge in the sight of God and these witnesses that this woman, Jeanine de la Fontaine, did willingly participate and practice the black arts of witchcraft?"

"I do," Colbert replied solemnly.

The bishop conferred with the man at his left before continuing. "Mademoiselle de la Fontaine, you have heard the charges. How do you plead your case?"

Jeanine did not hesitate. "I am innocent."

The council murmured as the bishop made comment and waited while the clerks penned her response. He stared at Jeanine with a stoic expression, and for a moment, she had the distinct impression that he'd already decided that she was guilty as charged.

"Monsieur Colbert, are you prepared to offer evidence to this council and give proof to the practices of this woman?"

"I am, your Grace. I have witnessed her actions myself and come here this day to expose her schemes."

"I will hear your testimony now," the bishop announced and leaned back into his chair.

Colbert looked hard at Jeanine before continuing. "This woman was to have been my bride. Her father, Monsieur François de la Fontaine, may bear witness to this truth. The details were agreed upon, the contracts signed, and Mademoiselle de la Fontaine was known to be in preparation for our wedding." He paused as if to defy Jeanine to deny what he said.

"It was during this time of preparation that I learned of mademoiselle's journeys into a most undesirable part of our town. Daily she would venture down to the docks and disappear into the rundown shop of the Jew, Simon Grosz."

"And upon learning this, what did you do?" the bishop questioned.

"I feared for the lady's virtue and followed her inside. It was there that I found she had transformed herself into the appearance of a man."

The council, as well as the physicians, began muttering among themselves. The clerks wrote furiously and appeared not in the leastwise to concern themselves with the implications of what had been stated.

"She was transformed, you say," the bishop more stated than questioned. "How so?"

Jeanine allowed her thoughts to drift to a place of protection and security.

She pictured herself sitting at the feet of her grandmère. She could almost feel the old woman's gentle hand upon her head. *Oh, Grandmère,* she thought, *my lies have brought me to destruction. I stand accused of all manner of falsehood by a man who would see me dead because of my rejection of him as husband.* She could imagine her grandmother smiling upon her, bidding her to calm her fears and place her trust in God.

"And you saw her actually cast a spell in your presence?" the bishop now asked Colbert.

Jeanine turned to see his reaction. He narrowed his eyes at her, and there was little doubt in her mind that he would gladly spark the fire that would consume her life.

"She thought to kill me," Colbert replied. "She cast a spell, but God was with me. I moved aside and the Jew Simon Grosz received her vengeance instead."

"He lies!" Jeanine called out.

"Silence, Woman. We will determine what falsehoods are spoken," the bishop told her. "Monsieur Colbert, what happened to the Jew?"

"He began clutching his chest, and it was evident that the pain he experienced was most grave. He collapsed to the floor at that point, and while the witch—I mean, mademoiselle—was distracted, I yanked off her disguise and broke the spell of transformation."

"I see. What became of the Jew?"

"He died."

The council stared at Jeanine with open hostility. She felt light-headed and dizzy, as though she might faint. It seemed that her case was most hopeless. Just then the doors opened behind her, and to everyone's surprise Victor Pindar entered the room with Simon Grosz at his side.

"I would like to address this council," Victor announced. Jeanine's breath caught in her throat. He hadn't deserted her.

"And who might you be?"

"I am Victor Pindar, and this gentleman is Simon Grosz." Victor paused and grinned. "The dead man of whom you speak."

The gasps of surprise were welcome sounds in Jeanine's ears, but no more so than the sight of Simon. She wanted to run to him—to both of them. Simon was alive! She eyed him suspiciously for any signs of his failing health, but he only smiled at her as if to reassure her of his strength.

"You are the Jew?" the bishop asked curiously.

"I am he," Simon admitted, coming to stand in front of the council.

"Monsieur Colbert, you told this council that the Jew had fallen victim to the practices of witchcraft."

"Can you not see? The witch brought him back to life. She has powers that far exceed our imaginings," Colbert declared, then crossed himself for emphasis.

"What say you of this, Mademoiselle?" the bishop asked Jeanine.

"I am innocent," Jeanine answered as evenly as she could. Her heart was pounding with anticipation of her freedom. Surely now that Simon was here, the council could see Colbert's lies for themselves.

"Mademoiselle de la Fontaine," the bishop began, "will you tell this council what purpose you had for consorting with this Jew?"

Jeanine swallowed hard. The easy thing would be to lie, but she'd pledged to God and to herself that no more lies would pass through her lips. She glanced at Simon, whose very existence could be threatened by her telling of the truth. He nodded knowingly, as if to assure her that honesty could harm neither of them. Turning back to the council, she faced Colbert's sneering expression. There was pure hatred in his eyes as she answered, "I went there for the purpose of learning."

"Learning? Pray tell, what would you have a Jew teach you?"

"Simon is a physician," Jeanine said flatly. "I went to him in order to help him with his work for the poor. Many of the dockworkers and their families had fallen ill with no hope of affording proper care. Simon offered them his assistance in whatever manner he could, and I in turn offered my help."

"What help did you suppose yourself capable of?"

Jeanine finally allowed her gaze to travel to where Victor stood silently watching. He was dressed in a dark green cotehardie that reached just below his hips to meet black hose and boots. His dark hair was still windblown from his ride to the estate, but his eyes were eager to encourage her. He looked to be completely healed of his wounds, and in the healthy glow of his face, she found an expression of compassion that she had never known.

Her strength was renewed. God had not allowed her to face the council without support. Not only was He in His heaven watching over her, but He had sent her family and her one true love to stand beside her throughout her ordeal.

"I felt myself called to learn of Simon's medical knowledge."

The bored-looking physicians seemed to take new notice in this declaration. The leader, an aged man with thick mounds of wavy gray hair, held up his hand to enter the conversation. "You say you desired to learn of the Jew's medical knowledge? What possible wisdom could he have in this field?"

"He is a physician. He trained at the university in Montpellier."

"That may well have been the case, but Jews are not allowed to practice medicine under the laws of our country. Laws, which I might add, are most clearly given for a purpose."

"This man is most gifted, and he helps those who cannot afford the care of legal physicians such as yourself." Jeanine felt her anger mounting. It was enough that they should attack her, but to impugn Simon as well was more than she was willing to stand. "This man has saved hundreds of lives and should be held in your esteem instead of your contempt."

"I see. And do you consider yourself a physician as well?" the doctor asked her in a cynical voice.

Jeanine paused, looked over her shoulder at her family, and took in a deep breath. "I do."

The council again began murmuring together, and this time, the physicians joined in. The bishop held up his hand for silence. "By what authority do you make these claims? Have you proof of your work with the Jew?"

"I claim no authority except that which is given by the Lord God in heaven. As for my work, how could I yet prove it while standing here before you? I could recite the dealings of the body. Speak to you of humors and the anatomy that designs each human being. I can tell you of binding wounds and setting bones, of surgical procedures to save the lives of the dying, but what proof can I offer you?"

"I stand as her proof," Victor offered, coming forward with long, even strides. "I submit myself before the physicians of this board. I was injured in a storm at sea. I sustained some form of head injury—I'm certain Mademoiselle de la Fontaine could be more precise about the details."

He pulled back the thick dark hair that had fallen in an unruly manner across his forehead. "Here at the temple I received a desperate blow, and here is the place where the pressure was relieved when the blood pressed in against my brain."

The leading physician stood up and came to examine Victor's head. "Trephining is a most delicate surgery that requires a great deal of skill and training. Would you have me believe that this woman acted out such a procedure? I'd sooner believe the Jew capable of this."

"Ask her yourself, but I know she saved my life." Victor's gaze found hers and lingered for several moments on her face. He smiled, and there was such tenderness in his expression that Jeanine felt herself flushing. He knew what she'd done, and he didn't appear in the least disturbed by it. What manner of man was he? Could he truly accept this passion of hers?

"Is it true?" the bishop finally asked when the physician seemed to become more fascinated by Victor's new scars than in interrogating the defendant.

Jeanine nodded. "Oui. I performed the surgery with the assistance and direction of Dr. Grosz." She heard her mother gasp and longed to turn and offer further explanation, but Antoine chose that moment to seal her doom.

"Your Grace, can this be anything other than the proof you need? She admits to holding life and death in her hands. She admits to performing acts of surgery upon the flesh of this man. What more do you need to show evidence that my accusations are true?"

The bishop nodded. "You make a valid point, Sir, but I have yet another question to ask of this woman." He paused. "By whose authority have you gained your power?"

Jeanine's chin tilted upward in confidence. "By the Lord God Almighty."

"Blasphemy!" Colbert declared. "She speaks blasphemy. The devil is her god."

"You are wrong, Monsieur," Jeanine said, shaking her head. "I serve only the Lord God in heaven."

"She lies, I tell you," Colbert said, taking a stand between Jeanine and the bishop. "The church gives no recognition of women as physicians. Our own laws declare it illegal for women to practice medicine, and Holy Scriptures demand our obedience unto the laws of the land. How, therefore, can this woman speak the truth and accredit her acts to God? She is the devil's handmaiden, I tell you."

At this, Jeanine's father protested loudly, as did her brother. Victor had stepped away from the board of physicians and made several menacing steps toward Colbert.

"Enough!" the bishop demanded. "The council will speak on this matter in private. I believe we have heard sufficient words on this day." He turned to the board of physicians and continued. "We will retire and hear your thoughts on this matter. I shall give my decision within the hour." At that, he and the other members of the clergy rose to their feet and exited the great room.

Jeanine let out a long breath, not even aware that she'd been holding it the entire time of the bishop's departure. She watched as the physicians followed the clergy. All seemed to eye her with contempt, and not even one offered her so much as a single word of acknowledgment. Colbert waited until they had gone to motion his men to take Jeanine in hand. Victor quickly came to her side and met Colbert head-on.

"She stays here," Victor said, taking hold of Jeanine's arm. "You have seen her imprisoned for the past month, and that is more than enough."

"She is a witch," Colbert said, glaring in defiance.

"I stand to defend this woman's honor," Victor replied, drawing Jeanine ever closer. "I should call you out for your words and run a sword through your heart."

Colbert laughed. " 'Twould be your own death, Monsieur." He eyed Victor for a moment as if trying to decide whether the battle would be worth the effort, then waved his arms in acceptance. "Have it your way. Let her say her good-byes and farewells. 'Tis of little consequence to me."

Victor turned to Jeanine and led her to where her family stood anxiously waiting. Jeanine longed to remain at Victor's side, but at the sight of her mother's open arms, she fled one haven for another. "Oh, ma mère," she sobbed against her mother's frail shoulder, "I am so sorry for the lies I told you."

"Hush now. All is forgiven," her mother whispered.

Jeanine felt her father's sturdy hand upon her head. "Has he harmed you, Daughter?"

She raised her tear-filled eyes and shook her head. "Non. He feared the excommunication promised by the priest should he lay a hand upon me. Of course, that warning did nothing to close his mouth from the rude and wicked things he said to me."

Victor and Étienne had come to stand directly behind her, and Jeanine turned to meet their dear faces. "I am so sorry to have brought this upon our house. It was only my desire to help people. Truly, I sought only to serve God through the work of my hands." She wiped at her tears with her sleeve. "I was foolish not to realize that by lying I was also serving Satan's purpose. No matter what happens this day, I will not forget what you have done." She said this as if collectively for the group, which now included Simon as well. But it was to Victor that she directed her gaze.

Already she could hear the commotion of the physicians and clergy as they made their way back into the great hall. They had been gone only minutes, instead of the promised hour. She began to tremble, seeing the stern, unyielding expressions on each of their faces. Her doom was certain, and in that moment, she realized that they would demand her death. Colbert's men pushed Victor and her family aside and took Jeanine roughly in hand to bring her before the table where the men were now assembling.

"Jeanine de la Fontaine," the bishop addressed her with an arrogance that left her cold, "by your own admission you have willfully performed the acts of surgery and the concocting of potions. Because there is no evidence in Scripture that God would allow a woman the power of life and death in the actions of a physician, it may only be assumed that your power is from Satan, himself."

"No!" Jeanine cried out and the men at her sides tightened their hold.

"Silence!" the bishop demanded. "You have admitted to consorting with a Jew, a man whom we all know to have no faith in the risen Christ. You have admitted to taking on his teachings, and therefore you have made yourself a heretic in the sight of the church. You have willingly participated in the manipulation of human flesh and held power over those in your care, and therefore have provided evidence to this council that you are given over to the powers of your dark lord, Satan."

"No! 'Tis a lie! I denounce Satan. I serve God alone," Jeanine declared, struggling against the hold Colbert's henchmen kept on her.

The bishop ignored her. "It is the decision of this council that you be burned at the stake upon the dawning of the morning sun, for the practice of witchcraft. May God have mercy on your soul."

Jeanine felt her chest tighten and the room began to swirl around her. They were going through with this. They were really going to put her to death, and all because she had tried to heal the sick. She felt her vision dim and a sensation of heat overwhelmed her. In her mind's eye, she felt the flames lick at her face as she lost consciousness and fell limp between her captors.

Chapter 14

Victor longed to dislodge the unconscious Jeanine from the grip of Colbert's henchmen, but he knew he had little hope of doing so. He stepped forward just as Jeanine's mother and father rushed to the bishop to plead for their daughter's life.

"Your Grace, she's not a witch," Madame de la Fontaine declared, sobbing out her words with the broken heart of a mother. "She is but a girl, and her heart is pure."

"She is just a child," François de la Fontaine added. "Our only daughter."

"Unless it is your desire to burn at her side, you will leave this council and accept her fate. She has admitted to her guilt, even if her intentions were otherwise. The church cannot accept such behavior in its people, and your daughter cannot be allowed to live only to corrupt the souls of others."

Colbert watched with seeming indifference. He turned to find Victor openly watching him, then motioned to his men to leave Jeanine upon the floor. They did so, unceremoniously dropping her to the cold hard stones before throwing Victor a glance that dared his interference.

Victor clenched his teeth tightly and prayed for heavenly intervention. He wanted very badly to pull the sword at his side and run each of the men through before separating Colbert's head from his body. But instead of acting upon those feelings, Victor held his ground. For Jeanine's sake, he would find a way to rescue her. Mindless of Colbert's watchful eye and self-satisfied expression, Victor moved past the guards and went to where Jeanine lay.

Tenderly, he turned her and lifted her still form in his arms. He carried her to the place where her family had sat to watch her mock trial, and there he cradled her until her mother came to him.

"I think you have come to care a great deal for my daughter, non?" the older woman questioned. Her eyes were red from crying, but her face was ashen white. Fear etched itself deeply in her countenance.

"I do," Victor admitted. He looked down upon Jeanine's delicate features and wondered why it was that she had ever fallen in love with him. There had been nothing between them save her desire to keep him from death. By her own admission, many others had been saved by her hand, so what made him different? Why had she gazed upon his face and lost her heart?

Madame de la Fontaine stroked her daughter's face and called to her. "Jeanine.

Jeanine. Wake up, my little angel."

Jeanine stirred in Victor's arms, and her eyelids fluttered open. She smiled up at Victor as if finding herself in his arms was a commonplace thing. She closed her eyes again, and Victor was glad for the moment to compose himself. Her trusting smile had pierced his heart. She could count on him to save her life, even as she had saved his.

"Jeanine, wake up," her mother said again, and this time she gently patted her daughter's cheeks.

"What?" Jeanine questioned drowsily, opening her eyes again. She looked around at the people now gathered, and realization began to dawn upon her. Her face took on an expression of sheer terror, and Victor found himself helpless to soothe her fears.

"They are going to kill me," she declared and pushed away from Victor. He eased her onto the bench beside him, but kept a hand on her arm as if to calm her.

"You must have faith," her mother told her, tears flowing anew. "We must have faith."

Étienne came to put an arm around his mother, even as his father joined them and announced, "Colbert has put us from his lands. We may witness the execution on the morrow, but we will not be allowed to remain with her through the night. Jeanine is to be taken back to her tower room and there. . ." He could say no more.

Margarite de la Fontaine began to sob in earnest, and Étienne gently handed her over to his father. "We must take Mama from this place," he advised his father. "Trust Victor and me to work through the details."

"Might I offer my assistance?" Simon questioned in a whisper.

Étienne nodded. "We will need all the help we can get."

Colbert came up at that moment. "Take this Jew from my house, and all of you go. I want no interference in this matter. Monsieur de la Fontaine, I will expect payment in full on the morrow for your debts." He acted as if to leave them, then turned around and motioned to his henchmen. "Escort them from the estate."

François cast a quick glance upon his daughter. "I love you, my child. God will be with us."

Jeanine nodded. "I love you, mon père."

"Do not lose faith," her mother managed to say between mournful wails.

"I won't, ma mère. I love you." Jeanine suddenly became the strong one.

Étienne leaned down and kissed her upon the forehead. "I will return."

"I love you, Étienne," she said, and Victor noted the desperation in her voice. It wasn't fear; it was urgency to say that which might never be said again.

Simon was already being led from the room when the second guard took hold of François de la Fontaine and gave him a powerful push toward the door. "Leave the witch now," he ordered.

Jeanine's father tried one final time to appeal to Colbert, and Victor took that moment to turn to Jeanine. He took in the huge worried eyes, so dark and velvety in their brown depths that for a moment he could forget her plight. He reached up a hand and touched her cheek, and instantly he claimed Jeanine's attention.

"Five geese flying," he whispered, his lips barely inches from hers. He saw her eyes widen in surprise just before he kissed her soundly upon the mouth. "I will come for you," he said, pulling away.

Jeanine's hand flew up to touch her lips. She was obviously overwhelmed with her feelings for what had just taken place. Colbert's angry denial of Monsieur de la Fontaine's pleadings caused Victor to realize he hadn't much time. "I love you."

"Oh, Victor, I love you, too. You are my heart."

"Do not be afraid," he told her confidently. "I will find a way to set you free."

❧

From the moment Victor had declared his love for her, Jeanine found a peace of mind that made facing her own execution not quite so fearful. She had marveled at his confirmation of feelings that she had long only dreamed might be given her. Now, as she hugged her arms to her body and watched for the first light of dawn, Jeanine knew that God was with her and that she had nothing to fear.

"Death cannot take love from me," she whispered and leaned back against the cold stones of the wall. "Not God's love, nor Victor's, nor that of my family. I have known much love in my short life, and should all else fail and my death be required, I will face my fate with the assurance that God has been ever faithful."

Since the time Colbert had seen her thrown back into this room, Jeanine had contemplated Victor's words and her own future. "I trust you, Father God," she prayed. "I believe in Your power to bring me out of this nightmare, but if it is not Your will, I accept that as well." She glanced back out the tiny slit of a window. The black skies remained as confirmation that her presence on earth might yet continue awhile longer.

"I don't want to die," she whispered, but this time her eyes remained dry as she lifted her gaze upward. "I give You my heart and soul and mind, Father. I give You all that I am or ever hope to be. I commend my spirit into Your keeping, even as I did as a small child. I beg Your mercy for my family and ask that You might comfort them in this hour, even as You have comforted me."

She smoothed down the thin linen cloth of the unbelted white houppeland that she'd been given to face her execution in. Her head covering had been taken from her, and her curly brown hair had been left to flow freely around her. Colbert intended to humiliate her in her final hour, but in truth, Jeanine found no embarrassment in her condition. She had remained faithful. She had refused to lie, even though it meant her life.

She glanced out the window again, and her heart lurched. The tiniest thread of color imposed itself upon the far horizon. Her time had come.

As if on cue, she heard the bar lift, and the guard pushed back the door. "You are to come," he said solemnly.

Jeanine nodded and followed the man down the spiral stairs. She wondered if her family would be allowed to come to her and whether she could offer any comfort to them. Walking slowly behind the sober-faced guard, Jeanine kept remembering Victor's last words. He had used her code with Simon. Five geese flying. She forced herself to think of her grandmother's stories and of the significance of such symbolism. Concentrating on these things, Jeanine found the strength to go forward.

She was led into the courtyard and just beyond the stables, and it was here that she found Colbert and the priest awaiting her. The skies were barely touched with blue, and the sun had not yet appeared above the horizon.

"I have come to hear your confession, my child," the priest said sympathetically.

"Thank you, Father, but I have already made my peace with God," Jeanine said defiantly.

"Demons cannot make peace with God," Colbert said, sneering at her.

Jeanine smiled ever so slightly. "You should know, Monsieur."

She walked past them and caught sight of the post that had been erected for her execution. A small platform had been nailed approximately five feet off the ground. This would allow for the bundles of wood and straw to be placed beneath her feet, while Jeanine stood on the platform, hands bound to the post at her back.

She swallowed hard, fear threatening to take away her composure. God is with me, she reminded herself. Nothing Colbert or his men can do can take that from me.

Chapter 15

The priest came to stand beside Jeanine, and without asking her permission, he made the sign of the cross and offered up prayers on behalf of her soul. "Do you renounce Satan?" he asked.

Jeanine looked fiercely at Colbert and answered, "I do now, as I always have."

"Do you accept the one true God?" the priest continued.

"I do."

"Do you now seek absolution from your sins?"

Jeanine heard Colbert snort as if to hold back laughter. "I have already been absolved," Jeanine replied. "I have given my spirit over to God, and it is well with my soul."

The priest seemed momentarily stunned by her response. He made the sign of the cross again and lifted a crucifix to Jeanine's face. *"Sis mortuus mundo, vivens iterum Deo."* Be thou dead to this world, living again to God. Jeanine smiled, recognizing the Latin words and remembering Simon's diligence to teach her the language as an aide to her medical training. The bittersweet memory flooded her soul, along with a deep regret that she might never live to know Victor's love in full. She scanned the horizon for any sign of her love or her family, but there was none to be found.

"Let us finish this before there is trouble," Colbert demanded. "Who knows what treachery her family has planned?"

The church council assembled at the table Colbert had prepared for them. There was a good distance between them and the execution platform, but Jeanine knew they would have little trouble confirming that their orders were being carried out in full.

Colbert grabbed her arm roughly, and Jeanine shuddered at his touch. He laughed. "You could have found yourself considerably better cared for, had you not denied me."

"I would have naught but misery in your presence," she replied.

He stopped, eyed her contemptuously for a moment, then shrugged. "You have made your own fate. You chose to live by your hand, and now you will die by mine. It seems just fair that I should have the final say in this matter."

"You have no say in this matter at all, Monsieur," Jeanine countered. "God in heaven holds the keys to life and death. You, Antoine Colbert, are but a pawn in His game. You think to outwit God, to force your will upon Him and His people,

436

but you are gravely mistaken." She faced him bravely, not caring how he might respond to her. "I have known the love of family and friends and of a godly man. You cannot take that from me, even if you take my life."

"You are a foolish woman," Colbert declared. "You might have saved your life had you but yielded to me. I feel nothing but contempt for you now." He spat in her face and turned to walk away.

"And I feel nothing but pity for you, Monsieur," Jeanine called after him. She saw his shoulders stiffen and knew her words had hit their mark. Her sense of peace offended him. No doubt he had hoped to have her beg for mercy and fall upon him for salvation.

The guard was again at her side. He motioned her forward, and when they stood beside the execution post, he gently lifted her thinly clad body and positioned her bare feet on the platform. On a ladder that had been placed behind her, Jeanine could glance around to find still another guard preparing to bind her hands with leather thongs. Below her, a bevy of servants worked at a feverish pitch to mound dry wood and bundles of straw.

Colbert had taken his place with the bishop, and Jeanine refused to give in to the look of triumph upon his face. God would save her. Whether it be in the midst of flames as He took her spirit up to heaven or in the miraculous rescue that Victor had promised.

The priest again appeared below her to offer up prayers on her behalf. Jeanine felt desperation edging out her confidence. *I can do this,* she promised herself. *I can stand strong in the face of this false accusation because God knows my innocence.* She took a deep breath and caught the priest's sympathetic expression.

"What of my parents?" Jeanine dared to ask.

The priest shrugged. "It is better this way, non? 'Twould be difficult for them to observe their child burned alive."

Jeanine swallowed hard. Victor and Étienne had promised to return, but there was no sign of them or anyone else who might offer her love in her final moments. Sweat formed on her brow, and her stomach churned with revolting anxiety.

"Let us finish this thing," Colbert called out. "The sun is now in the sky." Colbert's guards formed two straight lines behind him.

The bishop nodded and offered the final words. "Jeanine de la Fontaine, for the sin of consorting with the devil, you are hereby sentenced to death by the purging of your soul and flesh in fire. As the Scripture of our Lord tells us in Revelation, 'Blessed are they that do his commandments, that they may have right to the tree of life, and may enter in through the gates into the city. For without are dogs, and sorcerers, and whoremongers, and murderers, and idolaters, and whosoever loveth and maketh a lie.'"

Jeanine felt the words pierce her soul. She had been one to make lies a daily part of her life, and now she was paying the penalty. But even as she thought this, God filled her heart with peace, and she recalled the words of Psalm 6: *Siegneur, ne me reprenez pas dans votre fureur, et ne me chatiez pas dans votre colere*— "O Lord, rebuke me not in thine anger, neither chasten me in thy hot displeasure." *Ayez pitié de moi, Seigneur, parce que je suis faible*—"Have mercy upon me, O Lord; for I am weak." The words seemed to flow through her mind with ease, and Jeanine began to murmur them loud enough for the man who bound her hands to hear her.

"Heal me; for my bones are vexed. My soul is also sore vexed: but thou, O Lord, how long? Return, O Lord, deliver my soul: oh save me for thy mercies' sake. For in death there is no remembrance of thee; in the grave who shall give thee thanks?"

The man tied her hands loosely. His touch was infinitely tender. He leaned forward and whispered, "God have mercy on you, Mademoiselle."

"Merci," she replied, touched by his kindness.

Turning her gaze back upon the bishop and Colbert, Jeanine faced her impending execution. She watched as a burning torch was brought forth by one of Colbert's men. He halted before the bishop, who appeared to bless the man and the fire.

Then, even as she watched the scene unfold before her, Jeanine heard something in the distance. Turning her head to the south, she saw the unmistakable rise of dust marking the approach of riders. The noise increased, and the thundering sound left little doubt that the number of riders was great.

"Burn the witch!" Colbert cried out and motioned to his guards to take up their positions. But it was too late. Much to Colbert's surprise, Victor Pindar and Étienne de la Fontaine appeared on horseback from behind the stables. The army approaching from the south seemed to be their signal to reveal their presence.

"Burn her!" Colbert raged and moved forward to take the torch in hand for himself.

The man behind Jeanine quickly cut her bonds and pointed to Victor's approaching mount. Victor rode up beside the execution platform and motioned to Jeanine. "Jump!" he declared, as the bondman saluted him.

"I do not understand," Jeanine said, turning to the man who was now climbing down the ladder to take up arms on behalf of Victor.

"Jump to me," Victor demanded and held out his arms.

Jeanine hesitated a moment, but as Colbert touched the torch to brittle wood, she knew there was no other choice. She threw herself out, pushing off the platform with as much force as she could muster.

"Stop them!" Colbert screamed. His guards advanced on Victor's horse, just as Jeanine flung herself into Victor's awaiting arms.

There was no time for Victor to settle her properly on his mount. He spurred the horse into action and moved away even as the clang of swords rang out against their scabbards.

"Hold tight," he yelled in her ear, to be heard above the din. The army who had come to their rescue was moving into position to offer them protection and coverage.

"Who are those men?" she asked, clinging desperately to Victor's neck, her legs flailing wildly behind her and slapping at the horse's side.

He laughed. "Tell you later." With one fluid motion, he slipped his hand beneath her legs and hoisted her into position in front of him. "Better?"

"Much," she admitted.

Jeanine buried her face against Victor's neck as they raced ahead to meet the front line of their defense. Étienne was quickly beside them with a roar of raging men following up behind.

"Better pick up the pace," he called to Victor, "or you'll never live long enough to become my brother in law."

Victor chuckled, and his amusement lessened Jeanine's fear. They both seemed so confident of their ability to take charge of the day that it gave her cause for hope.

"I'll stay here with the others," Étienne added, "and I'll meet you both at the agreed-upon place."

"God be with you," Victor answered, and Jeanine glanced up to watch Étienne fall behind them to join the ranks of the small army.

For several minutes they rode in silence. Jeanine knew from the direction they'd taken that they were headed south, farther away from Bruges. Still stunned by the suddenness of her rescue, she was further surprised when Victor slowed his mount.

"What is this?" she questioned. "You have slowed. Colbert will catch us."

"I think not," Victor replied. "The king's men will busy him."

"The king's men?" Jeanine questioned.

"Aye."

"I don't understand," she said, shifting her weight. She was painfully aware of her light linen gown billowing out around her. Modestly, she tucked the edges of the skirt beneath her as best she could.

"You hardly need to," Victor told her. He slowed the horse even more and stared down into her face. "It is enough that you are safely here in my arms."

She felt her face grow hot, even as she became aware that he was going to kiss her. His kiss was tender and searching, as if seeking answers for questions that he'd not yet voiced. She wrapped her arms around him and pressed closer. *Would that such feelings could go on forever,* she thought.

"Thank you for saving my life," she murmured, as he pulled away. It was the only safe thing she could think of to say.

"I was indebted to you," he said, eyeing her curiously. "I remember you as Dr. Font, but I cannot imagine how I mistook you for a man."

She laughed, and it sounded good in her own ears to be filled with such joy. "You were most gravely injured and heavily drugged with our concoctions. It is not hard to imagine that you saw me as a man. It is a wonder you saw or remembered anything at all."

"I remember you blessing me. It was the one thing that stuck out in my mind. Then that night when you were fleeing your marriage to Colbert, you offered up the same blessing upon me again."

"I remember," she said, feeling suddenly shy. "I wanted very much for you to know me. To know how much I cared."

Victor halted the horse and looked at her with great perplexity. "How is it that you came to care for me?"

She smiled. "I was drawn to you from the moment of our first meeting. I appeared upon the *Crispin,* in disguise of course, and my brother led me to your litter. I found you there, dying from your wounds, and never have I felt the things for another that I felt for you that day."

"But why? Certainly the face of a dying man could mean nothing to you but yet another patient."

She shrugged. "I know not why my heart chose you. I only know that the feeling never left me."

"What feeling is that?" asked Victor, still appearing to scrutinize her words for solutions to the puzzle.

Jeanine threw caution to the wind. If he found offense in her words, then at least she would have been honest with him. If he rejected her then, it would be painful, but certainly less so than were there to be lies between them. "The feeling that we were destined to be together. That I would always love you. That I would find my greatest happiness with you."

"I see." Victor grew strangely silent. He urged the horse forward, still lost in thought.

"When did you come to care for me?" Jeanine finally asked, desperate for the silence to be filled.

Victor laughed, and tiny lines formed around his eyes. Jeanine thought they made him look even more handsome than he already was. "I'm not sure I can say exactly. It might have been when you came into my room that night. You were so brave and noble about the entire matter, giving me over your prized possessions, all in order to save your father from certain destruction."

Noises from behind them alerted Victor that he'd been too lax in his duties. "Hold fast. We're being pursued."

Jeanine's heart picked up speed. She dared to glance over her shoulder and found several mounted men, including Antoine Colbert, bearing down upon them.

Dear Father in heaven, she prayed, *help us to escape our enemies.* Psalm 6 came to mind once again, and she remembered the final verses of the passage with hope: *"The Lord hath heard my supplication; the Lord will receive my prayer. Let all mine enemies be ashamed and sore vexed: let them return and be ashamed suddenly."*

Jeanine didn't care that Colbert be punished for his actions against her. She longed only that she be allowed to escape without harm to herself, Victor, or her brother. Then, too, she thought, there were the men of the king's army. She whispered a prayer for their safety and asked God's blessings on all who had befriended her cause, but even as the words were thought, she noticed that Victor's horse was tiring under the strain of two riders. Colbert was gaining ground.

Chapter 16

I t was evident to Victor that outdistancing Colbert would be impossible. He chided himself for his lax attitude and assumption that he could simply ride in and take Jeanine without any trouble coming upon them.

"I'll have to fight him," Victor told Jeanine and reined back on the horse so hard that the animal cried out in fear and reared wildly. Jeanine tightened her grip on Victor, but already he was maneuvering to put her from the horse. "Go into the trees. Stay out of sight. If you remain out here, someone might take you from me."

Jeanine slid down the side of the horse, her face a ghastly shade of white. "Oh, Victor, no! I cannot lose you now."

"Have faith, Jeanine. I once was quite handy with a sword. I have no reason to believe myself incompetent now."

Colbert and his men had slowed a safe distance from Victor and Jeanine. Victor cast a quick glance from them to Jeanine and back again. In the distance he could see pursuing riders. Either Étienne had come to his defense, or they were friends of Colbert. Either way, Victor didn't want to wait and see. He reached behind him and pulled his sword free. He thrilled to the sound of the metal as it passed from the scabbard and into the air. The ring persuaded him that he was capable of meeting any match.

Ahead, he could see Colbert's expression change from satisfaction and victorious pursuit to one of fear and assessment. Colbert halted his horse's progress and appeared to contemplate the matter. The men at his side matched the action of their leader and brought their own animals to a stop. The rotund man scratched his belly, then drew his sword and laughed at what surely appeared a hopeless attempt on Victor's part to protect Jeanine.

"Dear God," Victor prayed, "if ever Your help was needed, 'tis now. Remember me, Your servant, this day. Give unto me the victory that I might glorify Your name. Amen." Confidence surged through Victor. He glanced over his shoulder and saw that Jeanine had made her way to the trees. The time had come.

Victor balanced the sword carefully in his hands, then swung it around in a circle over his head and gave a fierce battle cry. Sinking his heels into the horse's flanks, he held fast as the animal leaped into action.

Colbert and his men were so intent on Victor's display, that they failed to notice Étienne and six other mounted men approach from behind. The men were nearly upon them just as Victor came within proper fighting distance of Colbert. Wielding his weapon, Victor brought the sword down hard, as if to cleave Colbert in half. The sound of metal upon metal rang out in the early morning countryside as Colbert's sword intervened and kept the older man from death.

Étienne and his men busied Colbert's guard while Victor faced off with Colbert. The horses whinnied and pranced nervously as the men lunged and pressed their war upon each other. At one point, Colbert lurched sideways to deflect Victor's blow. Hopelessly off balance, Colbert tumbled from the side of his horse and narrowly escaped being stepped on by the beast as it fled the battlefield.

Victor swung his own mount around and jumped from its back. The match was now to be on foot, and Victor could see that Colbert could barely lift his weapon. His weight and age were clearly against him. Victor thought to offer him mercy. It was evident that the rest of Colbert's guard were being soundly defeated.

Sweat poured from his face as he called out, "Do you yield? Will you leave us to go in peace?"

Colbert laughed haughtily. "Never! I will kill the witch myself after I run you through." He lunged, but Victor easily dodged the sword.

"It is not my desire to take your life, Monsieur," Victor replied, "but I will not allow you to kill my intended bride."

"Bride, ha!" Colbert gasped for air before continuing. "She will never be yours."

He raised up his sword and brought it down hard, but Victor jumped to the side while slicing his own weapon through the air. The sword caught Colbert's left arm, and a thin strip of material fell away. Blood immediately oozed from the wound, but this only served to infuriate Colbert.

"She has been condemned in the eyes of the church. Condemned to death," Colbert said, his thick chest heaving up and down with every swing of his blade. "Who will marry you, should you live? They will only seek you out, and then both of you will die."

"She is no witch, as well you know. You have lied in the sight of God and His witnesses," Victor said, thrusting the blade forward. He pierced the sword arm of Colbert and felt the edge of his sword hit bone.

Colbert screamed in anguish. His arm appeared useless as his sword fell to the dirt. Victor took that moment to halt the fight. He stood panting lightly, watching Colbert intently.

"Will you yield now, Man? You are wounded, and I have no desire to cause you further harm."

Colbert refused to acknowledge him. His loud wailing and groans made it evident that he was completely spent. Victor glanced up to find Étienne looking down on him from atop his horse.

"Sorry we let him slip through. The home guard was a bit of a challenge," Étienne offered by way of explanation.

" 'Tis my fault as well for slowing the horse. I should have kept my thoughts on what we were about, instead of romancing your little sister," Victor admitted.

Colbert's wound was bleeding profusely, and Victor motioned to Étienne. "Tear a strip from one of his men's tunics. We should bind the arm."

Étienne nodded and turned his horse to ride back to where Colbert's men were now disarmed and bound. Victor thought only to assure himself of Jeanine's safety, and without concern for Colbert, he, too, turned his back upon the older man.

He walked less than two paces when the hairs on the back of his neck prickled and Jeanine's scream rent the air. Turning, sword poised, Victor met Colbert as he charged. Colbert flailed the sword aimlessly in his left hand, while Victor's weapon remained sure and steady. There was no stopping the man's onslaught, and Victor winced as his sword buried itself deep in the man's chest. Colbert dropped his own blade and reached dumbly for the sword now sticking out of his body. He opened his mouth, then fell over backward.

Victor pulled his sword out and knelt beside the man. "It need not have ended this way, Colbert. You had but to let us depart in peace."

"Curse you and the witch," Colbert said. "Be gone from me and let my own attend my wounds."

"You need a physician." Victor stood and caught sight of Jeanine waiting faithfully by the trees. He wiped the bloody sword against his boot and made his way to where she stood, still covering her mouth with her hands.

"Colbert is wounded—mortally, I fear," Victor told her gravely.

Jeanine fell into his arms, a sob breaking from her throat. "I thought he would kill you. I thought—"

"Shhh," he whispered against her ear. " 'Tis well with me, but that man will bleed to death if he doesn't have a doctor's care soon."

Jeanine straightened. "I will go to him."

Victor stared at her in silence. "Dare you say that you propose to see to his wounds?"

"I am a physician, whether legal or elsewise. If his wounds are that grave, there is scarce time to return him to his estate, much less bring a doctor from Bruges."

Victor smiled, his heart warmed by her ability to tend her enemy. "Come then." He put an arm around her and drew her along.

Victor had nearly reached Colbert's side when the wounded man screamed out in pain, "Get the witch away from me!"

Jeanine ignored him and squatted down beside his quivering form. "Monsieur, you are wounded. Let me attend to you."

"I would rather die," he said hatefully. Gasping for air, he tried to roll away from her touch.

"You will die if I am not allowed to help you. This wound is severe."

" 'Tis your doing, Witch. My death will be upon your head." Colbert shifted, groaning miserably as his life's blood drained from his body. "My men will testify to your treachery."

"What can they do to me?" Jeanine asked softly and got to her feet. She stared down at Colbert as if anticipating an answer. "You have condemned me to death already, yet God has interceded on my behalf. With God so obviously for me, what can you or any mere man do to cause me harm?"

Colbert spat at her and again insisted that one of his own men be allowed to tend his wounds. Victor finally agreed and called to Étienne. "Release the man who is least injured and bring him to tend his master."

While Étienne took up this task, Victor reached for Jeanine. "Come. We must make for safety. Colbert is right in saying that others will soon be summoned to find us."

Jeanine nodded and fixed her gaze on him in such a way that Victor wanted very much to crush her to him and kiss her long and lovingly. He found her trust so rewarding, so faithful. She reminded him in many ways of his sister. Loyal, true, trusting.

"Where will we go?" she asked, and Victor knew instantly it wasn't offered as a question of doubt.

"We have it all worked out," he assured her. "You have only to trust me."

She smiled warmly and looped her arm through his. " 'Tis no difficult task to do that. I would follow you to the ends of the earth."

"And well you may," he teased, pulling her back to where his horse mindlessly nibbled on the grass. He lifted Jeanine up on the horse, then climbed on behind her. "Étienne, let us be off," he called. "These good men will see to Colbert's wounds and give us the time we need to get ourselves to safety."

Jeanine eyed the six riderless horses. " 'Twould make more sense, my love, if we were to take up one of the other horses to aid our cause," she said.

"They would only add thievery to our list of wrongs," Victor told her seriously. Then turning her in the saddle so that she fit more neatly against him, he smiled. "Besides, I like this so much more."

Jeanine pressed her face against his neck and sighed. "Oui, it is most acceptable."

Chapter 17

Jeanine felt her sense of security slip from her as they neared Bruges. Victor had tried to reassure her that all was well under control, but she still feared for her life and his. Ever in the back of her mind was the worry that they could never find peace again in their lives. She had been condemned as a witch. No matter where she went, that past would haunt her and rise against their happiness.

Victor maneuvered the horse into a narrow alleyway and waited while Étienne slid from his mount and reached up for Jeanine. Jeanine grew fearful for a moment, thinking that Victor intended to leave them while he went elsewhere. To her relief, however, he dismounted and tossed the reins to a gangly boy who had materialized out of a darkened shop doorway.

"Do you know what to do with these beasts?" he asked the boy.

Jeanine saw the boy nod. "You can count on me, Monsieur. Simon told me where to hide them."

"Good enough," Victor replied. He motioned to Étienne and pushed Jeanine toward the open door. "We'll go here first and change our clothes. I wouldn't want you to catch your death from the light weight of that gown."

Jeanine felt her face grow hot. So he had noticed the thinness of the houppeland. Embarrassed, she longed for nothing more than a heavy cloak or cotehardie. To her surprise, she was offered both once they were inside the shop. A woman not so much older than Jeanine came to them. " 'Tis well worn, but I have a gown for the lady. Come with me."

Jeanine glanced up at Victor and then to her brother. "Go on," Victor encouraged. "And be quick about it. We haven't much time."

Jeanine hurried into the back room with the woman, and rather than strip off the white linen gown, she pulled a very plain, sideless surcoat over her head. The dark brown material fell against her execution gown in stark contrast, but Jeanine didn't care. The woman handed her a simple woolen cap before offering to braid her hair.

"You are very kind to help me," Jeanine murmured. "Thank you."

"You saved the life of my father," the young woman said, pulling the thick bulk of Jeanine's hair into some semblance of order.

"Me?"

"Oui. He was on the *Crispin*. His leg was badly crushed. You had to remove it, but at least he didn't bleed to death or take on poisoning of the blood. 'Tis a small way to offer you thanks."

"I remember him well," Jeanine responded thoughtfully. " 'Twould be my great pleasure to see him again."

"You will when the time is right. He has agreed to help see you to safety." She finished Jeanine's hair and waited while Jeanine secured her cap in place. "I have a cloak for you by the back door. It should allow you to slip through town unnoticed."

"Again, you have my thanks," Jeanine said, taking hold of the woman's shoulder. "I feel quite blessed to call you friend."

The woman blushed and waved Jeanine off. "You'd best be gone now. No doubt they'll be searching for you."

Jeanine rejoined Victor and her brother and found both men sporting heavy cloaks. " 'Tis a good thing the mornings still merit such protection," she said, pulling the cloak around her.

"We must hurry," Victor told her. "We have a bit of distance to cover before we reach our shelter."

"Then let us be gone."

⁓

Hours later, after weaving their way behind many establishments along the dock, Jeanine, Victor, and Étienne made their way to a small run-down inn. It wasn't until they were given a single room on the upper floor that Jeanine suddenly thought of her mother and father.

"Étienne, what of our parents?" she questioned, concern clearly evident in her voice. She threw off the cloak and turned to face her brother.

"They are safe," he assured her. "Simon has taken them to another of your patients' homes."

"My patients?" Jeanine grinned. "You mean Dr. Font's patients, no doubt."

Étienne looked at her and shook his head. "It was you on the *Crispin*, was it not?"

She remembered that moment clearly. Fear for Étienne's safety had caused her to place herself in jeopardy of being discovered. "Oui. It was I."

"I cannot believe it," Étienne replied. "I did not even know you."

"That was the idea," Jeanine admitted.

"I feel the fool," he said, chuckling.

Victor had gone to the window to check the alleyway behind the inn. "You feel the fool?" he called over his shoulder. "The woman worked on me as a physician, and I thought she was a man."

"I am very good at what I do," Jeanine said, feeling the joy of her freedom for the first time. "I like to believe my patients were more focused on being healed than on my ash-stained face and hands."

"Still, it should have been evident," Victor said, coming up behind her.

"Mayhap God clouded your eyes," she offered lightly.

"Whatever the way," Étienne said, still amazed, " 'tis good that you used your abilities, for elsewise, this man would be dead."

Jeanine turned and beheld the look of affection in Victor's eyes. " 'Twould have been my death as well. For my heart scarce beats, but what it thinks of him."

Noises outside the door caused both men to put a finger to Jeanine's lips. It would have been amusing to her, had their looks not have been so grave. The rousing protest of the landlord instantly alerted them to danger. Étienne pulled Jeanine one way, while Victor pulled her the other. Finding herself torn in two different directions, Jeanine hardly knew what to do. She couldn't cry out, and yet to stand in place would see her gravely injured.

The men seemed not to notice, until the voices moved down the hall and they each turned to see why their progress was halted. Jeanine stood, arms outstretched, one man at the end of each tightly held hand.

"Shall you make a wish and cleave me in two?" she asked in a hushed whisper.

Étienne was the first to let go. He laughed very softly and shrugged. "With her father, I've been her protector for a score of years. Old habits are difficult to put aside."

Victor nodded. "I have been blessed by your aid in keeping her from harm. It seems she is one of those people who requires many keepers."

"I take offense at such talk," Jeanine protested. "I've managed to see to myself lo these many years while working on the docks. You have no faith in my abilities."

Victor grinned, and Étienne chuckled. "We have a great amount of faith in your ability to get yourself into trouble," her brother assured her. He bowed low and made a sweeping movement with his arm. "I give her gladly to you, Monsieur. You will never know a moment's peace."

"Mayhap you are right," Victor admitted, "but 'tis my belief she will make up for that loss in other ways."

"Mayhap I will throw you both over for someone else entirely," Jeanine said, crossing her arms against her chest. "I am hardly a woman to be considered lightly. I have a strong faith and a powerful Father in heaven who listens to my cries. Should you think to abuse me overmuch, I will simply put it to Him to be dealt with."

"Let it always be so," Victor said, reaching out to pull her into his arms. "It is my deepest wish that I might never abuse the love and faith you have put in me."

Jeanine relished the way his arms closed around her. She felt safe here. Secure from the worries of the world, and even though she still had far to go in order to reach true safety, she was happy here.

❧

The following morning a light rapping at the door sent Victor hurrying to pull the sleeping form of his wife-to-be from her peaceful slumber on the tiny bed. He and Étienne had slept at the side of the bed on the wood floor and had positioned themselves so that they blocked any hope of entrance should someone try the door.

Jeanine gazed about sleepily, as if to discern what was happening as Victor pushed her down to the floor and silently drew his sword. The rapping came again, and her eyes widened in fear. Victor pressed a finger to his lips and motioned her to remain hidden, while Étienne went to the door.

"Who disturbs my slumber?" he called out in a gruff manner.

" 'Tis only I," came an ancient-sounding voice. "I have brought you food to break the fast."

Jeanine instantly sat back up. " 'Tis Simon," she said in a whisper.

Victor nodded to Étienne and remained fixed with sword, while the younger man opened the door. It was indeed Simon, and he had managed to come alone.

They hurried him into the privacy of their room and quickly shut the door. Jeanine got up from her hiding place and came to embrace the old man. "I do not know when I have found more pleasure in a visitor. Simon, I am so grateful God spared your life."

"As am I," Simon admitted and handed a cloth-wrapped parcel to Victor.

"So what word have you for us?" Étienne asked.

"They are searching for you, as is to be expected. There are criers on the streets announcing your escape, as well as the charges that stand against your sister." He turned to Jeanine with an expression of sorrow. "They still mean to see you dead."

Jeanine nodded. "We knew it would be so."

" 'Tis madness," Simon replied. "They have listened to no one but the devil himself. You will be sorely missed when you are gone from this place. The people love you well."

"Most do not even know I exist," Jeanine protested. "I posed as a male physician. Dr. Font is who they love."

Simon smiled. "They now know well the true identity of Dr. Font. I have spread the word that they might know and realize what has become of their good doctor."

"And they were not offended by the fact that I am a woman?" she asked, taking a piece of hard cheese and bread that Victor offered her.

"You prevented their deaths, nursed their sick children, brought new lives into the world—they scarce seemed concerned that you were not as you appeared."

"They are good people," Jeanine replied before sinking her teeth hungrily into the cheese.

"Are the plans we made going to work?" Victor asked suddenly.

"At this point, all looks well," Simon assured him.

"What of the men who aided our escape?"

"They escaped without a single death. Two men were injured severely, but I saw to their needs and they now await your escape from Bruges."

"And no one suspects who they were?" Victor questioned. His worst fears were that those men might be found out for who they really were.

"Non," Simon answered. "Colbert has everyone believing that Jeanine summoned up some evil force. Even the bishop is convinced that it must be so, especially when there was no man left behind to prove the human natures of their attackers."

"So Colbert lives?" Étienne asked.

"Oui, but his wounds are grieving him greatly, I've been told. He swears a legion of demons attacked him as he tried to bring Jeanine back to her just punishment. The men who were with him at the time of his injury completely agree with this story. They have done much to spread the story of an army of evil."

"But I do not understand," Jeanine said, pausing in her eating to question Victor. "You told me those men were from the king. Was not their standard visible to the bishop and Colbert?"

Victor looked upward for a moment and let out a deep breath. " 'Tis true they are the king's men. I simply left out the matter of which king they served."

"You mean to tell me—"

Victor gave her a sly smile and bit off a chunk of bread. He chewed it very thoughtfully before replying. "My family stands well with the king of England. He thought it rather amusing to do something so irritating to old crazy Charlie."

"The king of England sent men to rescue me?" Jeanine said in an air of disbelief. "Why did you not tell me before now?"

"It seemed not to be of importance," Victor replied as if what had been accomplished on her behalf had been less than significant.

"Not of grave importance? The king of England sends his men to Flanders to interfere with the edict of the church, and you think it not of grave importance?" She appeared quite indignant, and Victor could no longer lead her the merry chase.

"I didn't say that the rescue wasn't of importance. I merely meant to imply that where our help came from wasn't as important as the fact that it came. Then, too, it was of great import to keep the identity of those men secret. They appeared as mere working men rising up to aid the cause of one of their own. They are safely awaiting us on a ship that sails for England tonight. If all goes as planned, you and I and your family, as well as Simon, if he will come, will be on that ship when it leaves Bruges."

Jeanine stared at him in wonder. "You worked out the details of all this? On my behalf?" Tears filled her eyes.

"Well, I could hardly allow Colbert to deny me of a wife before I even had a chance to ask for her hand in marriage."

Jeanine looked at him with such love and admiration that Victor thought his heart would burst. All his life he had sought to find satisfaction in his work. With his imagination, he designed fine buildings. With his purpose and direction, he was able to hire good men to help him transfer those dreams from paper to stone and mortar. But in the twinkling of an eye, this young woman had given him the satisfaction and fulfillment that had somehow evaded his life.

"I know not what to say," Jeanine said softly and wiped at her eyes with the edge of her sleeve.

"You might agree to marry me," Victor said, reaching his hand up to touch her wet cheek.

"But who will marry me to anyone?" Jeanine asked quite seriously. "The church has branded me a heretic and a witch."

"Trust God to find a way," Victor told her. "He has yet to let us down, eh?" She nodded. "So does that mean you will marry me?"

"Oui," she whispered softly. "I will marry you."

Victor smiled and threw a glance at Étienne and Simon. "See? You rescue the fair damsels and they will happily give themselves over to you in marriage."

Étienne laughed. "But what of the man whose life is saved by a woman?"

Victor sobered and gently stroked Jeanine's cheek. "You lose your heart forever to a woman like that. For you see, she not only saves the body from death, but she saves the heart as well."

Chapter 18

B
ut why will you not come with us?" Jeanine asked Simon for the third
time. "You are not safe here in Bruges."

"I know that full well," Simon admitted, "and it is not my intention to
stay in Bruges. I seek only to see you safely away, and then I will see my own
pilgrimage realized."

"Where will you go?" Jeanine asked, barely able to hold back her tears.

"I will return to my homeland to the east," Simon said solemnly. "I long to
see what family of mine might still exist there. I have a brother and two sisters,
and together they have many children—maybe even grandchildren by now. I
desire to see them again before I die."

"Speak not of death. I had thought to have lost you once before, and now it
seems I am losing you in truth," Jeanine said, reaching out to touch Simon's shoulder. "You are a dear friend. I know our faith is different, but I will pray for you to
reach your family and to know the joy of being reunited with your loved ones."

"And I will pray that the Lord God of Israel will guide you to a better
place—to a homeland where you will not face persecution."

The moonlight shone brightly overhead, and Simon smiled and pointed
upward. "Imagine them there," he told her, and Jeanine stared quizzically at
the skies.

"Imagine what there?"

"Five geese flying," Simon said with a grin. " 'Tis just as you and your family will be. Five geese fleeing persecution and certain death. Five geese flying to
safety and hope."

"Oh, Simon," she sobbed and clutched the old man tightly in her arms. "I
shall miss you so very much."

"And I will miss you, Dr. Font," Simon told her and stroked her head tenderly.

"I am Dr. Font no longer," Jeanine said with a sigh. She pulled away just as
Victor arrived on the dock.

"Come," he told her. "Your parents are safely on board, as is your brother. We
must leave now or risk discovery." Jeanine nodded and reluctantly let go of Simon
as Victor added, "We've still room for one more."

Simon shook his head. "Non. I am traveling to my family. May it be well
with you. Take good care of my little doctor here. She fears she will no longer
find a way to practice what she has learned, but I truly doubt she will stand

defeated and idle for long."

"So do I," Victor said with a low chuckle.

Simon smiled and nodded. "Godspeed, my friends," he said softly. "Godspeed."

            ∽

They were some time out to sea when Jeanine, unable to sleep, came up to the main deck. Her life had so completely changed in only a few short months. It was hard to imagine what might come next. She tried not to fear the future, but even Victor couldn't give her decisive answers as to what they might find awaiting them in England. Victor had great confidence in the friendship his family held with the king, but more so, he reminded Jeanine of the kinship they had as Christians with the King of Kings.

Standing at the deck rail, Jeanine stared out to sea. The moonlight reflecting off the still waters made the sea look like polished black glass. The lightest of breezes put wind in their sails, but their ship was small and even now the king's men were rowing the ship toward the English shore.

Contemplating her life seemed a sensible thing to do. Behind her was France, the condemnation of the church, her medical practice, and Antoine Colbert. Before her stood England, the promise of absolution and forgiveness, the hope of marriage to Victor Pindar. *He loves me.* Suddenly she felt overwhelmed with emotions at the mere thought of Victor going to so much trouble to save her.

The wind picked up a bit, and without warning someone came to stand behind her. She knew it was Victor without turning to look. She felt so sure of him—of his presence, of his love. What a wonder it was and how she thanked God for His goodness in bringing them together.

"What are you doing here?" he asked softly, pulling her against him.

Jeanine reveled in the pleasure of his arms around her. "I thought I might clear my mind," she finally answered.

"And have you?" he whispered against her ear.

Jeanine sighed. "I have."

"And what did you determine in this clearing of your thoughts?"

"How blessed I am," she admitted. "Blessed that in spite of my sin, God brought about good in my life. He put us together, albeit in a very strange way, and He drew from us both the feelings and truths that would forever bind us together."

"We are blessed," Victor agreed and hugged her even more securely to him.

"No matter what my future holds," Jeanine told him softly. "No matter what happens, I will always love you, and I will always thank God for what He has done in bringing you to me."

Victor turned her very gently, and putting his hands to either side of her face, he said, "It will all work out. You must have faith. Just as your geese fly south in the winter and return again in the spring, you must have faith that God will restore life and happiness to you."

"But I am happy, Victor. I have you. My family is safe, and even Simon will be outside the reach of the punishing hands of Antoine Colbert."

"But you are worried," Victor said, sensing her deepest secret. "I see it in your eyes. I hear it in your voice. I want to take that fear from you. I want to see you happy, free from the burden you carry. Give it to me, Jeanine, and if not to me, then give it to God."

Jeanine sighed. "How can you know me so well in so short a time?"

He smiled and kissed her forehead. " 'Tis the knowledge that love puts upon one's heart. And, 'tis God's way of joining us together as one."

"I pray that may be so."

"It will be," he promised.

The breeze blew up, chilling Jeanine through the thin cloak, but it wasn't for this reason that she trembled. Victor stared down at her with such intensity that she could scarce stand up to the power of his love. He lowered his lips to hers, and when they touched, Jeanine wrapped her arms around Victor's neck and gave herself over to the splendor of his kiss. In his arms, it was easy to imagine that all would be well.

In the distance, Jeanine could hear someone calling out, but she was so lost in Victor's hold that she refused to focus on the words. It was Victor who pulled away and laughed at her dreamy-eyed stare.

"Did you hear that?"

"Ummm, what?"

"Silly little goose of mine," Victor said, laughing. He turned her in his arms again and pointed. "Look there—see the moonlight catching the white cliffs? My home—our home."

Jeanine's breath caught in her throat and tears again came unbidden to her eyes. " 'Tis beautiful."

"Aye, that it is."

Then as if for the first time, Jeanine realized that in England she would not even be able to speak the language. "Victor," she said, desperation edging her voice as she turned abruptly. "I cannot speak English."

Victor laughed lightly, then surprised her as his laughter turned into a hearty roar of delight. "You will hardly be alone," he said, trying to regain his composure. "So if that is your only fear, put it aside and leave it behind you. English was proclaimed the official language less than forty years ago. There are more people speaking French in England than you would imagine. You should feel quite at home."

Jeanine felt her spirits lift. "Truly?"

"Truly. Even my Eleanor prefers French. She says 'tis a fairer language by far than English. So you will find it easy to converse with her, and she will love you just as I do."

They stood in silence for several moments, watching and waiting as the boat drew ever closer to England. Jeanine prayed fervently for the faith to believe, all the while thanking God for His goodness to allow her freedom from the death Antoine Colbert had planned for her.

"Are you still afraid?" Victor's concern was evident in his tone.

Jeanine nodded. "I cannot lie and say I am not. Lies did nothing but harm me in the past. They will have no part in my new life. Aye, I am afraid, but I know, too, that there is hope and promise in our future. I will not allow fear to take charge of my life, if that is what you think. I only hope that God will direct me in such a way as to make useful my skills. I do so long to help people."

Victor's eyes seemed to twinkle as the moonlight caught them just right. "I believe, my dear Dr. Font, you will have little trouble in that regard. There are always people to be helped."

"Oui, but not always do they desire to be helped by one such as me. Women are not often accepted as physicians, and I cannot help but believe this is true even in your homeland."

Victor grinned mischievously. "Perhaps if you were to borrow some of my clothes, and put ashes and mud upon your face, and send out coded messages. . ."

Jeanine laughed merrily as Victor whirled her around. If anyone thought them strange, no one said so.

"We are truly five geese flying," she said when Victor set her down lightly upon the deck. "Flying to another land where we will start anew."

"Flying to freedom and God's future for our lives," Victor added.

"And to our love," Jeanine murmured.

"And to our love," Victor agreed.

Epilogue

Jeanine laughed gleefully at the sight of Victor being chased by his nephew. The boy held a very muddy piglet and was quite intent on his uncle sharing in his good find. Lady Eleanor, a graceful, dark-haired woman who appeared to be a miniature of her brother, joined in the laughter at the escapades of her son and brother.

"Marcus will no doubt catch up to him before long," she said, grinning broadly at Jeanine. "And when he does, there is no telling what havoc we shall see."

"Do you suppose the priest will be shocked?" Jeanine questioned, leaning closer to her new sister-in-law. "I mean, having just joined us in matrimony, will he find it difficult to accept that the groom is off frolicking with his nephew rather than with his bride?"

Eleanor shook her head. "Not Father McKay. He's known Victor since he was a boy. He'll simply see this as acceptable behavior for my brother."

Jeanine smiled and threw Victor a kiss as he narrowly skirted Eleanor's herb garden and made a mad dash for the garden wall. The pig squealed in terror as Marcus fairly flew by, jumping up and over the end of Eleanor's favorite roses.

"Truce! Truce!" Victor demanded from atop the garden wall. "I yield to your mercy, Sir Marcus."

The boy laughed at his uncle's ridiculously overdramatized bow and put the frightened piglet on the ground. "I could have caught you."

"And well I know it," declared Victor. "Which is precisely why I yielded the fight. 'Twould do me little good to come to my bride smelling of the pigsty."

"But that is exactly why Étienne told me to do it," Marcus giggled. "He thought it would be a great joke."

Victor jumped down from the wall and caught Jeanine's laughing expression. "No doubt he did, and I can imagine a few great jokes we might yet play on Étienne."

Eleanor was the one to put an end to the conspiratorial glances Victor and Marcus shared. "Not today. Today is for Jeanine's pleasure and goodwill. Today we celebrate the king's declaration of her absolution from the charges of witchcraft and heresy." She paused and added, "As well as your marriage, in case you forgot."

Victor rubbed Marcus lightly on the head and strode toward his sister with determined purpose. "That is not likely." He kissed Eleanor on the cheek, then left her to tend her son while he walked on to where Jeanine stood watching him.

Jeanine's laughter died in her throat as he seriously, passionately fixed his stare on her. He said not a word as he swung her up into his arms and headed for the small castle keep that monopolized the Bramston estate.

"Victor, you can't run away with her just now," Eleanor called after them, and Jeanine giggled at the expression on her husband's face.

"Just watch me," he replied, never breaking his stride.

"Victor!" Eleanor demanded his attention.

He turned on the steps of the keep and grinned mischievously down at his bride. "They will plague us all day and night, if we allow them to." Then to his sister he replied, "Go tend to your party. We will make our own."

"You cannot just leave like this," Eleanor said, coming forward. "What will I tell her family?"

Just then Étienne rounded the corner to catch sight of the scene. "What goes here?"

Eleanor looked up hopefully. "You must stop him. My brother is acting quite uncivilized."

" 'Tis nothing uncivilized at all," Victor answered them and winked down at Jeanine. "I merely feel the need for a doctor."

"If that is the case, mayhap she should be carrying you," Étienne said with a laugh, and everyone joined in.

Jeanine had never known such happiness as when she was in Victor's arms, and she trembled at the thought of the passion they shared for one another. She prayed that their marriage would be good, and she hoped that if it were at all possible, her grandmère might know of her happiness. Gently she fingered the brooch of sapphires and rubies that Victor had returned to her, along with her grandmother's combs, only the night before. *Perhaps Grandmère does know,* Jeanine thought happily.

Suddenly five geese appeared on the horizon and made a steady flight to the north. "Look!" Jeanine gasped in disbelief. "Victor, look!"

The gathering grew silent and stared heavenward as the birds, ever mindless of their human audience, journeyed past the keep. Victor grinned down at Jeanine, and she knew he understood the meaning of the sight in full. Five geese flying was a sign, her grandmère had assured her not so very long ago. A sign of hope—a sign of love.

A Letter to Our Readers

Dear Readers:

In order that we might better contribute to your reading enjoyment, we would appreciate your taking a few minutes to respond to the following questions. When completed, please return to the following: Fiction Editor, Barbour Publishing, Inc., P.O. Box 719, Uhrichsville, OH 44683.

1. Did you enjoy reading *Castles?*
   ☐ Very much—I would like to see more books like this.
   ☐ Moderately—I would have enjoyed it more if _____

   _____

   _____

2. What influenced your decision to purchase this book? (Check those that apply.)
   ☐ Cover   ☐ Back cover copy   ☐ Title   ☐ Price
   ☐ Friends   ☐ Publicity   ☐ Other

3. Which story was your favorite?
   ☐ *A Kingdom Divided*   ☐ *If Only*
   ☐ *Alas My Love*   ☐ *Five Geese Flying*

4. Please check your age range:
   ☐ Under 18   ☐ 18–24   ☐ 25–34
   ☐ 35–45   ☐ 46–55   ☐ Over 55

5. How many hours per week do you read? _____

Name _____

Occupation _____

Address _____

City _____ State _____ Zip _____

E-mail _____

If you enjoyed

Castles

then read:

❧

Wildflower Brides

Four Romances Blossom Along the Oregon Trail

The Wedding Wagon by Cathy Marie Hake
A Bride for the Preacher by Sally Laity
Murder or Matrimony by Pamela Kaye Tracy
Bride in the Valley by Andrea Boeshaar

If you enjoyed

Castles

then read:

KANSAS

Four Prairie Romances Dusted with Faith

Beyond Today by Tracie Peterson
The House on Windridge by Tracie Peterson
Threads of Love by Judith McCoy Miller
Woven Threads by Judith McCoy Miller